The SECOND COMING of the
STAR GODS

Also by Page Bryant

Psychic in the Devil's Triangle (1975)

Encounters in the Devil's Triangle (1977)

Crystals and Their Use:
A Study of At-One-Ment with the Mineral Kingdom (1983)

Earth Changes Survival Handbook (1984)

Terravision: A Traveler's Guide to the Living Planet Earth (1987)

Earth Changes Now (1988)

The Magic of Minerals (1988)

Awakening Arthur: His Return in Our Time (1990)

The Aquarian Guide to Native American Mythology (1991)

The Spiritual Reawakening
of the Great Smokey Mountains (1994)

Starwalking: Shamanic Practices
for Traveling into the Night Sky (1997)

Star Magic (2001)

The
SECOND COMING
of the
STAR GODS

A VISIONARY NOVEL

PAGE BRYANT

HAMPTON ROADS
PUBLISHING COMPANY, INC.

Cover design by Marjoram Productions
Cover art © PhotoDisc/Hisham F. Ibrahim/Getty Images

Hampton Roads Publishing Company, Inc.
1125 Stoney Ridge Road
Charlottesville, VA 22902

434-296-2772
fax: 434-296-5096
e-mail: hrpc@hrpub.com
www.hrpub.com

If you are unable to order this book from your local
bookseller, you may order directly from the publisher.
Call 1-800-766-8009, toll-free.

Library of Congress Cataloging-in-Publication Data

Bryant, Page.
 The second coming of the star gods : a visionary novel / Page Bryant.
    p. cm.
 ISBN 1-57174-343-X (alk. paper)
 1. Cheops, King of Egypt--Fiction. 2. Egypt--History--To 332
B.C.--Fiction. 3. Kings and rulers--Succession--Fiction. 4.
Human-alien encounters--Fiction. 5. Gods, Egyptian--Fiction. 6.
Pharoahs--Fiction. I. Title.
 PS3602.R95S43 2004
 813'.6--dc22
                                2003024197
                        ISBN 1-57174-343-X
                        10 9 8 7 6 5 4 3 2 1
              Printed on acid-free paper in the United States

Acknowledgments

No book comes into existence through the efforts of the author alone. This one is no exception. I would like to thank my husband for his loving support and saintly patience during the months that my time was spent writing. I also thank my friends and supporters of my work through the years who encouraged me to take the leap of writing a novel, including Jaine Smith, Helaine McLain, Donna Dupree, Judy Cooke, Evans Bowen, Mary Hunning, Nikki Craft, my daughters, Mary Page and Jamie, my first astronomy teacher, Barry Perlman, and my astronomy mentor who gave me my first telescope, Mike Harvey. I am particularly grateful to the works of Graham Hancock, Robert Bauval, Adrian Gilbert, John Anthony West, Zachariah Sitchin, Alice Bailey, H. P. Blavatsky, Dr. Robert Jastrow, Chet Raymo, and John Major Jenkins.

My deepest thanks to my editor, Richard Leviton. Without his sound advice and dedication to accuracy and detail, *The Second Coming of the Star Gods* would not be what it is. Richard guided me, sometimes gently and sometimes vigorously, in the writing of this, my first novel, with honesty and genuine concern for the story being both interesting to my readers and informative regarding spiritual concepts and truths, history, and terminology.

Finally, I thank the Star Gods, who I believe brought the vast body of astronomical, astrological, medical, architectural, mathematical, and esoteric knowledge to planet Earth eons ago, and whose existence will someday be proven.

Table of Contents

Preface

The Second Coming of the Star Gods takes place in Lower (northern) Egypt in the Fourth Dynastic period, commonly referred to as the Pyramid Age. By then, Upper (southern) and Lower Egypt were united into one country. The Pharaoh of the time, Khufu—also known as Cheops—ruled over the entire land and was called the Wearer of the Double Crown. Generally, it is Khufu whom Egyptologists and archeologists consider to have ordered the construction of the Great Pyramid of Giza, some would say the most sacred monument that sits in the Earth's exact geographical center. However, this long-held version of Egyptian history has recently been brought into question, based upon the actual age of this pyramid and the Sphinx.

The works of John Anthony West, Graham Hancock, Robert Bauval, Adrian Gilbert, and others have proposed convincing astronomical, meteorological, and even archaeological arguments that, if correct, will not only change the popular view of the age of these monuments, but also lay to rest the opinion that the pyramid was constructed as a tomb for a rather ego-centered king. Curiously, no mummy or other evidence has ever been found to show the pyramid was used as a burial site. Rather, the evidence seems to point to the enigmatic structure having been a place of initiation for the members of the priesthood into the esoteric mysteries.

My story is written from this perspective: the pyramid complex and the Sphinx were already an ancient presence in Egypt's history by the time, and perhaps long before, Khufu was king. While the correct age of these monuments, once established beyond question, would surely change the "facts" of when they were built, it would not change the truth of the secular and religious beliefs and hierarchies. These monuments were the Throne of the powerful priesthood of Heliopolis, the site of the great Sun Temple, and home of the order of astronomer-priests and priestesses in human history. The elite of Heliopolis (now absorbed by modern-day Cairo) attracted some of the world's most celebrated sages and philosophers, such as Herodotus and Pliny, all of whom claimed to have learned what they knew about the mysteries of the universe, magic, and ritual from the Heliopolitan Orders.

Due to his position as Pharaoh, along with other kings before and after him, Khufu was not only the political leader of Egypt but was also the head of the priesthoods throughout the land, much like the monarch of England is also the head of the Anglican Church. But while the English monarch is but a figurehead, this was not the case in ancient Egypt. Khufu was far from a figurehead: he was a priest trained in the sacred and what we would call today the scientific knowledge that had long comprised the arcane religion that was the source of knowledge—the belief system, if you will—that formed the very foundation of daily life, including the people's sense of values, ethics, culture, art, and religious practice.

The Second Coming of the Star Gods is framed with my personal opinions and views of the answers to these questions: Where did this incredible body of knowledge come from? With whom did it originate? Who built the Great Pyramid of Giza and why? If not Khufu, who? If not a tomb, what?

The story gives thoughts, feelings, and personality to the lives of a few historical figures and the times in which they lived. Many of the characters were people who existed and who held their respective positions under Khufu's reign, a few during the reign of Khufu's predecessor, his father, King Sneferu. Others of my characters are fictional, created to personalize what life may have been like within the orders of the priesthood in the Temple of the Sun in Heliopolis and within the royal family, and the tasks and responsibilities that rested on the shoulders of the Pharaoh. These fictional characters, for the most part, correspond to known historical roles, though little is known of the actual people.

A case in point is Taret, High Priestess of the Sun Temple. My idea for Taret came in a channeling I experienced while conducting a teaching tour in Egypt in 1987. The transmission concerned a long-forgotten holy order of female priestesses, called Star Priestesses, who were the feminine counterparts of the male priesthood of the Temple of the Sun. I have taken the liberty of assuming the existence of this holy order of women, and named it the Holy Order of Nut, after the sky goddess of ancient Egypt. Khem and the Nubian Tiye, my two principal characters, are fictional versions of likely figures who had important roles to play at a crucial moment in Egyptian public and spiritual life.

Khem and Tiye are girls, aged fifteen, which will seem quite young to modern readers for characters who are so self-assured and committed to their fate. Both are educated, intelligent, and keenly intuitive. Given the fact, however, that the average human lifespan of the times was much shorter than now—fifty then would have been very old—the matter of their maturity becomes clear. What life may have been like for the youthful Star Priestess apprentices within the social, academic, cultural, and religious community that comprised the great temples like the Temple of the Sun is purely fictional, though I hope plausible. I have taken literary license in assuming that the personal fears and emotions that haunt teenage girls today would have been of concern and importance to Khem and Tiye.

I have also provided the Pharaoh of the time, Khufu, with a personality of intense feelings and commitments as well as the conventional wisdom of one who must lead a country. The Heliopolitan High Priest Meri-ib, Taret, Ani, and the scribe Sheshat provide insights into what those trained in the sciences and practical application of astronomy, astrology, and the magical arts might have held important and how their knowledge and skills shaped their personalities and provided a mission and course in life. I have sought to determine who and what such individuals were, what they thought and felt about life and its challenges, both personally and spiritually, and what their values consisted of, individually and collectively. For surely many like these once lived.

The same is true for the fictional character Sokar, Khufu's half-brother, a man deeply troubled by what he considers a justified anger and hatred towards his own fate. He is the villain, typical of all good-versus-evil stories. Sokar makes some common mistakes due to feelings regarding his self-importance being invalidated in the scheme of things. Sokar misuses sacred knowledge by seeking magical knowledge and power for personal gain. Sokar proves that magicians, though they spend a great deal of time in the realms of the supernatural and possess superhuman powers, can be motivated by human emotions, human thinking, their own perspective of the nature of what is true and what is not, as well as their social, cultural, and religious systems, their upbringing, and other human vulnerabilities.

Magicians and shamans, Egyptian or otherwise, ancient or modern, live in two worlds that parallel one another, i.e., the physical world of natural laws and forces and the world of spirits and deities. Sokar's fate shows that there are indeed consequences to the wrong use of sacred knowledge and the personal power it bestows.

The holy city of Heliopolis (the Greek name) and its famed Temple of the Sun God *Ra (Re)* was indeed a real place, as are the various temples and monuments, cities, and a few of the historical characters in the story. Various events such as the significance of the heliacal or predawn rising of the star Sirius that heralded the beginning of a new calendar year, the annual flooding of the Nile—the season of Inundation—the existence of the Sphinx Temple, the buildup of sand that concealed the body of the Sphinx, the coronation of the king, and the various ritualistic and religious practices dealt with in the story—all these are historically accurate and verifiable.

Creating characters for my story and giving personality and feelings to some of the historical characters of the Fourth Dynasty was a joy for me, as was creating the story itself. Underneath that joy I kept focused on the reason the story was written: to open up the world of the Egyptian star religion to readers in a form that would be an enjoyable reading experience and to inform my readers of the profundity of that religion, and of the magical knowledge and practices that were an integral part of its existence. I also wanted to show how the same metaphysical, spiritual, and ethical truths still affect our lives and spiritual paths to this day.

This ambition proved to be somewhat difficult in that many of the terms I chose in presenting these "teachings" are more modern or perhaps even "new age" words and expressions than the language and words of the ancient Egyptians. For example, I had no way of knowing for certain what words the Egyptians would have used for karma, shamanic journeying, astral travel, the astral plane, and visions and dreams. Therefore, throughout the story, I have elected to use contemporary terms in many cases, although their term "Duat" seems to refer to what we call the astral plane. The identities of the various gods and goddesses that appear in the book are accurate in terms of their powers and their role in Egyptian religion, though, for the most part, I have called them by their more well-known Greek names, e.g., Isis instead of Sothis, Osiris instead of Sahu, Horus instead of Horakti. This was done in hopes of providing my readers with a more familiar terminology and to avoid any confusion about what is being discussed.

The story is fictional, for it must be so. Whether or not the gods and goddesses of ancient Egypt came to the Earth, literally, from another and distant star system, my personal belief in this possibility—indeed probability—gives "life" to the circumstances and consequences such a scenario would support. *The Second Coming of the Star Gods* provided me as a teacher and storyteller an opportunity to unleash my imagination and to apply its fruits to a real time, a real place, with real and fictional characters.

In ancient Egypt, Inundation occurred between the months of June and September—no specific date. The floodwaters would not reach the Cairo area until September. As for the Egyptian calendar and Sirius, astronomers observed that the annual inundation of the Nile commenced at the heliacal rise of Sirius, the first day the star appeared before sunrise. No exact date is given. Every 1,461 years a new Sothic (Sirius rising cycle) began when the rising of Sirius occurred on the exact date of the new year. So, the rising of Sirius, Inundation, and the Egyptian new year are the same as far as I can determine.

However, what with the frequent discovery of new evidence, the reader will have to decide if my story embodies as much reality as it does imagination. In these times in which we are currently living, our knowledge of the ancient Egyptians, Mayans, Native Americans, and others has valuable and direct applications to help us appreciate the value and power of what is going on in our world. It provides us a way to deal with the current cosmic, galactic, and planetary energies and alignments. It is in that spirit that I present this story of the Holy Order of Star Priests and Priestesses, the star kings of ancient Egypt, and their mystical worlds.

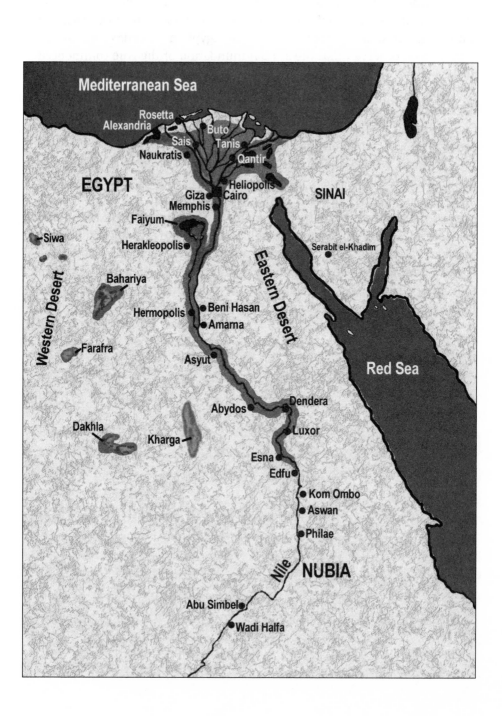

Chapter One

Journey to Heliopolis

The long journey would soon be over. Rashid and his family had secured space on a cargo vessel sailing north from Abydos to the city of Heliopolis in the Delta. For days the trip up the Nile had provided Rashid and his wife, Bata, and their children, Khem and Atef, with endless sights of what life was like outside their beloved Abydos. They saw desert dunes on one side, oases and fertile fields on the other during their daily sojourn on the thirst-quenching river. The travelers saw peasant men herding camels, sailed by countless villages with their meager huts nestled along the water's edge, and smelled the smoke wafting from cooking fires through groves of date palms, mixed with odors of animal dung, roasting fish and fowl, and the hot, parched dust of the arid land. Children played joyfully in every village. Women pounded clothes on rocks at the river's edge, while engaging in lively chatter about the latest news. Water buffalo walked in circles, endlessly pushing turnstiles to irrigate the crops. Village after village floated by, each a stage upon which the drama of the daily lives of the *fellahin*, the most common among the Egyptian people, unfolded.

Rashid was a fisherman by trade. In the cool winter months he helped build homes to supplement the family's income. Bata and Rashid were good parents who loved their children. They led quiet, honest lives. Aside from her duties as a wife and mother, Bata was a fine embroiderer and spent much of her spare time stitching colorful images on fine linen garments that were brought to her by women of the wealthier class.

Abydos was a flourishing metropolis that had long been an established religious center. The city belonged to Osiris. Temples erected in his honor dotted the landscape, but none was more impressive than the Grand Temple that served as a sort of cenotaph for the god.

Osiris was a good god. He had watched over Egypt for a long, long time, maybe forever. It seemed that He had been especially good to Abydos as it was the place where legends say his head was buried. Since Khem was very young she could remember the stories about Osiris told to her and Atef by their father. Rashid had always felt the need to make his children aware of the divinities, as they are the source of all things in life, including life itself. Above all else, Rashid had said, Osiris is the god of resurrection. To Khem this meant that no matter what might come, life continues.

One memory that stood out in Khem's mind was of being lifted to her father's shoulders during the Festival of Osiris so she could see the procession of priests pass by. Her eyes had drunk in the sight of the Osirian barque, the *weskhet*, bearing its sacred cargo to the temple to be purified. Ahead of the *fellahin* went the jackal-god, *Wepwawet*, the herald of Osiris. Scores of priests, court jesters, and common celebrants went before the royal barque, their songs and antics telling the stories of Osiris's conquests. Gods don't always have it so easy, she had thought. People want to harm or even kill them. Their lives are not always filled with the luxury and sanctity that one would expect to be accorded a deity. Though somewhat confusing, this was what had endeared Osiris to her from the earliest times she could remember.

Though the common people could not witness the purification of the god, as that took place within the Holy of Holies deep inside the temple, when the festival was over, Khem felt a strange sense of security just knowing that Osiris was cleansed and all was right with the world for another year. In her young mind, whenever trouble arose within the sphere of her life or when she became anxious over things that disturb a child's peace—a broken doll, a stubbed toe, a tear in her favorite sheath—she would remind herself that, come what might, Osiris reigned. He protected her and made things right. It was a thought that never failed to calm her fears and soothe her hurt feelings. Never did she suspect that such reassurance from the god himself did not cross the minds of others her age. To her, it was natural. It was a practice that would eventually determine the course of her life.

It was shortly after a festival day when, at the age of seven, Khem had a dream that made an indelible impression on her. Unbeknowst to the young dreamer, the dream contained the seeds of her future, the very future toward which the boat was now carrying her.

Rashid stepped out of the passenger cabin and stood at the prow of the small ship. The breeze caused by the boat's movement and the northerly airflow whipped gently through his black hair and caressed his tanned skin. Even on the water the day was hot. Throughout the day the sun's rays had reflected on the water like dancing diamonds on the river's surface. The dancing now ceased as on the western horizon the orange solar ball was sinking slowly behind the dunes. Deep in thought, Rashid wondered if he was doing the right thing. What would be his daughter's fate? She was his only daughter. Though he took great pride in his only son, Atef, Khem was his heart.

The decision to let Khem go into training at the Temple of the Sun in Heliopolis had been made. Now he and Bata must remain resigned to the decision to turn their daughter over to the High Priest at the Temple and to the High Star Priestess, Taret, who had beckoned the child telepathically with an authority that Rashid could not comprehend. The gods had called, and it was a summons that could not be ignored.

As Rashid's thoughts drifted back to earlier times, and he pondered his fatherly loss, Khem interrupted his bittersweet musings. With a tug on Rashid's arm she cried excitedly, "Come, Father! Come look at the great beast that has been killed!"

Rashid had been so lost in his thoughts that he had failed to notice the horde of noisy hunters hoisting a bloated hippo carcass from the river. Snapped back to the present, Rashid followed as the girl pulled him to the rear of the boat where they watched until the hunters and their giant quarry faded from view. The sight brought back memories to Rashid, memories of his own dream unrealized. There was a time when, as a boy, he had dreamt of being a great hunter. There would be no quarry too elusive, no beast too strong, none too smart to escape him. But, alas, these were but dreams. His days had been spent hauling his catch from the bounty of the river in order to provide for his family, an honorable task for an honorable man.

"One more night, Father, and we will arrive in Heliopolis."

Khem knew she would not get much sleep this night. Her head was filled with expectation and images of what it would be like to live in the Temple. Even at the tender age of twelve she had known it was her destiny to learn the wisdom of the stars. Now, three years later, she knew being at the Temple of the Sun, training as a Star Priestess, was where she had to be.

As twilight came, Bata and Atef joined Khem and Rashid on deck. The Nile was a mirror reflecting the pink and gold of the sunset. There was a cool breeze and the pre-night air was sweet. No one spoke. Each was deep in thought about what the next day would bring. It was the day they would arrive in Heliopolis, the day Khem would turn herself and her life over to the gods. Objections and anticipation, if they were present, did not show on the faces of the four. There were only quiet thoughts. . . .

Khem woke at the crack of dawn. As she washed her face and brushed her hair, she pondered fragments of a dream of a tiny lion cub rolling around on a grass mat, a shiny bronze mirror, and a small aging woman clad in a plain linen sheath with a circular gold pendant hanging on a chain over her heart.

Neither Khem nor any member of her family had ever been to the Delta region. The Temple of the Sun was familiar to her in the way a fabled place is when one has heard about it countless times. Bata scurried about the cabin gathering the bedclothes and stuffing them into a large cotton garment bag. She had not slept much, and fatigue, born from insomnia and charged emotions, showed on her face.

"Hurry, Mother!" Khem urged. Bata seemed to think that moving slowly would make time stand still. As a mother, she clearly resisted what lay in store. She hated losing the daughter she loved so dearly, but she knew that the command of the gods had to be obeyed.

Reluctantly, Bata slipped a fresh clean sheath over her head and began combing the night tangles from her hair. Though Khem had combed her own hair earlier, she had done so in haste, so her mother did it again. From a cosmetic bag, Bata took a long strip of ribbon. Pulling the girl's long locks into a bundle at the nape of her neck, she tied the ribbon to secure it, leaving the ribbon's ends hanging loosely, entwining with the dark silky hair. Khem took newly woven papyrus sandals from her own clothes sack and slid them on her feet. Bata then busied herself with lining her own and her daughter's eyes with green kohl, dabbing a touch of sweet lotus perfume oil behind their ears.

"What's going on in here?"

The sound of Rashid's voice broke the rhythm of the dressing ritual and jerked Bata back from the edge of the tears she had wanted to give in to since the moment dawn had chased off the night's shadows. "We are almost ready," she replied. Before the words were out of her mother's mouth, Khem ran and flung herself into her father's arms. "Father, we are almost there, are we not? Can you see the city? Has Atef awakened? Are the—"

"Wait! Slow down! I can only answer one question at a time, my daughter."

"Oh, I am sorry, Father," Khem replied quickly. "It is time. I know it will not be long before we arrive. We must not miss a moment! We must hurry to the deck. I want to see the city, Father. I must!" Her voice became higher pitched as the anticipation of their arrival in Heliopolis shot waves of adrenaline through her. This was the day she had looked forward to and dreamed about for three long years, the day she would go to the Temple to learn about the stars.

The stars had always fascinated Khem. They were her friends. Since she was a child she had known that the sky gods held the future of the land and its people in their power. She must learn about the Star Gods. She had to know about the great Celestial River and the mysteries of the night. She knew it was what she had been born to do.

"Atef is waiting in the dining cabin," Rashid said. "He has accepted an offer from the head oarsman to have a morning meal. Come, let us go eat."

Food was the last thing on Khem's mind. But when she sank her teeth into the sweet figs, she realized how hungry she was. When they finished the meal, the four washed their hands in the clay washbowls that had been placed on the table. Rashid left a few faience beads to pay for the food, and folded the leftover loaves of bread and a few dried dates into a napkin he pulled from his clothes bag. These would come in handy as a snack later.

The river, Atur, was particularly wide in the place the boat was approaching, and it rounded into a slight bend. Ahead, the city loomed into view. The sight of it so overwhelmed Khem that she could only fix her eyes in silent wonderment. As she stared, hypnotized by the sight, memories of a dream she had dreamed a long time ago, indeed the dream that had revealed her fate to her, replayed itself in her mind. The dream had come when she was seven. She was now fifteen. The images had been vivid. Each figure and symbol and even the sounds had burned themselves into her memory in a way no other dream or waking experience ever had during the few years of her life.

Drifting off to sleep after she and Atef had had a fun-filled day playing with a day-old water buffalo calf, Khem had entered the dream world that carried her into a never-before-seen-realm, the domain of Nut, the Sky Goddess. As she awakened into her night vision, Khem found herself being led down what seemed an endless passageway suspended in space, with giant stone columns on both sides. This passageway was not solid, but composed of countless stars afire with power. No one can walk on this, she had thought, sure that she would fall through the star road and be swallowed up by whatever monsters might lurk below.

Two women, one on each side of her, guided her down this path of stars. Each was clad in the softest of linen sheaths, the seams of which were stitched with gold threads. Their skin was the color of rich cream. As the Star Priestesses guided Khem across the star bridge, suddenly a golden throne appeared; first it was empty, the next moment it was occupied by a beautiful goddess in an aura of shimmering gold light.

The deity's garment was white with a gold-colored sash around the bodice beneath her breasts. Her transparent skin revealed myriad stars inside; her eyes were like emeralds; her straight black hair hung loose to her shoulders. On her head was a crown fashioned into a five-pointed star.

Encircling her delicate neck was a magnificent pectoral of sparkling gem-stones. In her right hand was a staff carved from sycamore wood. Alabaster pillars, each topped with a pyramidion carved from black Star Stone, flanked the sides of the great throne.

As the resplendent image of the sky goddess stabilized in Khem's mind, four more female sky spirits appeared, two on each side of the great throne. On the right stood Neith, the goddess of the East, and Uatchet of the North. Nekhebet, the mistress of the southern sky, and Hathor of the western, completed the Holy Four. At the feet of the five star women was an image of the Earth shown suspended in space. Khem felt as if the beauty and power of the divinities would take her breath away, and for an instant a wave of fear threatened to shock her awake and return her to the darkness of her bedchamber.

A telepathic beam of calming energy brought the girl lovingly into the mental embrace of the Great Goddess and the fear was banished. The dreamer, at once a part of and yet separate from the holy presences, heard a voice speak to her. As she spoke, the voice resounded from all directions, penetrating every cell of her being:

> I am Nut, Goddess of the Star World. Welcome to my place in your mind, my little one.

The words vibrated through Khem. She felt herself being drawn into the sanctity of the goddess's aura, a place of warmth.

> Great dangers are about to befall the land of Egypt, the ancient soil that first received knowledge of the will of the Ennead. It is your destiny to know these things. The sleeping King knows not his enemy; an enemy who is flesh of his flesh, brother and priest. Know and remember the name, Sokar. It is he, who comes from the Underworld, he who manufactures the very bones of the king, he who knows the magical formulas of the sacred oils. It is Sokar who seeks to wear the crown of Egypt upon his head, he who wishes to hold the Great Scepter. He is darkness and light. His light beckons all things to grow; his darkness destroys and causes all to die unless his will be served.
>
> It is you, my Star Child, who must someday help those who will reveal the presence of the enemy. We, the goddesses of the heavens, will watch over you and protect you. We will guide you to the place and time of your destiny. Be it so.

As the deity's words vibrated through the dream capsule in Khem's mind, the air began to crackle with millions of volts of electricity. A horrific clap of astral thunder immediately turned the child's dream into a nightmare and rent the image of the Sacred Five. Before Khem there now appeared a powerful male figure.

He was big and strong, his muscular headless body as hard as a rock and clothed in a kilt of pure gold. Two cobras were coiled around his ankles, their hoods spread wide with hissing sounds spewing from their gaping jaws. As the dreamer watched in horror, the man-demon sprouted huge falcon wings from the blades of his wide shoulders. A scream lodged in Khem's throat so tightly it threatened to choke the life out of her. As quickly as the image had appeared, it vanished, leaving her momentarily suspended in a netherworld of darkness that, instead of frightening her, soothed her and restored her uneasy sleep to a peaceful slumber.

When Khem woke up the next morning, the powerful dream visions had faded. There were only the emotionally charged remnants of a journey, of spoken words and silent words, of figures with no form, fragments.

That fateful dream had occurred again recently; the same vision of the sky goddess and her consorts, the same prophetic words, the same demonic god-man suddenly appearing. This time Khem would not forget it. It would be an otherworldly scene she would replay in her mind time and time again, each time pondering its meaning. She knew it spoke of dangers that would someday befall her beloved Egypt, of things destined to be. She knew it in her soul.

Standing now at the prow of the boat as it plowed steadily through the waters of the Nile, Khem turned to Atef, the excitement of their arrival in Heliopolis causing her voice to sound shrill.

"There it is, Atef. There is Heliopolis. We are finally here."

Atef stood head and shoulders above his sister. He was almost eighteen, and though three years older than Khem, he had felt a strong closeness to his sister all through their childhood; a protectiveness that sometimes had a parental quality. There was no rivalry between them. Theirs was a relationship that was mutually supportive and loving. Khem looked up to Atef. She admired his physical strength and agility, and loved to watch him shoot at targets with his bow. He almost never missed, and that made her proud. More than once, much to Atef's dismay, she had volunteered her brother to show off his talents as an archer for her and her friends' entertainment. She wanted to go with him wherever he went, and often proved to be an unwelcome pest for Atef when he was in the mood to safeguard his privacy.

But for all her veneration of Atef, it was his loyalty to her and their parents that was the apex of her love. She knew of his deepest secret ambition to become a scribe of Thoth at the temple in the very city that now lay straight ahead. She also knew that it was her brother's loyalty and love for their father that had led him to sacrifice his dream for the future. The fishing business was hard work, and Rashid could not do it alone. The money they earned depended upon the amount of fish that could be scooped from the river in a day. Two could earn more than one, and to Atef it was that simple. He had chosen to remain in Abydos to work with his father to catch and sell fish in the city's streets.

Khem's acceptance—indeed, her "summons" to the Temple of the Sun, where she would train to become a Star Priestess—had done its part to enhance the family's status, if not financially, at least socially. The word had gotten around Abydos that Khem would soon be leaving for Heliopolis. Well-wishers had come by in the last few days, bringing small gifts like fig loaves, kohl, an ivory comb, and ribbons for her hair.

As the boat drew closer to the city, Khem's excitement shifted into solemn anticipation. The roofs of some of the buildings in the municipality, along with the tops of date palms and various other trees, were now visible above the walls that surrounded the city. Sycamores, some huge, grew plentifully along the riverbank, their branches providing blessed shade from the blistering sun. The trees towered over the marshes, a rich feeding ground for the herons and storks that dipped their beaks in search of bugs and fish. The city's smells reached her nostrils. Sounds of humanity, barking dogs, and braying stock animals sent waves of eagerness through her. She wanted to see it all.

The boat's crew began to prepare the vessel for docking, forcing the family to retreat into the main cabin out of harm's way. The thick canvas sails were lowered, and the large ropes that would secure the ship to the river pilings were dragged from their storage bins. As the craft drew closer to land, Khem could see the dockworkers waiting on the shore to help tow in the boat. The boat eased into its berth between the flat river barges and an assortment of private vessels. The boat secured, the captain motioned for Rashid and his family to leave the cabin and go ashore.

Rashid and Atef gathered the clothes sacks and the reed basket containing Bata's needles, tapestry threads, and other notions. Khem watched as a thick plank was lowered from the boat to meet the land. The large vessels were a frequent and familiar sight along the lengthy course of the Nile. Vessels like these brought luxuries not native to the country to the wealthy, to Pharaoh, and to the court. Common people traveled as passengers on the cargo boats, making the vessels a major business enterprise.

By the time the family stepped onto the land, the sun was hanging like a blast furnace over the city, its glare washing out the colors and making the desert and the man-made structures melt into one. The moment Khem's feet touched the soil she felt connected with the city. She was where she was supposed to be, and she knew it.

The ambiance of Heliopolis was similar to that of Abydos. Doubling as private residences, workshops built of mud bricks were everywhere. On the ground floor craftsmen produced their wares. Some buildings contained kitchens and bakeries; others served as cattle stalls and storerooms. On the second floor were the owner's private apartments. The two levels of the white-washed structures were connected by an outer stairway leading up to a flat roof. Wooden pillars on stone pedestals supported the roofs.

Khem and her family made their way through the crowded streets. The gardens alongside many of the houses contained palms, pomegranates, sycamores, acacias, and various other shrubs, some of which concealed gazebos covered with trailing vines. As the family neared the city's main square and the wealthier neighborhoods, the landscaping became more elaborate with pools for fish and graceful lotus and other water plants. Some dwellings clustered around a common courtyard. The more prosperous homes had sun-dried brick walls surrounding them, while others were built from quarried stone.

The noonday air was filled with smoke from the cooking fires throughout Heliopolis. Vendors hawked their wares, food merchants beckoned passersby to sample their morsels, and the sounds of people chattering and children playing added to the ordered confusion. Business traders hurried by, hauling their goods from one part of the city to another. Always eager to replenish her needlework supplies, Bata could not resist stopping in front of a small cottage where a woman sat behind a display of fine needles and colorful threads on a large reed mat.

Khem's eagerness was apparent. Tugging anxiously on her mother's hand, she exclaimed, "Come, Mother! We must get to the Temple!"

"Be patient, my sister," Atef injected. "The Temple will not go away!"

Atef had known of his sister's coming to Heliopolis for some time, and he had no doubt that it was right. Still, he had pondered the changes in the family and in his own life that her leaving would bring. He would miss Khem. He also had more than a slight twinge of envy that Khem was able to follow her calling. Atef's desire to enter Temple life burned in him, but it would have to wait. There would be time, he told himself, though secretly he had doubts.

Bata rejoined her family at the stall of an animal vendor who kept birds in reed cages. They were for sale, along with an assortment of long-legged, skinny cats who would be used as mousers. An aging dog slept at the edge of the stall. Her curiosity aroused, Khem skipped over to the menagerie. Her eye caught sight of a tiny lion cub tethered to a wooden stake. Khem kneeled down and held out her hand for the cub to sniff. She had never seen a lion before. She was mesmerized. Reaching out to touch the coarse fur yielded a quick response from the baby cat, which rolled over to let the girl rub its belly.

"Oh, Mother, look at this baby. It is so beautiful."

Bata was not as trusting as her daughter, and led Khem away from what she perceived as potential danger. "You will be scratched! Come!"

Rashid and Atef exchanged glances at her remark that revealed to them how difficult it was for Bata to relinquish her position as mother in her daughter's life. Khem's entering the Temple would be a big change for all of them, but especially for Bata.

Rounding the eastern corner of the city square, the family saw a small palace that served as the king's residence during the ceremonial season. Khufu was a good king who ruled the people with diplomacy and quiet reserve. His name meant "protect me," and the majority of people felt that he was their protector, and in that way a father figure, and a guardian of their beloved land, Egypt.

Khufu had protected the country from invaders and was a force to be reckoned with by any would-be plunderer. The son of Sneferu and Queen Hetepheres I, the Pharaoh envisioned Egypt as the earthly domain of the gods. He had vowed to establish the country as an empire fit for the divinities to whom he was devoted. Khufu understood his own psychic connection with the god Osiris, and rumor had it that the burden of his position and the responsibilities that went along with that commitment bordered on being an obsession with him.

Looking up at the secondary royal residence now, Khem wondered about the man who lived in the palace. Would she ever get to see him? What was it like to live in such a splendid place? Was the king really a god? How many wives did he have? What was it like to live in a harem?

As the family walked past the palace, Atef pointed to a feature of the facade of the great house, the Window of Appearances.

"That is where Pharaoh shows himself," he said.

Looking up, Khem imagined that she could see Khufu there, wearing the Crown of the North upon his head. "I have heard that he gives gifts to those who do special deeds," she remarked, imagining what sort of delightful trinkets such gifts might be. A short distance away from the palace stood the sixty-foot-high wall that enclosed the Temple of the Sun. Seeing it for the first time, Khem stopped and stared, her thoughts focused only upon savoring the moment.

Seeing the wall sent a thrill through her and at the same time stirred a foreboding. It was a feeling the girl had never once associated with her future in Heliopolis. The feeling passed as quickly as it came.

The gates to the great complex were guarded by soldiers and by the stone representatives of the gods. On either side of the multistoried doorway stood a huge granite statue of Horus, the Great Lord God of Heaven.

Rashid went up to the pylon gate. It would not be appropriate for either his wife or children to approach the guards. Taking a deep breath, he approached the head sentry. Reaching into a pocket of his ankle-length *galabayya*, he pulled out a small papyrus scroll that was rolled into a cylinder and tied with a thin strip of leather.

Handing the scroll to the guard, Rashid stepped back respectfully while the man read the summons requesting the presence of Rashid's daughter at the Temple of the Sun, where she would begin her apprenticeship as a priestess in the Holy Order of Nut. The document had been signed and sealed by Meri-ib, the High Priest himself. "Nothing will ever be the same again" was the thought that passed through Rashid's mind now, as it had so many times since the summons had arrived. He watched as the guard read. Satisfied of its authenticity, the sentry beckoned for the gates of the huge entryway to be opened. Rashid waved to his waiting family and they proceeded past the granite Horus statues through the gates.

The first thing they saw was a long avenue of stone sphinxes. At the end stood the embodiment of the temple's power: the pyramidion set atop a great obelisk whose sides were inscribed with writings from the sacred texts. The giant stone needle and its meteorite capstone captured Khem's attention like a magnet, causing her to have the sensation of levitating. Next, Rashid and his family proceeded down the line of sphinxes past the obelisk, and passed through the next set of gates into a massive plaza. Once inside, it was apparent that, like the city, the Temple was a busy place, a self-sustaining, living entity. Priests, servants, and couriers continuously passed along the avenues, all busy with their duties.

All wore loose, long white robes with the insignias of Ra and Horus embroidered at the center of the chest or on the upper arm of the short right sleeve. Some were barefoot, while others wore papyrus sandals that laced around the ankles, or slip-ons that made a soft clapping sound against their heels when they walked. A few, perhaps those of higher ranks, wore gold sashes over cloaks with green emblems of the royal Crook and Flail stitched on the back.

These must be Pharaoh's personal priests, Khem thought. She turned in time to catch her mother's admiring eye as Bata inspected the embroidered symbols.

The chatter among the people in the courtyard was lively but subdued, the ambiance of tranquil order. Khem drank in the scene's minutest details. They moved slowly toward the center of the plaza and a large rectangular pool with steps on each end leading down into the water. The largest papyrus plants Khem had ever seen grew profusely in the pool, along with various types of water lilies. The courtyard was paved with limestone and surrounded by red granite columns whose shafts and capitals were carved to resemble giant papyrus plants, adding a stately air to the plaza. Attached to the west side stood another small palace used by the king and his family as a dressing chamber during festivals and ceremonies.

The guard at the main gate had instructed Rashid to proceed to the upper-level courtyard. So he and his family ascended the wide limestone stairway at the far end of the pool. At the top they found themselves in another court, framed by a colonnade opening onto the temple's hypostyle hall. In the center were seven huge clay pots each containing a palm with graceful fronds that together formed a potted garden. These surrounded a colossal stone statue of the hawk-headed, human-bodied Horus. Its great head was adorned with a disc that had been molded from gold; the god was clad in a golden kilt of equal brilliance and he held a staff in his left hand.

The monument cast a solemn mood over the courtyard, which was a much less busy place than the lower plaza. The hypostyle hall led into the Holy of Holies. Numerous shrines and storage rooms that held the temple's treasures and cult objects surrounded this inner sanctum. Dozens more structures, mostly warehouses and offices for the priests, scribes, and servants, occupied the upper part of the complex.

As the family stood gazing at the impressive Horus figure, fascinated by its size and power, an elderly priest walked up to them. The cleric was accompanied by a tall, thin, younger man dressed in the typical servant's garb of a plain coarse linen ankle-length skirt with a fold of material thrown over his shoulders.

"Good day, my countryman," the priest spoke to Rashid. "I am Senna. This is my loyal servant, Pepi. The Chief Priest, Meri-ib, is expecting you, as is the High Priestess, Taret." Then, turning to the girl, the man smiled. "And you must be Khem."

Khem stepped forward and politely allowed Senna to take her hand. As her eyes met his, she saw a gentleness that relaxed her in his presence.

With a sweeping gaze that acknowledged Rashid, Bata, and Atef, the priest said, "You must be tired and hungry from your journey. Come. Pepi will show you to your quarters."

The servant reached down to pick up the pieces of baggage, but Atef quickly grabbed them himself. He was not used to having a servant for such menial tasks.

Without further ado, Senna said, "You, Khem, come with me. I will take you to the dormitory where you can get some rest and meet your chamber servant."

The moment had come. Khem was being separated from her family. She knew, as they did, that her future had just begun. Her past was behind her from this moment on, and she stood at the threshold of all the tomorrows of the rest of her life.

As her family was led away by another servant, Khem followed Senna from the courtyard down a corridor with rooms on either side. As they passed each door, Khem could see that the rooms were all the same.

"This will be your home, Khem. All the women who are in training to become Star Priestesses live here," he said.

Though Khem hid it well, Senna detected her apprehension. When the pair arrived at the end of the hallway, Senna stopped in front of a doorway whose door was a curtain of clay beads that hung from the timber lintel that formed the top part of the wooden archway. The priest drew the beads aside and beckoned to Khem to move inside.

The small room was lit by light that streamed in from a single window and an open doorway that led onto a tiny veranda. The doorway had the same type of beaded curtain, which had been pulled off to one side so air could get into the room. Off the main room was another smaller one that contained a grass mat bed on the floor, a chair and table, and a washstand with pitcher and washing bowl. Senna explained that this was her servant's room.

The floors inside the dormitory were of hardened sand covered by thick grass mats that gave off a slightly sweet fragrance. The larger room was sparsely furnished with a wooden table beneath the windowsill and beside it a matching chair. In a corner stood a stack of three large papyrus storage baskets, their flaps easily opened for clothes and other personal belongings. The wooden bed frame held a linen mattress case filled with soft reeds and grasses. An oil lamp sat on a tiny table on the bed's left side.

As Khem stood looking around, Pepi came into the room and, bowing first to his master, Senna, and then to Khem, he placed her clothes bag on the floor by the bed. Making several trips, the servant brought a clay pitcher filled with fresh water and a washing bowl, both of which he put on the dressing table. He freed the curtain from the wall inside the patio door, the beads clinking as they swung over the opening, and he placed a tray of barley cakes and a bowl of figs on the bedside table, then put a soft roll of marsh reeds covered with a linen pillowslip at the head of the bed.

"There now," Senna said. "Do you have what you need to make yourself comfortable?"

Khem nodded approvingly, but said nothing. It would take some time to adjust to her surroundings, and to know what, if anything, she needed.

"Thank you, Pepi. Go. Fetch the servant girl. It will soon be time for us to go. This young woman needs rest."

Turning to the newcomer, Senna took her by the hand and led her over to the edge of the bed and sat her down. Looking into her eyes, the priest said, "I am happy that you are here, Khem. It is a good thing to be called into the service of the Great Ones. They never choose anyone without reason. Perhaps you think you know the reason, or perhaps you are here on faith. In the end it matters little. The *Neteru* have led you here, and the gods will reveal their purpose to you in due time. Until then, apply yourself to the studies of the sacred texts. Learn from Taret, and listen well. Knowledge of the stars is an admirable but difficult pursuit. Put all other things aside, and grieve not for the past. Your life here will be a good one. It will meet all your needs. You will see."

They were interrupted at that moment when Pepi reentered the room with a petite brown-skinned girl in tow who looked to be about Khem's age. Bowing to Senna, Pepi grasped the girl's hand and pulled her gently towards the priest, who smiled at her in the same fatherly way he had greeted Khem.

Pepi spoke. "This is Akhi. Come, child."

The priest put his hands on the servant girl's shoulders and turned her to face Khem. "This is Akhi, your servant girl, Khem. She will attend to your needs. I am sure the two of you will get along fine."

"We will leave you now." Senna motioned to Pepi that it was time to leave. "I will see you at the evening meal, my child. Now get some rest and freshen yourself. Good day, Akhi."

The priest walked out of the room, leaving the two girls alone in an awkward silence. Khem would have felt better if she had just been introduced to a new friend or roommate. But a servant? She had never had a servant before.

Akhi stood motionless, waiting, Khem wasn't sure for what. "I will unpack your bags, my mistress. You rest."

Khem did not need much encouragement. She was tired. Besides, taking a nap would provide a welcome opportunity for her to be alone with the thoughts and feelings racing around in her mind....

Later when she woke up, the Sun was casting a long shadow on the wall across from her bed. Sitting up, Khem saw that Akhi had unpacked the clothes bags and put their contents away in the storage baskets. A small pot of tea was brewing over a small brazier placed on the floor near the doorway that opened onto the veranda.

Akhi poured a cup and offered it to Khem, who drank the sweet beverage thirstily. It revived her quickly. The servant girl then busied herself pouring water into the washing bowl on the dressing table. She had already laid out a fresh sheath and placed it with Khem's sandals, which she had slapped together to clean them of street dust. An array of cosmetic jars was arranged on the dressing table alongside the washing bowl, comb, several kohl pots, and bottles of perfume oils.

"I thought you might wish to unpack these things yourself, mistress," Akhi said, handing Khem a small bag. Inside were gifts from family, friends, and well-wishers in Abydos, and a few more personal items, some of which she had had since she was a child.

Opening the bag, Khem began taking the contents out one by one. Hair ribbons, a necklace of beads, a small scarab pendant tied to a strip of linen, a palette of kohl, and the gift of a papyrus and a palm pen from Atef. He told her that when she learned to write she could use these to send him letters. Dipping into the bag again, Khem brought out a little package wrapped in a piece of the finest dyed linen. She carefully unwrapped the bundle, revealing a six-inch green statue of Hapi, the Nile god; her paternal grandmother, Henna, had given Khem this on her third birthday.

Khem loved the Nile. The river was magical and mysterious. Placing the statue on her bedside table, she reached back into the bag and pulled out a waist sash that her mother had embroidered with beautifully colored papyrus plants and lotus blossoms. The ends of the linen belt had been frayed, forming an exquisite fringe. Khem hugged the sash close to her chest, her heart flooding with love for Bata. The feelings reminded her of her family, and made her wonder where they were.

"I must find my mother and father and Atef. I wish to see them," she exclaimed anxiously.

"Do not worry, my mistress. You will see them at dinner. It is time now for you to bathe and ready yourself."

Akhi's voice had an edge of firmness that caused Khem to respond promptly. She let Akhi disrobe her, and proceed to wash away the day's dust and sweat, first from her hands and face, under the hair on the back of her neck, down her body, and finally her feet. It brought back memories of the baths her mother had given her as a child.

Akhi helped Khem slip a clean dress over her head and handed her the special sash, which Khem tied around her slim waist. She then strapped on the newly cleaned sandals. The servant girl then bade Khem be seated in the chair that she had placed in the center of the room, and proceeded to comb her mistress's long black hair until it shone. She slipped a ribbon underneath the heavy locks and behind her ears and tied it into a dainty bow on top of her head. Taking a kohl pot from the dressing table, Akhi applied the makeup to Khem's eyes, and put a dash of red ochre on her cheeks. "There. You are ready."

The girls looked at each other, warmth passing between them. They knew their respective roles had been established, and it felt all right.

Just then a light tap came on the wall outside the door. Akhi opened the curtain and stepped aside with a slight bow as Senna walked into the room.

"I have come to escort you to dinner, Khem," he said. "Your family has arrived and they are waiting for you in the dining hall. Come."

The priest reached out his hand in a polite gesture, and together the two departed.

The dining room was a long rectangular hall off the lower courtyard, featuring a short-legged wooden table that stretched almost the length of the room. Soft cushions were placed on both sides and at each end of the table. Upon entering the room, Khem immediately spotted her parents and Atef, and quickly made her way to embrace them. The three greeted Senna in a friendly manner.

Looking about the room, Khem saw that there were several other girls who looked to be about her age, as well as a few older women. As Khem and her family and Senna settled themselves at the table, a short, muscular Nubian servant woman came into the room. Clapping her hands twice, she announced in a strong voice: "The mistress Taret, High Priestess of the Holy Order of Nut, has arrived."

Following the lead of the others present, Khem and her family stood up in anticipation of the entry of the chief priestess. The room fell silent when through the arched entryway came a slender, almost slight, aging woman dressed in a long, flowing white robe topped by a full-length cobalt-blue cloak that hung gracefully from her shoulders. Clasped at her throat was a gold Eye of Horus. The woman's hands and feet were as small as a child's, her face creased with the lines of her years. Her brown eyes were large and resembled bottomless pools of dark water. The Nubian who had announced the High Priestess guided her to a low, cushioned saddle chair where the woman seated herself.

"Please be seated," Taret said, her voice soft, full of the sound of resolve suitable to her office. With a wave of her hand, the Nubian servant beckoned toward a side door. Serving women entered, bearing bowls and trays of food.

The table was soon filled, and the women placed helpings of dates, figs, roasted fowl, fish, and loaves in the bowls before each person. Most of the conversation was limited to small talk between those seated closest to each other. Talking with her parents, Khem learned that they had been provided with resting quarters for the time they would be at the temple. Her parents had rested, but Atef had elected to spend his time wandering the city in the temple's vicinity.

Khem studied a woman seated to the right of the High Priestess. She was plump with a pleasant round face and dark hair and dark features. She wore a wig of shoulder-length hair with a headband across her brow.

She wore rings on every finger except for the thumbs; heavy gold and silver bracelets clinked on her wrists; a long ankh pendant hung on a gold chain around her neck. The woman (Khem had heard her called Ani) was engaged in conversation with Taret. Khem felt a strong attraction to Ani. As she stared at her, the priestess returned her gaze, causing Khem to look away, embarrassed that the woman had caught her staring.

Looking about the room, Khem continued to take stock. Three girls, who she assumed were apprentice priestesses, were engaged in a lively discussion punctuated by whispers and giggles. One girl who sat directly across from Khem was picking at her food. She seemed to be lost in her thoughts and had an air of sadness about her. Khem wondered who she was and what was wrong.

Two other women sat at the opposite end of the table from Taret. Khem could hear bits of their chatter about the coming Full Moon and got the impression they were discussing a ritual that would soon take place. She also heard that Pharaoh, also referred to as "King," was coming, but could not catch the details. A sixth young woman seated to Khem's right was talking with Bata. The girl, Kasut, had also come to Heliopolis from Abydos.

When everyone had finished eating, the serving women cleared the table and brought in cups of beer. Not long after, Taret and Ani rose from their seats and left the room. As soon as they had gone, the Nubian servant came over to Khem and relayed the message that she was to meet with Taret the following day.

Khem knew that her parents and brother would be boarding a cargo vessel for their return trip to Abydos at dawn. She had been so wrapped up in the excitement and joy of the trip and her arrival at the Temple that she had not allowed herself to think of her family's departure.

The family said good evening to Senna and left the eating hall to stroll through the lower courtyard and out onto a large patio that faced the western desert. The setting of the sun had painted the sky purple and gold. A slight breeze rustled the leaves of the giant sycamore whose branches shaded the area.

Khem and Bata seated themselves on a bench beside the tree's huge trunk. Rashid and Atef sat cross-legged on the ground in front of them. Each of them knew that these would be the last moments they would spend together for a long time. Few words seemed appropriate. It was Bata who finally spoke.

"I dread leaving you, my daughter, but I know I must," she began.

"Oh, Mother," Khem interrupted, only to have Bata press her forefinger to her lips to silence her.

"You have no need for a mother now. You have grown into a young woman. I will miss you, but I will sleep well, knowing that you are in good hands. Osiris will watch over you. This I know."

Reaching into a linen purse, Bata took out a small bronze mirror that had been polished to a high luster. Its handle was fashioned like a papyrus stem, and the reflection disk was nestled in a cradle formed by two bronze leaves that spread out on either side.

"It is beautiful, Mother."

"Yes. It belonged to my mother, Memu, who was dead long before you were born. She would have wanted you to have it. Like you, my daughter, she was a seer. She knew that someday I would birth a daughter who would follow the way of the stars. Take it. May it show you beautiful visions of yourself each time you look into it." Tears welled up in Bata's eyes as she placed the mirror in Khem's hands.

"Thank you, Mother. I will treasure it always."

The moment seemed like the right time for the family to part company. Nothing more could or needed to be said. Bata's cheeks were wet with tears as she clasped her daughter. Rashid embraced her too. Then, taking Bata gently by the hand, they walked away, leaving Atef and his sister alone.

"I will miss you, Atef. Please do not forget to put out seed for the birds . . . and . . . and don't forget to water the fig trees . . . and . . ." The girl's voice trailed off as she sobbed.

"Do not concern yourself with such things, my sister. You have much more to think about. This is a good time, so do not worry."

With those words, Atef kissed each of his sister's cheeks now wet with salty tears. Never before had Khem experienced the shedding of tears of joy and sadness at the same time.

By the time she had wiped away the tears, Atef was gone. For an instant, fears, doubt, and apprehension came over her, but they were soon replaced by a sense of freedom.

Night had come to the desert, and the sky was filled with twinkling lights alive with the breath of the gods. The Moon, nearly full, was coming up over the horizon. A peace came over the girl seated alone in the darkness. Tomorrow would come all too soon, and she was tired.

She stood up slowly and picked up her mirror. As she held it in front of her, its shiny surface caught the reflection of the light of the Moon. Was it her imagination or did she hear a voice say, "I, Thoth, am watching you"?

It did not matter. Her heart was full. She was at peace. The moonlight lit her steps as she made her way into the courtyard and up the steps to the upper level and her room. Tomorrow she would deal with whatever came, but now all she wanted to do was sleep.

Chapter Two

The Holy Order of Nut

The Sun Temple of Heliopolis glittered in the sunlight. Erected on a mound for the worship of the Sun god Ra, the compound served as the major religious center of Egypt. The great obelisk, the first one Khem had ever seen, rested on the original rise, called the Primeval Mound, regarded to be the first land on Earth. Legend had it that the obelisk's capstone, carved out of iron meteorite, had fallen onto Egypt's soil eons before. The fall of the "sky stone" had been ordained by the Sky Gods. They had designated Giza as the place where the celestial realm of the gods would be replicated on Earth.

Since those early days, the temple had become a city unto itself. The priesthood consisted of more than a thousand men and women whose duties included recording the daily movements of the planets, Sun and Moon, keeping the calendar, and healing the sick. There were specialists among the different orders, one of whom was Chief Dream Priest Seku and those who worked with him to interpret dreams for Pharaoh and other high-ranking members of the royal court in the dream sanctuary. Ani, the Star Priestess Khem had been so curious about on her first night at the temple, was also a Dream Priestess whom Seku had trained. So adept was she at dream interpretation that the Chief Dream Priest had put Ani in charge of the sleep room where dream therapy and magic were available to all Egyptians.

The Temple of the Sun was the only temple that included among its priesthood the Holy Order of Nut, an elite group of women of various ages and social backgrounds. Commonly called Star Priestesses, the women were trained in astronomy, the keeping of the records of the risings and settings of the Sun and Moon, the activities of the "wandering stars" or planets, and the timing of rituals and other religious events. The priestesses also served as diviners of the important sky omens. They were the keepers of the star knowledge, and the protectors of the earthly realm of the Sky Gods. The only male who worked with the women was the aged Chief Star Priest, Caliph.

Of all the holy orders at Heliopolis, none was more celebrated or signif-icant, and at the same time more secretive, to the religious well-being of the country and the Egyptian people than these celebrants who were believed to be the direct descendants of a more ancient order. Its original members had been the human recipients of the stellar religion given by the Star Gods some five thousand years earlier. The sacred teachings and myths, as well as the magical formulas, spells, and practices that accompa-nied them, had been passed down orally through the lineage for fifty centuries. The order, known as the Followers of Horus, was housed at the Temple of the Sun, and their ancestors were the architects of and the reason for the temple having been built in the first place. The first priests of this order provided the design and oversaw the construction of the Sphinx and the pyramids on the Primeval Mound at Giza.

Now in the tenth year of his reign, Khufu was visited by Meri-ib, the High Priest of Heliopolis. Meri-ib had left Heliopolis and traveled to the capital city of Memphis to deliver a message in person, a not-so-common event. The Chief Priest had had a powerful vision during his annual seven-day ritual fast in which he prepared for the ceremonies that heralded the arrival of a new year. While in meditation in the central chapel, Meri-ib experienced the most profound spiritual encounter of his life when the god Thoth appeared before him.

The deity, who manifested as an ibis-headed male human, held a scribe's palette in one hand and a notched palm leaf pen in the other. Upon his head rested a silver disc topped by a crescent that symbolized the Moon. Thoth's long, curved beak glistened like polished ebony in the dim light of the inner sanctum. He was clothed only in a linen kilt secured around his waist by a dark metal sash.

The apparition struck Meri-ib dumb. Time stood still. With words that silently passed from the god's to the man's mind, Thoth transmitted knowledge to Meri-ib that contained a task the likes of which no human had been commanded to perform in thousands of years. Now, sitting across from the King of Egypt, the High Priest related the words that Thoth, Lord of the Holy Words, had spoken to him on that day:

I, Thoth, the Elder, the Master of Time, Consort of the Goddess Nut, come as a messenger of the great god Osiris. The time approaches when the Star Gods will come again, one by one, to bring new teachings and to once more activate the power of the Field of Monuments, the connector between Heaven and Earth. The ancient Star of Knowledge will be transmitting its divine force to the sons and daughters of Nut, the Sky Goddess, who shall in turn trust that lore to the incarnation of Osiris on Earth, the honorable Pharaoh, Khufu. It is he who must bring the original initiation chamber out of the prison that time has created and rescue it from the desert sands.

The entire world must be set in order for the return of the Star Gods. The star gates will open once again for you to receive transmissions from the Star Gods who are the spirits of the Pole Star of the North, the constellation Orion, the great star Sirius, and the stars of Ursa Major. The time has come for the Protector of Egypt, the Star God Osiris, Conqueror of a Million Years, to walk again upon the soil of Egypt so that the sacred land and its people will gain new, deeper knowledge about who and what they are and the nature of their mission in life.

The vision burned itself into Meri-ib's mind. He told Khufu that the apparition's hand had transformed into a gold Rod of Power, which the deity then passed over the Chief Priest's head.

Then, as suddenly as it had appeared, the apparition of Thoth vanished. Meri-ib could not move. Nor could he bring his mind to bear upon the reality of what had occurred. Slowly, as his wits returned, he was not sure if what he had seen and heard had been real or imaginary. The High Priest told Khufu that as he rose from the floor of the sanctuary, he observed a white feather in the center of the altar. It was this feather that he now removed from inside the sash around his waist and handed to the king. All initiates knew (as king, Khufu was an initiate) that a white feather was the object placed on the scales that weighed the deeds of the dead at the time of the Judgment of Souls, a ritual supervised by Thoth, and presided over by Osiris.

Khufu was silent. Taking the feather from Meri-ib, the Pharaoh eyed it as if it were the god himself he held in his hand. A few moments passed, then Khufu got up from his chair on the dais and walked down the alabaster steps to a window where he gazed out at the desert. In the distance he could see the outline of the stepped pyramid at Sakkara. This monument, and others, were part of the most sacred landscape on Earth. This was his domain, and he would protect it. Khufu knew his station in life, and he had vowed to uphold the peace. Thus far he had done so. He had no doubts about his rights or his ability to reign.

But this was different. This had nothing to do with how well Khufu was doing his job. It had nothing to do with the constant threat of outside invaders or with the country's economy. This was a direct order from the gods. The king was aware of the cloistered Followers of Horus, the descendants of the Old Ones who were the first humans to receive knowledge directly from the Star Gods, and who had safeguarded the texts and rituals for thousands of years. But those rituals had long since ceased to be performed.

The coordinates of the constellation known to the Star Priests as Horakti, the Sphinx, had changed over the eons since its earthly counterpart had been constructed. This had resulted in the cessation of the initiations and ceremonies of old. Since that time, the Followers of Horus had served primarily as the keepers of the secret knowledge and texts that contained the ritual formulas that, when performed by qualified Star Priests, would empower them with the souls of the Star Gods. This merging of gods and humans had occurred among the ancestral Star Priests during Zep Tepi, the First Time. That blending had given humanity the knowledge and power needed to make a giant leap forward.

An abrupt change in the course of human events took place. Humans were no longer primitive, mere naked barbarians. The fusion of the Star Gods and humans, facilitated by the rituals known only to a few, had created a civilization and a Golden Age that became the foundation for present-day Egyptian life.

While Khufu gazed out the window, Meri-ib waited patiently. It was not every day that one got a message that the Star Gods were about to return to Earth and communicate openly with humans through the persons of the most ancient of the Holy Orders. In addition, the task would be formidable, to unearth the Sphinx that the desert had claimed centuries ago so that it might once again serve as the Temple of the Stars.

Khufu had known, since he became king, of the secret prophecy that was part of the oldest tradition of the Followers of Horus, that at the end of the First Time, even when the Star Gods had withdrawn from direct contact with humans, a time would yet come when the star gates would once more open, and the gods of the sky would transmit more knowledge and power. That time, so it seemed, was imminent. Khufu must do his part. Only he could issue the command that would recruit the labor force needed to complete the task Thoth had requested.

Turning away from the window, the King faced Meri-ib.

"It will be done." Khufu's commitment was clear in the tone of his voice. "My foremost responsibility is to see to the well-being of Egypt and her people. If the time approaches for the return of the Star Gods, for a line of communication to be open between us on Earth and them, then we must prepare for this at all costs. I will speak to Manetho tomorrow. I will have the vizier report to you, Meri-ib, when a plan is in place."

The High Priest felt a deep peace wash over him. He knew that what lay ahead would require tremendous effort on the part of many people, but he had confidence in Khufu. He was, after all, the One, the earthly incarnation of Osiris.

Bowing to Khufu, Meri-ib prepared to take his leave. "I will await Manetho's arrival in Heliopolis," he said. With that, he turned to go.

"Are you not forgetting something, my friend?"

Khufu held out the fragile white feather for Meri-ib. Reaching for it, the High Priest thought for a moment and said, "You keep it. It is yours, Your Majesty. It will give you strength for the task ahead. Good day."

Khem awoke to a room filled with fresh morning air. The sound of crows calling outside the window sent Akhi out to chase the noisy birds away. The servant girl hurried back into the room and went straight to the clothesbaskets and removed a clean sheath for her mistress, who was now sitting on the side of her bed. Akhi put her mistress's chamber pot on the floor and went to the dressing table and began pouring water into a washing bowl. When her morning personals were done, Khem pulled her nightdress over her head and sat for Akhi to bathe her.

Today would be special. Khem was excited about meeting the High Priestess, Taret, but she was most excited about the fact that she was about to become one of an elite group of Star Priestess apprentices of which there were never more than a dozen at any time. Like the others before her, she was chosen from among all the young girls whose identity and location had been made known to the High Star Priestess by a dream. When each girl reached the age of fifteen, she was summoned to the House of Life in the Temple of the Sun at Heliopolis to begin training. No one was accepted unless there was a vacancy created when an apprentice graduated into service at the Temple, or died. The young woman whose place Khem would fill was now working with Taret.

As the plans for the day swirled in Khem's mind, her excitement was momentarily overshadowed by the knowledge that her parents and Atef were, by now, preparing to depart on their journey home. Khem knew that she must keep her mind focused on preparing for the events of the day, but it was not easy. She would surely miss her family, and she knew there would be times when she would be homesick and lonely for them and Abydos. Akhi put a bowl of dried dates and fresh-baked bread before her mistress, but Khem was too nervous to eat. She wanted to make a good impression on Taret.

Khem picked up the mirror that Bata had given her the night before and held the smooth, shiny disk up to her face to see how she looked. It was not her appearance she was interested in so much as whether she looked composed. She must not be flustered or apprehensive during her audience with Taret, lest she appear not up to the task of becoming an apprentice priestess. She knew that not everyone made it, and she did not want to fail. Khem found her reflection acceptable, composed, and she hoped she could stay that way.

Suddenly, as she was about to put the mirror on the table, the image Khem saw was not her own. The mirror's surface had become cloudy, then another woman's face formed, her features undulating in a mist. In a second the face was gone, and Khem once again saw only her own image. The face she had seen was no one she knew. The woman appeared young, her features typically Egyptian. Her shiny black hair was styled in a single thick braid twisted into a cone-like roll on top of her head. Her dark eyes sparkled. Even though the woman in the mirror was a stranger to Khem, she seemed familiar.

The vision startled her. It had vanished so quickly, she thought she must have imagined it. Putting the mirror on the dressing table, she asked Akhi anxiously, "Where is Senna? It is time."

"He will come, mistress," Akhi replied, just as a knock came at the door. Drawing back the curtains, the servant girl bowed to Senna.

"The mistress Taret is ready, Khem. It is time to go," the old priest said. "Come."

The old man and Khem left the room and began their walk to the House of Life. It was good to have Senna accompany her, Khem thought. Senna had been a priest in the Temple of the Sun for most of his life. He had entered Temple life shortly after the death of his young wife and their infant son, who had both drowned when the flatboat ferrying them across the Nile had sunk. Khem had overheard Senna telling her parents the tragic story at dinner the night before. He had long served as overseer and protector of the apprentice priestesses, and they all loved him. They were the children he had lost to the Nile.

Senna and Khem walked through the upper courtyard and down the wide stairway to the lower level. They then rounded the corner and went into the House of Life. When they reached the entrance of the audience room where Taret waited, Senna patted Khem on her arm in gentle reassurance.

Khem walked through the double doors that opened into the audience room. The long room was lined on each side with palms in huge clay pots. A handwoven carpet ran up the middle of the entire length of the rectangular chamber. Brightly colored scenes of the gods and goddesses adorned the walls. On a raised platform at the far end, the High Priestess sat on an ornately carved wooden chair, its front, back, and arms inlaid with lapis star-shaped designs. Two similar chairs were placed on each side of it.

Khem's eyes went immediately to Taret. The woman seemed even smaller than Khem had remembered. Her robe was draped gracefully around her, covering her feet. Its loose sleeves came to her wrists as her tiny hands rested on the arms of the throne. A gold headband with a five-pointed star mounted on a short, gold stem fit snugly on her head. A shoulder-length wig added a youthful air to the woman's appearance.

Seated to Taret's right was the plump priestess, Ani. The chair to Taret's left was occupied by a woman who looked to be a few years older than Khem, but younger than Ani. At first, Khem did not see her face for she was bending over to reach into a wooden box next to her chair to retrieve a roll of papyrus and an ink palette. Khem's heart skipped a beat and she gasped. It was the face she had seen in her mirror. Before Khem had a chance to think, a woman came forward from a group of several standing at the foot of the platform and motioned for Khem to follow. As they neared the dais, Khem bowed her head the moment her eyes met Taret's.

"You are Khem," the High Priestess said. "I have known of your coming to Heliopolis for some time now. The goddess Nut informed me. The goddess has also told me that she came to you in a dream during which she entrusted you with a prophecy that is of great importance for it bespeaks a grave injustice regarding Pharaoh Khufu."

At Taret's words, images of the dreams came back into Khem's mind. It was not until this moment that she knew the woman in her dreams had in fact been Nut, the Sky Goddess. Taret continued speaking.

"You are to keep such things in your heart, and speak of them to no one outside the Order. For now, there are other matters at hand. You are here to begin a significant journey. There will be knowledge entrusted to you that has been part of the spiritual foundation of Egypt since the First Time. You will learn the ways of the Star Gods and of the power invested in the Sun, Moon, and stars. You will be expected to live a chaste life. The more pure your body and heart, the more power the great Star Gods will entrust to you."

Turning to Ani, Taret said, "Ani will be your tutor. She will answer your questions and help you get acclimated to your new home here at the Temple. She will also assist you in your studies." Pausing for a moment, Taret then turned to the priestess on her left. "This is Sheshat. You saw her last evening. She is my chief scribe. She records the words of Nut and the other Sky Mistresses as they are spoken through me."

Khem's eyes met Sheshat's. Why had this woman's face appeared in her mirror? What did it mean?

Sheshat returned Khem's look, her lips curling in a slight smile. Khem looked away and listened to Taret greet the remaining apprentices and invite them to come and formally meet the new arrival from Abydos. The first girl had sat across from Khem and her family at dinner. Khem remembered how there had been a sadness about her, and how she had played with her food, eating little.

"I am Bakka."

Khem thought the girl was beautiful. Her dark skin and big eyes were the main focus of her beauty. Her hair was longer than Khem had ever seen on a girl. It hung below Bakka's waist, straight and shiny. Though the girl was pleasant, she seemed melancholy. Bakka stepped aside to allow the next apprentice in line to offer her greetings.

"I am Kasut. My room is next to yours."

The girl reminded Khem of a friend in Abydos. "Hello, Kasut," Khem responded in a friendly manner.

The third priestess was Neba, in training for five years now, and awaiting approval from Taret for initiation as a full-fledged Star Priestess. Neba had become known to be a seer.

Kasut came up again, this time with another woman in tow.

"Khem, meet Meretneith. We call her Meret. She is Ani's star pupil— no pun intended!" Kasut said, smiling. Khem extended her hand to Meret while Kasut continued. "Meret is a dream-talker. The Star Gods speak to her through her dreams." Letting go of the priestess's hand, Khem remarked that it all sounded very interesting and she was anxious to learn more.

Khem and the apprentices mingled and talked for a long while, getting to know one another. They spent the morning and had lunch together before Taret interrupted their socializing. "Please, all of you come and be seated. There is something you must be told."

The apprentices sat down on soft floor pillows arranged in a semicircle in front of the raised platform where the High Priestess sat with her attendants. Taret's expression became serious. She sat perfectly still with her eyes closed for what seemed like several minutes, her head falling slightly forward. Then, raising her head slowly, she began to speak, her voice much lower than before.

"I have come to inform you of an omen that shall soon appear in the sky over Egypt. It will be seen for many nights. It will set the heavens ablaze with its glory. A great comet is sent by the god Horus to bring the first of the Great Ones to return, the Star Goddess Isis. This comet shall be both omen and vehicle for Isis' return. It will happen at the time of her annual journey to herald the rising of the waters of Mother Nile. It is ordained by Ra, god of the Sun, that the comet brings to the Earth the seeds of tomorrow. You must divine the true meaning of this portent. Therefore, there must be a meeting of the Holy Orders of Osiris and Nut, the Star Priests, and Star Priestesses. This meeting must take place at the hour of sunset of the coming day. In time, you will be joined and advised by one of the Old Ones, one of the Followers of Horus. So be it."

Though Khem had only just arrived at the Temple of the Sun, she sensed the gravity of Taret's words. She also noticed that Sheshat wrote down all that the High Priestess said.

Her transmission over, Taret sat still and quiet, allowing her conscious mind to become centered. Following Ani's lead, the apprentices sat quietly as well while Taret's servant girl escorted the High Priestess to her private quarters. When they had gone, Khem turned to Kasut.

"The comet will be the first one I have ever seen, at least that I remember. I was told that there was one in the sky on the night I was born."

"Comets are the messengers of the Star Gods," Kasut said. "Their appearance is foretold through dreams."

While they talked, Khem spotted a girl she had not noticed before. She did not look like the other apprentices. Her dark skin and her features were distinctly Nubian. Her hair stood out from her head in a coarse, black halo. She wore a wide copper armband on each of her upper arms, and large gold earrings hung from each ear. A neckband encircled her neck, along with several gold chains.

"Who is that girl?" Khem asked Kasut.

"Which?"

"The one wearing the gold arm bands."

"Oh, that is Tiye. She is Nubian. She recently came from Ombos in the South. I have heard that she trained with an old female magician in the village, and that she is an adept of Moon magic. That is all I know. I have not spoken to her since she arrived."

Kasut seemed as curious as Khem about the strange-looking Nubian, but Khem detected distrust in the other priestess when she spoke about Tiye, as Egyptians were not generally open to associating with Nubians due to cultural and religious differences. Khem was even more surprised by Tiye's presence at the temple. She was curious to learn about this girl, and this curiosity motivated her to introduce herself.

"I am going to speak to her. Will you come with me, Kasut?"

At first Kasut seemed hesitant, then she agreed and the two walked to where the Nubian was talking to the only man in the room. As they neared the pair, Tiye stopped talking and turned to face them. Her eyes were dark and piercing. A wall went up around her, which the other girls sensed right away. Kasut stopped short in approaching the girl, but Khem continued on, and when she got close enough, she bowed her head politely and said, "I am Khem. I have just arrived from Abydos. I understand that you are also recently come to Heliopolis and that you are from the South."

Tiye looked at Khem, and then past her at Kasut, eyeing both of them suspiciously. "I am Tiye from Nubia."

Tiye looked different from anyone Khem had ever seen. Her royal blue linen skirt hung down to her ankles. Two linen straps crisscrossed her upper body and back, revealing her breasts. Of the several necklaces that hung around her neck, one caught Khem's eye. The gold pendant was suspended on a chain of the same metal. In the pendant's center was a large piece of green jasper carved into the likeness of a human head. Four gold crescent moons hung in a row across the bottom of the necklace.

Aware that Khem was staring at her jewelry, Tiye took the piece in her hand and held it out to give Khem a closer look.

"It is beautiful," Khem said as she studied the carved jasper. "It must have a meaning."

"Yes, it does," Tiye replied, her tone somewhat guarded. "It was a gift from my mentor and teacher, the magician Khaba. It is an image of the Moon spirit."

Khem felt a strange attraction to the necklace. It seemed alive. Just then, the priest that Tiye had been talking to spoke to Khem and Kasut.

"Allow me, please, to introduce myself. I am Mentu, the Oracle Priest."

Somewhat taken aback by the priest's high rank, Khem wondered why he was present at a gathering of apprentices. She knew that it was the job of the Oracle Priest to tend to the daily needs of the statues of the deities. Containing the spirit of a deity, the statues needed the same care and activities as any living being. Therefore, the Oracle Priest's duties involved washing, feeding, and even entertaining the icons. Sometimes the washing took place with a purification bath in a sacred pool inside the temple; other times it was a matter of pouring purified water over the image. Then a dozen or so priests would proceed into the main courtyard inside the complex. The public was not allowed to enter beyond the gates at such times.

Once inside the sanctuary and as the Sun rose, one of the high-ranking clergy would break the clay seal on the door of the special room where the god's effigy was kept. The statue was then removed from its niche, divested of its garments, cleansed, and new clothing put on. It was perfumed and set back in its place. Next, the Oracle Priest presented the god with food and drink. At the close of the ceremony, the sanctuary would be resealed and the priest would depart, carefully erasing his footprints and any other evidence of his having been there. Few priests had a more important job than this.

Perceiving the apprentices' unspoken question, Mentu explained that Taret had summoned him to hear the announcement by Nut regarding the appearance of the comet.

The mention of the celestial visitor turned Khem's attention away from Tiye and her intriguing jewel, and focused it on the special meeting that Taret had announced would take place on the following afternoon. Such a meeting was not rare, Khem learned, but its timing was curious, close to the annual New Year celebration. This time of year coincided with the flooding of the Nile. To call a meeting of all the Star Priests and Priestesses must surely be an indication of the importance placed on the anticipated comet.

"Have you ever seen a comet, Mentu?" Khem asked the Oracle Priest.

"I have not," the man replied thoughtfully. "But—" Before Mentu could finish what he was about to say, Tiye spoke out abruptly.

"A comet is an omen of misfortune and evil. Khaba told me this. She often spoke of a great star with long, sparkling hair that she had seen in her dreams." Tiye's voice had an edge that revealed an apprehension regarding the comet. Her eyes flashed as she spoke. "Khaba's dreams always came true."

The comment suggested that Tiye knew more, but the Nubian said nothing further. Her expression changed from intensity to a superficial friendliness. Turning to face Khem and Kasut, she said abruptly that she had to go.

With Tiye gone, Khem and Kasut bade Mentu their parting pleasantries and joined a group of apprentices chatting about the meeting Taret had called. The two walked up just in time to hear Meret describing the details of a strange dream she had had the previous night. Everyone listened intently as Meret talked.

"There was a big bird, a falcon, I think, with great wings. It wore a hood over its head. I do not remember ever dreaming of a falcon before." She was obviously puzzled by her dream, so she listened with interest as other apprentices offered their ideas as to what it might mean. Khem listened for a few minutes before wandering off.

She was soon to learn that no one took Meret's dreams lightly, and that her own not staying to listen was a mistake. Meret was a dreamer for the gods, and she had been in training under the tutelage of Ani, the Chief Dream Priestess, since her arrival at Heliopolis three years before.

The hour was late and Khem was anxious to return to the privacy of her room so she could set up her altar. She had not had the time to do so since settling into her new quarters. A quick glance around the room revealed that those assembled were starting to depart. Taking her leave, Khem took Kasut by the hand and gave it a friendly squeeze. "I must go now. I have some things to attend to before I sleep. I will see you in class tomorrow." With that, she turned to go.

"Wait, please!" Kasut said. There was obviously something on the girl's mind, so Khem paused and looked at her, curious as to what was suddenly so urgent. Kasut took a deep breath.

"Perhaps you will think me silly, but I am feeling very uncomfortable with the Nubian, Tiye. I cannot say exactly why, or even put my feelings into words. But even though she is gone from the room, I can still feel her presence. Have you any of these feelings?"

Kasut's words were puzzling. Khem had found the Nubian girl intriguing, and certainly different in her physical appearance from any of the other apprentices. But she had not had a negative reaction to Tiye. Seeking to reassure her new friend, Khem made light of Kasut's concern. "She is just different, Kasut. When we get to know her, I am sure that she will be like the rest of us. Do not be concerned."

Kasut nodded her head slowly in a gesture of agreement that Khem was probably right.

"Come," Khem said. "We will walk back to the dormitory together."

As the two apprentices walked, the conversation turned to girl talk about dresses, servant girls, and jewelry. They reached Kasut's room first, where they parted company.

Khem went to her own room next door. At the entrance, she found a small package on the floor. Picking it up, she proceeded into her quarters. She put the bundle on the table beside her bed and sat down. Then, taking it into her hands again, she unwrapped the papyrus. Inside was a small amulet. Holding it up to the light of the oil lamp, Khem saw that it had been made from faience into the shape of the Eye of Horus, the *udjat*. There was no note telling her who had left it or why. She knew that it was an amulet for protection, and her mind searched for an answer as to who might have given it to her. Little did she know that Nut, the sky goddess and the same deity who had appeared to her in a dream long ago, was working to bring the amulet to her from the subtle dimensions of the spirit forces.

Just then, Akhi came out of the anteroom where she had been resting and practicing her lyre. The servant girl had been given the instrument when she was a child, and she had been teaching herself to play it for a long time.

"Look, Akhi. I found this outside my door. Do you know where it came from, or who left it there?"

"No, my mistress, I do not."

Khem laid the amulet on the table and walked to the corner of the room to a niche in the wall. Though it was not all that spacious, this was where she would make her altar. She began busying herself with the task.

In the center of the niche, Khem placed the small statue of Hapi along-side one of Thoth and another of the goddess Hathor. She placed a tiny bronze lamp that she would light twice each day as an offering to the nine deities that made up the Grand Ennead of principles, the "Company of the Gods." To protect her from the Evil Eye, Khem put a tiny, sacred cowrie shell her father had taken in payment for fish on the day she was born. It had come from the Red Sea. She picked up the mysterious amulet and laid it beside the other objects. "There. It is done," Khem said to Akhi, who had been watching her mistress respectfully.

"It is time for you to go to bed, my mistress. You must rest." Akhi could see that Khem was exhausted. It had been a long, full day.

When Khem lay down, she did not drift off to sleep right away. Lying on her bed, looking at the ceiling, she replayed the day's events in her mind. Of all the images that passed through her thoughts, it was that of Tiye that stood out. Khem recalled the pendant the Nubian wore, and wondered about "Moon magic." She also recalled Kasut's reaction to Tiye, a flicker of doubt arising as to whether making light of the girl's fear had been appropriate. Was it fear Kasut had felt? Or was it a personality conflict, or a prejudice? Before she decided what the truth might be, Khem fell into a restful sleep.

Chapter Three

Pharaoh's Dream

Morning came to the desert, and with it came the heat. Khufu had not slept much, and what sleep he did get was filled with fitful dreams. The day before had been stressful and tiring. He had spent most of his time in the audience hall at the palace with his vizier, Manetho, presiding over civil cases and listening to petitions for money from the royal coffers to pay the importers. He had had a hard time keeping his mind on the matters at hand because he was preoccupied with the message Meri-ib had delivered the day before.

Khufu recalled the white feather that Meri-ib said had been left on the altar in the central chapel at the Temple of the Sun. There was no denying that Thoth was the messenger who requested that the Sphinx be excavated from beneath the desert sand under which the ancient monument had rested for centuries. Was the Lion King still intact? Was it—? He wasn't even sure what questions he should ponder. No one had seen what truly lay buried under the sand. All Khufu knew was that the time had come to unearth the Sphinx to make ready for the return of the Star Gods.

Khufu told Manetho about Meri-ib's visit and his vision of Thoth, and the vizier was stunned. The Pharaoh wasn't sure it was the monumental task of clearing the sands away from the Sphinx that had shocked him the most, or if it was the prophecy regarding the return of the Star Gods, but Manetho accepted the task without hesitation. It would take planning and many men to complete, but how much time and how many men, he did not know. With all this weighing on his mind, Khufu retired early and fell asleep almost immediately.

As soon as slumber came, so did the dream. Sitting now the next morning with his wife, as servants brought them breakfast, his mind was deep in thought. The images had been so real and replayed themselves in his mind:

He was standing beside the huge head of the Sphinx when he felt the ground giving way as if the Earth were swallowing him. In the next instant he slid into a large hole like an unending tunnel. He fell deeper and deeper into the dark chute, then was dumped into a subterranean chamber. Getting to his feet, he looked around, trying to figure out where he was. Five hallways led out of this room. The walls of the room were inscribed from the floor to the ceiling with symbols and scenes from the sacred texts. There was a large granite stone altar upon which a five-pointed star had been carved. A flash of light temporarily blinded him.

When his eyes cleared, he saw perched in the center of the altar a giant falcon, its talons big enough to tear a mountain. The huge bird fixed his eyes on Khufu, and as Khufu stared into the falcon's eyes, its pupils turned into flames that engulfed the room. Just as the flames were about to consume Khufu, he awakened with a jolt, nearly throwing himself out of bed.

The dream was bad and puzzling. It had been strangely real, especially the chamber. The wall paintings, stone altar, falcon, the fire—all had been eerily authentic. The dream left him feeling he had had a profound experience.

A soft scuffle of reed sandals on the limestone floor brought Khufu back to reality. The royal wife, Meritates, put her hands on Khufu's shoulders and began giving him a light massage. "You seem to be lost in your thoughts, husband," she said gently.

Khufu extended his hand to his shoulder and patted hers. Then he walked out onto the patio adjacent to his bedchamber.

The Memphis palace was beautiful. The big patio with sunken pool and well-tended flower garden was his favorite place. Meritates followed the king and sat on a bench in the shade of a large palm tree. She knew not to encourage her husband to speak about what was on his mind, though she could tell something weighed heavily on him.

"I have sent for Nemon, my cousin," Khufu finally said slowly.

Nemon was the master builder and a reliable member of the royal court. "He is in Abusir overseeing the construction of a new temple."

Khufu trusted Nemon, and now he would turn to him again. If there was anyone who could devise a plan for unearthing the Sphinx, it was Nemon. "Egypt approaches an important time. There is much to be done to prepare."

Meritates could tell by Khufu's words that whatever was going on weighed on his heart as well as his mind. Just then, a small boy ran onto the patio and flung himself into his father's arms.

"Cephren! You are getting heavy!" the Pharaoh said, admiring the boy who, though barely six years old, had grown as quickly as a reed of late. "Have you had your breakfast?"

"Yes, Father. Let's go for a sail on the river today, can we?" the lad asked excitedly. "It is a wonderful morning for a sail."

"I would like that," Khufu answered, "but I must attend to matters that cannot wait, my son. But you have my promise that we will go sailing very soon, and we will fish too."

Meritates stood up and went to her son. Taking the boy by the hand, she said, "Come, Cephren. Your father has much to do." With that she smiled lovingly at Khufu and led the child back into the palace.

The dream from the night before still vivid in his mind, Khufu clapped his hands to beckon his valet, Hui. The servant was advised that the royal scribe should come to the king's private audience hall immediately. There were messages to be dictated. One would be to Nemon, another to Meri-ib.

Nineteen miles away to the north in Heliopolis the morning sunlight streamed in through the window in Khem's bedroom. Akhi busied herself helping her mistress get ready for the day. This was Khem's first day in class. She was anxious to begin her studies and had looked forward to this day for a long time. However, it was the sunset meeting of the Star Priests and Priestesses that Taret had called that occupied her thoughts this morning.

Out of a small inlaid jewelry box, she took a necklace Atef had given her on her thirteenth birthday. It was a four-pointed lapis star hung on a linen ribbon. After tying the star around her neck, Khem picked up her mirror and admired herself. Deciding that she looked exactly the way she wanted to in order to make a good impression, she let out a deep sigh in an effort to release some of the tension that was building up. It was time to go. Grabbing her scribe's palette and pen, Khem hurried from her room into the hall where Kasut was waiting.

Senna and his servant, Pepi, greeted the two girls who made their way to the classroom. The old priest often sat in on the classes and sometimes contributed to the day's teaching.

Khem and Kasut went inside and took a seat on the floor. The apprentices were all present. In a few minutes Ani arrived. Today's topic would be the Isle of Fire.

Ani settled herself on a bench-like chair on the dais and began telling about a distant, magical land that lay in a place beyond the Earth. It was called the Isle of Fire, a place of everlasting light where the gods were born. It was from there that the gods came to Earth. It was also there among the deities that a great bird lived, shaped like an eagle and as large, its spectacular plumage red and gold. The bird, known as the *Benu*, had originally come from Arabia in the East.

"Once every five hundred years the *Benu* appears, always after the death of its father. It makes a large ball of myrrh in which it places its father's dead body. It then begins a journey to Earth, its final destination being the Sun Temple in Heliopolis. Once the *Benu* arrives, it buries the myrrh egg that contains its father's body. Its task is completed as the *Benu* has again planted its seed on the Earth. It was the *Benu* that brought magic to Egypt."

Khem listened to the story, imagining the bird. To her it was a real thing, not just a story; just as she had this thought, Ani's words confirmed that belief.

"Those things happened a long time ago during the First Time. Some say that the Isle of Fire exists, and that it is on an Earth-like planet that revolves around a sun in a distant star system. Others say it is but a story told by the gods to describe things that we humans could not otherwise understand.

"When the *Benu* brought magic to Egypt, the formulas and rituals were recorded in a tome that the human priests who first received it called The Tablet of Destiny. This volume is still in the hands of the descendants of the Followers of Horus. No eyes but theirs have looked upon the holy texts that contain knowledge of everything that has ever been or will ever be. The priests who comprise the ancient holy order are not only the guardians of the sacred tablet, but they are the only ones who know where it is kept.

"What is known is that the last time the *Benu* came to Heliopolis it was seen by many. It appeared in the night sky like a blazing ball of fire. The *Benu* did not bury its ball of myrrh this time for it contained untold magical powers. The powers of life and death, healing, prosperity, immortality. No man or woman on Earth was yet able to use such powers in selfless ways. This the gods knew for they had witnessed firsthand the abuse of the powers by humans. Therefore, the gods instructed the chaste Followers of Horus to take possession of the great ball, which the priests called the 'Star Stone' because they looked upon it as a 'stone' from the heavens, and to hide it in a safe place. They were to instruct the initiates among them in its secret formulas and rituals.

"The priests placed the Star Stone inside a secret chamber within the Holy of Holies here at the Temple of the Sun. No one except them has looked upon it since. A replica of the sacred stone, which is said to be shaped more like a cone than a sphere or an egg, was made and placed upon the top of the Great Pyramid. From that time the pyramid was known to the priests as the 'Mansion of the *Benu.*'"

Ani's words induced Khem into a waking dream in which she entered the Holy of Holies. There, in the center of a great altar carved from the finest red granite lay a piece of black, cratered stone. An aura surrounded it as if the stone were ablaze. The vision was so vivid it gave Khem the feeling she was inside the inner sanctum and was seeing the sacred stone.

She was intrigued by the Followers of Horus. She remembered stories about the people who had lived in Egypt a long time ago. The tales painted them as a superior race unlike ordinary Egyptians. Her father had said that they were not Egyptians at all, but of divine origin. Now she knew from Ani's teachings that they had likely come from another star system. Khem's musings were interrupted and her attention brought to focus on the teacher again as she heard Ani in midsentence.

". . . No other god but Horus. The common people were Followers of Osiris. But it was Horus the Divine that humans held above all others."

Khem did not know much about the god Horus, so she listened with keen interest.

"Horus, the falcon god, is the great lord of Heaven. All of the parts of his body hold celestial power and significance. His outstretched wings are the sky from horizon to horizon, the sky that is home to all that exists. His right eye is the Sun, his left eye the Moon, his speckled breast the feathery clouds. The ancients called him *Hor*, a word meaning 'far away.' It was *Hor* who led them to the Earth.

"Since the beginning of time, the falcon has been the sacred totem of Horus. When the god arrived on Earth, knowledge of him spread throughout Egypt. Sanctuaries were dedicated to him, and the priests incorporated him into the Ennead. So great was *Hor* that those who followed him carved his image out of the Mountain of Stone on the desert floor upon which the god had first set foot. This monument was created to forever watch the place from which Horus and his followers had come. The people called the watcher monument *Harmakhis*, Horus of the Horizon. *Harmakhis*, the Sphinx, never takes his eyes away from the horizon, though the stars have changed their places since the day that *Hor* came."

Khem realized that Ani was speaking of the curious head of stone that, though she had yet to see it, she knew existed at Giza. She now felt an urge to see *Harmakhis* for herself.

"There is much to learn about Horus, and you will do so in time. It is time to pause now for the noon meal. After taking food and drink, Meret will speak about dream journeys."

With that, Ani left the room. All that Khem had heard was still running through her mind, and she was lost in her thoughts.

"Khem?"

Kasut's voice broke into her daydreams of the faraway place among the stars from which Horus had come, coaxing Khem back into the present. Rising to her feet, she went with Kasut to the dining area.

Khem didn't have much appetite. Her mind was engrossed in images of a distant planet in whose skies two suns rose each morning, whose people were in harmony with the laws of the universe. Seeing the ways of the people of Egypt, one of the Gods of the Two Suns had come to bring magic. The people would no longer be in darkness because Hor, the God of Light, had given them the formulas and rituals that would lift them out of the darkness into the light. Humanity would now be able to think and intuit—Khem's thoughts were vivid. She felt herself leaving her body for the place of the Two Suns.

Her inner journey was interrupted when a servant leaned over her to place a tray of dried fruit on the table. It was difficult for Khem to keep her mind focused on what was going on around her. Ani's teaching had opened up a part of her that was not constrained by flesh or time, a part that knew how to fly on wings of imagination. Khem was now feeling a freedom within her that Ani's words had triggered. If she had had any remaining doubt that she was where she was supposed to be, it was gone now.

Khem barely spoke through the meal. She tried making small talk a couple of times, but her thoughts kept going back to the teaching. When she had eaten what she could, she slipped out of the dining room and made her way to the upper courtyard, where she stood gazing at the huge statue of Horus. As she looked into the god's eyes, she felt a connection that up until now she had felt for no other deity.

It was time for the afternoon class to begin. Khem made her way back to the classroom where the others had already gathered. Ani was not present, but Meret was. Khem felt drawn to Ani's protégé and wanted to know her better. In the very short time she had been at the Temple, the people she had met, especially Tiye, had intrigued Khem. Looking around the room, she noticed that the Nubian was not present; neither did she remember seeing her at the morning session. This was puzzling because she knew Tiye was also a Star Priestess apprentice. Khem's thoughts were interrupted as Meret began speaking.

"Like each of you," she began, "I am learning about the stars and their power. Since my arrival here, however, I have been working with Ani, the Chief Dream Priestess. Dreams are an important part of our lives, and understanding them is an important part of our training. They are the means by which I commune with the Star Gods, and they with me. Eventually, each of you will experience such contact. Although great distances separate the stars and the Earth, the mind is not constrained by distance or time. In your dreams you can take journeys your body cannot. You can travel to the stars in your dreams. Your dreams provide a means by which the Star Gods may transmit their energy to you. But you must learn how to know when a dream has been given to you by the gods, and when it is but a dream message to you from your own inner self."

Although Meret's words had to do with knowledge Khem had not been formally taught, Khem intuited the truth of what Meret was saying because of her childhood dreams when Nut had come to her in a dream. What Meret said now made Khem think about the headless demon-man who also had appeared in that same dream. Recalling it made her uneasy.

"The dream vessel within you must be clear for the Sky Gods to transfer their consciousness into yours. Keeping your vessel clear of negative thoughts and fears is imperative. Your physical body must also be pure, which is why the Star Priests and Priestesses are celibate. When a Sky God has a message to deliver, they select a dreamer whose energy can be elevated so that images can be transmitted and take form, undefiled by the dreamer's personality. The divinities choose their messengers carefully. Usually one who is considered for this is monitored from birth, and then a dream is planted into the dream vessel at the right time to reveal to the chosen their destiny to study and serve at the Temple of the Sun."

Meret's comments made a deep impression on Khem. It was one thing to have a notable dream, a transmission from a deity. But it was quite another to consciously prepare and maintain yourself physically, emotionally, and spiritually to serve as a channel for the Sky Gods.

When the afternoon session ended, Khem and Kasut left the classroom together, both mulling the teachings. After a while, Khem said, "You sure are quiet, Kasut."

"I was just thinking," Kasut replied. "I can remember a dream I had a long time ago. It is vague and I cannot recall much about it, but I do remember walking on a road of stars. There was a woman on either side of me as I walked. I don't know who they were or remember what they looked like." Kasut stopped walking and looked at Khem. "There was also a woman who looked like a queen. She sat on a throne. I remember her looking into my eyes. I will never forget her eyes." Kasut's voice trailed off.

Khem was shocked. Kasut's dream was similar to hers. She then related her dream to Kasut as it filled in details Kasut had been unable to recall. As Khem spoke, Kasut's eyes widened and she was unable to speak. It was obvious they had had the same dream. The revelation unnerved Kasut, though both were intrigued and puzzled. The girls realized their dreams had been their "call" to Heliopolis and the Temple of the Sun.

The two friends walked slowly down to the lower courtyard, discussing the dreams and how it was meant they should be at Heliopolis together. After a while, Kasut said that she was tired and left for her room to rest before dinner. Before returning to her own room, Khem paused at the foot of the Horus statue. She thought of Ani's teaching of how the god came to Earth during the First Time from his home on the Isle of Fire.

Standing there, Khem caught a movement out of the corner of her eye. Turning to see what it was, she saw two priests she had not seen before. One was dressed in the garb of a lector priest. His long, straight skirt went down to his ankles, a broad, white sash was draped diagonally across his chest, and he wore papyrus sandals. His companion was striking in appearance, tall for an Egyptian. His skin was dark bronze, his eyes large, his lips full, his body firm and muscular. He wore a wide copper band on his upper right arm. Unlike other priests, he did not have a shaven head. His shoulder-length black hair was thick and straight. Like a lector priest, he wore a kilt with a wide linen sash wrapped around his trim waist, its ends tied into a neat fold on the side that hung halfway down the long kilt. Khem had never seen a man with such large hands and feet and whose body was so imposing. His expression was stern and reflected a pride that came across as arrogance.

Engaged in conversation, the two men were walking slowly. When they reached the statue where Khem was standing, the tall one stopped and looked her way. She could feel his eyes on her though she did not look immediately in his direction. The man put his hand on the forearm of the lector priest, motioning him to stop. Khem did not wish to encounter these men, so she walked to the wide staircase that led to the mezzanine and the wing where her room was. Even though her back was turned to the men, Khem knew she was being watched. Unable to not turn and face the men, Khem was startled by the familiar appearance of the tallest, most exotic of the two.

"That's *him*," she thought, the image of the man startling her. "That is the man in my vision, the man who the sky goddess warned me would try to divide the people of Egypt and threaten the sovereignty of the Throne."

She wasn't sure what to do, if anything. What if her vision was wrong? What if she had misinterpreted or misunderstood what she had seen? But this could not be so, for the High Priestess Taret had known of her vision that had occurred years before they had met, and that was a confirmation of its validity.

Once in her room, Khem lay across her bed to rest. Her body was tense, her mind filled with images and thoughts from the day. Nonetheless, she soon fell asleep.

By the time she woke up, the sun had begun to set. Khem sat up on the side of the bed, hungry. She went to her dressing table, where Akhi had placed a bowl of figs. Picking a plump one, she popped it into her mouth. Then she put on a clean sheath. It would soon be time for the evening meal and she did not want to be late.

"You are awake, my mistress. I was afraid you would sleep through dinner. I had to do errands, but I see I did not need to worry." The servant girl began smoothing the wrinkles from Khem's bed linens.

Khem went to the main dining hall and found Kasut waiting for her at the arched entryway. The evening mealtime was as much a social event as it was a time for eating. Entering the hall, the two girls joined other apprentices already seated with Senna. Khem was more interested in eating than in participating in what was going on around her, though she heard one girl discussing the meeting scheduled for the next day. How could something as important as that have slipped her mind? Khem wondered.

In response to the girl's comments, Senna said that he remembered another time when just such a meeting had been called. It was when the king's half-brother, Sokar, had entered Temple life. The event had caused a stir, not only because of the rarity of a member of the royal family entering the priesthood, but that when he had done so, Sokar had been taken under the wing of the High Priest himself.

Khem listened, forgetting her hunger. After the meal, she retired to her room where she undressed and climbed into bed. The light from the small oil lamp beside her bed made flickering patterns that danced on the ceiling and lulled her into a dreamless sleep.

Chapter Four

Visions of the Past, Present, and Future

When Khem entered the classroom the next day, she noticed Tiye. It was the first time she had seen the Nubian since they first met, and she found her no less exotic now. The young woman sat alone, cross-legged on a floor pillow, her back leaning against the wall. She is not very friendly, Khem thought. At the front of the room, Ani cleared her throat, indicating that the lecture was about to begin.

"When Horus, Lord of Heaven, brought the Tablet of Destiny to the people of Earth, he left it in the hands of the priests of the Followers of Horus, where it remains to this day. Part of the teachings written on the Tablet were of the worlds beyond our own and of the gods of those worlds. Some of the gods of the celestial orbs have a link with the Earth and work with humanity in matters of a highly spiritual nature. To the masses, these matters are part of the mystery of life, but to those trained in the secret tradition, they are known and understood. It is time for you to receive a part of that knowledge, the part that concerns the Morning Star."

As Ani spoke, Khem sensed that the teacher had entered into an altered state of mind. Her eyes had a look of someone seeing into another time. She knew Taret had trained Ani, and she wondered with all that Ani knew, what Taret must know. Khem felt respect for these elder priestesses whom she barely knew.

"The mystery of the Morning Star is tied to the god Horus. You will recall that in the last session I spoke about the *Benu*. When the *Benu* came to the Earth the last time, it came in the form of the Star Stone, a meteorite.

The stone served as a vehicle for the Lord of Heaven, Horus, to come and bring the wisdom teachings to the people, although they were later deemed incapable of using the knowledge in the proper manner. Greed and avarice were too deeply entrenched in the human heart. So, from that point on, the core of the sacred wisdom was withheld from the masses and placed in the hands of the priests of the Followers of Horus, who in turn taught it only to those whom they judged worthy.

"For a time, Horus lived with those from his own star system who had followed him to Earth. However, the time came for the god-man to return to the Isle of Fire on the World of the Two Suns, for as long as he was away, there was but a single deity who could rule. Since there were two Suns in that world, there were two Sun gods. Therefore, it became necessary for the missing god to return and restore the Twin Light. Before his departure from Earth, the god met with the Followers of Horus to let them know the time had come for him to leave. He promised he would return someday. Until that time, the initiates were instructed to disperse the teachings only to those qualified to learn.

"The god Horus said that a sign would appear in the sky to mark the time he had spent on Earth. Sometimes it would appear at dawn, at other times in the night. The heavenly light would shine with great brilliance and beauty. Its appearance in the morning and evening would also remind the Followers of the contents of the deepest mystery, the mystery of cycles, of day and night, life and death, the mystery contained in the Cycle of Osiris, which is the mystery of death and resurrection. The sign would likewise represent the *Benu*, who is in reality the soul of Horus.

"The sacred sky light would be seen changing its place from the morning to the night, dying in the flames of the Sun and then being reborn from them for as long as Earth shall last and until all that lives has become enlightened. The light will forever pave the way for the Sun, be a herald in the darkness. Horus said that the light would be known as the Morning Star and Evening Star, and only the initiates would know that these were the same light.

"This knowledge is part of its mystery. Only the initiates were taught that it was not a star at all, but the representative of Horus and the promise of everlasting life. They would know the holy light as 'The Crosser.' When The Crosser is not visible in the morning or night, it reminds us of the darkness of ignorance that engulfed the Earth before Horus brought the teachings."

Ani was finished. For now, there would be no more words. Khem thought back to the times she had seen the Morning and Evening Star. Now she knew they were one and the same. She would never see them the old way again.

Before leaving, Ani drew the apprentices' attention to the bronze water bowl she had placed on the table. She announced that in the afternoon session, Taret would teach them how to see visions of the past, present, and future. Khem was filled with expectation, as it would be the first time she would hear Taret teach.

When the noon meal was over, the apprentices returned to the classroom. Shortly after, Taret arrived and took her place on the dais, Sheshat at her side. The High Priestess, though petite, was imposing. A silence fell over the room and all eyes focused on her. Her voice was soft, and Khem had to strain to hear what she was saying on the art of divination.

"All physical things have an aura, a subtle, luminous energy field that surrounds them, be they animate or inanimate. Awareness of an aura comes as a result of the daily practice of heightening your ability to sense it. What the uninitiated do not know is that events that have already occurred, events that are occurring, and those that are yet to occur also have an aura that exists on the subtle plane where the energy of events is present and accessible. Seeing such an aura is best facilitated by water, due to its magnetic properties."

Taret motioned to Sheshat to place a small olive wood table with the water bowl in the center of the dais so everyone could see it.

"Water is a tool that can enable an individual to project her consciousness into the dimension where space and time, as you know it, do not exist. Glimpses into that place allow one to see events from the past and future. Such glimpses happen upon occasion to everyone. However, since the First Time there have been prophets and seers capable of doing that regularly, to go beyond the physical into the astral. It is the duty of a Star Priestess to develop your skills for this to the highest state."

Taret's words gave Khem pause. She had never considered herself a seer, but thinking about it now, she had often known something was going to happen beforehand. One time came to mind.

She was no more than six years old. There was a boy in her neighborhood who was born crippled. One day, while watching the unfortunate boy playing on the bank of the Nile, Khem "saw" him floundering frantically in the water, after which he sank. A few days later, while hobbling along the river's shore, the boy slipped and fell into the water. No one saw the accident, and it was not even known about until the boy's lifeless body was found floating at the river's edge the next day. Khem had known it was going to happen, but only after the fact did she realize she had seen something before it happened.

"Each of you should select for yourself a bowl that you can use for the purpose I am about to demonstrate," Taret continued. "The bowl you choose should never be used for anything other than its intended purpose. This bowl has been in my possession for many years. I purchased it on the very day I received the teaching I now pass on to you. It has served me well, for I have taken care to protect it, and to treat it with the same respect that you would a faithful helper."

Taret's reverence for the bowl was evident. Her words brought to Khem the idea that objects were helpers and, in that way, a relationship between them and the user was indeed a bond as honorable as any union between two humans.

"Once you have chosen a scrying bowl, it must first be washed in the waters of Mother Nile on a night when the Moon is full. Nile water is the very life-blood of our beloved Egypt. It will give of its life force to cleanse the vessel you choose to be your helper. Mother Nile will also cleanse you. Wash your hands in her waters, then take some and touch it to your eyes so that you might see only truth."

Taret touched her forefingers to her eyelids, which she closed. Then, touching her lips, she said, "Taste of the Nile, my sisters, so that you will speak only truth." Placing her right hand over her heart, she said, "Bless, too, your heart with the waters of Mother River as a prayer that you will always be able and willing to discern the truth.

"Take your bowl to a place where you can be alone. In an act of awakening your vessel into your service and in the service of the gods and goddesses, perform a ceremony. Place the egg of a crocodile in your bowl. Burn the egg and give its ashes to Mother Nile as an offering that new life may be created from the life destroyed. The egg is the symbol of life, the ashes of its death being that from which new life will be born. In this ritual you will have reenacted the greatest mystery of the law of immortality. You will have awakened the power of life and death in your vessel. It will then belong to the *Neteru* and be ready for you to use.

"When you have need to see into the past or into tomorrow, when you are doing so in answer to the bidding of the gods and in service of the gods, fill your bowl with water. When the water is still and reflects no light, look into it. Let not even your breath ripple the water. In this way you will see that which you desire to behold. What is revealed will equip you with insight. Remember, you are responsible for what is revealed. Use that knowledge against no one, human or god, or in a manner or for a purpose that is unseemly for a priestess of the Holy Order of Nut, goddess of the sky."

With that, Taret stood, bowed her head to those present, and left. For a few moments, the room was quiet. No one moved to leave. Khem glanced at Tiye. Returning her glance, the Nubian curved her lips in a slight smile.

Khem was surprised. Maybe she was opening up to her after all. Taking the chance that she was reading the gesture correctly, Khem went to Tiye, who rose to meet her. Bowing her head gracefully, Khem said, "I am pleased to see you again, Tiye."

The cultural differences between the two girls were a barrier that could not be denied. Having lived her life in Abydos, Khem was familiar with Nubians. Her father had often traded with them, exchanging fish for household goods. But the social status of Nubians was for the most part lower than that of Egyptians, so Khem had never interacted with them. None of this mattered now, though she sensed that Tiye was defensive about it. Perhaps she expected to be shunned. The thought caused Khem to extend herself to Tiye. She wondered if others had made such an effort or if the Nubian had experienced prejudice since entering the Temple.

"It is nice to see you too," Tiye answered. "I have thought about you since we met. Mentu tells me that you come from Abydos. I have been there many times with Khaba."

"You must miss Khaba to speak of her this way," Khem said, her remark drawing an immediate response.

Tiye glanced at the floor, and when she looked back up at Khem her eyes were brimming with tears. "Khaba died last year."

"Oh, I am sorry. I did not know," Khem replied, a bit embarrassed. But before she could make any further comment, Tiye changed the subject.

"The meeting that Lady Taret has called at sunset, you will be there, yes?"

"Yes, of course."

"I have heard priests say that what is to be revealed will greatly affect the future of Egypt."

Tiye's remark surprised Khem with its candidness and because it implied the Nubian was friendlier with the priests than she was with the apprentices or elder priestesses. Khem recalled that at the time of the first meeting, Tiye had been talking with the oracle priest, Mentu.

"I am anxious to hear what is said. I do not know what to expect."

Khem's words were not entirely true. Taret had made it clear that the meeting was being convened for a transmission that would concern the prediction by the Followers of Horus regarding the appearance of a comet at the time of Inundation. Inundation marked the beginning of a new year and the annual flooding of the Nile. The event was always heralded by the predawn rising of the Nile Star, known also as Sothis, the original name of the goddess Isis, wife of Osiris. Although Khem did not understand the implications of the comet's appearance, she was aware of the significance of the time of year.

Egypt's existence depended upon the Nile. Its flow was greatly reduced throughout the time of drought from late February through June. The first waters of the river's annual rise, called the Green Nile, were foul. The Green Nile was followed by the Red Nile, whose waters took on the color of the thick, reddish slime carried downstream by the flood. The river's highest level occurred between the end of September and the first ten days in October, the time of Inundation, one of Egypt's three seasons.

Tiye seemed uncomfortable at mention of the comet. Khem was not sure how to read the Nubian's attitude. "Tiye," she began cautiously. "I get the feeling there is something about the comet that frightens you."

The Nubian jerked her head around and looked at Khem, giving the young apprentice the feeling that the question had angered her. However, Tiye's face softened quickly. "No, it does not frighten me. Khaba knew of its coming. She told me about it a year ago before she died. They were the last words she spoke to me."

The pain of Khaba's death was written all over Tiye's face. Khem could tell that speaking of her teacher was difficult. "I am sorry, Tiye," Khem said softly, reaching out to touch the other girl's arm.

"It is all right. You could not have known. Come. Let's go eat."

The two sat down to a dinner of fish, dried fruits, and barley bread. Khem knew that Tiye wanted to talk, and it made her feel good that she perhaps might be comfortable enough with her to open up, but she did not try to lead the conversation. Sipping on a cup of beer, Tiye seemed lost in her thoughts and it was a while before she spoke.

"I never knew my mother. She died giving birth to me. My father wanted nothing to do with me. I suppose he blamed me for her death. I was born with my mother's rope wrapped around my neck, and the womb veil covered my head. I was suffocating, but the midwife, Khaba, removed the rope from my throat and pulled the veil up and over my head. I lived."

Tiye took a bite of food before going on. "Khaba took me. She raised me. She was the only mother I ever knew." The bittersweet words caused her eyes to well up again with tears. Khem said nothing, for no words would come. In a moment, Tiye's expression changed from sadness to one that told Khem how deep was her love for Khaba.

"Khaba told me that children who were born with the womb veil over the heads have the Sight. They are born to serve the *Neteru*. My mother— I called Khaba mother—taught me everything she knew. She taught me to use the Sight. She taught me medicine and how to work the magic spells."

Khem realized that what Tiye had learned must be considerable. She had heard of Nubian sorceresses. She knew that Egyptians would sometimes consult a Nubian oracle for healing and potions, and to have spells worked.

"Khaba would sometimes have dreams," Tiye said. "But to her they were more than dreams. They were omens of things to come, things that bade evil for all of Egypt and Nubia. Her last dream was of the dawn sky filled with Sky Gods, one in the body of the Guardian Star, Sothis. Another was in the body of the comet. Another in the full Moon."

Khem was fascinated. "What does it mean? Who are the Sky Gods?" she asked anxiously.

Before Tiye could answer, Khem said, with a faraway look in her eyes, "Come to think of it, the Moon will be full this season. That is very interesting." How could Khaba have known? she thought to herself. She has been dead for a year.

Tiye shook her head slowly, indicating that she had no answer. "Khaba said only that the comet would represent or foretell the presence of an 'invader,' one who would stalk the White Crown of Egypt, who would stalk the throne in the darkness."

Her eyes wide, Tiye finished the last sentence in a halting whisper as if she feared that even to speak the words would bring Khaba's prophecy to pass. She glanced around, making sure no one had heard her. Her uneasiness was contagious, for Khem too felt a foreboding. Could Khaba's visions be linked to her own about the man who would threaten the throne?

For several minutes the two sat picking at their food in silence. Then Khem spoke. "It sounds like Khaba foresaw a threat to Pharaoh."

"I can think of nothing else it could be." Tiye spoke in a serious, almost threatening tone. Grasping Khem's upper left arm tightly, and leaning closer to her face, she said, "You must tell no one what I have told you. Promise me!" Her dark eyes narrowed into piercing slits, telling Khem that she meant what she said. No one must know.

Khem promised she would say nothing. The two finished the meal without saying anything further. Across the room, Kasut, also finishing dinner, motioned to Khem that she wished to speak to her. Excusing herself, Khem told Tiye that she would see her at the meeting.

"Since there will be no classes, I plan to go into the city tomorrow. Would you like to go with me? I want to see if I can find a scrying bowl."

Khem had been so engrossed in her conversation with Tiye that she had not given any thought to Taret's teaching. Now the High Priestess's words came back to her. "Yes. I would like that."

The two girls parted company, each expressing the desire to get some rest before the meeting.

When Khem returned to her room, Akhi was embroidering blue lotus flowers along the hem of a dress. "That is lovely, Akhi. I did not know you were a seamstress."

Obviously pleased, the servant girl held up the sheath for Khem to see. "There. It is finished," Akhi said, satisfied with her handiwork.

"You must have been working on this for many hours. Where did you find the time?"

"I wished to surprise you, my mistress. I am happy you like it."

"Oh, I do," Khem said, taking the dress and admiring the intricate designs. "Thank you."

After a short nap, Khem got up and washed her face and hands. She applied kohl to her eyes and brushed her hair. She would wear the sheath Akhi had embroidered to the meeting. As Khem changed clothes, the servant girl entered from the veranda where she had picked sweet-smelling calendula. "Here, my mistress. Let me put these in your hair." Akhi tucked the tiny golden blossoms under the ribbon Khem had tied around her head. She was ready for the meeting.

Chapter Five

The Meeting

As in many of the buildings throughout the complex, the massive double doors at the entrance of the main audience hall of the Temple of the Sun were of Lebanon cedar. On either side, a single, tall date palm grew out of a circular area of ground left exposed in the limestone walkway in front of the doors. When Khem got there she saw that the priests and priestesses had begun to arrive from their various stations within the Temple.

This day's conclave, though not a first, was a rare occasion. Such a meeting was called only for the purpose of revealing an important prophecy or truth. It had been rumored that Meri-ib, the High Priest over all the orders in Heliopolis, would be present. The rumor was confirmed when Khem spotted the hierophant rounding the corner, followed by an entourage of servants, priests, scribes, and advisors.

Meri-ib was a small man. His clean-shaven head was encircled by a narrow gold headband with a winged disk in the front. His long skirt just touched his reed sandals. A leopard skin overrobe lay across his bare chest, secured at the waist by a linen sash, dyed gold. The man exuded power.

When the High Priest went into the hall, the others followed. Khem stood back to wait for Tiye. She felt a connection with her since their conversation earlier in the day, and was anxious to be with her during Taret's revelation about the comet.

Khem heard a commotion and saw three men proceeding towards the entrance. Her mouth opened in surprise. One was the priest she had seen in the lower courtyard a few days before at the Horus statue. She would soon learn he was Sokar, half-brother of the Pharaoh. His servant, Kheti, was at his side. Though she had seen him only once, the man was even more imposing than Khem had remembered. Sokar looked exotic, dressed in a short white linen kilt with a wide gold sash tied around his midriff; his bare legs and chest showed a muscular body that had been rubbed with olive oil, and he wore a gold circlet on his head.

This time, it was not only Sokar's physical looks that drew attention to him. On his left wrist, clutching a wide leather band, perched a hooded falcon. The bird's head was big, its chest broad, its body two feet long, covered with brown feathers with touches of blacks, grays, and whites. Its short hooked bill protruded into a needle-sharp point, as did its talons. The bird was magnificent, and so was the man upon whose arm it perched. The priest next to Sokar paled in comparison.

Khem later learned that the other man was Nedjemou, the chief of the physicians and priests. He was dressed in a white linen robe with a cotton rope tied around his waist; his overrobe was also white. He carried a staff with a gilded head of the god Anubis carved on its top, its eyes and inner ears black. Numerous priests and priestesses trained under Nedjemou, who also had an office in the palace in Memphis as personal physician to the Pharaoh.

Khem watched as the men strolled past her and Kasut, who had joined her, and entered the hall. Once the men were out of sight the two girls looked at each other, their eyes wide with disbelief. It was uncommon to see a man like Sokar, and the hawk only added to his bold mystique.

As the priests and priestesses continued to file into the Hall, Khem was beginning to think Tiye was not going to show up. Another priest Khem had never seen walked towards the door.

"That is Caliph," Kasut said. "He is the Chief Star Priest."

Khem looked closely at the man, the oldest of the priests she had seen or met so far. Short and squat, Caliph shuffled and used a wooden staff to support himself. His skin was olive-toned, and his small eyes had a far-away look to them. Khem sensed wisdom in him.

Kasut and Senna joined Caliph in the meeting room, while Khem waited outside in the corridor. Finally, Khem spotted Tiye. "I have been waiting for you, Tiye. I was beginning to wonder if you were coming."

The Nubian muttered something about having fallen asleep, but Khem knew her reluctance to hear about the comet was the most likely reason why Tiye had delayed coming. But she was here now, and that was all that mattered. The two apprentices entered the audience hall together.

In addition to the usual floor pillows, this day the hall was furnished with fine cedar chairs in semicircular rows facing the raised dais. The room was very large. The walls were painted with beautiful scenes from the sacred texts, primarily of divine figures who represented the constellations: Orion, the Hippopotamus, the Thigh, the Lute Bearer, and others. On the wall behind the dais was a scene of the great Stone Head protruding from the desert floor; it was painted in shades of blues and whites that gave the image a dreamlike appearance. Large free-standing columns stood in rows three feet out from the side walls, their tops painted in the bright green colors of the sacred papyrus. The stars of the zodiac were painted upon the dark ceiling, covering it entirely.

The platform at the front of the hall was carpeted in squares woven from reeds that had been dyed a deep, rich red. To one side of the dais was a large, rectangular cedar altar table that was carved in such a way that its four legs formed the body of Mehturt, a Sky Goddess who was associated with the primeval waters from which Ra, the Sun god, was born. The wall behind the dais also had a beautiful gold winged disk painted on it. Leaning against the left side of the back wall was an ebony ladder that represented the Ladder to Heaven. The Ladder was a means of reaching the sky world and was used by Osiris. A gilded statue of Ra stood on one side of the Ladder, one of Horus on the other. These two deities had lifted Osiris up to the sky on the Ladder. The rungs of the Ladder, originally made from the sinews of Kasut, the Bull of the Sky, were here fastened to the Ladder's sides by leather thongs said to have been cut from the hide of the god Utes. Two large thrones occupied the center of the platform.

The priests and priestesses sat down on chairs and floor pillows in separate groups of men and women. Khem and Tiye sat in the back row, which provided them with a view of the entire hall. This is a magnificent place, Khem thought as she looked around. Then her eyes fell on Sokar. By now, she knew who he was. He was seated on the end chair a few rows to her right. He had placed the falcon, still as a statue, on a small wooden perch next to his seat.

Moments later, Taret entered from the back of the hall, and slowly ascended the dais. She was followed by her scribe, Sheshat, and two senior Star Priestesses who, once Taret and Sheshat were seated, went to the altar table. They lit incense in a bronze burner that diffused the scent of myrrh throughout the room. The women also lit the wicks in the two matching bronze lamps that sat on each end of the altar, before proceeding to the four corners of the great room, where they lit the tall floor candle that stood in each. In no time the scent of burning oil and candle mixed with the myrrh, creating a heavy fragrance that hung in the close warm air. The scene was different from anything Khem had ever experienced. She liked the pomp and formality of it all. It was apparently not the same for Tiye. The Nubian sat still, her eyes focused on Taret. The High Priestess waited patiently while the priestesses performed their duties.

As the Sun set, the hall gradually took on a soft glow. Their duties finished, the priestesses sat behind Taret. Just then four more members of the Order of Nut entered and walked in a procession down either side of the rows of chairs and up onto the platform where they stood to Taret's left. Khem guessed that these represented the four Sky Goddesses, Hathor, Neith, Uatchet, and Nekhebet.

For several minutes there was only silence. Then Taret stood up and spoke, straining to make her voice loud enough to be heard throughout the hall.

"Greetings to you all, my brothers and sisters of the Orders of Nut and Osiris, my fellow priests and priestesses, humble servants of the Sky Gods. It is the will of Nut, the One Who Gives Birth to the Stars, who has called us to gather here at this time. The Mistress of Heaven never speaks vain words, so it behooves us to listen carefully.

"It is my duty as the High Priestess of the Holy Order of Nut to speak for her so that what is known in the heavens by the gods will be known on Earth by humans."

Pausing briefly, Taret's eyes slowly swept those present. The sun had set now, and the large chamber had cooled off considerably. Khem eyed the falcon, perfectly still on its perch. The bird had an aura of power.

"In this part of the day that belongs to the god Atmu, the god of the setting Sun, I am prepared, as always, to offer myself to Nut to speak for her. My body is her body, my voice her voice, my words her words."

That said, the High Priestess's body relaxed. The servant girls who had lit the oil lamps earlier stepped onto the dais. One carried a narrow long-legged table which she put directly in front of the chair where Taret was seated.

Khem leaned forward to see what was happening. She watched as another servant priestess came forward carrying an alabaster bowl resting in the center of a gold-colored cushion. The girl moved very slowly, so Khem surmised that the bowl contained sanctified water.

The bowl-bearer paused in front of Taret for a moment and then, lifting the cushion slightly above her head and outward, she offered the bowl and its contents to the four directions, beginning in the east and slowly turning sunwise. She lowered the pillow carefully and turned to face the High Priestess and made a gesture as if she were presenting the bowl for Taret's approval. With a nod of her head, Taret signaled for the servant priestess to place the bowl on the table in front of her. This done, all the servants bowed to the Chief Priestess and left the platform. When they were seated, a priest stepped onto the dais and placed an oil lamp with long bronze legs directly in front of the table where the bowl rested and lit the lamp; the soft flame flickered to life.

Khem's curiosity peaked as she watched Taret lean forward in her chair and peer into the water, her lips forming unspoken words. Khem realized a conversation of sorts was taking place between Taret and a spirit known only to her.

Taret leaned back in her chair, her hands resting on its arms. Focusing her eyes on the flame in front of her, the High Priestess stared into the light. Her eyelids grew heavy, her head nodded and then hung gently. Then Taret raised her head and slowly opened her eyes, but they were eyes that saw nothing in the physical world. They were the eyes of a being, and its presence now filled the hall. Khem watched the priestess's body undergo subtle changes. It was as if she became larger, more imposing. Her posture was stiff, and her hands gripped the arms of the chair so strongly her knuckles were white. Taret began to speak, her voice flowing from her entire body in a way that was deeper and louder than Taret's usual soft voice.

"I am Nut, Keeper of the Stars. I am Nut, daughter of Shu, wife of Seb, mother of Osiris, Isis, Seth, and Nepthys, mother of the gods and of all living things, giver of food to the living and the dead. I am the feminine principle in creation. My body gives rest to the Sun so that the light of Ra might have the power to be reborn each dawn. It is to me that the great king Khufu and all the kings before him pray, saying, 'O my mother Nut, spread yourself over me so that I may be placed among the imperishable stars and never die.'"

The words, coming out haltingly at first, began to flow. Taret's body, now a vessel for the Sky Goddess, was stiff and erect, her eyes open wide and never blinking.

"I, Nut, am come to you, the priests and priestesses of the holy orders, servants of the Star Gods, so that I may, through this my humble servant Taret, speak to you of things to come. Know this: events on Earth correspond to changes in the sky. As it is above, so is it below. When there is an event that will affect the destiny of the children of Egypt, there will be a sign. Such a sign is a signature of my son, Osiris, the great Lord of Life, for it is ordained by him. Pay close attention to the time of the fiery omen, you servants of the Great Ones in the Heavens.

"At the time of Inundation, when the waters flow freely and the face of the Moon god, Thoth, is turned full to the Earth, the Moon shall be joined by a sky traveler who has made a journey into your precinct of the cosmos. This messenger of the Star Gods brings tidings of change, of the reopening of the star gates so that the Star Gods may come again to the holy land of Egypt. Their second coming is at hand. Knowledge that will change human life will be communicated to you who are seated here. But you must first ward off a great evil. You must recognize the face of falsity, a voice as sweet as nectar but that in truth is as bitter as alum. So be it."

With those words, the spirit force that had overtaken Taret's mind and body departed, leaving the High Priestess limp and silent. The energy in the room changed immediately. Khem thought that it was darker and warmer. Taret sat still, her eyes closed. No one in the room stirred or made a sound.

In a few minutes, Khem saw Taret lift the forefinger on her right hand and realized it was a signal to the servant priest and priestesses that the transmission was over and that she was back in her body. The priest who had placed the lamp came onto the platform first. Snuffing out the flame, he picked up the tripod and the lamp carefully so that no oil would be spilled and removed it to the side of the main hall. He was followed by the two priestesses who took away the table and scrying bowl. When the servants were finished, Taret looked out over the audience and said, her own voice returned, "The goddess has spoken." She then descended the dais, followed by the representatives of the four sky goddesses and Taret's two attendants. The entourage then made its way to the entrance of the main audience hall and was gone.

A wave of relaxation swept through the hall, which began humming with conversation. Heads came together with excited whispers regarding the meaning of the "great evil" the Sky Goddess had spoken about. Khem had been so enthralled by what was going on before and during the oracular speech that she had been oblivious to anyone's presence except Taret and those who facilitated the transmission. Now she became aware of Tiye next to her. Khem was surprised to see her smiling, and it was a smug smile at that. Whatever reaction she expected, it wasn't a smile, and she flashed Tiye a quizzical look.

"Khaba was right," Tiye said complacently. "The comet is the one that will accompany the Moon, and it foretells a great evil."

Khem knew that Tiye was more convinced than ever that the comet would bring unavoidable evil. She had heard the Sky Goddess's words as a warning, but not as a guarantee of pending disaster. The two girls were joined by Kasut and Meret who were making their way to the doorway.

"Did you hear that?" Kasut asked excitedly. "The spirit of Nut spoke in a riddle. What does it mean?"

"It means that there is trouble to come," Tiye snapped, causing Kasut and Meret to recoil.

"What! What trouble?" the girls asked in unison.

"Did you not hear the goddess's words? 'The face of falsity,' she said, and 'a great evil.'"

Tiye's tone was one of consternation. She had heard only the negatives that were issued in the form of a warning at the end of the transmission. Khem had to agree that the warning had been couched in a riddle. It fell to Khem to get in hand the situation brewing between the apprentice priestesses. Tiye was an alarmist and Kasut was apprehensive.

"I do not think there is cause for alarm," Khem said, trying to put a mild sternness in her voice to change the energy of this encounter. "The goddess has spoken of wonderful things, of a time when the Star Gods will reveal greater mysteries of the heavens, even of life itself. This is reason for celebration, not fear."

The other priestesses nodded their heads in silent agreement, but Tiye was not so easily deterred from her concerns.

"Have you forgotten? Did all of you not hear?" Tiye said. "There is a *condition*—two conditions in fact—that must be met before any new knowledge or communication between humanity and the Star Gods can take place."

Tiye was right. It was perhaps too easy to make light of or overlook the final words the goddess had spoken, but this was not the time to discuss the transmission any further. It would require some thought, Khem surmised, and with that the girls made their way to the door.

Khem and Tiye bade the other two priestesses a good evening and headed for Khem's room for a cup of wine. Khem was surprised Tiye accepted the invitation, as she did not seem to be very sociable. When the two came to the double doors that led out of the main hall, they saw the High Priest Meri-ib engaged in conversation with Sokar and overheard a snippet of what was said. With an air of smug arrogance, the falcon perched on his forearm, Sokar spoke of the Pharaoh.

"So, my half-brother has a great announcement to make at the Festival of Inundation, has he? And what might that be? It is the season for announcements, so it seems."

The expression on Meri-ib's face was polite placation. Khem and Tiye looked at each other, and before they were out of earshot, they heard the High Priest reply, "So it seems."

Sokar bowed haughtily and walked towards the doorway. Once outside the main hall he was met by a young woman Khem had not noticed at the meeting. She was beautiful, bronze-skinned, with long, straight hair and almond-shaped eyes.

"Who is she?" Khem whispered to Tiye.

"She is called Mafdet," Tiye replied. "She is the daughter of Menkar, a wealthy merchant."

Khem felt a shudder in her body at this. Try as she might to ignore the feeling, she sensed danger.

When the girls arrived at Khem's room, it occurred to Khem that she did not know where Tiye lived. Tiye told her she lived outside the Temple, boarding with a family who had agreed to sponsor her apprenticeship. It was an unusual arrangement, but Tiye found it to her liking. She was not one to mix much socially, and she liked the privacy that life outside the Temple afforded her. Tiye preferred the city's bustle more than the Temple's isolation.

They sat cross-legged on Khem's bed sipping wine and nibbling on bread and goat cheese. It was nice to relax, and they were enjoying the chitchat, and this made Khem reluctant to steer the conversation back to the speech, though it was obviously on both their minds.

"I was thinking," Khem said. "It was not the comet that was said to be an omen of evil or danger. At least that is not what I heard."

"No," Tiye replied. "But there is evil connected with its appearance. Like Khaba said, there always is with comets."

It was apparent that the Nubian was not going to focus on anything positive about what had come through Taret. Khem was beginning to think that Tiye was a pessimist, but as she listened to her friend talk, she changed her mind.

"Khaba taught me many things. She taught me magic. She taught me spells and formulas to influence people and events. She said important events, whether they are good or bad, are always preceded by an omen that tells of what is to come. Khaba said star omens always tell of things that concern everyone, even all of Egypt. She once told me about a star that fell from the sky many ages ago, and landed on a place in the desert that from that day became a sacred place. It was there that a great mound of earth existed, and upon that mound this very temple where we are now was built many centuries later."

Khem's father had told her the same story about the Primeval Mound. It had fascinated her then, as a little girl, and it fascinated her again now. Her thoughts went back to the Star Stone she had heard about in class.

Tiye continued. "Khaba said that when the star fell from the sky it made a loud sound that caused some people to die from fear. The Star Stone had great power, even the power of immortality."

Khem was intrigued by Tiye's knowledge. She knew that what the Nubian had learned from Khaba no doubt qualified her as a magician. Meanwhile, the hour was late, and Tiye had to venture into the city to get home. Her servant girl had come to Heliopolis with Tiye, and now awaited her mistress. She was chatting with Akhi in the anteroom. Tiye prepared to go.

When they left, Khem got ready for bed. Removing her sheath, the one Akhi had so beautifully embroidered, she laid the dress across her bed and admired it again. She then took the flowers from her hair, now wilted, and laid them on her dressing table. They were still sweet and their fragrance permeated the room. Her thoughts competed with fatigue, and slipping on a night dress, Khem went to the wall altar and lit the oil lamp. The flame sputtered to life, casting a soft, soothing glow in the room.

Khem picked up the statue of Thoth and held it up to the light. The small ibis-headed god felt warm in her hand. Thoth had the wisdom of the stars; he was in charge of the Moon. That led her to remember the Full Moon coming up at Inundation. It would be the first time she would see it after becoming an apprentice in Heliopolis. Aside from the rites associated with the flooding of the Nile, there would be a Moon ceremony as well. Khem looked forward to its celebrations.

Placing the statue back in its place, Khem offered a prayer to the divinities:

> Hail, Great God, Lord of the Heavens, You, who gave Light to the Dark Breath, and who brought order from Chaos. You, who have always been; You, who are now; and You who will always be; Bless me your humble servant.

Chapter Six

The Stone Head of the Desert

Pharaoh's courier had just delivered the message that Khufu had eagerly awaited. It was from Nemon, the master builder. The messenger had made the trip from Memphis to Abusir, where the architect was overseeing the construction of a temple being erected to the Sun god Ra. The contents of the communiqué indicated that Nemon would arrive in the capital city on the following day. The message brought Khufu great relief.

Khufu had thought of nothing but Meri-ib's vision since the day the High Priest had come from Heliopolis to the palace and informed him of his encounter with the god Thoth in the central chapel of the Sun Temple. Standing now at the window of the main court room of the palace, the Pharaoh reached into the waistband of his tunic and took out the white feather. He had held it and looked at it a hundred times before; each time it had brought the reality of the task of unearthing the Sphinx squarely before him.

Khufu contemplated the opulent environment of his court room. Decorated lavishly with gold and gemstones, beautiful scenes painted by Egypt's finest artists, carpeted floors—rich to be sure, but he had never known anything else. Turning to the throne, he remembered the day of his coronation when the artisans had brought the great Seat of Judgment into the main audience hall. It was made of solid gold that had been inlaid with a winged sun disk made from lapis. The ends of the arms of the chair were fashioned with the head of the Sphinx, the stone king of Giza.

Khufu ran his hand over the smooth Sphinx head. The gold was cool and almost soft to the touch. His mind filled with images of that day when he had ascended the throne and accepted the Scepter of Egypt. He had been carried on a gilded litter through the streets of Memphis. He could still hear the cheers of the people ringing in his ears when he let his mind go back to that time. The great hall had been decorated with rare blue lotuses making an avenue through which he walked alone to the throne. It had been the shortest and the longest walk of his life.

His memory of receiving the Crook and Flail and sitting on the throne for the first time was vivid to him. He remembered his oath of office, and the strange sensation that had come over him as he spoke the words of his pledge to Egypt and its people. It was as if he had stepped out of his body and for a moment had watched himself being crowned. He remembered the "pop" he heard inside his head when he returned to his physical body.

Khufu knew the responsibilities of being Pharaoh. His father had been king before him. What he could not know was that as he took on the mantle of kingship, along with it came initiation into the great mystery, the moment when, in the Duat, the spiritual realm of the gods, the heritage of the Star Gods would be passed to him as it had been to those before him and he would be handed the Rod of Power.

He recalled that the initiation had taken place in a dream before his coronation. He had retired to his private quarters early after a state dinner in the palace's main banquet hall. The food had been sumptuous, the entertainment fit for a king. Acrobats, musicians, chanters, and dancers had provided the finest amusement and inspired a range of emotions from awe at the quality of the drama to laughter at the antics. He loved the fanfare that surrounded kingship. He knew how to be king, and he was comfortable with the role. It was in the role of being an initiate as every ruler before him had been that Khufu was not completely confident. He wasn't sure he could fulfill the obligations to the ancient knowledge and practices with which he had been entrusted.

The Pharaoh was the leader of all the initiates, the priest of all priests and priestesses, the spiritual and religious leader of Egypt. It was not by his choice, but by birthright that it was so. Still, no man who had worn the crown of Egypt was more devoted to bear the burdens and meet the responsibilities, secular and sacred, of the kingship than Khufu. He knew his mission in life.

The precoronation "dream" had not been a dream at all, but an experience that had carried Khufu into a dimension of time and space in which he had never been before. He had found himself surrounded by a dozen white-robed magicians, gold medallions around their necks. In the center of each medallion was an overlay of copper with the Eye of Horus inlaid with lapis. A mist swirled over each initiate, and Khufu knew that he was seeing the souls of these Great Ones. In fact, there was nothing he did not know while he was in the presence of these beings. His intuitive faculties were fully awake.

The Great Ones encircled the candidate, moving ever closer to him, until the circle was closed and the beings melted into one entity of light. At this moment of closure, Khufu felt a powerful current go through him, activating him. He was aware of the energy lifting him above the swirling soul current that had been the twelve Great Ones. It was like being thrust into a vacuum in which he was uninhibited by his body or mind. He was pure soul, a conscious part of all that exists, one with the Star Gods. As the vortex of light held him in suspension, Khufu experienced his physical body being dismantled, atom by atom, in a purifying rite that would change him forever. He was no longer just a human. He was now a god—a Star God. He knew he belonged to the heavens and that someday he would take his place among the stars.

As the dream experience ended, Khufu returned to his physical self on his bed. His mind had been invested with a knowledge of the cosmos that was known only by the Star Gods, and they had entrusted that wisdom to him. Remembering the experience now made Khufu feel the weight of his responsibility to the Star Gods. He knew that when the celestial hierarchy chose a time to transmit knowledge to humanity on Earth, all the astronomical configurations and terrestrial conditions had to be just right. In order for this to be so, the gods had chosen the Stone King of the Desert for the transmission, the site where a great Hall of Records would be created. These records would contain the star wisdom and formulas for humans to connect with the gods.

No matter how many people already knew, and would soon know, about the Second Coming of the Star Gods, Khufu alone knew what the gods required once they were here, and why. So it was now his task to unearth the Sphinx and to see to the erection of a temple to hold the treasures of star wisdom.

Absorbed in the memories of his initiation and how knowledge of his soul's identity had come to him, Khufu pondered the logistics of preparing for a construction that would no doubt rival the challenge the earlier builders of the Great Pyramid and the Sphinx had faced. His thoughts were interrupted when the chief steward entered the room.

"Your Majesty, Nemon has arrived."

"Good. I have been waiting. Show him in, and leave us in private," Khufu answered calmly.

Moments later the ruler's cousin strolled into the audience hall. Nemon was vibrant, high-spirited, and intelligent. He embraced life, and most Egyptians, including Khufu, respected him as a man of vision. Khufu was confident Nemon would get the job done.

Approaching Khufu, Nemon bowed deeply in respect of his cousin's high office. The two embraced, and Nemon delivered his customary friendly slap on Khufu's back. Since they were boys the two had been close, although their respective careers had robbed them of time they would liked to have spent together.

"To what, pray you, do I owe the honor of this command visit, your Majesty?" Nemon asked, his eyes sparkling with expectation.

Khufu's mood turned serious as he went to the window and gazed at the desert. Choosing his words carefully, for there was only so much he could reveal and still manage to get his point across, he said, "A few days back I was paid a visit by Meri-ib, the High Priest of Heliopolis. Meri-ib had a . . . vision—no, he had a visitation."

Nemon's curiosity peaked. He looked at Khufu expectantly, waiting for him to go on.

"The visitation was a spirit who informed Meri-ib of a time in the near future when the Star Gods will return to the Earth for the second time in human history. Their coming has to do with providing the old lineage of Star Priests, the Followers of Horus, with new knowledge that will change the course of human evolution."

Nemon was spellbound. Like all Egyptians, he had always known of the visitation of the Star Gods during the First Time. That story was part of Egypt's legacy.

"Meri-ib has received certain instructions that must be carried out, and the project must be undertaken immediately."

"What project, my cousin?" Nemon inquired eagerly.

"You are of course familiar with the Stone Head at Giza?"

"Yes," Nemon replied.

"It is known that what is seen above the ground is not the entire monument. But, as you also know, it has been covered by sand for so many centuries that there is no one alive who has looked upon it in full. We only have the ancient texts to go by."

"Yes, your Majesty. There are even drawings of the whole monument in the texts, so I have heard, but that may be hearsay for I have not seen them," Nemon said.

"There are some original designs, but they are very old, and it is not known if they were produced by eyewitnesses or represent fabled accounts," Khufu admitted.

Nemon assumed that Khufu's knowledge was based on information provided to him by the priesthood, so he asked no questions. He had begun to guess where the conversation was leading, but he let Khufu continue.

"The Sky Gods have petitioned the High Priest, head of the Temple of the Sun, and me, Khufu, Pharaoh of Egypt, that the time has come for *Harmakhis* to be released from its prison of sand. This is why I have sent for you, Nemon."

Khufu fell silent to allow his words to sink in. Nemon walked to a nearby chair and sat down, heaving a deep sigh. After a pause, he looked at the king with conviction. "It will be done, your Majesty. I will begin to work on a plan right away, and I will get back to you before the Sun has set on *Harmakhis* again," Nemon said. "Now, unless there is something else, I must go. I have a lot of thinking to do."

In Heliopolis, the sun had reached its zenith. The air was hot and dry, the streets dusty, the city bustling with people going about the day's business. Khem and Kasut had left the Temple after the morning meal. Followed close behind by their servants, Akhi and Nita, they had ventured into Heliopolis to purchase some needed items. Akhi and Nita got along well and appreciated making the journey into the city for pleasure instead of errands. Although most lived in the Temple complex, many servants still had lives outside, and some had families.

Khem and Kasut headed towards the market square, where merchants of all kinds brought their wares to sell. The young priestesses were looking for bowls suitable for scrying. They walked along the street, stopping to look at goods displayed in the stalls and to sample the foods.

Kasut stopped to look at the palettes of kohl. The oval-shaped palettes for eye shadow were spread out on a low-legged table along with phials of green malachite and galena, tiny bone and metal spoons, face paint, and yellow-red henna leaves for coloring nails, hair, and the palms and soles.

Khem left Kasut and wandered over to another part of the bazaar, where a vendor had pigeons and other birds in cages. She recognized the merchant as the one she had seen on the day she arrived in Heliopolis. She was eager to see if the lioness cub was still there. To her surprise, the man remembered her and flashing the girl a toothless grin, he disappeared into a small tent. He returned cradling the cub in his arms. The cat had not grown much and it looked lethargic. It must be the heat, Khem thought, but she sensed it was more than that. The vendor explained that the cub had been orphaned and had come close to dying from starvation before it was found. It had been transported by cargo ship upriver to Heliopolis from the south and had been unresponsive to the food scraps it had been fed along the way.

"How old is it?" Khem asked.

"Barely eight weeks," the man replied.

The cub's ribs stuck out, causing Khem to wonder if the cat was getting fed properly even now. Khem asked if she could hold the cub. He happily handed it over to her, the tiny cat offering no resistance. Holding it carefully, she was surprised to find it heavier than she expected. Though it was pitifully thin, muscles rippled in its body. Its paws were large, its claws caked with dirt and dry dung, and its coat was coarse to the touch.

"Oh, you poor thing," Khem cooed. "Look at you, you are all dirty."

The baby lioness relaxed, its gold-colored eyes looking up at Khem. There was something about those eyes that made her heart ache, a sort of lonesome, forlorn look. "I bet you would like some milk, wouldn't you, my little friend?" Khem turned to the man and asked if the animal had had milk today.

"Oh yes, some," he replied in a way that told Khem that milk, or any other nutritional food for that matter, was not something to which the cub was accustomed. Its short life, judging by its condition, had been traumatic. Khem felt sorry for the orphaned cat.

"Where can I get it some milk?"

The man pointed toward a food stall a few paces away where eggs, breads, fruits, and meats were for sale. Giving the cub back to the man, Khem got a small vessel of goat's milk and a piece of dried meat and returned to the animal stall. Taking the cub in her arms again, she walked to a nearby acacia tree and sat down in its shade. The vendor provided her with a siltware bowl into which she poured a little of the fresh milk. She dipped her finger into the bowl and touched it to the animal's lips. At first it jerked its head back and sniffed the milk. It then began licking furiously.

"Oh, you like that, do you?"

Khem put the bowl on the ground as the little cat stuck its head into it. Within a few minutes she refilled the bowl three times, and still the cub lapped it up hungrily. Unrolling the meat from its palm leaf wrapping, she put it up to the cub's nose.

"Ouch!" Khem exclaimed as the lioness bit into the meat, nicking her finger.

The cub's demeanor changed almost instantly. The food, maybe the first real meal it had ever had, and the loving attention had worked a miracle. As if it knew it was with somebody to whom it belonged, the lioness lay down and rolled on its back. Khem patted the full pink belly and smoothed its coat with gentle strokes. The cat licked its face and paws with its rough tongue, and then, flipping over, laid its head down on its paws, ready for a nap.

"There you are, Khem. I lost you. I did not know where you disappeared to."

Khem looked up to see Kasut headed toward her.

"Oh, what is this?" Kasut knelt and cautiously reached out her hand for the cub to sniff.

"Isn't she beautiful?" Khem answered excitedly. "I saw her on the day my family and I came to Heliopolis. She was almost starved to death. I have just fed her milk and meat. Look."

Khem rolled the now-docile cub over on its back, exposing its belly for Kasut. Kasut rubbed the cub, then cupped her hand over its face and playfully shook its head from side to side. The lioness rolled over, stood up on all fours, waddled over, and climbed up onto Khem's lap. The two girls giggled.

"It thinks you are its mother," Kasut said. "Now what will you do about that, my friend?"

Khem looked at the animal lovingly. She was beginning to think she would not be able to walk away and leave the cub.

"Come, Khem," Kasut said. "We haven't finished our shopping. We haven't found our bowls."

Shopping had become unimportant to Khem. All that was important now was figuring out how she could keep the cub. She knew that some Temple residents had pets, but none had lions. What would Akhi think? How would she react? What would the vendor want for payment? She had some money, but had no idea what a lioness cost. What would she do when it grew up? All these thoughts were running around inside Khem's head as she considered her options. She did not know what would befall the animal, but she could guess that it would be doomed to stay with the vendor if he did not sell it soon, or be abandoned in the desert or, worse, be bought and skinned for its pelt. Khem shuddered at the thought.

"Wait, Kasut," Khem pleaded. "I cannot leave this animal. I must have her for myself."

Kasut stared at Khem with a shocked look. "You can't be serious," she said.

"I am quite serious." She marched over to the animal vendor who was collecting money for a cage of several large pigeons. "Is the lioness cub for sale?"

"Yes, of course. Do you wish to buy it? I will make you a good price." The vendor could smell a sale and that inspired him to become quite charming.

"How much?" Khem asked, not falling for the politeness.

"For you—" he hesitated, then appeared to come to a decision. "I will trade for you—remember me and my family in your prayers."

Khem smiled. She had not realized how apparent it was that she was an apprentice priestess.

The transaction completed, Khem realized what she had done. She was happy yet apprehensive. Whether it would work out or not depended as much on Akhi as it did on her. She didn't have long to wait to find out. The two servant girls spotted Khem and Kasut and came over. Akhi and Nita saw the lioness cub, and much to Khem's relief, both girls stooped down to pet the animal.

"Isn't she beautiful?" Khem said, with all the enthusiasm she could muster. Thinking the cub was cute was one thing, but what would Akhi's reaction be when she found out that it now belonged to her mistress? No point in waiting to find out, Khem decided. So, with no doubt in her voice, she announced to Akhi that she had bought the cub and would raise it at the Temple.

The look on Akhi's face was surprise and disbelief. At first, Khem thought she would surely balk at the idea. However, in a moment, the servant girl's expression changed and her face broke into a smile. "Are you jesting, my mistress?" Akhi asked, expecting Khem to laugh and say that it was all a lark.

"No, Akhi. She is really mine," Khem replied. "I have fallen in love with this little one. I could not resist." Khem took the lioness in her arms, cradling it like a baby. It was all going to be all right.

"Here, my mistress. I will carry her."

Khem smiled to herself as she handed the cub to Akhi.

Khem and Kasut had not found the bowls they had come for, so Akhi and Nita volunteered to take the cub and return to the temple so the girls could finish making their purchases. With the lioness in tow, the servants set out for home.

Khem and Kasut strolled the avenue until they came to a potter's stall. Bowls, water jars, and cooking vessels of all kinds were spread on the ground and two women sat on short wooden stools. The younger of the two, probably the older woman's daughter, stood up and greeted the priestesses shyly. The shoppers walked around looking at the clay wares, picking up several of the vessels to see if they would do.

Kasut found her bowl almost immediately. It was of plain clay, its rim etched with *wadjets*. Khem admired it, and considered a similar one decorated with lotus blossoms painted in soft blues and greens, but decided against it. The girls were about to leave to seek out another potter when the young girl attending the stall took out two vessels from a large reed basket. Both were made of alabaster: one was small and looked more like a vase than a bowl; the other had a lovely pink hue to it and was a shallow, oval-shaped dish. Its simple yet elegant design was perfect, durable, even pretty to look at, Khem thought. Taking a coin from her purse, she paid the asking price, and the two headed back to the Temple, bowls in hand.

Chapter Seven

The Star of Isis

Khem's feet were hot and dusty, her sheath wet with sweat. It had been a hot day and now that the sun was beginning to set, she was ready to change into a thin linen caftan and take off her sandals so her feet could feel the coolness of the limestone floor. She had walked faster than usual on the trip back to the temple. She was anxious to get home and make sure that Akhi and Nita had gotten home safely with the lioness cub.

On the way, all sorts of thoughts passed through her mind. She had begun to have doubts about whether she would be allowed to keep the animal in the Temple. She knew of no rule against it, but then it might be the first time anyone had assumed that a lioness would be welcome. Would she be able to feed it? How big would it get? She had been so lost in her thoughts that she had barely said a word to Kasut.

When Khem got to her room it was empty. There was no sight of Akhi or the lioness. At first she was alarmed. Where could they be? Was there trouble? Trying to remain calm, she sat down on her bed and kicked off her sandals. Then, just as she stood up and began to pull her sheath over her head, Akhi came in from the patio with the cub cradled in her arms.

"I did not know you were home, my mistress," Akhi said in a surprised tone.

When the cub saw Khem, its ears perked and it let out a sound that was more like a rattle than a meow. The little cat already seemed to know her. Akhi put the lioness on the floor, and it bounded over to Khem playfully, latched on to one of her sandals, and began chewing it. The two girls watched, laughing, before it dawned on Akhi that the shoes being chewed were Khem's best.

"No! No!" Akhi shouted sharply, causing the cat to stop its chewing and hunker down in anticipation of being smacked. Both girls realized the cub had probably been punished during its short life, and they felt sorry for it. They also knew that the cub would have to be trained very soon or they would surely have an unmanageable animal on their hands. Khem removed the shoes from the cat's reach. It was apparent that nothing could any longer be left in a vulnerable place.

"I have brought some milk and fish for the cat. She must be hungry again by now. You finish changing, my mistress, and I will feed her," Akhi volunteered happily.

"Yes, thank you, Akhi," Khem replied, grateful for a moment's respite. What would she do without Akhi. She had, in a few short days, come to depend on the girl and thought of her as both friend and servant.

Khem changed her clothes. Where would the cub sleep? It certainly could not be left to roam the room at will, at least not until it was older. Akhi had anticipated the problem. The servant disappeared into her bedchamber and in a moment returned carrying a large crate of acacia wood.

"It is perfect, Akhi," Khem cried. "You have thought of everything."

Settling the cat in its box after it drank a dish of milk, Akhi began tidying up. She picked up Khem's sandals and assessed the damage. Finding the shoes all right, she collected the soiled sheath and poured some water into the washbowl on the dressing table. "You will feel better if you wash the dust and sweat from yourself," Akhi said.

Khem went over to the table and, taking a linen cloth, began cleaning the day's soil from her body. She preferred to wash herself, and Akhi had not insisted otherwise. Lifting her hair to wipe the sweat from her neck, Khem stopped and turned to Akhi.

"The lioness must have a name. What shall I name her, Akhi?"

Before Akhi could answer, Khem exclaimed, "Bastet! Her name will be Bastet. She will be named after the Sun's daughter. She will be a lioness goddess. I will call her Bast for short." Khem was pleased with her choice.

Sleep came swiftly to Khem that night. If the lioness stirred, Khem heard nothing. Not long into her night's rest, the priestess awakened in the dream world where images unfolded within an undulating cloud. Khem found herself standing in the center of a beautiful, ornate Throne Room. She was clothed in a long white robe with a heavy gold pectoral around her neck. Her robe had long sleeves that almost covered her hands; it was a garment unfamiliar to her, but made her feel like a bona fide priestess. The floor on which she was standing was inlaid with a gold five-pointed star, which emitted an energy that flowed upward through the soles of her bare feet to fill her body.

Suddenly, the dreamer felt an urge to turn sunwise three times. The mere thought made it happen. She felt her body lifted on a gentle current of energy, and she began to spin slowly in the air, provoking a powerful spiritual presence. A throne suspended in midair appeared before her. Upon it sat a woman in a gown woven from pure gold. As Khem looked at the goddess-like figure, she was frightened. The woman's head was not human. It was a cat head, and it drew the priestess's eyes to her own like a magnet. Even though the figure's lips did not move, Khem heard the cat woman speak: "I am Bastet, daughter of the Sun god. The time of Inundation approaches. It will be a time of great change, a time when you will be empowered. Look to me. I will guide you. I will sanction you. I will awaken the warrioress within you, Star Daughter."

Her attention locked in the gaze of the hypnotic green eyes of the cat goddess, Khem's dream began to fade. The five-pointed star upon which she stood turned into a whirling vortex of cool mist that slowly engulfed her body, sucking her downward into a tunnel, and she knew no more.

After this, Khem slept deeply through the night. When morning came, the sun's rays were warm and the room was already starting to heat up. Shaking the sleep from her head, Khem sat up in bed. The linens were soaked with sweat. Bounding playfully out of Akhi's room came the lioness cub, and in an instant she had jumped onto the bed to lick Khem's face. The moment she saw the cub, the memory of her dream came back. She could see the cat-headed woman, her svelte body, and those emerald eyes that had held her in a timeless dimension. The deity's words replayed in her head as the cub's paws grabbed at her hair.

Akhi took Bast in hand, reprimanding the animal sternly. "You must not be on the lady's bed," she scolded. "You are a naughty cat!" She then put Bast in her box and began to lay out Khem's toiletries and fresh clothes. Khem sat deep in thought, pondering the meaning of the dream.

The business of the morning shifted Khem's attention away. When she finished dressing she sat for Akhi to brush her hair and braid it into a plait, then coil it into a cone atop her head.

Once dressed, Khem ate a meager breakfast of bread and fruit. She was anxious to get to class and hear the teaching and get some information on Taret's talk from two evenings before. There was so much going on it was hard to think it all through as thoroughly as it deserved. There was also the matter of the lioness. She would have to inform the powers that be about Bast, but not yet. . . .

A few weeks had passed and Khem was settling into her Temple life. She was happy. Aside from her studies and the social life that was just beginning, she could feel herself changing inwardly. She clearly felt that there had been a shift in her, and she was now more psychically open. Her dreams seemed more vivid and momentous now than the ones she had had before coming to the temple, with the exception of the destiny dream. She realized dreams had always played an important role in her life.

On her way to class Khem encountered Senna sitting by the lotus pool in the lower courtyard. She was happy to see him and she wanted, finally, to tell someone about Bast.

"Good morning, Senna," Khem greeted the priest, who rose to his feet when she walked towards him. "I am happy to see you."

"And you, Khem," Senna replied. "I have missed seeing you. You wouldn't be avoiding an old man now, would you?"

"No, my dear Senna. I have been going in a thousand directions, it seems. Life here is full!"

Khem found the old priest to be kind and his presence in the dormitory made her feel secure. Besides, she missed her father and Senna helped fill that gap in her life. She vowed to herself that she would spend more time with him. Hesitant at first, she asked Senna if she could tell him a secret.

"I love secrets. Tell me, child," Senna answered, looking at the priestess with expectation.

"Well, it is not exactly a secret, but you are the only person other than Akhi and a couple of others who know . . . yet anyway."

Khem decided to just blurt it out. Looking around to make sure no one could hear what she said. "I have gotten a pet, Senna. It is a wonderful pet," Khem said in a loud whisper.

"Oh, is that all?" Senna answered, somewhat disappointed that the girl had not told him a juicier tidbit than that. "Many of the priests and priestesses have pets, and so do some of the apprentices."

"Yes, I know. But this is no ordinary pet, Senna," she explained, wanting to get to the point but still apprehensive as to his reaction.

"No ordinary pet? What do you have, daughter? A crocodile?" Senna teased.

"No, I do not have a crocodile. I have a lioness cub," Khem stated a bit defensively.

"A lioness cub, did you say?"

"Yes, a lioness cub," Khem replied, eyeing the priest carefully for any nuances his face might reveal. "Her name is Bast."

"Why, that is quite a pet. And where, pray tell, did you get this Bast?"

Khem proceeded to tell Senna about her excursion into Heliopolis, and how she had found the half-starved kitten. "I am sure I saved its life." Khem's voice took on the air of one who felt the need to justify her action. "Will I get into trouble? Do you think Taret or Ani will forbid me from keeping her?"

The priest thought for a long moment before replying to the question, realizing that the girl was relying upon his response to test the waters as to what objections she might encounter. Finally, he said he did not feel there would be a problem so long as the animal was not dangerous.

"Oh no, she is just a babe. She will not hurt anyone," Khem replied. She anticipated Senna's next remark. "She will be big someday, I know. But she will be well mannered. Akhi and I will see to that."

"I am sure you will, child, I am sure you will."

Khem felt better. Senna had not been upset, so she doubted that anyone else would be either. In any case, she would deal with objections if and when they arose. For now, she was anxious to be on her way to class.

When Khem entered the classroom, the first person she saw was Tiye. She excitedly told her about Bast and invited her to see the cat after the teaching session. Khem sensed that Tiye was preoccupied and tense. "Are you all right, Tiye?"

"I had a dream last night that I cannot get out of my mind."

Khem could tell that whatever Tiye's dream had been about it had frightened her, and left her shaken. She also suspected that no sooner had Tiye said that than she regretted having mentioned the dream. Khem wondered if the Nubian trusted her as much as she had thought. "Tiye, you can trust me," she assured her friend. "I will speak to no one. Tell me what you dreamed."

Tiye took on the smugness that was a natural part of her demeanor. It was a part of Tiye's personality that Khem was learning to accept and to not take so seriously. The Nubian snapped her reply, her head cocked to one side. "It meant nothing. It was just a dream."

"If you say so," Khem quipped, trying to appear as if the matter was dropped. "Will you come and see Bast?"

Tiye said that she would and walked away and sat down on a floor pillow. Khem let her go. She didn't think it would be wise to press her any further about her dream.

Ani will be teaching today, Khem thought, as she found her own place to sit. Kasut came into the classroom and joined her. Before long, Ani came in and climbed the few steps up to the teaching platform. Khem had not interacted with the Dream Priestess, but was keenly interested in the work the woman did in the dream room of the temple.

When Ani began speaking, she announced that the newest apprentices would soon begin studying with the priestess Dak, the chief amulet maker.

Amulet making was something Khem knew little about, and the prospect of learning it excited her. Ani then made a second announcement.

"Today I will speak about the star Sothis, the Nile Star."

When Khem heard the words "the Nile Star," she felt a tingling sensation that made goose bumps rise on her skin. She was already mesmerized as the teaching began.

"The Sun hides the stars in its light. In the same way, the sacred texts hide the great mysteries of the cosmos. It is imperative that you understand that events that occur in the heavens are revealed to our eyes on Earth by a sign, a sign that mirrors a great celestial milestone. It is about such a milestone that I wish to speak to you now."

"A very long time ago, at the beginning of the First Time, the union of three potent celestial powers took place. It was an event that involved the unity of the cosmic forces. These are the force of magnetism, the law of attraction, and the force of pure light. Together, these three form the one law, the law of unity or cohesion. This cosmic union took place as a direct and natural result of the evolution of the universe as a living entity. To mark this event, a sign was revealed in the heavens that would remind the people of Egypt that these forces were forever joined."

Reaching around behind her chair, Ani brought up a large piece of papyrus that had been painted with geometric designs. Khem saw they comprised a map of the heavens. Ani continued. "The celestial trinity represents the most powerful forces in nature, as well as of life and death." Pointing to the star map, Ani identified the stars in the trinity. Then, pointing to the star Sirius, she said, "This is Sothis, the Star of Isis. This great sun is the Mother Goddess clothed in her star body. She embodies the power of cosmic magnetism."

Ani next put her finger on the group of stars that comprise the constellation Orion. "This is the great god Osiris, husband of Isis. He is the force of pure light, electric." She then pointed to the design that represented the Daystar. "And this is the divine son of Isis and Osiris, the god Horus, the Lord of Heaven. Horus is a manifestation of the cosmic life force and he is the balance of the two energies."

Khem was not sure she understood all the implications of the power that the celestial trinity embodied. She did understand that the stars Ani had identified formed the foundation of Egyptian star mythology. Every Egyptian knew the stories of Isis, Osiris, and Horus. She now realized for the first time that the union of the three was portrayed in the sky. They *were* the Sky Gods.

Putting the star map back on the floor, Ani continued her line of thought. "It is a special time of the year, when Sothis is the great provider to the people of Egypt."

Chapter Eight

Partners in Magic

Sokar was in his apartment in the Temple of the *Benu*. A smaller temple than the Temple of the Sun, the *Benu* sanctuary housed its own High Priest, Horakis, and other highly skilled sky-watcher priests, the Followers of Horus. It was also where the sacred Benben stone was kept. The Benben was said to be a piece of the original Star Stone now secure in the possession of the elite priests. Exercising his royal connection as the Pharaoh's half-brother, Sokar had chosen to live at the *Benu* temple for reasons known only to him.

It had been a long day and Sokar was ready to relax. Entering his luxurious quarters, he immediately called for his house servant to bring a robe and water to wash his face and hands. The Sun always seemed to burn the brightest and hottest just before the New Year, he reflected.

After changing his clothes, Sokar went into his private sitting room. On a perch near the double doors that led onto a large patio with a water garden in its center sat the sleek-feathered falcon, whom Sokar called Horus. Sokar extended his right forearm to the bird and Horus stepped from his perch, his wings flapping to maintain his balance. Sokar strolled out onto the plaza and let the falcon climb onto another perch there. He had had the falcon since it was a young chick. It was his friend and served Sokar as a magical partner, his familiar.

Sokar's mother, Nefer-er, had died many years earlier. She had been a concubine of Pharaoh Sneferu, Khufu's father. Her dream was to become the primary wife after giving birth to the king's first son, but it was not meant to be. Sokar had been raised in the palace and treated well. But he was bitter. He felt that he, not Khufu, should now be king. He was the first-born son, and being raised in the luxury of the palace did not make up for his bitterness. He was not Pharaoh. Khufu was.

Sokar had been educated as a scribe at the Temple of Ptah in Memphis, and had entered the priesthood soon after graduation. He had done well, but being a priest, even a high-level one, was not what he wanted to be, and the Temple of the *Benu* was not where he truly wanted to live. He wanted to occupy the royal palace in Memphis. He wanted to be Pharaoh. It was his birthright. He had a plan that, if successful, would put him precisely where he wanted to be. He would let nothing and no one get in his way of being Pharaoh.

Sokar's jealousy and bitterness, however, made him a target for being recruited, unconsciously, into the service of the dark forces. Be they right or wrong, motives that are fueled by negative emotions are motives that will eventually put one on a collision course with the forces of light. In every case, a battle will ensue between the opposing forces. Regardless of who emerges as the victor, one is likely to carry the scars of the battle for decades to come, if not lifetimes. Such battles, though they may originate on subtle planes, will ultimately play out on the Earth, with humans being the free-willed disciples of one force or the other.

The battle Sokar's anger had drawn him into had begun during the First Time. It was a conflict that involved the Sirian Star Gods, Osiris, first Pharaoh of Egypt, and his evil brother, Seth. So great was Seth's envy of Osiris that he was drawn deep inside his shadow self where the power of his hatred drove him to murder Osiris. Like the old axiom "like attracts like," Sokar's disdain for his half-brother Khufu drew him to the god Seth. In the same fashion, the anger and pain of a feud that happened a millennium ago was still being played out on Earth. All that was needed to keep it going was for human counterparts of the "original sin" drama to come together with the same feelings.

Sokar was being manipulated and controlled by Seth, and his soul knew it. But his ego did not know it, resulting in the blindness that often accompanies a lack of self-knowledge. Sokar was Seth's puppet in the Duat, his physical body a vehicle for Seth's bidding, his heart carrying enough negative emotions to override any joy or fortune his life had brought him.

Sokar's anger drove him and his jealousy of Khufu empowered him, as did his pain, desires, and dreams of taking his rightful place as Pharaoh of Egypt. There was no way Sokar would let go of his negativity, for he was sure that would mean giving up on achieving his true destiny, and giving in to the fate of being a minor royal, and a bastard one at that. Never! Such is the kind of human the forces of darkness manifest through.

Khufu, like Osiris, was Pharaoh. He was the one beloved by the people of Egypt, the one who would ascend into the starry realms at his death. Not Sokar. Like the god Seth's life, Sokar's life had been one of thirsting for power and all the spoils it brings—position, wealth, adoration, fame, and self-deluded freedom. He had lived his life his way by his choice. Like Seth, his need for power had made Sokar self-righteous, believing in the rightness of his actions and feelings. He would stop at nothing to prove the truth of his convictions to everyone, including himself.

Sokar could not remember a time when his anger at his father, Pharaoh Sneferu, did not burn inside him. He often recalled standing beside his mother's sarcophagus at the age of twelve, and feeling his ire rise that his mother had died a mere loyal concubine, one who had earned a life of luxury in the royal harem because she bore the king a son, albeit a bastard, but not as the queen of Egypt. To avenge his mother's fate and to claim his rightful inheritance had become a vendetta for Sokar from that moment on. His resentment that his rightful fate had passed him by had slithered like a cobra into the core of his being and lay there coiled and ready for when the time was right to strike. For Sokar, that time was now.

Throughout his life, Sokar had done everything with the belief that sooner or later it would serve his purpose of becoming king.

Of all the memories of his early years, it was the time he spent with Men-kar the Elder, his teacher in religion, that Sokar recalled the most vividly. It was not the part about the Neters that had captured his attention so much as it was the magic capabilities many of these deities possessed. They were power-defined giants among ordinary men, immortals among mortals. It was their *heka*, or magic, that made them victorious in battles, that gave them the strength to overcome illness, to survive attacks from monsters in the underworld of the Duat, that allowed them the freedom to travel in other worlds. Indeed, it was their knowledge of magic that assured them immortality, the ultimate goal and reward of every Egyptian. After all, the Egyptian religion prepared one to die from the physical world into a heaven in which all lived forever.

Sokar knew what he wanted to do with his life. He was supposed to be the king of Egypt. He also knew that the chance of that happening to the son of a royal concubine was slim at best. His mother had tried to discourage him from dreaming such dreams because she knew it would never be, even though Sokar was Sneferu's first-born son. Had she been the primary wife, there would have been no doubt that Sokar would inherit the throne after his father's death. However, nothing could keep the illegitimate prince from dreaming of becoming Pharaoh.

It was at this point in his life that Sokar had committed himself to laying claim to his rightful place. If he learned magic and developed his skills as a magician, he would be all-powerful like the gods. He could overcome all obstacles on his way to the throne. Through magic he would become the human incarnation of the god Horus.

These were the motives that powered Sokar, the reasons why he poured all of his intellect and physical prowess into learning magic. He would seek out the most learned magicians for apprenticeship. To date, his commitment to himself had led him down many roads and into the company of many scholars, but none had influenced him or taught him more practical magic than the wizard Dedi.

Dedi was already an old man when Sokar met him. It happened when the magician had been commanded to appear at court to perform his magic for the Pharaoh. Dedi's reputation was legendary; he was even credited with restoring the severed head of a goose, bringing the bird back to life. Sokar had been present at court that day and was mesmerized by the mysterious man. He vowed that he would apprentice with Dedi, no matter what it took.

As it turned out, Dedi was just as curious about Sokar. He saw in the young man the potential to become a skilled practitioner of the magical arts. Elders always have an eye for the few who hold promise for carrying on the knowledge and tradition of the mystery schools. In Dedi's case, it went further than that, in that he was not a member of the orthodox priesthood. Rather, he was a member of what could only be called the underground priesthood, independent magicians who worked as physicians and healers, casters of spells, and makers of powerful, effective amulets. Magic was their business, and they were among the best at it.

Sokar spent only two years with Dedi, but he learned all the necessary concentration techniques and the proper voice tones used in reciting spells. Sokar learned from a master, and a master he too would become. And he had. Now was the time his mastery would pay off.

On this particular evening, Sokar's thoughts focused on what Dedi and others had taught him about animal spirits. He recalled the crocodiles that lived in the sacred pool on the temple grounds at Komombo in the South, and how they were free to roam back and forth from the temple's pool to the Nile. He remembered what Dedi had told him about the power possessed by this unholy creature and about the crocodile god, Sobek.

As Sokar mused, Kheti, his house servant, magical assistant, and confidant, appeared and began dropping fish eggs into the garden pool. Sokar studied the man, feeling deep gratitude. He needed Kheti for he could never accomplish his goal of usurping the Throne of Egypt alone. Kheti was dependable in every way, and Sokar trusted him completely.

"Kheti, pack an overnight bag. We will be making a journey to Memphis tomorrow. See to securing passage on the river as well," Sokar said.

"Yes, my lord."

Sokar's "father" had been the chief domestic in the palace when Sneferu was Pharaoh. His mother had been an attendant to the queen. His parents had had a good life, their positions and wages allowing them to own land in the rich Delta region. That land had been turned into a productive and profitable vineyard. It was not uncommon for priests to have businesses outside the temple, but it was rare for a servant family. Sokar's mother, Nefer-er, in her position as one of the queen's attendants, had become one of Sneferu's many concubines.

When she became pregnant, Nefer-er assumed that the Pharaoh would take her and their child into the royal harem, though she had hoped for much more. But the king had never acknowledged the boy as his royal heir. It was then that the only man Sokar had called father, Amen, had married Nefer-er, even though everyone knew that Sokar was Sneferu's son.

When Sokar learned from his mother the truth of his birth, he grew angered. Though he was but twelve, he had sought audience with the Pharaoh to petition for acceptance as a legitimate member of the royal family. Sneferu had refused to meet with the boy to discuss the issue, which led to Sokar's hatred of the king and his resentment of Khufu, who now sat on the throne. After the old king's death and after Khufu had learned Sokar's true identity, he had acknowledged Sokar as his half-brother. That had angered Sokar even further, for it proved beyond doubt that he was Sneferu's son, albeit illegitimate, and that he deserved to be recognized as such and reap the benefits of being a royal heir.

Kheti tidied his master's quarters while Sokar sunned himself, his thoughts drifting to his earlier years. After Nefer-er's death, Amen had left his position as chief domestic and retired to his vineyard in the North. He had not lived for long afterwards, and some said he had grieved himself to death. Sokar inherited his parent's holdings and could have been content to build upon his wealth, which would have provided him with an honorable and secure life. But that was not what he wanted. So he made the decision to lease his land and live on the revenues. This arrangement left him free to remain in Memphis, and later Heliopolis.

He devised a long-term scheme that would assure him the throne. The first part of that plan was to enter the temple in the capital city and get an education. That completed he would enter the priesthood. It was a life that served his purpose well. Like most priests, he could have a life and business interests outside the temple, while his being a priest gave him a reason to be on the inside politically. The priesthood was powerful, privy to what was going on politically, and arguably it had as much power collectively as Pharaoh himself. Sokar wanted to know Khufu's every move, his every decision. He only need bide his time before he found a way to do away with Khufu. When he did he would be king.

Aside from the political and economic power that being a member of the priesthood gave Sokar, there was another benefit that would turn out to be the most rewarding of all—his training in magic. . . .

From his brief conversation with the High Priest of Heliopolis on the evening of Taret's transmission, Sokar felt that something was up with Khufu. Although he did not yet know what it was, he knew it probably had to do with the appearance of the comet and the New Year's celebrations, and that it was not only significant, but secret. He believed Meri-ib knew what was involved with the announcement Pharaoh was rumored to make soon. He had to know, and the best way to know was to go to the source, Meri-ib. Going to the Chief Priest in person would probably avail him nothing, as he had learned from talking to him prior to the meeting. But he *would* find out what he wanted to know, and he would not have to be in Meri-ib's physical presence to do it.

Sokar went to the falcon's perch. Stroking the big bird's head with two forefingers, he admired him for the majestic being he was. His sleek feathers gleamed in the sunlight, and his head twisted to and fro as he attended to every movement around him.

"I have a job for you, Horus. You are going to pay my friend Meri-ib a visit," Sokar spoke softly. The magician excelled in the ancient arts. Perhaps, as his instructors had told him, he had been a magician in other lifetimes, or maybe some are born with the ability and he was such a one. Sokar knew a relentless power within motivated him. The power of anger and hatred. He had wanted to learn, and be the best. Now he was the best, and he knew it.

Leaning his face down to the falcon's head, Sokar whispered, "We must prepare ourselves, Horus. Night will come all too soon. The night is when people dream."

The great bird cocked his head to one side and looked into Sokar's eyes. In the fleeting moment when their eyes met, electricity passed between them. They were more than a team, more than practitioner and familiar. Horus was Sokar's astral partner. The hawk would do Sokar's magical bidding, and there were no barriers, no boundaries he could not and would not cross.

"I must prepare for our operation, Horus. You are in good hands. Kheti will see to your needs." As he stroked the feathers on the hawk's back, Sokar's thoughts burned in his mind. "I will come for you at the midnight hour, my friend. Be ready." With that he clapped his hands loudly to summon Kheti, who trotted gingerly onto the patio and bowed to his master.

"Kheti, I wish you to gather my special white robe and sandals and a vial of natronade and one of jasmine perfume oil." After a short pause, he added, "And an incense burner and some myrrh."

Kheti replied immediately, his body doubled over in a deep bow. "Yes, my lord, right away."

The servant was always eager to please Sokar, and this command was no exception. He had been with his master long enough that he knew when a request was of a personal nature or one that involved Sokar's magical work. He never asked questions, he only obeyed, which was why Sokar relied upon and trusted his companion.

"There is no hurry," Sokar replied, easing Kheti's inclination to immediately fulfill the request. "I will not need those things until sunset."

"Very well, my lord. They will be ready."

Sokar indicated that he was ready to eat, so Kheti departed to the pantry to prepare a meal. Returning soon to the sitting room adjacent to Sokar's bedchamber, he put out a lavish spread of barley bread, stewed figs, boiled onions, charcoaled lamb bits, and a flask of wine.

Sipping on the wine, Sokar focused on the woman he had met recently, Mafdet. She was the daughter of a wealthy merchant, Menkar. Sokar had resisted becoming involved with women except for the occasional encounter with a concubine to satisfy his male urges. He knew the price of a sexual encounter, how it could drain one's magical power. This was a time now when he did not intend to risk losing an ounce of his fortitude on any level. However, Mafdet was an extraordinary woman, beautiful and intriguing.

They had met when the girl came to the temple to visit her best friend, a Star Priestess apprentice. Sokar had been attracted to her right away, and he sensed that the feeling was mutual. He had seen her just that once and he had escorted her to the meeting called by Taret. He had resisted the desire for further contact with the young woman, but now he was beginning to think she might be of use to him in more ways than one. His thoughts were interrupted when Kheti came in to collect the leftover food and the dishes.

"I will be leaving for the city in a moment, Kheti. I will return by mid-afternoon."

"Yes, my lord," the servant answered. "There is a change of clothing on your bed."

Sokar enclosed himself in the privacy of his bedroom and dressed for his walk into Heliopolis. He planned to go to the Temple of the Sun, where he would meet with the chief scribe, Haroun. Haroun's duty was to copy sacred and magic texts. There was a particular spell Sokar needed, and he needed it now. Haroun would be easy to deceive. He was aging and his eyesight was poor. Sokar would request to see certain texts and then he would copy what he wanted from other secret books at liberty without Haroun's knowledge.

The city was even busier than usual today. A large cargo vessel had come up from the south carrying a load of goods. The bustle around the docks was unusually hectic and added foot traffic to the city's streets. Sokar walked the short distance from the *Benu* Temple to the Sun Temple and entered through the gates. Making his way to the House of Life, he didn't stop to talk to anyone, as he did not want anyone to remember having seen him there.

The House of Life was separate from the main complex and differed from the monastic part of the temple. It was not only where the priests were trained in how to read and copy the texts, but it was also an academy for scribes and for the children of the wealthier class. Sokar himself had trained there during the last two years of his formal pre-priest education. It was also where the elite Star Priests and Priestesses worked after they graduated from training.

Sokar went directly to the Room of Scrolls, where the original documents copied by the scribes were kept. He was met at the door by a scribe he recognized as having been a pupil at the same time as he. The man, Her-bak, had remained at the library and was now in charge of the mathematics division. The formula Sokar was looking for could only be found in the most highly classified texts. Among these were the original funerary scripts on papyrus scrolls or calf leather, kept in jars and boxes.

Sokar greeted Her-bak and stated his purpose. "I need to speak with Haroun." Her-bak replied that the chief scribe was in his department. Sokar proceeded without tarrying, all the while projecting thoughts of being forgotten by anyone he encountered. Telepathy came easy to the magician-priest, and he used it now to erase the memory of his presence from Her-bak's mind.

Arriving at Haroun's study, Sokar tapped lightly on the cedar door. A voice from inside bade him enter. The aging scribe leaned over a massive manuscript the likes of which Sokar had never seen. Haroun stood and greeted his visitor graciously. "Welcome, Sokar. To what do I owe the honor of your presence?"

"I am pleased to see you, Master Haroun," Sokar replied, bowing deeply. "I have come to make a special request. I have received word that a friend of my dead father has died. His family has sent word that I should make a special petition to the great lord Osiris on his behalf. I wish to copy a suitable verse from the Book of Coming Forth, as I do not seem to have what I need among my personal texts."

Haroun listened to Sokar's request with interest, seeing no reason why the priest should be denied. "Yes, I see," he finally replied. "I will get you a copy of the funerary text. Wait here."

Before Haroun turned to go, Sokar stepped forward and looked into the old man's eyes. The scribe felt a wave of apprehension wash over him, and for a split second felt as if he were in grave danger. As suddenly as he had captured Haroun's mind in a grip of fear, Sokar let go of it and spoke in a gentle voice.

"Do not bother yourself, Master Haroun. I will get the text myself."

Before Haroun could object, Sokar walked toward the shelves that contained the scrolls. A large clay vessel marked with hieroglyphs held a papyrus scroll upon which were written spells to make spirits appear and to perform viewing from a distance. Sokar had seen this scroll once when he had assisted Haroun with copying the texts for the priests at a temple in Abydos.

Taking the jar down from the shelf, Sokar read through the contents of the scroll. Around the corner in the main room, Haroun stood frozen in the grasp of Sokar's will. The spell Sokar was looking for jumped out at him from the very page he was focused on at the moment. He scanned the hieroglyphs, his finger tracing every line as he read. Sokar had found what he came for. Rolling up the scroll quickly, he placed it back in the jar and put the jar back on the shelf.

When Sokar returned to Haroun's room, the aged priest was still standing in the spot he had been in when Sokar had gone to seek the manuscript. Walking up to the scribe, Sokar put his hand on the man's forearm and said, "Thank you for allowing me to read from the Book of Coming Forth, my old friend."

As the current from the magician passed into the body of the chief scribe, the man snapped to his senses, having no memory of the lapse in time. Sokar's comment about his being allowed to read the text was confusing and distracting. He had no memory of Sokar's excursion into the room where the sacred texts were kept. He only felt a disorientation from which he quickly recovered and that he promptly dismissed from his mind.

His mission accomplished, Sokar made his way out of the House of Life with as little fanfare as he could muster and returned to his private quarters at the *Benu* Temple. Kheti had been busy gathering the items Sokar requested earlier. The words of the formula for viewing from a distance running through his mind, Sokar went about the ritual of preparing for the magical operation he intended for later that night. He was meticulous when it came to preparations. He knew the success of any magical operation depends on how well one prepares. His conviction that he had been wronged motivated his doing everything he could to assure the success of his scheme to become king of Egypt, and it empowered his magic as well.

As soon as night fell, Sokar would journey to the bank of the Nile, where he would go through a self-blessing and self-purification ritual, a prerequisite to magical work. Kheti always went with him for this. There was nothing about his master that Kheti did not know, and he was in agreement that Sokar was the rightful heir to the throne. He had been with Sokar since the Pharaoh's son had been sent to school. Educating his bastard was the only thing Sneferu had done for Sokar. The would-be prince had had a good life, no doubt, but it was not the life Kheti felt he deserved. Kheti was a loyal and trusted ally, one who would stop at nothing to support and protect his master. He also knew what would be in it for him. He would be elevated from his position of slave to one of prominence in the royal court.

As the Sun began to set, Sokar got ready to go down to the Nile. The protection afforded by the darkness was desirable. There was a place on the riverbank where Sokar always went, as it was shielded by tall bulrushes, and the water there was shallow.

The short walk to the river took the pair to an area of the city through which they could pass relatively unseen. The water was still, giving the river a glassy appearance like a giant mirror that reflected the light of the newly risen and nearly full moon. Sokar wore a long, loose-fitting white *galabayya* and leather sandals. Priests did not, as a rule, wear leather, but Sokar was not a priest tonight. He was a magician.

Kheti followed close behind his master carrying the bag that contained the myrrh, incense burner, and other paraphernalia needed for the purification ritual. No magical operation, especially one that would take place over an extended period of time, could proceed without a cleansing ritual, and there was no better or powerful place to do such a ritual than at the Nile. The Nile is more than a river. It is Egypt's lifeblood, Sokar knew. Washing in its waters for ritual purposes, particularly during Inundation, was common among priests and magicians.

Once they reached the riverbank, Sokar took off the leather sandals and stepped into the protective privacy of the bulrushes in the ankle-deep water. He pulled the *galabayya* over his head and stood naked in the moonlight before the deity that was Sokar's astral counterpart: the god Horus. It was not Horus in his aspect as son of Isis and Osiris or even as a god of the sky that he worshipped. What attracted Sokar to Horus was the god's aspect as embodiment of divine kingship.

If Sokar was to become king of Egypt, and in doing so assume his rightful position, he must have the help and blessing of Horus. Sokar also knew the god as the warrior deity and avenger, for it was Horus who had avenged the death of his father, Osiris. Sokar was a warrior of magic, and he was an avenger who *would* avenge the wrong done his mother and him.

Kheti followed behind Sokar as he entered the water, staying close enough to be of service when needed. Sokar asked for the natron and began cleansing his mouth and ears. Natron, a natural substance, was used in sacred and profane purification rituals. As the natron filled his mouth with its familiar taste, the desire to purify himself was foremost. Sokar knew that if he was to enlist the assistance of the gods, he must follow certain procedures. Self-cleansing was but one. After swishing the natron mixed with water around in his mouth, Sokar spat it out. He then wet his forefinger and dipped it into the substance and began swabbing his finger in each ear. Both were acts to assure powerful speech and clear hearing, important to magical practice.

The cleansing rite completed, Sokar motioned for Kheti to hand him the glass vial of perfumed oil. Opening it, he poured a small amount of the jasmine-scented oil into the palm of his left hand. He then dipped a finger into the thick liquid and touched it to his brow, anointing his third eye between his eyebrows, then blessed each eye, his lips, ears, throat, heart, abdomen, and the base of his spine.

Kheti had witnessed and assisted in this ceremony many times. Now he resealed the bottle of perfume oil and handed his master the *galabayya*, which the magician slipped over his head, the soft, fine cotton falling down over his body. Both men walked slowly out of the Nile, the soft, cool mud squishing between their toes as they went. Once they had reached the harder silt that was the shore, Kheti put the bag that carried the ceremonial paraphernalia on the sand and took out a bronze incense burner and a chunk of myrrh. Next, he retrieved two stones and some dried river grass from the bag. He then began striking the stones together until a spark set the grass afire.

The light from the flame lit up the men's faces. It danced in the creases of their bronze-colored skin and reflected in the pupils of their eyes. When the fire was burning steadily, Kheti added a few small pieces of dung. Sokar sat a foot away from the fire and stared into the flames. He had come to the point in the ritual in which Kheti was no longer a servant but a partner in magic.

Staring into the fire, Sokar intoned the words of a conjuration of the avenger aspect of the god Horus. Soon the fire burned down, and the magician-priest was in a deep trance. Kheti watched as his master's face took on a stern look. This was his cue.

Reaching again into the bag, he brought out a small wooden box inlaid with mother of pearl that gleamed in the dim light. The box contained a powder whose ingredients were known only to a few initiates. Kheti sprinkled a pinch of the powder over the myrrh in the incense burner. He then took a silver spoon and picked up a few of the coals from the fire and placed them in a brazier. The smoke curled into the night air giving off a heady fragrance. Setting the brazier on the ground, Kheti took another pinch from the box and cast it onto the glowing embers.

In an instant the smoke from the powder became a mist and in it formed the figure of a man with the head of a hawk. The spirit merged with the body of the entranced Sokar, the two becoming one. Kheti had witnessed this merger before, and it always filled him with wonder and fright. He watched as Sokar's body stiffened and then shook with power. The magician went limp and fell on his side as if asleep. Kheti remained still. He knew the avenger's spirit had entered his master.

After about twenty minutes, Sokar began to stir, appearing drowsy, as if waking from a deep sleep. Kheti placed a flask of wine in Sokar's hand. The liquid would help his master regain consciousness and reorient himself to the present time and place. Sokar never seemed afterwards to have any memory of what had taken place, and this time was no different. Kheti helped him stand up, then busied himself with dowsing the embers and collecting the ritual objects.

The two men walked back to the Temple of the *Benu* in silence. Once in his private quarters, Sokar changed his clothes and went to the falcon and held out his arm for the bird. The hawk's muscles rippled and tightened, his talons gripping the man's arm so strongly they threatened to pierce the flesh. Sokar looked into the bird's golden eyes and, squinting his own into narrow slits, telepathically planted the seed idea in the bird's mind: Visit Meri-ib soon in a dream.

Chapter Nine

How Magic Came to Egypt

Lioness cubs don't like being kept in cages. The moment dawn broke and light began filling Khem's room, Bast was ready to eat and play, in that order. In the time the cat had been at the temple, she had gotten plenty to eat and was filling out. Her ribs didn't show anymore and her fur was softer and shiny. Akhi said it was the oil in the fish the animal was being fed. Khem had also discovered that the little cat liked barley beer. No one could leave a cup unattended or it would be lapped up in an instant. Bast was also partial to milk, and Akhi had observed that she would eat just about anything.

Khem was anxious to get dressed and start her day. She and Tiye had been sent a message to meet with Ani and Taret in the High Priestess's private audience room at nine o'clock. She supposed that the meeting had something to do with the study of magic for which the two girls had been selected. Khem had expected her time at the temple and her studies to change her life, but she could not have anticipated how much and how fast.

Bathed and dressed, Khem gulped down a cup of water and a sweet cake. But with every step, Bast was at her heels grabbing the ends of the linen sash tied around her waist.

"Stop! Bad cat!"

Khem swatted at the cat as she scolded. She was in no mood to deal with the pesky lioness this morning. Akhi had repaired the curtain beads twice since Bast had come to live with them, and rumor had it that one sandal had been dragged into the box and chewed to ruin. Akhi rescued

Khem from Bast. Taking the cat in her arms she put her in her box so she could see to her mistress's needs without further interruptions. She saw that Khem was tense, and Akhi was anxious to make it easier for her to get ready for the day.

When Khem reached the doorway to Taret's quarters, Tiye was already there waiting for her. The two had an almost instantly calming effect on each other.

"We have been chosen for a reason," Khem stated flatly. "And we will soon know what it is."

Taret's scribe, Sheshat, came to the door where Khem and Tiye were waiting. "Taret will see you now," she said, beckoning to the girls to follow her into the audience room of the High Priestess.

The room was simply but elegantly decorated. The walls were painted to depict scenes of the divinities interacting with humans, the ceiling with the zodiac. Small palms graced the corners, and saddle chairs were arranged in a circle in its center.

Taret entered accompanied by Ani. The physical differences between the two were striking. Taret was petite and aging, while Ani was tall, younger, more robust. The two represented more than fifty years of knowledge and experience, a fact that commanded the respect of the apprentices.

"Please, be seated, my sisters." Taret spoke softly. When all were seated, the High Priestess went straight to the point of the meeting. "Your studies are progressing well. I have watched you, Khem and Tiye, with interest, and what I have seen and the guidance I have received from the Star Gods have led me to choose you both for a special program of study. The magical arts were brought to Egypt by the Star Gods to enable Egyptians to become gods themselves. The ancient formulas have been taught only to those chosen to receive the knowledge and because they exhibit qualities that are both necessary and desirable—a kind of fortitude, let's say."

Taret's words were a welcome vote of confidence to Khem and Tiye, who both listened with interest. Tiye was attentive, but Khem knew that the now-familiar arrogant look on her face said Tiye already considered herself a magician and wasn't sure she had anything new to learn. Khaba had taught her and, as far as Tiye was concerned, she had taught her *all* Tiye needed to know. She was adept at the healing arts, the interpretation of omens, predicting the future, diagnosing illness, casting spells. All she had learned was passing through her mind now with thoughts of her beloved Khaba. Nubian magic was known far and wide for its potency, its origins steeped in ancient tribal traditions.

Taret read Tiye's thoughts. She looked at Tiye and said, "I am aware of your skills, Tiye, and that is precisely why I have chosen you to learn

Egyptian high magic. It will not only add to the knowledge you already have, but will surely make you the finest female adept in the land."

The High Priestess's words took Tiye aback, but before she could utter any response, Taret spoke again. "On two occasions since you arrived in Heliopolis I have been visited in my dreams by the Nubian named Khaba. She has petitioned for your acceptance as a student of high magic and, I must say, she made a very good case in your behalf."

Tiye was stunned. She blinked hard trying to hold back the tears that welled in her eyes. Taret's mention of Khaba and a petition on her behalf were humbling and heartwarming. She missed Khaba terribly, and now she felt closer to her mentor than ever before. Tiye said nothing. She didn't have to. The look on her face said it all.

Taret turned to Khem, her eyes sparkling, her lips curved into a subtle smile. "I suppose you are wondering why you have been chosen, Khem."

Nothing could have prepared her for what Taret said next.

"I have known you in many lifetimes, my child. You have been my daughter, my sister, my teacher. We were together in the ancient temples during the First Time when we learned to walk among the stars."

Khem's mouth dropped open but no sound came out. Her eyes, wide with shock, were fixed on the small woman seated across from her.

"I realize you have no conscious memory of these things or those times long past. But when you learn to read the Scroll of Life, you will know all that has been. You will learn how to walk awake through your dreams. You both will, and you will learn to dwell upon the more subtle planes with as much ease as you now live in the physical world of Egypt."

The High Priestess stopped talking. She knew the apprentices needed time for her words to settle. After a few minutes she said, "Ani will be your teacher. You are in good hands, and I leave you to those hands now."

With that, Taret rose from her chair. Sheshat also stood up to go and the two disappeared into Taret's private quarters. When they were alone, Ani looked at the apprentices with a glance that told them that she once had been in their position and understood the numbing effect of what Taret had just said.

"I am pleased to have the opportunity to be your tutor," Ani said finally, her eyes shifting from one priestess to the other to make certain both knew they were respected. "Magic is serious business. It cannot be approached with the intellect alone. It must be understood, not just known, and to truly understand, you must rely upon your intuition. Ultimately, you must bring all of yourself to bear upon your craft—your mind, body, and soul, the *khat*, *ab*, and *ba*. Magic is *heka*. *Heka* was used by the Creator to make the universe. Special people, places, animals, and some objects possess *heka*. The gods and the stars use *heka*. When magic is taught and entrusted to you, you will never again be the same."

It was apparent that the meeting was over, and for the apprentices it was none too soon. Their minds were spinning. Ani told them they would be notified about the time and place of their next meeting. It appeared that, rather than through classes, the priestesses would be trained by Ani in an informal environment. They took their leave from the audience hall to get some food and sit beneath the shade of the large sycamore in the lower courtyard.

The courtyard was empty. It was noon and everyone was in the main dining hall or in private eating rooms. The basket of bread and fruit they had gotten was unopened. Neither of the priestesses was hungry after all. Their minds were still on the meeting with Taret and Ani. Khem knew that Tiye's mind was also on Khaba.

"I was thinking," Tiye said, finally able to put her thoughts into words, "that the dead can communicate with the living. Taret's dream about Khaba proves that. So, I could dream Khaba into my life again, couldn't I?"

Khem understood what Tiye was getting at, but she wasn't sure how to reply. She wasn't convinced that the use of sacred knowledge for self-serving purposes was proper. Yet she was not certain the Nubian's motives were self-serving. After pondering this, Khem said cautiously. "I would suppose so, yes. But don't you think that Khaba's *ba* would have to be in agreement with that?"

Tiye had not thought about that. She had been so overwhelmed at the prospect of being able to have Khaba in her life again, even if only in her dreams, that she had not considered the details.

As an afterthought Khem said, "It must also work the other way around too, Tiye."

"What do you mean?" Tiye responded, a puzzled look on her face.

"Well, if the dead can come to the living, can the living go to the dead?"

Tiye shrugged her bare shoulders in a reaction that made it appear as if the whole matter was not important. But both girls knew it was.

"What about you and Taret? Have you thought that you have known her in past lives?" Tiye asked.

"No," Khem replied, as Taret's words came to her mind. She wondered if she would ever have Taret's conscious recall of other lifetimes. Since she was a child she could sense a familiarity with certain people and places. She recalled the first time, sitting atop her father's shoulders, she saw the procession of priests in Abydos at festival time. Though quite young, she remembered how natural it had been. Even so, past lives was not a subject that Khem had given much thought to. The truth of it was a foregone conclusion to her, and it had not come up before now. Now it caused her to muse about her own fate, why she was in Heliopolis, why she was in training to become a Star Priestess, and why she was with Taret. *Again?* To her there was no question. It was all predestined.

Taking the food out of the basket, Khem gave Tiye her share. The two, now hungry, ate their meal in silence, each lost in her own thoughts. When they were finished, Khem collected the bread and scattered it on the ground for the sparrows.

Both girls were expected to attend an afternoon class. Khem and Tiye were about to leave the courtyard when Khem spotted Akhi with Bast in tow on a braided rope. The lioness was learning to walk on a leash very well. So many things were happening in her life that Khem had had little time to spend with her cat. Eyeing Khem, Bast tugged on the rope to get to her, pulling at Akhi.

"Akhi! Bast!" Khem greeted the girl and the cub, surprised to see them.

"I thought she needed to walk," Akhi said.

"That is a wonderful idea, Akhi," Khem replied gleefully, kneeling down to play with the cub. Tiye stepped back a few paces, not sure whether the animal posed a threat. Khem assured her that Bast was harmless. Tiye relaxed and came over to get a closer look.

Bast sniffed Tiye's outstretched hand, then put her paw on the girl's forearm. Tiye's face lit up in a wide smile. It occurred to Khem she had not seen the Nubian smile like that before. It showed a side of Tiye that she had never seen, and she liked what she saw.

Akhi tugged on Bast's leash, gently pulling the cat back toward her. "Bastet, you come," Akhi ordered. "We must finish our walk." The lioness reluctantly but obediently fell into step and the two sauntered off.

When they were out of sight, Tiye turned to Khem and said, "Where did you get the lioness? How long have you had her? Does she live with you in the temple?" Her questions came in a volley. On the walk to the classroom in the south wing, Khem told Tiye all the details of how Bast had come into her life.

Chapter Ten

The Man Who Would Be Pharaoh

Khufu was cooped up in the audience hall of the palace. He had been hearing common civil suits all morning, and was finding it difficult to keep his attention focused on the business at hand. He had settled a dispute between two shepherds fighting over which was the rightful owner of a stud water buffalo, and he had decided an appropriate penalty for public drunkenness. None of this was important to him now. Not today. This was the day he expected to hear from Nemon, the day the chief architect had promised he would give Khufu a plan as to how the Stone Head could be unearthed from its prison of desert sand. Khufu was impatient, anxious for news from his cousin.

The king's vizier, Manetho, was on hand, and the palace guards had been put on notice that when Nemon arrived he should be escorted to the audience hall straight away. Inundation was only weeks away, and time was short, especially for what Khufu knew would be a monumental task. There was some reason for concern that the chief architect would be able to travel from Abusir to the palace in Memphis. The *khamsin* winds had begun blowing from the South since dawn, and their force was beginning to increase. Khufu had sent for his master astronomer, Nebseni, for a report on the chances of whether the winds would become more intense. The *khamsin* had been known to bring life to a standstill.

Nebseni had said that the celestial configurations and astrological indications pointed to this being a mild blow. The only cause for concern was that the Moon was waxing, which could add some strength to the atmospheric currents. The astronomer-priests like Nebseni also predicted the weather, and the people, government, and priesthood relied upon their accurate predictions. The king trusted Nebseni was right, that the winds would not prevent Nemon from coming.

In the middle of a case involving a domestic dispute, Khufu was told that Nemon had indeed arrived. The Pharaoh passed judgment on the matter at hand as quickly as he could and ordered the hall cleared. He commanded servants to prepare a meal for his guest. Unknown to Khufu, however, Sokar and Kheti had also docked at the Nile and were en route to the palace. . . .

Nemon strolled into the audience hall in his usual jovial manner. Bowing to Khufu, he then greeted his relative in a more personal manner as always. The king was relieved that the *khamsin* had not kept Nemon away, and he was anxious to get down to business.

"I am happy that you have come, my cousin. Have you a plan?" Khufu asked, getting straight to the point.

"Whoa! Not so fast, cousin," Nemon teased the king. "I have needs, you know." The architect was referring to the fact that he was thirsty and ready to eat. Khufu clapped his hands to hurry his servants. Two domestics brought in a low-legged table and placed it before the king and his guest.

"Manetho will be joining us," Khufu informed a valet. "Show him into the room."

Nothing went on in Egypt that the vizier did not know about, and no decision was made without his counsel. Being the Pharaoh's chief advisor meant it was his job to oversee the project to unearth the Lion Man of the Desert.

When Manetho arrived, food was brought in, along with vessels of wine and beer. The three dignitaries sat on soft floor pillows, as servers filled bowls and platters with stewed onions, roasted pigeons, skewers of lamb, and loaves of bread. Outside, the wind blew and sand blew through the arched windows. Khufu's mind shifted to the *khamsin* again, sensing the wind was rising. A devastating *khamsin* could cost the Sphinx project precious time that he did not have. So he hoped Nebseni was correct.

When the meal was finished the palace servants cleared the table and refilled the wine cups. Presently, the chief scribe, Hui, came into the hall. Khufu had sent for him to record the minutes of the secret meeting. No one must know of the project until a plan had been devised and a public announcement made. Egyptian prophecies had told of the Second Coming of the Star Gods. This would be the most significant event in Egyptian history since the days of the First Time. It was a blessing from the gods themselves that this should happen while Khufu was king, assuring him immortality. It would also provide him an opportunity to deepen his initiation into the Mysteries.

Khufu knew he had come from the stars and that upon his death he would return to the stars. But to be king at the very time the Sky Gods returned to Egypt and to play a role in the preparations for that event was the biggest responsibility any leader could have. Khufu considered it the epitome of his destiny.

His hunger and thirst satisfied, Nemon summoned his valet, who brought in a large papyrus scroll which the chief architect opened and rolled out on the table. On it was a drawing of the Giza complex of three pyramids and the Stone Head.

Khufu's reign had been filled with tasks that required huge numbers of laborers and man-hours to accomplish, but it had established Egypt as the star temple of the world. First there had been the restoration of the Great Pyramid, the Pyramid of the Rising and Setting Sun, a project started by Sneferu. The alignments of the massive pyramid with the heavens made the monument the most soul-empowering initiation chamber on Earth.

Nemon collected his thoughts as he studied the papyrus. "We can only assume that the legends of the Stone Head are true, that he is truly the Lion Man of the Desert. This would make the body, in proportion to the head, approximately 440 royal cubits at the base, and about 280 royal cubits high. If I am correct in my assumptions, I figure an army of a thousand workers could clear the sand from around the Sphinx's body in little more than one Moon cycle."

Hearing Nemon's words gave Khufu the feeling that comes when a tremendous burden has suddenly become lighter. The news was good. The project could be done, and it could be done by Inundation.

"I will begin recruiting a work force immediately," Khufu said emphatically. "There will be no hesitation."

The three dignitaries agreed on the strategy of how to proceed. Manetho would see to the enlisting of laborers the following day. Nemon would turn the overseeing of the construction of the temple in Abusir to his right-hand man on the project, and return right away to the capital city to take charge of the work force. Pharaoh would be available to provide whatever financial and spiritual support was necessary. The three would make a good team. They had worked together successfully before, and they would do it again.

The meeting over, Nemon prepared to leave. Turning to Khufu, a twinkle in his eyes, he said, "Well, cousin, you can make your proclamation to the people. The project is sealed in the very soul of the god Thoth."

"Yes," Khufu replied thoughtfully, his mind searching ahead for the right time for the public announcement. "I will. I will go before the people at the time of the full Moon."

This decision relieved Khufu even more. When a ruler is called to a task by the divinities, he must not fail. The knowledge of the return of the Sky Gods was the most profound announcement any Pharaoh would make to the Egyptian people since the First Time. Now that there was a viable plan for unearthing the Sphinx, and he knew approximately how long it would take, Khufu must get word to Meri-ib right away. He knew that the High Priest would be anxiously awaiting word from the palace.

Servants came into the audience hall and began clearing away the table and incidentals left from the meeting. There were still civil cases on the court's docket that would need to be heard later that afternoon, but for now Khufu would retire to his private chambers for a rest and libation. As he started to go, the vizier and an aide returned to the hall.

"You should know, your Majesty, that your half-brother, Sokar, and his valet, Kheti, have been sighted in the city. They are presumed to be en route to the palace and will most likely arrive momentarily."

"Sokar," Khufu muttered the name under his breath. He had not seen or heard from his half-brother for a season or more. Why was he in Memphis? What did he want? If he guessed right, Sokar was not paying a mere social visit; there would be a purpose to his coming. His timing was interesting. Khufu was well aware of the magician-priest's intuitive prowess, so it did not surprise him that his sibling had shown up at this auspicious time. Sokar might not know what specifically was going on, but he was psychic enough to sense that *something* was in the wind.

Thinking of the wind brought Khufu's attention back to the *khamsin.* He had been so engrossed in the meeting with Nemon and Manetho that he had forgotten the winds that were threatening to get worse. Now, looking towards the window he could see that sand was blowing harder than it had been a couple of hours before.

"Has there been any further word from Nebseni on the *khamsin?*" Khufu inquired of Manetho.

"No," Manetho replied, "there has not. I will inquire if it pleases your Majesty."

"Yes, do that and report to me as soon as you have any word." Khufu knew that a lengthy *khamsin* would delay the Sphinx project and he did not want to miss the date of the full Moon. He knew how important the proper astronomical configurations were to the success of any undertaking, and especially to one like this.

Khufu's thoughts shifted to Nemon again. He could always count on Nemon. His cousin was more than his chief architect. He was also his trusted friend. Nemon's soul was related to the god Ptah, the architect of the universe and patron god of Memphis, the god whom Khufu served.

The Pharaoh walked over to the wooden statues of Ptah that stood on the west wall of the audience hall. The god was portrayed as a mummy, and his hands protruded from the wrappings and held a staff that combined the djed pillar, the ankh, and the *was* scepter. Touching the statue gently, Khufu said, "From Your heart came the thoughts that brought the world into being. From Your mouth were uttered the words that made all things exist."

Though respectful of Ra and all the other gods, Khufu was closest to Ptah. He felt a heart connection with the deity the likes of which he felt for no other. He had spent much time in the few years of his reign studying the texts written by the Ptah priests at Memphis, particularly the creation myth that attributed the birth of Ra and all the Neters to Ptah. He thought about the once-all-powerful god Sokar, whose name his half-brother had been given at birth. Sokar the god was the consort of Sekhmet, the lioness wife of Ptah. To be given a name of a god was regarded as an omen, and the one so named followed the same life path as the deity, learning the lessons of the deity.

Khufu had seen Sokar only once since his coronation. That had been at the birth feast for Khufu's son, Cephren. In a way he understood his sibling's unspoken bitterness at not being accepted as the legitimate heir to the throne. But none of the decisions regarding the circumstances of Sokar's birth and his subsequent position, or lack of it, within the royal family were Khufu's doing. He had tried to maintain an honorable relationship with his sibling over the years. He even called him brother. Still, there was little contact between the two who as adults had their own paths.

Somewhat reluctantly, Khufu gestured to his attendants that he would see Sokar. He didn't understand his own reluctance, nor did he ponder it too closely now. He only knew the feeling was there.

Sokar entered the room with aplomb. He was an almost perfect male specimen, Khufu thought, when he saw his half-brother dressed in the garments of his office as priest. His fine linen skirt was held in place at the waist by a wide sash; a leopard-skin pelt draped over his wide shoulders and hung down his back. His muscular biceps were encircled with thin gold bands, and a large ankh-shaped gold ring graced the middle finger of his right hand.

Kheti, who stayed several paces behind his master, exhibited pride in being included in the presence of the Pharaoh. The relationship between Sokar and Kheti gave one the impression of equals rather than master and servant. It was clear that Kheti was dedicated to Sokar, that there was nothing he would not do for him.

Sokar went directly to the foot of the throne where Khufu was seated and bowed deeply. The expected gesture was exaggerated, but then so was everything Sokar did. The king nodded his head in recognition of his visitors.

"Greetings, your Royal Majesty, representative of the great god of the Sun, brother of Osiris, patron of Ptah," Sokar said dramatically.

"Welcome, brother," Khufu responded politely. "It has been a long time. Tell me, Sokar, what brings you to Memphis?" Khufu saw no point in prolonging the pleasantries, and Sokar was the kind of man one had to deal with head on.

"My dear brother," Sokar said with an air of sarcasm. "I must know about my sister-in-marriage, the lovely Meritates, and the heirs Osiris has blessed you with."

"My family is well, Sokar. And you?"

"Splendid. I am as splendid as the lustrous land of Egypt, as content as a suckling babe."

Kheti followed the exchange between the two men attentively. It was evident that the same father had sired them for they bore a physical resemblance to each other. But that was where it stopped. The half-siblings were as different as night from day. Khufu is weak, Kheti thought. He is not strong like Sokar. Sokar is the rightful king. There was nothing the servant would have liked more than to be able to help make that a reality.

Sokar walked to a window that provided a view of the desert plateau. After a moment of silence, he turned to face Khufu, who sat waiting for his guest to state the purpose of his visit.

"It is very dry. If the *khamsin* continues, it will be even drier. What do you think? Have your astronomers made a forecast about the winds?" Sokar asked, his comments deliberately diverting him from stating his purpose.

Khufu found Sokar's remarks about the *khamsin* surprising. "The astronomers are not overly concerned. But, tell me, brother. Is it to speak about the *khamsin* that you have come?"

Sokar's lips curved into a sly smile. Strolling back to the foot of the throne, he deliberately made light of Khufu's inquiry. "No, of course not. I only hope that there will be no delay in your plans."

Khufu was caught off guard by what Sokar said. What plans? He could not possibly know of the impending public announcement of the plan to unearth the Sphinx, and he certainly could not know anything about why such a plan was in the works. Khufu did not know that his half-brother had been present at the spirit-inspired transmission Taret had given a few nights before. Trying to hide his astonishment, the king asked calmly, "What plan would that be, brother?"

"For the New Year celebrations. I assume you have festivities planned as always?"

Khufu felt relief. So Sokar did *not* know about *the* plan. But the magician-priest sensed something or he would not be here. Sokar was fishing for information, because if he did know about it, he would go to any length to become involved with the Second Coming of the Star Gods. He would want to be their emissary and keep the knowledge they would give to himself for his own ends rather than have it benefit all Egyptians.

Feeling more relaxed now in Sokar's presence, Khufu replied that the usual preparations for the New Year celebrations were being made. "Will you be joining the festivities here in Memphis, my brother?" He asked this secretly hoping that Sokar had other plans.

"Of course," Sokar answered. Seeing no need to prolong the visit, he said, "I must take my leave for now. Thank you for your time, my brother."

With that he bowed to the Pharaoh and motioned for Kheti to follow him as he went towards the door. Before leaving the hall, however, the magician paused and, turning to face Khufu, he said, smiling broadly, "Perhaps I will see you before the New Year. Maybe I will see you in my dreams."

The remark puzzled Khufu. Was Sokar making a joke? Or was he making a threat? Or a promise? That was the most perplexing thing about Sokar. One never knew for certain what the motives were behind his words.

He would put Sokar out of his mind for now. There was much to be done to prepare for the Full Moon ritual at the temple in Memphis, as well as for Inundation. He must send a courier to Meri-ib, then he would finish the court's business scheduled for the afternoon. As thoughts of his responsibilities passed through his mind, Khufu felt a momentary heaviness that stirred doubt and fear within him. It wasn't often he didn't feel up to the task of being Egypt's king, but he was feeling it now.

"Mighty Ones, Ptah, Sekhmet, Nefertem, Lord Horus, Ra, Osiris, and Thoth: give me strength," Khufu whispered. "Help me do your bidding, O Holy Ones."

Slowly, a peace came over the Pharaoh, a soothing, yet empowering stillness of mind and heart. He would do what he had to do, what the divinities needed him to do. He would make ready the land and prepare the people. He would lead both into a new era of knowledge and spiritual renewal. Nothing and no one would stand in the way.

Chapter Eleven

Ra, Mighty Monarch of the Gods

Khem sat up in bed with a start. The sun was not yet above the horizon, and the room was still bathed in the last vestiges of moonlight that cast an eerie glow on her surroundings. She felt she was being watched, and uneasiness slipped over her as she strained to see if anybody was there. Seeing nothing and no one, she lay back down and tried to go back to sleep.

As she lay there, between sleep and wakefulness, her meeting with Tiye, Taret, and Ani came to mind. Drifting on a dreamlike current, Khem found herself suspended in a darkness where she had no sense of herself, a sort of netherworld of nothingness. Then, a distinct voice spoke from within what seemed to be the center of her head.

"Egypt is made in the image of heaven."

The words deepened Khem's concentration. As her consciousness sharpened, she felt a slight jolt and heard a crack inside her head, then found herself floating above her bed, looking down at her body, still and seemingly lifeless.

Consumed by thoughts of that meeting with Ani, Khem stood at an ornately carved cedar gate and before stone walls that surrounded an enclosure. She became aware of someone standing beside her: Tiye. In the next instant, the two priestesses were clothed in white linen sheaths, with leopard skin shawls draped loosely over their shoulders. Taret and Ani appeared behind them wearing long gowns, silver single-starred circlets on their heads. The foursome stood facing the huge gate, and it began to open slowly.

The four directions of the interior were marked by torches whose flames bathed everything in iridescent greenish-blue light. In the center of the enclosure was an immense brilliant quartz crystal. As they approached the crystal, it began to disassemble itself into luminous globules that gradually took the form of a female. The nameless woman-god fixed her eyes on the four priestesses, her dark pupils flashing, her lips moving in slow motion. Words resounded in the priestesses' heads.

"Egypt is more than a copy of the starry sky. It is an earthly reflection of cosmic harmony, the music of the spheres. To know this harmony you must take the vows that will allow you entry to the solar barque that sails upon the celestial Nile. The time of Inundation shall bring a tide that will create a ladder that extends from Earth to Heaven. It directs the currents of things between above and below."

The voice fell silent. The female figure transformed herself into a solar barque from whose side extended a gold gangplank. Khem and Tiye went to the threshold of the boarding plank to climb onto the vessel. Once they were aboard, the ship sailed on a river of stars through the night sky. A comet came out of nowhere and slammed into the side of the vessel. The torn ship began to sink into the star-laden waters.

Khem's dream body fell back into her physical one with a convulsive jerk that awakened her in her bed. Struggling to break free of the dream bonds that held her mind and body, Khem started becoming conscious of her physical surroundings. She opened her mouth to call for Akhi, but no words would come. Panic shook her out of her predicament, and finally she heard her voice ring out in the darkness of the room.

"Akhi! Come! Akhi!"

The servant girl was startled awake. She sensed the fear in her mistress's call, and it propelled her feet to the floor so quickly that she became disoriented as she rushed into Khem's bedchamber.

"What is it, my mistress?" Akhi asked loudly as she came upon Khem sitting up on the side of her bed.

Shaking her head in an effort to clear her mind, Khem said, "I had a bad dream." The memory of what she had dreamed had already faded. "I can't remember it now. I will just lie down and rest for a while longer."

Akhi could see that her mistress was all right, but she offered to sit with her until she went back to sleep. Khem declined. She wanted to lie alone to think. Maybe she would remember the dream. . . .

By the time the sun's rays filled the room with their warm light, Khem had at last gotten some much-needed dreamless sleep. Feeling refreshed and renewed both physically and emotionally, she got up and began preparing herself for the day. There was a class session in the morning before she and Tiye would meet with Ani.

The classroom was bustling with chatter when Khem arrived. She sat on a floor cushion next to Kasut. Kasut and and two other apprentices had been engaged in a lively conversation regarding the coming full Moon. Khem listened with interest. It would be the first full Moon since she came to Heliopolis, and she eagerly looked forward to being a part of the ritual. She felt a strong attraction to the Moon, and thought it the most beautiful object in the night sky.

Taret, who entered the room with Sheshat, would present the day's teaching.

Taret looked out over the audience of apprentices, which was her signal that she was ready to begin. Taret spoke in her usual soft, low voice.

"The ancestral Egyptians wrote many prayers to the gods. These included petitions of praise to the sun god Ra. It is important that you understand the spirit of Ra is the pure creative power that gives life and form to all things. The Sun is but the physical vessel that contains the creative force."

The teacher's words revealed a truth to Khem that she had not thought of until this moment. The Sun and Moon, and even the stars, are not the gods themselves. They are but the vehicles within which the deities dwell, just as people dwell within their homes, though they are not the homes themselves.

Taret continued teaching. "The Sun god, like all the divinities, has many aspects. Each is expressed during the times the Sun makes its daily trek across the heavens. At dawn, the Sun is the body of Khepera. Khepera takes the form of a scarab beetle that sometimes is the head atop a human body. It is at daybreak that the Sun's energy is the most creative. At sunset, the Daystar's energy embodies the great god Ra, god of Heliopolis, City of the Sun. There is much to be learned about Ra, for the god has many aspects. He was first known as Atum, who lay silent within Nun, which is Chaos, his body wrapped in the bud of a lotus. The power of the solar light was locked safely within his great being. Then the time came for Atum to break free from his cocoon and come out of the darkness so that his brilliant light might be revealed. He was no longer Atum. He was now Ra.

"Ra, the glorious Sun, formed the first pair of gods whom he named Shu, a male, and Tefnut, his sister. Shu and Tefnut in turn gave birth to the twins, Geb and Nut, who became the parents of Osiris, Isis, Seth, and Nepthys.

"Ra is the Great Father of all things. What is important to understand is that the universe Ra created for his children was very different from the universe that exists now. That universe was known as the First Time. It was an age when the gods lived on Earth among humankind, including Ra himself. Ra was the first king of the Earth, and he ruled his kingdom from Heliopolis. His daughter, Ma'at, was his co-ruler, for she was the deity who possessed the power of truth and wisdom. Each day Ra would rise and board his great solar barque and travel through the twelve divisions of his kingdom during the sunlight hours."

Taret's tone changed from that of a storyteller to teacher. "There came a time when Ra tired of his task of ruling the Earth. So he made the decision to give that responsibility to Thoth, the Moon god. The transition, Ra's passing of the Rod of Power to Thoth, involved a process you need to understand.

"The Rod of Power is a wand that has been in the possession of the gods since Time began. It is kept in the archives of one of the temples in the home star system of the gods. When the Rod is passed from the hands of one deity to another, there is a shift in energy that filters down to the Earth from the heavens. The energy shift always results in a changing in power on Earth, a change in the rulership of Egypt. When Ra passed the Rod of Power to Thoth, the most significant event that occurred on Earth was the ascension of Osiris to the Great Throne to become Egypt's first king."

Taret's description of Osiris's rule was captivating. She was not talking only about a god, Khem realized. She was talking about a human. Could it be the gods were humans who had lived in Egypt long ago?

"Osiris did many things for Egypt. One of the first of his acts was to deliver Egyptians from destitution. He made the people realize that their brutish manner of living had to change if they and their country were to survive. Osiris did this by showing the people a better way to live. He taught them, with the help of his queen, Isis, inner cultivation. He defined and passed laws by which the people could live. He brought religion and taught Egyptians to honor the gods. He had great temples erected to the deities, and cities grew up around these sanctuaries.

"Osiris made himself accessible to the people. He traveled all over the land and ultimately all over the world, civilizing it. He convinced the people that they did not need to bear arms against one another. You surely know that this was no easy task, but Osiris had tremendous charm and was very persuasive. He earned the people's trust. They did what they did for him, and it was good for them, and it was good for the land. When Thoth took Osiris's place, progress continued. He established a common language so the people could communicate more freely. He also invented letters, and gave humans the first principles of astronomy and all manner of music."

As the High Priestess spoke of the great things accomplished by Osiris,

Isis, and Thoth, Khem knew that Osiris was an emissary of Ra, and that his coronation as Pharaoh of Egypt had been a reflection of a shift of power in the realms of the Star Gods.

"Power, for those who thirst for it, corrupts," Taret resumed. "For them, power is a narcotic. To Seth, the uncle of Horus, power became the ultimate ambition, power over the land and the people. Seth became the enemy of Horus, indeed, the enemy of all the gods. He was the would-be usurper of power from Osiris. Seth wanted to be king of Egypt.

"Seth schemed day and night to find a way to overthrow Osiris. Once, while the good king was on one of his many journeys out of the country, Isis was left in charge. Seth devised a treacherous plot in collusion with the Ethiopian queen, Aso. He secretly measured the length of Osiris's body, then commissioned the building of a beautiful, ornate chest the exact size as Osiris. When Osiris returned, Seth commanded that the chest, which was really a coffin, be brought into the room so that everyone could admire its exquisite beauty. Seth took advantage of the admiration and promised to give it to the man who should find the chest to fit his body perfectly. All the men tried but none fit. Then Osiris lay in it and his body was just the right size. As the king lay in the chest, Seth and his coconspirator slammed the lid shut, trapping Osiris inside. The chest was then carried to the river and tossed in, where it began making its way to the sea.

"When she heard of the dreadful deed, Isis became distressed beyond words. Determining the location of her husband's coffin by divine inspiration, she went to the place called Byblos. There the chest had come to rest at the foot of a tamarisk tree. Much to her dismay, Isis found that the tree had grown massive and enfolded the chest within its great trunk. Fascinated by the tremendous size of the tree, the king of the country, Melcarthus, had part of the trunk cut off and used as a pillar to support the roof of his palace.

"Once Isis arrived in Byblos, she changed herself into a swallow and hovered around this pillar, lamenting her loss. In time, Isis revealed her true identity to Melcarthus, who granted her wish that the trunk be cut open and the chest removed and taken back to Egypt. Once there, Isis hid her husband's coffin in a secret place. But while hunting on a moonlit night, the evil Seth discovered it. He took Osiris's body from the chest and hacked it into fourteen pieces and scattered them all in different places. These things happened in the twenty-eighth year of Osiris's reign."

Taret concluded the story of Seth by telling how Isis searched for and eventually found all the parts of her dead husband's body except one, the penis. Each part she gave to a different city, in which a tomb was erected to contain it. It was in this devious way that Seth became the ruler of

Egypt. "Now there are many implications to this ancient story, but there is one in particular that I wish to discuss at this time. You will recall that the murder of Osiris occurred in the twenty-eighth year of his reign as Egypt's king. The science of numbers holds this number to have great significance as it is related to the length of the lunar cycle.

"Although the Moon has many aspects that are represented by various deities, its energy is best understood through the god Khonsu, the adopted son of Amun and Mut. Khonsu is depicted in art as a male youth with a crescent and full Moon upon his head. In his hands he holds a crook and scepter. The name Khonsu means 'the wanderer.' A fitting name for a Moon god, is it not? As a lunar deity, Khonsu assisted Thoth in recording the passing of time. He served the people as a healer of the sick and a protector against evil spirits, for such is the nature of the Moon's power. Khonsu was also an exorcist who knew that evil spirits are at the root of many sicknesses. He was a great physician who healed countless people. When Khonsu left his physical body, the baboon image of him became the most sacred of his symbols.

"The Moon, like Khonsu, has many faces. The New Moon, symbolized by the crescent, represents growth, rebirth, and resurrection. The waxing Moon is expansion, blossoming forth. The Full Moon is fulfillment and completion. The color blue is related to the lunar light, the Moon itself being white and reflecting the light of the Sun like a mirror.

"Through star calculations, then, we can understand the heavens because through that we learn everything is related and ordered. So, from the actions of Seth we know that when power falls into the hands of those dominated by a force they see as superior to themselves, their path will inevitably lead to evil."

Chapter Twelve

Powerful Men Meet

The High Priest of Heliopolis was getting a late start. Since dawn he had been making his daily prayers and offerings to Ra in the central sanctuary. Meri-ib liked being in the sanctuary. It was the heart of the temple. Being there made him feel protected from the outside world; he had no cares there, just the blessed peace that comes from being in communion with the gods.

Now that he was back in his private quarters, Meri-ib was studying passages from the texts his chief scribe had recently transcribed. The newly discovered inscriptions were older than first thought, and contained teachings about the Star Gods that the priesthood found exceptionally relevant to the star-based beliefs of Egypt.

This morning, however, Meri-ib was finding it hard to concentrate. He was anxious to receive word from the palace. He knew that Khufu had planned a meeting with Nemon regarding the plausibility of unearthing the Stone King. The reason for the monumental project dominated the High Priest's every waking thought, as it had since his visionary encounter with Thoth in the Holy of Holies a week before. The Second Coming of the Star Gods to Egypt was more than a cause for celebration. It was an event that would no doubt change lives of all Egyptians.

Meri-ib was grateful for his relationship with the Pharaoh. There were some political differences between the two men and the *nomes* or districts they represented, but Meri-ib respected Khufu's position. He knew full well that the crown was more than an emblem of kingship, more even than a position claimed by birthright. No, the crown embodied, and in some ways replaced, the human king's personal thinking. He thought for the gods. The crown was his destiny and attested to the power of his personal character. A god did not confer the crown. Rather, a god and the power and purpose of any given deity are transmitted through the crown and the man who wears it to the people. Meri-ib knew that the Pharaoh never carried out any act, civil, political, or sacred, without asserting that the Neters were the inspiration. The High Priest was sure that the unearthing of the Sphinx would be no different.

As Meri-ib was pondering Khufu and his role as king, a knock came at the door. The message the Chief Priest had been waiting for had arrived. He must prepare to go to Memphis right away. Without wasting a minute, he summoned his personal servant and busied himself with the details of what could very well be most important journey of his life, certainly the most significant of his position as High Priest of the Sun Temple.

At mid-day Meri-ib and his entourage boarded the temple's barque and began the short trip to Memphis. The breeze on the Nile was welcome compared to the strong *khamsin* that had blown in from the South for two days. Thankfully, the people, animals, and land had been spared what could have been a devastating storm.

Upon arrival, the High Priest was received immediately into the palace's audience hall and into the presence of the king. Khufu was seated on the throne, his fan bearers keeping up a steady rhythm with their magnificent plumed fans to provide as much comfort for the king as possible. Khufu's expression told Meri-ib that the news was good.

"Your Royal Highness, Khufu, great and noble emissary of the Neters," Meri-ib spoke, bowing to the wearer of the crown. He honored Khufu not only as the son of Ra, the perfect and divine being, but also as the One Who Measures the World. Khufu was not only king, he was a priest. As a priest, he and all the kings before him had been tutored to understand each was the living incarnation and return of the source of the Divine Word made tangible to the people. Such was the meaning of royalty.

"And you, Meri-ib, High Priest of the Sun Temple, Lord of Heliopolis, the city upon which the Neters smile," Khufu said, graciously returning Meri-ib's greeting.

There were no more powerful men in Egypt than these two. Between them they held the earthly and spiritual life of the land and the people in their hands.

"I am pleased that you have come. Welcome again to the palace. What pleasures you after your journey, my lord priest?"

It was customary at this point to fill the cup of any and all visitors, and

Khufu was a gracious host. Barley beer, flasks of cooled water and wine, and round cakes were brought in while Meri-ib and his scribe were made comfortable. Both men were anxious to get to the point of their meeting so the preliminary small talk was quickly passed over for the business at hand.

"You have spoken to Nemon, your lordship? I am sure he has things well in hand," Meri-ib said.

"I have indeed, and he does. The chief architect has informed the court of the need for a thousand able-bodied laborers to complete the task in a few weeks of time."

"And you have executed the order for the recruiting of workers, I assume."

"Even as we speak, a royal decree is being sent by messengers to villages throughout the North. I expect the labor force to be assembled in a matter of days."

Now that the physical details of the Sphinx project were discussed, the greater matter of the significance of what was to come needed attention. Khufu was the first to broach the subject.

"Only the Creator, the great Atum, can make something out of nothing, or cause something as phenomenal as the Sky Neters coming to the Earth to occur. There is a reason for the Second Coming, Meri-ib. But that reason has not been made entirely clear to me. Have you insights that may shed light on the matter?"

It was an uncommon thing for a Pharaoh to seek counsel as Khufu was doing now. He was, after all, a god incarnate. With the possible exception of the cloistered High Priest of the Followers of Horus, more so than any other, he, Khufu, would be privy to the inner meaning of such auspicious events.

Meri-ib replied thoughtfully. "I too am awaiting a more revealing vision, your Majesty, and I must admit that I have entertained thoughts of requesting an audience with the old priest Shemshu-Hor."

The two men did not need to discuss the matter any further. That it was time to consult the oldest of the sages, the prophet of the prophets, was settled. He surely would know the deeper meanings of these things.

In her room at the Temple of the Sun, Khem was waking up from a nap. She was more nervous about their first lesson with Ani than she had realized, and after eating, she became sleepy. The drowsiness that came over her had made her feel as if her body and mind were being overtaken by a presence. She had given in to the feeling and had lain across her bed for what she expected to be a short, uneventful nap, but it had turned out to be more.

Images of a dream vision came into her mind. She remembered being in a room with four walls painted with scenes of the Neters in their celestial environment, the ceiling graced with stars against an indigo background. In the center of the chamber stood a large black granite altar upon which lay a scroll. Several words were visible: "Treatise of the Heart." In the corner of the room appeared the figure of Isis, the Great Mother, and she spoke:

"Your Earth, with all that lives on it, is a part of a living whole. Its movement in space is a part of the celestial breath, just as every particle in your body is part of your breathing. You now move into a time in your life when you will learn to entrust your breath to the Earth Mother and be unified with her and the Star Gods. Learn the laws of magic well, my daughter. Abide by them for all your days."

After the goddess had spoken, Khem awakened. She was certain the experience had been a dream visitation from Isis and she felt the deity had come prior to her study of magic to let Khem know the importance of this step in her life, to express the depth of responsibility involved. Khem had been aware of magicians and their craft since childhood. It was part of Egyptian life. But she had never considered it would play a role in her own.

She thought of Tiye. Tiye is a magician of some renown already, Khem reflected. Khem had not wondered why Tiye was chosen as Ani's protégée, what with her cultural and magic background, but why she herself had been chosen was still a mystery to her, even in light of what Taret had said about having known her in past lives. It was all too new to make sense. . . .

Khem snapped back to the present when Bast jumped onto the bed, ready to play. Khem noticed how much the cat had grown over the last few weeks. Her body was filling out and her coat was more like fur than the fuzz it had been when Khem found her in the marketplace. Akhi had done a good job mothering and training the cub, and Khem was feeling guilty that she had not spent much time with the little animal. She had envisioned herself and Bast as companions, but it had not worked out that way, not yet anyway. It was time to change that, and change it she would. "There is no time like the present," she said aloud, her words catching Akhi's attention.

"What did you say, mistress?"

"You have done a good job, Akhi. I think Bast is ready to go places with me, maybe even to my classes soon. She is very well trained and polite, don't you think? It is time for Bast and me to become the companions we were meant to be."

Akhi was surprised by Khem's sudden determination. She was not going to put a damper on her enthusiasm though she had some reservations as to the wisdom of the decision. "It will be well, my mistress."

It was time for Khem to meet Tiye. The two were to convene in Ani's audience room adjacent to the lower courtyard. By the time Khem reached the plaza, Tiye was waiting for her with an anxious look.

"What's wrong, Tiye?"

"Nothing," the Nubian replied. "It is just that the last time I was taught about magic it was by Khaba."

Of course, Khem thought. Tiye would be reminded of her dead teacher at this occasion. She tried to offer some words of support. "Yes, but you must remember what Taret said. Khaba is still your teacher, Tiye. She is just teaching you in a different way now."

The comment seemed to comfort Tiye and together the two apprentices entered the foyer of Ani's quarters, where her domestic steward met them.

"The mistress Ani is expecting you," the servant greeted the girls pleasantly. "Please, be comfortable. Here, sit. I will let her know you are here." The man bowed to the priestesses and disappeared into an adjoining room. In a few moments he returned and beckoned them to follow.

The audience room was nearly twice as large as Khem's apartment. The floor was covered with a woven reed carpet, the walls painted with scenes of Egyptian life. A servant girl met the two and bade them sit on the large floor pillows placed around the room. Beer and dried fruits were provided on a small table nearby.

Ani came into the room and greeted her apprentices with a friendliness that neither of them had experienced from her before. Ani had never been unfriendly or aloof, but she was an imposing figure, perhaps in part due to her size. She was tall for an Egyptian. She looked even taller in Taret's company because Taret was so petite. Seeing Ani now in her domain was the first private encounter either of the girls had had with her, and they both felt on edge. The priestess detected their uneasiness and offered them refreshments.

Taking a date, Khem passed the dish to Tiye, who also took a piece. The threesome were soon comfortable in each other's company, Ani asking Khem if she was feeling the Temple was her home now. Khem said that she was. Through it all Tiye was quiet. Soon, Ani got down to the business of their meeting.

"As you know, the two of you have been chosen for training in the magical arts. A choice such as this is not made lightly, I assure you. Magic is a word associated with supernatural powers. But in truth, it is any act that causes something to be different from the way it was originally. In reality, the law of causality is not missing from a magical act. There exists in magic a bond between cause and effect, and that bond is the Neter involved. A magician spurs the deity into action through her appeal of incantations and formulas. In this way the Neter becomes the instigator, or the cause, of the magical effect."

Tiye did not find this surprising. Khaba had often spoken of the spirits who worked with her, one in particular called Tet, a healer spirit. However, this was all new to Khem. She knew that the Neters had a special relationship with priests and priestesses because she herself had encountered certain of them in dreams. What she did not realize until now was just how intimate a relationship there was between a Neter and a magician. Her thoughts went back to her dream before this meeting. Was Isis the Neter who would work with her?

As if Ani had read her mind, the teacher informed the neophytes that, as their work proceeded, they would be working closely with Neters. "You, Tiye, will be working mostly with the spirit Khaba. This is the way the old woman will continue to keep you under her protective wing."

Ani's words were not entirely unexpected because of what Taret had already told her. Tiye didn't give any visible response, but it made her happy.

"Both of you, at first, will be working under the jurisdiction of the great goddess Isis."

Khem was startled. Nothing happens spontaneously anymore, she thought. Everything seems to be preceded by a vision or dream now. It was a different way of life yet it seemed natural and right.

Ani continued. "The goddess Isis possesses knowledge of *heka*. She will, in time, come to each of you in a dream and reveal to you your secret magical name, your *ren*. When this has occurred you must inform me of your dream right away. This will signify the time you will gain entrance into the magic realms of the Neters. Your ren will be the key that unlocks their great doorway. It will ring out like a bell and announce your arrival."

Ani's words sent a chill through Khem. She had spoken the truth and Khem knew it. There was no turning back. Tiye knew the same thing, but instead of chills, stinging tears gripped her, tears born from fear and anticipating Khaba's presence again. Death isn't final, Tiye thought.

Ani offered her guests a cup of barley beer. The liquid was cool to Khem's throat, which was dry. Everything in her life these days represented a milestone. It was making her strong, but there was still enough child inside her that she could fill with wonder with talk about Neters by people who had a relationship with deities as real and intimate as any between humans.

Khem and Tiye left when Ani said that she would expect to hear from each of them within a few days regarding their dreams. Khem was once again taken aback by the casual manner in which Ani had spoken of the forthcoming dreams, as if their occurrence were a sure thing. The two friends walked slowly through the lower plaza, then sat down on the edge of a palm-lined lotus pool. The air was thick with fragrance from the blossoms. The water reminded Khem of the bowl she had picked to use for scrying, and she asked Tiye if she had gotten hers yet. The Nubian replied that she would use a shallow clay vessel that had belonged to Khaba.

The priestesses had been sitting only a short while when Kasut came up. Khem had not spent much time with Kasut lately, and she was glad to see her. She could see that Kasut was still not comfortable with Tiye. Khem sensed her friend's shyness and wanted to do something to give the two an opportunity to get to know each other better. She decided that a good way to do that would be to invite them both to come to her room for a visit with Bast. Nothing like an animal to break the ice, she thought. Besides, she wanted to show off her lioness.

The three girls walked up the stairway that led to the upper level where the dormitory rooms were located. At the top of the stairs they ran into Bakka, the apprentice who had sat across from Khem and her family at dinner on her first night in Heliopolis. The young girl had been present at the classes and Khem had seen her at mealtimes, but Bakka seldom interacted with or spoke to anyone. Encountering her now, Khem observed the girl emanated a melancholy just as Khem had sensed that first night. No one seemed to know much about Bakka, only that she had come from Memphis and was the only daughter of a wealthy food merchant named Ali.

Bakka had come to the Sun Temple some six months before, shortly after the death of her mother. There had been some gossip that the beautiful young woman had been forced by her father to enter the priestcraft to get her away from a young suitor she wanted to marry. Entering Temple life was a matter of great significance to most of the apprentices, and Khem had been shocked to hear rumors of Bakka's plight as her reason for joining.

The three stopped and warmly greeted Bakka, who seemed nervous when the priestesses spoke to her. She cast a wary glance at Tiye, causing the Nubian to put up a silent barrier that made her seem aloof.

"Hello, Bakka," Khem spoke, her face lighting up in a friendly smile.

"Hello," Bakka replied shyly, her eyes looking down as she spoke.

"We are going to my quarters to see my lioness cub, Bast. Would you like to come?" Khem hoped the girl would accept the invitation.

Bakka seemed to regret that Khem had issued the invitation. She gave off the kind of surprised look that one experiences when an excuse to refuse doesn't come to mind fast enough, and when refusing would be awkward. The girl's eyes reflected her hesitation at joining the group, causing Khem to insist. Reaching out and clasping Bakka's hand, Khem said, "Oh, please come. You have to see Bast. She is so beautiful."

Bakka relented and the four proceeded to Khem's quarters.

Once inside, the girls found Akhi feeding the cub, who was hungrily lapping a dish of goat's milk. The company engaged the animal's curiosity. It bounded over to Khem, its paws prancing as Khem knelt to scoop her up. Khem could feel the cat's muscles flexing as it squirmed in her arms. The cub was anxious to sniff the other women, so Khem put her down. The cat immediately ran to Tiye. Very curious, Kasut tried to entice the animal to come to her, but Bast only had eyes for Tiye.

Khem was intrigued by the way the lioness went to the Nubian's feet and rubbed her head and body on her ankles and calves in what seemed like an attempt to caress her. After a few moments Tiye bent over and petted the cat on the back of the head. As her hand touched the animal's body, Bast fell gently to the floor and rolled over on her back for Tiye to rub her belly. Khem had not seen the cub act that way with anyone except her and Akhi. She was struck by the energy that passed between Tiye and the lioness, and watched Tiye and the cat lock eyes for several seconds. In those moments, their eyes looked strangely similar: large golden disks with vertical black pupils like slits of ebony.

Kasut saw the same thing, but her reaction was fear. The priestess grabbed Khem's arm nervously and whispered loudly, "Did you see that?"

The spell between girl and lioness broke, but Tiye continued stroking and playing with Bast. The play brought out a side of Tiye that Khem had not seen before, childlike and innocent. Sensing the revealing nature of her play with the cat, Tiye drew back her hand and stepped back from Bast's paws still reaching out to grab her ankles. Khem took the cue and picked up the cat and turned to Kasut and Bakka. Bakka was afraid, and it showed in her eyes and posture.

"She will not hurt you, Bakka," Khem assured the girl. "She is just playing." The little cat rolled her head backwards and squirmed wildly to free herself from Khem's arms.

"I think it's time for you to finish your lunch, Bast."

Khem called for Akhi, who entered from the anteroom and relieved her mistress of the furry wiggling bundle. With Bast in tow she picked up the bowl of milk and went out onto the patio. Just as Khem was about to invite her guests to have something to drink, Tiye announced she had to go. She had a long walk into the city, and she must be home in time for the evening meal with her host family. Although Khem understood her need to leave, she felt her departure was abrupt.

As soon as Tiye had gone, Bakka said that she too had to leave. Bowing slightly to Khem and Kasut, the girl turned and walked to the door. Once there she paused and thanked Khem for inviting her and was gone. Khem was prepared to encourage Bakka to stay but thought better of it and let her go with a pleasant farewell. The girl's demeanor was troubling to Khem. She felt that Bakka needed a friend.

Khem and Kasut sat and talked for a while, sipping their beer. Bast curled up in Khem's lap, lulled to sleep by her soft rubs and gentle scratches along her back.

"Bakka seems sad, does she not?" Kasut inquired, turning the conversation to their colleague. "And Tiye is very strange to me. I do not know how to approach her."

"Tiye is an intense person," Khem admitted. "But she is quite likeable once you accept her as she is." Her assessment of the Nubian told Kasut that the two had become close. "As for Bakka, I do sense a sadness about her. Do you know anything about her?"

"No, nothing, other than the gossip about her being here at her father's insistence."

"Yes, I have heard that too. If it is true, it must be difficult for her to be here."

Kasut remembered what she had witnessed between Tiye and the lioness, and wondered if she had imagined a recognition between them.

"You did not imagine it, Kasut. I saw it too."

The lioness cub began to stir, its eyes opening and its jaws gaping wide in a lazy yawn. "She must know we are talking about her," Khem said with a smile, and rubbed the cat. "It seemed that Tiye and Bast were lionesses at that moment."

Her own words shed light on what she had seen transpire between Tiye and Bast. Understanding spread across her face, along with a smile.

"That's it, Kasut," Khem said excitedly. "What we saw was a soul connection between Tiye and Bast. We saw the image of the lioness goddess in their connection."

Chapter Thirteen

Hawk-Man Dreams

Meri-ib tossed and turned in his sleep all night, his dreams haunted by fragmented images of a huge hawk whose eyes looked through him into his soul. The big bird had changed back and forth in its appearance, from human to bird. When it appeared as a man, the hawk's stern facial features framed dark eyes that pierced his mind and made him feel so vulnerable he felt his memory had been robbed, as if there was no knowledge in his mind to which the hawk-man did not have access. When the image manifested as the hawk, it would spread its wings and fly around the High Priest's bed, swooping down as if it intended to capture his sleeping body in its talons and carry him away to a land of no return.

Meri-ib woke up numerous times during the night, each time sinking back into his fitful dream where he was once again in the presence of the hawk-man picking his brain. When dawn had finally come, the priest awoke to the bright rays of sunlight. Morning had never been more welcome.

Meri-ib lay in bed, his fine linen sheets soaked in sweat, and fought to clear his mind of the dream fragments that had left him feeling uneasy. All he could recall were visions of the man and the hawk, which made him feel him uncomfortable and invaded.

Meri-ib finally dragged himself out of bed. He felt groggy and moved slowly. His body felt as tired as if he had not slept at all. Calling for his chamber servant, the priest asked for water for drinking and washing. The water helped him wake up when he splashed it on his face and neck. Changing out of his bedclothes into a fresh long kilt also helped. By the time he drank a cup of cool water and ate a bowl of syrupy figs and a small cake, he felt better.

His thoughts turned to the Pharaoh and the secret Sphinx project. The plan to unearth the Sphinx would not be revealed to the public until the Full Moon. It had to be that way so that he and Khufu would have time to inform all the High Priests of the numerous temples in the upper and lower precincts of what was about to occur and why. Talk of a Second Coming of the Star Gods could cause panic, or at least invite rumor and power struggles that could threaten the throne. Humans could be ruthless in their quest for power, and this event would certainly put the Pharaoh and others in authority in jeopardy unless they had the matter in hand.

This was precisely why he and Khufu had decided to seek audience with the cloistered High Priest of the Followers of Horus. In itself, that was an uncommon occurrence. The elite priesthood was housed in the smaller Temple of the *Benu* in Heliopolis. Its members seldom ventured beyond the temple gates or interacted with other religious orders inside or outside the complex. Very few people had access to the order's members, particularly to the High Priest Shemshu-Hor. The old priest was aging and, at last account, almost blind. But Meri-ib knew that there was no one in all of Egypt, or the world, in closer contact with the Sky Gods than he. Meri-ib sent for his chief scribe, Haroun. It was time to send a letter to Shemshu-Hor to request an audience for himself and the king. . . .

Sokar had risen before dawn. Magical work stimulated him and he could not sleep. His mind was on Meri-ib. Had the High Priest had a dream? Had the hawk entered the man's unconscious mind to plant the seed that would result in his taking Sokar into his confidence? With the possible exception of the vizier, no one knew more about Khufu's activities and palace intelligence than the High Priest of Heliopolis. The political and religious strength of the Temple of the Sun came close to rivaling the power of the throne, and made the High Priest a political insider.

Sokar wandered out onto the patio that adjoined his bedchamber. The area was bathed in warm sunlight that aroused the birds to song. The morning air was dry. A breeze took the edge off the heat. Sokar liked the serene beauty of his garden; having his breakfast here was a good way for him to begin the day.

Horus the falcon perched in a covered area of the plaza on a cedar wood. His head was covered by a leather hood placed on him nightly. Removing the hood, Sokar watched as the big bird ruffled its feathers from head to toe and stretched its wings like a human just waking from a night's sleep. The hawk's black eyes squinted and blinked rapidly at first as it adjusted to the sunlight.

"I trust your dreams were interesting, my friend," Sokar spoke to his familiar. The telepathy between the man and hawk was as keen as any that existed between two magicians. Sokar was eager to tune into Horus's mind to learn if he had been able to enter the dream-mind of the High Priest of Heliopolis. Had Horus found out what Meri-ib knew about a special announcement that Khufu was rumored to soon be making? Was something special going on at the New Year festivities?

Holding out his right forearm for the hawk to perch on, Sokar admired the magnificent winged creature with pride and kinship. He saw himself in the hawk. Like him, Horus was proud and kinglike. Horus knew he was a king within the feathered tribe, and Sokar knew he was meant to be a king among men. Horus is completely comfortable with who and what he is, Sokar thought to himself. Just like me, Horus is strong. He is at home in the realms of the gods.

Sokar walked to the lotus pool at the center of the patio, and leaned his arm and shoulder down so Horus could step onto the rim of the pool's wide edge. Seeing his reflection in the water, the hawk cocked his head to one side and stared at the image with acute interest. That slight cocking of his head always let Sokar know the bird's mind was open to him. Now was the time for Sokar to make his transition from man to hawk. Sokar was adept at the art of shape-shifting, and this was the way he was able to make the connection with Horus's mind.

Closing his eyes for concentration, Sokar began to inhale deeply. His muscular chest heaved and expanded with each of the seven breaths that gradually drew all his subtle bodies, and his physical one, into one inner self. The transformation made him into an astral being. Once inside himself, the magician then only need "think" himself a hawk and he would become a hawk.

Kheti came out onto the plaza to bring his master's breakfast. When he had taken but a few steps, the servant stopped in his tracks. There, on the tiled rim of the lotus pool, were two hawks standing side by side staring at their reflections in the water. Kheti didn't go any further. He knew better. He had witnessed Sokar's shape-shifting many times. He knew when the magician was working, and he never interfered.

The two hawks stood still as stones for what seemed to Kheti like hours, though he knew it was only a few seconds. Suddenly, the hawk on the right spread its wings and took a stance and preceded to leap into the air. When the bird took off, its feet left the pool's rim and landed on the limestone floor of the patio, its bird feet transforming instantly into human feet. In a flash, Sokar's physical body re-formed. He was human again.

Kheti allowed a few moments to pass for Sokar to regain his wits before he approached his master and offered him grape juice and sweet cakes. Placing the food and drink on a table by the chair, Kheti held out his arm for Horus. The hawk was as familiar with Kheti as he was with Sokar, and was trusting of both. Kheti took Horus back into the sitting room and placed him on a perch with a feed bowl attached to it with leather strips into which he placed a dead rat. Kheti always found Horus's feeding time a distasteful chore. He couldn't bare to watch the bird eat so he busied himself with attending to Sokar's needs.

The magician-priest was sitting in a relaxed position sipping his juice and absorbing the warm rays of the morning sun. "Well, Kheti. It seems as if there is indeed something afoot in the kingdom."

Although Kheti did not ask any questions, he knew that Sokar was referring to information he had learned from Horus during the shape-shifting. The valet was well aware of the hawk's ability to enter into a person's dreams, and he could guess that the latest dreamer might have been Meri-ib or perhaps the Pharaoh. He awaited his master's comments patiently, for he knew Sokar would tell him everything, sooner or later.

"It has to do with the Stone King of the Desert, the Sphinx," Sokar said slowly, his mind struggling to put together the pieces of mental fragments that Horus had picked from the High Priest's subconscious.

After a long pause, Sokar continued. "Whatever it is, it is buried so deep in Meri-ib's mind that it is in the form of bits of images and a few words. I am certain that it concerns a matter of paramount importance, but all I have at this point is pieces, fragments that I know fit together somehow."

"What are the fragments, my lord?" Kheti spoke out. He felt that the conversation had reached a point where he could proffer a question without overstepping his boundaries or risk invoking Sokar's ire.

Sokar looked at Kheti over the rim of his drinking cup, his dark eyes reflecting his deep thoughts. Finally, he answered. "The Stone King, the season of Inundation, a royal proclamation, an architectural design, thousands of laborers, a full Moon."

Kheti listened intently as Sokar revealed the bits Horus had retrieved from Meri-ib's mind. After pondering how the images might fit together, he said, "I do not know what it all means, but the Stone Head is of little portent, my lord. It has no body, no soul. Perhaps it was of importance in times long past, but its purpose may have already been served, and those times are long gone."

Sokar's thoughts went to the myths. A great magical power had once existed in the place where the Stone Head was located. Its aura had extended over all the region. There was a power that had existed since the beginning of time. More pieces of the legend came to mind, the coming of the mighty god Khepera to Egypt. Thinking about Khepera made Sokar think of the age-old symbol of the scarab, the sacred beetle of Egypt. "He who becomes"—that was what he had been taught the name Khepera meant. Khepera represents the rising Sun, reborn in the East every dawn. Egyptians had always seen the scarab as pushing the Sun across the morning sky.

"All in all," Sokar said aloud, "Khepera embodies the power of rebirth."

"Begging your pardon, my master," Kheti responded.

"Never mind, Kheti, I was just thinking."

It was apparent that Sokar did not want to pursue the matter or explain himself any further, so Kheti took the cue to drop the subject. Little did the servant know that what he had said about the Stone Head of the Desert had led Sokar's thoughts to a legend that would indirectly help knit the pieces of the puzzle together in time.

"I will be going to the Temple of the Sun later this afternoon, Kheti. I will need a scribe to accompany me, and of course I will expect you to come along too."

Kheti bowed to his master and took his leave to recruit a scribe.

Across the city at the Temple of the Sun, Khem was getting ready for class. The dream she was expecting had not come yet, but she had gotten a restful sleep. Awakening, she had felt rejuvenated, filled with expectation of the day's teaching. Taret had said that she would be presenting more information about the Moon and the goddess Hathor. Khem felt a closeness to the lunar goddesses, and assumed that was because she was a female.

When Khem went into the classroom it was already bustling with conversation. Priestesses were scurrying about finding seats and settling in for the lesson. Tiye had arrived, and Khem joined her.

"Did you have a dream last night?" Khem inquired expectantly.

"Yes, I did," Tiye replied, but before she could go into any detail Taret entered with Sheshat. The two women seated themselves on the low dais, and the room quickly quieted down. Taret began speaking.

"There is much to learn about the Moon. This is best gained by understanding its aspects and deities. Of these, it is the goddess Hathor I wish to speak about at this time."

Khem and the others listened attentively as Taret discussed Hathor from several perspectives, including her paradoxical attributes as goddess of love and joy, and death and the Underworld. Khem took that to mean that the Moon itself was paradoxical. The teacher-priestess said Hathor is depicted in art wearing the horns of a cow which symbolize the Moon, and between the horns rests the lunar disk.

"All of these facts are of importance," Taret assured her audience. "However, it is a particular aspect of Hathor's power, and subsequently of the Moon's power, that is of primary concern now and in the future in your work as Star Priestesses. There is much hidden within the personage of Hathor, my star daughters. The seeming contradiction of joy and love, death and the Underworld, will no longer be such when it is understood that Hathor's rituals involve practices that trigger a sort of divine madness that frees one to follow her ways from the mundane world. With the proper training, initiates are able to enter into other planes of existence and walk with the gods.

"True enough, Hathor's power is symbolized by the Moon. But the Moon is not the *source* of her power. The source is the star Sirius, the Nile Star, the star that ushers in the New Year as it rises on the first day of the month of Thoth."

Taret then said that only the initiates know this, that it is a part of the truths given to Egyptians during the First Time. "The first day of the month of Thoth is also the birthday of Hathor. It is a festival day, not only a time to celebrate the goddess's birth, but the day of the year when her power is transmitted through the Moon and is accessible in its greatest potency to all her followers. Hathor has the power to bring change, to bring love and joy. But she also has the power to bring death to those who misuse the power of love, to those who seek to bring separation, to those who would dishonor the dead in any way for any self-serving reason."

The teacher's tone had become ominous. It was clear that the High Priestess placed tremendous stock in the proper use of power and a clear understanding and respect for natural law. No student of hers would ever be able to plead ignorance of those all-important factors.

Taret continued. "The worship of Hathor has been a part of Egypt for a long time. Her cults have always been filled by priestesses, and very few priests have ever been included. Women have held the positions of authority and exercised responsibilities in the cults. It is important to realize that within one of Hathor's powers, the energy of pure joy, her deepest mystery is concealed. Hathor priestesses have known that sound and movement have a profound yet subtle effect on the various levels of the human mind and body. Thus they are specially trained in music and dance in which they generate and release this subtle power.

"Hathor priestesses are servants of the goddess, living embodiments of

Hathor. They understand that movement and sound are expressions of her principles. As if they were one, the goddess and her holy women bestow beauty, joy, grace, and rapture. They are the musician-priestesses who perform the sacred dances in temples throughout Egypt. Their music and dances are entertaining and beautiful, and they are magic. They invoke cosmic harmony and love that allow the law of unity to exist. They raise energy that can empower and heal.

"While performing their rites, Hathor priestesses dress like the goddess herself with a *menat* —beaded collar, and a sistrum or rattle. The *menat* and sistrum are the magical tools presented to Hathor's initiates upon their acceptance into her cult. There are some among you suited to become a priestess of Hathor. Perhaps you already know who you are." She looked at Kasut and Bakka, but said nothing.

When the teaching ended, the apprentices gradually left the room. Khem and Tiye left together.

"I am anxious to hear about your dream," Khem said, excited about what Tiye might tell her.

"It was the strangest thing," Tiye began. "Have you ever had a dream begin before you fall asleep?"

"Before you fall asleep? What do you mean? How could that happen?"

"I went to bed and pulled the netting around the canopy. I was just lying there trying to fall asleep when I saw a figure starting to form at the foot of my bed. At first I thought I was seeing things, but the figure became very solid and clear."

Khem's eyes widened as she listened to her friend's story. "Who was it?"

"That's just it. The apparition became so clear yet it was not anyone I knew."

"Who did it look like?" Khem urged.

"It was a beautiful woman, with long, straight black hair. She was wearing a headdress that looked like it was made from two gold wings that fit on her head like a crown and hung down each side, framing her face. The headdress had a crown in its center formed out of cow's horns. A reddish-gold disk rested between the horns, you know, just like Taret was describing about—"

"Hathor!" Khem broke in.

"Yes, like that. The woman was dressed in a gold robe. Even her skin looked like gold to me." Tiye's expression showed that talking about the woman, she was seeing her again. "I stared at her, at the soft glow that surrounded her. I know I was awake. But the next thing I knew it was morning! When I woke up I remembered my dream. The woman I had seen in my room before I went to sleep was then in my dream. There was a lioness by her side in the dream, a full-grown lioness."

Khem remembered what she had seen transpire between Tiye and Bast.

"Did the woman speak to you?" Khem asked expectantly.

"Yes. One word. *Nefer.*"

Khem was taken aback by the Nubian's experience. She had never known anyone who had fallen asleep and had the vision continue in a dream. "*Nefer?*" Khem repeated.

The two walked in silence the rest of the way to the dining hall. When they had gotten their food they sat down on pillows and put their bowls on the short-legged table in front of them. Khem brought up Tiye's dream again. "If I remember correctly, *Nefer* is a hieroglyph sign that means 'good,' or is it 'beautiful'? Maybe it is both."

"I thought about that," Tiye answered. "But to me it has another meaning. It is the name for the crown of my part of Egypt, the South."

Tiye's mention of her being from the South took Khem by surprise. She had come to know the Nubian so well, it seemed, she had ceased to notice their differences.

"And it represents the heart and windpipe of an animal, any animal," Tiye mused.

Khem again thought of Bast and the lioness in Tiye's dream. "I think the lioness in your dream was you, Tiye," she blurted out, catching Tiye off guard. "The woman must have been Isis. Ani said she would come to each of us in a dream."

"Yes, I know," Tiye replied, her eyes taking on a faraway look. "I believe it was Isis and that she gave me my magical name."

"*Nefer,*" Khem said with excitement. "Your magical ren is *Nefer.*"

"Ssssshhhhh!" Tiye snapped, looking around nervously to see if anyone had heard their conversation. "Someone might hear!"

Khem lowered her voice and spoke apologetically in a hushed tone. "I'm sorry. I will keep your secret."

Magical names were the key to a person's soul, Khem remembered, the experience making her realize how careful one had to be with who knew or had access to this information. If someone had a mind to, she could use it to cast spells or make one psychically vulnerable.

Finishing her meal and sipping on a cup of wine, Tiye asked Khem if she had dreamed of Isis yet.

"No," Khem said softly, expectantly. "Not yet."

Chapter Fourteen

Sokar Is Appointed Co-Ritualist

Sokar and Kheti walked through the streets of Heliopolis stopping at a vendor here and there. Kheti purchased a clay pot filled with natron to replenish his master's ceremonial supply and for his and Sokar's use in personal grooming. Natron made a good cleansing agent for the teeth and hair. The servant also bought three pigeons he would later kill and prepare for the evening's meal. The succulent birds were Sokar's favorite food. Kheti also purchased two skins of wine; one palm, one date.

Sokar was headed to the Temple of the Sun to see Meri-ib. He intended to offer his services to the High Priest as co-ritualist for the major rite at the New Year festival. What better way to be close to Meri-ib and on the inside of what was going on?

When they arrived at the Temple complex, Sokar paused at the Great Mound upon which the huge obelisk stood shining in the sunlight. He said a prayer and left an offering at the site where the gods first came to Earth. Looking up at the tapering needle-like monument, the tip of which was shaped in the form of a pyramidion, or *benbenet*, the magician reached into the sash around his waist where he kept his special ceremonial objects. Unwrapping the linen parcel, he took out a small chunk of myrrh. Holding the fragrant resin in his hand, he lifted his head towards the Sun and, closing his eyes, began to murmur.

> Honor to You, O Sustainer of the Spirit.
> May every Egyptian utter a prayer to you on their lips this day,
> O Great One. O God of Renewed Existence, O Ruler of Heaven.
> You who made Eternal Life, I give praise to your radiant light.

Sokar then kissed the lump of myrrh and placed it on the ground next to the obelisk. He and Kheti then proceeded through the gates of the temple into the lower courtyard, bustling with priests, officers, and servants. Sokar immediately spotted one of the High Priest's scribes and made his way over to the man with a friendly smile on his face. His smile was disarming, warm, and genuine, and put most people at ease right away. He knew the scribe would probably know Meri-ib's schedule for the day.

"Good day, sir," Sokar greeted the scribe politely. "Would you know if His Honor the High Priest is free of duties this afternoon?"

Thinking for a moment, the scribe replied, "I think the lord priest is in his quarters with his chief scribe, Haroun."

"Thank you," Sokar said, bowing. He went to the wing of the temple where Meri-ib's private rooms were located. Although he had no appointment, he felt sure Meri-ib would grant him an audience. He was after all a member of the royal family and the priesthood.

When Sokar arrived at the High Priest's quarters, two temple guards met him. Security was always a primary concern, and the protection afforded for Meri-ib was second only to that of the Pharaoh.

Sokar announced to the guards his desire to meet with the Chief Priest, and was met with a formal rejection. Meri-ib was busy with Haroun and was accepting no visitors. Undaunted, Sokar said, "I understand that the Lord High Priest is occupied with important matters, and that he is unaware of my coming. I ask you, in kindness, to see to it that the noble representative of the gods is informed of my presence. I am Sokar, half-brother to King Khufu, son of the honorable Sneferu, priest of the Temple of the *Benu*, and servant of the great god Horus. I wish only a few moments of Master Meri-ib's valuable time."

Eyeing Sokar carefully, the guard in charge disappeared without a word into the inner foyer of the quarters and soon returned to announce to Sokar that the Chief Priest would receive him presently and that he should wait until then.

When Sokar was finally summoned into the outer room of Meri-ib's audience chamber, he had grown extremely impatient. He disliked being kept waiting almost more than anything. But his ability to conceal his displeasure was impeccable, and he used it now when he greeted the High Priest. He smiled broadly, exerting the charm that was as much his trademark as being known as the Pharoah's bastard.

"Sokar, I regret to have kept you waiting, but I did not know in advance of your coming," Meri-ib stated, his words designed to convey disgruntlement at having to receive an uninvited guest.

"You would have known if I had known, gracious servant of the great god Ra," Sokar replied apologetically, bowing deeply to the Chief Priest. "I am here in an obedient response to a beckoning by the divinities. I am come to do their bidding."

Meri-ib's curiosity was baited by Sokar's remarks. The magician knew he would be, and as always, played it to the hilt.

"What, I ask you, are you talking about, Sokar?" Meri-ib asked, his eyebrows rising inquisitively.

Sokar's demeanor took on a pretend seriousness intended to enchant. "I have been visited in my dreams for many nights. I have been beckoned by the great god Horus, son of the luminous Isis and Osiris, to come to you, my Lord Priest."

"For what purpose?" Meri-ib asked, his curiosity rising.

"I have been made aware, intuitively, of course, that the upcoming season of Inundation is to be of particular and tremendous significance."

The priest felt a shock thrill through him. What did the magician-priest know? Surely the gods were not informing people, other priests, about the Second Coming. He being the High Priest would know about such things, would he not? Meri-ib felt apprehension.

"The god has asked me as a priest of Heliopolis to come to you personally and offer myself to you in service in the holy celebration of Ra, to honor the Sustainer of the Spirit of all that lives, and the Lord of the Gods. I wish to stand by your side, Lord Meri-ib, in the Holy of Holies, and perform with you the sacred rite as your co-ritualist and humble servant of the gods. I come to offer this in obedience to my god, Horus."

Meri-ib stood in silence, his eyes fixed on Sokar. He knew he was caught in an awkward position. To accept Sokar as co-ritualist in the holiest rite of the year would require him to spend a great deal of time with the magician-priest, and that as his assistant, Sokar would have to be informed of all that was going on regarding both the holy and secular activities planned for that day. Meri-ib was also aware, though he could not prove it, of Sokar's jealousy of Khufu, and he did not particularly like or trust the king's half-brother. He felt he would take any opportunity to gain power. Yet Sokar was telling him that Horus himself had ordered him to offer to fill this all-important role. How could he in good conscience refuse Horus? What reason could he give?

Meri-ib turned away from Sokar and walked to a chair and sat down, his thoughts racing. Sokar stood silently, confident he had made his case, knowing anything else said at this point might jeopardize his advantage.

The High Priest sat quietly. Finally, his chest heaving under a heavy sigh, he looked at Sokar and said, "I must give your offer some thought. I cannot make a judgment at this very moment." Knowing the magician-priest would not give up easily, he promised that when he had made his decision, he would send a courier with a sealed message to that effect. Meri-ib's tone and his body language reflected his quandary. On top of it, the dream he had had the night before in which the hawk had changed into a man and back into a hawk again had left him drained. He did not feel he could make a decision this important regarding the Inundation ritual on the spot.

Sokar knew it was not appropriate to push the issue any further, though he would have preferred an answer. He would wait for Meri-ib to make up his mind. It would not be wise to use telepathic magic on him to get what he wanted. At least not yet, not here.

"You are most gracious, Lord Meri-ib. Do not tax yourself now. You seem tired. I will await your reply."

With that, Sokar bowed to the High Priest and left the room. Kheti was waiting outside the door of the audience room. He could tell by the look on his master's face that the visit had not been entirely successful, but thought better of asking questions.

As the two made their way out of the temple complex, Sokar walked in long strides, his chin jutting out arrogantly, his posture erect and stiff. Kheti had seen him this way before, and he knew it meant that something Sokar considered of paramount importance was not working out exactly as he planned.

Once on the city streets again, Kheti requested permission to return to the Temple of the *Benu*. He was still carrying the cage of pigeons and the bottles of wine he had bought earlier, which reminded Sokar that Kheti needed to return home to prepare the evening meal

"Yes, Kheti. We can go now. My task is done."

The two men walked the short distance to the *Benu* Temple, Sokar in the lead. Once inside his private rooms, he retreated to his bedchamber to rest while Kheti prepared the meal.

Sokar told Kheti to see to it that he was not disturbed while he rested. He also requested a cup of wine to help him relax and nap. Confident that his wishes would be carried out, he closed himself in his bedchamber. Alone, the magician went to his altar to his scrying bowl. Made of alabaster, the bowl was beautifully carved with lotus blossoms around its edge.

Taking the bowl in his hands, Sokar filled it with water. Then, placing the bowl back on the altar, he lit a beeswax candle and a chunk of charcoal; once it started to heat up, he placed the charcoal in a small brazier alongside the bowl. He dropped a piece of myrrh resin onto the glowing charcoal. The fragrance of the incense filled the room. The smell of myrrh always put Sokar in the receptive frame of mind that made his meditative and magical work go more smoothly.

Settling down onto a large floor pillow, Sokar closed his eyes and went through a deep-breathing exercise to relax his body and calm his mind. Once this was accomplished, he let his mind go. Using his keen visualization skills, he pictured Meri-ib's face. Holding the image in focus, the magician made a mind-to-mind connection with his quarry, planting the seed that Meri-ib would decide favorably upon letting him serve as his assistant for the New Year Ritual to the god Ra. Sokar could feel the mental energy flowing from his own consciousness to that of the High Priest. He was acutely aware that Meri-ib was also a highly trained priest capable of detecting transference of mental power into his mind.

To guard against being found out, Sokar disguised himself in the Duat by creating a decoy persona that would make him appear in Meri-ib's mind as the god Horus. That way, the chances were good that the High Priest would think that it was the wishes of the god that he accept Sokar as his assistant. He also knew Khufu had no idea of what he was up to, so to cover his tracks he felt it was time to inform his half-brother of his desire to serve with Meri-ib. He need not go to the trouble. He was sure that Meri-ib would send a courier, if he hadn't already, to the palace within minutes of Sokar's departure from his quarters.

In the capital city, Khufu's day had been busy. He had turned all civil hearings and other state matters over to Manetho earlier that morning. As Pharaoh, he needed to focus his time and energy on the Sphinx project. He considered nothing more important.

Just after the noon meal, a courier arrived with a message for the king regarding the matter of Sokar's visit to the High Priest of Heliopolis and his request to serve as Meri-ib's main assistant for the New Year ritual. Sitting alone in his private office, Khufu mulled over the situation. He did not know if his half-brother's involvement with the ceremony was a good thing or not. What he did know was that Sokar never sought to interact with anyone unless he had a reason, and that reason was always one that had to do with his own power and position. Still, Sokar as co-ritualist had advantages.

If Sokar was an intimate participant he could be watched more closely and his whereabouts known. On the other hand, Khufu was aware of his sibling's rivalry and had long suspected that Sokar felt himself the rightful heir to the throne of Egypt. These were important times. Nothing could go wrong. It was certainly not the time for Khufu to have to defend his kingship against any rival, living or dead, family or outsider.

The Pharaoh's thoughts went again to the visitation by the god Thoth

that Meri-ib had had days before. He had thought repeatedly of the apparition and the implications of its appearance, for Egypt, himself as king, and
the people. The god he served was Ptah, and the sun gods Ra and Horus,
but Khufu had always felt a deep respect, even a soul connection, with
Thoth. It was Thoth's link to astronomy that made the king feel something
special between himself and the god who would someday affect his life.

He, Khufu, Pharaoh of Egypt, initiate of the star mysteries, servant of the
Sky Gods, would prepare a temple the likes of which Egyptians had never
seen: a temple that would receive the Star Gods when they returned to the
Earth. The great temple would be a fitting place for the Great Ones to perform
their rituals and give their wisdom to the priesthood, who would in turn
benefit the Egyptian people in untold ways. It would be the most marvelously
progressive event for Egypt since Osiris brought them civilization.

The finest materials would go into the temple's construction. The
most elite and learned of the priesthood would be in service to the Returning Ones. What wisdom would they learn? The most highly trained scribes
would be at their disposal. The temple's scrolls would become filled with
new truths. Mysteries would be solved, and texts from the Star Gods
would be written down and studied for millennia to come. No, nothing
and no one would stand in the way. No one could be allowed to turn this
event into a power struggle.

The Sky Gods had made their decision to come to the Earth now when
Khufu was king. There had to be a reason for that. Why had the star deities
chosen this time? Was his being Pharaoh at *this* time a coincidence? He
could not accept that. The deities obviously trusted him to provide for their
needs and to see to it that their teachings and their arrival were used properly for the benefit of all Egyptians. The Pharaoh wondered if the Second
Coming would happen if someone else occupied the throne, such as Sokar.

Sokar. As long as he had been king, Khufu had felt a need to always
look over his shoulder. He sensed his sibling held a grudge against him.
Although Sokar had never come out and said he felt that he should have
inherited the kingship, Khufu knew it was so. Khufu had had nothing to
do with his father's decision, with Sokar's lot in life, or with the internal
politics of the royal family during his father's reign. Upon Sneferu's death,
Khufu had been notified of his forthcoming ascension and, as far as he had
been concerned, that was that. Sokar apparently felt differently, and his
feelings had resulted in Khufu's dealing with the magician-priest politely
but with extreme caution.

Perhaps every ruler has some concern about his place in history. When
one was king, one had everything: wealth, power, wives, children. There
was nothing left to attain but to be remembered, not only for having been

king, but for what occurred and what one achieved on the Throne. There was no doubt that the Sphinx project, the great temple that would be built, and the Second Coming of the Star Gods would assure Khufu's immortality. That gave him satisfaction, but it also made him feel a responsibility he must handle with complete dedication.

What should he do? Should he advise Meri-ib to deny Sokar his request? Or should he advise the opposite? The decision weighed heavily on his mind. At times like these he always turned to the gods for guidance. He would go to his altar room and make prayers to Isis, the Great Mother of the World. Khufu trusted that she would guide him in the right direction.

Accompanied by his ever-present bodyguards, Khufu left his study and proceeded to the altar room. As a sanctuary it was beautiful, its walls painted in elaborate images of the nine major deities of Lower Egypt. Large columns stood along each wall. The altar itself was gilded, and held fifty candles whose light filled the room with a soft glow.

When Khufu entered the room, the strong fragrance of incense filled his nostrils. He loved the heady aroma, a mixture of myrrh and musk. It never failed to put him in a reverent frame of mind. Going up to the altar, he lit a cone of incense and offered it to the image of Isis that stood nearby. Then, bowing in respect and humility, Khufu began to pray:

> Hail Isis, Mother of the Gods,
> Hail Lady veiled with the cloak of the Sun,
> Whose light illumines the Earth.
> Hail Isis. I thank you for your guidance.
> Enlighten and empower me so
> that I may be a good king to the souls of Egypt,
> that I may teach by example.
> May you grant me wisdom, patience, and all other skills
> I need to have so that I may be an honorable ruler.
> As you nurture me, may I nurture the people.
> As you are patient with me, may I be patient with them.
> As you give me love, may I give love freely.
> Great Isis, grant this my prayer.

His prayer finished, Khufu lifted his head and looked up into the face of the beloved goddess. He found it distasteful to approach the deity on issues regarding power. He was in a position where there was no greater power a human could attain. He was a king among men. Did he have any reason to fear Sokar was out to usurp his power? Was he being unfair to his half-brother by distrusting him and his motives for wanting to serve as Meri-ib's ritual assistant? He had to know for sure.

Divination was a skill Khufu had learned as a young man while in training for the priesthood. He had devised his own method using specially made faience scarabs made by a Nubian magician named Dedi known far and wide for his magical skills. Dedi charged every sacred object he made with the power bestowed upon him by the god Sobek, with whom the magician enjoyed an intimate relationship.

Khufu reached inside the linen bag that Manetho had given him on the day of his coronation. The bag was embroidered with hieroglyphic symbols sewn with gold threads. Pulling open the drawstrings, he took out the seven scarabs. He looked at the objects and felt their power in his hand. Khufu rarely consulted the scarab runes, and when he did it was only for matters of consequence to the Throne and Egypt.

Each of the scarabs was painted with a symbol: ankh, wadjet, Nile, ibis, crocodile, stars, the god Seth. Only the initiates knew the deepest and true meanings of the symbols. Khufu knew the energies embodied in the runes from several perspectives, and he knew how to read them for advice and foretelling the future.

Cupping the scarabs in his hands, Khufu knelt on the floor. Picking up a scroll from the altar, he unrolled it in front of him, then held his cupped hands with the scarabs inside to his forehead and whispered aloud. "Spirit of Khepera, instill once again your power into these scarabs. Tell me, God of the Rising Sun, is it right that my brother Sokar serves the great Lord Horus as the High Priest Meri-ib's co-ritualist for the New Year festival?"

Khufu's petition was direct and to the point. There would be no misunderstanding about what the scarabs would reveal. He would abide by their answer. Rolling the scarabs vigorously around in his hands, the king opened his palms and released the runes, and watched as they tumbled onto the tapestry. Four out of the seven landed upright, exposing the beetle's backs. The other three fell and rolled over, showing the symbols of the crocodile, the Nile, and the stars. Khufu gazed at the three upturned scarabs, their symbols burning themselves into his mind.

The king picked up the rune nearest him. The crocodile. The symbol's meaning gave him apprehension and suspicion. The scarab was telling him that there were dangerous "unseen" threatening forces afoot that would be difficult to control. It also foretold of someone entering Khufu's life with negative results. It could be a person unnoticed or disregarded, suddenly emerging like a crocodile from the water. Only the god Sobek could mount a defense against crocodile forces.

Khufu picked up the rune next to the crocodile. The Nile. Like all Egyptians, Khufu loved the Nile. The river was the life source of Egypt. It brought life in all its forms to what would otherwise be a barren land. The Nile is a positive symbol, he thought, as he turned the rune over and over.

Its message was that all difficulties encountered could be resolved by his flowing like water around them. The scarab told him that he must look for solutions to problems by allowing events to unfold, never by seeking to control them.

After musing over the combined meanings of the two scarabs, Khufu picked up the third rune with stars. This symbol made the issue cosmic in nature, indicating great matters were at hand that could only be defined as fate. On another level, this scarab symbolized a new beginning: the Second Coming of the Star Gods. He knew that no matter what perils the crocodile represented, which Khufu interpreted as Sokar or some other potential usurper, or what the outcome might be between the people involved, the gods would have their way. Spiritual affairs would supersede human ones. Khufu, like Mother Nile, would have to flow around whatever obstacles rose out of the water, and flow around them he would.

The star scarab was the key. The Second Coming, and all that surrounded it, including the Sphinx project, would be a milestone in the life of Egypt. That he was sure of, and no one would stand in the way of that happening. Not Sokar, not anyone. With will and determination, Khufu would advise Meri-ib of his approval to let Sokar serve as his co-ritualist for the Inundation rite.

Now that he had made his decision, Khufu was relieved. He collected the scarabs and placed them in the linen bag, dropping them in one at a time. He drew the drawstrings and looped the bag over his waistband. One can never know for certain if one has made the right decision, but Khufu knew that he had made the only decision he could if he wanted to keep his commitment to Khepera to follow guidance from the runes. He had learned since becoming Pharaoh that decisions do not always come easy. However, once a decision has been made, it must be acted upon aggressively.

Rising to his feet, Khufu stood in the silence of the sanctuary. This place was a source of strength for him. He breathed its power into his lungs with long, deep breaths. When he was at peace within himself, the king left the altar room, pausing briefly in the doorway to look back at the beautiful statue of Isis. "Thank you, Great Mother. Thank you." He returned to his study and called for a scribe. There was a message he needed to send to Meri-ib, High Priest of the Temple of the Sun in Heliopolis.

Chapter Fifteen

A Mysterious Death in the Temple

Feeling the need to spend time alone, Khem retired to her room after the evening meal. Bast lay sleeping peacefully at the foot of her bed, while Khem cleaned her altar and replenished the supply of incense that Akhi had bought. The altar was the heart of her room; it connected her with the divinities. That morning, while rummaging through some of the gifts she had been given on the eve of coming to Heliopolis, she had come across a small statue of Isis. Though lovely, the figure had not held as much meaning for her then as it did now. She had put it on her altar along with the other objects she held dear.

Looking at the statue in her hand, Khem remembered Ani saying that Isis would work with her in the Duat in her magical training. The thought reminded her of a story she had heard many times when she was a child. It was the story of Isis's great magical powers. Lying back against the pillows on her bed, Khem ran the legend through her mind while clutching the statue tightly.

Isis had vast powers, but she wanted more. She knew there was no one who possessed greater knowledge of the occult arts than her grandfather, the sun god Ra. So she devised a scheme that, if successful, would get her what she wanted. Noticing that the old man was dribbling saliva from his lip, she collected some of it and mixed it with some soil where Ra had walked. She then took the clay and fashioned it into the shape of an arrow and buried it at a place where she knew Ra would pass the next day on his journey from horizon to horizon. When he reached the crossroads where the arrow was buried, it changed into a serpent and bit the god on his ankle.

Ra fell to the ground sorely wounded, writhing in agony as the serpent's poison spread through his body. Though he called for help from the other gods, none could heal him of his awful wound. Finally, Isis came along and, seeing Ra's condition, whispered in his ear that she could free him of the black magic if he would reveal his magical name to her. The goddess knew the name would give her the secret of his power. Urged by his pain to give in, Ra relented.

Reluctantly, after giving her a list of his titles and attributes, Ra finally allowed his magical name to be transferred from his heart to hers. His only condition was that Isis promise she would reveal his true name to no one except her son, Horus, and that Horus should keep it a secret forever. The deed completed, Isis uttered the formula that freed Ra's body from pain and restored him to health. From that day on, Isis was the most powerful of the deities. She alone possessed knowledge of all things.

There were things about the story that had always troubled Khem. She thought that what Isis had done to Ra was mean-spirited. She did not know enough as a child to realize that Isis had used black magic to get what she wanted. She had only understood that the old man had been hurt and that it was Isis's fault. So she had not liked the goddess very much, and that was why she had left the little statue of her in storage instead of putting it on her altar. Even now, though she knew more, she was not clear as to how she felt about what Isis had done. And she still didn't know if she trusted the Great Mother because of that deed. But she was willing to trust Ani's knowledge and judgment.

If Ani said that it was Isis who would be working with her, then there must be a reason. Besides, everything else she knew about the Mother of the World was positive. That was what she had no other choice but to concentrate on now. It had been her decision to enter into Temple life, and she intended to see it through. That meant she would have to deal with whatever obstacles she encountered.

That decision made, Khem went to her altar. The light from the oil lamp cast a soft glow upon the objects assembled there. Her eyes fell upon the statue of Hapi, the Nile god. The little green figure always made her feel warm inside. She loved the statue, she loved Hapi, and she loved the Nile, the river that had brought her to her destiny.

Khem looked at the gift that had appeared at her door, the *udjat*. Looking at it now, she felt curiosity about its donor. It bothered her that she still did not know. Sometimes its presence made her feel uncomfortable, but most of the time she treated it as one of her personal possessions, and gave it no particular importance. That was how she felt now as she looked at it.

Khem gazed at her scrying bowl. She had not yet used it, nor even filled it with water, though now she felt an overwhelming urge to do so. Khem put the statue of Isis on a chair and went to her dressing table for the pitcher of water. She filled the little dish with water, noting it looked less like water than a surface of sparkling energy as it reflected the light from the lamp. She looked into the bowl. The water was still. Khem saw her own face looking back at her. It was one of the few times she had seen what she looked like so clearly, and she was captivated by what she saw.

I am pretty, she thought to herself, immediately embarrassed by her vanity. She looked at her lips and then her eyes. The kohl made them appear larger than they were and added an exotic look to her face. She had not thought of herself as exotic before seeing herself now. She had changed. She looked older, but the aging was not physical. It was an inner change reflected in her appearance. Khem approved of what she saw, and the self-acceptance made her feel confident and secure.

As the image of her face held Khem's attention, the reflection began to fade. In its place formed the head and face of a lioness. The beast's jaws were strong like iron, its nostrils wide, its pupils sharp and black. Its fur seemed to burn like a soft-glowing coal, and its mane seemed to be of raging flames from the fires of the Underworld.

As quickly as the lioness's image appeared, it was gone. Startled, Khem reeled backwards and tripped over the pitcher of water she had put on the floor. She went down on her buttocks, her right hand bracing her fall. The commotion woke up Bast and brought her bounding over to Khem, lying amidst pieces of the shattered clay vessel.

Thinking it was time to play, Bast licked Khem's face and clumsily put her paw on the girl's head. Sitting up and raising her hands to ward off the cub's playful attack, Khem got to her feet and began to pick up the pieces of the broken jar. The spilled water had soaked the papyrus mat. Bast busied herself with sniffing the wet places on the straw carpet.

Her composure regained, Khem thought about what she had seen. Had she really seen the image of a flaming lioness or had she imagined it? Now in the light of reality she wasn't sure. Looking at Bast, she was struck by the exactness between the cub and what she thought she had seen. The lioness, tiring of sniffing, romped around the room, grabbing Khem's feet.

Having snapped back to where she was and to what was going on, Khem put Bast in her box for the night. She blew out the oil lamp and climbed into bed, her thoughts spinning with images of the lioness in the scrying bowl. Had she seen it or not? She convinced herself that it didn't matter and fell asleep.

It was hours into her night's rest when Khem's dream-self awakened in the world of night visions. The dreamscape was bathed in the gold and orange light of the Sun setting behind a range of mountains. One of the peaks was the site of a huge cave, its mouth gaping open, drawing her like a magnet. She approached the cave opening, though cautiously. She had never been inside a cave and found the prospect unnerving but irresistible. As she stepped inside, the cavern gave her the feeling she had entered the womb of the Earth. She felt the coolness and smelled the mustiness.

Khem knew she was being watched and turned to see a lioness-headed woman. It was the goddess Sekhmet, daughter of Ra, wife of Ptah. The figure's torso was human, clothed in an orange-colored sheath with straps that crisscrossed her chest, exposing her breasts. Her head was that of a full-maned lioness that expressed fierceness and gentleness. Her head-dress was a solar disk surrounded by the uraeus, the protecting serpent. Khem was not frightened by the lioness-woman, though a part of her thought she should be. In a gesture of welcome, the goddess spoke, her words flowing telepathically into the dreamer's mind.

"I am Sekhmet, Lady of the Mountains of the Setting Sun. It is I who protect the king from harm, for I am she who is powerful. I am a part of Bast, the cat Mother Goddess of joy. I am a defender, a deity of war and destruction. As Bast and Sekhmet, I embody Isis."

The lioness-headed woman transformed into Isis. The radiant image bathed Khem in a warmth that enlivened every fiber of her being. The spirit's eyes were stern yet compassionate, exhibiting the goddess's inner strength and outer force. She held a lotus scepter in her right hand. "I am come into your presence, star daughter, in peace. I am the Queen of Heaven. Into the stars I will take your name, you who desire to know my nature. On my soul your ren will be emblazoned in letters of light. You will know me as Isis of the Stars. Together, Sekhmet and I will carry you."

As the goddess stopped speaking, Khem heard a name: *Neqet.* As soon as the ren resounded in her head, her dream vision deepened. Once again, the Mother Goddess spoke. "In the eastern part of your bedchamber, *Neqet*, erect a special altar to me. Purify and consecrate the shrine when the Moon is full. You will feel my presence and partake of my power in this place. Purify and dedicate yourself and each object you choose to place on my altar. Make an offering of flowers and incense to me every day. As my priestess, you will always find me there. My shrine will emanate my love for you. So be it."

Slowly, the vision of Isis faded, leaving Khem alone inside the cave. Khem lay still and relaxed in bed. When she was fully awake, she recalled every detail of the dream. She had a strange urge to recite a prayer to the Great Goddess:

Great Isis, I call out to you against all perils of the worlds of darkness.
Great are you of all the gods, so beautiful you are.
Give to me your spirit and your power.
Great Power of Isis, protect and guide me.
May I partake of your glory forever.

The prayer uttered, Khem felt peace flow through her. She felt empowered and tempered. Her body felt like a lump of clay ready to be molded into any shape the Neters desired.

Akhi came into the room. The servant girl went directly to the reed cage where the lioness cub lay asleep. Opening its door, she put down a dish of water. Khem sat up and stretched her arms over her head, her mouth gaping in a wide yawn.

"The day be good to you, my mistress," Akhi greeted Khem smiling. "Have you slept well?"

Khem returned the girl's greeting and stood up, wrapping a loose-fitting linen robe around her naked body. She always seemed to feel cool when waking up from a deep sleep that had taken her on a dream journey. Sitting down on her bed, Khem recalled the name *Neqet*, the sound of it running over and over in her mind. It suddenly came to her that the name was one of Isis's names. She thought it meant "magician." The name formed on her lips: "*Neqet, Neqet.*"

"Yes, mistress. Did you say something?"

"No, Akhi," Khem answered, turning to face the servant girl. "I was just speaking my own thoughts."

While Akhi prepared breakfast and laid out fresh clothes, Khem went to Bast. Akhi had saved some pigeon bones for the cat, and seeing them now, Khem took them and coaxed Bast to come. The animal chomped her teeth on the bones and began chewing. Khem let Akhi finish feeding the cat while she stripped and bathed herself.

Now that she and Tiye had been given their magical names, it was time to inform Ani. She couldn't wait to tell the Nubian what she had experienced. Tiye had told her the name she had been given: *Nefer*. So now it was *Nefer* and *Neqet*. Khem liked the sounds.

When she finished washing and had put on her clothes, Khem sat down to a meal of porridge made from ground barley and sidder berries, which she washed down with a cup of cool water. The lioness cub, contentedly chewing a bone, reminded Khem of Sekhmet in her dream. She thought about Sekhmet's reputation as a warrioress, her presence in the cave, and the cave itself, and all these images seemed like an unlikely prerequisite to Khem's meeting with Isis. Has Bast somehow changed me? How, if at all, had she changed? What meaning did this lioness have in her life?

Bast turned her head to one side as if she had heard Khem's thoughts. The cat's face was beautiful. It was strong, like the face of Sekhmet and Bastet, but a gentle strength. She loved it when Bast looked at her. . . .

At the classroom, Khem was met by Kasut, her eyes red from crying.

"What's wrong?" Khem inquired.

"It is Bakka. Her servant girl found her dead in her bed this morning."

"Dead! How? Why?" Khem responded, her shock making her voice shrill.

"It appears that she died in her sleep," Kasut answered. "I do not know."

Khem could not believe what she had heard. Being told of her death left Khem numb yet curious as to why.

The two went into the classroom and sat down. Neither spoke of the matter any further. Khem saw Tiye come in, and she motioned to her to join them. When Khem began to whisper the dreadful news to Tiye, she acknowledged that she had already heard. The information was already out on the streets of Heliopolis. Bakka's father was a prominent citizen, so her death was news. She was a wealthy and beautiful young woman, and her mysterious death would surely arouse controversy and speculation. Khem remembered the gossip she had heard about Bakka's not wanting to be at the Temple, and how she had supposedly wanted to marry. She also recalled how sad the girl had seemed every time she saw her, and how she resisted most attempts to be drawn into friendships. Bakka had always sat silently and alone in class, showing little interest in the teachings.

The classroom quieted down when Taret and the scribe Sheshat assumed their seats on the dais. The air of silence that always fell over the room when the High Priestess arrived was different this morning; it was thick and heavy, and it was obvious that everyone's mind was on Bakka.

Taret's presence was calming. As she looked around the room thoughtfully, her expression gave those assembled an awareness that the apprentice's demise was also on her mind. Her voice pitched lower than usual, Taret said, "I am certain you are all aware of the death of Bakka Gabri. It saddens me to tell you that there are no answers as yet as to why or how this death occurred. We will gather at the sunset hour to say a spell for the dead." Taret spoke no further about Bakka. But acknowledging the heaviness of the occasion, she canceled the teaching session and dismissed the class.

The priestesses began filing out of the classroom. Once outside, some congregated in the lower courtyard and talked quietly about the shocking event. Khem bade Kasut farewell, telling her she would see her at the sunset ritual. She motioned to Tiye to join her on a bench under the large sycamore. It probably wasn't an appropriate time to bring up the subject, but Khem was anxious to tell the Nubian about her dream. Besides, she thought that talking about the dream would take their minds off Bakka, at least for a while.

"I know it is a bad time to talk about this, Tiye, but I must tell you. I dreamed about Isis last night," Khem blurted out, not giving her friend much of a chance to refuse to hear what she had to say.

"Tell me about it," Tiye responded eagerly, making Khem feel relieved that she had not offended her friend by bringing up a subject she might think unimportant under the circumstances.

"You really want to hear?" Khem asked anxiously.

"Of course! Why wouldn't I?" Tiye shot back, growing impatient at her friend's hesitation. She was as anxious to hear about the dream as Khem was to tell her.

"It was strange," Khem began. "I don't know what I expected the dream to be like, but it was certainly different from anything I had thought." Tiye shifted on the bench, her gesture signaling Khem to get on with the story. "I found myself in the mountains. At the base of one of them was a huge cave. I went inside. It was there I saw her."

"Isis?" Tiye asked.

"No, not at first," Khem answered. "I saw Sekhmet."

"The lioness-headed warrioress?" Tiye responded, her eyes wide in disbelief.

"Yes," Khem said. "She was so beautiful, Tiye, so powerful, yet gentle. I knew she would not hurt me, and I was not afraid."

Khem went through her dream step by step. When she was finished, Tiye sat quietly in contemplation of the dream and how different it was from her own.

"So, your ren is *Neqet*, and mine is *Nefer*," the Nubian finally commented.

"Yes," Khem replied. "How do you feel about the dreams, Tiye?"

"I think it is time for us to tell Ani."

"I agree," Khem said, and together they set out to the Dream Priestess's private quarters. Neither was sure that, in light of Bakka's death, the time was right for them to go to Ani. But they had been told to inform her immediately. . . .

Meri-ib was mulling over the news of Bakka's death at his noon meal. He knew the girl's father would be coming from Memphis to the Temple of the Sun to claim his daughter's body for burial. He also knew that Ali would want answers about what had happened, how and why Bakka had died. As of now, Meri-ib had no answers. He had only the fact that an apprentice was dead, and that she had apparently died in her sleep. The High Priest was in a quandary also about the answer Sokar expected from him regarding whether he would be chosen as co-ritualist. It was fast becoming a day in which he had to come up with answers, and he felt the pressure mounting.

Sipping beer and contemplating his position, Meri-ib had his thoughts interrupted by his scribe, who announced a courier had arrived from Memphis with an urgent message from the palace. The priest waved his hand in an impatient gesture, telling the scribe to bring the message right away. As Meri-ib read, he felt relief and concern. He had his answer: Khufu recommended that he accept Sokar's offer.

The Chief Priest rolled up the scroll. "Thank you. You may go," he said slowly, waving his scribe to go. "Leave me to my thoughts." Meri-ib knew he had his work cut out for him. He would have to do his best to perform the rites for the New Year as he always did, while at the same time, to protect his and Khufu's secret announcement of the Second Coming until the king could tell the Egyptian people after the holy rites were over. He was confident in his knowledge and years of magical training and experience such that he was not about to underestimate Sokar's ability to find out what he wanted to know and to have things go his way. Well, almost everything, Meri-ib thought with a touch of smugness. After all, Sokar is not the Pharaoh.

Meri-ib's apprehension led him to go to the central chapel near the heart of the Temple. There he would do a Ritual of Protection. He would call upon the four sons of Horus—Mestha, Hapi, Tuamutef, and Qebh-senuf—to give protection. Hapi would provide the High Priest with what he needed, would help him maintain the integrity of his selfhood in the Duat in whatever magical work he did. He would call upon Hapi to protect him, the king, and the upcoming New Year's celebration.

Meri-ib put on his ceremonial robe and put his leopard-skin pelt over that. He had been in the inner sanctum of the Holy of Holies earlier in the morning when he had performed one of the three daily services. This time he was going for himself and for what he held special.

Walking down the long corridor to the door of the lesser Holy of Holies, Meri-ib was deep in thought. Motioning to the guards to open the door, the Chief Priest walked inside. The light was dim in the chapel. Small shafts of sunlight pierced the darkness, forming patterns on the tile floor. The sanctuary was silent and smelled of the many cones of incense burned there over the years. Its tranquility always elevated him out of the details of his day-to-day life and his tremendous responsibilities. This is where the gods dwell, he thought; the Great Ones find a home here in this chapel.

In the center of the sanctuary stood a black granite altar like the one upon which Meri-ib had found the white feather that bore witness to the appearance of Thoth. Facing the altar now, he knelt humbly for the approaching god. Images of the Nile formed in his mind in his reverent anticipation of the presence of Hapi. Like all Egyptians, he loved the Nile.

The river was a miracle-worker that renewed fertility every year without fail, turning the fields green, then golden for the harvest. Inundation always united the people in the joy of thanksgiving and celebration, a time defined by Hapi, a pot-bellied, bearded man with pendulous breasts and a headdress of aquatic plants to attest to his fecundity. In Meri-ib's mind, Hapi always appeared holding a tray of offerings that represented the many gifts that Mother Nile gave to the land and people.

As the Chief Priest knelt, he visualized the green god, then in the center of his head, he heard a voice pronounce Hapi's presence. "I, the god Hapi, speak truth to you, Son of the Nile, holy leader of the sacred land of Egypt. I have come at your request. What do you ask of me?"

Taking his cue from the god's words, Meri-ib responded. "I, Meri-ib, High Priest of Heliopolis, and humble servant of the divinities, beg for your protection for the Egyptian people, the honorable Pharaoh Khufu, and myself, against any perils that might befall the land or the people from the magician Sokar."

The priest saw no reason to elaborate why he was making this request. He knew the gods were aware of what was in a man's mind. His petition completed, he awaited a reply. Countless times he had experienced the silence between an invocation and a deity's reply. Though usually but a moment, it could seem like an eternity. Meri-ib felt his skin caressed by soft, wet river water as a coolness flowed through him. The prayer chamber began to echo with the deity's voice.

"I, Hapi, am a magician of Osiris, the Great God. I will protect all who deserve protecting. If you are associated with the Master, your flesh will be defended, and your magical operations will be successful. I will intercede for you and for the king against all perils. I will forever put beneath your feet all who would harm you as long as you walk in truth. I will hold your bones and the bones of the king together, and I will keep the components of your bodies, minds, and souls in safety and in peace. I will strengthen each of you if you speak in truth and honesty. To warrant this protection, you must say a special prayer to the god Ra when his light shines on the horizon in the East, and again at his setting in the West. You will be a master of the universe and a beautiful one before the Great Hawk. You and Khufu must follow the path of beauty and remain in the Company of the Gods and stray not."

The room fell silent. Hapi had spoken. Meri-ib knew that the god's words were filled with promise, and for that he was grateful and relieved. But he also realized that the deity's transmission contained a couple of symbolic references and they must be pondered carefully. There was no room for misinterpretation. "If you are associated with the Master," the god had stated. Who was Hapi referring to? Was "the Master" a human? A deity?

Meri-ib lit a cone of incense and placed it on the bronze brazier on the altar in the room's center. The sweet-smelling fragrance filled his nostrils and wove a circle of smoke around his head. Abruptly, a flash of knowing came to his mind. Of course! The master is Shemshu-Hor, lead priest of the Followers of Horus. It was he with whom Meri-ib must associate more closely. As the idea saturated his mind, the truth of the master's identity sent a chill of confirmation through his body. He remembered the decision he and Khufu made to contact the Horus priest. It had been a correct one.

Chapter Sixteen

The Face of Death

The news of Bakka's death spread through Heliopolis like wildfire. Rumors became as plentiful as bees buzzing in a hive. It was even being suggested that the unfortunate girl had been murdered. The population of the Temple of the Sun awaited the arrival of Bakka's father, Ali, to claim his daughter's body and learn any news about the reason for her untimely death.

Khem and Tiye were on their way to Ani's quarters. It was time to inform the teacher about their dreams. Although there was a lot of tension within the temple complex, the priestesses felt it was appropriate to follow the instructions they had been given and let Ani know the goddess had appeared to them in their dreams.

When the two arrived at Ani's quarters, her chief house steward informed them her mistress was in a meeting with Taret and Meri-ib. The girls exchanged nervous glances. The meeting no doubt had to do with Bakka's death. Their report to Ani would have to wait.

Meanwhile, word had reached the palace at Memphis that one of the apprentice Star Priestesses had died. When Khufu heard this he was troubled. He had known Ali for many years, even before coronation. The merchant was a wealthy member of the society of the Lower Kingdom, and his influence reached beyond the boundaries of Egypt into other lands. The event added sadness to the preparations for the festival, while the mystery of how she died was a puzzle that would have to be solved soon. Khufu's thoughts were interrupted when his chief steward announced that a messenger had arrived from Heliopolis.

"I will receive him immediately," Khufu said, eager to hear what information the messenger brought. Any message from Heliopolis, no matter what it concerned, would be more important now than at any other time. As the courier made his way into the Throne Room and bowed to the Pharaoh, Khufu felt a momentary wave of apprehension.

"I bring word from Chief Priest Meri-ib, your Majesty. He wishes you to know that he has sent word to the cloistered priest, Shemshu-Hor. The priest of the Followers of Horus will be brought to the Temple of the Sun in Heliopolis the day after tomorrow. He will arrive at noon when the sun god Ra is smiling upon Egypt. The master Meri-ib requests your presence as head of the great house and ruler of Egypt."

The message delivered, the courier bowed again to Khufu and awaited the king's response.

"I will be there before the sun god rides highest in the heavens."

In Heliopolis, Meri-ib, Taret, and Chief Scribe Haroun were in audience with Ali Gabri. The grieving father had arrived distraught at the news of his daughter's death. He wanted to know what had happened and why. While the heads of the Temple were relaying the details of how Bakka had been discovered dead by her house servant at sunrise, they were informed of the arrival of Chief Physician Nedjemou. His report was not good. The post mortem examination had revealed that the girl had died from drinking poison.

Ali's shoulders slumped when he heard this, the man no longer able to conceal his sorrow. The revelation that his daughter had committed suicide was too much to bear. Guilt pierced him like a knife. He had had no idea how devastating his demand that Bakka enter Temple life would be. He knew of her love for her suitor and her desire to marry, but had not approved of her plans; he had insisted she give them up and become a Priestess of Nut. It would be an honorable life for a motherless girl. She would be educated, and she would live a life of service to the divinities that would bring honor to the household. Now that would never be. Now there would only be shame to bear for the rest of his days. How he wished he could turn back time.

Taret put her hand gently on Ali's shoulder to comfort him. "You must not blame yourself. You could not have foreseen the depth of your daughter's despair."

Meri-ib and Haroun remained silent. This was a moment that needed a woman's sympathetic presence. However, if Taret's words were meant to soothe, they failed. Ali was inconsolable. In a flash his grief turned to anger.

"No. You are right. I could not have known. But you, you who are the closest to the Neters, you who are great seers—*you*, all of you should have known!" Ali blurted out furiously.

The three stood in wide-eyed silence. Meri-ib started to speak, but a wave of Taret's hand and a quick nod of her head stopped him.

"The Neters do not always choose to inform us about things between them and the soul of an individual," Taret said gently, trying to bring reason and calm to an unreasonable situation. "Bakka made a choice. To say that it was a proper or improper one would be to judge her action from our perspective tempered as it is by grief and pain."

What Taret said seemed to abate Ali's rage. He looked at Taret, unable to respond. The man's heart was broken, and at that moment, so was his anger. Nedjemou the physician took advantage of the lull and told Ali that Bakka's body was being prepared for burial and would be ready to claim by sunset. The mention of this morbid detail stirred the man's grief again.

"Thank you," Ali replied, his eyes as dark and cold as iron. "I will send for my daughter." Then, to the three Temple leaders, he said in a matter-of-fact tone, "You will hear from me. I assure you of that."

After meeting with Taret, Ani returned to her quarters and learned of Khem and Tiye's visit. Although she was anxious to know about the priestesses' reason for calling, Ani was preoccupied with the "Spell for the Dead" she was to perform for Bakka. While the specific funerary rites would be decided by Bakka's father, there were certain things her religious beliefs demanded that she, as the dead girl's teacher, must do. She must gather the ritual objects and go to the mortuary where Bakka's body was being prepared for burial. The Spell needed to be said over the physical body of the recently deceased so as to form a telepathic link with the disembodied consciousness. She had to assist Bakka in focusing her consciousness on her journey through the Underworld to rebirth.

As Ani gathered what she needed for the Spell, she thought it would be appropriate for her newest students of magic to accompany her to the mortuary. She sent for Khem and Tiye. Ani's messenger located the two priestesses in the lower courtyard and told them to go to Ani's quarters right away.

At the morgue, Bakka's slim body was pale, rigid on a block of black granite that looked like an altar. The dead girl was clothed in a plain white linen sheath that went to her ankles. Her feet were bare. A grayish-blue ringed her eyes, lips, and fingernails. She does not look like she is only sleeping, Khem thought, as she had often heard said about the dead. It was painfully obvious that Bakka was dead, not sleeping.

Taking an oil lamp, Ani lit the flame and some incense in a tiny brazier. Then, with Khem and Tiye looking on silently, she touched the dead girl's brow with a sweet-smelling ointment of lotus essence. When Ani spoke, her prayer filled the room:

> Hail to this one called Bakka,
> May you now rise and stand,
> May you be cleansed and purified,
> May your *ka* be purified,
> May your *ba* be purified,
> May your *sekhem* be purified.
> May you go to your mother, Nut,
> In the region of unification
> Where she will receive and sanctify you.
>
> This is Bakka,
> Behold she is arrived at the Duat.
> Hail to Bakka,
> May she dwell with the spirits
> And live forever with the gods.
> Hail to Bakka,
> May your limbs, your bones,
> and your organs
> and your head
> come before the Great Ones.
> May they guide and protect you.
> May you be with them.

The Spell finished, Ani looked at Bakka's lifeless body. The waste of a young, beautiful life made her feel sad. Khem and Tiye felt the same sadness. Seeing Bakka lying there cold and still reminded Tiye of the time she had looked upon Khaba's lifeless body that had just the day before been so full of life. Death was that way, the Nubian thought bitterly. It robbed one of life like a thief in the night. It replaced warmth with cold, smiles with tears, motion with the immobility of a stone. It was hard to forgive death for taking someone you loved. What with all the promises of rebirth and even eternal life, death was still a robber of joy and a bringer of pain.

The three left the mortuary without talking and headed to Ani's private chambers. There the priestess ordered her house servant to bring cooled wine for refreshment. She beckoned Khem and Tiye to sit.

"I assume you came earlier to tell me of your dreams," Ani said. The comment was a welcome shift of the somber mood that had prevailed since the mortuary.

"Yes, we did," Khem answered for them both. "We didn't know if the time was appropriate, what with Bakka's death, but we decided that we should follow your instructions and tell you as soon as the dreams had come."

"You decided correctly," Ani answered, choosing not to indulge in any discussion about Bakka. "Now, tell me. I am anxious to hear."

"You speak first, Tiye," Khem encouraged her. "Your dream came first." But before Tiye could begin, Ani injected that she was only interested in knowing the rens that had been given to the dreamers, not the details of the dreams.

"*Nefer*," Tiye said.

"*Neqet*," Khem followed.

A look of understanding came across Ani's round face. For a moment she made no reply, her silence leaving the priestesses in awkward suspension. Finally, she looked at the two young women, her face lighting up in a pleasant smile.

"Interesting," she spoke thoughtfully. "Very interesting."

Khem and Tiye were not certain that Ani's reaction was a positive one, but their teacher's next words told the tale.

"*Nefer* means 'good,' 'beautiful,'" Ani said, looking into the Nubian's eyes. "It is also a symbol associated with the part of Egypt that is the place of your birth. You must make for yourself an amulet of the *Nefer* and wear it at all times, Tiye. Wear it as a necklace or a bracelet, as you wish. You must perform this task by the time the Moon is round. The amulet will protect you from evildoers in the physical and subtle worlds; it will also serve as your key to unlock the mysteries of *heka*."

Tiye listened intently. The instructions were such as what Khaba might have given her. Her mentor's face flashed into her mind, giving her a warm, excited sensation. It had never occurred to her that anyone would ever, could ever, take Khaba's place, nor was it a thought she entertained seriously now. But it did go through her mind and caught her off guard. No. No one is like Khaba, she thought, dismissing the idea as wishful thinking.

Turning to Khem, Ani repeated her name, *Neqet*. "*Neqet* is one of the names of Isis, Khem. It means 'magician.' The goddess surely claims you as one of her own."

Khem felt a tingle run through her body. She had never thought of herself as "belonging" to a goddess, or to any deity, except maybe the Nile god Hapi, whom she had felt close to since she was a child. It was a good feeling, but strange and unfamiliar.

"Now that each of you have been visited by Mother Isis, it is time to go forward," Ani said. It was clear that the priestess had the information and confirmation she required to accept Taret's appointment of the two priest-esses as neophytes in magic. The rens were good omens, and omens were everything. They were the signs by which the lives of all in the priesthood were guided; they were messages from the Neters.

"You have earned the right to know my ren, but not until our next meeting," Ani said. Her announcement was immediately followed by a word of warning. "You must never reveal my ren to anyone without my knowledge and consent." Her stern tone was one that the apprentice magicians would hear many times, one they would come to know and respect without question or hesitation.

"You, Khem, must also make an amulet for yourself by the time the Moon is full. Make it the symbol of the *Nefer*, the same as Tiye. The *Nefer* will link the two of you together in a psychic bond for all time. It will serve as your key to the inner planes, and provide you with the power to unlock the mysteries of *heka*."

The Temple of the *Benu* was smaller than the Temple of the Sun and very beautiful. Rows of slender obelisks flanked the entrance, and on them relief carvers had chiseled symbols and images of reverence and love for the gods who kept order and harmony between humans and the environment. The heavy gates were open and the priests were just now entering the hypostyle hall, whose ceiling rested on giant columns and whose capitals were painted to depict the sacred papyrus plant. Sokar did not take part in every morning ritual, but he was going to today. He wanted to be as visible as he could. Besides, he felt the need to pay attention to his spiritual life and discipline as his relationship with the Neters was of paramount importance, especially now.

Every priest had a role in the ritual procession. Some carried plates of food, others jugs filled with wine and water, others boxes of toiletries for attending to the gods Khepera, Horus, and Ra, and some carried incense. The procession made its way to the temple's central chapel. Each room succeeded the next, each ceiling lower than the one before it, assuring that less and less light came in through the ventilation holes. This style of construction added mystery to the temple. Stopping before the chapel's closed doors, the priest standing next to Sokar broke the clay seal and drew the bolt that had preserved the god's privacy during the night. The leaves of the door swung open, allowing the line of priests entry into the inner sanctum.

Outside, the Sun was rising over Egypt. To mark the occasion of a new dawn, the priests began to intone the morning hymn, the sound filling the chamber.

> Praise to Ra,
> Praise to Horus,
> Praise to Khepera, the Lord of Sunrises.
> Your light is radiant light.
> Praise to Ra, and to the rising up of radiant light.
> May Ra open up the doors of the four corners of Heaven.
> May he be the source of radiant light in the two horizons.

As the chant went on, Sokar awaited the performance of his own role as the *medjty,* the Keeper of the Robes. After the hymn he would see to the god's physical needs. He had done this so many times before this morning, yet each time was still special. Beneath Sokar's demeanor of pompous arrogance and the anger that he felt at not being king, there was a heart dedicated to the sanctity of the Neters and a mind full of the knowledge of magic.

The central chapel was a gloomy place. A single candle struggled to light the room's expanse. The senior priest approached the granite container and broke its seal, revealing the statue of Horus. Stretching out his hand, the priest began the ritual that gave the god back his soul and reshaped his earthly form. While the priest recited the prayer, the aroma of incense filled the air. When the recitation was finished, other celebrants came forward and placed food and drink on the altar. All assembled understood that it was the essence of the breakfast that would be consumed by the god and not the physical food. The offerings were from the yields of the vines and fields of the estate that had been bequeathed to the Temple of the *Benu* by King Menes many years before.

Sokar began his task of disrobing the statue of the garments that had been placed on it the morning before. While another priest held a large bowl of water, Sokar washed the statue and rubbed it with scented oil, then dressed it in fresh fine linen clothes. Every day, a new four lengths of white, blue, red, and green cloth were accorded the god. Sokar began painting the god's face, then anointed it with oil, reciting the prayer that would sanctify the statue.

When the ritual was finished, Sokar sprinkled the statue with water and laid the customary five grains of natron and resin on the floor in front of the altar and lit more incense. The rites completed, it was time to leave. The last priest out closed the doors and the procession departed to perform the same rites for the gods Khepera and Ra.

Ceremony always rejuvenated Sokar, and today his energy was already at a high level in anticipation of Meri-ib's response to his request to assist him in the high ritual at Inundation. Knowing what was going on with Khufu was of tremendous importance to him, and Sokar knew there was no better position than as the High Priest's chief aide to be privy to all the plans for the most significant day of the year.

When Sokar returned to his private chambers, Kheti greeted him with the message scroll he had been waiting for. He saw that the scroll was affixed with Meri-ib's personal seal. Breaking open the seal, Sokar read the communiqué quickly:

> I, Meri-ib, High Priest of the Temple of the Sun at Heliopolis, servant to the great god Ra and the Egyptian people, do hereby accept your request to serve as my humble and able co-ritualist for the celebration of the reappearance of the Holy Star and the flooding of Mother Nile. May the Great Ones walk with you.

Sokar felt a thrill. He had won. At least the first round. He felt like celebrating.

"Kheti!" he called to his manservant. "I wish you to prepare a wonderful dinner on the night of the full Moon. Spare no expense. Ribs of beef, pigeon stew, boiled fish, fruits, cakes, the finest wines from my vineyard."

"You will be having guests, my master?"

"Yes, Kheti. I will be having guests. Very special guests."

Chapter Seventeen

Murder in the Temple?

Khem was preparing for the morning class. Bakka's death and reports of her distraught father were occupying everyone's mind. An entourage of servants had been sent to claim Bakka's body for burial in Memphis. Word was that Pharaoh had sent a representative from the court to the funerary rite. Although Khem had not been close to the dead priestess, she would miss her. There was a bond among the neophytes that superseded social relationships, or the lack of them.

When Khem and Bast arrived at the classroom, they were met by Tiye. It was the first time the lioness had come to class and Khem was nervous about how she would behave. The animal lay down and curled up on a large floor pillow, her head resting on her paws, watching what was going on around her. It was as if she had always been around people and knew precisely what to do and how to act. The cat's calmness was a relief to Khem.

Once all the apprentices were settled, Taret and Sheshat entered the room. Taret seemed tense, and looked as if she had not slept well. Khem suspected that Bakka's death had taken its toll on the Chief Priestess, and wondered if there was something going on that no one knew about except Taret.

"The lesson today is important," Taret began. "With the approach of the Full Moon, there will be, as always, a celebration ritual. I know that some of you have never participated in this rite. Therefore, I have decided that it is time to discuss the lunar ritual, and ritual in general. It will be new to some, and a review for others."

Khem perked up. Ritual was something she had looked forward to learning about and participating in long before coming to the Temple.

"There are two keys to a successful rite. Correct use of posture and correct use of breath. That is the first. Proper posture automatically promotes proper breathing. It also assures the ritualist will not be distracted by the environment, or by her body. I will consider each of these keys one at a time.

"To achieve the correct posture, two things must be taken into consideration. The first involves the small of the back. It must be tucked in slightly at the waist level so that the spine rests in an 's' shape. This forces correct breathing from the lower abdomen. It is also important that this posture be cultivated so that it becomes the normal one at all times. If the chest or the shoulders are slumped over, the breathing will be shallow, and that will promote physical and emotional tension, unclear thinking, even illness.

"The second key is relaxing the body. Every part of the body, with the exception of the lower abdomen, should be at ease. The ritual begins when the proper posture has been assumed and the breathing is natural and without difficulty. Remember, when a ritual is performed, it is truly a drama that enables one to enact in the outer world a reflection of the inner action where the gods reside. Ritual solves problems inwardly so that outer events will follow. And follow they do.

"Ritual is a magic tool, Star Daughters. It is an act that allows you to open the doors of the star gates, which in turn leads you into holy matrimony with the kings and queens of Heaven, and ultimately with the universe. Rites assist you in becoming conscious with the sacred. This requires a high level of perception. Only with such depth and awareness can you overcome the unreal and experience truth. Ritual invokes the power of the divinities, and you must invoke them often. Ritual allows you to experience yourself as a being of light, and helps you learn to live in the magical world, the *Neter-Khert,* through your Body of Light. Every act you do with conscious intent is a magical act. This includes ceremony."

Khem trusted the truth of Taret's words and she made a commitment to herself that, someday, she would be as learned and powerful a Star Priestess as Taret.

"Humans consist of more than a physical body, or *khat.* The *khat* is surrounded by and connected to the other subtle vessels, each more ethereal. The first of these is the *khai'bit,* the shadow. This is the double, and is an exact duplicate of the physical body. Then there is the *ka,* the emotional vessel. The heart, *ab,* is next, and then the *ba,* the soul. The *ba* is linked to the *ka* through the *ab.* Then there is the *sahu,* the spirit body.

Through the *sahu* you are divine. Finally, there is that which is the subtlest, linked to the most subtle of all the ethereal vessels, the *khabs*. The *khabs* is your own divine component. It is a star.

"Collectively, all these bodies could be called a Body of Light. When a ceremony or any other magic act is performed, the Body of Light is your prime tool. It is composed of swirling, undulating energies that reflect your thoughts and feelings. All the subtle vessels are linked together by a magnetic connector known as the silver cord. The cord enables your consciousness to be centered at any time in any of your bodies. The ritualist knows how to shift consciousness to the subtler vessels, each of which senses the environment of the dimension which is its natural domain.

"The general environment for the Body of Light is the magic world. This should suggest to you that, like a human, the magic universe is divided into several regions that correspond to each of the subtle vessels and within which each vessel operates. You are able to travel in the magic world by shifting your consciousness into a corresponding vessel. Now let's review the Moon.

"Women are naturally in tune with the Moon and its cycles by way of menstruation. However, though we women can more easily align ourselves with lunar energy, the Moon ritual and initiation is just as essential for men. We regard the Moon as having a male nature, and relate it to the gods Thoth and Khonsu.

"The light emitted when the Moon is full has specific properties unlike that of the moonlight at any other time. Full moonlight is magnetic. It makes a strong impact on all your subtle bodies and your physical one. The Moon's light clears the psychic mind so that entrance into the magic world is easier.

"When the Moon is round, it is like a great white all-seeing eye that has observed all that has occurred on Earth since it began. What the Moon sees, it remembers for all time. When you are preparing to perform the Full Moon ritual, what you wear is very important and should be chosen with care. Your garments will enhance your sense of being a priestess, and set you apart from the everyday world. The use of special clothing, like all sacred, magical objects, is a tool that must be valued. Your clothing must be white like the Moon, of the finest, most delicate linen yet simple in design."

Khem imagined herself dressed in a loose-fitting robe. She remembered a dream in which she had seen herself dressed this way. Recalling it now made her feel like a priestess—no, like a magician.

"To perform a Moon ritual, in fact, to do any ceremonial work, you must learn the single most important technique—creating a light body. You do this through your *ba*, the soul. This subtle body is the vehicle in which you travel into the heavens, as well as into other dimensions of time and space. The symbol for the *ba*, known only to the initiates, is a hawk with a human head. Learning how to travel in your Body of Light is the key to freedom in the Duat. It is the key that unlocks your soul from the bondage of flesh and Earth. There are many ways to create a Body of Light, and soon you will know them all. For now, however, the *ushabti* is the easiest to use because it is an image of your own self, an image of you transformed into a role designated by you. The *ushabti* will travel *for* you and be your magical companion.

"You must understand that there are many uses for the *ushabti*. Some are known and practiced by seasoned magicians. What you will learn now is the most basic use."

As Taret was about to give the instructions, a noticeable change came over her face as she was overshadowed by her spirit helpers.

"*Ushabti* figures are best made of clay. You must make them for yourself, and they must look as much like you as possible. You can make the figure into whatever image you desire, depending upon its purpose. A Moon *ushabti* will do your bidding to honor and draw power from the Moon, that you can later get from the figure to use for your purposes. The power taken in by a lunar *ushabti* can bring change to any situation, regulate the menstrual cycle, and heal a body after childbirth. Make your figures from the clay of Mother Nile. When you have molded the *ushabti* into your image, invest it with your power by holding it in your hand. Fix your eyes upon the figure and say the following words." Taret the recited the formula:

> I, a Priestess of the Holy Order of Nut,
> the Sky Goddess, Servant of the Star Gods,
> co-ruler and spiritual counterpart of Meri-ib,
> the High Priest of the Temple of the Sun,
> empower this *ushabti*.
>
> I bid you to perform a deed for me,
> for I have created you and I now give you life.
> It is your task to go and be with the spirit within the Moon,
> to tap into and bring its power to me.
> Dispel, I pray you, all illusions and all negative energy
> that may blind my sight to the beauty and power
> of the White Eye of the Night.
> Be it so.

Khem thought she could see a stream of energy flowing from the teacher's hands into the clay doll she was using for the demonstration. This was confirmed when Taret said that when holding the figure, let your *sekhem*, or life force, flow from your body into the *ushabti* while the words are recited.

Taret ended the teaching by asking that each of the apprentices make their own Moon *ushabti* for the upcoming Full Moon ritual. She bowed her head in respect to her audience and stood up, motioned to her scribe, and the two left the room. In the hallway, Khem asked Tiye if Khaba had ever taught her about *ushabtis.*

"Yes," Tiye replied, the question obviously sending her mind into times past. "She called them *heka* dolls. I still have one that belonged to her. One she once used for healing me when I was ill with a fever."

"You do?" Khem asked, fascinated.

She was a neophyte compared with Tiye, to whom few of the teachings seemed new. Khem felt a new dimension opening up in her relationship with Tiye, and she knew the Nubian would be her friend and colleague, and one of her teachers.

The supper hour came none too soon for Sokar. Kheti had spent the better part of the day preparing a sumptuous meal for his master and his special guest. He had invited Meri-ib to dine, but the invitation had been refused. Too much to do to prepare for the upcoming ceremonies, Meri-ib had said through a courier. So Sokar invited the lovely Mafdet to join him instead, and he wanted the occasion to go well. Sokar rarely socialized unless he had something to gain, but the girl's father had much social and political influence, and Sokar felt that the more in-roads he could make into the elite circles in Heliopolis, the more contacts he would have to keep himself informed of doings in Memphis.

Mafdet, carried on her litter, was accompanied by her servant girl. No young woman of her class was allowed to travel the city's streets unattended. After making sure her servants were seen to in the servants' quarters, Sokar invited his guest onto the patio for a cup of date wine. The sun was sinking slowly, casting long shadows, and the air was becoming cooler. Sokar liked this time of day. It made him feel relaxed and eager for good food and conversation.

Mafdet was young. Her upbringing and her physical beauty enhanced her mannerisms and appearance and gave the illusion she was older than her fifteen years.

"I am pleased to spend an evening in your company," Sokar said charmingly. "Tell me, how is your father, Menkar?"

"My father is well, as is my mother, Mebak-her."

"Yes, of course," Sokar responded, eager to hide his oversight of the girl's mother in his social inquiry. "And you, Mafdet, how have you been spending your days?"

Mafdet's eyes were like black diamonds that sparkled at the least stimulus, and an opportunity to talk about herself was indeed stimulating. "I manage to stay quite busy. My father has hired a tutor to teach me to write, and I am learning to play the lyre, and to embroider."

"My, my, you have been busy," Sokar responded, pretending to be interested in the girl's activities. "It sounds as if your life is indeed full."

Kheti came onto the patio carrying a tray filled with a whole dried fish, sweet cakes, and fruits. As he placed the food on a low table, the servant observed Mafdet. What is it about this particular girl that has caught Sokar's attention? She is pretty, surely, but Egypt is full of beautiful women. There has to be something else. As always, Kheti was confident he would learn what.

Sokar and Mafdet were quiet as Kheti put the food down and replenished their wine. Then Sokar picked up the conversation. "With all the studying you are doing, perhaps you should come to the Temple."

His comment got an immediate response. "I had well considered doing that, for I know the most learned of the scribes and musicians are in the Sun Temple." Then her voice took on a serious tone. "But since my friend Bakka's death, my father and mother have forbidden it."

Sokar had forgotten about the apprentice's strange death until now. "You were Bakka's friend?"

"Yes," Mafdet replied. "Our fathers have often done business together. We had known each other since we were children."

Sokar could see that Bakka's death had upset Mafdet, but he felt the need to explore the situation more deeply. "Bakka took her own life, did she not? It is of no blame of the Temple." He detected by the look in her eyes that his words seemed to arouse confusion.

"It is said that she took her own life . . . yes . . . that is true. But—" Mafdet hesitated.

"But what?"

"But, Ali, Bakka's father, is convinced she was murdered." It was clear that Mafdet was uncomfortable hearing these words, even if it was she who spoke them.

"Murdered!" Sokar's shock was genuine. He had not heard such a rumor. "What on Earth makes him think so?"

Mafdet's discomfort with the new direction of the conversation was apparent. "I have heard it said that Bakka's father thinks his daughter was killed by an evil spirit from the Underworld. That she was not trained properly by Taret and the others. That she did not know how to protect herself in the magic world."

Sokar walked slowly to the lotus pool. Resting his right foot on the pool's edge, he gazed out upon the desert. Then he turned to face Mafdet. Bakka had just come to the Temple. Her training had hardly begun. There would have been no reason for her to be involved with magical operations, he thought to himself. Murder didn't make sense. The truth of the matter was that Bakka had taken her own life because she didn't want to be at the Temple. The idea that an apprentice was murdered by an evil spirit she didn't know how to handle was ludicrous.

It was obvious that Mafdet did not want to discuss the matter further. To change the subject, she asked Sokar about the hawk on the perch in a corner of the patio. She had never been this close to a hawk before. Mafdet was taken by the creature's beauty, but she was wary of getting too close. Standing back, she said, "It is beautiful."

Sokar was proud of his familiar. The connection they shared was one of brothers, though to casual onlookers, the bird was a pet and nothing more. Mafdet was skittish about such things as magic and Sokar knew this was a part of his life he could not share with her, not now or ever. That would stop any future relationship between them, but he was drawn to her. There were times when Sokar had entertained the idea of having a magic partner, a magical "mistress" of sorts, someone other than Kheti to share his life and his power with. No, Mafdet could never be one.

He found himself losing interest in her. Still, she was here, and he needed to make the evening as pleasant as possible. Taking the girl by the arm, Sokar said, "Come. Let us have food. Kheti has prepared a delicious meal."

With a sharp clap of his hands, Sokar summoned his servant to bring the main course. He led Mafdet to a chair by the dining table. In a few moments, two house servants followed Kheti onto the patio carrying plates of pigeons stewed in sweet figs, onions, and barley bread.

The Sun had almost set below the horizon, so Kheti lit the torches that stood in the four corners of the open-air veranda. The flames put out a soft light that cast dancing shadows on everything, including Mafdet's face.

"So, your plans are to continue your studies and develop your musical skills. Is that all?" Sokar inquired.

"I have many more plans than these," the girl said with calm determination ringing in her voice, looking directly into Sokar's eyes. "The terrible shock of Bakka's death will go away sometime. Soon, I hope. And then I will have my way. I will enter the Temple and become a priestess of Hathor."

Her words took Sokar by surprise. This *was* a woman with a mind of her own after all. She knew what she wanted and would get her way because she could bide her time. He had underestimated her. She was someone to be reckoned with, and he would keep that fact in mind. Sokar eyed his guest with a new respect.

Hathor is linked with the star Sirius, he mused, which is about to rise and give birth to the new year. The significance of the upcoming events surrounding Inundation was growing as the days went by. Sokar was beginning to realize that he had been right all along, that in some way this lovely young woman might after all be a part of his future.

Chapter Eighteen

The Moon-Mistress of the Night Sky

It was the day before Full Moon. The palace in Memphis was busy with the usual affairs of state. Khufu had breakfasted with his family, and was preparing to go to the Throne Room. He expected Nemon to arrive from Dashur later in the day. The Pharaoh had received word that Manetho had made all the necessary arrangements for the labor force needed to unearth the Stone Head. So all that was left to do was wait for Nemon to come with his plans and the work would begin.

Khufu had not slept much or well for the past few nights. His sleep had been restless. He did not feel up to his usual level of energy. He was sure the stress of the task before him was the reason. To doubt or fear the outcome of the Sphinx project would be a mental and spiritual disaster, and Khufu dreaded suffering panicky apprehension. To doubt himself or Manetho or, the gods forbid, Nemon, would be to lose his grip on the reins leading the project to success.

There was also the business of the imminent meeting between Khufu, Meri-ib, and Shemshu-Hor, the High Priest of the Followers of Horus. The king would have to travel to Heliopolis in secrecy. The meeting must be kept secret. He was feeling apprehension regarding the meeting. Although he, Khufu, was political royalty in the eyes of every Egyptian, and his station in life could not be denied, Shemshu-Hor was religious royalty, the elder of the most ancient lineage, an ambassador on Earth of the Star Gods. Not even a Pharaoh could deny the respect due to this human, or dare use the prestige of the Crook and Flail to engage in a power play with one so wise and respected.

The Throne Room was bustling with activity. Khufu had turned all civil matters over to the able-minded Manetho, so he could seclude himself in his private chapel adjoining the Throne Room to wait for Nemon.

Alone in the chapel, Khufu sat on a plush floor pillow and contemplated the statues of Ptah, Ptah's consort, the goddess Sekhmet, and their son, Nefertem—the Memphite Triad. Ptah's attributes came to mind, this god who was the inventor of the techniques for craftsmen and masons. As king and initiate in the ranks of the priests of Ptah, Khufu was second only to the High Priest of the Temple of Memphis and the Master Builder. Khufu realized that during the groundbreaking ceremony for the Sphinx project, Hap, the sacred bull, should be brought to the site to add its blessings and to oversee the great task.

Yes, the Sphinx project was an occasion over which Hap must preside. It would encourage the workers and insure that Ptah would bless the project.

A light tap on the outer wall of the chapel aroused the Pharaoh from his thoughts. It was the signal that Nemon had arrived. The Throne Room was quickly vacated of everyone except for Khufu and his scribe, the vizier, Manetho, and Nemon. Nemon was his usual jovial self, his personality lifting everyone's spirits. All eyes and ears were focused on him as he opened the discussion with a personal comment. Nemon began:

"From many years of reading the scripts, I have come to believe that there can be little doubt that the Stone Head of the Desert is the representative of Horus, Son of Ra. Facing east, the great Sun god beams his rays upon the face of his son and heir as he rises each day. This leads me to think that the Sun not only energizes the world with life each day, but quickens the one who occupies the throne with the power to rule with strength and wisdom. The king is the living Horus, is he not?"

Nemon reached into a linen bag attached to the waistband of his kilt and withdrew a papyrus scroll and unrolled it on a table beneath the throne. When they looked at what was on the scroll, Khufu and Manetho gasped. The drawing depicted the full body of the Stone Head with the pyramids in the background. It was the first time either had seen an image of the colossal monument in its entirety.

"This is the complete monument as it exists under the sand," Nemon commented, while Khufu and Manetho stared at the image. "To remove the sand, if my calculations are correct, we should begin around the head and at the back end, working toward the middle. That way, any structural damage will be discovered and repaired immediately so that the integrity of the massive figure will be maintained. I figure the work force should be divided, half digging in the front, half in the back."

Manetho spoke. "I will monitor the work force. The men, some

Nubians, will work for me. The last of the laborers will arrive by boat from Abydos by sunset tomorrow."

Khufu said nothing. He was still absorbed in the image of the Stone Head's full shape. It seemed familiar, though not like a recent memory. It was more of an ancestral memory coming to the surface, eliciting a strange, almost ecstatic, feeling.

"Well, my cousin. What do you think?" Nemon said, forcing Khufu out of his silence.

After a short hesitation, the king replied, "I think what you think. Let the project begin at sunrise the day after tomorrow."

Turning to Manetho, Khufu ordered him to assemble the work force for the Sphinx project at the east side of the Stone Head at sunrise the morning after tomorrow. He commanded his scribe to send a courier to the High Priest of Memphis, ordering him to have the bull brought to the site by dawn on that day. Then, ascending the dais and seating himself on the throne, Khufu decreed that, at noon the following day, he would make a public appearance to announce the Sphinx project to the people.

Only one more night until the Full Moon, Khem reflected. She noticed that Bast seemed to be responding to the energy of the class that day. The cat was very active, but there was something else. The lioness had an air of maturity, seeming somehow older and wiser. Bast's eyes were like gold flames, her pupils doorways into unknown passageways. As Khem looked at Bast, she was reminded of the vision of the lioness-headed woman in her scrying bowl.

Khem's mind shifted from Bast to the *ushabti* she would make after the Sun went down. She would have to go to the bank of the Nile to collect silt. But first things first. There was the morning class, and she and Tiye had a magic lesson with Ani in the afternoon. This was one of those mornings when her mind was so full of thoughts racing to and fro that it was difficult to focus on one.

At the classroom, Tiye said, "I stopped along the riverbank on my way and filled a pot with mud. We can use it to make our Moon *ushabtis*."

"That will be good," Khem replied.

The two girls went into the classroom and sat down. Taret and Sheshat, her scribe, were already seated on the raised platform, signaling the time for the teaching to begin. Khem noticed that Taret also exhibited an aura of tense expectation. The High Priestess began.

"As I have told you before, moonlight is powerful energy. Today, I wish to speak about certain things closely associated with the Moon's light. One is water. Water absorbs moonlight. It holds the light. When the Full Moon rides high in the night sky, it empowers the waters of Earth. When you see charged water in your mind's eye, it exhibits a silvery color that makes it shine. This silvery substance—and it is a *substance*—is actually psychic energy emitted from the Moon. Such water is rich with the essence of fertility. It makes things grow and reproduce. Moon-charged water is useful for plants of all kinds. Water is an essential ingredient at a temple site, and is placed here in the form of lotus and papyrus pools.

"There are certain plants and trees connected with the Moon. Palms of all kinds, pine, sycamore, white and blue lotus, papyrus, persea, roses, and all night-blooming flowers. The bark, cones, sap, fruits, and flowers of these are useful for medicinal and ceremonial purposes. Moon food is sacred, especially fish, for they live in the water that absorbs the rays. This is why fish is not eaten except on special occasions.

"Moon rays propel human consciousness into the dream vessel. They also give life to and nurture the vessel. On the crests of Moon waves the Neters are able to enter into the dreamer's mind and heal the various maladies that plague body, mind, and heart. Healing occurs when the dreamer's energy is restored. In fact, Moon energy is one of the most potent of healers.

"Silver is associated with the Moon, as is emerald. Both make wonderful offerings to the Moon. Lying in the moonlight is good for the mind and body, a purification ritual practiced by initiates since the First Time. What we come into contact with, physically and in the Duat, causes our physical body to exude various substances, the most common being sweat. For the most part these substances are harmless and evaporate. But others, such as those emitted due to stress, anger, and other strong emotions, do not. Those that do not can become poisonous and must be cleansed away. The ground will do this for you by drawing out any negative energy that might be clinging to you as you lie down upon it.

"Of all waters, the water from Mother Nile is celebrated the most for its powers of purification and healing. Mother Nile is a living entity, an intelligent being that has assured, and will continue to assure, the survival of all lives in Egypt. Down through time, priests and priestesses and *fellahin* alike have washed their sins away in the Nile's living waters.

"Remember, moonlight purifies your body and restores its balance. This empowers you. So, it is a good idea to place a clay vessel filled with water under the Moon's light. The water will drink in the Moon's energy. It can then be used for bathing or drinking before and after sacred rituals. Water charged with moonlight can also be used to cleanse ceremonial objects."

The High Priestess ended her teaching at that point, with a reminder to the students to create their *ushabtis* to be ready for the upcoming Full Moon. "When the refreshment hour is over, we will gather again for a brief discussion of the Full Moon ritual."

Over a light meal of sweet cakes and figs, Khem and Tiye made plans to get together after their lesson with Ani to make their *ushabtis* and to take care of the other Full Moon preparations. They also decided that Tiye would spend the night with Khem at the Temple rather than returning at a late hour to her host's home in the city. When the apprentices reconvened for the short class session Taret had requested, the room was buzzing with talk about the upcoming ceremony. As always, when Taret came in a hush fell over the room.

"As you all know, there are many rituals that comprise the backbone of our religion. But none is more important to women, especially to priestesses, than the one that marks the Full Moon. The Moon is the timekeeper. It regulates the constant flux of incoming celestial energies to the land. It makes the seeds sprout and keeps the ground fertile, the harvest bountiful. It brings on the blood of women and coaxes the unborn from the womb. The Moon is the patron Sky Goddess for the Children of the Night, for you, the Star Priestesses of *Al Kemi*, Great Egypt."

Khem's feeling for the Moon deepened as Taret spoke. She now *understood* the Moon. The link she felt between her human self and the womanpower of the Moon helped her understand more of what being a female *and* a priestess was about.

"To gather as priestesses of Nut in the ritual arena of the Temple of the Sun is to reenact the ritual in honor of the Moon through the forces of Hathor, the Moon goddess, and Thoth, the Moon god. This has been taking place since the First Time. Many among you lived during those earliest days, and now you have returned in new bodies. From this you should see the path of a Star Priestess is long, sometimes taking lifetimes to complete."

Taret concluded with instructions to gather at the pool in the ritual area of the Temple at sunset on the morrow, the night of the Full Moon. None were exempt. All should dress in white and wear a piece of silver.

Later, just outside Ani's private apartment, Khem held a tight rein on Bast, who was becoming accustomed to walking on her leash and sitting for an hour or more in class. Khem was a little surprised at how well the lioness was doing. Bast seemed to know how she must behave, as if she had done it all before. I wonder if animals reincarnate, Khem reflected.

As usual, Ani's chief house steward met the two priestesses at the door. He left to tell Ani that the students had arrived.

Ani entered full of energy, reminding Khem how "charged up" everyone was. She too had been feeling exhilarated, but had attributed it to her general excitement at being at the Temple. "Now that you are here, shall we begin?" Ani said. She made no comment about the cat that settled at Khem's feet and fixed her eyes on Ani. "When we were last together, I told you it was time for you to know my ren. I will give you that now. *Urthekau.*" (Khem translated it in her mind: "She who is knowledgeable or rich in magical spells.")

"*Urthekau* is one of the many names of the great goddess Isis," Ani continued. "It is Isis that I wish to speak to you about now. I am a faithful daughter of Isis. I have been her servant for as long as I have been a priestess."

Khem and Tiye were receptive to what Ani was saying in light of their dream experiences with the goddess. Khem wondered if Ani could clear up her confusion about the goddess's seeming use of black magic to learn the magical secrets of her father Ra.

"Isis is a mysterious deity. She possesses many secrets. She is ever active in working magic with the power of her wisdom. To partake of Isis's wisdom, you must understand her for the complex goddess that she is. Her nature expresses many paradoxes. These things you will learn in time. The great goddess will come to you in proportion to your ability to perceive and receive her. Know that your perception will grow and become refined over time.

"To begin developing a relationship with Isis, you must know her celestial lineage. Just as Isis is associated with the Moon, so is Isis also connected with numerous stars and constellations and the air element. The three star groups are Gemini, with Castor and Pollux, Libra and its brightest star, and Aquarius and its brightest star. These embody aspects of the power of Isis.

"You are familiar with the depiction of her as a winged goddess. This image is the key to one of the greatest mysteries given to the priesthood at the end of the First Time. It regards the mystery of birth, death, and resurrection. The Law of Cycles. The presence of the wings is the visual, symbolic key that the soul, the *ka*, is nourished in the Underworld by the air spirits, what you will come to know as light beings. These Great Ones control the breath in all things, in seed and jasmine flower, in every animal and human so that all might live and breathe and grow and change. It was Isis's wings that gave Osiris the gift of resurrected life, immortal life. This is the truth of the winged Isis, the Great Female Eagle of the Sky.

"Her mystery in the twins Castor and Pollux is that they represent her light and dark sides. The uninitiated see one as light, the other as dark, but such people remain ignorant that each side possesses the light and dark.

Not to see this is the illusion. Humans think either/or, rarely in terms of both. The nature of 'both' is that it devours either/or. They become one. Think about this. The Star Gods put the keys to the mysteries in the stars. Where else? And by what else would the truth be written if not in the stars?

"The stars of Libra have to do with justice, ethics, principles, all necessary qualities a Star Priestess must have to become an initiate. The stars of Aquarius have to do with the starry river, the celestial Nile, poured onto Earth. The streams of water poured forth from the celestial water vessel manifest in Egypt as the River of Life, Mother Nile. The stars of Aquarius are the source of the river that unites Heaven and Earth."

Up to this point, Ani had made no mention of Bast. Khem and Tiye thought that curious. Now Ani gazed at the lioness curled up near Khem's folded legs. "Cats have always been associated with Isis. Cats, such as this little one, have an affinity for the sexual and the mothering power of Isis. I will speak about this later. There is no star in possession of a greater portion of Isis's power than Sirius or Sothis, the Nile Star. Sirius is the 'Home of the Soul of Isis.' The Soul of Isis is represented on Earth in the goddess of joy, Bast, and in her opposite or shadow side, Sekhmet, the lioness-headed Neter.

"Sirius with Procyon and Betelgeuse form a triangle in the sky, a celestial pyramid, if you will, that points to Earth, just as our pyramids point to the sky. As above, so below. Soon, Sirius will rise in the predawn sky and blaze forth as Earth's aura refracts its light. This heavenly event, year after year, age after age, ushers in a new year and the cycle of life. Immortality is thus reassured.

"Isis is also associated with the Moon. The Moon and Isis are manifestations of cosmic energy. The Moon's feminine nature *is* Isis; its male aspect is Thoth. To know the nature of cosmic energy and the difference between it and any other kind, you must know the attributes of these Neters.

"The Moon is the subject of your first magical degree. Prepare well for the upcoming Full Moon ritual. To help you do this, meet me, both of you, at the sacred pool in the dream temple when the Moon rises tonight. We will have a ritual cleansing. I will baptize you in the water so that you, Khem, will have the energy of your soul, of *Neqet*, awaken within you, and you, Tiye, will have *Nefer* awaken. Go now. I will see you there."

Chapter Nineteen

Baptism in the Lotus Pool

Khem and Tiye went to Khem's room for a snack after Ani's lecture. Then, as they were getting ready to meet Ani at the sacred pool, the room filled with sweet-smelling night jasmine. The fragrance was so heavy it made them dizzy and they felt themselves slipping into an altered state. The room glowed yellow-orange with a circulating light like a vortex. In a flash the light formed into a transparent woman with a lioness at her side. She said:

"I, Isis, will cleanse you of all impurities. I will wash you in my light. I will free you of all that clings to you, so you will be pure to walk in my path."

The vision faded, leaving Khem and Tiye speechless. Even Bast stared at where the woman spirit had been as though she could see her.

When they arrived at the pool, Ani was waiting. She greeted them and asked them to disrobe as the ceremony would be done in the nude. Ani descended into the pool first. The water, still warm from the hot sun, rippled in circles out from her bronze body as she made her way to the center. Ani cupped her hands and dipped them into the water to wash her face. Lifting her face to the Moon, she stretched her arms upward and began speaking.

"Praise to you, Goddess of the Night, You Who Never Lose Your Glory. Beautiful is your radiant light. I beseech you to favor me, allow me to come into your presence. I, *Urthekau*, am in your hands. I come before you to present to you your daughters, *Nefer* and *Neqet*, who are in the process of being born into your realms. I bring them before you for the purification of their bodies, minds, speech, hearts, and spirits. I pray you, O Shining Eye of the Sky, to accept these Star Daughters into your being."

Ani's petition to the Moon goddess finished, she bent her knees so her body became submerged. Ani basked in the warm pool redolent with the fragrance of lotus. She began her return to the edge of the pool, halfway ascending the marble steps. She held out her hand to Khem, beckoning her to enter the pool. Khem took Ani's hand and stepped into the waist-deep water. The reflection of the moonlight made Khem feel as if she were afloat in a sea of light.

They moved to the center of the pool and Ani looked into Khem's eyes. She dribbled water on Khem's head and said, "In the name of the Moon gods and goddesses, I, *Urthekau*, bless you who have chosen to walk in their path. In the presence of the Moon, I cleanse you and name you *Neqet* in obedience to the will of Isis."

Khem felt blessed and empowered. It was a good feeling. As she let the strange sensation sink in, Ani's hand pushed down on her head, gently forcing her beneath the water until she lifted herself back up. Ani kissed Khem's brow, then left her standing in the center of the pool.

Ani waded back to the steps and held out her hand to Tiye. The Nubian was reluctant to respond. Ani knew she was thinking of Khaba, and that taking another teacher's hand in ceremony would sever her connection with her mentor. "Come, Tiye, Khaba is *in* me. I beckon you come. Now."

Ani sounded different to Tiye, her voice not entirely her own. Mixed with Ani's was Khaba's. As she realized this, the Nubian's reluctance fell away. Taking Ani's hand, she felt electrified as she descended the steps to the center of the pool. Ani cupped her hands, dipped them into the water, and lifted them above Tiye, her lips murmuring a prayer to the lunar Neters. The water, though warm, sent a chill through Tiye as it trickled down her back. "Take this, your able daughter, *Nefer*, into your light, Moon god and goddess. Bless her as I, *Urthekau*, bless her. Keep her peaceful in mind and heart as she walks in the footsteps of our Great Mother of Magic, Isis."

Ani turned and looked into Tiye's eyes. "I cleanse you, *Nefer*, in the name of Isis. In her you will find your true power." Ani took Tiye's right hand and extended her other to Khem. The three stood silently under the soft light of the Moon.

Ani was the first to loosen her grip and break the circuit. Then, turning away, she returned to the steps. Once there, she climbed out of the pool and called the two supplicants by their magical names and beckoned them to come out.

Ani's servant girl had been standing in the shadows of the garden. Now she helped the girls dry off and slip into their sheaths. She handed Ani an embroidered bag. Reaching inside, Ani retrieved two small ankhs carved of lapis; a braided gold string threaded the loop of each. "I have something for each of you," Ani said. "These represent life. Your lives—your magical lives—have just begun."

Meri-ib was finding it difficult to fall asleep. His mind kept going over the carefully laid plans made for Khufu and Shemshu-Hor's journey to Heliopolis for the secret meeting. It wasn't easy for the Pharaoh to go anywhere in secret, for so many needed to travel with him. Even though in this case his entourage had been reduced to Khufu's personal valet, two servants, and a small brigade of palace guards, it would still be hard for the king to pass unobserved. The plan was for a rumor to be let out that the royal wife would be coming to Heliopolis to make a special offering to Ra. That way, the sight of a royal litter and palace barque would be less likely to arouse suspicion or draw the crowds that always flocked to see the beloved monarch.

Shemshu-Hor was another matter. The problem was that it was unusual for the leader of the ancient order even to go outside the confines of the Temple of the *Benu*. So his appearance would certainly attract attention. Even the most common of the city's residents would know that an appearance of Shemshu-Hor at the Temple of the Sun must be significant.

Meri-ib decided that since Shemshu-Hor's being seen in public was so rare and thus unexpected, that fact ironically would allow him to make the journey unnoticed so long as he was not with an entourage. No one would be looking for him. Meri-ib assigned two of his trusted guards to escort the Old One to the Sun Temple by noon the following day. Now all was in the hands of the Neters.

Meri-ib finally fell into a light sleep, but soon found himself in a dream, robed and walking down a long, narrow hallway. The place was unfamiliar, but seemed to be part of a temple. The hall seemed endless. He heard the soft padding of his own sandals on the limestone floor. He felt he was walking through fog. At the end of the hallway, against a wall painted with figures of Horus, stood an ebony table with a papyrus scroll on it. The dreaming Meri-ib unrolled the scroll and saw what seemed like thousands of identical Horus figures, each drawn in a simple black design. The designs merged, forming a single image of the hawk-headed god.

Suddenly, the image came to life as a huge hawk that flew off the page into Meri-ib's face. The bird's talons dug into Meri-ib's flesh. Then, as quickly as it had appeared, the hawk vanished. Meri-ib saw his own blood dripping onto his hands and down the front of his white garment, and this startled him awake.

Meri-ib was relieved to be awake, but he could not dismiss the experience as only a dream. He had not become High Priest of the Temple at the hub of the country's religious center without valuing dreams. What if it bore ill tidings for the secret meeting between himself, the king, and Shemshu-Hor? He had had a nightmare on the eve of a crucial event. Meri-ib lay on his bed. Dreaming of being attacked by a hawk that, moments before, had been but an image drawn on a papyrus scroll—was it a positive sign? He had, after all, dreamed of a god: Horus. Surely that was something. Though his experience with the god in his dream had been shocking, it *was* powerful. How had the dream made him feel? Meri-ib was surprised to find the dream had not left him frightened. He felt almost peaceful and empowered—not what he expected, and that seemed strange.

Meri-ib got out of bed and walked to the small window and looked out. The last bright stars were still shining in the predawn sky. Ra would soon rise on Egypt, freed from the body of Nut to once again send his light to reawaken and revitalize the land and people. The next time Meri-ib saw nightfall, the sky and Earth would be bathed in the silvery rays of the Full Moon, the meeting would be over, the decisions made. He would then know more about the Second Coming of the Star Gods.

Still deep in thought, Meri-ib prepared to go to the central chapel for his daily prayers. He was not about to alter his routine or delegate his Temple duties. Not today. That surely would invite undue attention. He would follow his usual morning procedure, which included the daily ritual to Ra. After all, his close relationship with Ra had empowered him, helped earn him the position of High Priest. After these duties were done, he would return to his private apartment to await word of the arrival of Khufu and Shemshu-Hor.

In the classroom, Taret was dressed differently than usual this day. Her garment was a tight-fitting white sheath from beneath her breasts to her ankles. Two straps crisscrossed her chest, leaving her small breasts exposed. The dress was embroidered with hieroglyphs and multicolored beads. She wore a long wig with hair falling thickly from the crown of her head to her narrow shoulders. The individual tresses were twisted into spiral plaits. Atop the hairpiece sat a circlet with a golden disk resting between polished cow's horns. Plain palm sandals completed her attire. She began:

"It is important to understand the nature of cycles in order to truly understand the nature of the Moon spirit. Everything in nature is cyclic. Cycles provide life forms with a sense of rhythm, and rhythm is important because it goes to the core of human feelings. Since time began, the Moon has served as the primary 'regulator' of Earth's cycles. Being in or out of harmony with the Moon's rhythm affects a person's health on all levels. Your health is affected when you are out of balance with Nature's rhythms.

"One of the most important of nature's rhythms is the cycle of day and night. Light stimulates growth and regulates the mating and migrating cycles of animals and birds. It affects all that goes on in the body and emotions. How much energy you have, your moods, your sexuality, your menstrual cycle, everything that has to do with physical existence is determined by the Moon.

"The simplest way to maintain balance with the Moon is to set up your life so that it coincides with the Moon's phases. The dark of the Moon, for example, is the time for introspection, meditation, and to spend as much time as you can being quiet. The Full Moon is the time to bring projects and other activities to completion, to do psychic work, to make use of the surge of power the Full Moon arouses within you. The times between the dark and the full Moon are best to prepare for future activities and to take care of menial tasks.

"The word 'light' defines the power that distinguishes day from night. But there are other, invisible lights that can only be seen with psychic sight. There is a 'temple' within the head. The inner sanctum of that temple is here." Taret placed the forefinger of her right hand to the center of her brow. "This is where the light receptor and transmitter reside. It can see all kinds of light. It has the power of vision and connects you to all that exists on the land and in the sky. The light you receive is transmitted to all your subtle bodies.

"Healing is aided by exposure to light. Sunlight, for example, is best for healing ailments that slow the body's processes and fatigue. Like your inner temple, the Moon is also a receiver and a sender of light. Moonlight heals anxiety and other kinds of emotional tensions, and is good for healing the heart, lungs, aches and pains in the head, joints, and feet, and plays a major part in the timing of childbirth."

Taret continued, her tone now more serious. "Evil destroys. It kills. Like 'good' light, 'evil' light is invisible to the human eye. Though it cannot be seen, it is always present everywhere. The most significant thing about evil light is that it makes the invisible visible, causing it to glow with an eerie violet-colored aura. Magicians know how to capture and use good light. But they also know how to capture evil light and store it in quartz crystal.

"There are many kinds of evil spirits and demons, such as those that cause illness. When a magician is in league with these, she can place a crystal filled with evil light in the place where the spirits or demons are suspected to be and, in moments, they can be seen with the human eye. Black magicians have been known to store evil light in crystals and place them on a person's body while they sleep. Evil light causes the body to turn red and burn. It can cause blisters, swelling, and even cause the skin to peel off. So, to understand the good and evil properties of light is important because learning this involves ethics, the subject of another teaching soon."

Khem shot Tiye a look of fear. She had never heard of evil light. Nor had she given much thought to black magicians. Tiye's expression told Khem that she too was uncomfortable with what Taret was saying, though it was not new to her.

Chapter Twenty

The Living Ascension

The arrival of the king of Egypt at the Temple of the Sun in Heliopolis had gone as planned. No one other than the temple and palace guards and a few trusted servants were aware of Pharaoh's presence, even as Khufu, his chief scribe, and Meri-ib awaited the arrival of Shemshu-Hor, High Priest of the Followers of Horus.

"Once we are clear about the Star Gods' intentions," Khufu said, "we will proceed immediately with Nemon's plan to unearth the Stone Head."

"I assume the labor force has been assembled?" Meri-ib inquired.

"Yes. Everything is in place. All that is left is our counsel with the Old One."

When Khufu mentioned Shemshu-Hor, a look of deep respect came across his face. He might be king of Egypt and an initiate of the Greater Mysteries, but there was not a man alive in more intimate contact with the Neters than the aged priest.

"No one knows how old he is, but some say he is the oldest human alive—older than a century! If true, he could not be an ordinary man." For reasons unknown, Khufu thought of Sokar, and abruptly changed the subject. "Have you had any contact with my half-brother?" Khufu inquired of Meri-ib.

Raising an eyebrow at the mention of Sokar, Meri-ib looked at Khufu and replied. "No. I sent a courier to inform him of my decision to have him serve as my assistant for the New Year ritual." Meri-ib remembered Sokar's having sent him an invitation to join him for the evening meal, and related this. Khufu listened with interest.

"My half-brother is well versed in social protocol, I assure you. He did, after all, grow up in the palace. Perhaps sharing an evening meal with you was his only intention."

"Perhaps so. Perhaps not," Meri-ib replied, his tone leaving little doubt as to which answer he suspected was true.

As the two men chatted, a servant came with jars of wine and a splendid tray of dried fruits. Only a few minutes passed before Meri-ib's chief house steward entered, bowing deeply, first to Khufu and then to his master. With a nod of his head, the steward let Meri-ib know that Shemshu-Hor had arrived.

"Show him in," Meri-ib commanded.

When the old Chief Priest entered the room, a powerful aura of energy came in with him. It had been a long time since Khufu or Meri-ib had seen the Old One, but seeing him now reminded them both that he was truly a living god.

The old man's limbs were stiff, though not to the degree one might expect. He was dressed in a long robe-like linen garment, the front of which was rounded off so that it fell in little folds, embracing his wraith-like figure. A panther skin was draped across his shoulders; the head and forepaws of the animal hung down, the hind paws tied together with blue ribbons over one shoulder. The skin on the elder's face was etched with deep crevices. His thin, gray hair hung down to his shoulders in uneven twisted locks. He supported himself with an ebony staff polished to a high luster. The hand that held the staff appeared withered, but, like the rest of his body, it still suggested strength.

The two guards who had escorted Shemshu-Hor made sure their charge was comfortably seated before backing out of the room to stand outside the door of Meri-ib's study. Once they were alone, Meri-ib approached the Old One and formally welcomed him in a reverent tone. "Welcome, Shemshu-Hor, Chief of the Followers of Horus, patron of the great god Horus, son of Isis and of Osiris, Lord of the Heavens. Honor to you, Lord of Countless Years. I am conscious of the god that is here in you. We are in the company of the honorable leader of Egypt, the Great One, Khufu, Son of Sneferu, wearer of the Red and White Crowns, servant of the Memphis Triad, highest among all Egyptians."

With that introduction, Khufu walked over and stood by Meri-ib's side, the two men facing the elder. The old man did not acquiesce to the rank of either who had sent for him. Whether it was a gesture of political or religious intent did not matter. That was the way it was, and neither the High Priest nor the king took offense.

Khufu and Meri-ib sat down. Khufu's chief scribe sat near the three behind a short-legged table upon which he placed a box of writing tools and unrolled a papyrus scroll.

If Meri-ib or Khufu thought that one of them would be required to brief the old priest with the details of why he had been summoned, they were mistaken. Before the Pharaoh or the priest could say a word, Shemshu-Hor spoke, his voice cracked with age.

"The god *Heru-Ur*, the Elder Horus, has spoken to me of what is about to take place on Earth."

The Old One's words captured Meri-ib's and Khufu's attention immediately. Shemshu-Hor was completely relaxed, his tone almost matter of fact.

"There are times when the development of humanity reaches a critical point. This is such a time. The Neters have decided it necessary, because humanity is ready to provide a great demonstration of the wisdom of the ancients, for the Neters to manifest themselves to the people."

It was easy to anticipate the Old One's next words. They knew he was going to speak about the Second Coming of the Star Gods. However, the statement that followed was not what they expected.

"My ancestors, the Sky Neters, last came to Earth during the First Time. Horakti led them here to this place, Innu, the seat of the Pharaoh. To me, it will forever be Innu. Here, Horakti caused a great temple to be built, and here objects of great power were gathered, objects that linked the people with their ancestors in the sky. The land looked different then. It was green and fertile. It was sanctified land. It was the earthly place of power for nine Star Gods who chose this place because it was part of the First Land that emerged from the primeval waters at the moment of creation. The land where the First Time began, where the gods commenced their rule on Earth.

"The original human priests of Innu took on the responsibility of guarding and nurturing the great tradition, the theology of Innu from which was born Isis and Osiris. The priests also possessed the powerful stone that fell from Heaven. Most believe it was lost, but it is still kept safe, in the Mansion of the *Benu* in the holy of holies in the central chapel—here, in the Temple of the Sun. In Innu, the mysteries of the cosmic cycles were first told to men.

"Times have changed all around Innu. Egypt and her people have changed. Even the stars have changed their places. But the wisdom has not changed. It never will. The gods who are in the sky brought the relics. They brought the wisdom to you all.

"You, Khufu, king of Egypt, wearer of the Double Crown, are the keeper of the Crook and Flail. The time will come when you, like the pharaohs before you, will begin your journey to take your place among the stars. This will happen for you in a manner different than with any other king. The Star Gods will come for you. The Neters on Earth will assemble for you. They will take you to the starry realm of Osiris, your Sky Father, to show you that place while you still live so you can see it through the eyes of a mortal man. They will place their hands under you and make a ladder so that you may ascend. The doors of the sky will be thrown open to you."

Khufu was stunned. He was aware of the ramifications of being Pharaoh and of the fact that at his death, like all the kings before him, he would be reborn as a great star, that he would forever traverse the sky as a companion of Osiris. This was to be the ultimate reward for him as a human. He would become a god. He was assured of immortality. However, this was supposed to happen only after he died. Surely he had heard the Elder wrong.

Shemshu-Hor paid no mind to Khufu's shock, and continued. "When the time is appropriate, you will go into the heavens. Your ascension is ordained by the Star Neters. The sacred ladder, suspended from its iron skyhook, will be lowered from the heavens to Earth. The sky window will be open for you. The gods will receive you into their realms, where you will sit upon your iron throne. This event will be remembered for all times. You will be known as 'The King Who Did Not Die to Become Immortal.' All Egypt will witness you ascend and become a star. When your sky journey is over, you will return to the Earth to live among men and reign over Egypt. You will bear witness to all who live that those who carry the Pharaoh's lineage are living gods."

The old priest had spoken for the Neters with self-assurance and trust in the truth. Shemshu-Hor sat there quiet, his eyes closed.

Standing up, Meri-ib, his head filled with questions he could not even form into words, walked over to a wooden chest upon which stood a figure of Osiris. He stared at the statue for a moment, then turned to face Khufu and the Old One. "Are we to assume that this living ascension is part of what we believe to be the Second Coming of the Sky Gods to Earth?" Meri-ib's voice reflected his bafflement. The question roused Shemshu-Hor from his contemplation. Opening his eyes slowly, he looked at Meri-ib.

"When the Star Gods came to Earth it brought real time, First Time, into being. It was revealed that they would leave the Greater Mysteries in the hands of the priests of Egypt. They promised they would return at a time when humanity was ready to be responsible for expanded knowledge. That time has come. The original priests and their descendents have served the people through time, passing the knowledge from one genera-tion to the next. They have served the Neters and the people well. The people have grown towards the Light, so it is time. The Second Coming of the Star Gods is indeed at hand."

Meri-ib and Khufu exchanged glances, but neither spoke. Khufu was deep in thought about the Old One's statements. The Sky Gods' imminent return was astounding, but now his world had been turned upside down. To anticipate becoming a star *after* his death and joining the long line of star kings before him was what he had accepted as part of kingship. Life led to physical death, and Khufu accepted both as the path that led to eventual immortality. But now, to contemplate being lifted up into the starry realms while he was still *living. . . .*

"My Lord, Chief of the Followers of Horus, I am humbled by your words," Khufu finally said.

The old man looked at Khufu with understanding. "I have served the great god Horus for a long time. Every Pharaoh who has sat upon the Throne of Egypt in my time, and before, has been the living incarnation of my beloved Horus."

For the first time since entering the room, the old man stood up slowly, bracing himself with his staff. Facing the king, he said, "Horus, as you well know, was the first man-god king of Egypt, the son of Isis and Osiris. You are Horus, and through you Horus walks the Earth. As king, you are ordained to do Horus's bidding. His bidding is that you prepare for the coming of the Star Gods, brothers and ancestors of Horus."

The priest's strength began to wane and, for a moment, his body swayed as if he would fall faint. Khufu reached out and took the old man's arm to steady him, but Shemshu-Hor resisted.

"No, no bother. I am well. Listen, for my time runs short. You are given a task, my Lord King. You, chosen by the Neters, are to free the Stone Head from the desert's prison. This you know. When the Stone Head is uncovered, you will see that it is a lion-man, Horakti, who faces East. It was carved from the rock in the small, fertile valley when the one it is the likeness of walked the Earth during the First Time. When this work is completed, build a temple oriented to the Nile Star at the foot of the paws of Horakti. Build it on the ruins of the Temple of the Lion that once stood there, the temple built after the First Coming. The Lion Temple will rise from its own ashes like the *Benu*. Its design will be revealed to you in a dream, tonight. In the new temple, the power of the Nile Star will shine upon an altar carved from granite. Upon the altar place a gift that will come from the gods. It will bear witness to future generations of the Second Coming.

"Only to you, Khufu, king of Egypt, will the nature of the gift of the Second Coming be revealed. In your dream. When the temple is complete, and that will take many years, your work on Earth will be done. You will forever be remembered as the king who gave the Lion-Man back to Egypt, who built the temple that captures the light of the Great Star of Mother Nile. This light will empower the priesthood to awareness. You as the king will lead the people with truth. So great will you and your times be, that you will have the most phenomenal structure ever built named after you. Yes, you, Khufu, future Lord of the Horizon."

There was nothing more to be said. It was all clear. The Star Gods civilized humanity, gave their knowledge of the Mysteries, then monitored the people of Earth. Through the gifts of the Neters, humans had reached a critical point. Now, the Star Gods are preparing to come to Earth again while Egypt is under his reign, Khufu thought. The unearthing of the Stone Head of the Desert, the Sphinx, would be followed by the building of a Nile Star temple to honor the brightest of the stars and capture its power. As king he would ascend to the heavens before the eyes of the people. He would then return to Earth, alive, and live for many years. And all of this would help bring people closer to becoming living gods themselves. Khufu felt stunned by it all.

For his part, Meri-ib knew the tasks before them were clear, tasks that must be accomplished at any cost. Like Khufu, he was astonished by the Old One's prediction of the Pharaoh being taken alive by the Star Gods into the domain of Osiris. As a priest of Ra and Horus, Meri-ib rejoiced at the Second Coming and all it represented and all the benefits it would bring. He envied Khufu the experience of becoming a living star-man. Meri-ib knew he was at this moment in the presence of two extraordinary humans.

When Shemshu-Hor's attendants arrived, they helped the old man stand and walked him carefully to the door. He turned to face his hosts. "May the peace of the Neters be with you both. May the Great Ones come peacefully into your dreams, my beloved Son of the Star Gods."

Khufu was the first to speak after he left. "Upon my return to Memphis, I will have an audience with the chief architect. I will tell him the things from our meeting, that it is time for the work to begin."

"Will you tell him *everything*, my Lord King?" Meri-ib inquired. Who, if anyone, would be told about the living ascension?

Khufu did not answer.

As the King was preparing to leave, Meri-ib brought up a subject neither of them had thought of before now. "What and how much do I reveal to Sokar? He is to be my ritual assistant and will be spending time with me. Does he hear the announcement of the Sphinx project and the Nile Star temple from your lips along with all Egypt? Or do I tell him prior to that? Do I inform him of the Second Coming? It is information that he would surely feel he is entitled to. How much should he know of *this* meeting?" The High Priest did not trust Sokar. He knew of his thirst for power, and guessed at his envy of Khufu.

Khufu frowned at the mention of Sokar. No doubt his was an enviable position and Sokar would covet the Throne now more than ever, especially were he to learn what was to take place. The Pharaoh's assurance of immortality was the Throne's attraction. To be remembered throughout time as the only man to ascend *alive* into the domain of Osiris—that is a prize Sokar would want for himself, Khufu reflected.

"My half-sibling is a man not to be underestimated, Meri-ib. Tell him of the Sphinx project right away. I see no harm in that. Besides, not making him wait for the public announcement will appease him, for a while. You may tell him about the Second Coming of the Star Gods, but keep back the details for now. What he will learn from you will keep his mind occupied. We can only pray that his intuition will not reveal the rest of the story until the matter is well in hand and the throne is secure."

"As you wish," Meri-ib replied, bowing.

"I will be in touch when I have met with the chief architect. May the Neters walk with you, Meri-ib."

Chapter Twenty-One

Khufu Gathers His Resolve

Sokar was sitting in his private quarters at the *Benu* Temple when Kheti delivered him the message scroll that had arrived by courier moments before. The magician-priest immediately saw Meri-ib's wax seal, and knew it was from the High Priest of the Temple of the Sun.

When he unrolled the scroll and read its contents, Sokar was pleasantly surprised. Meri-ib was requesting audience with him on the following morning, the morning after the Full Moon. The message implied that they would discuss the upcoming New Year ritual. But Sokar sensed that there was something more to their meeting, and he always relied on what he sensed.

"Kheti," Sokar called with a sharp clap of his hands. "Send a message to the High Priest, Meri-ib, that I shall indeed join him at midmorning tomorrow."

"Yes, my master," Kheti responded, and was off on this and other of the day's errands.

Khem and Tiye spent the afternoon getting ready for the Full Moon ritual. The baptism ceremony had made both of them feel centered. They were eager to participate in the rite that involved all the Star Priestesses at Heliopolis.

Khem was tying a collar, that Akhi had embroidered, around Bast's neck. It was beautifully done with tiny cat figures sewn in gold threads all around it. Tiye sat combing her hair, braiding it into small, tight, curly plaits. It was a style the Nubian wore on special occasions. When the braids were undone, her coarse hair fluffed out in a large spray that framed her head like an elaborate headdress. Both of the priestesses wore plain, ankle-length white sheaths with gold linen sashes around their waists. The ankhs that Ani had given them would be their only jewelry.

"Have you ever noticed that the Full Moon makes you feel drowsy?" Khem asked Tiye. "I have been sleepy all day."

"Sometimes," Tiye answered, her tone intending to make light of Khem's question. There were other, more serious things on her mind. She had been thinking about Khaba all day. She remembered the first time the old woman had talked to her about the Moon. She had said that the Moon was feminine. Her ancestors had told her so.

Everything she knew she had learned from Khaba, until now, when she was learning from Ani and Taret. The thought of Ani made her realize for the first time that she was beginning to accept Ani as a teacher. It made her feel happy and yet more lonesome for Khaba.

Akhi came into the room and told Khem that a courier had delivered a spoken message from her brother, Atef. He would be arriving from Abydos by cargo boat in a few days, and would be in Heliopolis for the New Year Festival at Inundation.

Khem was thrilled. She had been so busy with her life at the Temple that she had had little time to miss her family. Word of Atef's visit made her realize how much she loved and missed her relatives, especially Atef. She wondered why her brother was coming to Heliopolis. Was something wrong, or did he just want to visit with her because he missed her?

"The Moon is full," Khem remembered suddenly. "We had better finish getting ready for the ritual."

Khufu had returned to the palace in Memphis and was preparing to go to the Throne Room where he would meet with Nemon later that afternoon. The king was much relieved that he had traveled to Heliopolis undetected and was back in the palace safely. His mind was cluttered with a hundred thoughts of the pivotal meeting between himself, Meri-ib, and Shemshu-Hor. Just being in the company of the old priest made the occasion memorable, but the Old One's words would change his life.

Khufu was anxious to speak with Nemon. His cousin filled many roles: relative, chief architect, trusted friend. Many people surrounded Khufu. Most were political and economic advisors; there were also the vizier, personal valets, servants, litter bearers, fan bearers, and others who performed duties to the throne. Manetho, the vizier, was perhaps the closest to him, and he trusted him implicitly when it came to affairs of state. But when it came to having a man he could truly call his friend, Nemon was the only one.

Wherever Pharaoh was, he was surrounded by splendor. In the Throne Room and outside it, fan-bearers accompanied him, fanning him with fresh air, waving bouquets of flowers near his head so that the air around him would be filled with floral perfume. In spite of the pomp and splendor, the wealth and position, being king was a challenge that required an extraordinary man. Counselors, many of whom had served his father, surrounded him, as did the army generals, clerks, and court officials. He had to deal with all without offending any.

Khufu knew he had enemies. He knew they were more likely to be his own relatives than outsiders. There was always an uncle, brother, cousin, or half-brother, like Sokar, who felt he had a more legitimate claim to the throne, or who thought he could do a better job than Khufu. Such would-be usurpers were often hard to detect, for in the king's presence they were submissive. Yet they knew how to aggravate misunderstandings between ruler and advisors or generals, hoping to cause rebellion. Khufu knew his half-brother was waiting for the right time and circumstance to stake his claim. He suspected there might also be others who felt the same and who would not hesitate to take action.

The burdens Khufu bore as Egypt's king often made him lonely. After all, how many could he trust? Yet it was difficult to spend much time by himself when he needed to. When these times arose, he went to his private chapel next to the Throne Room. There his seclusion would not be questioned or interfered with. The time a man spent with the Neters was *his* time, sacred time.

Now was one of those times, and Khufu needed to be alone while he awaited Nemon. The prospect of the dream that Shemshu-Hor predicted was weighing on his mind. It wasn't that he was worried what the dream would reveal; rather, it was the sequence of events—the meeting, the Sphinx project, building the Nile Star temple, the dream, the Second Coming, Sokar, the prophecy of his own ascension. He needed to speak from his heart to his beloved Ptah, to ask for guidance and purification.

When Khufu entered the chapel, the room was redolent with incense and the fragrance of lotus blossoms that grew in a small fountain pool. The Pharaoh knelt before the gold statue of Ptah, and lit a fresh offering of incense. He took out the white feather that Meri-ib had given him and that he had carried in his waistband since that day. The feather in his hand brought Thoth to mind, Thoth, Tongue of Ptah, god of wisdom.

The changes in Khufu's life, indeed in the life of Egypt itself, had begun with the appearance of Thoth to the High Priest of the Temple of the Sun. This single white feather, symbolized the power of that, of the future of Egypt and himself. After what had transpired in his meeting with Shemshu-Hor, the feather was now symbolic of his living ascension, the event that would give him wings to fly into the sky.

Khufu began to pray. "My beloved Ptah, Creator God, You who create works of art, and who are the master builder, praise be to you. Take me under your protection, give me your guidance. I pray you find my soul worthy of your nourishment. I beg you to purify me. May I be strengthened for my tasks. May I be refreshed by these prayers. May I have bliss before you, and may I gain control over the evil within me. May I have victory over my enemies, real or imagined. May you, Ptah, give me your influence and support my passage here. Be it so."

His prayer finished, Khufu went over to a plush floor pillow and sat down. He felt peace fill him. This was the first time in a while he had had time to think clearly. Khufu could think only of his son, Dejedfre, the High Priest of Memphis, who would rule Egypt after him. What will the Egypt he inherits be like? What will his legacy be? A country at peace or war? Would he have usurpers like all the kings before him? Would he be victorious and have a long and healthy reign? How will it be to follow in the footsteps of a father-king who became a living star-man? Khufu knew he would never have the answers to these questions. Dejedfre's fate, as his own, was in the hands of the Neters.

The king left the chapel. Entering the Throne Room, he saw that Nemon had arrived, and was chatting with the vizier. Whatever the matter at hand, Khufu thought, Nemon's mood was always jovial.

Seeing Pharaoh enter, Nemon bowed respectfully and addressed his cousin, formally first, and then with the customary shoulder embrace. Khufu ordered the room cleared except for Manetho, his chief scribe, and Nemon. The matters to be discussed were still too secret for most ears. It was time for Manetho and Nemon to hear of the meeting in Heliopolis.

"You are both aware that the Sphinx project is being undertaken at the bidding of the Star Gods," Khufu said. "What you do not know is that the Second Coming requires more of us than the unearthing of the Stone Head. Much more. I have met with the old Chief Priest of the Followers of Horus. He has informed me and the High Priest of Heliopolis of many things that have far-reaching implications. For now, suffice it to say that when the Stone Head is revealed, a great temple must be built at its base. A temple dedicated and oriented to the Great Star, Sothis, Star of Mother Nile. "I only know, now at least, that the temple will be—must be—built. The design, the style, these I do not yet know. I was told by Shemshu-Hor that these things will be revealed to me in a dream tonight. This is all I can tell you now. I have been informed that the labor force has been gathered and is ready to begin. Is this true?"

"Yes, your majesty." said Manetho. "The force is gathered. The *Apis* Bull is in its stall near the site. We await your command to begin."

With a sigh of relief, Khufu said, "Very well. Let the work begin at sunrise tomorrow. I will meet with the people of Egypt at high noon from the appearance balcony of the palace. I will tell the people about the Sphinx project. I request your presence by my side, both of you."

Manetho looked at Nemon out of the corner of his eye to see his reaction. Nemon smiled pleasantly and assured Khufu that he could count on him to be there. Manetho followed suit, saying, "Of course, your majesty." The business concluded, the two men left.

The sun was beginning to set. Outside the window of the Throne Room, shadows were starting to fall across the desert. Soon the Full Moon would rise over the dunes, the buildings of the capital city, and the rest of Egypt.

Khufu gazed out over the city, his city, on the east bank of the Nile. He saw the row of pyramids and felt the same about them as he had as a boy. They were the soul of Egypt, the living spirit of the people. Alone, the king confronted a deep, almost intimidating, truth. He had not been able to sort out his own feelings regarding his encounter with the Old One.

The responsibility the Star Gods had placed on his shoulders was for a reason: they trusted him, and would reward that trust with his becoming a god-man while alive. He would not have to suffer the fear or the pain of death before "seeing" the heavenly world. What greater reward could a human be given? What would better guarantee he would be remembered through the ages? To have the most impressive monument ever built, the Great Pyramid, called by his name—surely that would mean men would speak of him until the end of the Earth.

Looking out at the pyramids that already stood, there was no question these empowering monuments would stand until the Last Time and stand where they had stood since the First Time. The pyramids and the Sphinx were humanity's link to the Star Gods and Man's monument to itself.

Khufu felt he was at a time of death. How could he ever be the same person, knowing what he knew now? His old life had ended, and his new life, his new birth, was beginning. He did not know where his new life would take him, but the Sky Gods evidently saw something in him that he did not yet see. It wasn't just *he* in whom the Sky Gods saw something. It was all of them, the entire cast of characters—Meri-ib, Shemshu-Hor,

Nemon—they recognized as able to get the job done. The insight made Khufu feel less alone. For however many enemies or usurpers he might have, he also had staunch supporters who knew the significance of the times that Egypt was about to experience.

Chapter Twenty-Two

Khufu and the Dark-Robed Figures

Khem and Tiye went out onto the small patio adjacent to the main room of Khem's quarters. The sunset spread reds and gold across the sky like a god's pectoral. Egyptians normally went to bed at sunset and, for the common people, tonight would be no different. But not for the priests and priestesses. It was the Full Moon.

As the two girls stood taking in the smells and sounds of dusk, Khem said, "This is the hour of Nepthys, goddess of sunset and dusk."

"Yes, it is," Tiye replied.

"I always felt sorry for her," Khem went on. "Though she is beautiful, she always had to live in Isis's shadow. She was unhappy in her marriage to Seth, and envied the happy relationship that Isis and Osiris shared. She wanted the same for herself."

"What happened to her?" Tiye asked. Being Nubian, she was not all that familiar with the gods and goddesses of the North.

"She seduced Osiris by pretending to be Isis. She got away with fooling him because of the dim light of dusk."

"Oh. Is that all of the story?"

"No, not exactly. Seth caught her with Osiris and scared her away. Osiris never realized who she was and when she left he turned over and went back to sleep!"

"Sounds like a man!" Tiye responded, a teasing smile lighting up her face. Both laughed heartily.

The air was cooling down quickly as the sun set. When Khem and Tiye went back inside, Bast bounded over playfully and rolled over, grabbing at their feet. Khem had wanted to take the lioness to the Full Moon ritual, but thought better of it. Maybe next time. It was time for her and Tiye to join the other Star Priestesses.

Nervous with anticipation, the girls were ready. It was an event that Khem had looked forward to since coming to the Temple, her first ceremony with Tiye and the others. She did not know what to expect. The two reached the open-air hypostyle ritual area and saw that most of their fellow Star Priestesses had arrived. Night had fallen over the desert and the Moon was like a white round pearl.

The ritual arena was beautiful, Khem thought. It was the first time she had been there, but it was everything she had expected. The entranceway had a huge pylon adorned with flag-staves where, on festival days, fine linen flags waved, each appliquéd with figures of the Neters of Heliopolis. At the far end of the structure were steps to an altar of the gods laden with flowers. In the center of the high altar was a crystal vase filled with Nile water.

The Star Priestesses wore white garments either long, loose-fitting, robe-like dresses or tighter-fitting, ankle-length sheaths. Each wore a wreath of Nile reeds on her head. The group was coordinated by Taret's scribe, Sheshat; she and Ani would be co-ritualists with the High Priestess, who had not yet arrived. Female musicians were present to bring joy to the celebrants.

It was time for the ritual to begin. The priestesses formed a line, and slowly began their procession into the arena. When each of the twelve had taken their place, Taret appeared and, with Sheshat and Ani close behind, made her way to the steps of the high altar. Sheshat walked up the altar steps and lit a cone of incense in a brazier. Ani climbed the stairs next, and lit the ceremonial fire from twigs that lay in a piece of granite hewn to form a bowl. Fragrant fumes soon filled the night air.

Sheshat and Ani stood on each side of the high altar as Taret slowly walked up the steps. When she reached the top, she did a self-blessing ritual. She dipped the fingers of her right hand into the crystal vase, and touched the precious water from Mother Nile to the top of her head and said, "Bless me, Thoth, God of the Moon, for I am your child." She dipped her fingers into the vase again and put them to her brow. "Bless my mind that I may think good thoughts." Repeating the same process and touching different parts of her body, Taret continued: "Bless my sight so that I may see your path and mine. Bless my throat that I may speak truth. Bless my heart so that I may be open and loving to you and to all that lives. Bless my belly from which all my feelings pour forth. Bless my womb from which all life comes into the world. Bless my feet so they may walk in your path. Bless my hands that they might do your work."

The energy was beginning to build. Khem felt a surge of power each time Taret touched a part of her body during the self-blessing. It was as if invisible hands were touching her own body, as if all the celebrants were being cleansed and made fit to come before the god.

Taret dipped her hands in the large vase and let the water trickle over the surface of the altar. Taret faced the altar and lifted her arms upwards towards the Moon, then made an invocation to Thoth:

> Praise to Thoth, the Moon beautiful in his rising.
> Lord of bright appearances who illumines the gods.
> Hail to thee, Moon, Bull in Hermopolis,
> Who spreads out the seat of the gods,
> Who knows the mysteries,
> Who recalls all that is forgotten,
> The remembrance of time and eternity,
> Who proclaims the hours of the night,
> Whose words abide forever.

The energy intensified. Khem looked at Tiye, and knew by her expression she was feeling the effects. The bodies of the trio assembled before the high altar reflected the light of the Moon and the dancing shadows of the ceremonial fire. To Khem and the others, the women had lost their ordinary humanness. They had become *hekau*, magician-priestesses of the great god Thoth.

A naked girl appeared carrying a basket of white lotus flowers. Her long, straight hair hung over her chest covering her breasts. An aura of innocence and purity about her made her seem otherworldly. The girl proceeded into the column-flanked arena and dropped a white lotus flower in front of every celebrant, ending with Taret. Then she left, but another beautiful young girl appeared in her place, clothed in a wispy drape of linen that flowed loose and free. Her hair was done up in braids piled on her head. Her eyes were painted heavily with kohl. This second girl carried a sistrum. Moving to the center of the ritual arena, she played the rattle-like instrument, swaying her body in erotic movements as she danced. The shadows cast on her writhing body added sensuality and mystery to the gathering. Khem had never experienced anything like this. In a few moments, the lone dancer was joined by a dozen more, all dressed the same, playing simple sistrums and cymbals, moving in a circle.

Taret, speaking so as to be heard over the music, offered a prayer of invocation and praise to the Moon goddess, Hathor:

All hail, jubilation to you, Golden One, sole ruler of the world,
Mysterious One who gives birth to divine beings,
who forms the animals, molds them as she pleases,
who furnishes men and women.
O Mother, luminous one who thrusts back darkness,
who illuminates every human creature with her rays.
Hail, great one of many names.
It is the Golden One!
Lady of drunkenness, music, dance,
of frankincense and the crown, of women and men,
who acclaim her because they love her.
Heaven makes merry,
the temples fill with song,
and the Earth rejoices.

By the time the invocation was finished, it was evident that the High Priestess was in an altered state of consciousness. The effect was contagious. Taret instructed the apprentices to open their hands and look at their *ushabtis*. They were to hold the images to their noses and exhale the breath of life into them. They would serve as a protector in dreams and visions. Then the Star Priestesses clutching the *ushabtis* in their right hands lifted their arms up to the Moon and allowed the energy of the ritual to excite their bodies into movement.

The Star Priestesses joined in the circle of Hathor priestesses, the women allowing themselves to ride the crests of the Moon energy that shone upon the circle of whirling, writhing women as it had done since the First Time. The priestesses danced and let the Moon's power flow through them until one by one, their power spent, they dropped to the limestone floor and lay in a rapture.

Khufu had retired to the sitting room in the royal apartments. His day had been long and tiring. To say that it had been eventful was an understatement. Earlier, after his return from Heliopolis, Khufu spent a couple of hours with Nemon and Manetho discussing everything that was pertinent to the Sphinx project and the plans for the Nile Star temple. He would wait until the design of the temple had been given to him before sharing the rest of the revelations. He didn't feel that he could put it all into words for others yet, not even Nemon. Khufu was still struggling to do that for himself.

Before going to bed, Khufu told Meritates, his queen, he needed to spend the night alone. His wife never questioned his decisions, nor did she balk at his need for solitude. The first royal wife was secure in her marriage and readily acquiesced to Khufu's request.

It took a while for him to relax enough to fall asleep. His body was tired, but his mind was filled with stress that threatened to cause insomnia. By the grace of the Neters, Khufu slipped into a sound sleep within an hour.

Sometime during the middle of the night, Khufu woke out of a sleep so deep he found it difficult to regain full awareness. He lay in the bed in the darkness of the room, his eyes upon the barely visible ceiling. The night seemed to drag on, a thousand thoughts in his mind. He did not remember dreaming, was sure he had not. Khufu fell asleep again, and this time he entered his dream vessel.

He was standing in front of a magnificent temple surrounded by a stone wall. The wall's gates were carved from acacia wood, covered with plates of gold fastened with black bronze and iron. Beyond the wall was an entranceway with three copper-plated gates. Khufu's dream vessel entered the temple. Inside, the sanctuary was dark. He saw a circle of twelve robed figures, their faces dimly lit by hand-held candles. They were not humans but Star Gods. In the center of the circle of gods was a huge piece of red granite. Each corner had a carved lion's head with emerald eyes. The center of this altar was inlaid with a gold Eye of Horus, the *udjat*.

The dreaming Khufu now stood before the altar, surrounded by the twelve Star Gods, their solemn faces ageless. A beam of light flashed into the sanctuary through a narrow entrance fifty feet away. The light remained for a couple of minutes before fading away.

Leaving his dream vessel the moment the darkness engulfed him, Khufu woke, his physical eyes looking up at the ceiling, still barely visible. It was the same kind of ink-black darkness he had experienced in his dream. Pulling the bed's netting aside, Khufu got up and walked to the window. Dawn was imminent. The dream still fresh, he began reliving the images.

The first was the circle of twelve dark-robed figures. He knew they were not Egyptian, or human. Their skin was pale, their eyes narrow, and he knew their heads, though covered by cowls, were clean-shaven. Unlike the typical Egyptian, they were tall and thin. They were Star Gods. Khufu knew that the temple was the one Shemshu-Hor had predicted he would dream about. He vowed to remember the images well so he could tell Nemon what his dream had revealed. It would be a splendid temple. It would be a place where the Star Gods would gather in a circle of light to draw down the energy of the Great Star of Mother Nile.

Chapter Twenty-Three

The Stars of Sothis

That morning, Khufu joined his family on the veranda of the private apartments. He felt rested and refreshed from sleep, but the dream pictures were foremost in his mind. Sipping on beer, Khufu requested his house servant to send for his chief scribe. There were messages he needed to send right away. It was rare for the king to conduct business during the times reserved for being with his family, but matters were pressing. He needed to send word to Manetho to join him in the Throne Room as soon as possible so that he, Khufu, could be briefed on how the labor force's first work day had gone. He also needed to send a message to arrange a meeting with Nemon so that he could inform him of the plan for the star temple that was now very clear in his mind. He would also send for his chief astronomer, Nebseni. . . .

When Khem and Tiye woke, that same day, the sun's rays were already lighting up the room. Tiye had had a bedfellow through the night, Bast, and she was still curled up at her feet. The priestesses had returned to Khem's quarters in the early morning hours following the Full Moon ritual. Riding the high that comes when one's energy is completely spent, the girls had fallen asleep immediately. Now, in the light of day, the ritual seemed to have been a dream. But a dream it wasn't. It had happened. Khem had participated in her first ceremony since coming to Heliopolis.

So, the priestesses were having a hard time waking up and getting started with their morning toilet. A busy day lay ahead, class, then a lesson with Ani. It also might well be the day that Atef arrived from Abydos. Khem was excited about seeing her brother, yet felt foreboding. She found it strange that he was coming "just" for a visit. There must be something else.

By the time Khem and Tiye left for class, with Bast close behind, the morning was half over. The apprentices, some red-eyed from lack of sleep, awaited Taret. She arrived, her usual gentle, soft-spoken self and not the commanding high priestess who had invoked the lunar deities. The day's teaching concerned the Nile Star, Sothis. Obviously timed to precede the new year that was approaching, Taret's information concerned the astronomical and religious significance of the great star and the importance of Inundation. Taret walked up onto the platform, accompanied by Sheshat.

"Of all the stars, one is at the core of the mysteries taught by the Star Gods. It is Sothis, Star of Mother Isis and Mother Nile. It could be said that all stars are alike, that they have much in common. They all shine. They all move. They are far from Earth. Sothis is different. It moves, of course, and it shines, and though it is far away, it is one of the stars nearest to Earth. Because it is close, our astronomers calculate its movement by way of the old texts in which the motion of the stars has been recorded since the First Time."

All her life Khem had heard bits and pieces of the story of the First Time. She knew things had happened then that had never happened before or since, things that had changed Egypt. She knew that since the First Time the priesthood had been taught by the Star Gods that their land was a reflection of the heavens, that what went on in the heavens also took place in Egypt. It had always been that way, but until the gods came to Earth, humanity did not know this. The Star Gods had told their most faithful followers, those who became the priesthood, that if special monuments were built on the land to correspond to the stars, and were oriented to the stars, then Earth and the stars would be connected for all time and humans would have greater control over their destiny.

"Many mysteries surround Sothis," Taret was saying. "Those mysteries are an integral part of the teachings brought to Earth by the Star Gods in the First Time. These teachings have been in the hands of the priesthood for centuries. Some of their mysteries are known by all the priests and priestesses, but there are truths that are known only to the Star Priests and Star Priestesses, the earthly sons and daughters of the Star Gods."

A short pause signaled that Taret was entering a higher state of consciousness; then she went on. "One of the greater secrets about the Nile Star that is known only by the Star Priests and Priestesses is that it is not what it appears to be to the eye. It is not one star, as you and I see it. It is *three* stars. Sothis is a star *system.* It was from the Sothis star system that the first of the Star Gods came to Egypt. Even though a trinity of stars makes up the Sothis system, the teachings known by all the priesthood concern only two. The existence of the third star is known only to a few members of the priesthood.

"There are many things about the great star you must know. This knowledge is integral to your training as Star Daughters. The first concerns many of the Neters. The Star Gods who came here from Sothis were extraordinary beings who are now remembered as 'the gods.' I will speak now about the Neters that have to do with Sothis.

"The Sothis star system is home to the god Anubis, son of Nepthys and Osiris. You are familiar with the attributes of Anubis as a god of the dead, and all that is relative to death and dying. But to understand Anubis as a Star God, you must realize that he is the *protector* of all the gods, particularly Isis. He is like a dog that protects his master.

"As a Star God, Anubis represents time. Time and its passage is one of life's mysteries. Time is in motion and it is motion; it is a constant. To the human mind, time has a beginning and an end, for humans cannot 'think' eternity, but to understand Anubis is to understand time as eternity. It is to understand the circle, and motion, literally, circular motion because time is circular motion. All moves in the heavens in a circular motion. Anubis is circular motion, a star ever circling around another star. He is a star in the Sothis system. Ponder these thoughts, Star Daughters. They cannot be understood with the mind alone."

Chapter Twenty-Four

A Prophecy Revealed

The Nile was sparkling in the midday sun. A southerly breeze wound in and out of the branches of the trees and the bulrushes along the river-bank, cooling the heat that clutched every molecule of air. Atef had arrived. Their walk through the city had taken Khem and Atef through the market-place, where merchants constantly enticed them. Bast had come, and a lioness on a leash was definitely not a common sight. Some people shied away, while others, particularly children, petted her or otherwise came to express their curiosity. It wasn't until the pair reached a secluded spot on the riverbank that an opportunity to talk in peace presented itself.

"How is Mother?" Khem asked. "And Father?"

"They are well. Mother is busy these days. She is embroidering a special dress, a wedding dress. It is taking a long time. She sits and sews for hours on end. She says it helps keep her mind occupied. Father? He is content, I think. He has much to do to prepare for Inundation."

"Did Father not need you to help him?" Khem inquired, puzzled by her brother's absence from the family business.

"Father has help, my sister," Atef replied. "He has coupled his business with the fish dealer, Rom-mi. Father has joined with a group of fishermen, and the haul is taken to Rom-mi's stall in the marketplace. It is too much to fish and sell, so this arrangement is good. Rom-mi dries the catch, Father is paid, and his work is cut by half."

"So you are not needed," she surmised.

"No. But I could not have abandoned Father. If he truly needed me, I would be there." Atef's tone was adamant. He had obviously given the family matter due consideration, and had made the decision not to work with Rashid any longer.

"Why have you come to Heliopolis, Atef?"

"When you left, I did not want to see you go. But I knew that coming here and entering the Temple was what you knew you had to do and what you *wanted* to do. So I was happy for you to leave home because it was to fulfill your dream of becoming a Star Priestess."

Atef paused and looked into his sister's eyes. "I have a dream too, Khem. I have had it for a long time. I wish to enter the Temple. I wish to become a scribe. I can already write, and I will learn more. I wish to learn enough so that I can transcribe the ancient texts. That way I can know the wisdom that is in them."

Atef's eyes sparkled when he spoke of becoming a scribe. Khem knew he was pouring out his heart to her. She sensed he was searching for freedom. He had made the difficult decision to leave the family and Abydos to follow his heart, and she was empathetic with him for that. He would work in the city with a fish dealer in return for room and board. When he began his training, he would continue working part-time, at least for a while. Fish dealers were always looking for help, and it was common for the younger workers to live with their employer's family. It was a good arrangement for all concerned.

"I am happy that you are here, my brother," Khem said embracing him.

The time for Khem and Tiye's private lesson with Ani had come. When Khem arrived at Ani's quarters, Tiye was already there. Khem chatted about her visit with Atef, telling Tiye how happy she was that her brother would be staying in Heliopolis, studying at the Temple.

Ani came late. She had been meeting with Taret to discuss a request made by the High Priestess to enter the dream clinic to have her dreams monitored prior to Inundation. Dreams were the vehicle the Star Gods used to communicate with members of the priesthood. Any dreams that came at the time of the New Year, especially due to the predicted appearance of the comet, would be of paramount importance to Taret.

"The last time we were together," Ani began, "I spoke to you about Isis's celestial connections. I know that Taret has taught you about *ushabtis*, their use, and how they are made. I will take those teachings a step further. What I wish to explain to you is part of the teachings given to initiates by Thoth and Isis, the supreme celestial magicians. It is related to *ushabtis* and the practice of magic.

"Magicians make use of their *heka* or magical power on every occasion possible. What separates a white magician from a black one are two things: intent and willingness to pay attention to sense and reason. Intent or motive not only determines the good or evil of a magical operation, but can also influence its outcome. Reason determines the method or procedure a magician will follow to bring about the desired results, as well as dictating that her needs and desires will not occur at the expense of anyone else.

"As a rule, magic is accomplished by the recitation of spells and incantations, as well as by the performance of certain acts. Magicians first purify themselves by fasting and ritual bathing. The garments and jewelry worn during magical rites also contribute to the power and success of the act. Such things as dresses or robes, belts, jewels, and animal skins, help the practitioner's connection with spirits.

"When it comes to working *heka*, a magician's powers are as effective at a distance as they are close up. Effectiveness is assured by the use of amulets of varying forms, and by figures, like *ushabtis*, and clay and faience models of humans and animals. An amulet is any object worn by a person for magical benefit, most commonly for protection. Amulets and figures, which can be made from various materials, are then 'charged' by means of touch, or by reciting words of power and spells over them, or sometimes by actually engraving spells upon them.

"Amulets are made from many things—wood, mud, wax, or any other substance one might choose, including lapis, malachite, turquoise, jasper, and other stones. Metals such as gold, silver, bronze, copper, and iron may also be used, as can the teeth and hair of animals, and even shells and herbs. There is also faience, colorful glazed earthenware. It is the most common. My magical work is done primarily with amulets. Amulets can be mounted in necklaces, bracelets, rings, pectorals, or other types of jewelry. As a rule, amulet-making is overseen by at least one member of the priesthood.

"Amulets, though made by individual magicians, receive their power from another source. The Neters. There are many kinds of amulets. One of the most common is the Eye of Horus, the *udjat*, worn to ensure good health. The ankh is worn for long life. Oyster shell amulets bring good health to women. *Cippis* are healing amulets; green turquoise amulets protect you against harm of all kinds. Hathor priestesses wear the beautiful *menyet* to attract the goddess's protection. Priestesses of Isis sometimes wear amulets carved from sycamore for protection. These are cleansed in a tincture of *ankhamu* flowers. There are also many kinds of amulets for the dead. Perhaps I will tell you about these another time."

Giving the Nubian a thoughtful look, Ani said, "You, Tiye, have a special talent for making and charging amulets for use by the living. I have been told this in a dream and have been instructed to encourage you to work with this *heka*. It is a good way for you to flex your magical muscles and to focus your *heka* power. Your power is very strong. It can be used for many things with much success, my star sister. Will you follow this guidance?"

Tiye was taken aback at first, but after a moment, she agreed. She would begin right away.

"Good. I am pleased," said Ani. "I will personally oversee your work. I wish for you to come to the dream room tonight. I will monitor your dreams, for I am certain there will be revelations concerning the matter of amulet-making."

Tiye had never slept in the dream room before and was anxious. But because she had come to trust Ani, she did not voice any objection.

Ani continued. "Black magic is feared by the common people and by priests and priestesses alike, and well it should be. Black magicians impose their will on others, and they use their knowledge and power to do so. You will learn much about these things. Now, I have said that in all magical practice magicians recite incantations and spells. These comprise the sacred language. It is not the *words* that are magical; it is the action or activity the words *imply.* This is very important. *Heka* words are not merely one word followed by another in succession. It is the pronounce-ment of each *sound* that puts precise energy into motion, the sound being what gives a word life. Sound, which magicians call toning, produces phys-ical and psychological effects. Such effects are evoked by the utterance of words that, spoken in common talk, would have little or no such effect. The *heka* power of words is increased by repetition.

"The greatest of all magicians is Thoth, the mind and tongue of Ra. It was he who authored the great Book of *Heka*, the source of all our knowl-edge of magic. He was the greatest of all priests, possessing the art of writ-ing, itself a magical skill, and reading. This brings me to a point that I wish to make to you, Khem.

"You have some knowledge of reading and writing. It is time for you to learn more, much more. Writing will come naturally to you, as will read-ing. These are skills that will set you aside from the average apprentice and will make you a valuable servant of the sorority of Star Priestesses. The scribe, Sheshat, will teach you. You must begin this very soon."

What a coincidence, Khem thought. On the very day Atef arrives in Heliopolis with plans to fulfill his dream of becoming a scribe, I am told to become one myself.

Meri-ib was sitting in his study reading a sacred text when he was notified that Sokar had arrived. Ordinarily having the king's half-brother as his co-ritualist for the New Year ritual would be an honor. To Meri-ib, this was no honor. It was potential trouble. A priest, especially the High Priest, chose his assistants carefully. Although rank had something to do with the choice, the decision was his own. If a particular person was preferred, rank and position could be overlooked.

Meri-ib had not chosen Sokar. Sokar had requested the honor and in doing so was taking advantage of his being a member of the royal family. That he was a qualified priest could not be denied. Both points were in his favor so Meri-ib had agreed with the king's reluctant blessing.

The New Year festival, including its religious rite, was the most important one of the year. It was the time when the Nile flooded. A high flood was always welcome, for it promised a rich increase in crops. A low flood was dreaded, for it forecasted a year of famine. It was imperative to appease and give thanks to the Neters, and the New Year ritual provided for that.

Though the time of celebration was the rise of Mother Nile, it was first and foremost a time of hard work for all, especially farmers, Meri-ib reflected. Even the highest flood would not overflow all the fields, and if these were not to remain dry, peasants must undertake the laborious task of artificial irrigation. The water of the Nile was brought to what would otherwise be barren fields by a trench. Then a kind of draw-well was erected to raise and empty the pails of water. It was backbreaking work when the river receded, for the fields must then be plowed and the crops planted so that best use could be made of the gifts the Neters had provided.

The days of hard labor and the New Year's celebration combined to make these days the most important in Egyptian life. Meri-ib, along with the chief priests of all the country's temples, shouldered the religious and spiritual weight of the season, and none would risk anything going wrong.

When Sokar came into the room, Meri-ib was struck by his appearance. The man was a near-perfect physical specimen, a robust combination of brains and brawn that set him apart from the average Egyptian male. He was dressed in a short skirt that consisted of a straight piece of white cloth, draped loosely around his narrow hips, leaving his knees uncovered. The edges came together in the center at the front and were tucked in at the top behind the bow of the girdle, which held the skirt together. The simplicity of the garment showed off his muscular torso, wide shoulders, and large biceps. A gold-hilted dagger was tucked into the waistband of his kilt.

Meri-ib's eyes went directly to Sokar's magnificent necklace, so large it covered the upper part of his chest. Of gold, it portrayed a hawk whose enameled wings spread wide and were inlaid with carnelian, green feldspar, and lapis. A gold earring adorned the lobe of Sokar's right ear. The man's presence commanded attention.

"My lord, Meri-ib, servant of the Great God Ra, it is good to be in your presence," Sokar greeted the High Priest, bowing graciously in required respect.

"And you," Meri-ib replied, returning the greeting. "I have summoned you here to discuss your role as my ritual assistant for the upcoming Rite of Inundation."

"I gathered as much."

"I have decided that you shall be the leader of the procession through the city, that you will precede the Bearers of the Oracle. You will also stand by my side as the representative of Horus. Does this suit you, Sokar?"

"It does, my lord and High Priest. I am honored."

"As well you should be," Meri-ib muttered under his breath, as he turned away from him. It was rare he did something he felt would put himself or any other in a risky position, but he was doing it now, and he did not relish the feeling it gave him. Keeping the peace might sometimes require a man to risk conflict, and it was in that spirit and with that motive that he had elected to have Sokar serve a role second only to his own in the New Year rite. Though Meri-ib would have liked to end the meeting at that point, he could not. There were other things he must tell Sokar.

"Sokar, because you are going to be my assistant, you should know that Pharaoh has made an important decision. It is based upon a vision that the time has come for the Stone Head to be freed from the sands. This day, a great work force has been assembled for this work to begin."

Sokar listened with interest, knowing he was hearing only what Meri-ib wanted him to hear. He knew there was more.

"The unearthing of the Stone Head," Meri-ib continued, "which there is every reason to believe is a lion-man, is happening now because of a prophecy that has been revealed by the oracle."

"Prophecy?" Sokar inquired, his interest piqued.

"Yes. It has been foretold that the return of the Star Gods to Egypt is imminent. Pharaoh will make an announcement to the people tomorrow."

Sokar's face was solemn, his dark eyes flashing as Meri-ib's words registered. He had sensed something was afoot, and now he knew it. But he would not let on to Meri-ib.

"I see no reason for a rehearsal of my role, my lord Meri-ib. I have witnessed the rite many times, every year for as long as I can remember. I will, unless your wishes are different, be at the Temple of the Sun at sunrise on the day of Inundation. I will be here when the light of the great star paves the way for the first rising of the first Sun of New Year."

Meri-ib was irked by Sokar's arrogance. It was hard to tell if the man's self-confidence was an asset or a mask that hid a cunning aggressor who would stop at nothing to gain control of whatever he set his sights on, including the Throne of Egypt. One thing was certain. He had no idea what Sokar thought about the Sphinx project or the Second Coming of the Star Gods.

"That is acceptable," the High Priest said, eager to bring the meeting to an end.

Bowing, Sokar turned and walked to the door, where he stopped and faced Meri-ib again, and said, "May you live a hundred years."

Elsewhere, the work force was gathered at the site near the Stone Head, most camping in lean-tos or sleeping on the ground. Cooking fires dotted the flat desert. Organizing an army of laborers had been a monumental task equal to the unearthing process itself. This was the day that Pharaoh would come before the Egyptians on the Balcony of Appearances at the palace in Memphis to announce the Sphinx project. He would do his best to convince the people of the importance of the task that would require the effort of many.

Khufu was carrying a lot around in his heart. Though all of it was cause for joy and celebration, he could not share it with many others yet. He must take it one step at a time lest he reveal too much too soon. Nor could there be mistakes, or cause for panic among the people. He could not allow cause for anyone to think him a weak and vulnerable leader in the face of one of the greatest challenges any king had ever faced, for now was the perfect time for his enemies to try and unseat him.

Chapter Twenty-Five

Sokar Honors the Star Gods

Sokar, still in Heliopolis following his meeting with Meri-ib, was dressing for the day ahead. He had spent most of the night awake, going over what Meri-ib had told him. It was rare that he felt that something of great significance was going on without his knowledge. He did not know *what* it was, and that was disconcerting. If he was ever going to be king of Egypt, he could not do it by being ignorant of what was going on, either in the religious center of the country or in the palace. It was time to find out.

Walking out onto his patio, Sokar faced the eastern horizon. Taking a deep breath and exhaling slowly, he lifted his eyes to the Sun and offered a prayer of praise. "Honor and praise to you, Sustainer of Life. Your beauty and power be praised, and renewed, God of the Solar Orb, Heir of Eternity, Ruler of the Heavens. Lord of All the Neters, whom the ancestors adore, you are strong, you, the Master of the Universe, may you endure forever." His prayer to the Sun God finished, Sokar turned his silent thoughts to the Star Gods. "Praise be to you, O Star Gods, you who never lose greatness. Adoration and honor to you. You are the Lords of Life. Trust me to show obedience to your will today and every day, so long as I shall live."

When Sokar returned inside, Kheti met him. Kheti had brought an amphora of fresh drinking water and was tidying up the bedchamber.

"Will you be going out, my master?" Kheti asked, sensing that Sokar's mood was unusually sober.

"Yes, Kheti, I will be going to the palace in Memphis. Khufu is to make an announcement I wish to be present for, provided I can secure quick transportation. See to a small barge for my purpose right away. I will meet you at the main dock in an hour. You will accompany me to Memphis."

Kheti departed immediately. He knew that although Sokar spoke only about his plan to travel to the capital city, there would be magical work to come very soon. He could read it in Sokar's eyes. He knew that look; it told him his master felt threatened, or about to instigate a magical operation, or both. Such times demanded Kheti play two roles, servant and magical assistant.

After Kheti left for the dock, Sokar finished getting ready for the journey. On his finely polished ebony dressing table sat a carved wooden chest that contained his jewelry. The magician eyed a gold pendant shaped like the head of a lion, its eyes flashing emeralds. Dedi had given it to him, the man who taught him magic five years ago. The old man, who now resided in the South, had the reputation of being the most highly skilled *hekau* in all of Egypt. His spells could heal the sick and favor one with riches and social prominence. Dedi had picked Sokar as a natural-born *hekau* upon meeting him at the Temple in Memphis when Sokar was in training for the priesthood.

Dedi was a good teacher, and Sokar had learned well. Hour after hour, day by day, for two years he sat in the magus's presence. Dedi stressed that if and when a magician made the choice to employ his knowledge and skills for a self-serving purpose, he had better have the power and courage to accept the consequences of his actions. For that, the magician had to believe completely in the action. Well, Sokar believed completely in his action. He *was* the rightful heir to the Throne of Egypt.

A smile slowly crept over his face as Sokar slipped the lion-headed pendant around his neck. "I wear this in your honor, Master Dedi, servant of the great god Anubis. . . ."

Word had spread fast that Pharaoh would be making a special appearance that day. The streets were filled with people and pack animals. The Sun was beating down and the air was thick and heavy. A crowd had gathered around the gates, providing a welcome opportunity for merchants to hawk their wares while mingling with the throngs. Sokar found a place under a palm where he had a good view of the Balcony of Appearances. Few would be able to actually hear the Pharaoh's words, but those who could would spread the word through the crowd.

At noon, the king of Egypt appeared on the balcony of the palace. Khufu's face was pleasantly solemn, his posture erect and proud. The double crown sat tall upon his head, his white garment topped by a magnificent leopard skin cloak. When the king stood before the people and crossed the Crook and Flail across his chest, a thunderous cheer went up from the crowd. His entourage included his family, the High Priest of Memphis, royal fan bearers, perfume bearers, and guards. Handing the symbols of royalty to attendants, Khufu spoke in a loud, strong voice.

"I, Khufu, Ruler of the Two Lands, Loyal Servant of the Holy Trinity of Neters, the great god Ptah, the goddess Sekhmet, and Nefertem, the living Son of Horus, Occupier of the Throne of Egypt, son of Sneferu, Caretaker of the Land, do come before you in peace. I come with news to warm the hearts of all Egyptians, news that will give praise and honor to all the Neters."

Poised and confident, Khufu continued. "This day marks the beginning of a great undertaking. Many have seen the gathering of the army of workers. Your fellow countrymen from the North and the South have begun to uncover the Stone Head of the Desert from the sands that have imprisoned it. These sands have hidden Horakti from the eyes of Egypt far too long. The time has come for this monument to oversee the eastern horizon."

A cheer rose from the throngs who could hear Khufu's words. The king paused to savor the moment and for his words to spread. Pharaoh collected his thoughts for his next pronouncement. Taking a deep breath, and feeling his pride and the power of the Neters flowing through him, he spoke.

"Our history is long and glorious, with victory over our enemies, poverty, famine, and, by the grace of Mother Nile, over the desert and the domain of Seth. All our victories have been bestowed upon us by the venerable Gods."

Khufu had to stop speaking as a roar went up from the crowd.

"Hail to the Star Gods. Praise to the Mighty Ones," the sea of voices called out over and over again. When the shouts of praise finally quieted, Khufu went on.

"Our mothers and fathers, our priests and priestesses, our legends, our sacred texts—all have told us of the time long ago when the Star Gods came to Egypt in the First Time. Egypt has come to a time when the Sky Gods will come again. This has been foretold to the High Priest of the Temple of the Sun at Innu. It is known by your king, the High Priests of the temples throughout the land know it, and now you know it, sons and daughters of ancient Al-Kemi.

"The Star Gods have commanded the unearthing of the Sphinx, and this is begun. This is happening for a reason. The Star Gods are to return to Earth. Very soon, a sign of their coming will appear in the sky, and all Egypt awaits their arrival. These things that I have revealed are ordained by the Neters of Heaven and Earth.

Instead of a roar of praise and rejoicing, a respectful silence fell over the crowd. After several minutes had passed, the people began to react. Some fell to their knees to offer prayers to the Neters. Others formed circles and danced and sang, their arms over each other's shoulders in celebration.

Sokar watched. He felt the impact of the energy generated by Khufu's pronouncements. Khufu wasn't just their king; he was their god. Common people are the most devoted to the gods, and their devotion is honest, Sokar thought. To them, to "see" the Neters in a human made that human the most important, the most celebrated human on Earth. That human was a man, Khufu, but not he, Sokar. Khufu. He was the man-god; he was the one who would be sitting on the Throne of Egypt when the Star Gods returned.

"It should be me."

"What should be you, my master?" Kheti responded, his question helping him pretend that he did not already know what the answer was.

"I should be the king," Sokar said, the words coming out between clenched teeth.

Kheti chose not to respond. To agree would seem like pity for his master, and he did not want to run that risk. From the time Kheti was a boy he had looked up to Sokar, had wanted to be like him, to please him, be accepted by him. If Sokar expected Kheti to reply, it wasn't evident. Sokar commanded the servant to fetch a litter. He would be returning to Heliopolis at once. . . .

Word had reached the Sun Temple of Khufu's appearance before the people in Memphis. Couriers had been dispatched far and wide to carry the Pharaoh's message throughout Egypt. Meri-ib was relieved that it was over. Now all Egypt would know what he had been the first to know.

The High Priest had been puzzling over Sokar's lack of response when he was told of the Sphinx project and the Second Coming of the Star Gods. It was unusual, even abnormal. Sokar's silence was proof for Meri-ib that his co-ritualist had withheld comment to hide his feelings. Sokar saw what he had been cheated out of by not occupying the Throne. Meri-ib knew that Sokar felt that he should lead the Sphinx project, be the human who welcomed the Star Gods back to Earth, who received their wisdom. With all that, how would Sokar feel if he knew Khufu would be taken alive by the Sky Neters into the starry realm of Osiris?

Chapter Twenty-Six

An Ambivalent Encounter

Since Khufu's announcement, the mood in the classroom was one of sober open-mindedness and expectation. Taret's attention was now on the Sphinx.

"Egypt is a land of monuments, monuments that attest to the lengths that human beings have gone to honor the gods in appreciation for their gifts. They commemorate events such as the First Coming. Horakti, the Stone Head, is such a monument. It was over time the site of initiations, of countless elevations in consciousness achieved by priests and priestesses.

"Now His Venerable Majesty has told the people that the great Horakti will be freed from its desert prison so that its whole body will be revealed once more. My guidance tells me that when the task is completed, the Great Sphinx will again be a place of initiation, perhaps the very place where some of you will take your holy vows that will seal your commitment and fellowship with the Star Gods."

Initiation. The word triggered in Khem a future event in an hour between darkness and dawn which she would have to endure. The challenges, pleasures, and pains of the neophyte behind her, she had come to the Throne of Isis. Soft music from a thousand harps and the trills of countless flutes praised the Goddess. Khem stood at the feet of the High Priestess, waiting to have the Rod of Power passed to her. Then the vision faded. The vision convinced Khem that she had foreseen a future moment of triumph and glory, and knowing this would sustain her through times of darkness ahead.

"Initiations take place in temples and pyramids, as well as in many sacred monuments in our land," Taret was saying. "In these structures one experiences elevation into the higher levels of consciousness because these places hold the divine energy. This energy is a living substance, enlivened by the soul of the initiates who shed it in sacrifice to Geb, the Spirit of the Earth. It is not adversely affected by time, and has been passed on from one initiate to another. The Great Stone Head of the Desert is endowed with this substance. The Head is not imprisoned by the desert. It is merely preserved there for the time when initiates will once again stand at its feet and take the vows that will secure them a place in the hierarchy of adepts who have lived throughout time.

"As I have learned that Pharaoh has declared the Stone Head be uncovered, I have remembered the many times I have seen it in visions and dreams. It is gigantic. Its body is that of a lion, its head a man; an eternal god has watched Egypt change. The Sphinx has been worshipped and feared, honorably associated with the original god, Atum-Ra. It has also been called by some the 'Father of Terror.'

"Remember, the monuments correspond to stars and are the terrestrial counterparts of the stars. The question is: What stars are relevant to the Sphinx? This is an important question, especially in light of my statement that the Star Gods came to Earth from the East. The Sphinx, ever-watchful of the stars in that direction, fixes its eyes on the constellation Leo, the Lion, which once marked the spring equinox.

"There are inscriptions in the sacred texts that attest to this truth. In the heart of the star lion lies a powerful star. It is the heart of the lion and humanity alike. This great star is written of as the House of the Sun, Regulus, the Star of Kings. This is a clue to the sacredness and power of Innu, our city of Heliopolis, home of the earthly House of the Sun, our blessed Temple. The Star Gods came *here*, to *this* place, and it is to Heliopolis they will return, from Regulus, Heart of the Lion."

Hearing this, Khem knew she would never again look at the stars the same. They were no longer mere lights twinkling in the night. They were the "homes" of her ancestors. The stars were her *ancestors*, she was a daughter of the Star Gods. She had only seen herself as a part of a human family, with parents and grandparents before them. She loved them and they loved her. They protected and supported her. Little had she thought that the same was true of the Star Gods. So when it came to ancestry, she now had to include her celestial ancestors, and extend herself beyond Earth and reach out to the stars as her family. I am a child of the universe, she thought. That sent a chill through her followed by a wave of warmth, and a deep sense of belonging. She was a Star Daughter.

The class over, Khem asked Sheshat if she might speak with her. The scribe complied, and the two stepped out into the hallway.

"I do not know if you are aware of it or not, but Tiye and I are studying with Ani. We are studying magic."

Sheshat's expression told the young woman she knew.

"We are doing well with our lessons. Ani is a very good teacher."

"Yes," Sheshat injected with a smile. "Ani is a fine teacher and a highly skilled *hekau*. You and Tiye are indeed fortunate."

"Ani has given me an assignment, Lady Sheshat, and I need your help."

"How can I help you?" Sheshat asked, her gracious tone putting Khem at ease.

"I must learn to write and read better. Will you teach me? Ani said I should ask you."

A wide smile came across Sheshat's face. "Of course I will teach you. When would you like to begin?"

Khem was so relieved she bowed to the scribe. "Oh, thank you, thank you. I am most grateful."

"I am pleased to be of help to you, my Star Sister. Suppose you meet with me in my quarters after the noon meal tomorrow. That is a good time, yes?"

"Yes," Khem replied. "I will be there."

When the two parted company, Khem looked around for Tiye, but there was no sign of the Nubian. She thought that curious. As a rule, the two would freshen up in Khem's room before going to the afternoon lesson with Ani. Tiye must have decided to leave so Khem could speak to Sheshat in private. She would see Tiye at lesson time. She also remembered that this was the night that Tiye was to spend in the dream clinic. When Khem and Bast reached Ani's quarters, there was still no sign of Tiye. She was starting to get worried when she heard voices. Turning toward the sound, Khem saw Tiye come towards her.

"Where have you been? I missed seeing you after class."

Her tone was more demanding of a response than she had intended, but Khem had been more anxious than she realized and she came across as if she was agitated.

Tiye picked up on the tone. Her black eyes flashing, she snapped.

"I've been tending to my business!"

Khem realized that she had offended, perhaps embarrassed, Tiye, and tried to backtrack on her comment.

"I am sorry. I did not mean to interfere. I was just worried when I did not see you."

Khem and Tiye entered Ani's foyer and waited while her house steward notified his mistress of their presence. The mood between the two friends was stressed and neither spoke.

The house steward bade them go into Ani's study. When they had taken their place on a floor cushion, and Khem had managed to convince Bast to lie down beside her, Ani came in. The priestess sat down and pulled a short-legged table in front of her; then she reached into a jeweled box beside the table and pulled out a faience figurine about six inches in length, and placed it on the table. "This is a dream *ushabti*. Take a good look at it, especially you, Tiye. You will spend much time making these in the future."

Tiye focused on the greenish-colored figure. It looked like Ani. Khem leaned forward and studied it, causing the Nubian to flinch slightly when their arms touched. Ani noticed the tension between the two.

"The negative feelings between you must be cleared up before we go any further." Ani left the room without saying anything else, leaving Khem and Tiye alone. That action made the girls realize that they had broken a basic rule of magic by allowing a negative mood to cast a pall over teacher-student interaction. Of course such could adversely influence the clarity and purity of the information received. Ani's purpose was to give the apprentices time to balance out their differences.

The air was thick and warm in the small room. At first, Khem and Tiye said nothing. After a few minutes passed, Khem said sheepishly, "I am sorry if I sounded abrupt with you, Tiye. I was wondering where you had gone. I was worried."

Tiye softened a bit. She didn't look at Khem at first, until she realized that she could not deny her friend's concern was genuine. Khem had become her closest friend and ally. It was not worth putting their relationship in jeopardy over something about which she could now hardly remember why she had taken offense. "I am sorry too. I reacted like a child. Forgive me."

Ani came back. Seating herself again, she called their attention to the tiny figure on the table.

"Although the subject of amulets is mostly for you, Tiye, it is important that both of you have knowledge of this most common aspect of magic. They are a necessity in magic, for amulets are made for protection. This is a protection amulet I have had since I was born. An old *heka* woman in Hermopolis gave it to my mother to save for me. It is a *mekt*. All protection amulets are called mekt amulets. Those that bestow desirable qualities such as wealth and good health are called *wedjats*. You have a gift for making *wedjats*, Tiye, especially ones that resolve a crisis.

"Your skill, any magical ability, comes with a responsibility. There are times when the amulet-maker must deal with the demons that invade a person's mind when they are sleeping, causing nightmares and attacks. Demons are most powerful at night. Amulet-makers must deal with spirits sent by black magicians to cause harm and terrors. So, though amulets may be common, their makers are extraordinary men and women who must have great magical knowledge and skill. Amulets can be made from natural things like cowrie shells, wood, rocks, pebbles from Mother Nile, animal claws, bird talons, herbs, roots, and many other things.

"You have an affinity for another kind of amulet-making, Tiye. There are no lessons that can teach you how to make these. You simply do them and this activates the natural energy within you that lies coiled like a serpent in your mind.

"Another amulet is fashioned in the image of deities. These are not the most benevolent of divinities such as are ones worshipped in the temples, but those who possess the power to attack and defend. The wearers of these amulets have the benefits of the fiercest of the deities. Let me give you an example.

"Taweret, the hippopotamus goddess, has been used as an amulet for a longer time than almost any other. Her name means 'the Great One,' a name meant to pacify her as much as it is to define her power. Other fierce deities include Anubis, who has command of an army of messenger demons and who is a primary enforcer of curses. There is Bes, often associated with the power of the breath of life. Such deities must be confronted by the one who makes amulets in their image. You must be willing to create a harmonious relationship with them. This can never be done if there is fear in your mind and heart, Tiye. Never."

If Tiye had ever felt the need for a mother to embrace her, it was now. A woman she respected was telling her she was a natural-born magician with powers that would allow her to interact with the Neters. Yet many of these Neters were formidable, even caustic beings, feared by all. But fear she could not if she was to be an effective magician.

As if she knew Tiye's thoughts, Ani added, "You must always remember, my Star Sister, you are not alone, and you will not do your work alone. You shall invoke the power and protection of the gods you worship, but even the fiercest among them will be your allies. All you must do is love and respect the gods and goddesses. Do not fear them, but adore them, and they will walk with you and do your bidding."

Tears welling in her eyes, Tiye hung her head and wept. Khem touched her friend's arm to comfort her. Ani took Tiye's face in her hands and looked into her eyes and spoke in the same voice she had used to coax her into the sacred pool on the night of her baptism. "I, Khaba, am always with you. Let the woman child in you shed your tears, and let the Star Daughter in you go forward and have no fear."

The words spoken, Ani released her hands from Tiye's face and turned to look at Khem, who was sitting quietly "You now know how heavily the responsibility of magic can weigh on the heart. But you must, both of you, keep in mind that though the burden may be heavy at times, the rewards are great. They are benefits that come from a deep and abiding commitment to our beliefs, gifts from the gods."

Chapter Twenty-Seven

A Night in the Dream Temple

The dream room was small compared with most of the others in the House of Life, the educational part of the Temple, Tiye discovered. The outer room was light blue, with images painted halfway up the walls of white lotus plants growing along the banks of the Nile. On a highly polished tile floor, palms in massive clay pots cast shadows on the soft brightness of the chamber.

The sleep chamber was a stark contrast to the outer room. Its walls were dark blue, its high ceiling painted with hundreds of white stars. Gauzelike linen drapes strung on long, carved wooden rods suspended from holes bored into the walls on either side of the chamber made it possible to partition off the sections in which people slept. The beds were cots with white linens and a wooden headrest carved with protection symbols. A small anteroom housed herbal and magical remedies used by Ani and her attendants.

An attendant escorted Tiye into a dressing room and there Tiye changed into an ankle-length loose-fitting gown. Tiye was led to a small area with a bed and night table. It was partitioned off from the rest of the dark room. This was where she would sleep. Before retiring, however, she would join others in the inner chamber to hear soothing music and sip an herbal tea to help relax them for sleep.

Tiye sat on a low stool and waited.

After a few minutes had passed, Ani came into the room and sat down. A servant girl brought in the herbal brew and poured it into a small cup, giving it to Tiye. Tiye took a sip of the sweet-tasting liquid.

"I am awaiting the arrival of Taret," she said. "She will also be spending the night here."

The fact that the High Priestess was going to spend the night in the dream temple would add to the energy of the experience and was an indication to Tiye that the important matters at hand had also prompted Taret to seek the guidance of a dream.

"As soon as Taret comes and is changed and made comfortable, she will join you. Until then, please, relax," Ani said, then left, disappearing into one of the anterooms.

A young woman came in, set up a harp, and began playing. Taret entered the room soon after. Tiye felt that she was somehow different, less imposing now, a woman like any other, here for her own reasons.

The ambiance of the sleep room was relaxing and Tiye found it uplifting. In their conversation Abydos came up too. Taret told of a journey she had taken there to the Temple of Osiris, where she had known a prophet involved with calendar-making. His name was Amen-tep; his wife, Neith—named for the great goddess—had been a priestess of Hathor. Elderly when she met them, the couple had influenced Taret's decision to return to Heliopolis and enter Temple life.

The chatter and herbal drink made Tiye drowsy. Before long, Ani came in, accompanied by two servants, one female and one male. The Dream Priestess indicated that since the sun was now setting, it was time for the sleepers to retire for the night. The servants would assist in getting the beds ready and provide whatever other services Ani might require as she monitored the sleepers.

One servant pulled the linen drapes shut to partition off the small area as Tiye settled into her bed. The air had cooled, and the bed was comfortable. All Tiye could think about was how unnatural it was to be sleeping somewhere other than in her own bed or in Khem's room. To sleep for the purpose of dreaming seemed contrived, she thought. She had always told her dreams to Khaba, who had taught her of their importance. What if she did not dream at all? What would that mean? She wished Khem was spending the night here too. She had come to depend on her as a confidant and best friend.

Tiye's last thoughts before falling asleep were of Khaba. The herbs had relaxed her so that her waking thoughts carried her quickly into the dream world. Her dream vessel floated out of her body and awoke in the midst of the village where she had grown up. It was midafternoon, and children were playing in the dusty street in front of a small adobelike villa. One of the girls was her. Suddenly, Tiye was no longer aware of floating above the scene. Rather, she *became* the little girl playing with a kid goat. An old woman with stooped shoulders came out of the house. She walked with a limp, leaning on a cane.

The old woman was Khaba. She had come out to sit in the warm sun and watch her adopted daughter play. When she saw Khaba, the woman started to walk towards her and transformed into a beautiful young woman. A bright, shining aura shone around her that put off a warm glow the child could feel on her skin. The woman faded and Tiye once again floated above the scene, then slipped into dreamless sleep.

When morning came, Tiye awoke to a buzz of activity in the sleep room. Girls were serving cups of milk and bowls of stewed figs, while valets assisted with the morning toilet and bath. When the personal matters were dealt with and breakfast over, the sleepers were invited to join Ani in the outer room, one at a time, to tell her their dreams. A scribe would write it down and Ani would give an interpretation.

The prophetic nature of dreams was a given. Ani had trained for many years to focus her intuition to unlock the meanings of dreams. She knew the gods inspired all dreams, yet ordinary people, even some priests and priestesses, could not figure them out. Dream priestesses could; they were mediators between the dreamer and her god. Dream interpreters had powers which were greatly enhanced by being a master of a dream's secret signs. Since these masters were also magicians, they could perform spells for the dreamer if a dream boded ill. All this involved a special relationship with Isis, guardian of magical words and spells. Where a dream foretold disaster, the dreamer was sometimes encouraged to make a journey to a temple dedicated to Isis to request the goddess's intervention.

"Now, Tiye," Ani said, when the Nubian was led in. "Please tell me, what did you dream?" After Tiye related the dream, Ani said, "That is all you can remember because the dream ended. Do you have memories of Khaba?"

"Yes."

"You remember what she looked like while she was alive, don't you? Well, now you have a new memory, of how she *really* looks, for now you have seen Khaba's soul. The woman you saw, that was Khaba, and so was the old lady. One was the physical Khaba, the one you knew and loved. The other was the *real* Khaba, the Khaba who has always been and will always be, the soul that has lived in all her human lives, the last being as a Nubian shaman."

Tiye was stunned. "Khaba . . . the beautiful, young woman was Khaba?"

"Yes. She is no longer trapped in a body filled with pain. She is no longer lame. She is free, Tiye. You must let her be free. You must no longer see her as she was as a human, but see her as she really is, for what she is now. She has revealed herself to you in your dream so you will know her. In her soul body she will work with you as your magical assistant and guide you when you make amulets and do your other magical works. This way, she will be able to carry on her own initiatory work in the Afterlife.

"Go now, Tiye, and think carefully about what has occurred here. Alter the image you have always had of Khaba so that you will become accustomed to seeing her as she is. I am certain you will be seeing her, and feeling closer to her than ever before. I will see you again soon."

Tiye left and Ani and Taret were alone. Because she was High Priestess of the Temple of the Sun, Taret's dreams were sacred. They could be prophecies that affected all of Egypt. "You do well, Ani. Your manner puts one at ease," Taret said teasingly.

"Thank you, mistress Taret," Ani replied with a smile. "Now, are you ready to tell me of your dream?"

Leaning forward in her chair, Taret looked into Ani's eyes. "It was strange. I was walking along the riverbank among the lotus and papyrus when I came upon a man standing waist-deep in the Nile. He was a large man for an Egyptian, but an Egyptian he was, even though I could not see his face. He wore a mask of gold made in the image of Khufu. The masked man was praying to Horus in his guise as avenger. I could hear his thoughts. He was praying for revenge."

"Is that all you saw?" Ani inquired.

"No. There was one thing more. While I was watching, the man turned into a hawk and with great, wide wings flew out of the water and disappeared into the Sun."

Ani pondered what Taret had said. She knew that the High Priestess was herself adept at understanding dreams, and that surely she had ideas about what her dream meant. Yet she also knew how difficult it is for a person to interpret her own dreams. "The symbol of the Nile is important. When you think about all that has been foretold regarding the unearthing of the Stone Head, the Second Coming of the Star Gods, the appearance of the comet—all this is centered on Inundation. And water represents the magical world and the star world. However, I think that the Nile's primary meaning here is to denote a time.

"The man up to his waist in the water means half of his body is hidden. His member, the symbol of his power, is hidden. This denotes a secretive person, a man who has great magical powers, more than others realize. There is a man who wishes to be seen as a king, who mimics the king, who sees himself as king, and not as who he is. He is a learned and skilled individual close to Horus the Avenger. One does not seek to avenge anything but what one perceives to be a wrong, real or imagined. This man is a shape-shifter; his counterpart is a hawk."

The image of Sokar came into Ani's mind. She remembered seeing him with the hawk at the meeting where Taret had allowed Nut to speak about the comet.

"I think your dream foretells of a would-be usurper of the Throne of Egypt. Yes, I am sure that is it. It will put you in danger if the identity of this man becomes known to you or anyone else, so your dream should be kept secret."

Chapter Twenty-Eight

Predictions from the Chief Astrologer

Meri-ib had received word that Lucius, the chief astrologer, would be coming to Heliopolis that afternoon. What piqued his curiosity was that Lucius was sent by Khufu with instructions that Meri-ib should "read between the lines" of the astronomer's report and apply the information he heard to the events of the meeting with Shemshu-Hor and the Second Coming.

Khufu had sent for his chief astrologer just after making his announcement of the Second Coming and the Sphinx project. Aside from the usual briefing on celestial events, star motions, and other calendar affairs, he needed Lucius's interpretation of the celestial events surrounding the beginning of Inundation, especially the comet.

Meri-ib had not spoken to Khufu through courier or otherwise since their meeting. Word of Pharaoh's announcement had reached him, and he was confident everything was proceeding as planned. What troubled him was the appearance of the hawk on the windowsill of his study. He could not shake the feeling that the bird was a spirit or omen. His connection to the Neters and his prayers seemed to lack their usual power and he felt drained.

When the chief astrologer arrived he was escorted straight to Meri-ib's study, where the High Priest was examining funerary texts.

"Welcome, Lucius," Meri-ib greeted the astrologist.

"And you, Meri-ib, High Priest of the Temple of the Sun and Keeper of the secrets of the heavens. It is good to see you looking so well."

"Well? Thank you, Lucius, but I don't feel so well."

"Oh, are you ill, Master Meri-ib?"

"No, I am not ill, at least not physically." Fearing his somber mood would lead to further questions, Meri-ib shrugged off his remarks. "I am just tired, that's all."

"I see. That is understandable, what with everything that is going on these days."

"Yes, what with all that is going on," Meri-ib commented, and changed the subject. Knowing full well that the Pharaoh had sent him, Meri-ib still asked, "Tell me, Lucius, what brings you to Heliopolis?"

"The time of Inundation approaches, your worship, by the grace of the Neters. I come to the Holy City to await the rising of the Great Star and greet the first of the flood waters when they arrive."

The conversation reminded both men that Inundation was an annual miracle of mercy. Egypt depended in countless ways upon the flooding of Mother Nile. The coming of the floodwaters to the parched land was a time of the promise of plenty and abundance to come. Egyptians never witnessed a more exhilarating sight, or one that stirred more confidence in the Creator than the rise of the Nile. Day by day, night by night, the turbid waters sweep onwards, diffusing life and joy into the land, turning a wilderness of desert into green fields of corn, yielding innumerable pomegranate blossoms, and filling the air with the fragrance of roses, oranges, and sweet-scented flowers.

The beginning of the rise is the time of green water, the color resulting from the upsurge of slimy, brackish water and algae that causes the river to lose its clearness, Meri-ib reflected. Then, a few days later, the water becomes turbid, red, transformed into a seeming river of blood. The flood usually reaches the Delta region by June but by September, it has begun to decline. By winter, the river is once more blue and within its banks.

"The predawn rise of Sothis is an important event, Meri-ib. This year it will be accompanied by the appearance of a comet. As I figure it, the comet will come from the east through the Lion. It is correct to relate the comet's coming with the unearthing of the Stone Head, as I confirm this. The comet, which always heralds a significant event, is also a sign this time of the Second Coming of the Star Gods. These are all good things, but according to tradition as noted in the sacred texts, the coming of a comet is not an omen of something good. It foretells the fall of a leader, our leader."

"Khufu? Khufu will fall?" Meri-ib exclaimed. How could I have overlooked this? It was clear now. This was why he had so strongly suspected someone, most likely Sokar, might take advantage of the occasion to overthrow the king. That was why he had been reluctant to allow Sokar to serve as co-ritualist. The comet was an omen of mutiny! Thank the Neters that Lucius had given him a reason to confirm his suspicions. He would have to take measures to assure the sanctity of the Second Coming and the stability of the Throne of Egypt. Meri-ib knew a battle lay ahead, to be fought in the magical realms. It would have to be fought and won before it became a war in the world of men for the Throne.

"When do you expect the comet to first appear?" the High Priest inquired.

"Within two nights," Lucius replied.

"Then time is of the essence," Meri-ib muttered under his breath.

"Beg your pardon?" Lucius asked.

"Nothing. Never mind. I was just thinking to myself. But I do have a question. Am I to assume that you have reminded Khufu the comet is an ill omen?"

"Yes, of course. That is precisely why he sent me to inform you," Lucius replied.

Khufu had sent the chief astrologer as a way of letting Meri-ib know that their suspicions about Sokar were right, but without running the risk of trusting the information to a courier. Every security measure must be taken. To Meri-ib, those measures would be taken through magic. . . .

The workers at Giza were busy. Digging had begun. Khufu had decided it appropriate for him to make an appearance at the site as moral support for the workers and so he could see for himself what was being done. Word had been sent to Nemon that the royal entourage would arrive at noon.

Egyptians said that when Pharaoh appeared in public, the man-god should shine like the Sun when it rose from the horizon. Thus, the Pharaoh was expected to be surrounded by all the pomp and splendor worthy of a ruler. He would travel by land to the royal barque, and then board it for Giza, where he would be met and escorted to the site. A great tent would serve as a portable palace and a place for Khufu to receive guests, hold meetings, and accommodate his dining, resting, and sleeping. The massive tent would also contain an altar room with statues of Ptah, Sekhmet, and Nefertem, the trinity of the Memphis capital. Massive amounts of food would be transported to the temporary residence before Pharaoh ever left Memphis.

The entourage emerged from the palace, Khufu's litter preceded by a dozen guards. Seven priests carrying braziers of burning incense followed. All along the route to the Nile, the *fellahin* gathered to catch a glimpse of their beloved king. Khufu's train was magnificent. The wooden sedan chair was flanked on each side by two gilded lions in stride. The poles that held the seat rested on the shoulders of eight courtiers. Two fan bearers walked alongside, fanning the king and waving bouquets near his head to make sure that the air around the god-man smelled sweet. This procession was significant because Khufu's chief wife, Meritates, and three of their seven sons, were traveling with him. The royal family was being carried on an equally splendid litter immediately behind the king.

Khufu was dressed in full royal regalia. His short skirt was covered by an elegant golden, pleated robe. His hair and beard had been shaved. The customary artificial beard was strapped to his chin, and a headdress fell over his shoulders in two lappets. The uraeus, the symbol of royalty, graced the front of the headdress, while the material that made the back was twisted together behind his head in a pigtail. The golden serpent reared on the king's brow to threaten his enemies, just as it had done to the enemies of Ra.

When the entourage reached the Nile, they boarded the boat, *Star of the Two Countries.* The large vessel was long and flat, made of yellow pine; the fore and aft were dark blue with a gilded lion head at the prow. A large cabin, its sides draped with plaited matting, provided shade and comfort for the travelers. Standing oarsmen steered while dozens of seated ones provided the power to move the boat. Smaller vessels carried the rest of the entourage. The flotilla was a magnificent sight.

Nemon was at the dock awaiting Khufu. "Welcome, Lord of Both Countries, Ruler of Egypt, the Chosen of Ra, Horus, Lord of the Palace. Welcome to Giza, Your Majesty." He bent down and kissed the top of Khufu's right foot. Pleasant greetings were also extended to the queen and the royal princes, who were escorted to the massive tent that would be their home for the next two days.

Nemon and his chief assistant, Men-ka-re, followed Khufu and his two generals to the meeting room in the tent, where they would be briefed on the project. As they passed by, workers fell to their knees in homage. The appearance of their glorious leader had the effect Khufu hoped for, which was to inspire the workers and secure their dedication to the project and loyalty to the Throne.

When the principals were inside the tent, they seated themselves comfortably on ebony chairs inlaid with ivory, whose feet were shaped like the paws of a lion. Several low stands held jugs of beer and wine and baskets of fruit and baked goods. Sipping date wine, Khufu and the officials listened while Nemon gave his report.

"I am happy to report that things are progressing on schedule, perhaps ahead of time. The men are motivated by more than the uncovering of an ancient monument. Word of the Second Coming of the Star Gods has spread like fire through a field of dry corn. I have never seen anything like it. There has been very little rowdiness, and few complaints about conditions, food, or anything else. It is as if there is an air of fear, positive fear, I would say.

"I swear to Your Majesty that I believe that the Star Gods themselves are working their magic for the success of this project. As for the digging, the sand is dry and powdery for several yards down. It may turn out to be that way more than halfway down. If I am right, with the number of men working, the project could be completed ahead of time."

That was good news. Khufu was inclined to agree with Nemon. The Star Gods seemingly had a hand in it. The next few days were critical to the project. The heat was becoming more intense. Many of the workers who had been recruited were farmers, and the flooding of the Nile was crucial to their preparations for planting. Delays would be unfortunate for all concerned, making Khufu willing to go to whatever lengths necessary to ensure a speedy end to the work.

Khufu's thoughts shifted to his dream of the temple he would build in the coming months. He was thinking about the symbol inlaid in gold on the altar, the *udjat*. He had not given the symbol much thought before, but it was making a strong impression on his mind now. The voices around him faded. By far the most popular of amulets, the *udjat*, the Eye of Horus, was the stylized eye of the falcon-headed god. Khufu had known the story of the *udjat* since he was a boy. A battle was fought to avenge the death of Horus's father Osiris, and Horus had his eye torn to pieces by his evil uncle, Seth. Just as Thoth had reassembled the pieces of Osiris's body, Horus's sight was regenerated. This regeneration was what made the *udjat* a popular amulet worn to insure good health.

Khufu, knew there was more to the symbol than its use as an amulet. The White Eye is the Sun, the *utchat;* the Black Eye is the Moon, the *mehit.* The meaning of the Two Eyes was an initiatory matter, part of kingship, and the ruler must gain control of it for it was the key to the king's function. He remembered something said to him after his vows at coronation. "May you gain control of the Eye of Horus and its lunar light. May you yearn for the waters that are in it. May you gain control of the power that streams from it."

He had never given the words much thought. They had been among the numerous pronouncements of blessings and "may yous" that were showered upon him at the time, so many he could not remember them all. He was in fact curious that he remembered this one now.

"Your Majesty? Did you hear what I said?" Nemon asked, interrupting Khufu's thoughts.

"Uh . . . no . . . I am sorry, Nemon. My mind was wandering," Khufu responded, embarrassed to have been caught not paying attention.

"Is there something the matter? Are you not feeling well?" Khufu's chief general, Shem-hotep, inquired, somewhat alarmed.

"No, no. I am fine. Just lost in my thoughts. Please, Nemon, repeat what you said."

"Yes, of course, Your Majesty. I was saying that the sand being dug from around the body of the monument is being taken to the base of the Stone Head, where it can be used for the foundation and mortar for future construction. Do you agree with this plan?

"Yes, yes, that is good."

Nemon knew that whatever was on the king's mind, it wasn't sand. He felt that it was time for him and the others to leave so that Khufu could have time alone. He beckoned to Her-bak, the chief mathematician, and Shem-hotep. "Come, let us go and inspect the site."

When they were gone, Khufu ordered his servants to see to it that he was not disturbed for an hour so he could rest. Lying back on his couch so he could stretch out his legs and relax, he thought again about the *udjat*. The coronation blessing equated the Eye of Horus with the Moon. May you gain control over the moonlight and the waters that are in it, of the rays that stream from it, it said. How does one gain control or possession of the Moon? To a common Egyptian, water means the Nile, but to an initiate, water is the element associated with the Duat.

The Duat. To the uninitiated, the Duat is the Otherworld, the Nether-world. To the priesthood, it is far more. To understand it, you must go beyond the Earth to the stars, in fact, even to a specific "address" in the sky, to a region that is the "Dwelling Place of Orion and Sirius on the banks of the Celestial River" to the cosmic Nile, that meandering waterway of light.

"That's it!" Khufu said aloud. "Water is the Eye of Horus in the great star way!"

Khufu felt on the verge of putting together the pieces of a puzzle. The part of the sky spoken of in the ancient texts has to do with the constella-tions Orion and Leo and the star Sirius. The Duat and the starry sky are related, Khufu realized. The doors, the star gates, that lead into the Duat are not open all the time. When closed, one can only get into the lower realms of the Duat, and not into the region of Osiris. So the Duat is open *only* at special times. When? Of course. At Inundation, at the rising of Sirius before the Sun.

There were still some things that puzzled him. What is the relationship between the Eye of Horus and the Moon? The Moon, like the water, is associated with the Duat. So the Eye of Horus is a magical instrument which gives one control over the astral forces and the star forces encountered in the subtle planes beyond the physical world, Khufu reflected.

That is the key to the star gate—the *eastern* star gate, he realized. It is the formula that tells the initiated when the star gate is open, when the Star Gods from Leo, Orion, and Sirius are sending their energy to Earth, when humans can "walk" into the sky to commune in the Duat with the star ancestors.

Star gates. Only initiates of the highest level knew about these openings between the physical and metaphysical worlds, the worlds of men and gods, and their locations in the heavens. He had traveled through these gates into other dimensions many times. This was why the Star Gods would come, could *only come*, at Inundation. Gaining control over the Eye of Horus would be a magical victory over the dark forces; one would then know how to "walk" into the domain of the Sky Gods. Perhaps this was what the wisest of the gods meant when he said Egypt was an image of heaven.

These discoveries put Khufu in a contemplative frame of mind. It was even a little depressing. He knew there was more, but what he had been able to put together thus far was enough to let him know he was doing the right thing as Egypt's ruler. There were clues that he now understood which told him that the Eye of Horus was the key to Egypt's future. It was about more than the Sun and Moon, was more than a powerful amulet.

The *udjat* was a kind of *consciousness*. The Eye of Ra, the Sun, was creative power coming from the Star Gods to Earth. The Eye of Seth, the Moon, was emotion which when uncontrolled could lead one to murder and destroy. So the Eye of Horus was a balance between love and hate, spirit and matter, darkness and light, the balance where magic took place. As a symbol, it was the consciousness of the initiate, rooted in matter but ever gazing upward to the highest spirit.

This was his predicament, he realized. He was, as king of Egypt, rooted in matter, but as an initiate, he was ever aspiring to the realm of the gods. Khufu knew he was about to go through a dark night of the soul. He didn't know when or how it would manifest. He felt the weight of his position. He had to force himself to turn away from fear and stay focused on ruling. He would give thoughts of his soul's journey no more attention now. He needed to talk, priest to priest, with Meri-ib, and what I would give to have another audience with Shemshu-Hor, he thought.

Chapter Twenty-Nine

Star Waves and Omens
of the Second Coming

Khem had learned that her brother, Atef, had spoken to Pepy, the chancellor of the instruction house, about enrolling in the school of scribes. At eighteen Atef was getting a late start, but Pepy had accepted him anyway. Atef had convinced him that he was intended for the profession of scribe. He would be under the tutelage of Pepy himself, a teacher who had the reputation for being a stern disciplinarian. Atef would live at the Temple in the boys' dormitory in the House of Instruction.

Khem had sensed her brother's eagerness to learn, as well as his apprehension. Temple life would be an adjustment for him from the life he was accustomed to in Abydos. Yet Atef was no stranger to hard work; becoming a scribe was just a different kind of labor. He would have to master the art of writing by copying passages from the sacred texts, as well as stories and poems. This would teach him to write and, in time, to develop his own style. He had come away from the meeting with Pepy full of ambition and with his first copybook.

Listening to Atef had inspired Khem. She was happy to have her brother close by. It made her feel more secure. The two siblings had talked about their parents and life in Abydos. She already knew about their father's new business partner, and was pleased to hear that was going well. Their mother was not faring as well. Bata had become depressed when Khem left home, even more so when she learned that both her children would be gone. Khem felt bad for her mother's suffering. She vowed she would travel to Abydos as soon as she could to visit with her and Rashid. . . .

Khem was waiting for Tiye in the classroom, anxious to hear about the dream temple, but that would have to wait until after class.

When Taret and Sheshat came in, the usual hush fell over the room. The High Priestess seemed preoccupied. Tiye guessed that Taret's dream experience might have revealed information that was now weighing heavily on her.

"You must all know by now that nothing and no one, not even the Neters, is all good or all evil," Taret said. "Good and evil dwell in all that exists. There are times when the good is more easily detected and stronger and is therefore given more expression outwardly. That person, thing, or place is judged good. If the negative is stronger and more apparent, then the person, place, or object is judged evil. I wish to speak about good and evil not from the perspective of being qualities within a human, object, or place. Rather, I wish to speak of them as currents of energy.

"The source of these currents is the stars. Good and evil define star waves. A star wave is a type of energy emitted by stars. There are stars whose waves are constructive or good, and stars whose radiations are destructive or evil. Either way, star waves affect Earth and all that lives here.

"Now think about this, Star Daughters. If there are both good and evil in all things, then all that exists is the recipient of star waves, positive and negative, constructive and destructive. This makes stars responsible for the dual nature of all things, including all life forms. Pure energy, star waves permeate the universe, crisscrossing it in waves constantly in motion.

"Star waves are explained, in a hidden manner, by way of certain of the personages of the gods and goddesses. These give them form, and personality, if you will, so that the uninitiated will understand their existence. Particular gods and goddesses are the counterpart of certain stars whose energy has the greatest effect on Egypt. I will discuss the god Seth, brother of Osiris, and the goddesses Isis and Nepthys, Nepthys also being Seth's wife. Seth is feared by many and his qualities or powers are clearly the reason."

Taret's mention of Seth struck a chord in Khem. Being from the South, she had known the evil god since childhood. She knew the story of how Geb, the Earth God, divided the land into two parts. One part, Lower or northern Egypt, he gave to Seth's nephew Horus; the other, Upper or southern Egypt, he gave to Seth. Each god ruled his own land justly; when the two parts of Egypt unified, the two continued to rule in peace. Sadly, this unity did not last. Their relationship lapsed into an irresolvable polarity. Horus became the most popular, causing Seth to become his jealous and vengeful mortal enemy. Khem's mother and grandmother had always told her that if she behaved badly, Seth would come after her!

"Seth is sometimes called the 'red god,'" Taret continued. "The *fellahin* believe that this name was given to the evil god because it represented the inhospitable desert to the east, but there was a deeper reason. You are familiar with the story of Seth, jealous of his good brother, Osiris. Seth tricked Osiris into climbing into a coffin. Seth murdered him and dumped the casket into the Nile. When Isis found her husband's body, Seth became angry and cut up the corpse and threw the pieces into the river, where he hoped they would be eaten by crocodiles, thus denying Osiris eternal life.

"These stories are horrid, and there are many more like them. They clearly link Seth with acts of evil and malevolence, deceitfulness, obsession for power, violence, murder, conflict, jealousy, dominion, envy—all the things that pit man against man, family member against family member, good against evil, darkness against light. Obviously, these are undesirable, negative traits. They are the manifestations of 'evil' star waves that emanate from evil stars, the 'Seth stars.'"

Taret's words surprised Khem. She had never thought of evil stars before. It made sense, though. Evil stars could be avoided. Understanding that their energy polarizes all that exists, and that through polarity, evolution occurs, was a breakthrough in Khem's understanding of reality.

"There are animals associated with Seth and evil traits," Taret continued. "These include the jackal, hyena, hippopotamus, boar, and leopard. These animals wreck crops, disturb flocks and herds, and sometimes humans. They typify the powers of evil and darkness and the Lower World. Now, listen to my words very carefully. The Seth stars are Capella, Alpha Ursae Majoris, Phact, Antares, and Alpha Centauri. Four constellations are Seth constellations: the Thigh (Ursa Major), Hippopotamus (Draco), the Scorpion, and the Bull.

"At this point, I have simply pointed out a few stars. There are more, but these have the greatest effect upon humanity at this time. Understanding the energy emitted by these is imperative, so let me discuss one in detail, so you will know what a Seth star is. I will speak about the Scorpion constellation and Antares.

"The Scorpion is a furnace of Seth energy. Like the scorpion, it can have deadly power. This does not mean that the scorpion is a contemptible creature. It means that if you do not *respect* its destructive power, it will fill you with its venom and you will suffer and quite possibly die. How can such venom be handled other than respecting that it exists? Suppose an enemy stalks you, but sees scorpions surround you, or perhaps a large one sits on your head. Your enemy will be distracted from doing you harm and be frightened away. Thus the scorpion is your guardian who protects you from your enemy. This is precisely why our beloved goddess Isis has an intimate relationship with the scorpion. It guards her and, at the same time, it is her weapon.

"Now consider the goddess Selket, the scorpion goddess. Her qualities tell about the power of evil. She protects the dead. She possesses the power of the heat of the Sun and you know what damage such heat can do. Within the Scorpion constellation, the great red fire Antares is the most powerful of all Seth stars. Like Seth, it too is red; like the fire of the Sun, it is red. Evil, like the Scorpion and the Sun, has a fiery nature, as do Isis, Selket, Seth, Anubis, and other of the Neters. Like the scorpion, evil is powerful and must be responded to and handled with caution.

"Good is sacred. It is as powerful as evil. Good creates, constructs, heals, and repairs. Good begets life; evil begets death. Both are necessary if evolution is to occur, for time to exist, and for change to be the sole constant in the cosmos. Just as there are Seth stars, there are those that generate positive power. An example is the faint northern star Ma'at, which has long been associated with the beloved Ptah. So we could say that good stars are Ptah stars. In his hands Ptah holds the *was* scepter, the *djed*, and the ankh, all symbols of control, stability, and life. These are qualities of good. The Memphis priesthood holds Ptah in esteem as the original creator who existed before primal chaos. By an outpouring of love, Ptah brought chaos, Nun, and Nunet, his feminine counterpart, into being. Nun and Nunet gave birth to Atum, the Heart of Ptah. Such is the nature of good. Through good, all else comes into being.

"Sirius is a Ptah star, and so is our sun. Learn to recognize the differences between good and evil. Learn of their similarities, for there are many. Good can disguise itself as evil, and evil as good. The uninitiated cannot be expected to know these truths, which is why they view good and evil as completely different, and treat one as desirable, the other not. This is why people wage a never-ending battle to overcome evil, but it is a war that will never, cannot ever, be won. Initiates learn to live in harmony with both. This is the difference between the common human and a magician. So be it."

Khem had seen these stars all her life. They were all beautiful, luminous "friends" she had looked up at and talked to as long as she could remember. She had never thought of them as bad. Nor did she ever think the evil she sometimes sensed inside her was due to the intrusion of Seth star energy. It was unnerving. It made Khem face the possibility of evil in herself, in everyone and everything. There were people she didn't want to think of as having evil in them. She certainly didn't want to think of herself as evil, but the way Taret explained it, a part of her was evil, and so was a part of everything and everyone she knew.

Khem realized that Taret and Sheshat had gone, as had most of the apprentices. Tiye sat next to Bast, rubbing the napping cat's head. "I didn't realize you were waiting for me. I am sorry. I got lost in my thoughts," Khem said, collecting herself. The lioness, now wide-awake, slapped her paws at Tiye playfully, trying to entice her into a round of roughhousing. Even though the cub had grown considerably, she was still a kitten who took advantage of every opportunity to play.

As the two entered the courtyard, Khem was anxious to hear about Tiye's night in the dream room. "You must be very happy to have spent that dreaming time with Khaba," Khem said. Sometimes she envied her friend's relationship with her mentor. Even though Khaba was dead, the bond between her and Tiye was very much alive. Khem had never experienced that kind of relationship, not even with her mother. She was getting a taste of it with Tiye. She liked the warm, secure feeling it gave her.

"It was good, yes. You should have seen Khaba in her soul body. She was beautiful. I cannot find words. I have to see Khaba differently now, but it will be hard. I only knew her one way."

Sokar was angry. He was prepared to go into the city to meet with one of Khufu's generals when he received word that their meeting was off. Shem-hotep was with the royal court at Giza. Sokar had known Shem-hotep for a long time. His father before him had been one of Sneferu's officials, which resulted in his family's spending a lot of time at the palace when Sokar was growing up. He knew Shem-hotep to be hotheaded, arrogant, and hungry for position and power. He was sure that the man did not become a general at such a young age without stepping over any number of men. This was what led Sokar to believe Shem-hotep would be a good ally to whoever could best serve his purposes of gaining power. That was what Sokar needed, an ally and insider. He knew Shem-hotep's kind for he had been around politicians all his life.

Time was of the essence, too. Egypt was on the brink of one of its most significant times. The Stone Head was being restored to its splendor; the Star Gods were returning. The country's leader must be strong, worthy of claiming the knowledge the Star Gods would impart. That would restore the power the kingship had lost to the priesthood. Becoming a priest was how Sokar had been able to maintain a position in society in a way more politically beneficial than merely being in the royal family.

So he must find out when Shem-hotep would be returning to Memphis, and make arrangements to meet. He would use the excuse that he had heard rumors that the villages with his vineyards in the northern Delta had been raided. Generals were always on guard against this kind of threat. . . .

Back in Memphis, Khufu needed to consult Lucius, the court astrologer, again. Something about the comet was troubling him. Egypt might be a chosen place, selected by the gods as their temple on Earth, Khufu reflected, but he had to know everything that was going on in the heavens all the time, and for that he looked to Nebseni. But he also had to know what it all *meant.* That was Lucius's talent.

Lucius entered the Throne Room. The old astrologer had served Khufu's father and had always exhibited a deep loyalty to the Throne. He was a man who looked and acted much younger than his years. He had trained in the South at the Osiris Temple many years before, and had worked closely with the royal family since coming to the capital city a quarter of a century before. Khufu had a high regard for him, but found him flamboyant and a bit pompous. Lucius wore a linen skirt, a leopard skin stole draped across his shoulders. Many priests wore skins, but this one was bigger than most. Its paws hung down to his ankles.

"Greetings, Your Majesty, Khufu, King of Two Worlds. I am honored to be in your presence," Lucius said, bowing deeply. "Heaven make a star of you."

"I welcome you, Lucius. Ra has made many journeys through the Underworld since we last spoke. Please, make yourself comfortable," Khufu said. "The heavens show us many wonders, but sometimes, the wonders confound even the most brilliant among us. I know Inundation is upon us, that the Great Star and the Sun will soon release their most potent powers upon the Great River, that all will be revived and reborn from Seth's deadly grasp. These things I understand."

"Yes, Your Majesty. Osiris is a good god. He assures life, health, and fertility for the physical realm," Lucius said. "Soon, Osiris will appear in the southern sky in the constellation Orion, and Isis will show herself in the rising of Sirius just afterwards. She will shed her tears for her stricken mate so that the emaciated Nile will flow in abundance. The cycle of life will turn once again, the gift of the Neters to all Egyptians."

"This year the stars will be accompanied by a visitor," Khufu said.

"I take it that you are referring to the comet, my Lord King?"

"Yes, the comet. I have known about it for some time. I am also aware of the speaking by the High Priestess of Heliopolis, and I have seen the celestial interloper in a dream. I wish to know your interpretation of the meaning of its presence."

"Yes, I see, my lord. I thought as much. Comets are strange. They never come into sight without reason."

"Strange? They come for a reason? *What* reason, Lucius?"

"I am sorry, Your Majesty. I did not mean to avoid your questions. I was just thinking out loud to myself. I was trained by a master stargazer who was asked the same question by another king of Egypt a long time ago when a comet appeared. My mentor, Rama-se, spent much time pondering and divining. The answers always came. A comet is a living being, like a star. It has a life and a power of its own. It houses a higher, greater being whose period of dwelling in heaven is over and who is in its descent once more to Earth."

Eyebrows raised in response to that. Khufu spoke. "So you are saying that the comet is a sign of the Second Coming?"

"Yes, exactly, my lord king."

"And nothing more? You are certain of this?"

"My lord, begging your pardon, but I do not know of anything more profound than the Second Coming of the Star Gods."

"No. No, Lucius, you misunderstand me. I trust what you have said. A sign would surely herald such an event. I suppose I was wondering¾"

"You are wondering if the comet foretells a threat to your reign as king of Egypt."

Taken aback by the astrologer's candidness, Khufu walked to the window, silently looking out over the desert. Then he turned to face Lucius again. "Yes. That is what I was thinking." For a fleeting moment he felt vulnerable and feared he would appear weak in his advisor's eyes.

"There have been those who have interpreted a flaming star in that way, my lord. And perhaps they were right in doing so for *that* king at *that* time under the prevailing circumstances. I see no reason to follow that interpretation blindly now."

"You honor its general validity, but see no reason why it should apply to me now?"

"It is an omen of the Second Coming, first and foremost. However, in light of past interpretations, there is room for caution regarding Your Majesty's claim, a rightful one, to the Throne. Besides, this is an auspicious time in Egypt's history and the power of the Throne surely is appealing to any would-be usurpers. You would be wise to take all precautions, in my humble opinion."

The news was bittersweet. Usurpers were a constant threat to the Throne.

"Yet there are more important things to be concerned about now, my lord king, things that are a cause for all Egyptians to celebrate. It is all mapped out in the stars."

"What do you mean?"

"The star Sirius, the Great Provider, is about to rise. The celestial Sphinx and the comet will soon appear, all these things at the same time, all preceding the flood waters that will bring renewed life to Egypt. As always, Nun receives the impulse of the celestial influences. Nun has always existed and always will, my lord, before the sky or Earth or the gods. The Second Coming is preordained. It will happen. Nun has received the impulse. Remember that. Nothing and no one can undo what the Neters ordain. You must trust that Egypt is in good and capable hands. If you must deal with a usurper, so be it. Man must always deal with man. You are king, and king you will continue to be, unless your fear drives you from the Throne."

Chapter Thirty

Strategy for Kingship

Sokar was restless. He had been waiting for Shem-hotep for over an hour. He was reasonably sure that Khufu's general was going to be easy to win over to his scheme to become king of Egypt. But the longer he waited, the more he entertained thoughts of whether he was doing the right thing by revealing his plan to the general. Was he telling a secret to a man who would go straight to Khufu? Time was pressing, so trusting Shem-hotep was worth the risk.

Looking at the hawk sitting on the ebony perch in the corner of the room, Sokar was reminded of how long it had been since he had connected with his familiar. Whenever he allowed his thoughts to be consumed by his life in the world, anger and resentment ruled him and caused him to neglect his spiritual life. He could be a priest and function in the material world, but a magician in the physical world he could be only by employing his magical skills to fulfill his destiny to be king.

How he hated his father Sneferu, even more than Khufu. He, Sokar, was stronger and wiser than Khufu; he was determined to prove it to Egypt. As Pharaoh, he alone would possess the new wisdom the Star Gods brought. Priests and prophets would come to him for counsel. He alone would dictate additions to the sacred texts, and they would bear his name. He alone would rule the world because of what he knew, and that would guarantee him immortality.

Sokar's thoughts locked him into a hypnotic frame of mind. Standing by the hawk, he locked his eyes with the bird's and both were caught in a psychic bond. Images began to appear in the hawk's dilated pupils as Sokar entered deeper into trance. He saw himself kneeling in front of a huge statue of Horus. The Double Crown of the Two Lands was being placed on his head. His face was serene, for he was a man who had fulfilled his destiny. Sokar was enraptured, floating out of his body, euphoric.

Kheti entered the room and Horus blinked, breaking the spell. "Master, your caller has arrived."

Taking a deep breath, Sokar centered himself. He did not want to appear uncomposed. "Send him in, Kheti. And make sure there is plenty of cool refreshment and that we are not disturbed."

"Yes, my master."

Shem-hotep came in with the confidence one expects of a general. His regal apparel consisted of a dress from the chest to ankles, held by a metal clasp behind his neck. His head was shaven, and he wore an embroidered necklet and gold armband and had anklets on each leg.

"Shem-hotep, welcome," Sokar said. He did not want to give the impression that this was a social encounter, but, at the same time, he must have the time to engage the general in a conversation that Sokar could lead in the direction he had in mind, to determine Shem-hotep's loyalty to Khufu.

Shem-hotep returned Sokar's greeting, and the two sat down in front of a low-legged table with wine and dried fruit. Pouring a cup for his visitor and himself, Sokar tuned into the man.

Shem-hotep went straight to the point. "So, Sokar. You have information you think I should know regarding Egypt's borders in the northern Delta?"

"Yes. I have interests in the Delta, as you may know. My land holdings there are significant, and I stay abreast of the comings and goings in the area because of its proximity to the sea."

"Of course," the general replied, eyeing Sokar carefully. A man in his position was suspicious of others who might pose a threat to his position. Like the Pharaoh, high government officials had to constantly look over their shoulders. Power was everything; it separated court officials from the common man, and there were plenty of ambitious upstarts ready to step into a general's place.

"And you have reason to suspect that spies have been infiltrating the region?" Shem-hotep said.

"I cannot say for certain. I can only say that my vineyard keepers have sighted on several occasions as of late the movement of a nomadic tribe, the Nine Bows, into the area. There has been minor plundering, a few cattle have been slaughtered, for food no doubt. The situation is probably not serious, not yet anyway. But it is enough to know that Nine Bows are there though they have no business there."

"Yes, of course you are right. I will have the situation monitored."

"Tell me, Shem-hotep. What is your reaction to the Sphinx project? It must be a busy time at court."

"Indeed. I have recently visited the work site, and all is going as planned. The king is pleased, as he should be. These are interesting and challenging times for His Majesty."

"And my half-brother is up to the task," Sokar commented, fishing for some indication of the general's personal opinion of Khufu and his ability as king.

"Khufu is an able ruler. But—never mind."

"Is there a problem, my lord general?" Sokar asked quickly.

"No. Not a problem. An observation, I suppose. I have complete confidence in His Majesty's competence, mind you. But I would like him to be more aggressive. It is the soldier in me, no doubt."

"Aggressive? In what way?"

"Oh, I don't know. Aggressive in a way that would keep the Throne more completely in hand. Khufu tries to please too many people beyond those who count."

"Those who count?"

"He is more interested in the spiritual well-being of Egypt than in the economic and political status, in my judgment."

"I see. Can you give me an example?"

"Well, the landowners and wealthy merchants have less of an ear with Pharaoh than the priests, especially the High Priest of Heliopolis. It makes me wonder whether His Majesty is loyal to the Memphis Trinity, our great god Ptah, or if Ra is the god he serves."

Sokar thought to himself, this isn't much. A small flame, but it could be fanned into a blaze.

"Old Sneferu would not have pandered to the priests before those who fill the royal coffers," Shem-hotep added. "From what I hear, the old king had an eye for wealth and beautiful women."

"Indeed he did," Sokar remarked smugly. "My mother was one of those beautiful women."

Shem-hotep realized he had made a blunder by his remark, and took measures to excuse himself. "Yes . . . yes, she was. I did not mean any affront to you or your mother. I beg your pardon if I have offended you."

"You have not offended me, Shem-hotep. You would have if I did not know the truth of your words about my father Sneferu. While the old king had his faults, not cozying up to those who would make him wealthier and more powerful or who could satisfy his many passions was not among them. Khufu should have taken lessons from his father, it seems. If Sneferu had made me, his first-born son, king, I would. . . . But I am not king, am I?"

"You would what?" Shem-hotep asked, taking the bait.

"Oh, I must not bore you with my musings," Sokar answered, faking an embarrassed tone.

"It never hurts to know what one would do if he were king. I daresay that there is not a man alive who has not imagined himself as king or who has not got some ideas as to how the country could be run better."

"Of course, you are right, general. If I were king . . . well, I would form agencies within the government to deal with matters of state and finance, even the military. I would form a larger army and seek to make Egypt into a conquering nation, not just one satisfied with defending its borders. I would expand trade, seek more land for the wealthier class to own and oversee. That might be a good place to start."

The look on Shem-hotep's face let Sokar know that he had struck a nerve when he spoke about Egypt becoming a conquering nation and about expanding the army. "A larger army would need a competent general who could lead with complete confidence and sovereignty. A man like you, Shem-hotep."

The general was clearly pleased with Sokar's confidence. A man did not become a general unless he had the mind of a strategist and the heart of a warrior. The idea of him, Shem-hotep, being chief military officer for the country was intoxicating. "I agree with what you say, my friend. I have had the same thoughts many times. Maybe old Sneferu made an error by over-looking you in favor of Khufu."

"Well, I certainly would be taking Egypt in a different direction. But I am not king. There is no great army that needs a chief general is there? But there would be if I were king. There could be a greater army, much greater, and you and I could see to that." The carefully chosen words penetrated deep into Shem-hotep's mind, where they seemed to represent an idea of his own that had lain dormant.

Shem-hotep felt a rush of energy as Sokar's gaze began to fade. It went away quickly but left him disoriented. In the few seconds between the psychic transmission and the conversation the two had been having, Sokar picked up precisely where he had left off, not wanting the man to become suspicious of his motives.

Sokar continued in a normal tone of voice. "In these times of life-changing events, the leader must not only be strong, he must have vision, a vision for the land and the people. Khufu has these things. He is a good leader. But a true ruler must have a vision for the land and the people and for himself. My half-brother is not a ruler."

"I agree," Shem-hotep replied. He had always found Khufu a starry-eyed idealist, no realist. Maybe he had met a man who *could* lead Egypt, who would share the power with him. He would be the leader of a great army, perhaps vizier. "I must go. There are matters I must attend to before I return to Memphis. I will be in touch."

"I will expect to hear from you very soon," Sokar replied, bowing slightly, his eyes closed. With a sharp clap of his hands, he summoned Kheti, who appeared immediately. "Kheti, show the chief general out, please."

Chapter Thirty-One

Man in the Shadows

Khufu was enjoying a light breakfast with his family when a courier came with a message scroll. Taret, High Priestess of the Sun Temple, Chief Mistress of the Holy Order of Nut, was requesting an audience with him as soon as possible. Khufu found the request curious. Why would she want to see him? He had never met Taret, although he knew of her and her position within the Heliopolitan priesthood. Thus the Pharaoh assumed that it had something to do with temple business. In light of the events taking place now and in the future, Khufu felt it was advisable to grant Taret's request. . . .

Khem had sat in class all morning as Taret again spoke about benevolent and malefic star waves, on the circumpolar suns, the northern stars that never set but spin endlessly around the night sky.

Khem met Tiye outside the room when the class was over. "It is good to see you," Khem greeted her friend. "There is so much to tell you, so many things I wish to ask you about."

Bast recognized Tiye and began to sniff her ankles and feet. Tiye kneeled and put her arms around the cat's neck, burying her face in the fur in a playful greeting.

A royal courier strode past them and rapped on the doorway of Taret's study. Taret's chief steward received the message scroll. It was odd to see a courier from the palace here in Heliopolis, much less to be calling upon

Taret. She was chief instructor of the Star Priestesses, High Priestess of the Holy Order of Nut, and leader of ceremonies, but nobody saw her as being politically involved in State matters.

At the palace, Taret was escorted to the Throne Room. She had never met the Pharaoh but, like every Egyptian, she felt she knew him. She was at ease now as she was led into Khufu's presence. Bowing deeply, Taret spoke. "Greetings, Your Majesty, Ruler of the Two Lands. Thank you for granting me an audience."

Khufu was struck by the woman's appearance. *How petite and soft-spoken she is, almost to the point of looking frail. Yet to believe she is weak or to judge her strength by how she looks would be to underestimate her,* he reflected. "High Priestess of the Temple of the Sun, Faithful Servant of Nut, Goddess of the Sky from whose womb the great god Ra is born, welcome to Memphis and to the palace, Mistress Taret," Khufu said, nodding his head respectfully. "I am pleased to make your acquaintance. I am sure there is a reason you have come. These are busy days. There are many things going on that require my attention. Still, it seems appropriate that, in light of your position as High Priestess of Heliopolis, I should hear whatever you have to say."

"Very well, my king. I will get to the matter of my visit. I am certain that Your Majesty is aware of the significance of dreams. I have had a dream that concerns you, Wearer of the Two Crowns."

"A dream that concerns me, you say?" Khufu asked, a look of cautious surprise coming across his stern face.

"Yes, Your Majesty. I felt compelled to come, in person, to give you a message that is for no one's ears except yours."

Motioning with a clap of his hands for the room to be cleared of every-one except one guard who should remain by the doorway, Khufu leaned forward.

"I dreamed I was walking along the riverbank in a thicket of lotus and papyrus when I came upon an extraordinarily large Egyptian man standing waist-deep in the Nile. A mask of gold covered his face. The mask was made in Your Majesty's image. The mysterious masked man was praying to the god Horus. It was not a joyful prayer. It was filled with hate and revenge. Suddenly, the man turned into a huge hawk. He spread his great wings and flew out of the water and disappeared into the glow of the sun. I know Your Majesty has more to do than listen to the dreams of an old woman. What I have seen bodes potential disaster for Egypt and you, my lord king. I am sorry if I have unduly taken your time."

"No, no, do not apologize, Mistress Taret. Your coming pleases me. Your insights are valuable to many whom I hold in high regard, and that makes them valuable to me. Now, pray tell me. What do you believe your dream means?"

"I have not only considered the dream from my own perspective, based upon my knowledge and experience. I have consulted Ani, the Dream Priestess of the Temple of the Sun. We differ somewhat on the details, but we agree about what the dream foretells."

"And what is that?"

"Out there somewhere in Egypt is someone who wants to unseat you from the Throne, someone who would depose you, Your Majesty. This man is a powerful magician, and most likely a priest. I sense this man is a skilled shape-shifter who can turn into any form he wishes. He is a worshipper of Horus the Avenger. His power bird is the hawk. He wants to wear the Double Crown, the lotus and papyrus of the North and South. He wants the people to see him as they see you, as their king. He will stop at nothing to get what he wants."

Khufu studied the small woman for a moment without speaking. Then, letting out a deep sigh, he said in a low voice, "I was afraid of this."

"Have you had such dreams, Your Majesty?"

"No, well, not exactly. I did have a dream not too long ago, and there was a hawk in it, a large hawk which attacked me."

Taret stiffened at this, her head falling back, slightly elevating her chin as she let her breath out heavily. "Psychic attack. Your Majesty, you and the Throne are under attack in the Duat. It is only a matter of time before it—he—comes out in the open. Does Your Majesty know of enemies?"

"The Wearer of the Double Crown has many enemies," Khufu replied. "I fear your description leaves me with but one choice as to who the revengeful masked man is. . . . Your coming to me with these revelations is duly noted, Mistress Taret. I am indebted to you. You will hear from me very soon. I urge you to speak to Meri-ib about what you have told me, but to no one else. Consider that a royal command."

"I understand," Taret answered, closing her eyes and nodding in affirmation of Pharaoh's order of silence.

Khufu sensed he could trust her and he had to rely on his feelings at this point. He commanded the guard who was present to secrecy at the promise of death if he disobeyed. When Taret had gone, Khufu retired to his chapel. He took out his scarab runes and let them fall in front of him. The runes fell with their painted sides down except for two: the cobra and the god Khepera, the grandfather of the Neters. The cobra meant he had an enemy. Yet, it was a symbol of power, first and foremost, and of the divine, the uraeus, the third eye of the King's forehead, protector and the destroyer of Ra's enemies, Khufu reflected. The serpent was dangerous only when it was attacked.

Khufu had long suspected Sokar was his enemy, although he had no concrete evidence. Now with Taret's information, Khufu could no longer deny it. Sokar was the masked man in Taret's dream, Sokar was the magician, the hawk, the shape-shifter, and the priest who had impersonated him in her dream.

Khufu picked up the rune painted with a scarab beetle, symbolizing the god Khepera. The beetle takes flight in the hottest part of the day, so the scarab is a symbol of the Sun. The rune indicates positive, divine intervention in the matter at hand. This told him that he was on the right course. The rune signifies concealed or protected knowledge, which he had just had. Both runes are positive, Khufu thought. The message is clear as are the outcomes, depending upon what action I take. If my enemy is Sokar, the cobra, he will become deadly only if he is attacked. So I must not attack. I must be discreet.

Khufu realized there was only one way to deal with a magician: with magic. The battle to save his kingship would be fought in the Duat. But he would need help, and get help he would. The runes were telling him that the odds were in his favor. When the cobra was not threatened, the danger would pass, and the serpent would take on its positive role as protector of the king as his third eye. He must keep his insight clear, his mind and body pure, his doubts and fears abated. He must trust his intuition and the guidance of those he trusted. The gods would protect him and the Throne from all evil, save the evil in himself.

Emerging from the chapel, Khufu summoned his chief scribe and dictated messages to Meri-ib and Taret. He wanted them both to come to the palace two days hence. He dispatched a courier to Shemshu-Hor, to tell the old priest that he should prepare to come to Memphis and establish residence at the palace in two days and plan to remain there indefinitely.

In Heliopolis, Meri-ib was pacing back and forth in his study, his mind going over the appearance of the hawk on the windowsill a few days before. He vacillated between believing there was nothing to it and thinking it was an omen of evil. The High Priest could not remember a time when he felt so out of sorts. It was as if his head was telling him to look at things one way, while his heart was telling him to see them another. He felt confused, and confusion was an emotion and a frame of mind he was not used to. A High Priest had to live in the physical and magical worlds, and be at home in both. Meri-ib had always trusted himself in these regards. Now he had doubts, though he wasn't sure what he doubted.

Meri-ib sat down at his desk and began a process designed to confront the doubt. Where was it coming from? Why? It had started when Sokar had requested to serve as his co-ritualist for the New Year ritual. He had not favored the idea due to his distrust of Sokar. He sensed Sokar was envious of Khufu, and that King Sneferu had passed him over as heir to the Throne because he scorned him.

Why was he personalizing that doubt? Why did he feel incapable of dealing with Sokar with magic? Perhaps it is because I fear having to make the decision to use black magic, that if I do, I will suffer bad results, Meri-ib thought. It wasn't that he feared that Sokar was a more powerful magician. His ethics about misuse of magic would make him weak in the face of one as driven as Sokar. The answer was clear: If the good of the whole is at stake, using magical power to destroy is ethical. So, Meri-ib vowed, if Sokar, or any other person, tries to overthrow the Throne, I will not hesitate to use my magical power on that person, and do whatever I need to defeat him.

Chapter Thirty-Two

An Initiation Chamber Beneath the Sphinx?

Khem was practicing her word pictures. She had had her first lesson with Sheshat, and was excited now to try to form her images neatly. There was no class with Taret today, but she and Tiye were to meet with Ani in the afternoon, and she was waiting for Tiye. They were eager to share their experiences of the past few days. Bast was sleeping at the foot of Khem's bed, her belly full of food.

The lioness had begun to change. Khem thought she was more mature, more independent, though it was not causing the cat to isolate herself. She had taken on a confidence that wasn't arrogant or aloof, but a kind of insightfulness. Apparitions did not disturb Bast, and she seemed calm when exposed to ceremony or other forms of energy enhancement.

Her mind diverted from writing, Khem said, "Akhi, I was wondering. Do you think animals dream?"

"Yes, I think they do. Why do you ask, my mistress?"

"No particular reason, I suppose. I was thinking about my dreams, and I noticed Bast seems to move though she is sleeping." As she spoke, the lioness cocked an ear towards Khem, somehow listening to their voices, though she was asleep. Akhi called it "catnapping."

"Look," Khem whispered so as not to wake up the cat. "She is sleeping, but she is also listening to me and you. She hears our voices. I know she does."

"Yes. I have always known that. At least I think I have," Akhi commented.

"I wonder how animals do that. I suppose they are natural-born magicians."

The napping lioness woke up suddenly and stared at the door, her ears straight up. A tap sounded outside the curtained doorway. It was Tiye. Bast often woke when she sensed someone would be at the door even before anyone came. The cat was no longer a pet; she was Khem's sister apprentice priestess, Khem realized.

Leaping to her feet, with Bast close behind, Khem went to greet Tiye. "Come. It is good to see you," she said cheerfully. "Akhi, please get Tiye a cup of beer."

Tiye almost fell backwards as Bast, nearly half-grown now, jumped up, flinging her front paws on the girl's waist.

"Bast! Down!" Khem scolded. The lioness meekly rolled over on her back, expecting her usual belly rub from Tiye.

"She and I have missed you," Khem said. "Come, sit down. I want to hear more about your dream of Khaba. You only told me what you dreamed, not what it meant."

"When I told Ani my dream, she said Khaba would work with me in amulet-making. I should get accustomed to seeing Khaba, you know, in my mind as she is in her soul body instead of how I remember her."

"Why?"

"I suppose it is how she really is, so I should see her that way, and then I will be seeing Khaba."

"No matter. It is exciting that Khaba will work with you."

"Yes, it is," Tiye said, her tone suggesting that she wanted to change the subject. Talking about Khaba was something she still had a problem with at times, as it still made her feel sad over her loss. She was trying to get past her mentor's death, and get used to thinking of her as alive in a way other than physical, but it wasn't easy. "How about you? What have you been up to?"

"Well, let me see. Oh—I have seen Atef. He has begun his lessons in the Instruction House. They take up half his day. Then he works with a fisherman in the city. I have had one lesson with Sheshat. See, here are my writing tools." Khem showed Tiye her palette and reeds. Tiye could tell by the way Khem handled the palette how much she treasured it.

"Someday maybe you will write a book of your own," Tiye said, half-teasing.

"Who knows?" Khem said. "Stranger things have happened. Speaking of strange things, I have seen the sign, Tiye."

With a puzzled look, Tiye asked, "I wonder if the comet could be an omen of two things?"

"What do you mean?"

"Could it foretell something good like the Second Coming and something evil too?"

"Like what?"

"I don't know. Anything evil, I suppose. The death of someone important maybe. A war, or, who knows?"

"I see what you mean. I never thought of it that way. It is confusing. Maybe we should ask for a dream."

At the palace in Memphis, Khufu was in a strategy meeting with Manetho. The king was filling him in on his visit from Taret, and the message of a usurper making his intentions known soon. Khufu decided not to reveal his suspicions about who the usurper likely was; he wanted to reserve that information until he had the counsel of the people he trusted the most—Meri-ib, Taret, and Shemshu-Hor, the three most skilled seers he knew. However, when he voiced his plan of consulting with the three of them, Manetho raised a point.

"I understand your choice, Your Majesty. But these are servants of Ra and Horus, great gods indeed. Memphis is the domain of Ptah. Would this not be an affront to the Triad, and to the High Priest of the Memphis Temple, the honorable Dejedfre, the crown prince, your eldest son?"

Consulting the High Priest of Memphis had been far from Khufu's mind. He had been so involved with Meri-ib that he had considered himself in a sort of partnership with the High Priest of Heliopolis ever since the advent of the Sphinx project and the prophecy of the Second Coming. This had been due to a visitation by the god Thoth to Meri-ib. That vision had ended with a white feather apported onto the high altar in the Holy of Holies in the Temple of the Sun. He still carried the feather.

"Of course, you are right. I have committed a grave oversight. I must send for Dejedfre immediately. Order a courier dispatched at once."

There were religious differences among Memphis, Heliopolis, and Hermopolis, the third religious center in the north, Khufu reflected. The Memphis Triad provided a different perspective on truth and reality and was heralded by the Priests of Ptah as being closer to the truth than its contemporaries in Heliopolis, the Priests of Ra, and in Hermopolis, the Priests of Anubis. The king himself was a priest and worshipper of Ptah, so it could be taken as a type of religious treason for him to form an allegiance with the High Priest of Heliopolis, especially to the exclusion of the High Priest of the Memphis Temple. The fact that the holder of that position was Khufu's eldest son made the affair political and could be a source of unrest within the ranks of the court and temple officials. Khufu could not afford that, particularly if Sokar or some other enemy posed a threat to the Throne.

Manetho left the Throne Room to see to the king's order.

When Manetho returned, Khufu asked about Shemshu-Hor. "Based upon our earlier conversation, you are aware of my intention of seeking the wise counsel of the Chief Priest of the Followers of Horus."

"Yes, Your Majesty," Manetho replied. He did not want to comment further on the wisdom of Khufu's decision until he had heard him out.

"These times are unprecedented for the hundreds of generations before us. In all the time that has passed since the First Time, how many human beings do you know—do any of us know—who have a religious and spiritual, even a biological, lineage that can be traced back for thousands of years? I can answer that question: One. One old man. An old man who only by the grace of the Neters is still among the living and only the Neters know for how much longer. Shemshu-Hor has a direct connection to the god Horus, and there is certainly a link between the son of Isis and Osiris and the Stone Head. And there is his connection with the Star Gods.

"With the events going on now, and those soon to occur, how can I, King of Egypt and Ruler of the Two Lands, not draw upon the wisdom of this man? How can I, or any of the priesthood, not seek the sage counsel of one who is, without question, the most evolved human in the world? The fact is, I cannot. I cannot ignore the man cloistered in the *Benu* Temple."

"I see Your Majesty's reasoning," Manetho replied. "What do you plan to do?"

Khufu walked up the three short steps that led to the throne and sat down. Resting his elbow on the gilded arm of the great chair, he leaned his head back and let out a heavy sigh. Then, leaning forward again, he said, "I will send for Shemshu-Hor to come here to the palace to live here from now until the Second Coming has happened and we know what Egypt's future is."

Manetho, though not entirely surprised by Khufu's decision, was not certain that the old priest would accept the invitation, and said so.

"Then I will command that he come in service to the country and the people. Even Shemshu-Hor is not exempt from a royal command."

Manetho knew there was no changing Khufu's mind, nor did he see any reason to try. Quite the contrary. He agreed that the Chief Priest of the Followers of Horus was more than a human. His life was a gift to all Egypt, and if the people could benefit from his serving as counsel to Pharaoh, then so be it. "No, Your Majesty, no one can refuse a king. Perhaps a command will not be necessary. How shall you go about letting your wishes be known to the Elder Priest?"

"I want you to go to him, as my representative, the vizier of Egypt. Tell him my wishes, and make arrangements for his transport to the palace, and that of his personal servants, a scribe, and any of his assistants he needs to accompany him. All of his needs will be met, and he will be well cared for. I wish you to depart for Heliopolis at sunrise tomorrow. Tell no one of your mission until it is completed."

Khufu had to wait now. Within a day he would have three of the wisest members of the priesthood on hand. In the meantime, Khufu spent the afternoon dealing with civil cases and minor affairs of state. The last matter brought to his attention was a possible border violation in the northern Delta. The report was presented to the court by his highest ranking general, Shem-hotep.

"I am come to inform Your Majesty, Lord of the Two Lands, that I have heard of possible marauding bands in the north. I request permission to take a delegation of soldiers to determine the validity of the report."

"Is this just a report? From how many sources does it come?" Khufu inquired.

"One report, Your Majesty," Shem-hotep replied, but without volunteering any name. "But a reliable one, I assure you."

"Reliable, perhaps," Khufu said, his tone serious. "But that is the problem. One report of a 'possible' roaming band does not warrant our time or expense to investigate. I must refuse your request." Ever mindful of the diplomatic peace he had to keep, Khufu followed his refusal with a compliment and a promise.

"You must understand, Shem-hotep, the Sphinx project must take priority. It requires virtually every available man. I cannot justify taking men away from this for a long and expensive journey to the North. Your services are needed here. Your position as a general and official of the court requires you to participate in the Second Coming. I will not risk losing a valuable asset to the court to some pillaging gang of trespassers who may very well exist purely in the mind of one reporter."

Shem-hotep was furious inside. The refusal not only embarrassed him, it also made him feel incompetent that he had misjudged the king's priorities. He disliked the feeling that the king of Egypt might think his judgment incompetent, though Khufu had not said so. Every man's opinion of him had to match his own or he would go to any lengths to prove his power. "Of course you are right, Your Majesty. I will respect your decision, although I would regret an invasion that got out of hand when it could have been avoided. Surely Your Highness knows that I only have what is best for Egypt in mind."

"As do I," Khufu replied. "With two men such as you and I having Egypt's safety in mind, the people can sleep peacefully tonight."

Shem-hotep knew that his audience with the Pharaoh was over. He did not know how he had been perceived by Khufu, for he had been given a vote of confidence as a recognized and valuable member of the royal court. At the same time, he had been refused the thing he did best, protecting, and if need be, fighting for Egypt. As best he could remember, he had never been denied a request for action presented to the king.

Shem-hotep reflected on his meeting with Sokar. It had seemed unusual for Sokar to seek him out to report a matter that was common at Egypt's boundaries. Why had Sokar himself not gone to the king? Had he not gone to Khufu because he realized how preoccupied the king was? Of course that was it. He pondered the strange rapport he had felt, how Sokar had opened up to him about not being king. Sokar seemed calm about it, though Shem-hotep wasn't sure how he would himself deal with that predicament. Probably not well. He would feel cheated, angry, and resentful towards Sneferu. What about Khufu as the ruler of Egypt? That had aroused jealous feelings of his own that he repressed. Should he be content with being the chief general? Sokar had said he would elevate him and put an expanded Egyptian army entirely in his hands if he were king. It was a tantalizing thought. . . .

Khufu was being briefed by Nemon on the progress of the Sphinx project. It was going better than anyone had expected. But something had come up. "Is this Sun hot enough for you, cousin?" Nemon teased. He always lifted Khufu's spirit.

"It is indeed," Khufu answered. "But the royal fan bearers make life much more bearable."

"I am sure they do. How sweet life would be if the Neters ordained that every working man should have fan bearers! But, alas, there is news regarding the project that Your Majesty should know. Perhaps we should speak alone."

Khufu knew Nemon would not request privacy unless he felt there was good reason to do so. With a clap of his hands, the king ordered the Throne Room cleared. "Now, tell me, Nemon, what is it you wish me to know?"

"The workers have been digging in the front and back of the monument and have made considerable headway. There is a place in the front, where we have gotten down to unearthing the paws of the lion-man's body. The sketch I showed you some time ago is accurate. The paws lie stretched out in front of the body as supposed."

Nemon paced slowly before the throne as he spoke. "The further we have gone down into the bedrock in the area between the paws, just below the head, the more we find an indication there may be a cavity. Judging by what can be seen and sensed, if the cavity is there, it is probably large, buried less than five meters deep. My guess is that it is man-built, most likely at the time the lion-man was carved."

"You think the Sphinx is hollow?" Khufu inquired.

"No. Well, not the whole body. There is good reason to believe there is a chamber beneath the Sphinx, and that the entrance is between the front paws. If, and I say 'if,' there is an inner room, it is probably an initiation chamber. And if there is one, there are likely others, perhaps a subterranean network of rooms and tunnels. It is conceivable that such a network could connect the Sphinx with the pyramids and with other monuments long in ruins."

Nemon's words painted a picture in Khufu's mind of an underground complex that might have been used during the First Time. "If the chamber exists, there could be artifacts, some brought to Earth by the Star Gods. Nemon, do what you have to. Spare nothing to determine if your suspicions are true. Find that chamber. If it is there, report to me immediately."

Khufu wondered if it was a coincidence that new evidence of the First Coming was surfacing at the time when the Second Coming was imminent. The turn of events made him more sure than ever that everything was unfolding exactly as it should.

Chapter Thirty-Three

Nepthys, the Passive Goddess

Taret was preparing to go to the classroom for the morning session. She had dreamed again of the man with the gold mask identical to Pharaoh's face. The man, again standing waist-deep in the Nile, this time turned into a hawk, flew into her, and knocked her off her feet.

"There is a message for you, Mistress Taret," Sheshat said. "From the palace, with the king's seal upon it." Sheshat left the room so Taret could read the message in private.

The communiqué requested Taret's presence with the king of Egypt on the following day; she should arrive by noon. The same message had been sent to Meri-ib. Transportation for the two would be arranged by the palace, and they should meet the royal barque at the main dock in Heliopolis at dawn.

Taret laid the scroll on her dressing table. She felt confident that whatever had prompted Pharaoh to summon her and Meri-ib to Memphis was about his leading Egypt in the right direction. Taret called for Sheshat. "I will be going to Memphis at sunrise tomorrow. Please notify Ani that she is needed to fulfill my teaching responsibilities in my absence. I do not know how long I will be gone. I will send a courier as soon as I know." Taking Sheshat by the hand, Taret gave her a friendly squeeze. "I trust you will carry on here and be of assistance to Ani."

Meri-ib had returned to his study after his morning oblations to Ra. Since he entered the priesthood, the central chapel had always made him feel relaxed. Going there was a good way to start the day. Here, at the Temple of the Sun, the inner sanctum was empowering, being the chamber that housed the statue of Ra and a piece of the Stone of Heaven given to the people of Egypt by the Star Gods ages ago. No object was more powerful. He rarely spent time in the Stone's actual presence, for it was in a special chamber seldom open. Still, the energy of the "sky iron" was so intense, he could sense it when he entered the chapel.

Meri-ib focused his thoughts on the obelisk at the center of the Sun Temple. Atop the needle of stone was a conical capstone, a replica of the original *ben-ben* fallen from heaven. He had not thought about the *ben-ben* in a long time. His mind wandered among his memories of the holy relic; he remembered having copied some passages from an old manuscript about the sky stone. The words had captured his imagination from the moment he first read them. They told about stars falling to Earth, an event he had witnessed many times over the course of his life.

The first "fall" he could remember happened when he was eight. He had been crossing the Nile from the West Bank at Giza with his father, who had taken him to see the pyramids for the first time. It was night before they reached home. The sky had suddenly lit up, followed immediately by a loud noise like a hundred claps of thunder one after another. Meri-ib had seen a smoky fire trail streaking across the sky. "A Star God has come to Egypt," his father had said.

Although he had been too scared to ask what it meant, Meri-ib had never forgotten this first falling star. Every time he saw one again, he thought a Star God had come to Egypt. Now he knew they were gifts from the Sky Neters. Thoughts of the Star Stones brought the comet to mind. Meri-ib had never seen a comet. In his training for the priesthood, he had learned about the celestial visitors, that they heralded important events, so he was looking forward to seeing the heavenly apparition that was surely the omen of the Second Coming.

The High Priest's thoughts were interrupted by the chief house steward. A messenger had arrived with a communiqué from the palace. He was summoned to an audience with Khufu.

When the Sun rose it left an orange gash in the eastern horizon that reflected as soft reddish-orange ripples on the Nile. The barque awaiting Taret and Meri-ib's arrival was a long, flat sailing vessel of yellow pine, with a crew of twenty oarsmen and a pilot. The journey was pleasant and uneventful. Meri-ib and Taret settled comfortably into the cabin. They chatted congenially, but avoided the subject of why they had been summoned by Khufu. "Last night, I think I saw the comet," Taret said. "It was quite hazy, not yet well defined to the sight. But I am sure that it was the comet. Have you seen it yet, Meri-ib?"

"Oh, yes, I mean, no, no, I have not seen it. As a matter of fact, I have never seen a comet. I am eager to see this one. There may never be another opportunity for me to witness such a spectacle."

"Why, Meri-ib, surely your years will be long and prosperous."

"Is that a prophecy, Lady Taret? If so, I trust your accuracy completely," Meri-ib said with a chuckle that elicited a smile from the High Priestess.

When the barque approached the main dock at Memphis, landing and securing the vessel took half an hour. The passengers remained in the cabin until the boat was securely docked and litters brought to carry them to the palace. The canopied litters would keep them cool and help shield their identity from the public. Once at the palace, the guests were shown to their quarters to refresh themselves and have some food. They would meet with Khufu the next day.

Khufu, though busy with the usual matters of court, was waiting for word from Manetho regarding Shemshu-Hor's coming to Memphis. The uncertainty of it had led the King to not inform Meri-ib and Taret of his being there until their actual arrival. Khufu finally got the message he had been waiting for. Manetho had returned from Heliopolis, and would report to the palace as soon as he had refreshed himself of the sweat and soil of his journey. Even the most elite travelers had to contend with the elements.

The King cleared the Throne Room, including the fan bearers who were normally so welcome on a hot day like this. Manetho came into the room walking tall, his body language giving away the success of his mission.

"Greetings, Your Majesty," the vizier said, bowing before Khufu, who sat on the great chair and eyed him pensively. "My journey has yielded fruit, my lord. The venerable Shemshu-Hor, Chief Priest of the Followers of Horus, is en route to the palace even as I speak. He is expected to arrive shortly."

Khufu felt a surge of relief and satisfaction. He knew now his plan to form a council of three of the wisest religious officials in Egypt was right. The lack of resistance so far told that the gods were on his side making sure that everything came together. "Wonderful!" Khufu responded, his face lighting up in a broad grin. "This pleases me, Manetho, more than you know."

"Yes, Your Majesty. I can see that it does."

Khufu sensed there was something the vizier wanted to say. "Tell me, Manetho. Did you encounter any difficulty in persuading the Old One to come?"

"No, ahhhh, that's just it. I had no convincing to do. Not even did I have to tell the Old One why I was there."

"What do you mean?"

"He was waiting for me, Your Majesty. He knew I was coming and he knew why. When I arrived, he was ready to leave the *Benu* Temple. I tell you he . . . he is not a mortal, my lord."

Khufu knew Taret and Meri-ib were already in the palace, and now Shemshu-Hor was soon to arrive. Looking intently at Manetho, Khufu commanded that tight security be provided for the three prophets. "No harm must come to them, Manetho. They are here at my request, and I must see to it that they are kept safe."

"Consider it done, Your Majesty. I will engage General Shem-hotep to tend to the matter. They will be in good hands."

The mention of the general reminded Khufu of their encounter when Shem-hotep had requested permission to make a journey to the north to make sure the border was secure. He knew that the man was not happy with being refused, so Khufu was glad to have an important assignment to put in the general's hands. It was good politics. "Good. Shem-hotep is quite capable of the task, I am sure. Now, all that is left to do is to see to it that a fine feast is prepared for tomorrow evening. We will celebrate the forming of the Council. All is well."

Sokar was planning a feast, giving Kheti the details of his plans. "I expect to entertain General Shem-hotep tomorrow. He will arrive in mid-afternoon. There will be others. I will inform you as soon as the guest list is complete. Spare no expense, Kheti. Make certain there are fresh food and flowers, musicians, and dancers. It is time for me to be more social, don't you think?"

Bowing to his master, the servant agreed. "Yes, yes, my master. It will all be very nice. Trust me."

"I always trust you, Kheti," Sokar replied. "Send couriers with invitations and arrange for litters to bring Meri-ib and others from the Sun Temple. The general will need to be escorted from the main dock."

Sokar had been feeling time was passing too fast, slipping away. His resentment at not being king had become a pastime whether he wanted it or not, though he had never before chosen to act on his feelings. He had never carried out any of the countless threats to seek revenge, but if he believed he was the rightful heir to the throne, then it was time at last to take action and right the wrongs.

One thing was for certain: a hermit could not be king. If he was ever to gain allegiance of those who could help him overthrow Khufu, he had to be more visible, politically, socially, and religiously. Being Meri-ib's co-ritualist at the New Year Festival was a good start, but he would have to do more.

Of all the allies he could muster, none would be more valuable than Meri-ib. He was sure the High Priest did not like or trust him. What he wasn't sure of was whether the man's negative feelings about him were an expression of a personality conflict or due to Meri-ib's allegiance to Khufu. He needed to know, for the answer would influence his strategy. Sokar was not fooling himself. He knew his chances of becoming king were slim if he took the diplomatic route. Besides, it would take too much time to change people's convictions and loyalties. He also knew that Khufu was a popular, well-loved monarch with the *fellahin*, and that they would never allow him to be overthrown without a war. He would have to win alliances from the *inside*, and to do that, he would rely on his intuition and, if need be, on his magical skill.

Khem and Tiye learned that Ani would be teaching in Taret's absence and that the subject would be Nepthys, the Goddess of Sleep.

"You have learned from Taret about one star among the Sirius stars, the Great Star. It is the Star of Women that I wish to speak about at this time. Understanding this star means knowing Nepthys, the Hidden One, goddess of night images. Find Nepthys's energy within you. Work with her to express her power.

"There are certain ways to recognize Nepthys. Isis's energy is extroverted, active, and expressive, but Nepthys's is introverted, passive, and still. This sort of power is found within Nepthys in the dark side of the Moon, and is closely associated with water and emotions. She embodies the feminine principle in nature. Nothing is more significant than her relationship to the part in you which is hidden in the darkness inside. It is evil, yet capable of the highest and greatest good. But not totally. You should know that being capable of dealing with the darkness inside, in others, and in the world is essential to becoming an initiate.

"I ask you to heed my next words most carefully. Whenever there is talk about the darkness, dark forces, dark stars, demons, and the like, all too often these are taken to be evil. It is true they are. There are reasons for the uninitiated to assign evil to that which is misunderstood, grotesque, and alarming. Consider the fantastic array of beings in the realm of the dead. Some of these are humans with animal, bird, reptile, and insect heads. Some have two heads, or a head that faces backwards. Some carry threatening objects like knives and torches. And demons often have terrible names like 'Blood-drinker' or 'One Who Eats Excrement.' But it is an error to think of these beings only as evil. They may be dangerous to humanity, but they are under the command of the high gods. Think about this and never forget it.

"The uninitiated are aware that the dead must encounter these terrifying things on their journey through the underworld, and we make provisions for this. Such beings are frightening, but paradoxical. Demons do seek to challenge and harm humanity, yet are manifestations and messengers of the divinities themselves.

"People use all sorts of things to deal with spirits. Amulets, talismans, spells. All these are good. They provide ways of defense when such beings are encountered, when a person experiences the evil threat as coming from outside herself. But in reality, there is no evil *outside* yourself. No objective demonic energy can disturb your peace or bring you harm. Only the evil within you can harm you. It is your own inherent evil that demons and spirits prey upon and use to attack and harm, making you think it is they who have harmed you when you have harmed yourself.

"Evil is a confusing matter. An integral part of an initiate's training is to know the truth about evil so the error of misplaced power does not cause you harm, so you no longer search for or place evil outside yourself. Meeting the foes within and conquering them is to do battle with Apep and other monster spirits. To know this is to live without fear overcoming you, and this can make the difference between being an initiate and only thinking you are one.

"Whenever times of change have been foretold, response to the prophecies generates apprehension and expectation that can be filled with fear. This is why our wise Pharaoh must choose the appropriate time to reveal any dire predictions. Pharaoh has told all Egyptians about the Second Coming of the Star Gods. On the surface, this sounds like a time for celebration, but surface feelings are not the problem when it comes to fear. Fear of the unknown can cause panic.

"Not one of us was alive during the First Time. We can experience those times only through stories in the sacred texts. It is said to have been a turning point in our way of life, which is why the event has long been celebrated. Since none of us witnessed it, we have been only *told* about the First Coming, but now we are about to *experience* just such a monumental event. Surely there are many among the *fellahin* who are afraid of what unknown changes the Star Gods will bring to the land and to their lives. Humans tend to resist change, even when it is needed and prayed for. That which is familiar is often settled for out of fear of unknown changes. It must not be this way.

"So when we, the Star Priestesses, hear the Pharaoh proclaim that the Star Gods are coming we rejoice and sing praises. Yet who among you can honestly say that you have not felt apprehension about those prophesied things? The comet, the Sphinx project, and the Second Coming are all powerful events. If you have felt apprehension, no matter how slight, then you know I speak the truth."

Khem could not deny she had some apprehension. She had wondered how her life would change. Ani's teaching made her realize that she had to admit to some fear about the Second Coming.

Ani brought her lecture to a close. "To deal with your apprehensions about what is to take place you must find the goddess Nepthys within you. She is the 'Gatekeeper' of those places deep inside yourselves where fear resides. If you search for and find them you will still only be seeing them in disguise, and you will be blinded by the light of ecstasy and celebration. These are things to think about. So be it."

Chapter Thirty-Four

Pharaoh's Dream

Sokar had his plan. Orchestrating an overthrow of the king of Egypt was not the way to go. It would take too intricate a conspiracy, too much time. Murder was too risky, for there was no guarantee the people would accept him as their ruler in the event of Khufu's death. Of course, convincing the monarch to step aside was out of the question, and any attempt to politically unseat him was a waste of time. He would never get away with it.

Sokar decided that the best tactic would be to declare himself the rightful king of Egypt and set about forming an alternate government. He would count on the fact that when the people realized what he would do for them he would win their support and loyalty, and they would switch their allegiance.

Sokar would declare himself in a public announcement, and set up his capital city in the Faiyum region of the Delta. It was not the ideal way to become king, but when he learned of the Sphinx project and the Second Coming, it left him no alternative, because he realized that Khufu would be entrenched in the minds and hearts of the *fellahin*. Any hope he might have had of overthrowing the monarch and winning over the people's favor was dashed by that.

But an alternate government—that was another matter. He would staff his court with those who supported him. He could not deny that Khufu was a popular ruler, but there are always people who are unhappy, who want power. A new government would provide many powerful positions for ambitious priests, landowners, and merchants seeking fewer taxes and more control. There were risks involved in this approach, not the least of which was that Sokar would likely fall short of the support he needed. But it was a risk he was willing to take. The feast he was planning for a few select candidates for his court would be a time to feel out the climate. He would have to be discreet about how much he revealed, but he knew what to say and how to say it.

Sokar had his guest list partially formed already: Shem-hotep, Khufu's general; Bakka's father, Ali, a man who wanted revenge on the religious establishment; the wealthy merchant, Her-mon, who imported woods and resins from foreign countries; several from the priesthood who were growing in power. Now, as he was moving in the direction he wanted, Sokar felt calm—and justified.

Night fell suddenly as it does sometimes in the desert. The torches burning on the patio of the royal family's private quarters sent curls of black smoke into the warm night air. Though most Egyptians retired just after sunset, not so the royal family. Their means and environment made it possible to light numerous oil lamps so they could keep later hours.

The royal wife and children had retired earlier, but Khufu lingered on the veranda to gaze out over the city and desert. It was one of those rare, coveted moments when he was able to spend time alone with his thoughts. He felt secure, in control of everything he *could* control. The labor at the Sphinx site was going well, even better than planned. Nemon was drawing up plans for the temple of Khufu's dreams, a temple he would build in honor of the Second Coming of the Star Gods. Here, in Memphis, under the secure roof of the palace, were three of the most influential religious figureheads in Egypt.

In these auspicious times, Khufu needed the wisest, strongest, most dedicated among the priesthood to advise and support him, men and women who had given their lives in service to the Neters. Three such were now with him. If he was fortunate, another would come to be part of what he would call the Sirius Council. It would be a council of sages, magicians, seers, and prophets who would receive the Star Gods' legacy and help carry Egypt to unknown heights. He would not take their knowledge for himself alone. It belonged to the people.

Khufu looked into the night sky. "How beautiful is your domain, Nut, most gracious Mistress of the Sky," he whispered. Khufu noticed a faint, wispy star in the East, its body followed by a trail of light. "The comet. It is the comet. It is here." He felt a rush of energy, then a chill. He had never seen a comet before. Its presence pulled him like a magnet. . . .

Morning came and it brought fragments of a dream to Khufu. It was no ordinary dream, but one of a divine encounter, so overwhelming that Khufu summoned his dream priest, Mohammed, at once. "I saw a man shining bright like a thousand stars," Khufu said. "He was surely a god. His headdress made me think so. It was a large, golden disk in a crescent-shaped cradle that crowned his head. At his side was a *Benu*. Two lions crouched at his feet, one on the right, and the other on the left. The god-man commanded me to build his temple. Then a second man appeared. He was big and muscular and had the air of a conquering hero endowed with great strength. The hero held a tablet of stone in his hand. Upon the tablet was drawn the plan of a temple. This is what I dreamed."

Khufu walked to a gilded table beside his bed and picked up an oblong basket, the contents of which were covered by a piece of white linen. The king stood before the dream priest and pulled the cover away so Mohammed could see inside. "I found this on the floor at the foot of my bed when I woke this morning."

Mohammed's eyes widened. He was startled to see a flattened lapis stone tablet twice the size of a man's hand, upon which a stylus had etched the floor plan of a temple.

"Go ahead," Khufu urged. "Take it. Look at it. Is it not unlike anything you have seen before?"

Mohammed took the tablet and turned it over and over in his hands. Handing the stone back, he paced the room for a few moments then turned to face the king. "It is clear the dream is significant, Your Majesty. The first god-man to appear in the dream announced that you are to build the new temple. The *Benu* and lions are symbols; the *Benu* symbolizes rebirth, and the lions are the guardians of unseen forces. The *Benu* suggests the temple will be a star temple. The lions point to the exact point in the sky to which the temple is to be oriented, where the Sun will rise on the day of the New Year. The hero-god has obviously given you the plan of a temple."

Mohammed's interpretation made sense. Khufu would probably have surmised the same himself. Still, it didn't explain how the lapis tablet had got in his room.

"I have never seen anything like it before," Mohammed said. "But in my training as a dream interpreter, I have heard of such things. They are called apports."

Khufu put the tablet back into the basket and covered it with the cloth. He would decide what to do with it later. "I suppose there are times when something has to be taken on faith," he said. "I will build the temple, and I will build it according to the plan on the dream stone. Speak to no one of this, Mohammed."

When the priest had gone, Khufu made preparations for the day. He would meet with Meri-ib and Taret to tell them of Shemshu-Hor's presence at the palace. He was anxious for their insights regarding the upcoming events. Khufu ordered the Throne Room to be made ready for the meeting. He turned all state affairs over to the vizier so he could give his undivided attention to the sages from Heliopolis. He would meet with Meri-ib and Taret first, then have Shemshu-Hor join them. There were many things to discuss.

As Khufu was about to leave his private chambers for the Throne Room, his valet announced that a courier from the Temple of Memphis had brought a message from Dejedfre. Dejedfre would arrive at the palace the coming day to have an audience with his father. He was coming in response to Khufu's bidding.

When Khufu arrived at the Throne Room, Meri-ib and Taret were already there and comfortable. Fan bearers kept the air circulating, and servants brought them wine and sweet cakes. Pharaoh entered, the air of royalty about him. The priest and priestess stood up immediately and bowed. Khufu was a well-built, bronze-skinned man, taller than most. He carried himself in a regal manner. Those who did not know him could mistake his self-confidence for arrogance. "Please," Khufu said, gesturing to his guests that there was no need to bow. "You do me too much honor. It is I who should be honoring you. Please be seated. Let my servants make you comfortable."

"We have been treated well, Your Majesty, and thank you for your hospitality," Meri-ib responded.

"Lady Taret, faithful servant of the Sky Goddess Nut, welcome," Pharaoh said. "Come, sit. We must talk."

Khufu ascended the steps of the dais and sat on the throne, his hands resting lightly on the lion's heads at the chair's arms. Fan bearers stood on each side of him waving huge peacock feathers. He began to explain to Meri-ib and Taret why he had called them to Memphis. "I trust my summons has not interrupted your lives and duties to the point of hardship. I would not have requested your presence without the respect of ample notice unless there was a compelling reason."

"Your Majesty need not have such concerns," Taret said in her soft but strong voice.

Khufu said, "Good. Your willingness to come is noted as obedience to the Throne. I will not be so presumptuous as to say that I have summoned you on behalf of the gods. I will say that it is *because* of the gods that I have sent for you."

This was Khufu's way of asserting his rightful position as god-king to members of the holy orders. To Meri-ib, he said, "I suppose this all started with you, Meri-ib. You surely are chosen among men. It was to you that the great god Thoth chose to appear. It was to you the task of unearthing the Stone Head was revealed. Through you, Lady Taret, the Star Gods foretold of their coming and gave you warning of my enemy. It was not I who chose you or sought you out. It was the gods. They sought you out and revealed these things, and you revealed them to me. This has drawn the three of us into a bond.

"I need to set up a special council to serve several purposes. The Star Gods' return is a marvelous and exciting event we all eagerly await. But once they have arrived, many things will change. New schools will need to be set up, new texts written and copied for libraries throughout Egypt. A chosen people we may be, but Egyptians are still human. The gods will not be able to interact with the masses. They will need ambassadors from among the learned—physicians, scribes, priests, priestesses, astronomers, astrologers—to work with. The council I propose will seek out these ambassadors.

"Then, there is our need for insight and prophecy so we might see our way clearly into the future. Your existing spiritual connections with the gods are invaluable. As the council is being formed at the rising of the Great Star, perhaps it is appropriate to refer to it as the Sirius Council. It will be unlike any Egypt has ever known."

Khufu's voice fell silent. His case was stated. Meri-ib and Taret also remained quiet while they considered what they had heard. They were being given the opportunity to serve the gods and the people in ways neither had done before, and they knew that accepting the challenge would mean leaving their positions at their beloved Temple of the Sun in Heliopolis.

As if he had read their thoughts, Khufu spoke again. "As your king, I could command your acceptance as heads of the Sirius Council but I will not. If you serve, it must be your free choice to do so. That is the only way I will know that your minds and hearts will be in your work."

Meri-ib did not hesitate to answer. He stood up. "I am deeply honored that Your Majesty has chosen me to be a part of the Sirius Council. I accept in the name of the great god Ra." He bowed deeply to Khufu, who looked at him with a gentle smile.

Taret listened to Meri-ib's acceptance. A part of her was overwhelmed at the honor being bestowed upon her, yet she was mulling over the years she had spent teaching the Star Priestess apprentices. It was her life. They were not mere students; they were *her* Star Daughters, *her* spiritual sisters. Not once had she entertained the idea of not being their main teacher.

What her life's work was meant to be had always been clear, but now? She rose to address Khufu.

"The events of these times warrant measures a mere mortal could not have foreseen. I am prepared to step aside from my position as High Priest-ess of the Holy Order of Nut to serve on the Sirius Council for the gods and Your Majesty, incarnation of the great god Horus. In doing so, may I serve all Egyptians and my beloved Egypt well."

Khufu sighed. He had accomplished a big part of what he had set out to do. "I am pleased," he said. "There is something else to be discussed that concerns the two of you and the Sirius Council. A council such as this provides for great minds to work together for the good of the country. I have thought long and hard about a particular person who I believe is the most highly evolved person alive. I have sent for this elder priest. He is here at the palace even as I speak. No council of servants of the gods would be complete without the presence of the wisest among us. I recently had an encounter with him. I am convinced I was in the presence of a living god."

Khufu nodded and a team of guards escorted the honored guest into the room. It was the Old One, the venerable Shemshu-Hor, Chief Priest of the Followers of Horus. The frail elder stood with the help of his ebony cane, looked at the king, and began inching his way toward the throne.

With a clap of his hands, Khufu motioned for a chair to be brought for the Old One so the four now assembled could sit together. Meri-ib bowed in respect and greeting to the chief prophet, but Taret was so taken by his appearance she could not move. She had heard stories of the Old One and his wisdom. She had even glimpsed him once when she first came to Heliopolis, when he had been carried on a litter at the head of a New Year's procession. He was a living legend, and she was humbled to be in his presence.

"I am honored to have you at the palace, Your Holiness," Khufu said.

"I am honored to be here," the old priest replied, his voice cracking with age. He nodded to Meri-ib and Taret in acknowledgment of their presence.

Khufu saw no need to explain to Shemshu-Hor why he and the other two elders were in Memphis. Khufu elected to get straight to the point, but before he could get a word out, the old priest spoke.

"The heavens are filled with highly developed beings. Star system after star system is alive with forms less evolved and more advanced than the humans on Earth. Some of the advanced ones have had a long relationship with Earth beings. They have brought knowledge here so we could turn from barbaric ways and become civilized. At the First Coming, the Great

Ones from the Sirius stars came to Egypt. They established a link. They walked and lived among men. They taught astronomy, mathematics, geometry, architecture, many more things. They were your ancestors, for it was they who seeded Earth with the germs of life long ago, long before the First Time. They were the progenitors of the human race. You may find what I tell you now hard to believe. With the forming of the Sirius Council, the time has come for you to know something about one of the mysteries of life."

The Old One stood up, supporting himself on his cane. Walking slowly to the foot of the Great Throne, he faced the group and said, "You need to know something. I am not . . . human. . . . I am a star being. I am from Sirius, chosen by my star siblings to remain alive here in Egypt. . . . All these millennia, I have been their living link on Earth. I have never had to experience death. When my time here is done, I will ascend to the starry realms of Osiris. After the Second Coming and when the time comes for the Star Gods to return to their stars, one will remain behind to take my place. I shall go home. The one who will stay behind has been chosen. She is a star woman from Sirius. . . .

"Until my star siblings come and she takes my place, I will remain in Memphis as the star ambassador to the Sirian Council. I, Shemshu-Hor, am at your service, Your Majesty, as I have been for all the kings before you. I have looked into the eyes of every one, heard their voices, grieved their sorrows and failures, celebrated their victories, and mourned their burials. While I remain on Earth I will never leave your side or the sides of my fellow Council members."

Khufu stood in silence, tears streaming down his cheeks. Without taking his eyes off the Old One, the king sank to his knees in homage to the Star God before him. Meri-ib and Taret knelt and bowed their heads too.

"Humans waste time and energy putting their gods on pedestals. Initiates walk *with* the gods, not behind or before them," the Old One said.

Chapter Thirty-Five

The New High Priestess
of the Temple of the Sun

Meri-ib's invitation to attend Sokar's feast was returned with the message that the High Priest was out of the city, and when he would return was not known. Sokar thought the High Priest's absence was odd, but decided it was nothing he would concern himself with, not yet anyway. Shem-hotep, Ali Gabri, and the merchant from Lebanon would come, and so would Mafdet and other young women. He had invited Tiye, but had not heard from her. Kheti had gone into the city earlier to get the provisions, and was now ordering servants and cooks to get everything ready.

Sokar took his hawk from its perch and went onto the veranda. He thought the bird pensive today. He sensed an apprehension in his familiar. Sokar put the bird on its outdoor perch and stood quietly by, fixing his eyes on Horus's. Within moments, his mind-cord extended from his brow to connect with the hawk. As he slipped into a light trance, images formed in Sokar's mind: Horus was sitting on a windowsill watching an old priest at a desk. Meri-ib. There was Khufu, Meri-ib again, then a woman. He wasn't sure who she was, though she looked familiar. The three were standing together with their hands joined. The images faded and no more formed. Sokar withdrew his telepathic link with Horus.

Sokar went to lie in the cool water of the lotus pool, pondering the hawk's visions. Who was the woman? Suddenly, her identity popped into his mind. Taret, High Priestess of the Temple of the Sun. Given that, what was the connection between these three people?

Guests began to arrive at Sokar's private apartment at the *Benu*

Temple. A consort of musicians played on the patio. The reception hall was filled with flower-garlanded tables of food and jugs of beverages. Baskets held plates; washing stands for guests to clean their hands and faces after eating stood in the four corners; ample floor cushions lay strewn about. The higher parts of the inner walls were hung with carpets, the lower parts left uncovered, revealing the woodwork.

It had been a long time since Sokar had entertained. Brought up in the palace, he was used to elaborate banquets and other social functions going on all the time. King Sneferu had never denied that Sokar was his son, and his mother was so beautiful she was sometimes permitted attendance at court functions as a trophy for the king to show off. Even though he did not take her as his legal wife, Sneferu accepted her as a servant in the royal harem. Sokar had been exposed to the royal lifestyle all his life, so he knew how to impress guests and make them comfortable. Sneferu had made sure that all his children, including his bastards, were reared and educated properly. He had showered them with affection and a pampered lifestyle only royalty could afford. So Sokar was socially well equipped for tonight.

Bakka's father, Ali, was the first to arrive, along with Mafdet and her father, another wealthy merchant. Ali had lost weight, and his features looked drawn and tight. It was obvious that his daughter's death several weeks before had taken its physical and emotional toll. Mafdet looked lovely. If I were king, thought Sokar, she would make a beautiful queen and fill my palace with fine, healthy children. General Shem-hotep arrived next, accompanied by a woman Sokar assumed was his wife, but who was in fact his older sister, Pipu.

Other guests drifted in over the next hour, and everyone enjoyed the wine and food. Sokar engaged in conversation with Mafdet. "You are looking especially lovely," he said to her. "You make me regret that I have neglected to be in more frequent contact with you."

"You flatter me, My Lord Sokar. I am sure your time has been occupied with far more important things than me," she replied coyly. Mafdet knew she was beautiful, and she used it to her advantage. She was not pushy or smug, just self-confident, and that came across in a sensual way that made her appealing.

"Your father seems well, but Ali does not," Sokar remarked.

"He is grieving. He has never stopped grieving," Mafdet replied.

"I am sorry to hear that," Sokar said. "Perhaps being here is a good sign."

"Perhaps," the woman answered softly, looking to where Ali was standing with her father.

Excusing himself, Sokar joined the two merchants, inquiring about their businesses. They were satisfied with their income, but they were concerned about the safety of their imports what with rumors of roving gangs. Sokar raised an eyebrow upon hearing repeated the rumor he himself had started, but he said nothing about that. "Tell me, Ali. Have you been well?" Sokar had heard from Mafdet that Ali blamed the High Priestess Taret and her cohorts at the Temple for Bakka's death, and that he refused to believe that his daughter had killed herself.

"Well? Yes, I suppose so. Why do you ask?" Ali replied, seemingly annoyed at the implications of the question.

Taken aback by the man's curtness, Sokar smiled. "Death has claimed both my parents, my friend. I know how difficult its pain can be."

Ali looked down, frowning. He did not want his feelings to show. Sokar continued in his attempt to soothe the man's pain and elicit a more revealing response. "I am certain that your daughter has fared well on her journey through the Underworld. Her youth and innocence make for a light heart."

"Had she not been exposed to demons and evil spirits she did not understand, she would be alive today!" Ali spit out the words with a force of bitterness that Sokar could feel the power of intuitively. His grief and anger were a recipe for vulnerability, Sokar thought. He mentally filed the fact for later use.

"There are many ways of looking at such a tragic event, Ali. Perhaps it would be to your advantage not to come to any conclusions or place any blame regarding your daughter's untimely demise until you have had time for your heart to heal."

"My heart will never heal," Ali shot back, his eyes flashing, his features grim. "Someday I will get my revenge." Then, as if a completely different person had come out from beneath his morose facade, the man changed into a calm, pleasant person. "Tell me, Sokar. How go your vineyards in the Delta? Are you not ready to abandon the city and Temple life and retire to your villa near the sea?"

Sokar eyed Ali suspiciously, surprised at the quick change. Ali was not in his right mind, no doubt due to his grief and the guilt of forcing his daughter to go to the Temple against her will. He thought it best to go along with the man's mood shift, and not to call any further attention to Bakka.

"Soon, Ali. Soon I shall be basking in the cool breezes of the sea," Sokar said jovially. With a friendly slap on Ali's back, he left to speak with Shemhotep, who stood on the patio sipping on a cup of wine while admiring Sokar's hawk.

"A magnificent creature, is he not?" Sokar said, walking up to the general.

"Indeed he is," Shem-hotep replied. "He is like a great warrior."

"No, not *like* a great warrior, my friend. He *is* a great warrior," Sokar said, his pride showing in a way that bordered on arrogance. Holding out his forearm for the bird to climb onto, he beckoned the general to follow him so they could speak in private. Out of earshot of the guests, Sokar asked of the mood at the palace. Shem-hotep said that all seemed normal, but that something curious had occurred earlier that very morning.

"And what was that?" Sokar inquired, trying not to reveal the depth of his interest.

"Well, I went to Khufu several days ago to petition for a small regiment to investigate the report you gave me about roving bands in the North. I did not reveal the source of the report, but I made it clear how important I felt it was to make certain that the northern borders are safe."

"And what did my half-brother say?"

"He turned me down," the general answered, his face turning red as he remembered. "Said the men could not be spared right now mostly because of the Sphinx project."

"I see," Sokar commented. He did not have to probe Shem-hotep to determine how the man felt about Khufu's refusal. It was written on his face.

"This morning, I received a message from Manetho that there was a matter of a highly secretive nature, something about a security assignment that Khufu wished me to be in charge of. I have been summoned to meet with him tomorrow. Seems it has to do with guarding the safety of someone important. I don't know who."

Sokar was very interested. Khufu would not go to the chief of his army for any ordinary security detail. Whoever Shem-hotep would be in charge of protecting must be someone of high rank within the royal family or the government. Perhaps some foreign dignitary?

Shem-hotep spoke again. "I have heard that Pharaoh has been secluded for the last couple of days and turned all the court business over to Manetho."

"Secluded?"

"I heard he has been meeting with a couple of priests, maybe members of the holy orders from here in Heliopolis."

As soon as the words were out of the man's mouth, Sokar recalled the images of Meri-ib and Taret he had picked up telepathically from Horus. "Not the High Priest of Memphis, but Heliopolis?"

"That is what I think, but I do not know. Why?"

"Oh, no particular reason. Just that it seems curious that Khufu would be meeting in secret or seclusion, as you say, with priests from Heliopolis and not Memphis."

"Well, if that's who it is, I have better things to do with my time than to see to the protection of a couple of priests."

"Perhaps you had best not jump to conclusions too quickly. It will be interesting to see who these priests are and why they need protection, and why they are at the palace."

The Sun began to set. Sokar gathered his guests together and invited them to join him on the patio, where it was cooler. Sokar knew that if he was going to get the opportunity to feel his guests out about their political views, he must do it now. He was concerned that Ali had had too much to drink and might become a problem, so he took Kheti aside and told him to keep an eye on the drunken guest. Facing his dinner group and seeking to point the conversation in the direction he wanted, Sokar held up a cup of wine and proposed a toast. "To the Second Coming of the Star Gods, benefactors of all Egyptians, and to our venerable king who has been chosen by birthright to receive them."

All the guests, except Ali, lifted a cup. As they drank, the merchant drawled, "Damn the gods, and Pharaoh too," shocking everyone. To curse the gods was blasphemous beyond belief. Sokar took immediate advantage of the situation. "No one would curse the Neters or the king without good reason. Perhaps we should hear Ali's reasons."

Having the attention of everyone focused on him made Ali more sober than he appeared to be, and made him feel the need to take advantage of the forum to voice his opinion. "The shame of damning the gods I will carry and I pray for forgiveness. It is very hard for me to look to the future since my Bakka's death. I have given little thought to the return of the Star Gods, though I should have for such an occasion. Still, I cannot be completely sorry for what I said about the king. These times cry out for stronger leadership. But that is only my opinion. I spoke before I remembered that Khufu is your half-brother, Sokar. I beg your pardon."

"Do not apologize," Sokar spoke up quickly, in an attempt to ease the man's feelings. "Leadership is a quality not everyone possesses. We all know that. What would you do differently if you were king, Ali?" It was a question the merchant had never been asked before, and to which he'd never given any thought.

Mafdet spoke up. "Leadership is about trust, the people's trust."

"You are right," Shem-hotep responded. "And the people adore the Pharaoh."

"But do they *trust* him?" Ali barked. "Is adoration the same as trust? I think not."

"I am inclined to agree," Sokar commented. Then, turning to Mafdet's father, he asked, "What about you, Menkar? What do you think?"

Menkar cleared his throat, nervous about voicing his opinion. "I never thought of Khufu as being a particularly strong leader. But I have assumed the Throne is in capable hands. Khufu is there by birthright, and there is nothing anyone can do to change that, whether he is as strong a leader as the country needs, or not."

The comment about Khufu's birthright was the one sore spot that Sokar could not let go unchallenged. "Oh, but is that the case? Is being king truly Khufu's birthright? This is a question I have pondered all my life. More than any of you here, I have asked myself the question. What kind of king would I have been if my father had honored me with my birthright? How would I compare to my half-brother as a leader and king?"

"And have you gotten answers?" Mafdet cooed softly, stepping forward to stand beside Sokar.

"Yes, as a matter of fact I have. I would strengthen Egypt's trade with other lands and her army. I would build great temples to the great god Horus and construct a palace in the South and seek the most beautiful woman in the land to be my queen and bear me heirs. The dispute over who is the rightful heir to the Throne could probably be argued forever. I only know what *I* believe. In these times, I think it is best for the people to have a choice in their leader. This is why I have a plan for that choice. I have an alternative. Egypt is two lands. There is room for two governments."

It was not a convincing speech and he knew it. Sokar did not expect everyone to take him seriously, but it planted the idea of his being the head of a *second* government. That was enough for now. Sokar gave a sharp clap and summoned the musicians to play in accompaniment to the lovely female dancers he had invited to entertain his guests.

When the dancing was over, the guests cheerfully voiced their approval. All the while, Sokar had kept his eyes on Mafdet, watching her body swaying gently in time with the dancers. He remembered she was studying music and decided to invite her to play. The young woman was reluctant at first. With a little coaxing, though, she gave in to Sokar's charm, and took advantage of the rare opportunity to play in front of people other than her family and teacher. She chose the lute. The guests at first listened to the girl's playing, but soon began drinking and talking. Mafdet had Sokar's undivided attention.

Her beauty captivated him, with her shapely body, bronze skin, and straight hair that hung in two tresses to her bare breasts. The soft features of her face were accented by green kohl under her eyes, and black painted eyebrows and eyelids, making her eyes appear larger than they were. Her lips were rouged. The sweet-smelling oil in her hair was aromatic and enveloped her. A single strand of gold graced her neck and gold armbands circled each of her upper arms.

She was a queen fit for any king, but Sokar could not let his feelings go there now. If he was going to follow through with his plans, he could not let anything or anyone divert his focus.

Earlier in the afternoon, Meri-ib and Taret embarked on their return trip to the Temple of the Sun. A long discussion with Khufu had determined their immediate fate. They would return to the Temple and resign their respective positions of High Priest and High Priestess, and select those who would succeed them. The resignations would be unprecedented in the history of the Temple of the Sun. The situation would need to be handled skillfully.

After returning to Heliopolis, Meri-ib and Taret set about making the necessary arrangements for their move to Memphis. It had been decided by the Pharaoh that the Council members, including Shemshu-Hor, would reside in the palace. The royal house would not only provide comfort and safety, it would make it convenient for Khufu to meet and consult with them on a moment's notice.

When Meri-ib awoke, he tended his morning duties in the central chapel. Afterwards, he returned to his study and prepared to meet with the most influential of the priests who worked under him. These were the ones from among whom he would choose a successor. There was Un'e, head of a noble family with an ancient lineage, and who lived outside the Temple in the city. Un'e was a wealthy landowner who had inherited his position as a priest from his father before him. There was also Ra-hotep, Temple Overseer of the Treasures; and Ant'en the Prophet, leader of the priests of various divinities. All were men of high birth, capable of assuming the position of High Priest. There were also numerous other servants of Ra to choose from, many of whom were qualified for the job. But Meri-ib faced a problem not unlike that of the king: he had to select his successor from the perspective of which individual was best for the job and whose selection would best appease the priesthood.

When the priests gathered in Meri-ib's study, he began explaining why he had called them together. "You are all aware of the recent events about which the Honorable Khufu has issued proclamations. While the unearthing of the Stone Head is a huge undertaking, nothing can compare in importance to the present and future of Egypt than the Second Coming of the Star Gods. I have heard it said that only through what is known can what is unknown be apprehended. This certainly applies to the Second

Coming. The sacred texts tell us that the First Coming was an unprecedented event that changed Egyptians forever. Based upon what we know, I surmise the Second Coming will have no less of an impact on our lives, indeed upon our civilization.

"The Honorable Khufu has requested my presence and service at the palace in Memphis. While there I will serve on a council that is newly formed, a council whose task it will be to advise the Pharaoh during these days leading up to the return of the Star Gods. I will be among the diplomats who will welcome the divinities back to Egypt. It is therefore necessary for me to resign my position as High Priest of the Sun Temple, effective immediately."

The three priests were caught off guard. Ra-hotep, the most outspoken, asked the first question, his tone reflecting his surprise. "My Lord Meri-ib, this is indeed sudden! Have you chosen a successor?"

"My successor? No. Not yet. That is why I have called you all here. One of you will take my place. I wanted to consult with you before making my decision."

The three men were silent. Turning to Un'e, Meri-ib voiced his concerns. "You, Un'e, are dedicated to the great god Ra. This I know. But I realize that you bear responsibilities outside your life as a priest. Your business makes heavy demands upon your time."

"Yes, of course you are right, My Lord Meri-ib," Un'e replied. "I do not feel that I can do justice to the position of High Priest, though the opportunity is tempting and flattering."

Meri-ib turned to Ant'en. "You, Ant'en, are a great seer, one who has served me and the other priests well. I have depended heavily upon your insights, your spiritual stability, and dependability. And you, Ra-hotep, you are an able combination of scholar and priest, perhaps the one who understands the workings of the Temple better than any other. You are a humble servant of the Neters, as are all of you."

As the priests listened to Meri-ib comment on their qualifications, each had his own thoughts. Un'e was certain it was not right for him to take on the most responsible position in the religious world, and he said so. Ra-hotep said that in light of the times, the prophetic capability of Ant'en made him the most able man for the job.

"And how do you feel about this, Ant'en?" Meri-ib asked.

"I am humbled, my lord," the man answered, barely audible. "I have dedicated my life in service to the Neters, and this is an opportunity for me to fulfill my heart's deepest desire. What think you of my worthiness?"

Walking over to Ant'en and putting his hand on the priest's shoulder, Meri-ib said, "The Rod of Power would be in capable hands if you agree to accept it in service of the gods and your fellow countrymen in the nome of Heliopolis. Will you accept this charge?"

Ant'en, looking down at the floor for a few seconds, raised his head and looked into Meri-ib's eyes. "I will, Master Meri-ib. I will assume the position of High Priest and First Prophet of Heliopolis."

"May the great god Ra pour his blessings upon you."

Taret was confronting the same business in her wing of the Temple. Unlike Meri-ib, there was no question in her mind which priestess she must appoint as her successor. Ani, chief Dream Priestess and amulet-maker. No one was more able or qualified, no one wiser or closer to the Neters. Taret summoned Ani to her private quarters. When Ani arrived, she sensed something in the air.

"Since the night I spent in the dream temple, many things have come to pass in my life," Taret said. "The gods have called me on a mission to Memphis, to the palace. I have had an audience with the king. The Honorable Khufu is faced with many challenges and decisions right now, more so than at any other time in his reign. He wants special guidance, prophetic vision to assist him in taking the right steps for all Egyptians."

"Khufu has called upon me and Meri-ib to come to Memphis to serve on what he calls The Sirius Council. I cannot disclose the details, but you will all know everything soon. For now, Ani, there is a matter that cannot wait. My acceptance makes it necessary to abandon my position as High Priestess. I am faced with choosing my successor. There is no question who that woman must be. I ask you to assume the position of High Priestess of the Holy Order of Nut, at the Temple of the Sun."

Taret sat down and looked at Ani, whose expression revealed her depth of thought. Then, bowing her head in respect to Taret, the Dream Priestess replied, "I accept your trust in me with deep appreciation, Star Mother. I accept your judgment that it is I who is chosen to follow in your footsteps. I trust your judgment and pray to the Neters for their blessings."

"I would be honored if you would allow me to initiate you as High Priestess in the presence of the apprentices tomorrow, Ani," Taret said.

Chapter Thirty-Six

The Star Woman's Vision

When Khem woke, the Sun had not yet come over the horizon. The room was still dark except for the faint light given off by the oil lamp on her altar. She lay still for a few more minutes, allowing her mind to become centered. She had been sleeping so soundly it was hard to wake up. She knew she had dreamed, but she could not remember what. This morning her thoughts focused on one thing: the comet.

Throwing the bed linens back, Khem climbed out of bed and walked over to the window, examining the predawn sky for the comet. There it was, midway on the horizon, its tail faint but long.

Lying down again, she recalled her conversation with Tiye, about the comet being an omen of something good and bad. They had asked for a dream to help them arrive at the truth of the comet's nature. Khem felt frustrated and disappointed at not being able to remember her dream. She wondered if Tiye would accept her invitation to share quarters in the Temple. The bond between them had grown and they were like sisters. Tiye had wanted time to think about it. Khem thought of her writing lessons with Sheshat. She loved practicing the word pictures. Remembering Atef, she wondered how his lessons were coming along. She had spent little time with her brother since he had come to Heliopolis, and she longed for when they would be together.

Soon it was light out and Akhi came in to brush the tangles out of Khem's hair. Then Tiye arrived.

"Tiye, good morning. I did not expect to see you before class," Khem said. "Come, sit down. I will be ready to go in a short while."

"Do not hurry," Tiye responded. "I wanted to come early and tell you about two things. I have made a decision about moving into the Temple, about living here with you, if Akhi does not think my being here would be too much work for her."

"Oh, no, you are welcome, Tiye," Khem responded quickly. "Having you here would please me and Akhi very much."

Tiye smiled, but said nothing.

"You said there were two things," Khem probed.

"Yes, there is something else. I dreamed about the comet."

"Tell me what you dreamed."

"Well, it was a short dream. I only remember an image of a woman, an Egyptian. She wore a thick, black wig with a plain silver headband that encircled her head at her brow. She held her hands out in front of her, like this." Tiye cupped one hand over the other, the right one palm down about six inches above the left, which was cupped upward. "The comet was racing towards her! She was going to catch it in her hands. And she did! She caught it and pulled it into her heart. It illumined her, and she became a blinding light and disappeared. That's not all. After that, I remember seeing the palace in Memphis, and then there were two. I saw two palaces. I think the comet woman may be one of the Star Gods, but I cannot be sure. I think that she and the comet are the same. What do you think?"

"Hmmm, that sounds right to me. Yes, I think you are right. If you are . . ." Khem's voice trailed off.

"What?" Tiye urged. "What were you going to say?"

"I was just thinking that, if you are right about the comet woman being a Star Goddess and the comet is a sign that foretells the Second Coming, then I wonder if your dream is telling you that at least *one* of the Star Gods coming to Egypt is a woman, a Star Woman. You know, like the Star Woman Khaba used to talk about."

"Oh, yes. I remember," Tiye answered. "That makes sense. But what could the two palaces mean?"

"That *is* curious," Khem mused, turning the idea over in her mind. "Maybe it means two kings, one in each palace. But that is strange."

Tiye shook her head and threw up her hands. "Dreams can be so frustrating sometimes. Did you dream?"

"No. Well, yes, I did, but I cannot remember what it was."

Later in class the apprentices were buzzing about the comet. Kasut asked Khem and Tiye excitedly, "Have you seen the comet? I saw it last night. It is lovely! It looks just like a star with a sparkly tail!"

"Yes," Khem replied. "I have seen it twice. You are right. It is very beautiful."

"I have not seen it yet," Tiye said. "But I am in no hurry."

Kasut gave the Nubian a puzzled look, not understanding her comment. Khem changed the subject by asking Kasut if she had seen Senna. It had been a while since Khem had run into the old priest, and she was becoming concerned.

"Oh, don't you know?" Kasut replied, a frown creasing her face. "Senna has fallen ill. Some sort of fever, I think."

"I did not know," Khem answered. She thought it curious that she had not heard about the priest's illness. "When did this happen?"

"A few days ago. He is in the infirmary for treatment," Kasut explained. "That is all I know."

Taret arrived with her scribe. She climbed the dais, sat facing her audience, and expressed her pleasure at being back at the Temple. She had missed her Star Sisters, but acknowledged these were unusually busy times and her services had been needed in the capital city. "I will tell you more about my journey to Memphis later, but, for now, it is important to get into today's lesson.

"I wish to speak about a truth given to Egyptians by the Star Gods at the First Coming. It concerns *ma'at*, which means truth, justice, right. These words define the way it is in the realm of divine forces and with the divine agencies themselves. *Ma'at* allows no chaos. *Ma'at* is the order in the universe.

"*Ma'at* manifests as a female goddess, the daughter of Atum-Ra. She is depicted as a beautiful, winged woman, her wings outspread, wearing an ostrich feather in her hair. Ma'at is a passive deity. She maintains all the gods so their powers work in a harmonious and orderly manner. This implies the gods are nourished and maintained by truth. Without *ma'at* there would be no order. In the realm of the gods there is no disorder. All is in balance and harmony with all else.

"That is the way it is in the realm of the gods, but our lives on Earth do not pass in the realm of the gods. We always struggle with order and disorder on every level. There was a time, before the First Coming, when humans did not know any better. They were unaware of a life of order and harmony. The Star Gods taught us. They showed us a better way, and left the goddess Ma'at among us.

"Since ancient times, the task of establishing *ma'at* in our society has been the Pharaoh's. Not since the earliest times has a king been faced with a greater need to maintain *ma'at*, harmony, and balance among all Egyptians than at this time of the Second Coming of the Star Gods. It is upon Khufu's shoulders. Egypt cannot afford social disintegration, and social order must be aligned with cosmic order. This great responsibility falls to the king because he is human *and* god. Therefore he lives as much in the eternal as in the temporal world. In these times, *ma'at* must be constantly renewed and reestablished in the face of the tendencies toward disorder. We must all find the divine, orderly principles within ourselves. We must transcend being a mere human.

"The great god Ra has told us that *ma'at* is ours, given to us so we might live in harmony. We must not lose sight of the fact that *ma'at* is adored only by those who are truthful and righteous. As priestesses of the Holy Order of Nut, we must see to it that the mundane world is continually re-attuned to *ma'at*.

"You may think that an initiate could not live outside *ma'at*, but you would be mistaken. That is what being an initiate and a magician is about. You can make the choice to live in disharmony with others, with the land, with yourselves, even with the Neters. You can choose to live by principles and morals that create disorder for you. If you live in a disorderly way, you affect everything around you. A magician knows that she can use magical knowledge to exist in that kind of environment, inwardly and outwardly. That is using your power for a self-serving purpose. That is a waste and therefore a misuse of power.

"On the other hand, an initiate uses her power to live continually in *ma'at*. She strives at all times to reestablish *ma'at* within herself and the world. She contributes to the *ma'at* of the whole—temple, city, the Order of Nut. This is the difference between a black and a white magician. Many have knowledge, few have wisdom. Many know, with their minds, the *value* of *ma'at*. Few have the wisdom to *apply* that value to their lives."

Taret stopped and looked towards the back of the room. Ani had just entered. With a slight nod of her head, the High Priestess motioned for the Dream Priestess to come to the dais. Ani's plump body was draped in a loose-fitting, soft linen sheath tied at the waist with a gold cotton braid. Her ample breasts added to her image of a body that appeared strong and healthy. She was a commanding figure. Taret spoke again:

"The King of Egypt, the honorable incarnation of Horus, Wearer of the Double Crown, finds himself in the position of having to exert every effort to maintain *ma'at* in these times of major change. Most kings would not humble themselves to ask for help for fear they would appear weak and unworthy of the Crook and Flail. Khufu is not such a man. Khufu is wise. He knows he must have prophets and visionaries he can rely upon to forewarn him daily of threats to *ma'at* as we prepare to receive the Star Gods.

"Pharaoh has summoned the venerable Meri-ib, High Priest of the Sun Temple, and me to reside at the palace in Memphis. We will serve on a council made of the Pharaoh, Meri-ib, me, and another whose identity I cannot reveal."

The room buzzed with excited talk.

"Yes, this means that I will resign my position as High Priestess. It is a decision that saddens me, for it means that I will be leaving you all, at least for a while. I have chosen my successor. It is Ani. I am needed in Memphis right away, so I will pass the Rod of Power to Ani here and now."

The buzzing intensified. Taret motioned for Ani to stand before her. A servant girl scrambled to Taret's feet and rolled out a woven-mat rug for Ani to step onto. Two other servant girls came and stood behind the High Priestess. One held a bowl of water, the other a gilded rectangular box.

Looking at Ani, Taret spoke about passing the Rod of Power. "The wand has embodied the power of the members of the Holy Order of Nut since its inception during the First Time. In our language, the word 'sky' is feminine; thus, the sky is Nut, whose starry belly we see suspended in the heavens above us. She is the great celestial cow who gave birth to the sky when nothing else existed. She is the mother of us all, from whose bosom all things proceed. We are her priestesses. She has chosen us, one by one, and we have chosen her. Whoever among us possesses the star wand represents Nut on Earth. This is a great honor and responsibility.

"The Star Priestess who accepts the Rod of Power must understand that, as long as it is in her trust, her life, body, mind, and soul are no longer hers alone. She must think for Nut and feel for Nut, for she is the human incarnation of the Star Mother. The transfer of power takes time for the receiver to adjust, so Ani will need your love, patience, and prayers."

Taret motioned for the assistant holding the alabaster water bowl to step forward. She bade Ani to kneel on the woven mat. Dipping the first two fingers of her right hand into the same water that had been used to wash the statue of Ra that morning in the Holy of Holies, the High Priestess tilted Ani's head up with her left hand and touched her wet fingers to her brow and said:

> I call upon the power of Isis
> to protect you from all things of harm,
> from all darkness,
> from those that mean you harm,
> from those who would deceive you
> and cause you pain.

Taret beckoned Ani to stand. She nodded at the servant who held the gilded box that contained the star wand, and the servant opened the box. Taret took out the slender ebony rod, its shaft embedded with diamonds, one end capped with gold inlaid with lapis hieroglyphs representing the name Nut.

The High Priestess held the rod with both hands and she held it out so Ani could place her hands around the capstone end. As the two priestesses stood joined by the rod between them, Taret said:

> I stand in the pure, holy light of my mother,
> the Star Goddess Nut.
> Her light flows within me and through me,
> and unites me with the divine.
> With this star wand I pass Nut's power to you.
> As the light flows from my brow to yours,
> let my mind be cleared and your voice be filled with her wisdom.
> As the light flows from my throat,
> let my voice speak true and yours speak for Her.
> As the light flows from my heart,
> let my soul continue to be loving and your heart be filled with her power.
> As the light flows from my stomach,
> may it flow into you and make your instincts be right.
> As the light flows from my groin into yours,
> may it cause all your desires to be holy.
> As the light flows from my legs into yours,
> may all your travels be blessed.
> As the light flows from my feet into yours,
> may your steps be sure,
> and may your footsteps be welcome in all sacred places.
> As the light flows from my hands into yours,
> may your works be pleasing to the Neters.
>
> May Nut and Isis abide with you
> and may you live within the glory of their light forever.
> So be it.

The Passing of the Rod ceremony completed, Taret released her hands from the rod, leaving it in Ani's possession. "You, Ani of Heliopolis, Star Daughter of the goddess Nut, Humble Servant of the goddess Isis, are now, until you or the Neters deem it no more, the High Priestess of the Holy Order of Nut and Star Mother of the Star Priestesses of the Sun Temple of Innu. May you reign in *ma'at*."

Ani bowed, then faced the apprentices who saw that the new Chief Priestess's face was wet with tears. Taret would be missed because they all loved and respected her. Now they accepted Ani, and would support her in every possible way.

Taret left immediately so Ani could assume her new role. Besides, there were many personal chores to attend to before she boarded the royal barque for her new home in Memphis the next day. It had come about so fast. One day she was High Star Priestess, the next, a member of one of the most, if not *the* most, special councils ever in Egypt.

In light of Ani's elevation to High Priestess, she would turn the responsibility of Khem and Tiye's private lessons over to another priestess, Klea, who would soon arrive from the Temple of Isis in Hermopolis. She was not a Star Priestess and would have nothing to do with that part of their training, but she was a fine magician.

Khem and Tiye settled on the bed in Khem's room to discuss their new teacher.

"What do you suppose Klea will be like?" Khem asked.

"I don't know," Tiye replied. "I do not look forward to her coming. Ani is my teacher, and I want it to stay that way."

"But don't you see, Tiye. Ani has many new responsibilities now and—"

"So she doesn't have time for us," Tiye broke in, her voice sharp.

"Well, yes, if you put it that way. I suppose she doesn't," Khem replied, trying to understand why her friend was upset. Then, it suddenly dawned on her what Tiye was feeling. "Oh, I know. You are worried that your link with Khaba will be broken if Ani is not your teacher and guide. That's it, isn't it?"

Tiye did not answer, but the look on her face told Khem she was right.

"Do not think that. It is not true. Khaba has come to you through Ani, but she will also come through Klea. You will see. Besides, how do you know that Khaba has not had a hand in Klea's coming? After all, Khaba did say she was working with you from the Afterlife, and you have clear evidence of this truth."

"I wonder if the comet's coming is an omen of Ani becoming the High Priestess and Taret leaving?" Tiye said, a frown on her face, as if anything the comet foretold or caused to occur could only be bad.

"If it does, I do not interpret that as a bad thing, do you?" Khem said, frustrated with Tiye's view. "Why don't you ask Khaba? I am sure she will tell you the truth."

Khem's words shocked her.

"What's the matter? Ani said you could talk to Khaba, but only if you 'see' her in her true form." Getting up off the bed and going over to her dressing table, Khem picked up the bronze mirror her mother had given her when she came to the Temple. "Here, take this. I once saw a woman's face in my mirror. It was Sheshat, and later I met her. The mirror is like a scrying bowl, and I have my scrying bowl too if you would rather use that. Go ahead. Contact Khaba and ask her about the comet. I am sure you can."

Tiye stared at the mirror in Khem's hand.

"No. It will not work. It is *your* mirror," she said finally.

"Nonsense," Khem snapped. "You are just afraid Khaba will not come."

Khem's words hit a nerve. "Perhaps you are right," Tiye responded.

It was unusual to catch the Nubian in a weak moment like this. It made Khem feel guilty for having taunted her. She realized that Tiye was not as volatile as she once was. She did not want to mistake her willingness to show her vulnerability as a weakness, for that would be an error.

After a few minutes passed, Tiye's attitude changed. "I think I would prefer to use the scrying bowl, if you do not mind," she said.

"Of course I do not mind," Khem replied sincerely. "Come, it is on my altar."

The little bowl was filled with water illumined by the light from the oil lamp. Khem stood back and let Tiye stand at the altar. Besides, there was only room for one to see into the bowl. Bast watched them.

Tiye removed the bowl from the altar, put it on the floor, and sat in front of it. Even though this made it possible for both to see into the bowl, Khem chose to let Tiye work alone. Though she had shared many of her feelings with Khem, she knew the Nubian's relationship with Khaba was private.

Tiye took several deep breaths and relaxed. Khem could "feel" her friend's energy change as her consciousness shifted into an altered state. Tiye's body swayed slightly as her eyes opened into another realm of reality. As she peered into the bowl, the water turned into a foglike liquid. Tiye projected the image of Khaba as the young, beautiful woman into the water. Then she spoke to it. "I am so happy to see you, Khaba. The comet is here. Will you tell me about it? Is there something to fear, something I should know?"

The image in the water faded slowly and was replaced by one of the fiery comet streaking across the night sky. Tiye watched as the celestial traveler's shape began to shift, changing into a Star Woman. The word *Zeno-sothis* resounded in Tiye's head. The comet was bringing a Star Woman to Earth, a woman from another star system. Tiye realized she would be the first Star God to arrive. The comet embodied the Star Woman's energy, and would release her essence into the Earth as it journeyed through the solar system.

Then Tiye saw the Star Goddess. She was large-boned and strong, and her violet eyes were piercing. Her olive skin was like bronze, her black hair had gray-white strands. She was clad in a long, flowing, gauzy-sleeved dress, a short mantilla trimmed with fringe on the shoulders; an apron fell loosely from her neck to her bare feet.

The image faded and the water grew still. Tiye next saw the royal palace in Memphis. Instantly, a great earthquake ripped the magnificent building in two, each half becoming an image of the Pharaoh's dwelling. Between the two palaces stood Sokar. A great hawk with its wings outspread perched proudly on his shoulder; its eyes, beak, and talons flashed with light. The vision startled Tiye and she snapped out of her trance.

Bast rose, the hair on her back standing straight up, and started towards Tiye, now holding her head in her hands. Bast rubbed against her and then lay down beside her. Khem sat beside Tiye on the floor.

"Are you back with us?" Khem asked.

"Yes, I am fine," Tiye replied. "It was a wonderful but strange experience. I saw Khaba. She looked like she did in my dream, young and pretty. I asked her about the comet and . . ." Her voice trailed off as the images she had seen reappeared in her mind.

"What was it, Tiye? What did you see?"

"What I saw was wonderful!" Tiye was breathless, her eyes wide in wonderment. "It was what I saw at the end of my vision that puzzles me. I do not know what it means, but I know *who* I saw."

"Tell me. Tell me everything, Tiye."

"I will. Just give me a minute to get my bearings."

Tiye and Khem got up off the floor and sat on the bed. Bast jumped up and lay down beside them. The animal sensed the excited energy. It was making her extremely alert.

"What did you see, Tiye?"

"It was the same image in my dreams, with two palaces. An earthquake divided the king's house into two identical palaces." Her eyes widening, Tiye grabbed Khem's hand excitedly, "And do you know what? Sokar—he was standing between the two palaces with a big hawk on his shoulder!"

"Sokar? What could that mean?"

"I don't know," Tiye answered. "But I know how seeing the vision made me feel."

"How?"

"Uneasy. It felt like he was a conqueror. He felt pleased with himself, arrogant. He had divided the palaces. Two palaces. Two kings. It has to mean that."

"You mean Sokar sees himself as king?"

"No. I mean Sokar sees himself as *a* king; he is one, Khufu the other."

Khem was stunned. If Tiye's interpretation was correct, it meant Sokar intended to put himself in a rival position with Pharaoh. This was powerful information.

"The part about the two palaces and Sokar is troubling, but the first part—oh, Khem, it is unbelievable. First, I saw Khaba in the water. She was young and everything. I asked her to tell me about the comet, and then I saw it. It was beautiful. It was so bright and sparkly. While I watched, it changed into a woman, a Star Woman named Zeno-sothis. You should have seen her. She did not look anything like us, like an Earth woman. She was lovely, and I know she is coming here with the return of the Star Gods"

The Star Woman was on her way to Egypt, Tiye thought. That knowledge was as real to her as the bed upon which she was sitting. "I know I will see her. Zeno-sothis is part of my destiny."

Khem felt a chill come over her body. She was sure the Nubian was right.

Chapter Thirty-Seven

Time to Consult the Oracle

Dejedfre had received the message that his presence was requested at the palace. The young High Priest of the Memphis Temple and crown prince of Egypt now sat in an enclave adjacent to the Throne Room, waiting for his father to finish his morning's business. He felt anxious, wondering why he had been summoned in an official capacity. Since he first learned about the Second Coming, his time had been occupied with preparations in the Memphis Temple. The priests of Ptah were dedicated to the great god. The House of the Image of Ptah and its citadel of the White Wall was one of the most beautiful monuments in Egypt, due in part to the fact that Ptah was the patron of all artisans. This made many Ptah priests artisans in their own right, and as High Priest, Dejedfre was called the "Chief Leader of the Artists." Many of the tombs and other monuments were painted by or supervised by Ptah priests.

Dejedfre was a priest, but above all else, he was an artist. His was interested in all the arts, but his talents lay in painting and sculpting. He took his role as High Priest seriously and performed his duties with diligence, yet he spent every free moment creating and supervising works of art. One of his finest completed statues of Ptah graced the main entrance to the royal palace.

Khufu and his son had never been close, partly due to the demands the kingship placed on Khufu. There were other reasons. One was that, like most fathers, Khufu had a concept of how his sons, especially his first born, should be. They should hunt and fish, and do all the things that fathers and sons do. But Dejedfre didn't enjoy hunting or fishing or play-ing warrior games. He was a scholar, and a fine one at that. It wasn't that Khufu did not appreciate his son's intellectual and esthetic skills, but not being an artist himself, he had little in common with the crown prince.

For his part, Dejedfre had never shown any interest in politics or matters of state, so Khufu was concerned about him as his successor. A reli-gious devotee himself, the king was proud of Dejedfre's position as High Priest of Memphis; still, he knew his son was filling a role his heart was not in and that being a faithful servant of Ptah obviously satisfied his needs.

When Khufu received Dejedfre in the Throne Room, he felt guilty. He did not want to get into a conflict with his son, as their audience was a matter of state and religion, ingredients that often did not mix.

"Greetings, Father," Dejedfre spoke before bowing deeply in respect. "I trust Your Majesty, Son of Horus, King of Egypt, is well."

"I am," Khufu responded, his tone hearty and friendly. "I am pleased to see you, my son. It has been some time, too long according to your mother."

"And how is mother?"

"She is well," the Pharaoh replied. "I suppose you are wondering why I have summoned you here, Dejedfre."

"I assume it has something to do with the announcement you made recently regarding the Sphinx project. How is that coming?"

Clearing his throat, Khufu answered, "It is going well, very well, as a matter of fact. But as important as the project is, it is not what I wish to speak to you about."

Dejedfre looked at his father curiously, allowing himself to show inter-est for the first time. He tended to put up a wall around his feelings when he was in Khufu's presence.

"The other more important part of my proclamation to the people—surely you know, concerns the Second Coming of the Star Gods."

"Yes," Dejedfre muttered. "I am aware of that. There is tremendous rejoicing about this among the priests of Ptah. It is our prayer that it is the great and wonderful Ptah who has chosen to return to Egypt."

"Yes, well, whichever of the gods shall come, it is an event that is sure to change the course of Egyptian culture and history. Do you not agree?"

"Yes, of course, Father."

"I am surprised that you as chief of the Temple of Memphis have not been in touch with the palace regarding this."

Eyeing his father warily, Dejedfre answered, "You mean why hasn't the Memphis Temple made an 'official' statement?"

"Yes. That is precisely what I mean."

"Because we take no 'official' stand on the issue. It speaks for itself, does it not? What can a handful of priests in Memphis, compared to the numbers within the priesthood throughout Egypt, say regarding the return of the Star Gods? Should we see ourselves as the appointed ambassadors to meet the gods? Does anyone even know when and where that will be?"

Dejedfre had a point. It was one that Khufu had not thought about. He had been so caught up in the event itself, he had only vaguely assumed that it would take place sometime in the summer, near or at Giza. Dejedfre's presence reminded Khufu he needed the Sirius Council. Such things could not be assumed. They had to be known. The High Priest's remarks had also opened the way for Khufu to inform his son about the Council. Not only should he know, he had a right to know.

"Your words are very wise, my son. You bring to my attention some things I have failed to take into ample account." Getting off the throne and stepping down from the dais, Khufu went to the window that overlooked the desert. This view always helped him think, especially when there was something serious on his mind. Then turning to face Dejedfre, he spoke in a calm, low voice. "I was informed of the Sphinx project and the Second Coming by the High Priest of Heliopolis. Meri-ib came to me some weeks ago after a vision he had of the great god Thoth. He brought me this as a witness of that communication."

Khufu reached into his waistband and took out the white feather. "A few days later, I traveled secretly to the Temple of the Sun, where Meri-ib and I met with the old hermit priest of the Followers of Horus, Shemshu-Hor. He confirmed Meri-ib's being told by Thoth of the necessity of unearthing the Stone Head and of the Second Coming. It was all true. There were other things revealed, which you shall know about in time. For now these are known only to myself and my most trusted advisors, the founding members of the Sirius Council."

Pharaoh turned back to the window and again looked out at the desert, his mind going into the memories of the recent events. "I was also paid a visit by Mistress Taret, the High Priestess of the Holy Order of Nut of Heliopolis. She told me about a dream she had where an enemy of mine will try to claim the throne. All this led me to summon the three Heliopolitans to Memphis. The Sirius Council was formed by me, and its members are serving as prophets and advisors during these auspicious times."

Dejedfre listened with interest, taking time to let it all sink in before commenting. After pacing the floor, the High Priest responded to the revelations. "The Priesthood of Heliopolis is an able-minded, competent body of men and women, I am sure. The formation of the Sirius Council is a wise move on your part, Father. You are aware of the importance of these times. I think the wisdom of your decision reflects your humbleness and your willingness to admit you need guidance. It would, of course, please me had it been the priests of the blessed god Ptah who had been elected to serve as counsel, but I respect your choice."

Khufu was relieved by Dejedfre's reaction and impressed by his wisdom. Dejedfre had chosen to not make a political, personal, or religious issue out of the formation of the Sirius Council. For that Khufu was grateful; it made him realize his son would be an asset to the Council. "It would please me and honor me if you would serve on the Sirius Council, Dejedfre. As High Priest of Memphis, you deserve this opportunity, and I have confidence in what your presence and wisdom would contribute."

The invitation surprised Dejedfre. He knew the big step his father had taken by making the offer. Still, it was something he must think about, so he said that he would give an answer the following day. Khufu accepted that condition.

Dejedfre changed the subject. "Tell me, Father, what is Shemshu-Hor like? I have known of him and the cloistered priests of the Followers of Horus all my life, but my eyes have never looked upon his face."

The question took Khufu back to times when his children were full of questions, asking about things they did not understand or found fascinating. Khufu sought words to describe the legendary Elder. "He is more commanding than any ruler could be, but in a quiet way. His presence draws you to him like a moth to a flame. He is sharp-featured, fragile in body, both soft and strong inside. The wisdom of the ages resides in him and manifests in his words. He is a man who can humble a king."

Dejedfre had many times longed to look upon his face. Every Egyptian knew that Shemshu-Hor existed. To the older people he was the hermit priest who had been alive as long as they or their fathers could remember, but who was rarely seen and never in public; a religious genius who had forgotten more than the most learned among the living had ever known. To the younger generation, the Old One was the one their parents and grandparents spoke about as the embodiment of the wisdom of the gods, and who perhaps was himself a god.

"I would consider it a great honor to meet the Old One," Dejedfre said. "I am impressed and surprised that Shemshu-Hor is part of the Sirius Council. I did not think he ever left his home in the Temple."

Khufu wasn't sure how much he should reveal at this point about Shemshu-Hor's whereabouts or the relationship he had with him. The prophet's safety and the secrecy of the Council's activity had to be preserved. Yet he wanted to tell Dejedfre everything, and he would in time. It was best to wait for his son's decision about joining the Council before saying more. "When your decision is made, I will expect your answer promptly," Khufu said, concluding the conversation.

"You have my word that you will be the first to know, Father."

The crown prince bowed in respect and left the room. For several minutes, Khufu sat quietly pondering their meeting. He felt better, more honest somehow, now that all was out in the open between them. Whatever happened now was in the hands of the Neters.

A court servant announced that the chief architect had arrived from Giza and wished to have audience with His Majesty.

"Nemon? Of course, show him in."

Nemon came into the Throne Room walking briskly, the usual wide grin on his face. "Greetings, Your Majesty, my cousin. I bring news."

"I take it the news is good," Khufu answered, as if saying it would make it so.

"It is interesting, that I assure you."

Nemon took off his overcloak and laid it on a bench against the wall. His broad chest and muscular arms were brown from the sun. A broad-banded kerchief covered his bare head. The chief architect strolled to the foot of the throne where the Pharaoh was seated. "You will remember that, a few days ago, I told you there was good reason to believe that there is an underground chamber beneath the Sphinx? Well, we now know it is there. I have been inside it. It is obviously an initiation chamber of some kind, Your Highness. I saw numerous statues, old texts, and boxes of ornaments of the gods and sacred objects that I only glanced at briefly. There is no question that the chamber contains a link to Egypt's past."

"How many people know about this chamber?" Khufu asked.

"The workers who did the digging and I, that's all. But I am sure word has circulated among the labor force. Why do you ask? Is there a problem of which I am unaware?"

"No, no. I was just thinking how the discovery could best be handled. I suppose it should be announced publicly at the New Year festival." The Pharaoh's public proclamation would make it official and stifle rumors.

"I think that would be the perfect time for the announcement, Your Majesty," Nemon commented. "By that time, we will know more about the chamber, its size, its contents, everything."

"Good. Keep me abreast of all you find out."

"I must say, cousin, for a man who just learned about the discovery of what may be Egypt's greatest link with her past, you seem to be less than overjoyed."

Khufu smiled. Nemon had a way of hitting the mark where his feelings were concerned, and he had read him right again. "Yes, Nemon. There is something on my mind, but I assure you it has nothing to do with the discovery of the chamber."

"What then?"

Khufu crossed his legs and leaned on the arm of the Great Chair, eyeing his cousin thoughtfully. Then, letting out a deep sigh, he said, "I know the Star Gods are coming. It has been foretold, and the omen is streaking across the dark sky, getting closer and brighter every night. Though I do not know exactly when, I know their return is imminent. The Sphinx project and now the finding of the chamber, the comet, my dreams, the dreams of others—they all point to it being *soon*."

"Surely it is time for you to consult the oracles," Nemon said.

"You are right," Khufu replied. "I will do just that." His mind immediately went to Shemshu-Hor. He knew he would get an answer from him.

Khem and Tiye were preparing for their first session with Klea, their new instructor in magic. Neither of them knew what to expect from the magician-priestess, but they were anxious to meet her. On their way to Ani's they stopped at the infirmary to see Senna. The old priest had been confined to his bed for two weeks. The girls felt guilty they had not visited him.

Senna was sitting up in bed sipping a cup of wine. He said it helped him relax. He looked frail, but Khem saw that he was in good spirits. They kept the conversation light, just catching their friend up on what they had been doing. In the course of the discussion, the subject of the comet came up. The mention of it caused Senna to make a curious remark. "My mother used to tell me that a comet was in the sky on the night I was born, and that there would be a comet in the sky on the night I would die."

Khem and Tiye looked at each other, not knowing what to say. The remark had thrown a damper on the visit for them, a fact that Senna quickly realized. "Oh, don't take me seriously. It is just the musings of an old man."

It was time to leave so Khem and Tiye headed for Ani's quarters. She was accompanied by a young woman in a simple garment without folds, and the garment was so narrow that every curve of her body was visible. The dress reached from below her breasts to her ankles, and two wide straps of linen passed over her shoulders to hold it up. The hem at the top was embroidered with a tiny blue lotus. Anklets graced each of her bare feet, and she wore a longhaired wig. Nothing about the woman's appearance was distinctive except for a piece of jewelry around her neck. Clay beads of various colors were strung to make a collar to cover the area from neck to breasts. It was the most unusual pectoral Khem and Tiye had ever seen.

"Khem, Tiye, this is Klea. She came from Hermopolis to be your teacher," Ani said.

"Ani tells me that I am inheriting two excellent apprentices," Klea said, eyeing the young women carefully. "I am pleased to hear that. I always have high expectations of my students, though some would say too high."

Klea's voice was deep and masculine, her demeanor so confident it almost made her seem arrogant. Her bright eyes twinkled with a mischievousness that made her seem much younger than she was. Khem liked her right away, but Tiye was reserved. It had been hard for the Nubian to get used to Ani and accept her as her mentor. Now she was faced again with having to become accustomed to another.

Ani excused herself, leaving the apprentices with Klea. The new teacher let them know Ani had filled her in on what they had been learning thus far and made a reference to Tiye's amulet-making skill. "I have been an amulet-maker myself for many years. I find it to be an extremely rewarding experience. In fact, I have devised a different kind of amulet I will tell you about," Klea said. "Most amulets are made of wood, clay, or faience, lapis, even gold. But I seldom make them that way anymore. I prefer to draw them on papyrus. Here, let me show you."

Klea went into an anteroom and returned carrying a bag made from tightly woven beads. Reaching inside, she brought out a box inlaid with cowrie shells. She opened the box and took out several small papyri tied into a roll by pieces of thin, red-dyed yarn. She undid the tie around one of the scrolls and, kneeling, unrolled it on the table between Khem and Tiye. The scroll was covered in hieroglyphs painted in black. "This is one I just finished. I have done a lot of these. It is a protection spell for a newborn baby."

Moving her index finger over the long, thin rows of symbols, Klea began reading the scroll. "This decree of protection was ordained by the goddess Isis. She says she will keep safe Djedmonte, whose mother is Nespernut, son of Hori, my servant. I shall keep him healthy in his flesh and his bones. I shall keep him healthy in his head. I shall keep healthy his right eye and his left eye."

Moving her finger down every line, Klea said, "See, it goes all down his body, and even mentions all sorts of other ailments the child will be protected from—coughing, inflammation, fever. There, look, it says he is sheltered from eye ailments and any kind of upset. Here on this line is the most important protection of all. The goddess promises to protect the boy from demons, drowning, and evil magicians."

Tiye was taken with this. It was similar to something she had learned from Khaba.

"What is it, Tiye?" Klea asked. "You seem to have had something dawn on you."

A bit embarrassed to speak up, Tiye hesitated. Glancing first at Khem, she turned to Klea and said, "Khaba, my dead mentor and adopted mother, could not write, so she never made any of these like you have. Families brought their babies to her, and she would hold the child and recite a spell of protection over them. It was almost the same spell you just read from the amulet scroll. It truly was."

"That is most interesting. You must tell me more about this woman, Khaba, sometime," Klea responded. She was grateful the experience had made Tiye more willing to open up to her. Turning to Khem, Klea said, "I understand you are bettering your reading and writing skills."

"Yes, I am," Khem answered.

"Perhaps Tiye will tell you Khaba's oral spells and you can write them on papyrus."

"Oh, yes, that would be most interesting!" Khem could hardly contain her excitement. She could tell by the look on Tiye's face that she was happy about the prospect too.

Word had spread that Sokar had entertained his guests well. Rumors of a budding romance between him and Mafdet, the presence of one of Khufu's generals, the music and dancing girls—it all had set tongues wagging. It was rare that a social gathering took place within a temple, but Sokar resided in special quarters not actually part of the temple in which religious activities took place.

Sokar had figured out that Meri-ib's absence from Heliopolis meant he was one of the members of the Heliopolitan holy orders meeting with Khufu. In light of the images he had gotten from his hawk, his guess was that Taret was the other. Khufu was obviously seeking the counsel of these, and maybe others. No matter. Sokar's own magical charm would generate the energy needed to set up his own government, announce it to the Egyptian people, and become the ambassador who received the Star Gods.

Sokar stepped into his bedchamber, where his altar was located. He admired the objects upon the large ebony structure he had imported from the South. These were his prized possessions. No one touched or used them except him, not even Kheti. On the eastern wall behind the altar hung a gold winged disk he used to invoke the protection and cooperation of the air spirits, the wind, in particular. On the altar was a silver chalice that represented the element of water. His father, King Sneferu, had given him the plain cup when Sokar became a priest.

Sokar's Mirror of Hathor, made of solid bronze, was the most exquisite piece. The face of the goddess graced the top of the handle, while the mirror itself was molded in the form of a full Moon disk. The reflective side was polished, the other slightly scoured. All magicians had a mirror that they used for various purposes, scrying, returning harmful thoughts back to the sender, or summoning the Earth spirits.

However, of all the magical tools Sokar possessed, none was more important to him than his wand. Used to summon fire spirits and to direct magical power, his wand was carved from a single foot-long piece of the finest ebony. The shaft was plain, tipped with a large, clear quartz crystal that had a smoky formation on the inside shaped like a pyramid. Sokar had found the crystal years ago in the marketplace in Abydos with Dedi, his mentor in magic.

The wand felt comfortable in his hand as he turned it. In the quiet of the bedchamber, he began the first of his magical procedures to manifest his alternate government. He knew that the initial step was to create an image on the astral plane of what he wished.

Sokar held the Mirror of Hathor. Closing his eyes, he took several deep breaths, inhaling and exhaling slowly. The stress flowed out of his body and his muscles started to relax. The Sun was beginning to set, making the light dim. Several oil lamps in the room cast only a soft glow that created an ambiance that helped put Sokar in the frame of mind to perform the task.

Sokar opened his eyes, held the mirror out in front of him, and peered into its smoky-gray surface. His own face stared back at him, his features outlined by the firelight in the room. But as he stared more, the mirror went from being flat to having depth, drawing him into it. Suddenly, his face transformed into a hawk's.

Now in an altered state, Sokar began creating an astral scene. He saw himself dressed in the garb of royalty holding the Crook and Flail. He was wearing the Double Crown on his head. He made a gilded throne appear. Each of its arms carved into the head of a hawk whose gold wings spread out on both sides. He saw himself sitting on the throne flanked by fan bearers and servants. He constructed a palace, with private quarters and lavish gardens with beautiful trees, flowers, and a large pool. He saw priests bowing to him and honoring him as a king, a hierarchy of generals with Shem-hotep as chief, and other court officials. Sokar savored his mental creation. He held it in his mind until he had poured enough of his power into it to make it a living form, planting it as a seed in the Duat that any initiate could see.

The magical work finished to his satisfaction, Sokar began to withdraw from his altered state and returned to the reality of the moment. As he glanced into the mirror, he once again saw his human reflection. He laid the mirror back on the altar, and walked over to a large floor cushion and sat down. He felt a little drained, and needed to rest and reorient himself.

While he had been doing his magical operation, the Sun had set and darkness had come. Sokar walked out onto the patio to let the cool night air revive him. The air smelled delicately sweet from night-blooming jasmine. Sokar saw the comet. He felt his body drawn to it and imagined himself meeting the Star Gods on Egyptian soil. He took the spontaneous vision as an omen of the validity of what he was doing. He would *make* a kingship for himself within the hierarchy of Egyptian royalty. He had set the wheel into motion, for him to become a king.

Chapter Thirty-Eight

A Time for Amulet Making

Khem and Tiye moved into the apartment that had once been Bakka's. The space contained two beds with a small table on each side. Each girl had a dressing table, clothing baskets, several floor pillows, and three small chairs. The floor was covered with woven reed matting. The space opened onto a patio with a small lotus pool shaded by a sycamore. There was an anteroom large enough for servant quarters for Akhi and Nerah, the servant girl assigned to Tiye when she decided to move into the Temple. It was a comfortable arrangement. The priestesses were happy to be room-mates, and Bast seemed content to have Tiye around all the time.

Tiye settled down on the floor to make her first amulet, a small statue of Hapi, the Nile God, which she would then charge with a spell of Protection from Drowning. Though Hapi represented the waters of the Nile, he was not responsible for Inundation. That was the province of more power-ful deities. To Tiye, Hapi was the Nile God, and with the flooding approaching, he was on her mind. Although the flooding was a time of celebration for the many gifts the river brought, it could also be a dangerous time when your life could be lost to the rising waters. If the amulet passed the test of power, she would request Klea's permission to give it to Atef, who frequently worked around the river.

As Khem and Bast looked on, Tiye began molding the clay into the form of an obese male figure with long, sagging breasts. Its largeness repre-sented abundance, the breasts the life-giving properties of Mother Nile. Tiye had never tried to sculpt anything before, and she struggled with the clay. After several frustrating attempts, she figured the only way to succeed was to relax and allow the figure to mold itself.

Turning the warm clay over and over in her hands, pressing and pinching it with her fingers, Tiye watched as the figure took shape. Once she was satisfied with it, she decided that Hapi should carry a tray of offerings to symbolize the gifts of the river. Then she sculpted a crown of the lotus of the Upper Nile and the papyrus of the Lower Nile, riverside plants that made her think of her home in the South. With a few more presses and pinches here and there, the statue was finished. Looking at the crude blue-green figure in her hand, Tiye giggled and held it up for Khem to see. Bast's ears perked up, her head tilting slightly. "Well, it is done," Tiye said, admiring her handiwork critically. "It looks pretty odd, does it not?"

"No, it is not odd, not to me. It looks like a . . . a top-heavy kind of lopsided statue of the god Hapi!"

Both laughed heartily, but Tiye was proud of little Hapi, her first amulet. "I have to give him life," she said. "I think I know how. I have seen Khaba do it."

Tiye's mood turned serious. Cradling the figure in both her hands, the priestess closed her eyes and inhaled deeply. Then, after several more deep breaths, she cupped her hands around the statue and held it up to her face. Taking another breath, this time deeper, she exhaled through her mouth into the figure. She repeated the process twice more. Moving her hands away from her mouth, she sat still, eyes closed. After several moments her eyelids fluttered and opened. Almost immediately Tiye's body went into a slight slump as she relaxed, the task complete.

Khem went to her dressing table and picked up a small wooden box and offered it to Tiye. "Here, you can have this to put your Hapi amulet in. Are you going to make another?"

"Yes, yes, one more," Tiye answered. "Will you stay with me, and Bast too? I feel you both give me energy."

Khem and Bast looked on while Tiye fashioned the next figure, a protection amulet shaped like the *udjat*. The Nubian was not only more physically relaxed now, but also more focused and sure of herself. Khem could tell that Ani was right when she said that amulet-making was for Tiye a natural skill.

When the *udjat* was finished, Tiye charged it the same way, except this time she held the amulet to her brow for a few seconds after breathing life into it, and mumbled a few words that Khem could not make out. "I will take these to Klea tomorrow," Tiye said, half-excited, half-hesitant. "I suppose I will soon know if I have done it right."

Khufu had sent for Shemshu-Hor. He wanted to let the Old One know about the entranceway to the chamber Nemon had discovered, and he wanted to find out about what had become the most important thing on his mind: *When* would the Star Gods return?

Khufu had received word from Meri-ib and Taret that their duties at the Temple of the Sun were taken care of and they were ready to come to Memphis. A royal barque had been sent for them, and their arrival was imminent. They would be joining him in midafternoon when the daily court matters and his private meeting with Shemshu-Hor were done.

When the First Prophet arrived in the Throne Room, several personal servants and litter bearers accompanied him. The Elder was too frail to walk very far on his own, so a special small litter that could be used inside the palace had been constructed for him. Because of the Elder's inclination to live a cloistered existence, Khufu had instructed the bearers to transport the old man in a closed litter, and his servants to make certain that the area of the palace where his quarters were located was kept private. Under no circumstances would anyone other than those in his attendance be allowed in or near his residence. Khufu had learned from Manetho that for many years a male servant named Remy had been Shemshu-Hor's chief attendant; he had been sent for and was expected to arrive later in the day.

A chair had been placed at the foot of the throne for Shemshu-Hor. Khufu was not sure, but he thought the old man seemed stronger, younger somehow, and more alert than he had at their last meeting. There was a sparkle in his eyes. "I take it you are well, Master, and that you are comfortable in the palace."

Looking at the king with a slight smile curving his thin lips, the Old One replied, "I am at home. Nothing is changed or out of place. Thank you, My King."

Khufu knew that the holy man was referring to the reconstruction of his familiar environment within the palace, as all his belongings had been brought from the *Benu* Temple, and his private room was now identical to what it was there. Still, Khufu knew how little material things meant to the Old One. "You will be pleased to know that I have sent for Remy to join you and attend to your needs," Khufu announced.

Although the elder priest did not respond verbally, the look on his face was one of appreciation.

"Meri-ib and Taret will be joining us momentarily." At that point, Khufu changed the subject and began speaking about the things that were uppermost in his mind. The old man sat still and quiet, his hands resting on a walking cane, his eyes closed, listening.

"Master Shemshu-Hor, there are things on my mind I wish to discuss with you, things important to me, and all Egypt." Khufu told him about the discovery of the secret chamber between the paws of the Great Sphinx. He told him everything he knew, but asked no questions. He was not sure what to ask. He was hoping the Old One would comment.

The Elder nodded. "When the Star Gods came to Earth the first time, they chose Egypt as the place and Egyptians as the people to receive their wisdom. They knew it would take many generations for the knowledge to civilize the people and to influence their actions and consciousness. They knew this was the right place and right time. In time, star knowledge given to the people changed their lives. They built great monuments to their benefactors, 'the gods.'

"In a few of the monuments, the Sphinx being one, underground chambers were made for initiations and to protect artifacts that proved the First Coming happened. They contained formulas, designs, and magical tools. The Followers of Horus were the only ones who knew of the existence of the secret Hall of Records. This is still true. It is time for more awareness. The Second Coming marks this, so one of the chambers has been revealed."

Every time Khufu was in the presence of the Old One, he came a step closer to understanding his ancestry. He still could barely believe he was in the company of a Star God who had lived among Egyptians since the First Time.

"So if I understand, you are telling me that when the event of the Star Gods—no, no, when the time is right for the Star Gods to return to Egypt, the location of one of these hidden chambers is revealed?"

"Yes, the chamber that is found is always at the place where the gods will come," Shemshu-Hor said.

So Khufu now knew that the Lion Man on the Giza plateau was the place to which the Star Gods would come. That told him why he had been led to unearth the Sphinx, why he was building a temple at its base.

In his quiet, raspy voice, the Elder spoke again. "There are seven sites in Egypt where underground chambers exist. Five in the North, two in the South. The Sphinx Hall of Records is the most ancient. It has been there since the First Coming. It is time for what is in the Hall of Wisdom beneath the Sphinx to be revealed to *all* the people. That will be when my relations return."

"*When*, Master? When will the Star Gods return? I must know, so I can prepare myself and the people."

The old man looked at Khufu with an expression that made the king feel that it was a question he should already know the answer to. "One will come when the Great Star rises, the others a little later when Mother Nile overflows."

He had his answer. The knowledge made him feel afraid, as when a boy he heard stories of demons and spirits like the fearsome Apep, and even his beloved Sekhmet in her role as a warrioress. Shemshu-Hor perceived this.

"Fear is a normal reaction to something overwhelming. Sometimes fear is a negative, destructive, even loathsome demon. But it can be a signal from the deepest part of yourself to stand up and take notice. Be aware of what is going on lest you fail to live up to your potential, fail to protect yourself, fail even to survive."

"Some days after the predawn rising of the Great Star at Giza. What can we expect, Master Prophet? I cannot imagine it."

"Humans cannot be expected to understand or even perceive some things that are otherworldly," the Old One said. "In human language, you speak about the coming of the Star Gods. But this is misleading. It suggests they will transport themselves here by a long journey. Such is not the case, Beloved One. We transport ourselves without physical mechanisms. When the time comes for them to be here, they will simply appear."

While Shemshu-Hor was speaking, Taret and Meri-ib had slipped quietly into the room and stood listening. Enthralled with the prophet, Taret spoke up. "If Star Gods *think* themselves here they will be here? Is that so, Master? And are you saying that all Egypt awaits the second appearance?"

Shemshu-Hor answered. "Yes, precisely."

"There are a few other matters concerning these times that need to be brought to your attention," Khufu said. With a clap of his hands, he summoned the guard to bring him his basket. Shemshu-Hor sat with his eyes closed, his hands resting on his cane. Meri-ib and Taret looked on as the linen coverlet was removed. Khufu took the tablet from the basket he had kept it in since it appeared as an apport.

"Look at this," Khufu said, handing it first to Meri-ib. "Have you ever seen anything like it?"

Turning the heavy object over in his hands and looking at it closely, Meri-ib passed it to Taret. She was surprised by its weight. As it had Meri-ib, the exquisite design carved on one side of its flattened surface impressed her.

"You must value this object immensely," Meri-ib commented.

"Yes, I do," Khufu answered.

Khufu described his dream of the shining man who wore the Sun-Moon headdress, flanked on either side by a *Benu* bird and two lions. He told of the second, larger, muscular male and how he, Khufu, had been commanded to build his temple. "My dream priest tells me that the monument is to be a star temple, that the lions are its guardians and point to the place in the sky to which the temple should be oriented. That is the rising Sun on the first day of the New Year."

"My intuition tells me the *Benu* indicates that the energy of the temple will be one of renewal and rebirth," Meri-ib said.

"Yes," Taret said. "I agree. However, I question whether the temple is to be oriented to the Sun. I sense it should be aligned to Sirius, which I sense will be the source of the temple's power to renew, heal, and prompt rebirth."

"Yes, yes, I concur with Taret," Meri-ib responded.

As Khufu listened, he recalled dreaming about a temple in which he saw what he believed were Star Gods standing in a circle around an altar with a gold *udjat* inlaid on its top. His mind focused on light beaming into the inner sanctum and that the source of the ray had been revealed to him as Sirius. When he related the dream to the Council members, each nodded agreement.

Thus far, Shemshu-Hor had injected nothing into the discussion. But the mention of the *udjat* caused the Old One to stir and open his eyes. Looking passively at the others, he asked permission to speak.

"Yes, of course," Khufu answered.

"The *udjat* is a very ancient cosmic symbol that has many meanings. The one important to these times concerns the founder of the ancient Order of the Followers of Horus. It typifies him as the offspring of the forces of Nature and the eternal cycle of rebirth and renewal. The infant Horus is the symbol for humans struggling to lift themselves from ignorance to civilization. This is why the Star Gods came to Earth, and why Horus gave out the knowledge that would change the world. It is why Horus founded the Order so its members would forever be stewards of the wisdom. And so it is to this day."

Turning to Khufu, Shemshu-Hor said that seeing the *udjat* in his dream was an indication that the original Followers of Horus would be the gods who returned with the knowledge to carry humanity to the next stage. "Meri-ib and Mistress Taret are correct. Sirius is the system from which the god Horus came and will come again. The Temple of the Great Star will capture the star waves of the light of the Great Star, and that light will empower the *udjat* which embodies the wisdom of Horus."

Meri-ib asked, "Are we correct that the *Benu* is a symbol of rebirth? And the lions—are they guardians? Or is there a deeper meaning we are not seeing?"

"The dream priest has interpreted the meaning of the lions as guardians pointing to a specific place in the sky. This is correct. But there is a subtle meaning."

The old man stood up and untied a small cloth bag from his waistband. Opening its drawstrings, he took out a stone tablet and held it. It was identical to the stone that apported from Khufu's dream.

"This is a piece of meteorite," the Old One said. "It is Star Stone, just like the capstone of the great obelisk at Heliopolis. When I came here in the First Time, I was given this with the design of a temple etched on it. I was told to keep it safe. No eyes should see it until the Second Coming, when an identical object would come into the possession of a human. I would then know it was time for the Second Coming, for events to unfold and prophecies to be fulfilled."

Shemshu-Hor explained that the iron meteorite, or *B'ja*, was the substance used in the Opening of the Mouth ritual to insure the Pharaoh's soul would resurrect into eternal life amidst the stars. The oldest of the holy texts made it clear that there were "windows" or star gates through which the deceased king would pass into the realms of Osiris. These star gates were made of iron and it is through the star gates that the Star Gods passed in their journeys. Now in the Throne Room of the palace of King Khufu, the two iron tablets came together, yet another omen of the Second Coming.

Shemshu-Hor sat down, resting his hands on his cane. The Old One looked at the king and the initiates. "The time for dreams, omens and signs, and prophecy is completed. The return of the Star Gods to Egypt is *now*. The Sphinx will once more gaze upon the direction of another Coming. A reawakening of the old ways and greater knowledge will come. That knowledge will carry humans into a golden age that will last for millennia. A star temple will be built to mark that time. Star waves from the Seth stars, the dark forces, will also release their power. Light triggers the darkness. The war between good and evil must be fought and won again.

"What is going on in the heavens happens on Earth. That is always so. The dark forces put obstacles in the path of the one who represents the star gods and humanity. That one is you, Khufu, King of the Two Lands, Ruler of Egypt. The dark forces are already at work. You have an enemy, and that enemy is your half-brother. He threatens your power as king. Your relationship is the age-old battle of light and dark, fought again, as it has been since time began, as it will be until time ends."

Shemshu-Hor spoke again. "The two lions in your dream represent you and Sokar. You, Pharaoh, must have the courage of the lion when faced with difficult adversaries. Like the *Benu*, you must rise from your defeats. You must be reborn from the deaths that life brings and start anew.

"Know also that the texts tell about two lion deities, twin lions, *Sef* and

Tuau, seated back to back with the Sun's disk between them. Their names mean 'yesterday' and 'today,' the First Coming and the Second Coming. The spiritual and material worlds and their constant interaction. Your dream vessel has given you the experience of yesterday and tomorrow, your future and Egypt's future."

The next day when Khem and Tiye met with Klea, Tiye had her amulets secured in a cloth bag. Both were eager to have Klea determine their power. Tiye wanted to tell Klea about seeing the Star Woman, Zenosothis, in the scrying bowl.

There was something about Klea that made her different from any other woman Khem and Tiye had met at the Temple. Younger than Taret or Ani, she was more bold and risquée. They sensed that beneath her light-hearted facade was a strong-willed, self-confident initiate who could not be fooled or intimidated.

Tiye took out the little statue of Hapi. She explained to Klea why she had chosen to make it, to whom she planned to give it, and why. She took out the *udjat* and handed it to Klea. Though Klea seemed pleased with the Hapi, she had a reaction to the *udjat*. After holding the amulet in her hand for a couple of minutes, she looked at Tiye and asked why she had chosen the *udjat*.

"It came into my mind. I saw it and I felt guided to make it as one of my first amulets. I felt it would protect the person who carries it, if I have charged it right."

"Well, you have charged it right," Klea responded. "Its energy is powerful."

The *udjat* flat on the palm of her hand, Klea put it near an oil lamp kept on her altar. "I would like to keep the amulet for a while, if you do not mind, Tiye." Klea wanted to speak to Ani about Tiye's amulet-making ability, which she assured the Nubian was exceptional. "The *udjat* and the Hapi have been charged with *your* power, but they have also been awakened to their own power, whose sources are old thought forms of psychic power."

Chapter Thirty-Nine

The Invitation

Nemon was adamant about having an audience with the Pharaoh. He had never been in a situation in which he felt the need to interrupt the court, but he did now. The digging around the Sphinx was going well, ahead of schedule. This allowed him to leave the project in the hands of his foremen so he could investigate the underground chamber. He had previously gone into it a couple of times, but had not taken a close inventory of its contents.

That morning, Nemon and his chief foreman, Harum, had gone into the chamber, each carrying a torch, and they went several yards beyond the point of their last visit. Nemon had noticed an impression in the wall of the tunnellike structure. What had once been a door was sealed, but when Nemon placed his hand on it, it gave way. In fact, the stone of the door broke into several large chunks as it hit the floor.

The light from their torches cast eerie shadows on the brightly painted symbols that covered the walls. Reminiscent of ordinary hieroglyphs, the symbols were yet unfamiliar. The ceiling was painted with the same glyphs intermixed with star designs. The floor had a large white circle in its center, inside which was a gold five-pointed star. Nemon believed they were standing in an initiation chamber. The air was heavy and stale. They knew they were the first humans in there in a long time, and it filled them with excitement and apprehension. Nemon examined the ceiling. One picture symbol stood out. It appeared to be a star, but had a long, zigzag tail. He called Harum's attention to the symbol.

"It is a comet."

Harum looked around the room, his eyes wide and mouth open in awe. The beauty of the chamber was exquisite. He could feel its energy enveloping him.

There came a sudden noise like the flapping of bird wings. It startled them both. The sound seemed to come from every direction, and they spun around in circles trying to see what they were hearing. The room took on a pale glow, and they knew they were no longer alone.

Their instinct was to flee, and both started towards the door. But a calm came over them and took away their anxiety as a stately, bronze-skinned woman appeared in the center of the starred circle. Ostrichlike feathers rayed out from the crown of an elaborate headdress. A garment of golden mesh hung loosely about her. The scepter in her right hand pulsed. Neither had seen a woman so beautiful.

"I am come to you from a time and a world long passed, from a time you can know only through the sacred text and called the First Time. The wisest among you have been brought into the teachings given to humanity by us. Tell your Lord and King, Ruler of the Two Lands, Manifestation of Horus, to come to this place to meet those Wise Ones who reside in the realms of Osiris. He should come when the sun rises tomorrow."

Her message delivered, the spirit woman gradually faded. Nemon and Harum stood silently, looking at the center of the room where she had been.

Nemon left to get word to Khufu. When Nemon arrived at the palace, the chief fan bearer of the Throne Room passed word to the king that his chief architect was waiting outside the door, insisting on speaking with His Majesty right away. Khufu ordered the room cleared and bade Nemon enter.

"Greetings, Your Royal Majesty," Nemon said, bowing deeply. "I am sorry to interrupt the court's business and Your Majesty personally, but—"

"It is all right, cousin," Khufu broke in. "What is on your mind? Is there trouble?"

"No. No trouble," Nemon answered quickly, and told him, adding, "It said you should come there at dawn tomorrow so that you can meet with the spirits of those initiates who reside in the realms of Osiris."

Khem was practicing her writing, waiting for Atef. It had been a while since the siblings had spent time together, and she was anxious to see her brother. Maybe he would bring word from their parents, and she wanted to see how Atef's writing skills had progressed. Bast heard Atef's footsteps approaching. The lioness had come to know Atef in the short time he had been at the Temple, and she liked him.

Atef looked tired, as though he had not slept. When Khem asked what was wrong, he explained that he had been staying up past sunset for the last several nights to practice his writing. "It is a lot to learn and I wish to excel," the young man said. "There are so many figures, Khem, so much to know."

Khem thought she detected pessimism in his voice, but she shrugged it off. Atef went on, telling her that he had begun copying one of the texts that had come from the desk of the former High Priest, Meri-ib. "It is about the stars," he said with a look revealing that what he was copying had stirred him. "I cannot read all the characters I have copied, but just today I came across one passage I did understand. It read, 'Man is a fallen god who remembers the Heavens.' What do you think it means?"

Khem thought for a moment. "I think it means humans used to live in the heavens and somewhere inside us we remember that."

Atef was surprised by the matter-of-fact manner in which she had spoken. "I suppose I never thought of men as gods, fallen or otherwise," he said. "It is an idea I wish to give more thought to and perhaps learn more about."

"Ah, my brother. Maybe you should have gone to the Karnak Temple to study to become a Star Priest instead of coming here to become a scribe," Khem said teasingly.

"Perhaps you are right, sister."

As the two chatted, Atef pursued the idea of remembering the heavens. "Do you have any memory of being anywhere other than here in Egypt?"

"No, not consciously. But I do know that my—*our*—ancestors are the Star Gods. I have some memory of that. But it is not like an ordinary memory."

Atef was confused by this and wanted an explanation, but he didn't know what to ask. Sensing her brother's confusion, Khem tried to explain. "Since coming to Heliopolis I have learned many things. New worlds and new ways of thinking have opened up to me. I have never felt that I belonged to the land. I have always loved the stars. I have always felt that the sky is my home. I know now this is because my ancestors came from the stars. They are your ancestors too, Atef."

Atef looked at Khem with envy. "You have truly changed. You seem almost wise," he said, causing Khem to break out in laughter.

"No, my brother. I have a long way to go before I become wise, if ever I do," Khem answered him honestly. "It is only that my world has gotten bigger. So will yours. You will see."

"I will be glad when I can read all the characters. Then I will be able to read the sacred texts and perhaps gain some understanding." Atef's voice took on a somber tone as his deepest desire welled up inside him. "Maybe we were destined to be here at the same time."

"Someday we will know, my brother," Khem replied. "Someday soon."

The altar in Sokar's private chamber burned bright with the light from two oil lamps. The aroma of jasmine filled the room. The magician had cloistered himself indoors all day, focused on the image-making operation he had begun. As he sat quietly on a plush cushion on top of the reed mat in front of his altar, Sokar's thoughts drifted to the South, to Abydos and Dedi. It had been a long time since he had had any contact with the old man. Perhaps it was time to send him a message. Maybe he could elicit the master's magical help in his effort to become king. He could not be sure how Dedi would react to his ambitions, and he did not want to take any undue risks that might foil his plan.

As these thoughts rolled around in his head, they were interrupted by Kheti's gentle voice.

"Yes, Kheti. What is it?"

"Pardon my intrusion, my master. "I have made something for your magic."

Sokar got up from the cushion and faced the servant, who stood there holding a wooden tray. Whatever object was on the tray was covered by a linen cloth, Sokar waited.

Kheti set the tray on a table and removed the cover. Underneath it lay a small, exquisitely molded miniature palace of clay. Lines on the model's surface made it look like bricks; tiny walkways connected the rooms. Plants and twigs landscaped the building that was enclosed by a high wall. Trees made from palm leaves and dried flowers graced the outside wall and the inner central courtyard. "It is a palace, master, your palace," Kheti said. "I have made it for your altar, and I have empowered it with life and prayers to help it become a reality."

The servant's shyness was even more noticeable than usual as he timidly, but proudly, presented the gift to Sokar. He had never done anything like this before and was not sure how it would be received. Would his master think him presumptuous? Would he view his creation as interference with his magic?

Sokar studied the model for a few minutes, which to Kheti seemed like an eternity, then shook his head. "Kheti, I had no idea you were an artist. Thank you, my faithful friend. You have made me a beautiful and useful object. Please put it on the altar."

Kheti flushed. His aim to please Sokar had been the main focus of his life for a long time. His master's acceptance of the gift made him exuberant. Carefully taking the model from the stand, he set it on the cedar altar between two lamps. "It will now be easier to visualize your palace, my master," Kheti said happily.

Early the next morning, the docks were bustling with vessels of all sizes being loaded for destinations up and down the Nile. Atef was reminded of his two journeys from the South, once when he and his parents had accompanied Khem to Heliopolis, the other when he had returned to enter the instruction house to become a scribe. Both journeys had been momentous. Last night, he had stayed up long past sunset to write a letter to his parents and was now bringing the letter scroll to the docks to go with the cargo ship to Abydos.

On a dock not far from where he was standing, Atef noticed a tall, thin servant clutching a message. The man seemed nervous, and he eyed Atef warily. The docks were not always a safe place for the high-born or their servants. Jewels and other valuables could be a target for river rogues and dock thieves. Atef asked the man if this was the vessel headed south. It was. "I am Atef, son of Rashid, fish merchant of Abydos. I wish to send this message scroll to my family."

"I am Kheti, chief servant of my master Sokar, the high-born half-brother of the Honorable Khufu, King of Egypt, Son of Horus, and Wearer of the Double Crown. I am also here to put a message scroll on board this ship and, yes, it is bound for Abydos."

Atef wondered why the chief servant of such a high-born would be acting as an ordinary courier. Kheti picked up on Atef's expression and said he had brought the scroll to the quay himself because he had to be in the marketplace very early. "No use in tiring out a good courier for no reason," Kheti said with a nervous laugh as he did not want to give the impression there was anything amiss or lacking in his master's ways.

Impressed by his encounter with the chief servant of the king's half-brother, Atef said, "I am pleased to make your acquaintance, Kheti. I am a student at the School of Scribes at the House of Instruction in the Temple of the Sun. I have been in Heliopolis but a short time."

The two men chatted until a member of the boat's crew came to collect the message scrolls. They were comfortable with each other, and started walking together towards the marketplace, continuing their conversation. By the time they had to part, Atef had told Kheti a lot about himself, including the fact that his sister Khem was an apprentice Star Priestess. Kheti acknowledged his master's respect for the High Priest and High Priestess, Meri-ib and Taret.

"Oh, don't you know?" Atef said. "Master Meri-ib and the Mistress Taret are no longer the High Priest and High Priestess. They have been replaced."

Surprise was evident on Kheti's face. He had not known there had been such a big change, and he doubted his master knew either. He bade Atef goodbye and hurried off.

When Kheti arrived at the *Benu* Temple, it was time for Sokar's morning toilet. Kheti entered the bedchamber and found Sokar removing the leather hood from his hawk. Hurrying to pour fresh water and put out clean linen towels, Kheti noticed that the model palace he had given his master was not on the altar where it had been placed the afternoon before. It puzzled him so that he momentarily forgot the news he had been so anxious to tell. He dare not ask the model's whereabouts for fear his gift had not pleased his master after all. Kheti did his chores in silence. He felt fearful. Magicians do not tolerate interference and that could bring retaliation upon him.

Sokar wrapped a clean skirt around his waist and slipped into his sandals. He then strolled over to his dressing table, where he opened an ornate box, took out a gold ankh on a chain, and placed it around his neck.

He looks like a king, Kheti thought.

"Kheti, I have need for a special stand to be placed in that corner," Sokar said, pointing to the far left area of the room. "I have a plan to do an empowerment spell over the palace you created. It needs to be in a secluded, safe place so that none of the energy will be siphoned off by the other objects on my altar."

Kheti's heart jumped for joy! His master had not destroyed the model, nor had he been offended or thought him presumptuous for making it. His desire to please Sokar was secondary only to his need to be his magical assistant. Kheti was himself a magician at heart, but working as Sokar's assistant was the only opportunity he had to experience his deepest wish.

"Yes, my master. I will take care of it right away," Kheti said graciously, barely able to hide his excitement that his gift was accepted. "Will you be going out?"

Just as he asked the question, Kheti remembered meeting Atef at the docks and what he had told him about there being newly appointed heads of the Temple of the Sun. "Oh, yes, Master. I almost forgot. There is news you should know about."

"And what would that be?" Sokar inquired.

"There has been a major change at the Temple of the Sun. Master Meri-ib and the Mistress Taret are no longer High Priest and High Priestess."

"What!" Sokar said, gasping with surprise. "When? How do you know this?"

Kheti told how he had met the apprentice scribe and what Atef had said. He assured his master that this was all he knew and that he knew no further details.

Sokar's mind ran in circles as he processed what Kheti had said. "When did this happen?" Kheti had no more answers, so he would have to find out elsewhere. "Did you say that this young man you met—"

"Atef."

"Yes, Atef. He is an apprentice scribe?"

"Yes, Master. His sister is an apprentice Star Priestess."

"They will know the details, this brother and sister," Sokar thought out loud. After a few minutes of pondering, he told Kheti to send a message to Atef and invite him and his sister for a visit to welcome them properly to Heliopolis, or something. "Tell them anything. Just get them here as soon as possible."

Kheti went to do his master's bidding, leaving Sokar alone in his bedchamber in deep thought. How could such a major change happen and he not hear about it sooner? Why had Meri-ib and Taret been replaced? Did it have something to do with their going to Memphis a short time ago? Who had replaced them? Why was he not considered for High Priest? Why weren't there rumors going around about the changes?

When Kheti returned he informed Sokar that he had sent a courier to Atef at the Sun Temple to invite him and his sister to the *Benu* Temple so he could show them around. It seemed like a good way to entice them. He was counting on their not having been there before, and that they would have an interest in seeing the premises. It was, after all, a beautiful and historic temple, unique in all of Egypt. Named after the bird of regeneration, it was the place where the powerful *ben-ben* stone was housed, and it stood upon the ancient Mound upon which the first sunrise had taken place, which today was the home of the cloistered Order of the Followers of Horus.

"Good," Sokar said. "We will await a reply."

He did not have to wait long. The courier had delivered the message right away and Atef had accepted. He and his sister would arrive after class that afternoon. Atef had assumed his sister would be agreeable, so he had spoken for her. That would be an assumption he would regret. She said she would go, but not until she had scolded Atef for not asking her first, as she had to change her plans for helping Tiye with the amulets.

At the *Benu* Temple, Atef and Khem were surprised how small it was in comparison with the Temple of the Sun. The various rooms and private quarters opened out onto an inner courtyard where a huge, gleaming obelisk stood, the *ben-ben* atop it. Hieroglyphs were inscribed all over the needlelike column. Atef was particularly moved by its grandeur.

As promised, Kheti met the pair at the gateway of the Temple, pretending an eagerness to show them around. He invited them to his private quarters for refreshments and shade. The midafternoon sun was hot and his guests were thirsty.

As the threesome started towards Sokar's apartments, Atef whispered, "Oh, yes, sister. I forgot to tell you that Kheti is the chief servant for the half-brother of His Majesty, the king."

Khem's mouth dropped open. She remembered encountering the prince twice before at the Sun Temple. One of those times was when he was with Tiye. She had not liked the man. But this was to be just a short visit. No harm in that, she thought.

Kheti introduced Khem and Atef to Sokar. The priest was an imposing figure, his hawk perched on his forearm. The bird's weight caused the bicep in the man's upper arm to bulge, giving man and bird an air of power. Atef had never seen a tame hawk before and was enchanted.

"Welcome to the Temple of the *Benu*." Sokar greeted them. Turning to Khem, he remarked that he recalled seeing her and her lioness cub at the Temple of the Sun, and he inquired about Bast. It was a great conversation opener, he knew.

"She is with my servant, Akhi. She is growing big!" Khem answered, excited yet trying to conceal her discomfort at being in Sokar's presence. She knew she was uncomfortable with Sokar, and was trying to remember something she knew about him.

Sokar insisted that the two sit and relax. "So, you are brother and sister, are you?" Sokar commented. "And both of you are in training at the Temple of Ra?" Sokar spoke pleasantly, trying to make Khem and Atef feel comfortable.

Khem felt they were not there to visit with Kheti at all, but that Sokar had arranged this. She knew he had a reason for wanting them to come.

Sokar took advantage of Atef's fascination with the hawk. He did not want to bombard the pair with questions about recent events at the Sun Temple lest he arouse their suspicions. "Have you any animals?" Sokar asked.

"No, well, not now anyway," Atef answered, the question triggering an old memory. "I once had a cat when I was little."

"I see," Sokar mused with a smile as he turned toward Khem. "A love of cats seems to run in the family. Your sister's lioness is very beautiful."

"Oh, yes. But my cat was just an ordinary cat, not a lion," Atef clarified quickly.

"No animal is ordinary, Atef. All animals are special in their own way," Sokar responded, his eyes now focused on Horus. "Humans can learn a great deal from animals if we observe them carefully and listen to what they have to say."

Sokar's words caught Khem's attention. She knew Bast communicated with her and other humans, and she wondered if Sokar might offer insights on the subject. "You listen, I mean, *speak* to animals? And you understand them?"

"Yes, of course," Sokar replied without hesitation. Looking fondly at the magnificent hawk sitting perched on his forearm, he continued. "All the time. Horus and I have a special relationship. Not unlike that between two humans. He and I talk to each other all the time." Then, with a quickness that caught Khem off guard, he asked, "Do you and Bastet not communicate with each other?"

"A-a-h-h, yes," Khem stammered.

"It is said that during the First Time animals could speak, just as humans do now, that they even had their own language."

"Why do you suppose that changed?"

"Some of the ancient texts tell that everything changed when humans began to abuse animals, to kill them for sport rather than food, and put them into slave labor. The texts say that the animals withdrew from friendly contact with humans. They still speak to one another, but in a language that most of us cannot comprehend."

Khem listened with interest, sure the hawk was listening too, and understood every word. She felt the connection between the magician-priest and hawk.

"Are you the only priestess at the Sun Temple who has such a unique companion as Bast?"

"Yes, at least I think so," Khem answered.

"I understand that the animal attends classes with you. No one has objected? Not even the Mistress Taret?"

"No, there have been no objections. Not even from the High Priestess."

"And how is the honorable High Priestess? These must be extremely busy times for her, and for the High Priest too."

Khem assumed by his inquiry that Sokar was not aware of the changes in the hierarchy of the Temple of the Sun. Without thinking, she blurted out that Taret and Meri-ib were no longer the highest religious officials in Heliopolis, that they had resigned their positions.

"That is most interesting," Sokar responded in as matter-of-fact a tone as he could. "I had not heard. Tell me. Who has taken their positions? And why did they resign?" He was at the point where he no longer cared if

Khem and Atef became suspicious of his motives for questioning them. He wanted answers.

Khem felt awkward and uncomfortable. What was it about this man that disturbed her? "Mistress Taret and Master Meri-ib have relocated to Memphis. I am not sure why," Khem answered, as vague as politeness would allow. She did not trust Sokar and did not intend to be drawn into the issue. "Ani, the Chief Dream Priestess, and the Prophet Ant'en have been elevated to fill the positions."

Sokar did not care who had been elevated. He wanted to know why Meri-ib and Taret had gone to the capital city. He doubted that Khem or Atef had much more information, so he reverted back to concealing his lack of knowledge about the issue. It seemed like the rumor mill had been strangely silent on the subject. This was no doubt due to the fact that it had all happened recently. He could surmise for himself that if the sages had gone to Memphis, it had something to do with Khufu and the upcoming events.

Sokar was anxious to get rid of his visitors. It would not be hard, for they were supposed to be Kheti's guests. There was a lot he needed to know, and he did not want to waste time. So, hustling the pair onto the patio, where Kheti was waiting with refreshments, Sokar excused himself and went off alone to think.

Later, as she walked home and reflected on the meeting, Khem suddenly realized who this man was. He was the enemy of the Throne from her vision.

Chapter Forty

The Apparition of a Spirit Woman

The sky was as black as kohl. The long-tailed comet hung like a diamond pendant in the night. When Khufu looked at the celestial portent, emotions flowed through him. What an auspicious time to sit upon the Throne of Egypt. He was sure he was fortunate among men. And there was Nemon's revelation: spirit woman—that was what Nemon had called her—come from Egypt's past to foretell a meeting between him and initiates from the realms of Osiris. The Duat, the starry realm of Osiris, the place in which all kings hoped to reside after death for eternity.

Khufu fixed his attention on the fuzzy starlike comet and recalled the words from the old texts:

> The gate of the Earth is open for you,
> may a stairway to the Duat be set up for you
> to the place where Orion is.
> O king, the sky conceives you with Orion,
> the sky has borne you with Orion.
> O king, be a soul like a living star.
> The gate of the Earth-god is open,
> may you remove yourself to the sky
> and sit upon your iron throne.
> The aperture of the sky window is opened for you
> The doors of iron in the starry sky
> are thrown open for me,
> and I go through them.

These words concerned immortality, *his* immortality. To Khufu, the Duat was the cosmic world located in the eastern sky, the realm of the Star Gods. Represented by the red glow of dawn, the Duat swallowed up the stars each morning. On his way to join the stars, the dead king must first pass through the Duat to assure he would be guided in the right direction.

Khufu thought of Atum, the father of the gods, creator of the universe, he who preceded Ra as the original deity of Heliopolis. The two were aspects and different names of but one deity.

Like me, Khufu thought, Atum wore the Double Crown of a united Egypt. Although there were numerous animals associated with Atum—the lion, bull, lizard, snake—Khufu held the lion to be the most significant. Lions had always intrigued him—their eyes could look through you into your soul or guard temple entrances from the evil powers of Seth. The twin-headed lion god, Aker, guarded the gates of the Underworld and protected the Sun god on his nightly journey through that perilous realm.

Khufu's studies had taught him that the first beings created by Ra were the twins Shu and Tefnut. Shu, father of Geb, the Earth, and Nut, the Sky, was the god of air and light. Tefnut, Shu's twin sister, was also his wife and the goddess of moisture who helped her husband support the sky. These deities were often depicted as lions who guarded the eastern and western horizons. For as long as Khufu could remember, his royal bed had carved lions on its posts to protect him while he slept. The beloved Sekhmet, lion-headed wife of Ptah, and Horus, lion-headed rising sun, were the source of his strength as King of Egypt.

Yes, Khufu thought, the lion is powerful. I must be like a lion and guard Egypt. Like the Lion Man of the Desert, I must not waver in my vigil as I await the Second Coming of the Star Gods. All the kings of Egypt are infused with supernatural strength, and I am no different. The Pharaoh is like Seth, the god of destruction, who kills all who would harm him, and like Sekhmet, the warrioress, who never hesitates to slaughter those who threaten *ma'at.*

It was easy to imagine the comet as the head of a great, golden-white lion whose mane flung behind it in blazing glory. Khufu let his imagination free and the sight was mesmerizing. Words came to mind: *The Lion Woman of Sirius comes. . . .*

Khem had returned to the Sun Temple. The thought had crossed her mind that she and her brother had been lured to the *Benu* Temple for reasons known only to Sokar and his servant. But, if it was information they were looking for, neither of them got it because she and Atef did not have any. She recalled Sokar's surprise at learning that Meri-ib and Taret had resigned. Actually, Khem had not given the matter much thought. She had accepted it as normal business of the Temple, perhaps having to do with the auspicious events of the Second Coming.

Even though the sun had set an hour before, Khem and Tiye were still awake and talking. Daily life had taken them in different directions lately, and they had not seen much of each other. Now they were catching up, discussing the comet. When the girls finally quit, it didn't take long for both to fall asleep.

They dreamed. Khem was tumbling gently among the stars, aware she was not alone. Tiye was there, but she looked different. She seemed larger, more muscular, with darker skin and eyes. Khem realized they were in a lush oasis on a far planet, with willowy trees and fragrant flowers. She felt a thousand eyes watching their every move.

From behind a row of ornate columns a lioness appeared, larger than any on Earth. She was a magnificent, stately, and proud golden beast with eyes that drew in the dreamers. The lioness strolled through the middle of the columns, gradually turning into a woman with a headdress of feathers and a scepter engraved with hieroglyphs.

The lion-woman spoke to Kehm: "You, Star Daughter, are from a long lineage, the same as myself. You are special and the ruler of Egypt will be told about you. He, the son of Horus, will need you and over time will depend on your visions. You will learn more about these things soon. Also know that at the time of the Second Coming, you will become a Sirian Star Priestess, as will your spiritual companion, the lioness Bastet. Your initiation will be given to you by the Lioness of Sirius. I will come to you again closer to the time of the New Year."

The spirit woman turned to Tiye. "Though you are not of our lineage, you possess the power to protect the Coming Ones from the forces of evil that might seek to block their efforts to further the evolution of humans. Your amulets shall become known far and wide for their power to provide protection from perils. One you make will help preserve the Wearer of the Double Crown. We of Sirius will empower you and help you. Look for me. You will both know me when I come to Earth. I will stay and live with you, and your people."

The transmission finished, the Sirian became a lioness again and Khem awoke. Gathering her wits, she searched the dark room to see if Tiye was still asleep.

"Tiye," she whispered.

"Yes, I am awake," Tiye answered back, her voice barely audible. "Is something wrong?"

"No, I . . . I was having a dream."

"Me too," Tiye replied. "Wait. I will light a lamp."

Tiye climbed out of bed and felt her way to the altar for a tiny lamp. Normally, Tiye would not have made much effort to speak. It was an hour before sunrise, and she was still sleepy, but she could tell that Khem was shaken.

"Are you well?" Tiye asked with concern. "Did your dream upset you?"

"No, thank you, Tiye. I am fine," Khem answered softly, her mind still preoccupied by the dream's images. "It was a strange dream, so real."

"Mine too," Tiye said. "I saw the woman so clearly. I remember every detail of how she looked and what she said. It wasn't like a dream at all. It was like real life."

"You dreamed of a woman?"

"Yes. A lion woman."

"She was a lioness? Is that what you saw?"

"Yes, a big lioness who looked like Bast. And then the lioness turned into a woman."

"That is what I dreamed too," Khem blurted out excitedly. "And the place, I, no, we—*you* were with me, Tiye. The place was so beautiful and lush. It smelled so good. It was like another Egypt but far away."

"Yes. Yes!"

"Did the spirit woman—she called herself a Sirian Star Woman—say anything to you?" Khem asked.

"Yes. She said my amulets would become very powerful, and that one would save the king."

"I think we should go to Ani about our dreams," Khem said.

"You are reading my mind," Tiye replied. "Or do you think we should go to Klea first? She is our instructor now."

"Yes, but Ani is the High Priestess, and she is our instructor too, and we know her better. Besides, she knows us better."

By the time Khufu got out of bed and began preparing for his important day, he was already beginning to feel the weight of his meeting in the chamber beneath the Sphinx. Nemon would soon arrive to accompany him there.

Although the desert was relentless in its encroachment upon all in its path, Nemon and the army of laborers under his command had conquered the mountain of sand heaped upon the Lion Man. Khufu had not visited the site since the beginning of the project and he was as anxious to see the full body of the Stone Head as he was to keep his appointment with the initiates. With the Sphinx project nearly finished, it would soon be time to plan the ceremony to celebrate the unearthing of this most significant of Egyptian monuments.

While Khufu broke his fast with a cup of beer and a few dried figs, his personal servants washed his body and laid out the clothing he would wear that day. A courier came to the door of the royal quarters and delivered a message scroll with the seal of the High Priest of Memphis. It came with the request for Khufu to read it himself rather than having it read to him. Dejedfre obviously considered the message confidential.

The king cleared the room and sat down to read the message. Unrolling the scroll and seeing its contents gave him a deep satisfaction mixed with regret. Dejedfre, the Crown Prince and High Priest of Memphis, was informing his father, the King of Egypt, that he must respectfully decline the opportunity to become part of the Sirius Council. After giving the matter careful thought, and in the face of the initial guidance Khufu had received as to who should form the Council, he felt he could serve Pharaoh, the country, and the Star Gods better by remaining head of the Memphis Temple and being available in whatever ways were needed at the time of the arrival of the gods and thereafter.

Khufu knew Dejedfre's decision was political and personal. After all, the Sirius Council was comprised of members of the Heliopolitan priesthood, although that was not based on any political decision on Khufu's part. Fate had brought the members together. Khufu sensed his son felt he had been invited to serve on the Council more out of sentiment as his son than for his knowledge. Sadly, this was not the case. Even so, Khufu detected wisdom in Dejedfre. He now knew he had a son he could rely upon in religious affairs of state, as well as in personal matters. Though he felt sad Dejedfre would not be on the Council, he was grateful that the situation had let him know his relationship was intact. Only time and energy were needed to improve it, and Khufu vowed he would make this happen.

Yet as he reflected, Khufu saw that he had been so wrapped up in what was going on that only now was he beginning to feel its impact. He did not regret or fear his part in it. In fact, he was in some ways astonished to have such monumental events happen during his reign. He had given little thought to his personal life or what it would be like after the Second Coming and he had settled into his work with the Star Gods. Would he even have a personal life?

The thought crossed his mind that he had not informed the Council of his summons to meet the initiates. Perhaps he should meet briefly with Meri-ib and Taret, and even Shemshu-Hor. There was time. Still, he would limit his summons to Meri-ib and Taret, and not bother the Old One until circumstances warranted.

By the time Khufu reached the Throne Room, Meri-ib and Taret had arrived, accompanied by their palace guards and personal attendants.

"Greetings, Your Highness, Wearer of the Double Crown, Son of Horus," Meri-ib and Taret spoke in unison, bowing respectfully.

"And to you," Khufu responded. "Thank you for your promptness. There is a matter at hand I wish to seek your counsel about, and time is of the essence. Come, sit."

Khufu related the details of Nemon's finding the secret chamber beneath the paws of the Sphinx, and of his experience in the antechamber with the spirit woman. He told them what she had said, belaboring the issue of his going to meet with the initiates. Meri-ib and Taret listened with interest. When Khufu finished, Meri-ib spoke.

"I am pleased to know about this momentous occasion, Your Majesty. It seems you have the matter well in hand, and I do not see where I have anything to offer in the way of advice or guidance. Not regarding this incident."

Taret, realizing the king expected her comments, concurred with Meri-ib. "The only thing I might comment upon concerns the secret chamber itself, my king. I sense its existence and whereabouts should be kept secret, at least for a while."

"I agree, Mistress Taret," Khufu responded. "The same thought has passed through my mind more than once. Of course the laborers all know, and there is no way to determine how far beyond the site the news of the discovery of the chamber has spread."

"I understand," Taret answered. "I was thinking in terms of any official announcement being made. This way the discovery, should it come out, could be passed off as a mere rumor that would run its course."

"Point well taken. There will be no formal announcement until after my activities today," Khufu said.

Ani's chief house steward was surprised to see Khem and Tiye at this early hour. He surmised they would not have come so early if they did not believe their visit was important, so he let Ani know they were there. She agreed to see them right away.

When Ani came into the room she seemed happy, if a bit surprised, to see them. They had not seen one another since Ani had taken Taret's place. Seeing the new High Priestess now made Khem realize how much she missed the Dream Priestess. The look on Tiye's face revealed the same feeling.

"Khem, Tiye, I am surprised to see you. Come, sit," Ani said, greeting the girls warmly. "Now, to what do I owe this visit?"

"There was this dream, last night. It was the same dream, Ani. We both had the *same* dream," Khem said.

"Yes, go on," Ani replied.

The opportunity to tell Ani about the dreams brought the excitement of the experience back to her. "Well," she began, looking at Tiye. "We remember seeing one another, being together in the dreams and being in this strange but beautiful place. Then there was a big lioness, much bigger than Bast, but like her. It walked down the middle of a row of columns. When it got close to us, to me and Tiye, it changed into a woman wearing a golden gown and a feathered headdress."

"Did the woman say anything to you?"

"Yes, she did, Ani. She said that I was part of her lineage." Then, turning to glance at Tiye she said, "But Tiye is not. She said she was coming here soon from the Sirian stars and that I would have a special role to play."

"Was there anything else?"

"Yes. She told me that Tiye and I would help protect the king, me with visions and Tiye with a special amulet to protect the Pharaoh. She said I would be initiated after the Second Coming, and so would Bast. That is all I can remember. Did I leave anything out, Tiye?"

The Nubian shook her head. "No, I don't think so."

Ani figured there was probably more but they had not recalled it. There was little symbolism involved, Ani thought, so there was no way to interpret what they had experienced other than literally. In light of upcoming events, as well as the fact that Taret and Meri-ib had gone to Memphis to serve as personal counselors to the king, the part that concerned Khufu was of paramount importance. Maybe it was even a matter of state security.

"This is all most interesting," Ani said, her voice barely audible.

"Tell us, please! What does it all mean, Mistress Ani?"

"It means precisely what it seems to mean. It will all come to pass just as it has been told to you. Fate has brought the two of you together. In the time you have been at the Temple you have had several visitations and visions. They are evidence of the roles each of you will fulfill for the Wearer of the Double Crown, Egypt, and the Second Coming of the Star Gods. It is time that the things revealed to you be made known to certain people. You two go about your business as usual. I will see you in class later this morning. Speak to no one about your dreams or your seeing me. Wait until you hear from me, and that will be soon."

Chapter Forty-One

The Secret Chamber under the Sphinx

Sokar had spent the morning attending to personal matters and performing his daily ritual to Ra. All the while, his mind was preoccupied with his conversation with Khem and Atef regarding Taret's and Meri-ib's resignation and relocation to Memphis. It had to be an important event, maybe an unprecedented one.

Thoughts whirled in his head, but Sokar came to focus on the first step he had taken to imprint the image of his alternate government in the Duat. He reminded himself that once a magical operation had been set into motion, there was no turning back. Sokar had no intention of turning back, even if he could. This meant that he had to know everything even remotely relevant to what was going on at the palace and in Khufu's mind. He had to know when to make his moves if his scheme was to succeed.

His thoughts still churning, Sokar sat on a rush mat in front of the wooden cabinet that held his palette, red ocher and black carbon pigments, and the pot for water. Opening the cabinet, he took out the palette and inkwells and placed them on the mat. He removed the box that contained his pens. He would work on a story he had been writing. His mind had been on more pressing matters, so Sokar had not given any time to his writing for many weeks, and he missed it. Writing for him had always been an enjoyable task, one that calmed him.

Sokar was writing an autobiographical story about a young bastard prince who struggled to define a place within his father's heart. As with his fiction, so would he write the story of his own fate, the way it should be.

But as Sokar tried to focus on writing, his thoughts returned to his ambitions. Most important now was to know what was going on with Khufu and his powerful new allies, and for that he had an ally—Horus. Sokar could not concentrate on writing now. He walked out onto the sunlit patio, where the hawk sat on a perch in the shade of a sycamore. He admired the bird, his bronze-colored, feathered familiar. Affection flowed from him to the hawk, generating the desire within the bird to do his master's bidding. This desire was an ingredient in their partnership as magical practitioners.

Fixing his eyes on Horus, Sokar began transmitting thoughts, each an image of Horus flying into the mind of his human "target," Taret. The bird had already had a few encounters with Meri-ib, and Sokar did not want to arouse suspicions that his mind was being monitored. Over and over again Sokar sent the vision to Horus, commanding him to make mental contact with Taret's unconscious and search her recent memories. After a few minutes, Sokar knew the hawk had received the transmission. It was time to back off and let the bird do his work. Sokar would wait a few hours, and then communicate with Horus by shape-shifting into a hawk himself. . . .

Noon had passed and the heavy, hot air was relinquishing its hold on his mind and body. Sokar decided to spend the few hours he needed to wait by walking to the marketplace. Though the air was still hot, a gentle breeze was blowing inland from the Nile, making the heat bearable. The odor of fish wafted in from the docks. Birds circled the docks, and dogs waited patiently for scraps that might fall when the fish were unloaded.

Sokar loved the city. He loved its noise, its hordes of people, the marketplace, and the buildings, especially the temples. Like most Egyptian towns, Heliopolis was built on an elevated site safe from the Nile's flooding. However, the City of the Sun was situated there as much for political reasons as for concern with Inundation. Heliopolis was a city of learning, and Sokar liked being among the country's most learned scholars and priests.

Sokar came to the last vendor in the marketplace, one selling exotic oils and fragrances. The young woman tending the wares caught his eye. Her beauty was striking: she had dark almond-shaped eyes, long, shiny black hair, an exquisite face. Sokar appreciated a beautiful woman as much as any man, and he recognized the extraordinary when he saw it, and this girl was that.

"It is a lovely day," Sokar said, his eyes fixed on the young woman. "Almost as lovely as you."

His charming voice caught the woman off guard. She was not accustomed to receiving compliments from members of the aristocracy, though she was used to being bombarded with comments from virtually every common man she encountered, and it was unusual to see highborn men shop, a task usually done by servants. The woman was embarrassed by Sokar's remark, and looked down to avoid meeting his gaze, mumbling an almost inaudible negation of the compliment.

Her stall was filled with things that interested Sokar, a fine assortment of stone vessels. Vessels like these were much sought after as symbols of luxury. Sokar, who fancied himself a collector, judged the smaller vessels would be useful for the ingredients of his potions.

Sokar picked up one and inspected its fine workmanship. "Very fine granite and exquisitely polished," Sokar muttered, as he rubbed the smooth stone with his free hand. He set it down and picked up a larger, hollowed-out piece of calcite. "I have never seen a more well-crafted vessel, nor a more beautiful stonecutter." His face lit up with a smile as he spoke.

"Oh, no, no," the woman replied quickly. "I did not make these. My father, he is the maker."

"I see," Sokar answered, raising an eyebrow. "And who might your father be?"

"Ak-na, Ak-na of Memphis."

"Ak-na of Memphis? I see. And does Ak-na of Memphis's daughter have a name?"

"Pipu. I am Pipu."

"Ah, Pipu," Sokar repeated. "A beautiful name for a beautiful woman."

Not wanting to overextend his attention at their first meeting, Sokar shifted his focus back to the vessels, picking up the small granite piece again. He decided to purchase it. "I like this one very much." Sokar reached into the sash around his waist and brought out a green turquoise amulet carved in the shape of the *udjat*. "Perhaps we can make a fair trade, Pipu. It is green turquoise, and will protect its wearer from all evil."

The woman had never seen anything like the amulet before. She held out her hand and allowed Sokar to place the *udjat* in her palm. "My father makes such decisions, but I am sure he would say yes if he was here. He is in Memphis."

Pipu's willingness to make a trade told Sokar that she was a good merchant, and was warming up to him, no longer shy. "Good," Sokar said eagerly. "We have a trade."

Pipu was still holding the amulet in her palm when Sokar put his hand on hers and closed her fingers around it. "Wear it in good health and happiness," he said gently, once again making eye contact with the lovely woman. "But I suspect you, if you are the one who wears it, will not need protecting, for even the worst of evil spirits would not wish to do harm to one so beautiful as you."

With those words, Sokar took the vessel and admired his prize. He turned his attention to a vial of eucalyptus oil, which he chose with a clay jar of juniper berries. He often used these in his magical work. He traded a few beads for them, and then asked her a pointed question. "Does your father spend much time in Memphis?"

Surprised by the inquiry, Pipu replied that he did.

"And does he spend time doing business with the palace or the temples"

"Only the temples," Pipu answered, feeling helpless to avoid the questions. "My father supplies several temples in Memphis and here, in Heliopolis, with oils and fragrances and sometimes with stone pots and bowls."

"I see," Sokar replied slowly, his mind reviewing the prospects of Ak-na knowing what was current in the religious community of Memphis. Maybe he would have tidbits of gossip and rumors for Sokar. Conceivably, Sokar might learn something about Meri-ib and Taret's departure to the capital city.

Sokar promised himself he would get to know Pipu better, and her father. A reliable connection with someone like Ak-na would not arouse anyone's suspicions and could prove useful. Treasures in hand, Sokar bid Pipu farewell with an approving smile.

"I am sure we will meet again, daughter of Ak-na of Memphis," Sokar said, bowing his head in a respectful gesture usually reserved for those of his own social status. He was confident he had succeeded in charming the woman and that she was attracted to him out of curiosity about who he was. He knew he had flattered her and that she would remember him if she saw him again.

Sokar continued through the marketplace. After trading for a pair of pigeons to take to Kheti, he started back to the *Benu* Temple when he recognized a merchant from Memphis. The man was a supplier of linen and other fabrics used by temple seamstresses and weavers to make garments for the priests and their families.

"Good day," the merchant spoke, recognizing Sokar.

"And to you," Sokar replied with his usual courteous bow. He did not know the merchant personally, nor did the man know him except for seeing him with Kheti, who had traded with him for fabrics.

The merchant eyed Sokar closely, pegging him for someone important, maybe even minor royalty. Highborns were usually good for a hefty trade or two, so he wanted to engage Sokar. Sokar was just as eager to chat with the vendor to see what he might say about things in the capital. With that aim, Sokar gave in to the man's motion for him to come see his wares.

"Come, see," the merchant said eagerly. "Look at this." He picked up a small, beautifully carved cedar box. Symbols were etched on its lid, attention having been paid to the minutest detail. The delicate container did indeed catch Sokar's eye. "It is from Punt. Look at it. Is it not beautiful? It would make a pleasing gift for someone special. Your woman, yes?" The merchant babbled in typical vendor verbiage. As he spoke he noticed the gold-plated neckpiece Sokar was wearing. "You can have the box, I will have the neckpiece, yes?" The merchant spoke with the confidence of a seasoned barterer.

Sokar's lips curved into a sly smile before he transformed his features into a semblance of vulnerability. He often assumed this look when he wanted to play games. "The box for the neckpiece," Sokar said. "Oh, that is a very generous offer of trade, my good man. But I am afraid you would cheat yourself. This neckpiece is not as valuable as it appears to be."

Leaning closer towards his quarry, the vendor looked at the neckpiece suspiciously. He had been certain the piece was worth what it appeared to be, but now he wasn't sure. He had lost the upper hand for the moment, and was falling fast into Sokar's grip.

"It is gold. The box is cedar," the vendor proclaimed, almost arrogantly.

"Ah, then if you are certain the neckpiece if made of gold, then surely you know that gold is more valuable than cedar, is it not? Perhaps at your stall in Memphis you have something that would be equal to the neckpiece since you are certain it is gold."

The merchant was surprised that his client knew he had a business in Memphis. "Perhaps so," he commented, his voice trailing off.

"I get to Memphis fairly often," Sokar added quickly, not wanting to lose the man's attention. "I will keep our barter in mind and I will look for you in the marketplace there now that I know you are interested in the neckpiece."

The promise of a profitable trade yanked the merchant out of his confusion regarding the value of the jewelry. Sokar took advantage of this greed to open a brief, but lighter, conversation. Picking up a trinket as an excuse to tarry a moment longer, Sokar said, "Memphis must be a busy place these days, what with all the laborers coming and going from Giza. You do know about the Sphinx project?"

The man nodded that he did, and set about tidying his table.

"And Pharaoh's proclamation of the Second Coming? That must be drawing many people to the city. Pharaoh's dreams must be filled with auspicious images of the future. I wonder if they are dreams of Egypt's future, or *his*?"

"His future? The king's future? It has never been more secure. Pharaoh is a good leader and no king has ever had better advisors in his court than Khufu."

This was the comment Sokar wanted to hear. It was obviously known, even among the *fellahin* on the streets, that Khufu had advisors. Of course all kings had advisors. The question was whether the merchant and others like him knew if there were new or special advisors. Was the man referring to anyone in particular?

"Yes, I hear that Pharaoh's advisors are very wise," Sokar responded. "Perhaps he has chosen those even more wise to help guide him in light of what is going on."

"Perhaps so. I do not know," the merchant answered, his tone indicating a lack of interest.

His response led Sokar to conclude that if Khufu did have special advisors, and if those advisors were Taret and Meri-ib rather than the usual members of the court, it was not public knowledge. As Sokar was certain that Meri-ib and Taret had gone to the palace, the fact that they were there was being kept secret. Also, hearing how a commoner responded to any mention or comment about Pharaoh and the general goings on showed him there was little or no concern in the population regarding Khufu's handling of the Sphinx project, the Second Coming, or anything else. Sokar would have to rely on Horus to learn what he needed. Sokar bade the vendor a good day and returned to the *Benu* Temple.

Upon his arrival home, he found the hawk sleeping on his perch. When Sokar approached, the bird's eyes flipped open in acknowledgment. Holding out his right forearm for the hawk to climb onto, Sokar walked from under the shade tree to the lotus pool, where he and his familiar would engage in their shape-shifting ritual and Sokar would collect the images Horus had retrieved from Taret's mind.

When Sokar came to the pool's rim, he lowered his arm so that Horus could step off. It was time for shape-shifting. Kheti would observe at a distance and keep watch, making sure the ritual partners were not disturbed. The bright sunlight made the hawk's feathers shine with bronze radiance. Looking at the splendid bird, Sokar marveled, as he had many times before, how magnificent a creature Horus was.

The moment reminded him of the story of Isis changing into a hawk and by fanning her great wings under his nostrils, how she revived the dead Osiris. There is no power greater than that which can restore life. Sokar respected that power, and knew that its origin went back to the First Time. He also knew how to bridge the worlds so that the veil between the physical and nonphysical was momentarily lifted, a magical operation he had been taught by Dedi.

Kheti stood inside the entranceway of his master's bedchamber, keeping vigil. The transfiguration never failed to stir his imagination and to terrorize him. The servant had a healthy respect for *heka*, and he had witnessed what most Egyptians could only imagine. There was a crackling in the air around Sokar and Horus. The *heka* energy aroused, it began racing through Sokar, empowering him. His body became rigid, his eyes fixed on Horus. The magician began to regulate his breath, imagining himself transforming into a hawk. Within moments the metamorphosis was actual and complete. On the rim of the lotus pool now perched two hawks.

The two minds locked telepathically, energy flowing between them. Sokar's mind filled with images of a ritual in which the Rod of Power of the office of High Priestess of the Holy Order of Nut was passed to another woman whose identity he could not discern. He saw vision fragments of Taret and Meri-ib on a royal sailing vessel. The two in the company of the king. A fuzzy image of an old man. Words started coming: "stars in the Duat . . . immortality . . . Star Gods." He saw Khufu lifted alive into the heavens, taking his place in a great circle of immortals, the look on the Pharaoh's face a serenity no human could hope to experience.

When Horus's mind had transmitted all the images, the bond between the bird and Sokar began to wane, and in moments the connection was broken. Sokar and Horus were once more separate life forms. It was up to Sokar to decipher the images. His eyes transfixed, his body still as stone, Sokar began to change once again into a human. Bronze feathers dissolved into flesh; Sokar's human head appeared to burst out of the open beak of the hawk, shattering the form of the feathered body.

Kheti stepped forward cautiously and offered Sokar a cup of cool water. Water would ground the magician after a magical operation that had required a tremendous physical and mental power, and emotional control.

Sokar gave Kheti a slight smile of reassurance that he was all right. "Let me be, Kheti. I need time alone to ponder what I have learned."

Although Sokar seemed to be drained, he did not suffer any adverse effects. He was empowered. He had once commented to Kheti that the moments spent in a hawk's body not only provided brief company for Horus, but established a bond between the two that only magicians could comprehend.

Sokar sat on the soft reed mat in front of his altar. Here he could be alone with his thoughts, in this personal place where he could commune with the gods. His body began to relax as he emptied his mind of irrelevant thoughts. The aroma of myrrh filled his nostrils. It was an ever-present scent in the small room where he had been taught by Dedi. Detectable in every temple, it was a fragrance that always called him into the world of spirits. The late afternoon sun cast shadows on the walls and floor of Sokar's chamber. The slowly dimming light and the fragrance helped him to relax. Relaxation was imperative. Feeling a floating sensation, the magician allowed the images from Horus's mind to return, one by one. . . .

Almost an hour passed before Sokar roused himself. He had sufficiently pieced together the images to make assumptions about what was going on in the palace. Taret and Meri-ib had been summoned. They were not a part of the usual rostrum of court advisors, but were working behind the scenes, most likely with Khufu. Sokar surmised the two were living in the palace. This was troubling for it provided them with a more protected environment whose boundaries would be difficult to breach, and it indicated the former High Priest and High Priestess had a relationship with the king of Egypt that was more confidential than Sokar would have previously guessed.

But who was the old man who emitted such an extraordinary energy? Sokar could not recall ever encountering one so ancient in the physical world. For this elder to be in the palace, and for him to be in images plucked from Horus's mind—surely he was associated with Khufu, Meri-ib, and Taret. A priest. He must be a priest, Sokar thought. An image of the old man re-formed in Sokar's mind. What could the old man, surely a priest, have to do with the return of the Star Gods? Sokar wondered intently, the question burning in him.

Then the answer hit him like a bolt of lightning.

"That's it!" Sokar said aloud, almost shouting. "Khufu has sent for high level advisors. Could it be that he has arranged for the counsel of Shemshu-Hor, the oldest and wisest man alive?"

He knew that was it. The return of the Star Gods to Egypt was an event that no man alone, not even the Pharaoh, could handle. He would need sage counsel, and there was none wiser than the High Priest of the Followers of Horus.

Sokar felt satisfaction. It was clearer than ever now what a powerful foe Khufu was. King of Egypt, god incarnate, a god-man who lived in two worlds, one earthly, one heavenly—whatever he did as ruler he did in the spirit of expressing the connection of these two dimensions. All the rites he performed or presided over reinforced his identity and power as the living image of Ra. It was an identity that gave him extraordinary power. Now with Shemshu-Hor advising Khufu, all Egyptians would see proof that he was divinely appointed to be the Pharaoh at the Second Coming. No other man would be accepted as king; no other government could rule but Khufu's. Seemingly.

Sokar was not one to deny the power of what he was facing. He was also not one to deny the power of his magic. It would not be easy to win the allegiance of a portion of the people, much less all of them. But I don't need them all, Sokar thought. I only need enough, and enough I will get.

In the dark hours of the next morning, Khufu dressed. He liked wearing the clothes of the *fellahin*. Although the garments were not that different from his own royal short skirt, they divested him from all the trappings of his position—the crown, the royal jewels, the finery—and made him feel free. Khufu did not regret his lot in life. However, there were times when it was necessary for him to go somewhere or do something without being recognized. The only way he could do that was in disguise, and he enjoyed the brief anonymity these rare excursions afforded. Khufu had a plan. He would meet Nemon at the entrance to the underground chamber. The two would enter disguised, accompanied by two bodyguards privy to their agenda. Like Khufu and Nemon, the guards would be clothed as laborers.

Nemon had made several trips into the stone cavity beneath the Sphinx since its discovery. The laborers were busy with their work, however, and since no public announcement had been made regarding the chamber's existence, no one had taken particular notice of any one person's coming and going. Once inside and safely beyond the eyes of anyone, Khufu would proceed to the ceremonial hall where Nemon and his foreman had encountered the spirit woman. As to what Khufu's eyes would meet. . . .

The project site was buzzing with workers, even at this early dawn hour. Khufu gazed at what was nearly the full body of the Lion Man of the Desert. He could scarcely believe his eyes. No one in his lifetime had seen anything other than its great head. Fierce, relentless *khamsin* winds blowing in from the south had over the centuries deposited tons of sand to hide all but the huge head from view. It was now clear the massive body had been carved from a single ridge of rock.

Nemon arrived, almost unrecognizable to Khufu, dressed as a laborer, his head covered with a cotton turban.

"This is the way it will always be," Khufu said. "This place, this great monument, will excite the eyes and thrill the hearts of Egyptians until time is no more."

The men stood in silence, their eyes studying the giant figure. Khufu was drawn to its enigmatic face and noted the form seemed to emit a kind of life force in waves. "This is truly a sacred place," Khufu said.

The king was feeling a deep belonging to the land and its past, one stronger than any he had ever felt before. Uncovering the Sphinx had restored life to the area. He could feel the presence of the gods.

Nemon interrupted Khufu's thoughts. "Come, Your Majesty. The sun is rising. Let us go into the chamber before someone recognizes us."

When the party reached the entrance, the bodyguards became nervous. Nemon was there for moral support and the guards for the monarch's protection, but neither would go past a certain point. Khufu would go in alone, just as the spirit woman had requested. Khufu was struck by the energy of the chamber. The walk down the hallway was made easier by the light from a small torch carried by the bodyguard who led the way. It was unlikely that Khufu or Nemon was in any physical danger, but if anything did happen, the bodyguard would encounter it first. For now, there were only the deafening silence and the dancing shadows cast by the torch on the limestone walls. Fifty yards inside the stuffy tunnel, the men came to the doorway of the room where Nemon and Harum had met the powerful apparition of the star woman. "This is as far as I go," Nemon said, his voice shattering the quiet of the tunnel.

The two men locked eyes for a brief moment before Khufu turned to enter the chamber. The doorway was so low he had to bend his head and upper body to get inside. The king went into the musty-smelling hall. His eyes adjusted to the dimness and he saw the hieroglyphs Nemon had spoken about. Khufu placed his hand on the stone. It felt cool to the touch. Some of the symbols were red, and had been formed with thick paint. Then, holding a lamp above his head, he saw the star-painted ceiling. Khufu moved the light so he could scan it. One area showed a comet streaking across the sky. Then he examined the floor, and its large, rectangular limestone tiles. On the tiles in the center of the chamber was a gold five-pointed star, rubbed dim due to the shuffling of sandaled feet over time.

Suddenly, the flame of his lamp seemed to put off an extraordinary amount of light. The glow illuminated the chamber, revealing the colors and strange symbols and the star-flecked ceiling. The yellow-orange flame became elongated until it was as high as a man. Khufu gasped and stepped backwards to protect himself from the bright flame even as he still held the lamp. The flame seemed to move a little away from him now, as if independent of the lamp.

A tall, slender male figure formed in the flame, then became six more figures. Seven males, clad in ebony panther skins, stood in a circle around Khufu.

At first, Khufu was frightened by the suddenness of their appearance. But his fear left and a calmness washed over him. Khufu knew he was in the presence of the initiates. One of the figures stepped towards him.

"We have come from the Winding Waterway, the Place of Contentment in the Horizon. I am Senmut who dwells in the eternal heart of the god Atum. I come by the power of the Light. I come in the name of the Keepers of the Great Mystery, the omnipotent god Osiris, the Warrior of Light who walks free and at will in the heavens. It is he who wears the Face of Justice, he who is the Whisperer of Truth, he who dispels the darkness."

The initiate acknowledged the others.

"These are my brothers. We are dwellers of the starry realms, chief servants of Osiris."

The speaker for the seven fell quiet while the others, one by one, spoke their names: An-tef, Ny-netjer, Teti, Setne, Ipuwer, Userhat.

"We are seven of the Ancients. Over time, we have come to know the gods and to speak for the gods. We have trembled beneath the power of their hands laid in blessing on our heads at the time of our initiation into the Great Mysteries, just as one day, so shall you, Khufu, Wearer of the Double Crown of Egypt, the Mother Country of the World. We trembled in the absence of the Star Gods when they left us on our own to fulfill our destiny, a destiny ordained by them. You whose eyes probe every being, whose soul illumines the Two Lands and fills it with strength and life—we are as tied to your destiny as the ox is to the plow. We are here with you filled with joy. No one among us regrets the path that led us to this place at this time.

"Egypt is the earthly temple of the stars. You, Khufu, must lead the land and people. No other shall take your place. Some may put demons in your path. Should this occur, we give you a Word of Power to protect yourself from harm from any quarter, on Earth or in the heavens. You are one of us, and we take care of our own."

Khufu waited for the word. He expected the *heka* word to come from Senmut. Instead, it resounded from the ceiling, walls, floor, as if every atom in the room was speaking it: *Anupu.*

Khufu knew that word. It was one of the names of the god Anubis.

Senmut spoke again.

"Contained within the ren of each of the Neters is a sound that when spoken in the correct manner will call forth the power of that deity. Remember this word. Utter it not unless you or Egypt be threatened."

Then another of the seven spoke, the one called Ipuwer.

"We prepare a place for you. After your life on Earth is over, you will join us in the realm of Osiris. Before then, your coming alive will occur at the base of the Great Pyramid, which will forever after be known by your name and as the Place of Ascension, your ascension."

Khufu found himself alone. The seven were gone, but a tall, bronze-skinned woman appeared in their place.

"Go in peace, Khufu, King of Egypt. Go from here to fulfill your destiny without fear of faltering."

In an instant, she also disappeared. The chamber was plunged into near darkness again, faint light coming only from the small oil lamp Khufu held. He stood as if his feet were planted in the limestone floor.

When Khufu finally emerged he looked at Nemon, and said, "I am ready to go now."

Upon returning to the palace, Khufu went straight to his chapel and knelt before the gilded statue of Ptah to offer a prayer and give thanks to the Neters for their guidance, protection of the land, the people, and him. He concluded with a commitment. "Tomorrow I will call a meeting of the Sirius Council."

Chapter Forty-Two

Reporting the Dream

Khem and Tiye now had an inkling of the role they would play in the Second Coming. Khem had given a lot of thought to how the gods work, how everything was unfolding at the right time and in the right order. She was becoming more aware of how every person meant to be involved in any special event is drawn into the energy of the event, so that when it happens everyone is in place, and all can unfold as ordained.

The dream she and Tiye had experienced when they saw the Sirian Star Woman came to mind. She found it hard to imagine how two *fellahin* girls who had come to Heliopolis to enter training at the Temple of the Sun now found themselves about to witness the Second Coming of the Star Gods, much less that they might serve a purpose that would help guide and protect the king of Egypt. Khem marveled at how she was alive at the most auspicious time in Egypt's history. She would one day be looked upon as a woman of visions. And Tiye, her closest friend, was becoming known as a skilled sorceress making amulets to protect a king. It was all a lot to digest. Khem pushed her thoughts aside. It was time to get ready for the day's class, and she was anxious to see Ani.

They met Kasut at the classroom. The three friends had not spent much time together lately, and Khem had missed that. Life at the Temple was hectic at times. Any opportunity for a break in the responsibility of it all was welcome.

Ani and Sheshat entered the classroom and mounted the teaching platform. The day's lesson would concern Egypt's signature monuments: the pyramids at Sakkara and Giza. Like most of the *fellahin*, Khem took the pyramids for granted. She knew only the basics regarding their purpose. The monuments had seemed irrelevant to her studies of the stars. But now, maybe not.

"Egypt has long been blessed with wise men and women," Ani said. "Among them, none has surpassed the wisdom of Imhotep, a man inspired by Thoth. He was an ideal scribe, the embodiment of the practical wisdom of the ages. He was an architect, physician, chancellor, astronomer, High Priest, genius. Imhotep birthed the design for the pyramid at Sakkara, a structure that connects Earth and sky. Such a structure could not be built just anywhere. It had to be built in a special place charged with energy. The sites of all the pyramids possess that energy. The most powerful of these sites is Giza, known since the earliest times as the Primeval Mound. It is a place of birth, death, and rebirth.

"Physically, the Great Mound is a natural outcropping of rock now part of the largest of the three pyramids. The Primeval Mound itself came into being as the result of a great flood, greater than any flooding of Mother Nile. Water covered all the land.

"The instructions for how to build the pyramid, and the command to do so, were transmitted a very long time ago by seven divine beings. When the word was given to begin construction of the first pyramid at Sakkara, these seven Holy Ones were present. One was Thoth. He masterminded the building of the first temple on Earth. All this happened during the First Time. When the stepped-pyramid was complete, the seven sages performed a ritual to protect the site. The ritual was empowered by sacred words that assured that no act of nature and none by man would ever destroy the pyramid.

"The seven sages are the keepers of the wisdom that existed prior to the most devastating catastrophe to befall the planet, the Flood. Thankfully, their wisdom survived. When the waters retreated, the seven sages set out to help those humans who had survived to make a new start. They brought about a new age.

"The seven sages and the Neters originally settled on Earth on an island they called the Homeland of the Primeval Ones. The Flood destroyed that island, and all but five male and two female humans drowned. These survivors, the sages, came to Egypt and began a new life. They brought the wisdom with them. The seven have been called many names: Lords of Light, Builder Gods, the Ghosts, the Ancestors. Understand these seven survivors—sages—were not immortal. They were physical, I assure you. When they eventually died, one by one, their offspring performed the funerary rites and took their places. Know that the seven wise ones and the Followers of Horus were one and the same and the inheritors of their wisdom exist to this day within the confines of the Temple of the *Benu*.

"Their wisdom consisted of the secrets of mathematics, astronomy, medicine, geometry, mummification—all the great mysteries. This knowledge has been passed down from generation to generation, and is now safely in the hands of the most learned of the priesthood. There exist texts recorded by the sages that contain information concerning the building of monuments. The building of the Great Pyramid and other monuments was a way to accomplish numerous objectives. The most important of these was to build a structure that *embodied* star knowledge.

"The greatest of the pyramids has many 'moods.' It shines brilliantly in the sunlight. I have seen the setting sun cause it to radiate warmth like a giant glowing ember. I have seen it shimmer with a light as blue as the sky. Down through time, initiates have woven their way through the pyramid's passageways and activated the star wisdom and power with which the structure was built. Four initiations into star mysteries take place in it in four different chambers. The initiations have to do with Sirius, the three stars in Osiris, and the stars Thuban, which is the North Star, and Kochab. Each of these suns has its own power and is associated with a Neter.

"Taret taught you about these great stars, beginning with Sirius. You know of its association with Isis, the annual flooding of Mother Nile, and with the power of regeneration and rebirth. The seven sages also taught that Sirius generates a tremendous power that has to do with cosmic regeneration, the assurance of immortality, a power that conquers death.

"The North Star concerns what could be called cosmic pregnancy. The force that is the source of life exists there. Thuban, Sirius, and Kochab are part of the starry realm of Osiris, god of resurrection and rebirth. The Great Pyramid is aligned to these three important stars. These celestial power centers provide the monument with its power of regeneration and rebirth.

"The teachings in the Old Texts regarding the Duat tell us that the Great Pyramid and other monuments in our land embody the 'powers' contained within this region of space. No region of the sky is more important to our religion, none more powerful. Our beloved Osiris is the Lord of the Duat, and it is in the Duat that the souls of all the pharaohs reside after death."

Ani finished her talk with a slight bow to the audience and left the teaching platform to approach Khem and Tiye. "I would like to speak to the two of you in my private quarters."

The apprentices assumed it had to do with the dreams they had reported to her. When they arrived, Ani's chief house steward invited them inside. The sweet fragrance of incense filled the air. The sound of a lyre could be heard. Ani beckoned Khem and Tiye to follow her to her study. It was the first time either of them had been in this room.

"I have given much thought to your dreams. I have sent a courier to Memphis to inform Taret. She should know, especially in light of her position to the Pharaoh."

Couriers bringing message scrolls to the palace were subjected to close scrutiny by the royal security guards. Each was met at the gates and checked for concealed weapons, scrolls that had been opened or tampered with in any way, and anything that seemed suspicious. Security was a much greater concern now than ever before.

Couriers delivering messages to Taret or Meri-ib were detained at the gates by order of the Pharaoh. Khufu did not intend for his secret advisors to be shut off from the outside world, but they could be targets for kidnapping by would-be usurpers or any of the enemies of the Throne who would go to extremes to gather palace intelligence.

When Ani's courier, Sinuhe, arrived in Memphis, he went straight to the palace. Messengers who dealt with high-level political and religious persons throughout the country were trained to be discreet in the performance of their duty. More than one had died at the hands of those who intercepted their messages.

Taret read the message through twice. Two apprentices had experienced a dream with implications for the safety of the king and the members of the Holy Order of Nut. She had no reservations about giving Ani her blessings in whatever measures the High Priestess felt were necessary to protect the Throne and Khufu himself. Taret's personal scribe prepared a response for the courier to take back to Heliopolis. Her business finished, Taret went to Meri-ib to let him know what she had learned.

When Sinuhe returned to Heliopolis, he delivered the message scroll from Taret in all haste. He had been a courier for royalty and members of the priesthood long enough to sense when a scroll held a message of importance.

Sheshat received the scroll and gave it to Ani. Ani knew at once she had gotten the answer she expected. Taret agreed that the girls' dreams should be taken seriously, that the visions forecast a threat to the king's safety. Why else would Tiye have to make an amulet that would "save his life"? If there was any chance that Khufu faced danger, even if its source was unknown and faceless, every precaution must be taken. As for Khem becoming a clear and dependable visionary, that was not surprising. After all, it was Taret who had foretold that.

In Taret's message she confided to Ani how she was struck by the appearance of the Star Woman in both dreams. It reminded her how close it was to the time of the return of the Star Gods, and it reaffirmed that it was the Sirians who were coming back to Egypt, the Earth "home" to many of their lineage. Taret's recall of past lives when she had known Khem gave her a special feeling for the novice priestess as it showed they shared the same star lineage.

Ani rolled up the scroll and instructed Sheshat to read its contents and then put it away for safekeeping. She also sent a message to summon Khem and Tiye to her apartment on the following morning. There would be no class, so there was time for the apprentices' next lesson on magic. It was time for the students to learn how to venture into the astral world.

Khem and Tiye felt apprehension. They knew that Ani had summoned them for one reason. She had heard from Taret. The apprentices waited in the reception room of Ani's apartment. Minutes seemed like hours and their thoughts raced. Taret's acceptance of the dreams as valid meant Khem and Tiye were being drawn into a web of danger and intrigue.

Ani invited Khem and Tiye into her study. She sensed that the apprentices were nervous. "There is no need for apprehension. Such a feeling can turn into fear."

The girls were caught off guard by this. It made them aware of their tenseness and it calmed them. Ani saw the relaxation come over the two. Their breath came rushing out in a single, long sigh, their shoulders dropped. Ani bade them sit down.

"I have received an answer from Taret. It is important for you to know what her comments are regarding the dreams. She takes the dreams seriously and literally though some parts are personal and pertain to no one but each of you. The Mistress Taret recognizes you, Tiye, as a skilled young sorceress. She realizes that you are not opening up completely to that reality. She finds the prophecy of your amulet-making acceptable, so much so that she accepts as highly plausible the forecast of your making an amulet to protect the Pharaoh. She places, as do I, complete trust in your magical skills, and sees the making of such a sacred object as serving two purposes: to prevent harm to the king and to prove your magical power. Taret and I believe this will help you move forward to become a celebrated amulet priestess. For that is your future."

Ani had not merely offered an opinion. She had voiced a revelation, as perceived by Tiye. Her words sent a wave of energy through the Nubian, the kind one feels when one's fate has been described, when direction and purpose have been revealed. Tiye knew her destiny had been ordained by the Neters long before she was born.

"I will continue to be your teacher, Tiye. Your lessons on magic will now be more focused. I know precisely what knowledge will contribute to your skill as an amulet-maker."

Ani extended warmth towards Tiye. The Nubian was not always open, at least not on the surface, to emotional expression, as Ani had intuited when the two first met. Still, that did not prevent her from feeling a motherly love for her.

Tiye made no comment. She needed to be alone to digest this. She was certain Khaba had known this time would come, had known her purpose in life. Perhaps this was why the Neters had put her and Khaba together.

Ani left Tiye to her thoughts and turned to Khem. In light of what was said to Tiye, Khem again felt apprehension. Khem was not afraid of what she might hear, but of how it would change her. Maybe it was easier to get through life not knowing her purpose, she thought.

"Taret has known even before the two of you met that there is a soul connection and a star connection between you and her. Not a human link; a spiritual one."

These words took Khem back to the time when Taret had told her that they were soul-related, and that Taret had known her in many past lives. Khem felt the same now as then, disbelief and joy.

"Taret and I see you as a visionary capable of peering into the heart of a matter, a person, or the future. You are needed. The Mistress Taret and I concur that you are the one among the apprentices we can and must depend upon."

Khem was fascinated by what she was hearing. She felt as if Ani was speaking about someone else.

"These are significant times for Egypt," Ani continued. "Both of you know that. Important times are always filled with opportunities as well as perils, triumphs, and failures. Neither of you need me to remind you of the king's importance to Egypt, that he is the incarnation of Horus, the living embodiment of the lineage and power of that deity. The dreams you and Tiye experienced clearly indicate a danger to the Pharaoh. This must not be overlooked. This is our conclusion. You, Khem, as a visionary, must use your aptitude to gain visions of what will occur with any person, in any place, that will pose a threat to the safety of the Wearer of the Double Crown now and in future years."

Khem felt the burden of responsibility Ani's words carried. She knew the safety of the king would soon become her concern. A sick feeling knotted her stomach. Khem's first impulse was to run, and she would have except for her knowing she could not run from her fate. She was an apprentice Star Priestess. This was her first test. Did she have what it took to be a member of the Holy Order of Nut? Was she strong enough to bear the weight? If not, she would not pass the test. Her training, her life in the Temple, her spiritual aspirations for this lifetime—all would be over.

"I will do as you and Mistress Taret ask of me," Khem finally said. "Your trust in me strengthens my trust in myself. I thank you for leading me to this discovery."

"No, Khem. It is not I or the Mistress Taret who led you to this point. It was the spirit woman in your dream. . . ."

Khem and Tiye were quiet on their walk back to the dormitory. Akhi had cool beer and fig cakes for them while she and Nerah filled the lamps with sweet-smelling oil. Both servant girls were devoted to Khem and Tiye and went to great lengths to meet their needs and see to their comfort.

Bast bounded over to Khem as she came through the doorway. Khem made an effort to play with the cat, but her mind was still in the meeting. Tiye was more available to play with the lioness, so Khem left the two to their romp and lay across her bed. It was hard to relax at first, but in a few minutes Khem felt the numbness wear off and feeling come back.

"Are you excited about amulet-making?" Khem asked.

"Yes," Tiye replied. "I have been thinking about what Ani said. I do not want to let my talent go to waste."

Both girls laughed. The humor lifted the heaviness they had felt, and their conversation flowed freely.

"When you think about it, Tiye, we are fortunate."

"What do you mean?"

"Well, we have been given a vote of confidence that none of our peers have. Ani, Taret, the spirit woman—that's quite an honor, I should think."

Khem's perspective made both girls look at their situation differently. They had been so focused on the responsibility of what they had been chosen to do and their fears of not being qualified for the tasks, that neither had looked upon it as good fortune. Chosen for roles that involved protecting the Pharaoh—surely that was an exciting challenge.

Chapter Forty-Three

Dedication of the Temple of Thoth

Khufu awoke to the light of the rising sun, a dream still with him. He was in a huge room, walls, ceiling, and floor of polished limestone. The walls were painted in exquisite murals depicting days in the life of an Egyptian king. One wall showed an elaborate Throne Room, the Pharaoh seated on the great chair; another showed King Zozer carried in a procession to the stepped-pyramid at Sakkara; others showed the Pharaoh hunting in the marshes of the Delta, presiding over the court, undergoing coronation.

In the center of the room was a circular table of pink granite, all the Egyptian kings before Khufu seated around it, even Khufu's father. A solitary figure stood in the center: Osiris in his Memphis counterpart as Ptah, Lord of Everything. The deity's presence created a vortex of power around the spot where he stood. Upon his head sat the white crown of Lower Egypt, and he held the royal Crook and Flail in his crossed arms. His skin was green, symbolizing regeneration, vegetation, and growth. The kings around Osiris-Ptah were chanting in unison: "Honor to you, O King of Kings, Lord of Lords, Dweller at the Crossroads of Eternity. Your crown reaches the heavens to the Brotherhood of the Stars."

Khufu had never heard those words before, yet they seemed familiar. The dream's meaning was clear. He was with all his predecessors in council. The phrase "Congress of Orion" echoed in his head. Congress of Orion. . . .

Sokar was planning a journey to Hermopolis, south of Heliopolis. It had been a long time since he had been there, and longer still since he had seen his mentor, Dedi. Word had it that the old magician was at the main temple in the city.

Sokar had spent a semester in the House of Life in Hermopolis during his training as a scribe. The scribes there were among the finest in Egypt. In fact, it was at the Temple of Thoth where Sokar met Dedi. The elder, not a formally trained priest, was said to be in the city now to perform a ritual of protection as part of the rite of dedication of a newly raised obelisk at the Thoth Temple.

Sokar had been immediately drawn to Dedi, whose reputation had preceded him. Sokar had long desired to study with the magician from Abydos, and his wish came to pass when he told Dedi that he wanted to become his apprentice. The reason he gave was the truth: there was no one of his stature among magicians, and Sokar would have only the best. He told the aging man of his royal lineage, and offered him accommodations and compensation if Dedi would come to Heliopolis and accept him as his protégé.

Dedi had accepted, and he had accepted accommodations in the guest wing of Sokar's apartments in the Temple of the *Benu*. Being a member of the royal family afforded Sokar numerous privileges and his luxurious private quarters were among the best. But the master magician would not accept compensation. He considered it unethical, for when one works with natural laws to accomplish magical feats, one cannot be paid for such works. The universe takes care of the needs of such men, Dedi believed.

Dedi had spent two years training Sokar, and from Dedi he learned shape-shifting. Being an apprentice to Dedi had been the most challenging time of Sokar's life. The relationship had taught him much more than magic. It had cemented his determination to become a magician and priest, for he realized that his feet must walk both paths to be a whole man.

Sokar never knew for sure why the magus agreed to teach him, but he knew it was not due to his being a royal, nor to anything material. Sokar liked to believe that Dedi saw his potential for magic. Dedi said he recognized that to be a magician was Sokar's destiny. Sokar accepted that as truth, and devoted himself to learning. Seeing his mentor again now might be his last time with Dedi on Earth, and his only chance to confide his plan in hopes of getting Dedi's assistance.

Sokar enlisted a small entourage from his household staff that included two servants to attend to his physical needs, a bodyguard, and Kheti. The trip would be made on the Nile because it was the most rapid artery for travel. Hermopolis was part of the triangle of Memphis and Heliopolis, and home of the cult of Thoth. Thoth's relationship with the

Moon was comparable to that of Ra's with the Sun, making Heliopolis and Hermopolis solar and lunar cities, respectively.

As a Moon god, Thoth was often depicted as an ibis, an ibis-headed man, and a baboon. He was concerned with the order and regulation of the universe. Thoth uttered the creative sounds that "spoke" the cosmos into being. This aspect designated him as a god of magic because Thoth knew the correct intonations of the incantations. Only a magician with a true voice could gain command of the forces of nature. Dedi possessed that true voice, as did the precious few initiates who had been privileged to train under him.

The most important event that ever happened, the hatching of the World Egg by Thoth in his ibis form, was said to have occurred in Hermopolis. Legend told of the Lake of Two Knives in Hermopolis, in the middle of which was the Isle of Flames. It was there the World Egg was hatched, there the god's emergence took place, there all that exists in the physical world came into being. . . .

It was midafternoon when the boat docked and Sokar's party made the trip from the port to the west bank. The metropolis was bustling with visitors who had come to witness the dedication of the obelisk and to enjoy the celebration afterwards. The monument had been ferried on the Nile from a quarry in the south, and placed in the entrance of the causeway leading to the Temple of Thoth. No one entering the city could miss it, as it towered high above all the roofs. The dedication ceremony would take place the next day. Sokar had not let anyone know he was coming. His presence would be a surprise, even to Dedi. . . .

Dawn splashed the darkness with pink and gold windows of light. Sokar was an early riser, an uncommon habit among highborn Egyptians. This morning appeared to be no different from any other, but it was. Kheti and the servants laid out the clothes he would wear, shaved him, polished his nails, and washed his feet. It was paramount to Sokar that he feel clean and be freshly shaven at all times, particularly when he needed to make a good impression.

After a light breakfast, Sokar dressed in a loose-weave loincloth wrapped around his trim waist and ending just above his knees. His skirt was held in place by a knot at his midriff, and a leopard skin was draped over his broad shoulders. Although wearing the animal hide was usually reserved for rituals, Sokar chose to wear it now to identify himself as a priest. He hoped that being a priest would gain him an invitation to take part in the dedication ritual. He put on the amulet Dedi had given him during his apprenticeship.

The crowd began gathering early at the gates of the temple. Everyone wanted a good place so they could see the procession of priests and the cult statue of Thoth when it was brought from the inner sanctum. Such viewings were known to bring blessings and healings of all kinds to those who saw it.

The obelisk was the center of attention. Like a giant needle, the red granite monument rose more than seventy feet from the desert floor. Its shape was derived from the *ben-ben* stone. Stone baboons graced its base on each corner. As a boy, Sokar learned how wild baboons shrieked with excitement at the rising Sun, so their representation here made the obelisk a Sun symbol. The shaft was etched with hieroglyphs praising Thoth, its apex gilded to reflect the rays of the omnipotent Sun. Looking at the magnificent stone needle, Sokar was struck by its power. He viewed it as a living being and thought the elemental spirit inside the Thoth obelisk must be ancient, strong, and highly evolved.

The crowd was growing steadily, the area around the temple gates taking on the atmosphere of a marketplace. Vendors were setting up food and drink tables; oil and fragrance merchants, even potters and stonecutters, were roaming through the throng enticing customers to buy their wares. Aristocratic families mingled with the *fellahin*. All were there for the same purpose: to witness the dedication, to give and receive love and blessings from their beloved Thoth. It would not be long before the procession began, so it was time for Sokar to make his move.

Security allowed the king's half-brother to pass the gates and enter the main temple complex. Leaving his servants and bodyguard to wait in the courtyard, Sokar and Kheti made their way to the vestibule of the office of High Priest Petosiris. Here, Sokar presented his credentials scroll to the guards and was allowed entrance into the High Priest's reception room. Sokar knew that the head priest would see him as he was a member of the royal family and a fellow member of the priesthood. It was common for priests in one cult center to be politically and religiously separate from the others, but a priest is a priest and was respected as such by all members of the country's religious fraternity.

"Greetings, Sokar," said Petosiris, entering the room. "It has been a long time since our paths have crossed. Tell me, how are these times settling with you?"

Sokar bowed low. He had not spent much time in Petosiris's company, but what time he had spent was enough to tell him that he did not like the priest. The man was self-righteous and an intellectual snob. No matter. Sokar was not here to judge the leader of the cult of Thoth. He wanted to wrangle his way into participating in the ritual. That would draw him into the inner circle, and then he would hear whatever rumors were going around concerning the Second Coming, the comet, or the rising of the Great Star. And it would make him look good in Dedi's eyes, and that mattered.

"My thoughts and visions are filled with the hope of peace and joy for Egypt's future."

Sokar's answer was not what Petosiris expected. He, like everyone else, knew Sokar was the bastard son of Sneferu and had a reputation as a magical adept. Petosiris felt uncomfortable in his presence and was anxious to know what Sokar wanted. "I assume you have come for the dedication of the obelisk."

"Yes. In fact, I consider it such an important occasion for obvious reasons that I wanted to contribute."

"Contribute?"

"Yes, by offering to take part in the procession. I feel a special devotion for the great god Thoth. There must be other of my fellow priests from other parts of the land who similarly have come to honor the one who brought the gift and power of magic to the sons and daughters of Earth."

Petosiris knew he was caught. There was no way he could turn down Sokar's offer without engaging in what would be an embarrassing refusal. It would be easier to extend an invitation than to deal with any repercussions, social or otherwise. "Yes, of course, Sokar. You are welcome to join the procession. There will indeed be priests from many other temples, some of whom you know. You know Dedi. I seem to recall that you are among his few apprentices, and, oh yes, you must surely know Meri-ib, the former High Priest of Heliopolis."

Meri-ib was in Hermopolis? Sokar decided to play dumb. "Meri-ib? Did you say 'former High Priest'? I wasn't aware. I have taken several journeys away from Heliopolis as of late. I only heard rumors."

"Oh, it is not a rumor, I assure you. No, Meri-ib is no longer High Priest. He resigned his post and . . . but then you are not interested in idle talk. Go now, Sokar, and prepare to join the other priests for the ritual."

Petosiris walked toward the door, clearly expecting his uninvited guest to follow. Their meeting was over. For Sokar to attempt to prolong it by asking questions would be awkward and surely cause the High Priest to become suspicious.

"I will expect your appearance in the main reception hall just after noon," Petosiris said, a broad, forced smile on his face.

Sokar left the room and rejoined Kheti beyond the door. Kheti could tell by the expression on his master's face that things had been strained between Sokar and the High Priest. He waited until they were out of earshot of anyone before making any comment. "All is well, my master?"

"Meri-ib is here."

"Master Meri-ib from Heliopolis?"

"Formerly of Heliopolis, you mean. Yes. Petosiris told me about the resignation. I pretended not to know. I hoped he would tell me more details, but he didn't think I was interested."

The priests of Hermopolis gathered in the inner sanctuary of the Temple of Thoth. Each was dressed in a long, white linen skirt fastened at the waist by a gold brooch. Their heads were shaven, leopard skin pelts draped across their shoulders. One by one they gathered around a stone basin and began washing their hands and feet, the customary cleansing rite before any ritual. The large group fell silent. At the entranceway into the sanctuary stood Petosiris, accompanied by Dedi. They too had come for the cleansing ritual.

Dedi had aged considerably since Sokar had last seen him five years before. White hair flowed over his stooped shoulders. His body was lean, almost emaciated. Leathered by time and the harsh desert sun, his skin was stretched over high cheekbones and deep-set eye sockets, giving him an air of wisdom and timelessness.

Sokar stepped into Dedi's path of vision. The aged magician did not seem to recognize him at first, and then a twinkle sparkled in his eyes. Sokar made his customary low bow. Petosiris proffered a slight smile, obviously waiting to see how his honored guest would react to the encounter. He knew all too well how impermanent such relationships could be, that often a teacher will deliberately sever his relationship with the neophyte in the interest of preventing a dependency. Dedi, in a shuffle of small steps, walked straight to Sokar. "Sokar, it is you?"

"Yes, Master, it is me. It has been a long time."

Sokar remembered instantly what it was like being in his presence, to feel the energy the aged one emitted. A small man perhaps, but Dedi's power was big. The elder's legs were shaky, so Sokar took him by the arm and guided him to a stone bench beneath a tree by a lotus pool. He did not acknowledge Petosiris's silent protest at Sokar as demonstrated by the squinting of his eyes. Dedi sat down in such a manner that the stiffness in his bones was evident.

"Tell me, Honorable One, has life brought you the good health and abundance you so richly deserve?"

Dedi's eyes had a faraway look as if he had not heard Sokar's question. After a few moments of silence, the old man spoke in a raspy, weak voice. "Time has become my worst enemy, I suppose. It has taken to passing mighty fast. I fear it will soon leave me behind."

"It is said that time waits for no one, Master. But if it ever does, you are sure to warrant the exception. Time claims no man of your power until there is no more work to be done."

Dedi looked at Sokar as if he were looking into his soul. "What about you, Son of Sneferu, half-brother to Khufu, son of Horus. What brings you to Hermopolis?"

Sokar was certain Dedi's inquiry was meant to cut to the core of their encounter. He would not, could not, lie to the old one. "I came for the blessing of the obelisk, of course. I also came to see you, Master Dedi. There is a matter I wish to take up with you. Perhaps we can meet when the ritual is over. For now, your host is waiting and is anxious to have you get into your litter for the procession. Will you meet with me later?"

Chapter Forty-Four

Hail to Thoth

Sokar was pleased with his initial meeting with Dedi. His former teacher and mentor had seemed happy to see him, and the feeling was mutual. It had been a long time since their paths had crossed. Yet Sokar knew the Elder's power had not waned; if anything, his advanced years made him even more powerful.

As of yet, there had been no sign of Meri-ib. Knowing ritual protocol, Sokar guessed that the former High Priest of Heliopolis was part of a small group of chief priests who were congregated in an anteroom off the main sanctuary. The room was reserved for the priestly elite, and here servants performed an elaborate cleansing rite prior to all major religious events at the Temple of Thoth. He would see Meri-ib when the elite came out of seclusion to lead the procession of the statue of Thoth. Sokar had never seen the statue of Thoth in the inner sanctum of the Temple of Zehuti in Hermopolis, but he had heard about it many times. It was said to be the most magnificent image of the god in all of Egypt. Its daily washing ceremony would be especially important today.

Sokar mingled with the priests, all awaiting the arrival of the High Priest and his entourage, which would include Dedi and Meri-ib. Sokar chatted with a lector priest from the Delta whom he had met while visiting his family vineyards in that area. Then the leaders of the procession appeared in the doorway that led from the inner sanctuary into the courtyard.

The first of the religious elite Sokar sighted was Petosiris, who, when he saw Sokar, walked over to him. The High Priest's expression revealed he was reluctant about something he was about to say. "I extend to you an additional invitation to process with the other First Prophets from all over the country, including myself." Then, with a touch of arrogance in his voice, "After all, you are a member of the royal family."

Sokar knew the man did not like him or feel he had to go out of his way for the bastard of a dead Pharaoh. There had to be a reason, therefore, to account for the forced courtesy. Dedi. Of course, it had to be Dedi who had issued the request. Sokar decided not to injure Petosiris's pride by letting on that he knew how and why he was being asked to take a bigger role in the procession. There was nothing to be gained by alienating anyone at this point. Sokar bowed to Petosiris. "I am pleased to be a part of this momentous occasion to honor Thoth, the great god of wisdom."

The two men joined the elite group. Sokar took a place just behind Dedi's litter. It was then that he saw Meri-ib, who seemed filled with energy in anticipation of the ritual. Sokar and Meri-ib acknowledged each other with a quick nod.

As the activities began, several Hathor priestesses preceded the entourage of priests bearing the statue. Sistrums jingled, and some people sang to celebrate Thoth. Behind the musicians came the priests, then the barque of Thoth. The solid gold statue glittered. The barque's fore and aft were adorned with bronze ibis heads; garlands of flowers draped its four sides. The statue itself was that of an ibis-headed man two feet tall.

The litter-bearers and the procession of priests and priestesses left the temple complex through the cedar gates, stopping at the base of the obelisk. The crowds, gathered to witness the dedication and see the statue, were being held back a hundred feet from the monument. The litter-bearers put their burden on the ground. Once the dedication ritual was over, the image would be carried on a rare journey through the streets of Hermopolis.

Petosiris came forward first to offer a prayer of praise to Thoth:

> Hail to Thoth,
> Your divine name
> never loses greatness
> Honor to You, O Thoth,
> Beautiful is your radiant light.

Petosiris approached the statue and gave an offering of wine. The High Priest then went over to Dedi, the guest of honor, and led the elder magician to the side of the obelisk to a low platform. Petosiris motioned for four priests representing the northern and southern parts of the country to escort Dedi onto the canopied dais which had been decorated with potted palms and huge bowls of fragrant flowers. Silence fell over the crowd and the religious dignitaries. The elder's presence commanded a respect afforded to few except for the Pharaoh. Dedi was known throughout the land, revered by most, and feared by those who had once underestimated his power.

Stooped, Dedi slowly lifted his arms heavenward. A current of energy shot from his trembling hands and linked him with the gods. In a low, raspy voice, he began the blessing of the Tower of Stone:

> O Great God Thoth,
> I am come to this place where you reside.
> I am a magician who speaks truth.
> You have let me see you many times
> when I travel in my Body of Light.
> Let your light come into this holy monument
> that stands in honor of you
> in thanks for your many gifts to humankind.
> May the great obelisk rise up to meet the heavens.
> May it be wherein your holy spirit resides.

Dedi lowered his arms, reached into a leopard skin pouch at his waist, and took out a tiny vial containing a powder. In a flash of movement that surprised everyone, the elder cast the powder toward the obelisk. An incredible amount of what appeared to be gold dust came from the pouch; enough to momentarily enshroud the monument. A gasp rose from the crowd, including from the priests and priestesses. As quickly as the strange powder had been thrown into the breeze, it was gone, leaving a residue of power.

The four escorts and Petosiris walked down the steps of the platform with Dedi, supporting him. The dignitaries would return to the temple while the rest of the priests and priestesses would accompany the statue through Hermopolis. It was time for Sokar to make his move to speak to Dedi. Just as he started to approach the elder, Meri-ib stepped into Sokar's path.

"Sokar, I am surprised to see you. But pleased, of course. I did not know you were a servant of Thoth."

"Meri-ib, Adorer of the Sacred Ones, Osiris, Isis, and Horus. It is a pleasure to see that you are well and have taken time away from your duties as First Prophet of the Temple of the good god Ra."

Sokar's pleasant response to Meri-ib caught him off guard. He was now in the position of having to admit his resignation, which would open the door for a discussion that he would prefer not to get into with this sly magician-priest whom he did not trust. He had always been leery of Sokar's hunger for power and sensed it every time he had been in his presence. "I see you have not heard."

"Heard what, Your Holiness?"

"I have resigned the office of High Priest of Heliopolis."

Sokar feigned surprise. He was more likely to get the information he sought by pretending the news was unknown to him. "Resigned? Did you say 'resigned'? Was this a sudden decision?"

"I suppose, but it was the right decision," Meri-ib replied with confidence, hoping that his tone would shift the direction of the conversation.

"Surely you are still in the priesthood?"

"Yes, of course. My work has led me elsewhere for now." Meri-ib hoped that his deliberately not offering any details would discourage Sokar, but his hopes were dashed.

"And where would that be, where has your work taken you?"

"Memphis." This time, Meri-ib's reply contained enough of a tone of restraint that Sokar knew he would say nothing more on the matter, so he changed the subject.

"These are auspicious times in our beloved Egypt. I am sure you have your hands full no matter where you are."

Meri-ib gave an affirmative nod and bade Sokar good day. It was clear he intended to keep his work secret. Sokar now knew the former High Priest was an advisor to Khufu, but what advice was he being asked to give?

As Meri-ib walked toward a group of priests nearby, Sokar saw that it was time for Dedi to return to his guest quarters in the temple to refresh himself before the afternoon meal. Sokar approached the elder and requested a private audience. Dedi agreed to forgo his rest to listen.

Sokar's mysterious air and his claim on Dedi's time did not go unnoticed by Petosiris. Like Meri-ib, Petosiris had long distrusted the bastard prince who he felt would go to extremes to get what he wanted, and he knew that was power.

Sokar guided Dedi into a small reception room adjacent to the main courtyard. The atmosphere was pleasant, and servants assigned to the elder brought the two cool beers and sweet cakes. Dedi dismissed them so he and his guest could have privacy.

"Tell me, Sokar. What is so pressing?"

"My future," Sokar replied without hesitation.

"I see," the old man replied. "And what is it about your future that troubles you?"

"Does it seem that I am troubled?"

"It seems as if you have the same thing on your mind that you have always had since I have known you. You are feeling cheated again, yes?"

Sokar was not surprised at the old magician's insightfulness, but that did not make it less disconcerting. "You know my heart too well, Master

Dedi." Sokar replied as he gazed out a window into the garden. After a few moments, he turned to face the elder, and began to pour out his feelings. His tone had a trace of the bitterness that had become his constant companion.

"Cheated, yes, that is the right word." Sokar paced as he spoke. "Cheated from my rightful heritage. But that is not what I wish to speak to you about, my old friend." Then, locking eyes with Dedi, he revealed his plan to create an alternate government, his government. It would be more than a jealous challenge to Khufu's authority; it would give the people the opportunity to be led by the rightful heir to the Throne. It would provide the people with a choice as to whom they chose to swear allegiance. Not every Egyptian was loyal to Khufu or approved of the way he ran the country. There was need for a greater and stronger army to protect the land from the constant threat of invaders. There was the matter of foreign trade, the expansion of Egypt's role into lands beyond her borders.

To most, Khufu was a good king though it often seemed to many that his loyalties were divided, that he was confused about whether he should give attention to the country and the people or to his religious life. Sokar explained how he suffered from no such confusion. "If you will give me and my plan your blessing and work a spell for my success, I will be forever grateful to you. I will see to your well-being for the rest of your earthly life."

Dedi listened. The elder sat quietly for a long while. Sokar had taken a risk by revealing his plan, but it was worth taking if he could enlist Dedi's support.

"I see. It sounds as if you have thought it through. It is all very convincing, I must say. To go up against Pharaoh is a monumental undertaking, no matter what your reasons or whether those reasons are justified. As a solitary practitioner of the magical arts, I devised my own code of ethics a long time ago. Mind you, they are not the rules of the priesthood or any religious or political faction. They are mine. I answer to myself. I know only my motives. I answer only to the gods. I will not help you, Sokar, but neither will I stop you or betray your confidence. I will not help you nor hinder you. But I will give you a word of advice."

"And what is that, Master Dedi?"

"Stirring up passions guarantees you will attract energies equally passionate. If your passions are uncontrolled, so will be the energies you attract."

Sokar recognized the wisdom of Dedi's words. Control was always the key to successful magical practice. Still, he wasn't sure about Dedi's neutral position. He had expected a simple yes or no. There was no other human he would take at his word. So when Dedi said that he would not help or hinder Sokar's aspirations, he accepted it. Sokar would not have to worry about coming up against Dedi's magical powers.

There was nothing more to be said. Sokar bowed in respect to his teacher. "May your days be long and the gods favor you. I am certain our paths will cross again."

Chapter Forty-Five

Danger for the King

When Ani and her scribe Sheshat came into the classroom, the apprentices had already seated themselves in anticipation of the day's lesson. Bast lay near Khem's feet, her ears perked. The cat missed nothing.

"As long as there have been people on Earth and temples in Egypt, priests have watched the sky from temple rooftops across the land," Ani began. "Long ago, from these observations, the priests succeeded in establishing a yearly calendar, the very one our calendar is based upon. As you know, the year begins with the predawn rising of the great star Sirius, the Star of Isis; it is also the first day of Inundation.

"The year consists of 360 days, plus five extra days for the 'birthdays' of Osiris, Horus, and Seth, Isis, and Nepthys. It is no accident that the predawn rising of Sirius and Inundation are this year simultaneous events. They mark an important time in the life of Egypt. Once in many generations, Isis gives the world the rising of the Great Star *and* Mother Nile.

"Events are related to one another. It is within this relationship that time exists. Think about it. Without events there would be no time, no need for time. So time enables us to distinguish events from each other and it brings about the *order* of occurrences, allowing events to be objective or external. Everything that happens has its own place in 'objective' time. This makes time a *constant* that flows from the receding past to a future that is forever coming.

"The continual motion of what I will call 'apparent time' makes time into Time, a living, changing, evolving entity. One could say, and the old texts do, that the morning Sun is like the birth and adolescent years of a child, noon the time of adulthood, the setting Sun the time of old age and death, when the Sun enters the Underworld. One cannot be born without experiencing many crucial changes along the path of life, as the Sun does. The hours of day and the changes the Sun goes through allow us to form a relationship with the being embodied as the Sun who undergoes these changes in time.

"Now, if what I have said is plausible, then the same is true regarding the transformations the Sun goes through during its journey through the Underworld at night. This journey can be likened to what you will experience when you go into the invisible realms where most of your spiritual work will be done. This dimension lies beyond the manifested world. Now let me tell you a story to make this more clear.

"Ra, the sun-god, sailed on his barque into the Duat, the treacherous world of darkness. Once there, he immediately encountered the demonic serpent, Apophis, the most evil of those who dwell in the darkness. Ra saw that the darkness was divided into twelve provinces, each populated by terrifying demons, snakes, and horrible monsters who threatened him. Knowing Apophis would harm him, Ra and his crew fought and defeated the great serpent. But defeating the monster only once was not enough. Ra had to confront him and the other terrible ones *every time* he went into the Underworld. He had to face and conquer these threats to the progress and safety of his journey daily, and he had to win, each time.

"In a similar way, each of you will experience challenges in your work that will take you into the Dark Realm where evil lurks, into the unknown world that is home to demonic forces and entities which you must face and defeat. You must do this in your magical work here on Earth, and you must deal with it on your journeys into the kingdom of stars."

Later in her quarters, Ani said to Khem and Tiye, "I have reason to believe that the king is in danger. Not his physical safety, but his claim to the Throne." Ani paced. She focused her eyes on an open window with a view of the desert. "I had a visitation here in my study last night. I stayed up to look for passages in an old text. I wanted to mark them for Sheshat to copy. In the dim light of the room a large hawk appeared. It was much too big to be a physical bird. It was a spirit bird. An energy came from it. I felt leery of who or what the bird was and why it was there."

"What did you make of it?" Khem asked nervously.

"The hawk disappeared as quickly as it had come. It just dissolved and was gone, but its lingering aura told me that I was being spied upon by a magician."

Tiye spoke up. "Khaba told me many stories about spirit animals—jackals, birds, a wolf, even a serpent. None were animals or birds or reptiles at all. They were bodies created by a human to provide physical forms for animal souls."

"Yes, that's right," Ani replied. "There was no bird here. The adept who did this only wished to make me *believe* I saw a hawk. That is a powerful person to reckon with. So this is a good time to teach you about such things.

"A priestess must be able to discern the real from the unreal. This is determined by your degree of awareness of what is inside you versus what is outside. Reality is inseparable from the consciousness that experiences it. I believe the hawk was sent to observe me, to assess my energy and power. No one would do such a thing unless the target was of importance. Someone is interested in what I am about. Someone wants to know if I am a threat, if I feel secure. I cannot deny my feeling that there is a plot going on. So be watchful, Khem, Tiye."

Khufu stood on the patio outside his lounge. Night had fallen, bringing a cool breeze with the fragrance of jasmine. One by one, the stars were being born from the darkness.

Khufu looked at the slowly streaking comet and felt that whatever power he was wrestling inside him was also in the comet—it was the comet's spirit. "That's it," Khufu said. "I am brought face to face with my spirit, my god self, my immortal being." The time had come when he had to recognize that he was a god-man. "I am the god incarnate. All of Egypt's kings before me have been. I share a common soul with them all. They are me. I am them." For the first time, Khufu was confronting not *who* he was, but *what*, coming to know it with every fiber of his being.

After all, the sacred orders always proclaimed Pharaoh's semi-divine nature. They styled all kings as "son of god" or "beloved of the gods." He thought of the priestly words he had read before he was elevated to the Throne: "Ra has placed the king as the head of the living, forever and ever, to judge mankind and satisfy the gods, to do good and destroy evil."

The night breeze caressed and soothed Khufu's body and evening fragrances tantalized his senses. The sky was so clear the stars sparkled like jewels and the comet cut a swath through the sky. Khufu had been so involved with affairs of state and his life and destiny, he had not taken time to be with the stars. Yet for as long as he could remember he had felt close to them. These celestial bodies were not simply far-off, lifeless objects. They were manifestations of divine beings involved with the world. All of us, he thought, live in a universe of living gods. The gods are out there, Khufu mused. Then, placing his hand on his chest, he said, "And the gods are in here. They are me. I am them. . . ."

Footsteps approached. Khufu turned to see his wife, Meritates. She was dressed in a loose-weave linen sheath that hung from an embroidered band that fit under her full breasts. As always, her shapely body caused Khufu's maleness to burn. A silver, jeweled pectoral graced her slender neck and lay around her upper chest. Her upper arms had silver armbands; her long dark hair hung down her back. The sight of her reminded him of how little time he had spent with her or his children of late. Seeing her glowing in the moonlight captured his attention.

Putting her arm around Khufu's waist, her eyes glancing upwards to the starlit sky, Meritates spoke softly. "It is a beautiful night."

"Yes, my love," Khufu responded. "The sky is filled with wonder, and this is the greatest wonder of all. It is quite a spectacle, is it not, more splendid than anything of this world. Even the crown jewels fade in comparison."

They sat down on a stone bench. "Are you out here only to marvel at the beauty of the stars or is something more on your mind, my husband?"

"Both. For certain there is much on my mind, but nothing that should concern you, my love." The king rarely discussed his kingly duties with Meritates. He did not wish to trouble her with such things. He did not realize that this reticence made Meritates feel left out of her husband's life.

"What concerns you and Egypt concerns me, my love. It is more troubling to me to be kept in the silence about what weighs on your heart, no matter what or who it concerns."

Looking into Meritates's eyes, Khufu saw the pain of being so close yet so far from him. He saw her love for him. The king cupped his wife's face in his hands as she returned his gaze. "I know that being the royal wife is not easy, that you must spend many hours apart from me. These are unprecedented times for Egypt, and I must keep an unceasing vigil as the Wearer of the Double Crown."

Meritates clasped her hands around Khufu's wrists. "And for you, Khufu, what kind of times are these for you? How heavy is the crown on your head? On your heart?"

She knew him well. Khufu could not hide his feelings from her, nor brush aside her concerns, her right to know. Loosing himself from her gentle grip, the king stood up and lifted his eyes to the sky. Meritates was unaware of his dreams, his visit to the chamber beneath the Sphinx, his Sirius Council, the prophecy of his living ascension. She did not know how these things affected him. He realized how selfish it was to keep it all from her. She should know, and now was the time to tell her. "I have advisors to help me make state decisions, as you know, my love. I have seen no need to trouble you with such things."

Khufu walked over to a papyrus growing in the mud pool, broke off a browning piece, and began twirling it around in his fingers. "Under normal circumstances, advisors would be sufficient to advise me and to also fill the emotional needs that come with being king." Turning to face Meritates again, Khufu dropped his gaze to the ground. "Not this time. I need you, Meritates, in a way I have never needed you before."

He was finally opening up to her, she reflected, and for that she was grateful. Still, apprehension about what she might hear filled her as over the next hour Khufu began to tell her. . . .

In Heliopolis, Khem was lying in bed watching the shadows cast by the tiny lamp dance on the ceiling. She had not been able to fall asleep.

Thoughts of the future, hers and Egypt's, spun fragmented visions in her head, each leaving her feeling something of import was trying to come through to her. Her visions consisted of a procession of priests and priestesses, dressed in the regalia of their offices, followed by the royal litter bearing the king and royal wife, the royal fan bearers, and members of the court. Khem also glimpsed a huge, elaborate temple whose walls and brightly painted columns gleamed in the sunlight. There had been a magnificent man wearing a striped head cloth pulled tightly across his forehead and tied in a tail at the back. Two long strands of the striped cloth hung down on either side, the brow decorated with a uraeus and a vulture. She knew only the Pharaoh could wear such a head cloth, although her intuition told her that the man was not Khufu.

The strain of trying to decipher the images finally tired Khem and she drifted off to sleep. Soon afterwards, she found herself out of her body in her dream vessel. She was floating above the Lion Man of the Desert, now fully uncovered from the sand, its paws stretched out in front of its colossal body. A hundred yards from its paws stood a beautiful temple, the same temple she had seen in her waking vision. Her dream vessel hung in suspension above the pylons, gateways, and halls.

Beyond the outer pylon was a large open courtyard, beyond which were further pylons, each of which had great cedar doors hung at their entrances. Past the series of pylons and courtyards were pillared hallways, vestibules, and sanctuaries, each protected by heavy wooden doors inlaid with bronze. Khem knew that the interior of the temple was a world in which no ordinary mortal belonged. It was a sanctuary for a god or goddess, into which only one's divine self would dare to venture. Leading into the innermost sanctuary was a threshold that no one other than the High Priest and the king could cross. Only they could face the deity within the walls of the Holy of Holies.

Just as Khem's dream vessel began floating down to the temple, the structure faded into another dimension into which her dream vessel could not go. The temple image was then replaced by the sound of a woman's voice with an otherworldly resonance that seemed to come from every direction at once. "I am the One who dwells within the Nile Star. I am the one called Goddess by women. I who separated the Earth from Heaven. I who showed the stars their paths. I who regulate the course of the Sun and Moon. . . ."

As Nemon made his report to the king and the court the following morning, he spoke in the customary formal greeting. "Your Majesty, Wearer of the Double Crown, King of Egypt. You are like Ra in all that you do, everything happens according to the wish of your heart. We have all seen your wondrous deeds since you have been crowned King of the Two Lands. Your tongue speaks only truth. The thoughts of your heart are carried out. The Lion Man of the Desert is free from its prison of sand, Your Majesty. Your wish has been fulfilled. The people of Egypt can look upon the body of the Sphinx for the first time in the days of all living generations. I, Nemon, Chief Architect and Builder, declare the Sphinx project done."

Pharaoh was pleased. The project had unearthed a significant part of Egypt's history. Construction of the temple he had been instructed to build could now begin. Inundation was imminent. The land would be nourished, the people would prosper, and a good harvest would assure all would be fed.

Nemon's proclamation finished, he honored Khufu by kneeling on one knee, his head bowed. Khufu motioned for the man to rise and he congratulated him on a job well done. "For your efforts on my behalf as King of Egypt and your efforts on my personal behalf, and on behalf of the Egyptian people, I, Khufu, Son of Ptah, bestow upon you a villa on the bank of the Nile in the town of Silsilis near Ombos, long a possession of the royal family. You shall be provided with the best food so that your pantry will never be empty. You will have a staff of servants, housekeepers, and your own priest. You shall, from now on for the rest of your earthly life, have exclusive use of the villa. It is a gift of gratitude from the Throne and from the Son of Ptah."

Nemon was stunned. "I am humbled by your generosity, Your Majesty. I do not know what to say except long live the king and the kingdom."

Khufu made his way to his quarters to join Nemon and other invited guests. This would be more than a social luncheon. It would be the first step towards the construction of the Temple of the Sphinx.

A dozen servants rushed to see to his comfort. Everyone was seated around a wooden table whose surface was carved with winged solar discs. Cool beer and the finest palm and date wines had been poured and fan bearers stirred the air. Nemon was seated with Taret and Meri-ib, both of whom he had met on the occasion of a visit to the Temple of the Sun. An old man Nemon had never met was led into the dining hall and seated near Khufu. It was Shemshu-Hor. Although Nemon had never been in the presence of the legendary leader of the Followers of Horus, he knew who he was.

"Well, I see you are all here . . . and comfortable, I assume," Khufu said.

"Yes, Your Majesty," the guests answered in unison. Though Shemshu-Hor did not speak, his mere presence communicated as effectively in silence as an ordinary person could in speech.

"I have called you all together for something that cannot be delayed. It is time to lay out the orientation of the Temple of the Sphinx and to have the stones brought to Memphis from the quarry in Silsilis. That town is the easiest from which to import stone to the capital. The hard sandstone in quarries near Silsilis is prized for its quality. It is of this stone the temple will be built.

"Master Meri-ib, it will be your job to perform the Stretching of the Cord ritual. Lady Taret, I ask you to gather a few—perhaps six, you make the seventh—priestesses from whatever temples in the country you most admire and respect for knowledge and power. These should be chosen by the time the Moon is full again. Summon these women to Memphis to the Temple of Hathor, where you will be housed. Also, Lady Taret, I request that you perform a special rite to invoke the spirit of the Great Star of Isis in her guise as the able Protector of the Crown, as Sekhmet."

It was not uncommon for priestesses to perform rituals, particularly those to celebrate and invoke goddesses, Taret reflected. It was a task she was honored to do, one she welcomed. It would provide her and six other priestesses the opportunity to serve a role in the Second Coming of the Star Gods, and a greater role than she would have dreamed. It would reinforce the important role of the priestesses in Egypt. "Yes, Your Majesty. I understand completely and am grateful to serve the Neters and Pharaoh in this way."

Khufu was satisfied with the preparations for what would become the most beautiful and sacred temple in the land. It would be a structure that did justice to the great power it would honor, and be forever a place where members of the priesthood could connect themselves with the gods once a year at the heliacal rising of Sirius. Khufu's plan was challenging, and when completed, like the Second Coming, it would likely change Egypt forever.

Khem could not forget the voice she heard in her sleep. It was the voice of the Star Woman, the spirit of Sirius. The sound took her into a dimension beyond the physical. These other dimensions were becoming as real to Khem as the physical had ever been. The spirits she encountered were strange yet familiar, their messages revealing and reassuring. Khem was becoming aware of how visions happen in sleep and other altered states, even in daytime thinking. . . .

Khem and Tiye were at Klea's for their lesson. Khem noticed Klea's worktable was loaded with objects. Some she had already coated with bright blue glaze, making them look like lapis lazuli; others had been glazed in green and looked like malachite. Klea was hand-modeling green clay into rings of various sizes. "Oh, I didn't hear you come in," Klea said.

She had been so engrossed in what she was doing, it wasn't until Bast went up to her and bumped her furry head against the woman's thigh that she knew she had guests. The lioness liked Klea. She was always good for some dried meat.

"We did not mean to startle you," Khem said apologetically.

"You didn't. Come, sit down, both of you, please. I am making amulet rings. Here, Tiye. Let me show you."

Klea led the Nubian to a small shelf on which several rings had been glazed, fired, and etched with symbols, most of which Tiye did not understand. "I like to make amulet rings. They are easy to keep on the person all the time and stylish too, don't you think?" Klea slipped a ring on her right index finger and held it up to admire. "It may not sparkle like a fine jewel, but it will do things for the wearer no jewel can do."

While Klea and Tiye talked about and admired the rings, Khem sat quietly, thinking about the words she had heard in her sleep: "I am the One who dwells within the Nile Star."

"I am making this one for a newborn child. It is for protection. Here, take it and energize it," Klea said, handing the ring to Tiye. "The mother will wear it during the day, and tie it in a loose necklace on the baby while he sleeps."

Tiye cupped the amulet. She then felt an urge to hold it up to her mouth so her breath would be upon it. Doing so, she closed her eyes and spoke: "Great Mother Isis, you who see and hear all. Protect the mother and child who wear this ring, keep them safe. May their day and night paths be guarded by you, Holy Mother. May they be safe in your care."

Next, Tiye took the amulet away from her mouth and opened her eyes. The room and everything in it seemed blurry for a moment, her head spinning. Taking a deep breath to steady herself, she handed the ring back to Klea.

"It feels very warm to the touch. You have charged it well, Tiye, very well. Here, take this." Klea picked up a blue piece that had not yet been glazed and fired. "Why not make an amulet for Bast? Animals need protection too, you know. To do this invoke the spirit of the goddess Sekhmet."

Lying on the cool floor, Bast lifted her head at the mention of her name.

"You can sit here. I will continue with the rings."

Klea did not wait for Tiye to answer. She could only give the assignment and the reasons for it. Tiye had to do the work, and learn from the experience. The only advice Klea passed on was that Tiye must invoke Sekhmet's energy and blend her own consciousness with it for the goddess's power to flow through her into the amulet.

Khem took it all in. She learned best from observing and listening. Lately, she had noticed that things she heard, a sentence or a single word, often triggered images she had come to think of as "waking dreams." They were becoming more frequent.

"Have you had any dreams or visions?" Klea asked.

"Yes."

"Will you tell me about it?"

"It was a dream, or maybe it was a vision, I am not sure. It was only a voice."

"A voice?"

"Yes. I heard it after a dream, I think. It was a woman's voice. She said she was the One in the Nile Star."

"Do you know what it means?"

"No. Not yet anyway. But I will, I'm sure of it."

Sekhmet's realm was not familiar to Tiye. She had heard about the warrioress many times, but had never experienced a contact with her. "She Who Is Powerful"—the goddess's name said it all. Being a daughter of the Sun God, Sekhmet had an aggressive aspect. She was the most contentious of the gods. Tiye had never been aggressive, at least not openly. But she knew there was a power coiled like a serpent inside her that she had controlled for fear of what it would do if she let it go. It was like an angry spirit. She had felt it when she was very young: a bully had constantly harassed small children, even harmed a few. She had wanted to strike out and destroy him. She had felt that again when Khaba died, had wanted to lash out at something, anything. Every time she had felt that power within her, she restrained herself and forced her feelings to a place deep inside. Now, maybe. . . .

Tiye was working with the amulet, molding pieces of the faience into a small lioness head. "I am trying to copy the way Bast looks," she said. Again the cat's ears perked up.

Klea picked up a piece that was especially well done. "It is valuable to know about the deity you are working with, but you know that. Let me tell you about my own experience with Sekhmet. When I was a girl I had a best friend. Her name was Selket. She was named after the scorpion goddess. A scorpion bit her mother just before Selket was born and many prayers were made for her survival. It was promised that if the mother survived she would name her baby, if it was a girl, after Selket.

"My friend was small and very frail when she was young. There was an older boy in the village who was attracted to her, but Selket shunned his attention. The rejection angered him and he was constantly stalking her and picking on her. One day he went too far. My friend was walking along the riverbank, when the older boy tried in vain to win her favor by offering her a cowry shell necklace. Selket would not accept it and that made him very angry. When Selket walked away, he picked up a stone and threw it at her. It hit her on her head and she died.

"I was so angered by what happened I wanted to kill the boy. I felt a surge of hot anger surge up inside me. For nights afterward I dreamed of a lioness. It would come into the village to the boy's home and attack him and kill him like he had killed Selket. You see, I dreamed of Sekhmet. She is a warrioress and avenger. My experience made me want to know more about her because I knew she was in me, was part of me. I knew I had to learn about her and be in harmony with her or she would destroy me, that something would happen again, like Selket's death, that would cause me to unleash her fury. I did not want to do that but I did want to know how to deal with her power inside me.

"So, Tiye, you too must learn that balance with the Sekhmet within you."

Chapter Forty-Six

Sekhmet, Lioness of the Desert

Khem and Tiye were returning to their apartment when they decided to sit for a while under the shade of a large persea tree in the main courtyard. Tiye had been deep in thought since leaving Klea. The experience the teacher had shared revealed something to Tiye about herself, something she did not want to admit.

Khem asked, "Were you and Klea talking about Sekhmet? I don't mean to be nosy, but . . ."

"Yes, yes we were. She told me a story about the death of her best friend when she was a young girl. She told me how angry she felt and how it helped her find Sekhmet inside her."

Khem thought about this. She remembered the image of the lioness-woman seen in her water bowl when she first came to the temple. It had frightened her because it was so unexpected. She remembered the goddess's power. She looked at Bast, recalling how she had found the half-starved cub. She thought about the project to unearth the Lion Man of the Desert. It seemed as if lions had become a prime symbol in her life now, maybe in the lives of everyone around her.

Tiye considered the lessons she could learn from the lioness-headed goddess. She could and would learn how to transform the anger within her into a positive force.

"I hadn't thought about the rage in me," Khem confessed.

"Well, I have," Tiye responded curtly. "You have lived a life very different from mine. You were sheltered and had no reasons, perhaps, for rage to well up. But you can be sure it is there. It is in all of us."

"But it sounds so negative."

"It isn't. Not really, unless it gets out of control. It is power. That is what her name means. Sekhmet, the Powerful One."

Tiye was taking her work with Sekhmet very seriously. She vowed to learn all she could about the positive and negative sides of the goddess, so that the amulets made in her likeness and that contained her power would be worthy of her approval. This was Sekhmet's time of year, just before the Nile would rise in harmony with the predawn rising of Sirius, the star that had been absent from the night sky for seventy days.

Although prayed for and welcomed by all Egyptians, the New Year was not the easiest of times. It was feared because of the diseases, pollution, and fevers brought by the heat and flood waters. All of this was laid at Sekhmet's feet because it was her merciless demons who plagued the people. Yet Sekhmet was celebrated. Once the perils of her wrath were past, she could be seen for what she was: the source of rebirth, renewal, and prosperity as the Nile waters saturated the parched land.

Tiye's thoughts were so immersed in Sekhmet she could think of nothing else. She liked being near Bast, for the lioness made her feel close to Sekhmet. "I will take Bast for a walk through the marketplace. Do you mind? I wish to purchase some oils to anoint the amulets when they are finished."

A Nubian walking through the marketplace with a lioness on a leash turned heads. Since Tiye did not dress like the other apprentices, her physical self reflected her heritage. To wear two gold armbands and a band on her right ankle was typical Nubian attire, as was her woolly hair, long wrapped skirt, and the gold earring she wore in the lobe of her left ear.

Tiye was proud to be from Nubia, the land Khaba called Kush. The old woman had been taught by Kunum, one of the most feared, yet respected sorcerers in Nubia, a man whose primary ability was healing. With her natural talent, Khaba turned his knowledge into magical skill and passed that on to Tiye. As far as Khaba was concerned, no skill could be achieved without magic. This had become Tiye's belief though the magic Khaba had taught her was different from what she was learning in her Star Priestess training. Her Nubian heritage was more primitive perhaps, Egyptian magic more sophisticated.

Tiye spotted a merchant stall with brightly colored awnings, and went to look at the vendor's variety of fine oils. The vendor was nervous at the sight of Bast.

"She will not hurt you. She is very tame. She likes people," Tiye reassured the man.

"Good, yes," the merchant replied suspiciously. He did not intend to take Tiye at her word, at least not completely. It wasn't every day that a woman leading a lioness walked through the market.

Her shopping finished, Tiye walked Bast to the bank of the Nile. There was always a nice breeze close to the water and shade trees to sit under. A marshy area close to the river's edge was teeming with life. Long-legged herons stalked tiny fish and insects, starlings and hawks flew overhead. Tiye loved the river. When she was a girl Khaba would walk her to the river so she could play in the shallows and build mud houses. In those innocent days Tiye could not see her future; her world was secure, and she was with her beloved Khaba.

The ground felt damp where Tiye sat down under a sycamore, its branches swept out over the river. The tree was full of birds which captured Bast's attention. She tried to keep her eyes on all of them at once, her ears perked and moving in every direction in response to every movement and sound. Tiye rubbed the lioness's head gently. Before long, the birds and bugs lost their intrigue and Bast fell asleep, her head propped against Tiye's knees. Looking down at the sleeping animal, Tiye thought how beautiful she was. Leaning against the tree, the Nubian let her thoughts drift until she dozed off.

Before long, Tiye's dream vessel freed itself from her body and went back to a time in her past. She saw herself sitting under the shade of a sycamore, Khaba next to her. Sounds filled her senses. Khaba was telling her a scary tale that captured her imagination.

"A long way from here in the north, humans hatched an evil plot to overthrow the gods. It was a wicked thing to do. They would use the same powers the gods had given humanity so they might grow great and strong and be prosperous on Earth. When the sun god Ra heard what the evil humans intended to do, he called the most powerful of the gods together for a council. It was decided that the goddess Sekhmet would come to Earth and stop the rebellion. No one and no force could stand against Sekhmet. She would seek out and conquer all the humans. So she walked among humanity and destroyed them, and then she drank their blood."

This part of the story had upset Tiye when she first heard it from Khaba, and it frightened her to hear it now in her dream.

"The killing of humans went on night after night. It was so bad there was blood everywhere in pools on the ground. Sekhmet became drunk on drinking human blood. Finally, the other gods could stand the slaughter no longer, though they could not think of any way to make Sekhmet stop. They were afraid she would not stop until there were no humans left."

Tiye heard herself ask "What happened then, Khaba?"

"Well, the gods knew of a special plant that grew on Elephantine

Island. It contained a powerful plant spirit that could alter one's mind. The plant was mixed with other herbs and sent to the god Sekti in Heliopolis. Sekti added human blood and put it in some beer until there were seven thousand jugs of it. The contents were poured on the ground at places where Sekhmet would pass. Seeing the mixture of plants and blood, the goddess drank it all. She was very happy. Her heart was filled with joy. Sekhmet changed her mind. She was satisfied. She would destroy no more humans."

The story finished, Tiye's dream vessel floated gently back into her where she leaned drowsily against the sycamore on the bank of the Nile. When Tiye opened her eyes, Bast was still napping beside her. Looking at the lioness's face brought back pieces of her dream. She had not thought of Khaba and her stories of the gods in a long time. Tiye recalled how Khaba had told her about an order of priestesses dedicated to Sekhmet. Their duty was to lead the annual celebration in her honor.

The Sekhmet priestesses would prepare a beverage containing the drug and herbs the sun god had given Sekhmet to stop her slaughter of humans. The women celebrated in an orgiastic festival. Khaba once went to Denderah to attend the most famous of these festivals. She had told Tiye about it, people dancing and shaking sistrums in celebration of Sekhmet as the Beautiful One, the Peaceful One. Remembering Khaba's tale made Sekhmet seem even more important to Tiye. Or perhaps it was Klea telling her the anger that had welled up inside her identified Sekhmet in her.

Tiye looked again at the sleeping lioness. How strong Bast is, she could kill in an instant. Yet, she possessed the qualities of the goddess Bast—a passive, devoted friend. Tiye felt the lioness was like the goddess. Tiye knew the animal had emotions, that she felt love, hate, anger, fear, and even grief, the same as any human, but usually acted on instinct.

Tiye realized she acted from instinct too. She felt more comfortable with her instincts than her intellect. She was smart and had learned a great deal since coming to the Temple of the Sun, but she knew she was instinctual, passionate, and that this was the source of her power, it made her who she was. At that moment Tiye made a decision that would affect the rest of her life: She would become a priestess of Sekhmet.

The comet testified nightly to the significance of the times. The New Year was drawing close. It was time to meet with Meri-ib. The High Priest had been instructed to conduct a Stretching of the Cord ceremony for Khufu's Sphinx temple. The comet had reached its peak of brightness and Khufu could feel the energy and excitement of the imminent events building.

When it was time to lay out the temple's orientation, the king, Meri-ib, and a representative of the Mistress of Divine Books would drive a stake into the ground. Orientation would be determined by the circumpolar stars at a specific date of the year. For the Sphinx temple the date would be the time of the predawn rising of the star Sirius. Khufu would then plow a furrow with a hoe four times and scatter the contents of a bushel basket containing various kinds of seeds to represent fertility and growth; then he would marry earth and water to shape the first brick. Four such bricks would be made, one for each of the four corners of the temple; then, carrying incense, Khufu would circle the temple site four times before giving it away to its Master, Osiris, who dwells in Sirius.

Pharaoh issued a decree to set the wheels in motion for an expedition to the quarry in Silsilis to be led by Nemon and Men-ka-re. Stonecutters, a chief artisan, quarrymen, draftsmen, and several thousand laborers would comprise the work force. Khufu instructed Nemon and his foreman to draw the bulk of the needed recruits from the laborers who had worked on the Sphinx project. Others would be drafted from work forces from various parts of the country. It would be an army of men, the greatest since the building of the pyramids at Sakkara and Giza.

As thoughts of building the Temple of the Sphinx passed through Khufu's mind, he recalled the dream in which he had seen himself inside a temple with a long, narrow shaft. At the time of the annual rising of Sirius, the light of the great star shone through the shaft upon a red granite altar. The sight had made a deep impression on Khufu. The temple he would build would honor the Star of Isis and be the *one place* where the starlight could illumine the souls of the priesthood, the Sons and Daughters of the Star Gods. . . .

Sokar had returned from Hermopolis in a reserved mood. He had not achieved his goal of enlisting Dedi's magical assistance in creating an alternate government, but the journey had not been a failure either. He had, after all, been invited to participate in the ceremonial procession to dedicate the newly erected obelisk to honor Thoth. He had reunited with his mentor, and he had learned from Meri-ib that he had vacated his position as High Priest of the Temple of the Sun in Heliopolis. He had also witnessed Meri-ib's reluctance to reveal his current position, but at least he knew for sure that he was in Memphis, no doubt in Khufu's service. Sokar figured that service also included Taret, since she too had resigned her position as High Priestess at the same time as Meri-ib. Sokar knew who his enemies were. He did not know who his allies were.

Sokar reviewed the past weeks back to when he had decided to abandon overthrowing Khufu in favor of establishing his own government. He recalled his meeting with Khufu's general. The man had seemed displeased with the king's shortsightedness regarding Egypt's vulnerability to invasions. He had wanted the Pharaoh to expand the army and dispatch a large portion of it to the Delta. Khufu had refused, citing there was more than adequate protection already provided. This general, Sokar believed, could be persuaded to join Sokar's camp, and the promise of being put in charge of the military of an alternate government would almost certainly buy his allegiance. So that's one ally, he thought.

Mafdet, the beautiful daughter of the wealthy merchant—she might be another. Sokar guessed she would relish the possibility of being queen of Egypt. There was the father of Bakka, the apprentice Star Priestess who had died. Sokar knew that wealthy businessmen were an essential part of any successful leader's support system.

There was Kheti. He trusted no one more than Kheti. Not only was he completely confident of his servant's loyalty, he knew Kheti believed Sokar had been passed over for the kingship he was entitled to. Only a few allies, admittedly, but it was a start.

Khem was resting when Tiye and Bast returned from their afternoon excursion to the river. It did not go unnoticed that Tiye was in a strange mood.

"I am glad you are here. I have been wondering if you were gone forever with my cat! So where did you go?"

"What? Oh, I—we went to the river's edge to get some exercise." Tiye was still trying to pull her thoughts back from a faraway place.

"Tiye, are you all right?" Khem felt concern for her friend. The query snapped Tiye out of her distant attitude.

"Yes, I am fine. I was just thinking. Can I talk to you about something, something important to me?"

"Yes, of course. You know you can."

"I do," Tiye answered, letting out a heavy sigh. "I have made a decision, Khem. It is the right thing for me. But I am not sure how it will affect my studies here at the Temple, especially with Klea and Ani. You must promise to keep what I tell you a secret, for now. Soon everyone will know. I have decided to commit myself to the goddess Sekhmet. I feel I am one of hers, one of the lioness-headed daughters of Ra."

Khem's mouth fell open. When she could speak, she was careful not to let her words pass judgment on her friend's decision. "You are going to become a priestess of Sekhmet? Why? What has happened for you to make this decision?"

"No, no, there is no reason for concern. I am very happy about this. It is just that it happened so fast, and unexpectedly."

"What happened?"

The Nubian told Khem about her and Bast going to the riverbank and resting beneath the sycamore, falling asleep, her vision of Khaba telling her the story of Sekhmet. "The thing that impressed me so strongly is that Sekhmet is *inside me*. She is *part of me*. Like her, I am good and bad, horrible and beautiful. I have never felt this way about any other goddess, not even the Great Mother Isis. When I woke up and saw Bast sleeping beside me, I felt as if Sekhmet herself was there."

Hearing her name mentioned, Bast lifted her head and tilted it to one side while looking at Tiye. Tiye looked at Bast, then turned to Khem.

"I have been called, Khem. Sekhmet has called me, and I must go." The conviction in her voice was clear.

After a long silence Khem asked, "Go? Go where, Tiye?" For the first time Khem felt apprehension. Would Tiye leave the Temple? Where would she go? What would become of their relationship? Their work with Ani and Klea?

"I will go to the Temple dedicated to Sekhmet here in Heliopolis."

"Are you going to tell Ani and Klea right away?"

"I have no choice. Yes, I will tell them," Tiye said thoughtfully. "I am not sure what Ani's reaction will be."

"Ani understands being called by the divinities," Khem said. "She will accept it."

It was time for afternoon classes and the girls found the classroom buzzing with conversation. Khem and Tiye were late, and by the time they arrived, Ani and Sheshat were already ascending the teaching platform. Inundation and the rising of Sirius were ever closer, and the subject of today's lesson was another related topic, Hathor and the Moon's influences on her priestesses.

"The time of the New Year is quickly approaching. This is a crucial time. The desert sun is unrelenting. Its heat is scorching to body and soul. The *khamsin* winds blow. Soon, Mother Nile will begin to rise in harmony with the predawn rising of the star Sirius. This is both a dangerous and beneficial time for all Egyptians, and honor must be paid to Hathor, the benevolent goddess, and to Sekhmet, the Dangerous One, who interweaves death and life in the seasonal cycle. Thus Hathor and Sekhmet, at this time of the year, become one.

"As the old year draws to a close, Pharaoh will perform rituals to appease the angry goddess Sekhmet. Pharaoh's rituals will appease Sekhmet, the land, and our people. Priests and priestesses throughout the land will recite litanies to the goddess in hopes she will not unleash her awesome power against the king. The litanies will not cease until the king is protected from all of Sekhmet's harmful influences, and all demons and diseases are expelled. When this is accomplished, the time of renewal can occur again. I repeat: this is Sekhmet's time, and she is near."

Tiye looked at Khem. Ani's words sent chills down her spine. The Nubian knew the truth of Ani's words. It *was* Sekhmet's time and, for Tiye, it was an exciting and challenging time as well.

"Let's consider Hathor," Ani continued. "A beautiful legend tells us that Hathor's name means the 'Dwelling for Horus.' This is because it was believed that the Sun god came to rest each night on her breast before being reborn at dawn. Another story says Hathor is the 'Celestial Cow' who gave birth to the universe and everything in it. Hathor is the goddess of many things, some of which seem contradictory. For example, she presides over Heaven and the Underworld. She is a Sun goddess and a Moon goddess. She represents the eastern and western horizons. She is also a sky deity, which makes her important to you as Star Priestesses.

"Of all her attributes, the fact that Hathor is a Moon goddess is of primary concern to the Holy Order of Nut. She is a giver and a taker of life. She is the goddess of joy, of ecstasy, music, dance, and song. While these are important, let it be known that Hathor, like Sekhmet, is linked to Sirius. The day of Sirius's rising is the day Hathor's birth is celebrated. You will all participate in that festival. Preparations must be made before the festival. Very soon, the priestesses of Hathor in Heliopolis will come to the Temple of the Sun and teach you the way of the dance. They will show you how to play the sistrum so that you may all honor the Moon goddess's birth.

"Now to another subject. In the Temple at Denderah there exist two star maps. One is rectangular, carved in the ceiling of the hypostyle hall; the other is circular, on the ceiling of a chapel on the Temple's roof. The signs of the zodiac are arranged in a concentric circle with the ecliptic pole at its center and seen in the udder of the hippopotamus constellation. Aside from the constellation, there are five planets, Jupiter, Mercury, Venus, Saturn, and Mars. In the rectangular zodiac the planets are situated differently. All of the zodiac figures face east-south-west, following the apparent course of the heavens.

"Sirius is represented twice in the zodiac: once by a papyrus stem supporting a falcon, situated in the Temple's axis and aligned with the constellation Gemini. It is seen the second time between the horns of the cow of Isis, in alignment with the stars of Cancer. This points out that when the Temple was built, there was a special relationship between its orientation and Sirius's place in the sky. When a building is oriented in such a way, in this case to a specific star, the power of that star is 'captured' by that building. That power in turn is used by priests for magical purposes.

"I have spoken about the way a building or monument can be constructed to draw in the energy of a star. The same holds true for a planet, the Sun and Moon, and the times of solstice and equinox. Capturing celestial energy is done with a mirror. This elementary practice will be a frequent and useful part of your work as Star Priestesses."

The class was over. Ani was growing accustomed to being a surrogate mother to the apprentices, so when she was told Tiye wanted to see her, she was happy to make herself available. Tiye approached Ani in her usual shy demeanor. She wasn't sure how to open the conversation, so she plunged headlong into explaining it. "Mistress Ani, I have something important to speak to you about. It is about my decision."

"What decision is that, Tiye?"

"I had a dream. I mean a vision. Oh, I don't know where to start."

"Come, sit down," Ani said, grasping the Nubian's hand and leading her to a bench. Tiye usually felt comfortable in Ani's quarters, but today she was nervous. "Whatever you wish to tell me you can do so with complete confidence."

"I have decided to become a priestess of Sekhmet."

Ani raised an eyebrow, her surprise visible. "I see."

"Let me explain."

"There is no need to explain. I know you would not come to an important decision like this without good reason."

"No, please, I want to explain. I must know how my decision will affect my work with you and Khem and my amulet-making with Klea."

"Very well," Ani responded. "Tell me. I want to know anything that affects you, Tiye."

"I had an experience. It was a dream, I think. In it Khaba was telling me the story about Sekhmet and her attack upon humans." As Tiye spoke, her gestures became animated. "But she is not bad. She was only doing what Ra told her to do, to keep the evil humans from overthrowing the gods. She has a kind and gentle side, and she is inside me. She lives in me, Ani. I know her, and I know her power."

Ani listened. She knew she was witnessing a girl's life changing. She sensed Tiye's emotion and commitment. Ani took both Tiye's hands, leaned forward, and looked into her eyes. "Yes, she is inside you. All the goddesses are inside you, and all of them are one. It is the goddess in her personality as Sekhmet who has awakened within you." As she clutched Tiye's hands more tightly, a smile spread across Ani's face. "It is a calling. She is calling you, claiming you as one of her own. And you are right to heed her summons."

Her eyes brimming with tears and her voice filled with emotion, Tiye said, "But my work with you and Khem to protect the king—and I do want to learn about the stars—and my studies with Klea. . . ."

"Do not fret, Tiye. You do not have to abandon your studies except for your training as a Star Priestess. But this is for only a short time. Your training with Klea can only be enhanced by your commitment to Sekhmet." Ani released and patted Tiye's hands and stood up. "Do not worry. It will all work out for good. You will see. Now, you go and get yourself ready for your session with Klea."

Chapter Forty-Seven

The Calling

After a long day tending to court matters, Khufu retired to his private chambers for a quiet meal with his queen. Afterwards, the couple adjourned to the garden adjoining the royal apartment. The king and Meri-tates had begun a nightly vigil of observing the comet's passage as it sailed like a sparkling ship through an ebony ocean.

As the miracle of the changing seasons and the dawning of a new year drew closer, Khufu's attention had become increasingly focused on the unprecedented events that would make this year the most memorable in Egyptian history since the First Time. As they often had over the past few days, Khufu's thoughts turned to Shemshu-Hor. He had not wanted to tax the elder's strength, but he needed another.

The couple strolled leisurely onto the patio. The twilight air was cool and fragrant. The marvelously groomed garden was filled with pomegran-ate, jojoba, and tamarisk trees, its paths lined with cornflowers and lupine. The four corners of the large lotus pool in the garden's center were flanked by fragrant wisteria arbors, the queen's favorite.

Khufu's life had changed dramatically in recent weeks. From an ordi-nary king—if any king could be considered ordinary—he had become the force behind the unearthing of one of Egypt's most ancient monuments, the one now making plans to build a unique temple, the one preparing for a living ascension. All were gifts from the Sky Gods, who had chosen his reign as their time to return to this planet of mortals.

As the purple and gold sunset faded and the sky turned indigo, Khufu and Meritates watched the comet appear. No Egyptian seeing this would ever look at the night sky the same way again, Khufu thought. He was certain the comet's brilliance and eerie beauty had made an indelible imprint on every mind.

The queen faced her husband, her eyes catching his in the twilight. A smile softened the lines in her sharp features and high cheekbones. "Tell me, my husband. Now that the temple plan has been laid, when will the construction begin?"

As a rule, Khufu did not discuss his responsibilities with her, but these were challenging times and details should not be withheld. He had not yet told Meritates about all his dreams or the profound event pending in his life. Before Khufu could speak further, a meteor streaked across the sky. The falling star appeared to cut a path of misty light through the comet's tail. The brief flash of the meteor's white-orange fire lit up the deepening darkness.

"Ohhhhhhh! A shooting star to make a wish upon, my love," Meritates exclaimed. Her almond-shaped eyes, outlined in cobalt kohl, gleamed. "What are your fondest wishes, my husband?"

Khufu sat still, his body coppery in the dim light, his white kilt and shoulder drape almost pink. Looking at the expanse of the night sky, the monarch took a deep breath, exhaling it with a slow sigh. "I suppose I have wishes. For you to be happy. That is my greatest wish."

A blush crept over Meritates's face, visible even in the dim light. "I am flattered by your words, my husband. But, come now. Surely there are greater wishes due a king. Besides, I am happy, happy being your primary wife and the mother of your sons and daughters. So, you are permitted another wish, many other wishes. What might they be?"

A faraway look came across Khufu's face. He had not thought of wishes this way in a very long time. He had always seen himself as prosperous in every way, as not having to wish for anything. Now that the queen had posed the question, he got up and strolled slowly over to the rim of the lotus pool to ponder his answer. The firelight from the torches danced on the water, casting shimmering reflections. "If I have a wish, it must be that I will be permitted to reign as king of Egypt until the Temple of the Sphinx is finished, until the first litany in honor of the Great Star has been recited within its walls."

Hearing himself say those words helped Khufu realize how important a project was the unearthing of the Sphinx and the building of its star temple. He had not seen until now that it would stand for his kingship, that with his living ascension it would put him on the "scrolls" of Earth's memory.

Khufu's comments left her confused. "Of course you will be king then. Your reign has only begun," she said attempting to reassure him. "Have you any reason to feel differently? Do you know something that you have not told me?"

The question provided the opportunity for Khufu to talk about other things he had not told his wife. He realized how isolated he was from his personal life, how he had unfairly kept Meritates in the dark. Placing his hands on her shoulders, he said, "I know I have been distant as of late from you, my beautiful wife, and from my children."

"Sssssshhhhhh . . . I know you have a country to run, my husband. Do not trouble yourself. We are doing well, though we miss your company. There will be more time for us when the country has passed through these important days."

Khufu could not let his wife underestimate what was going on any longer; she must know the truth. Khufu said, "You are right. These are important times for Egypt. You are aware of the Sphinx project, of course. The time is almost here for Inundation and the New Year. But there are other things you do not know."

Over the next hour, Khufu told his wife more about what had transpired during the past several weeks—the dreams, visions, and prophecies that had revealed to him the meaning of the times.

The queen listened, her eyes searching his face for clues that might reveal his feelings. Her love for the man flowed through her in a way different from before. He was more than husband, life mate, father of her children, more than king: he was a living god. The recognition humbled her. "I had no idea that your burdens have been so great, my husband. I have not been there for you. I have let—"

"Shhhhhhh." Khufu put his finger to his wife's lips. "You could not have known, and it was wrong of me not to have informed you of all this long before now. I did not consider your feelings, or your right to know. I did not want to disturb your world. I can only assure you that I acted, whether right or wrong, out of love for you, my wife."

Sokar sat cross-legged on the floor, twelve soapstone figurines on a grass mat in front of him. He had not taken the magical figures out in a long time. They were a gift from Dedi during his apprenticeship. Sokar valued them because they were from Dedi, and for their primitive beauty.

Sokar examined each—a crude hippopotamus, a jackal with one leg broken off, a crocodile with a mouth full of ivory teeth, sticklike male and female figures, a five-pointed star, the god Seth with its long nose and squared ears. No one knew what animal Seth was. It was a frightful beast with a forked tail and a doglike body that you would not want to encounter in the dark.

Sokar's thoughts turned to Seth. Seth devoured the Moon once a month, causing it to disappear from the sky. Seth, son of Nut, brother of Osiris, Isis, and Nepthys, the last also being his wife, was called the "red god" of the inhospitable eastern desert. Seth's very name was associated with malevolence and evil. The god's predicament intrigued Sokar. After murdering his brother, Osiris, Seth became engaged in a relentless and violent contest with his nephew, Horus, who sought to avenge his father's death. After struggles between the two, the gods were asked to decide which would rule the Earth.

That reminded Sokar of his relationship with Khufu. He knew that no matter how justified he thought himself to be, if he tried to overthrow his half-brother he would be seen as the embodiment of Seth. That he could not accept, to be labeled evil for seeking to claim what was rightfully his.

Sokar picked up a figurine in the form of the mace, the fiery eye of Horus. Kings who armed themselves with a mace always defeated their enemies, he believed. Some said the weapon embodied the Pharaoh's supernatural power. This gave Sokar the idea to make his own mace. It was a simple weapon, a stone head attached to a shaft of wood tapered slightly where the wielder gripped it. He would do this by magic, and instill it with supernatural power for his benefit. He saw himself wielding the magical object. Yes! This would impress in the Duat the image of him as a conquering king and would reinforce the image he had already imprinted there of his palace, himself seated on a throne.

Sokar called out to Kheti and ordered him to gather the necessary materials to create a life-sized mace, a foot and a half in length. "You will assist me with the spell, Kheti," Sokar said, his eyes sparkling as they always did when he felt the power building within him. . . .

Tiye returned to the dormitory following her meeting with Ani, convinced her decision to devote her life to Sekhmet was right. Meanwhile, Khem awaited her roommate's return, anxious to hear what had transpired between Tiye and Ani, and particularly the High Priestess's reaction to Tiye's decision. She was curious how the decision would affect their studies. Khem had no reason to disagree with Tiye's choice, though it was unexpected. She knew Tiye would not make such a change in her life unless she believed it essential. Khem also suspected Tiye's decision was influenced by Khaba.

"Did you speak to Ani?" Khem asked, as soon as Tiye came in.

Letting out a long sigh, Tiye answered quietly, "Yes, I did."

"And?"

"She understands that I must do what I have been guided to do. No, what I have been *told* to do," Tiye spoke with resolve. It had sunk in. She had made her decision and there was no turning back.

"When will you leave? Will you have to leave the Temple?"

Tiye was amused at her friend's anxious state. Eyes twinkling, she said with a smile, "No, I will not have to leave the Temple, at least I don't think so. Ani said I would continue my studies with Klea and that you and I will continue to work with our magic to protect the king. I will stay here. This is my home."

Tiye's eyes scanned the room lovingly as she spoke. Moving into the Temple dormitory, and her friendship with Khem had drawn her out of the shell she had retreated into after Khaba's death. She had not thought of the changes her decision would bring to her life. Khem sensed this and wanted to ease her concern. Patting Tiye's hand gently, she spoke softly. "It will all be fine, I am sure. Everything will work out exactly the way it is destined to be. Your decision—we are all in the hands of the Neters."

Khem heard herself saying the words, but she felt apprehension as to what that future would be. . . .

Tiye went out to the courtyard to join Akhi and Bast, so Khem stretched out on her bed, many thoughts in her head. The image of the lioness-headed woman in the water bowl came to mind. Sekhmet. The lioness woman she had seen was the same goddess Tiye would serve for the rest of her life and she came to *me* too. It was her face in my bowl. "Why did she come to me?" Khem said out loud.

"Who? Who are you talking to?" Tiye asked, coming back into the room with Bast trotting playfully at her side.

Khem sat up. "Oh, I was thinking about something that happened a long time ago."

"Tell me, if it is not too personal."

When Khem's story was finished, Tiye asked, "What do you think it meant?"

Hesitantly, Khem said she did not know.

"Do you think Sekhmet was calling you into her service?"

"I never thought about that. I don't remember getting a feeling like that at the time, or now either. I don't know. Maybe I should try to contact her."

"How about consulting an oracle? Like Klea. She will know."

The gentle breezes coming off the Nile were soothing to body and soul, which is why Sokar loved the river. It was his favorite place to do a ceremony. Time and time again he felt the force of the water empower him. Like the river, twilight empowered Sokar. It was the time when the world was suspended between day and night, a time when adepts could slip from the bonds of the physical into the magic dimension.

This magical operation would carry Sokar into the realm of Nun. Sokar would wade waist deep into the river to be with the god who lived in the Nile, the lakes, indeed, in all the waters of Egypt. He rarely worked with this deity, but when he did, he experienced supernatural journeys with often unsettling experiences.

Kheti prepared incense for Sokar's ritual, while the magician stood on the west bank of the Nile, reviewing the myth of Nun. Nun personified the dark, primeval waters that contained the potential for all that exists. Nun had no form, no surface; he stretched out in all directions. It was from Nun that Ra, the Creator, was born. After creation, Nun continued to exist beyond the boundaries of the universe and in the waters of Earth.

It was Nun's presence and creative power that Sokar now sought in Mother Nile. The magician knew he was treading on dangerous ground. Nun was a force to be reckoned with, and Sokar was aware of the negative forces the god represented. Nun's dwelling was all that lay outside the bounds of the universe. Nun and his allies could adversely affect him if he did not handle their energies properly. They could damage his health and bring down events that would destroy any chance he might have to elevate himself to king.

The thought of himself as a king took Sokar deeper into the place in his mind where he was already the Egyptian leader. Once he was enthroned, people would see in him their rightful pharaoh. What he would do for the country—economically, politically, socially—would quickly demonstrate his capability. The people would realize that he was a greater ruler than Khufu.

"No, it will not take long," Sokar whispered to himself. "The people will give me the majority rule for as long as I live. It will be I who ascend into the starry realm of Osiris at my death, I who will be assured of immortality."

Sokar's thoughts were interrupted by Kheti with a clay bowl out of which rose a fragrant smoke. Sokar stripped himself of his kilt and sandals, wearing only a gold sunburst medallion around his neck. His coal black hair fell loose around his broad shoulders. Taking the incense bowl, Sokar waded up to his waist in the river. A rite of cleansing was a prerequisite to every ritual. Holding the bowl skyward and closing his eyes, Sokar said a prayer to the Spirit of Mother Nile:

"Cleanse my body, O my Mother the River. Cleanse my mind and my soul. Connect my spirit with the spirits of my ancestors. Let this sacred smoke cleanse the air around me so that I may breathe in beauty."

Opening his eyes, Sokar motioned for Kheti to come into the water and take the incense bowl away. Then, the magician began to flex his mental muscles. Lifting his bare arms to the sky, he spoke: "Ancient gods and goddesses who walk among the stars. I pray you indulge me in my petition for my greatest wish. By your powers and your grace see the goodness and justice that would be served by my being a leader of Egypt. The kingship I create is for the people, the justice of doing it is for *me*."

Standing in the warm water enhanced Sokar's state. The river was doing its part to open the doors through which the gods could contact him. As the magical words fell from his lips, a force began moving through his body.

In his sensitive state, Sokar slipped into a strange realm. The Nile was as black as the night sky, the rippling water sparkling like stars. The river was not of the Earth. It was a sky river, the cosmic river of which the terrestrial Nile was but a reflection. A vortex more intense than any he had ever felt began to swirl up around Sokar, lifting him out of his physical body and into his Body of Light. He was now a being in the realm of the Sky Gods of the Great Night. Sokar swam in the celestial river.

This is a strange dimension. Nothing is familiar here, he thought. It is a world of sounds like tolling bells. Sokar realized he was inside a small pyramid. Was it the Realm of the Dead? Sokar felt a presence. A quick glance in all directions revealed nothing, still the presence was there. A transparent form began materializing: a female spirit not entirely human except from the waist up and her mistlike lower part tapered into nothingness. The magician was in awe. This was no deity.

The spirit began to communicate with him, in a "voice" that sounded as if it came from a deep well, the sound flowing from the mind of the apparition into Sokar's. The words were drawn out and distorted as if it spoke in slow motion.

"I am the ghost of a priestess gone from your world of flesh."

The female spirit, though hideous to look upon, was enchanting. He was not afraid. He was in her world, and she was in control.

"I know of your desires; the power of your desires has enticed me, has drawn me to you."

The words stirred Sokar to listen rather than use his will to retreat back into the physical dimension.

"I am attracted to the jealousy within you. I and those like me, women of death, roam the hidden places of Night, the night above you and within you and all who still live in bodies of flesh. I am dangerous to those who have no desires, no passion, those who allow fear to hold them captive so they do not act on their lifelong dreams and wishes."

The spirit's energy was weakening quickly. Her final words, planted in Sokar's mind, would recur many times in the days to come.

"You can petition the Neters to grant your wish, and they may do so, and they may not. You must justify yourself to receive their help. With me, you need no such justification for I care not. Grant me my wish and by the power of the dead I will grant yours. Yes, I can grant your wishes, assure your fondest desire. But you must in turn give something to me. In payment for my granting your desire to be a king, you must provide for me a living human body I can enter to live again in your world."

Sokar snapped back into the physical dimension. The air around him was electric. Slowly, feeling returned to his body and he became conscious of his blood circulating. He had never had a spirit bargain with him. No doubt his thoughts and desires had been monitored and attracted her to him. That gave him pause.

Sokar's thoughts were interrupted by Kheti clearing his throat to get his master's attention. "Ah, pardon me, my Master. I do not mean to disturb you, but there is a matter that requires your attention."

His mind still far away, Sokar replied in a stern, yet barely audible voice. "Yes. What is it, Kheti?"

The servant reacted nervously to Sokar's sternness. It was apparent the magician was lost in thought. "Your mace, Master," Kheti answered, holding the wood and small carving knife out to Sokar. "It is time for you to fashion the mace, yes?"

"Yes, yes, of course," Sokar stammered as he grasped the reality of where he was and why he was there. "Thank you."

Taking the wood from Kheti's hand, the magician dipped it into the warm river water in a symbolic act of cleansing and blessing. He gripped the soft wood in his left hand and began to carve. Chips and slivers fell into the water as he transformed the wood into a mace. When he was finished, Sokar faced east and held the object up to the heavens. "Mighty One of the East, Henkhisesui, accept this my magical mace and instill it with your power." Sokar turned slowly clockwise, facing the south, west, and north, respectively. "And Shebbui, Mighty One of the South. Hutchaici, Element of the West. Qebui, Mighty Element of the North."

Sokar handed the mace to Kheti, dropped his arms by his side, and bowed his head. Slowly, Sokar turned and waded to where Kheti was waiting with a linen towel to dry off with, and his kilt. Kheti gathered up Sokar's ceremonial materials and followed his master back to the *Benu*

Temple. After a meal of beer, stewed dates, and sweet cakes, Sokar went out onto the patio to breathe in the fresh twilight air, and to feed dried meat kernels to Horus.

The sky was dark enough that the brightest stars had just begun to pop out. It wasn't the stars that caught Sokar's attention, however; it was the image of the comet in the pupils of the hawk. The comet, still dimmed by the setting Sun, was stirring. It was an extraordinary object. He could feel its power. He knew its appearance meant something. His mind raced back over the events of the past few weeks, and the plans he had for his future and the future of Egypt. Perhaps it is human nature to seek to relate portents to one's own self and personal life, Sokar thought. "So, Splendid One, what meaning do you hold for me?" Sokar said aloud.

Sitting on his nearby perch, the hawk let out a shriek that echoed through the night air, and caught Sokar's attention.

"Ohhhhhhh, so you think you have the answer to my question, do you?" Sokar said to his familiar, the bird's piercing black eyes blinking at him.

Chapter Forty-Eight

The Sirius Council Meets Again

Khufu, his queen, and Sokar were not the only ones focused on the comet this night. Khem stood on her patio to watch it too. Tiye was in meditation, while Akhi had taken Bast for her before-bedtime walk. The stars sparkled in the indigo sky and the Milky Way arched as a bridge of stars. Khem imagined, as she had since her earliest childhood, a throng of souls walking the Star Bridge from Earth to Heaven. The comet—it is an emissary, yes, that's it, Khem thought. An emissary from some far-off kingdom of comets in the starry realm of Osiris. But an emissary of what? What is it like where you come from?

Khem felt the comet heard her. How many people have seen you? Khem knew this ever-brightening streak of light had been here before, had been seen by her ancestors. Khem remembered the moment she sensed her connection with the universe. That brought to mind the realization that all the stars were her relations, so she was a "relative" of this silver-haired comet.

Celestial siblings. We all have celestial brothers and sisters, Khem reflected. If I talk to the comet like I talk to Atef, it will hear and understand me. Khem was sure of that. She was sure the comet would communicate with her, maybe reveal the message she was sure it possessed. The comet was developing another tail. How beautiful you are, my sister, Khem sighed soulfully. What secrets do you hold? What will befall Egypt? Will it be good or bad? Will we survive?

As if the comet were answering, Khem heard: "Many things, now unknown to the people of Egypt, will soon be known and remembered for ages to come. The events of your times will reveal many mysteries. The fate of Egypt and her people is in the hands of Osiris, the Supreme Heavenly Judge."

Taret awoke from sleep to a red dawn. The predawn rising of the Great Star was close. She felt the power of the event building. She and Meri-ib were keeping a psychic vigil to detect any negative energy around the king. His safety on all levels was paramount.

A pitcher of cool water, along with sweet cakes and stewed figs, had been placed on a table in Taret's room. Though the High Priestess was not hungry, she knew she must eat to keep up her strength. She thought of Meri-ib. He had told her about his trip to Hermopolis and the dedication of the obelisk at the Temple of Thoth, he told her of his encounter with Sokar. Meri-ib had expressed his distrust of him, reinforcing Taret's suspicion of Sokar as a threat to Khufu's sovereignty. That led Taret to tune into the magician-priest, but the more she tried to "see" him, the more confused the images became. She saw Sokar, the man, but this quickly turned into the god Apep, dragon of the Underworld.

This sudden switch startled Taret. Aware of Apep's association with storms, darkness, even earthquakes, she thought the vision implied the existence of a rebellious, chaotic force within Sokar. Shaking her head to free her mind from the Apep image, Taret focused again on Sokar. This time the man's face transformed into the head of a falcon.

As quickly as the vision appeared, it dissolved. Taret knew she had made psychic contact with Sokar and she was certain the image of Apep was good reason to be suspicious of the magician and his allegiances. Apep was not a good sign. The Underworld monster was a devourer, the demonic enemy of Ra. The falcon was not a symbol easily interpreted. On the one hand, the hawk was associated with Horus, the divine child, son of Isis and Osiris, the god worshipped as a savior throughout Egypt. But the falcon was also a warrior, a patron of families, and, most importantly, the avenger of Osiris's murder, a positive avenger who set things right with the forces of good and evil.

Taret remembered that symbols should not always be interpreted literally. Visions appear in signs familiar to the visionary, so it was a matter of what the symbols meant to *her*.

To her, Apep was a symbol of evil, pure and simple. His energy was demonic. If that meant the monster was an ally of Sokar's, then Sokar definitely posed a threat. It was Khufu's authority that Sokar threatened. In light of what she knew of Sokar's jealousy of Khufu, the falcon represented Horus as the Avenger, which meant Sokar intended to get revenge for being passed over by Sneferu. It was clear Sokar intended to be king. How he would accomplish this, Taret did not know, but she was certain he would make his move during this most auspicious time.

Khufu awakened realizing this was the day construction of the Sphinx Temple would begin. Measurements had been taken, litanies and prayers recited, a labor force gathered. Now ground would be broken. The Sphinx Temple would be functional and beautiful, and built in honor of the Great Star of Isis, it would capture the light of the predawn rising of Sirius to empower Egypt's priesthood. This vision of the great temple made Khufu's heart swell with pride. It would be a flawless monument that told the story of the rising of the Great Star, the annual flooding of the Nile, and the changing of the old year into the new.

Just outside the entrance pylons, there should be a great obelisk, and then, flanked on each side by massive granite pylons polished to a high gloss, the entryway would lead into a large courtyard. The columns situated around the inner perimeter of the courtyard would be styled like magnificent papyrus plants. Further into the compound would be an outer and inner vestibule whose walls would be painted with scenes of the heavens. Next would be the shrine with a statue of Isis in her guise as the Mother of Egypt. Then the inner sanctum, in which a hand-chiseled block of red granite would serve as the High Altar; upon that, once in a year, the precious light of the Great Star would shine. This would be the first temple in all of Egypt dedicated exclusively to Isis.

Storage chambers and cult rooms especially for gods and goddesses who were related to Isis, including rooms for Osiris, Horus, and the goddess's sister, Nepthys, would enclose the inner halls. An outer corridor would surround the cult rooms. On either side of the temple, staircases would lead to the flat stone roof for a lovely view of the Nile and desert. The sacred lake would be dug on the premises, rectangular in shape, lined with stone, and accessed by a flight of steps. It would be the site for the annual re-enactment of scenes in the life of Isis, and her role in the resurrection of Osiris. The lake would hold the forces present when the Sun first emerged from the primeval waters. Priests would use the lake to purify themselves before daily rituals and other religious duties.

Today, Khufu would meet with the Sirius Council. Inundation was quickly approaching and plans needed to be made. He looked forward with anticipation to any information the Council members had regarding a challenge his half-brother or any other faction might pose to his authority. That Sokar presented a threat Khufu had long assumed, but how and when he would make his move was a question unanswered.

Khufu joined the members of the Sirius Council already gathered in an antechamber of the Throne Room. The journey to Memphis had been a trying one for Shemshu-Hor, who had returned to the monastery at the *Benu* Temple in Heliopolis to meet with his fellow Followers of Horus. The old man seemed to have aged, if that was possible, his shoulders more stooped than Khufu had noticed even days ago. The monarch greeted the Council members warmly. He not only trusted these advisors, he had grown fond of them as well.

The meeting began with Khufu telling them that the royal wife knew everything that had transpired, and that he trusted his mate implicitly. No one voiced any objection. The focus then turned to dreams. Khufu asked if any of the Council had experienced portentous dreams or visions.

"Yes, Your Majesty," Meri-ib began. "I have had but one dream since we last met, but I feel it bears mention." Meri-ib described his dream. He spoke about the image of the great comet that transformed itself into a wondrous celestial boat sailing the waters of the heavens. "In the boat were three goddesses I recognized as Isis, Anukis, and Satis. The three became one Star Woman, and changed again into a big, bright star that drifted upward out of the boat and came to rest high in the sky. And then the strangest thing, Majesty. The star was suddenly devoured by a serpent-like creature from the Underworld!"

Taret's attention was drawn to this. She recalled her vision in which Sokar had changed into Apep, god of the Underworld. Was this connected to Meri-ib's dream?

A sensitive man, Meri-ib was at the point of nervous trembling by the time he had finished telling his dream. Noticing Meri-ib's tenseness and the puzzled look on Khufu's face, Taret spoke up. Only old Shemshu-Hor sat passively. He understood what the dream meant.

"Majesty, perhaps I can shed some light on Meri-ib's dream." Taret said. "It wasn't a dream exactly, but I too had a similar experience."

Khufu and the others turned to face her.

"This morning, during my meditation, I was picturing a certain person who—let's just say is someone I don't trust. When I pictured the man's face, he transformed into Apep. When I tuned into him the second time, he became a falcon."

"What do you think it means?" Khufu finally asked. "And, Lady Taret, who is the man you do not trust?"

"Sokar."

"I see," Khufu answered solemnly. The revelation did not surprise him.

While the others sought to interpret the riddle of Meri-ib's dream and Taret's vision, Shemshu-Hor listened. Then slowly lifting his blue eyes and viewing them with a faraway look, he began speaking. "These visions are indeed a portent. The great comet is a celestial barque that brings the power of Mother Isis to Earth. The three goddesses combine the power of the Mistress of the Great Star, whose full power will be released at the moment of its predawn rising to mate with Ra. The star in Master Meri-ib's dream is the Nile Star, of course, marking the rising of the waters of blessed Mother River. But this year's rising could be different.

"The Goddess Star, and all it represents, especially now, are in peril from dark forces. The dark forces do not do their work alone. They must have earthly counterparts whose intentions are compatible with theirs. It is that person who channels his dark energies from their dimension into the physical world, enabling the negativity to manifest. The one called Sokar is the one whose motives will mate him with forces from the Underworld that seek to turn what should be Egypt's finest hour into the hour of her greatest darkness, ignorance, and spiritual despair."

"The gods are with us," said Meri-ib after a few moments of silence. "We would not have been given these visions unless it was meant for us to know *ahead* of time what threats we face."

"Yes, yes, you are right," Taret chimed in. "The gods have given us forewarning. Forewarned is forearmed, is it not?"

Khufu listened but was tense. He walked to the window and gazed out over the desert. The others left him to his thoughts. Minutes passed before Khufu turned and faced the others. His expression was of determination. "The message the gods have given us is clear. Sokar is in league with the dark forces, whether he is conscious of it or not. We cannot waste time or energy trying to figure out his motives. We must take steps to deal with this crisis, do whatever it takes. We must see to it that the upcoming events are not interrupted, or that Egypt's power is diminished in any way."

The Council members knew the only way open to them was magic—psychic warfare. Openly acknowledging that the palace was aware of Sokar's scheme would bring it before the people, and that could serve Sokar's purpose. No, it was best kept quiet and they should address the problem without delay. Taret, a skilled practitioner of magic, was the most adept at such endeavors. She would not resort to those tactics except in the face of great peril to those things she held dear—Temple, priestesses of the Holy Order of Nut, Khufu, Egypt.

"No one among us, not even Pharaoh himself, is better qualified than you, Taret, to engage in this task," said Meri-ib.

Khufu stepped toward the magician-priestess and spoke with passion. "As king of Egypt, it is within my power to command you to accept this task, Lady Taret. But I am aware that one should not be pressured to perform what may turn out to be the greatest magical work ever undertaken. Only one completely loyal to the Throne, who will act in defense of our beloved land at whatever cost, could take on such action. Loyalty and dedication to a cause cannot be ordered, and I will not try to do such a thing. It is your decision."

Khufu turned away and sat down on one of the minor throne chairs placed throughout the palace. The room fell quiet. All focused on Taret.

The hot air in the council room weighed heavily, beads of sweat formed on foreheads, even lulled Shemshu-Hor into a light sleep. Taret walked over to Khufu with an expression of calm resolve. Bowing slightly before she spoke, the priestess said what the king and the others hoped they would hear. Her voice was filled with strength.

"Your Majesty. I do not yet know all the details of what Sokar and his probable allies are up to or how he intends to achieve his goals, but I *will* find out. With my allies in the priesthood, I will do within my power what it takes to see the Throne remains sovereign and secure, that Egypt is not cheated out of the rewards and revelations in these glorious days in her history. This I vow."

Chapter Forty-Nine

Journey to Memphis

Tiye had been preparing for her journey to the Temple of Sekhmet in Memphis for days. Akhi and Nerah had cleaned and packed her clothes and other personal items in a traveling basket. The Nubian had attended her classes, including a private session with Klea, and had completed her assignments. These chores took care of her outer world responsibilities. She had had several "conversations" with Bast to assure the animal she would be gone only for a short while, and that when she returned she would have many things to tell her.

Tiye had prepared herself for the journey. She had "talked" to Khaba about her decision to become a follower of Sekhmet, and had felt a wonderful closeness to her teacher that made her loss easier to bear. She had made prayers to Sekhmet, and had begun to sense her presence in Bast. What a powerful energy this goddess is, Tiye thought.

Tiye boarded a cargo boat that made a daily trip to the capital city. The air was cool and the light spray was refreshing. Tiye felt the river was cleansing her, helping her prepare for the Temple. Storks and white herons waded in the rushes along the bank looking for fish and insects; kingfishers jabbed with their sharp beaks, swallows swooped and darted through the hot desert air.

At Memphis, Tiye asked a stranger for directions to the Temple. It was small compared with the Temple of the Sun. Later she learned the small compound was actually a mystery school. At the entrance were six standing figures, three representing kings, and three for Ptah, Sekhmet, and their son Nefertem, the lotus god. Beyond the statues the entranceway opened into the great hall; it was not "great" by most standards, yet the artwork made up for its small size. Scenes depicting Sekhmet in many of her four thousand names graced the walls.

Tiye touched her hand to the wall. She had not been trained as a scribe and did not read well, still she understood many of the images. One showed the goddess as Lady of the Flame; another as the Great One of magic; both acknowledged the awesome power attributed to her priests and priestesses, all of whom were magicians. As the afternoon heat became more intense, it made Tiye think of Sekhmet as the goddess of the scorching desert sun. She felt the hint of a presence. Sekhmet was here, and Tiye knew Sekhmet was aware of her.

Now that I am here, what next? Tiye had made no plans for what she would do at the Temple, but it soon became clear that a greater power had.

Standing by the lotus pool in the great hall and fingering the petals of a water lily was a woman in a long linen sheath. The above-the-waist straps crisscrossed her chest, leaving her breasts bare. Her coarse black hair was pulled back and coated in olive oil. The skirt went down to her ankles; her feet were sandaled in thongs woven from reeds. The outfit did not strike Tiye as unusual, but the gold medallion the woman wore did, a lioness's head with sunrays around it. The woman walked up to Tiye with a warm smile.

"Hello, my dear. Welcome to the Temple of the Great Goddess Sekhmet, the Lady of the Lamp, daughter of Ra, wife and sister of Ptah, mother of Nefertem."

Tiye's shyness overtook her for a moment, and before she could gather her thoughts and say something, the woman spoke again.

"I am Mutirkis. I greet you and welcome you," she said, her eyes searching for a clue as to whether the Nubian had wandered into the Temple for a visit or was here for a reason.

"Thank you, Mud . . . Mur . . . tikes," Tiye answered hesitantly, stumbling over the name. "I have come here to see the Temple."

"Well, come, I can show you around."

The two left the hall and went into a small outer sanctuary where Tiye saw a large statue of Sekhmet which stopped her in her tracks. Seeing Tiye's reaction Mutirkis said softly, "Isn't she beautiful? She is a powerful goddess to be sure."

"Powerful is the word," Tiye said breathlessly.

"There is another statue like this one in the innermost chamber of the Holy of Holies, and other different ones in the school."

Tiye was engrossed in the statue, and it took a moment for what Mutirkis said to register. "A school? There is a school here in the Temple?"

"Yes, but it is not really a school. It is the place where followers of Sekhmet gather to learn her ways and celebrate her rituals. Some among us are scribes who copy rituals and texts from the old scrolls. Others lead the rituals, and others wash the gilded statue and tend to its needs."

"That is what I want to do," Tiye suddenly realized. "I want to serve the goddess in that way. I want to take care of the holy statue every day, for the rest of my life!"

Mutirkis was stunned. Who was this young woman?

Tiye realized that her bluntness had shocked and confused the older woman. Could she trust Mutirkis? She would have to. She had come too far, both inwardly and outwardly, to allow her shyness to delay her or stand in her way now. Mutirkis led Tiye into the great hall and they sat down on an ornately carved limestone bench. Tiye told Mutirkis about herself, her experiences with Sekhmet, her decision to enter into the goddess's service.

Mutirkis hung on her every word. She felt Tiye's sincerity and detected the Nubian had experienced a "calling." She knew Tiye had made a commitment to Sekhmet.

"Come, child. There is someone you must meet," Mutirkis said.

Tiye followed her through the sanctuary into the corridor of a small wing on the east side of the complex. They came to a room whose privacy was protected by a door made of dozens of vertical strings of cowrie shells interspersed with wooden beads. Pausing before the doorway, Mutirkis called out. "Amenti? It is I, Mutirkis. I wish to see you regarding a matter of importance."

A low-pitched feminine voice responded immediately, bidding Mutirkis entry.

"Wait here," Mutirkis whispered to Tiye. "I will return in a moment."

When she returned a few minutes later, she said, "Amenti is the High Priestess of the Temple of Sekhmet. You must make your appeal to her if you are to be accepted into our life here. Come. She will see you now."

Mutirkis took Tiye by the hand and led her into the two-room chamber. The High Priestess sat on a wooden chair fanning herself. No breeze was stirring and the air was heavy. The room was scantily furnished, with just a bed and altar. Amenti was a slight woman in the prime of her life.

"Amenti, my lady, this is Tiye. She is an apprentice Star Priestess at the Temple of the Sun in Heliopolis and a daughter of Nubia in the South."

Amenti looked at Tiye, her dark eyes sparkling. It was a welcoming, friendly look that put Tiye at ease. Mutirkis excused herself and left the room.

"So, Mutirkis tells me you have a desire to enter the service of the

Ruler of the Chamber of Flames, the mighty Sekhmet, Guide and Protectress from the perils of the Underworld. Is this so?"

"Yes," Tiye stammered awkwardly. "Yes, I do."

She had not expected the High Priestess to be so direct. When Amenti
said nothing further, Tiye took it as a cue that she should explain herself,
and was surprised at her lack of inhibition.

"I see. Well, Tiye, this is an unusual request, but it is your extraordinary act of coming here and approaching me that tells me you are sincere
about your 'calling.'"

"Calling? So you agree Sekhmet has called me, Lady?"

"But of course," Amenti answered. "The goddess has called you, and she
calls no one without reason. She has plans for you, I am sure. In time we
will all know what they are. You must come here to live in the Temple. I
wish you to be here and settled in by Inundation. I will assign Mutirkis to
meet you when you arrive with your belongings and help you get settled.
The dormitory rooms are small, but comfortable. You will be part of the
contingent of women in charge of the daily washing ritual of the statue in
the Holy of Holies. Now, if that is all, I will retire for my afternoon prayers."

"Yes, that is all," Tiye replied, flustered.

Amenti's words brought Tiye's decision to become a follower of
Sekhmet into the light of reality with a jolt. It pleased her and made her
anxious. Plans spun in her head about what to do and how little time she
had. The feeling of "belonging" was coursing through her veins, and that
was the best part.

Khem received a message from Ani requesting she and Tiye meet with
the High Priestess the following day. Upon Tiye's return from her journey
to Memphis, Khem told her about the meeting. They assumed it had to do
with their work protecting the king.

Tiye was anxious to tell Khem about her trip. After the afternoon class
and the last meal of the day, the two talked long past nightfall. Tiye related
the details of her encounter with Mutirkis and Amenti, and described the
Temple's structure and atmosphere. Tiye's excitement was contagious.
Khem found herself wishing that she too had been "called" to serve
Sekhmet, and was upset that her friend after all would be leaving.

The next day at Ani's, they found Sheshat and Klea there as well. After
telling everyone to make themselves comfortable on floor cushions, the
High Priestess opened a scroll. "I have received a communication from
Lady Taret. The information it contains concerns all of you to one degree
or another, which is why I have summoned you here." It read:

"The Council of which I am a member has come into information concerning a plot. If successful, it would threaten the sanctity of the Throne, and possibly the safety and the sovereignty of the king during the rising of the Great Star of Isis and the time of Inundation. The Council has determined to address this problem through magic, so the people of Egypt will not be alarmed by danger or disruption of the Throne in these auspicious times. I will journey to Heliopolis in the coming day and meet with you who now hear my words. Until then, I remain yours in service of the Star Gods. Taret."

"I suspect that when the Mistress Taret arrives she will have much to tell us," Ani said. "We must be prepared for whatever we hear. I will inform you of her arrival."

Sokar awoke with a start. He sensed he was not alone in his bedchamber. He had slept off and on throughout the night, his rest plagued by dream fragments of his encounter with the ghost he had met during his Nile ritual. He had been tormented by the "guarantee" the female spirit had given him, and his need to succeed in his own magical knowledge and skill. He did not like entering into a pact with a ghost, the most feared of spirits. He knew how to work in allegiance with spirits on a one-on-one basis, but this was different. This spirit wanted him to provide a body. Who in their right mind would surrender a body?

Sokar reviewed his training on the multiple "bodies" that comprise a human. There is *aufu*, the physical body. The "blood and bones" self is mechanical and lacks consciousness. The brain operates *aufu*. There is *ka*, the body of "experience," the *double-ka* is mind. The *haidit*, or shadow, is the body through which the unconscious is experienced, while the *khu* and *sahu* are bodies appropriate for magical work. So there was no way an individual self could survive in the physical world without all the bodies intact.

Sokar said out loud, "No one will give up their body for me to be king."

Only the most skilled magician knew how to drive all the subtle bodies out of alignment with their physical, protective vehicle. Sokar could do that. All practitioners sooner or later have to decide whether or not to use their power to walk the dark path. Did the female ghost know he could fulfill her desire? Evidently. Power drew her to him in the first place, his power and determination to be pharaoh.

Sokar realized to fulfill the ghost's demand, he might have to convince or force someone to surrender his body. It would be easy to lure a slave or remote villager. Such people would not be missed, and even if they were, no one would suspect he was involved, and the person would still be alive, in a way.

So what are the risks? Do they matter? Sokar's mind was made up. He would go through with it, and start looking for a body to steal.

With Khufu's blessing, Taret boarded a small royal vessel, unmarked so as to ensure secrecy regarding her identity. Taret needed to enlist the aid of those she knew who could be of service in protecting Pharaoh and country from whatever perils might befall. Upon arrival in Heliopolis, Taret's first errand was to go to the Temple of the Sun to consult the oracle. She wanted to have this consultation before meeting Ani and the other priestesses.

Consulting an oracle was serious business. Cult statues were asked to forecast the future and to dispense guidance. Oracles were kept in stone shrines. Two shaven-headed priests carried them to the Holy of Holies when people needed to consult the statues; other times they were carried through town by priests in white linen, resting them at intervals on pedestals. This allowed the *fellahin* to consult the oracles for help.

The new High Priest was expecting her. When Taret arrived she was escorted immediately to the Ra Shrine in the Temple of the Sun. Taret had been in this part of the Temple only on rare occasions. She was led past the open court where commoners paid respect to the Neters and past the roofed-over court where the nobility worshipped until she came to the Holy of Holies, reserved for the priesthood. This sanctum's name was "His Great Throne Is Like the Horizon of Heaven."

Taret and her escorts ascended a stairway leading up to the chamber. The air in the closed room was stuffy but fragrant with incense, the light dim. Taret entered alone, the escorts remaining outside to protect her privacy.

The sanctuary was empty of furnishings except for the altar that held the shrine. Both were carved from granite polished to a high sheen. Carved from diorite, the impressive statue of Ra stood in its niche. The walls were painted with scenes of the Sun god and members of the divine family, while the ceiling depicted the night sky.

Taret reached into a pouch on her waistband and took out a heavy black stone, one of three pieces of meteorite she had been awarded at the time of her elevation as High Priestess. She held it to her lips and kissed it before laying it on the altar as an offering to the god. She knelt on a mat in front of the shrine, and spoke:

"I call upon the Light of Ra and the mighty power of the Sun to protect me and mine. Keep me safe from all that comes at me from the darkness, and from all manner of unjust attack. Let none who would do me harm cross the barrier of this Thy Sacred House. May your light and power stop them so we may speak in private with one another.

"I know You Who Know All are aware of the peril threatening the Pharaoh. You are friend to his allies, enemy of his foes. I, Taret, High Priestess of the Holy Order of Nut, daughter of Mother Sky and Advisor to His Royal Highness, Khufu, Horus incarnate, first born son of Sneferu, come to you. I ask you, Mighty Ra, to give me two signs. One that tells me we are right. One that tells me what animal spirit I may enlist to help us fight the battle."

Taret remained on her knees and allowed the energy of Ra to flow from his likeness into her. The power felt like a current of heat moving into her physical body. She felt it coming into her heart and spreading throughout her nervous system. When the current subsided, Taret again spoke aloud to the oracle:

"I glow with the Light of Ra! I speak with the Power of Ra! I go from this sacred place protected by the Justice of Ra!"

Taret stood and walked to the door. She knew the god had heard her, that the signs she had asked for would come, and soon. Taret faced the oracle and whispered a word of gratitude. Her escorts led her down the staircase and into the Court of the Nobility, where she was met by Ani and the others privy to her message.

"Welcome, my lady," Ani greeted her friend with a bow and a warm smile. "Welcome home."

Taret was pleased to see her. Ani held out her hands and clasped each of Taret's wrists in respect and welcome. Taret noticed the gold pendant Ani wore around her neck, a Sun medallion. It was Ra appearing to her already, his first sign to let her know her concerns were well founded.

Realizing that Taret was taken with her necklace, Ani said, "Is something wrong?"

"No, no, of course not," Taret answered, shifting her eyes off the pendant. "I was admiring your medallion. It is beautiful."

Taret and her entourage proceeded to Ani's private quarters for their meeting. Servants greeted them with refreshing palm wine and fruits, duck eggs, and roasted quail, all spread out on a low ebony table. They were hungry and used the meal as an excuse to put serious matters aside and catch Taret up on the goings-on at the Temple. She was particularly interested in how Khem and Tiye were progressing in their studies.

The meal finished, it was time to get down to business. The energy in the room became solemn. Taret's face revealed a deep-seated worry that, moments before, she had managed to conceal. "It is difficult to know where to begin." Taret spoke quietly, her eyes cast downward. "You are all aware of the suspicions many have had, including Pharaoh, for some time now regarding a possible threat to the Throne. Someone wishes to over-throw Khufu, or perhaps worse. Such turmoil is a cause for alarm for Egypt, for all of us. An Underworld battle lies ahead of us. I choose you, Ani, Klea, Sheshat, and your two apprentices to be in magical service to the king."

"If you are certain about the dire events about to unfold, you must know who is behind all this," said Ani.

"Sokar."

Taret spent the next hour telling them about Sokar. "Power. It is all about power. This man is no *fellahin* and must not be underestimated. He is one of us, a priest. He is also a highly skilled magician trained by a magus from the South named Dedi."

"Where do we go from here?" Klea finally asked.

"Klea, you and Tiye will work together," Taret replied. Then, turning to Ani she said, "And you must work with the dreams and visions of every-one here. We will rely on those to guide us."

Ani felt a weight settle on her shoulders when Taret spoke about the role of dreams and visions in this situation. She was confident of her abil-ity, yet knowing she and the priestesses would have to live in two worlds for a time, the physical and the astral, was daunting. It would require coop-eration and precision.

"It will be necessary to keep this work completely secret," Taret continued. "You must carry on with your daily routines so as not to arouse curiosity or suspicions."

These words upset Tiye. She was about to leave for Memphis, though no one was aware of that except Khem. She felt like she had been plunged into a situation that could now threaten or delay her plans. What should I do? she thought. Speak now or wait to see how Taret's plan unfolds and what it requires of me?

Taret continued. "Report all dreams and visions to Ani at once, day or night. Never underestimate the significance of *anything* that comes to you. The smallest detail could turn out to be extremely important."

Taret then turned to Khem and a soft smile lit up her face. "I have sensed your intuitiveness since first meeting you. You have the ability to perceive the presence of spirits and the nature of the energy they emit. You can do the same with places. This is a valuable asset that will serve you well as a priestess. It is also needed for the success of this operation. There will no doubt be times when you will be called upon to assess the energy of a person or place. Your assessment will be our foundation for action."

Sheshat would be an assistant, whenever and wherever she was needed, Taret said. She would have access to any of the magical spells and texts the priestesses might need. Klea was the magician. She and Tiye would perform the magical rites and enchantments, make the amulets, and gather the necessary divination objects.

Taret's mission was completed for now, so she announced her intention to return immediately to Memphis. Once she had relayed the details of their meeting to Khufu and other members of the Sirius Council, she would be in touch by courier as to how and when their plan would be activated. When she rose to leave the room, Tiye spoke.

"Lady Taret, there is something I must talk to you about."

"Yes? What is it, Tiye?" Taret replied, with a slight frown.

"I do wish to work with you, all of you, and I realize the importance of this whole affair."

"I am sure you do," Taret answered. "Is there a problem?"

"Well, yes, there might be. You see, I have made—I am about to make a big change in my life. I have decided to dedicate my life to the goddess Sekhmet. I will be going into her Temple in Memphis. I wish to leave Heliopolis very soon."

At Tiye's announcement, Taret realized she had received the second sign. She should enlist the lion as her animal spirit. "I see," the High Priestess said after a moment's reflection. "When a young woman is called to the priesthood, it is as a rule a lifelong commitment. However, the Neters have something else in mind. The gods know whom they wish to have serve them. If the Great One, Sekhmet, has called you into her service, then so be it. Besides, neither time nor distance is a factor in magical work. Go to Memphis, Tiye, but tell no one of your secret work."

Chapter Fifty

Khaba's Ghost Appears

On her return to Memphis, Taret requested an audience with Khufu and Meri-ib to brief them on her meeting with the select Star Priestesses and her visit with the oracle. "I have received the signs. The first confirms our suspicions regarding the identity of the enemy," she said. "The second shows me what animal spirit would be most appropriate to deal with this situation. It came when one of the Star Priestesses, a Nubian named Tiye, announced her decision to dedicate herself to the service of Sekhmet, the Powerful One."

Khufu and Meri-ib knew of the power of the lion, animal of the Sun, and manifestation of Ra, and they knew Sekhmet embodied the aspect of the lion associated with war and death. Even so, the thought of war disturbed Khufu. Concern for invaders and usurpers was something any ruler must keep in mind, but a civil war was unthinkable. Sokar must be stopped.

There was hope, though. Meri-ib, who knew the Sun's aspects, reminded the king and Taret that all things have a positive and negative side. "There is reason for concern, but we must not lose sight of the fact that Sekhmet's *positive* aspects are protection and rebirth."

"Yes, of course. You are right," Khufu said as he sat down on the throne and crossed his bare legs. "It depends entirely upon the intent, whether the energy is focused towards good or evil. Which it is depends on the priestesses and us."

Sokar sat alone in Heliopolis, deep in thought. He could feel his bid for power coming to a head. He would soon have to make crucial decisions, and he knew there was not a minute to waste. His encounter with the ghost still weighed on his mind. Sokar wrestled with the need to find a person who believed in his cause enough to give his body over to a ghost. Only one person was that dedicated to him and his cause. Kheti.

The thought brought on mixed feelings. Sokar was sure he could convince Kheti to do this for him, yet he cared for Kheti and would hate to lose his devoted companionship. But personal feelings should not stand in his way. His decision was made. When the time came, he would use his knowledge to take Kheti's body.

Tiye was preparing for Memphis, excitement mixed with sadness. She would miss her life at the Temple, her bond with Khem, best friend and fellow priestess, and Bast, for whom her feelings were unlike any she had ever felt for an animal.

Khem sat on her bed watching Tiye pack two baskets. Khem knew that Tiye's move did not mean their relationship was in jeopardy, yet she would miss their daily interaction.

Bast lay on the cool floor beside the entryway to the patio, her head resting on her front paws, watching Tiye's every move, sensed something going on. She looked at Khem, then Tiye, then Akhi.

Her baskets packed, Tiye dismantled her altar, placing her sacred objects in an embroidered linen bag Khaba had given her. Among these was a lioness amulet she had crudely carved out of turquoise when she was a child. Handing the piece to Khem, she said, "Here, I want you to have this. It is a keepsake that will bind us together."

Khem accepted the gift, knowing it would always remind her of Tiye and their friendship.

On Tiye's last day in Heliopolis, she and Khem took Bast to "The High Sand." This was where the first solid matter was created by the Sun god, according to the old texts. The priestesses obtained permission to visit the small island in the middle of a shallow lake. Small reed rafts tied to the shore provided transportation. In the center of the island was a carved obelisk, its capstone chiseled from meteorite.

The sand felt cool on their bare feet. Bast didn't like the raft and was happy to have her feet on solid ground, lifting her head often to sniff the air and watch the birds soaring and diving. The atmosphere of the place was different from other sacred sites they had visited. It was humbling to think that they were standing on the first piece of matter ever to appear on

Earth. And obelisks captured Khem's imagination. They were like giant needles whose roots went deep in the Earth, their points reaching into the sky. Khem detected a buzzing sound from the obelisk. "Do you hear that?"

"What?" Tiye whispered back, playing dumb to see if she and Khem were hearing the same thing.

"That noise," Khem replied. "Hear it? It sounds like a thousand bees!"

Bast got up and stood still, ears thrust forward, every muscle in her body tense and alert as the sound became louder.

"Yes, I hear it!" Tiye said.

Both sensed a current of electricity in the air coming from the obelisk. The buzzing became louder and then stopped. Then it seemed the obelisk became transparent and out of it stepped a woman.

"Khaba!" Tiye cried.

She appeared to be in physical form, but Tiye resisted the urge to embrace her. Khem was astonished.

"Khaba, you are here!" the Nubian exclaimed as she took a step toward her.

The spirit woman held out her hand. The gesture was followed by a clear, crisp voice. "Do not touch me, child. Only listen. Egypt's Crown faces great peril that you and your celestial sister must help avert." Khaba turned to Khem, still transfixed. "The heart of the First Born beats with pain, a pain that only misgivings of one's fate can bring."

The identity of the "First Born" flashed in Tiye's mind: Sokar!

"A battle is pending, not a battle with brawn and weapons, but of wits and magical prowess. You two will help Egypt fulfill its role. Watch your dreams, night and day. Guidance will be forthcoming. Believe what your visions tell you without hesitation. Know time is of the essence."

As Khaba spoke, the love Tiye felt for her burned in her. She was not sure she should respond.

Khaba smiled slightly. "It is all right, child. Take my hand. See that I am real, that your eyes do not deceive you."

Tiye, choked with emotion, took the extended hand. It felt so familiar, that old leathery skin. Khaba released Tiye's hand and stepped back, her attention fixed on her "daughter." Tiye looked on, tears streaming down her cheeks.

The girls watched as Khaba's ghost vaporized. Bast bounded over to Khem, jumping up at her. Khem grabbed hold of Bast's leash and gently pulled on it to get the cat to sit. Both girls were silent as they struggled to come to grips with what had happened.

Khem was the first to speak. She reached over and put her arm around Tiye's shoulders, and their heads rested together. "So that was Khaba."

"Yes," Tiye answered, sniffing and wiping away tears. "I cannot believe what I saw. Khaba was so real. She was alive. I touched her, yet I know she is dead. But you saw her too."

Tiye shook her head and squeezed Khem's hand. "What is important now is what Khaba said."

"Yes, of course you are right," Khem replied, the spirit woman's words coming back to her. "She said we must be aware of our dreams and visions."

Morning came and Sokar roused himself out of bed. Kheti came with a pitcher of water and dried fruit. Sokar was slow to get dressed and start his day. He wanted further communication with the ghost, to tell her his decision. Now that it had been made, it brought him peace. She had guaranteed him his fondest wish would be granted. Could he trust her? If not, what recourse would he have? Sokar would trust the ghost. He was now in a position to realize the dream fate had cheated him out of. It was his turn to cheat fate.

Sokar finished dressing and ate breakfast. His thoughts turned to Dedi. How would Dedi go about the task Sokar now faced? What magical spell would he use to convince Kheti to allow a spirit to occupy his body? A seasoned magician, Dedi taught his apprentices there were rare occasions when black magic was viable. Such incidents happened when the injustices one experienced were traceable to their source. It was then appropriate to return the negative energy to its sender. The one who had done Sokar an injustice, who had robbed him of his birthright, was his father, Sneferu. He could not get revenge on the dead king, but he could on Khufu.

What was important was the spell to vacate Kheti from his body. The image of the library in the Temple of the Sun came to him. It had the most extensive sources on magic in Egypt, with scrolls few eyes had ever seen. Even fewer were the priests who had the incantations committed to memory. He would find the scroll he needed.

Chapter Fifty-One

The Prophecy of the Blue Star

When Tiye boarded the small boat that would take her to Memphis it was a bittersweet moment. Khem and Bast had come to see her off. As the craft pulled away from the pier, Tiye watched her friend and the lioness become ever smaller as the boat began its journey and her new life began.

In Memphis the marketplace was crowded as usual. Vendors sold pigeons in stick cages, the morning's river catch, and other foods, flowers, incense, fabrics, pots, jugs, and cooking vessels. Tiye walked through the streets to the Temple of Sekhmet, her mind filled with images of the goddess, the "calling" coursing through her.

Mutirkis met her at the Temple entrance, her smile as warm as the midday sun. Grasping Tiye's hands, she bade her welcome, and showed Tiye her quarters. The small, stark room was dim and smelled musty. Mutirkis explained that it had been closed for several months after being vacated by another priestess who had left to care for aging parents. Yet the place felt familiar, its energy like the home she had shared with Khaba years ago.

A low brick platform ran along a wall as the base for the mattress. Several large reed baskets for clothing stood nearby. Cedar tables stood by the bed and against the west wall and held oil-burning bowls with cloth wicks. A brazier to provide light and warmth on winter nights stood in a corner. A wall painting depicted Sekhmet on a golden throne, her cobalt eyes gazing out as if from eternity. Amethyst, turquoise, and faience had been fastened to the deity's neck on the wall to make it appear she was wearing a beautiful pectoral.

The art was meant to convey the message that the Daughter of Ra and Lady of the Flames possesses a powerful energy that, in the minds of all Egyptians, had once been turned on humans who tried to overthrow the gods. The image of the warrior goddess depicted here left no doubt in Tiye's mind that she was capable of swift revenge upon any enemy of Pharaoh.

Mutirkis sensed Tiye's thoughts. "She's lovely, isn't she?"

Tiye's thoughts snapped back into the present moment. "Yes, she is," she replied. The goddess had a narcotic effect on her. It was a strange sensation, as if she was merging with Sekhmet.

After giving Tiye the schedule for the next few days, Mutirkis left her to settle into her new surroundings. There would be few demands on her time. Tiye needed time to get settled, and her thoughts were split between the excitement and challenges of her new life and her involvement with the covert project with her Star Priestess colleagues. And she was tired. It had been a long day already. After a light meal of figs and barley cakes, she lit a lamp, sending soft light and the faint, familiar scent of burning oil wafting through the room. The coverlet felt soft and cool in a way that only fresh sheets can. Tiye reclined and let the bed soothe her tired muscles. Before long she was too comfortable to get up and blow out the lamp, so she lay there peacefully, her eyes roaming the room.

When she looked at the painting of Sekhmet she felt compelled to keep her eyes on the figure. The deity was beautiful, yet had an air of ferocity that made Tiye think of a coiled serpent ready to strike. The goddess's power drew Tiye like a magnet. She knew Sekhmet dwelled within her, though she didn't know what that meant. Soon Tiye fell asleep.

A dream was quick in coming. Tiye floated above her body, then she was sucked into the image of Sekhmet on the wall. Now she possessed a new body, part human, part lioness. She felt a power coursing within her, and she was expanding, growing, vast, filling all space.

Is that what it is like to be a goddess? Am I in the world beyond life? Am I dead? The dreaming Tiye noticed a polished copper mirror suspended in midair. With a thought, it was in her hand. She held it up to her face and was startled by the image she saw: It was not herself but Sekhmet. The goddess herself was staring back at Tiye through eyes that were narrow gold slits. *I am She. She is me.* She heard words: "I am the One Who Knows the way in and the way out. I come in peace. I am the Great Mother, the Mother of Mystery, Protectress of the divine order, goddess of the passion in you, mightier than the gods."

Amenti was praying. "O Sekhmet, when you rise, the Light appears; when you go back, darkness comes! Grant that the King of Upper and Lower Egypt, the Master of the Double Land, the Son of Ra, the Lord of the Crowns, does not die from your arrow. Grant that your fever does not touch him, for he is the god from whom you come forth. He is Heru, the Offspring. O Sekhmet, who clothes her master in her Light, and who conceals him in her pupil! Come to the Living Image, the Living Falcon! Protect him from every evil fly of this year, so that it does not cling to him."

As usual, Amenti had risen before sunrise and completed her morning ritual in the inner sanctum. She was now about to breakfast on honeyed cakes and beer. On the small altar table in her bedchamber, a translucent alabaster statue of Sekhmet stood next to a basket containing semiprecious gems, and a miniature obelisk. It would soon be time to go to the House of Life, where apprentices were schooled in spiritual practices. The most important of these was internalizing the image of Sekhmet. When this was accomplished, increased access to the goddess would be gained.

As Amenti sat on a cushion sipping beer, her house steward, Ba-ba, came into the room. "Mutirkis is here, Mistress."

"Good. Show her in," Amenti replied, rising from the floor.

The two women exchanged greetings and sat down on floor mats facing each other.

"The Nubian, Tiye, has arrived," Mutirkis began. "She is getting settled in and has spent her first night in the Temple."

"I see," Amenti answered thoughtfully. "I expected her to return. I was not sure it would be so soon."

"Yes. She is very serious about her calling, my lady."

"That was my judgment too when I met her." The High Priestess's words revealed that she recognized Tiye as having been summoned by the goddess, though for what purpose she had no idea, nor would she question that just yet. Mutirkis lowered her eyes in thought.

"What the reason is for her calling," Amenti said with confidence, "we will know soon enough. Go, now, Mutirkis. Bring the Nubian to me. We must talk."

Ani, Klea, and Sheshat strolled from the classroom to the dining hall for the noonday meal. When they arrived, Khem was already there with Bast at her feet, panting to cool herself from the swelter. A gentle breeze from the Nile was bringing an unusual amount of humidity. Khem exuded sadness which the others noticed. No one needed to ask why. She was missing Tiye. Bast stood up in response to the arrival of the three women. Klea, fond of animals, held out her hand for the lioness to sniff, and scratched the cat's head.

After small talk, the four went into the dining hall. When they were settled comfortably on cushions around a low table, Ani motioned for a servant to bring the meal. "I suppose Tiye is getting settled in the Temple by now," Ani said, unable to avoid the subject on Khem's mind.

"Yes," Khem replied. "I suppose so."

Klea leaned forward, her voice lowered to a whisper. "Have any of you had any dreams since our meeting with Lady Taret?"

"I did," Khem volunteered, adding, "although it was a daytime vision. With Khaba, Tiye's old teacher." Khem shared the content of the message the old spirit woman had given them.

"Khaba warned of the forthcoming of a magical battle, one of wits, not weapons. She said that time is of the essence because the Crown of Egypt is in peril."

Recalling the vision experience gave Khem a chilling feeling, particularly when she thought of Khaba's comment regarding Egypt's First Born, whom she knew to be Sokar.

"Tiye and I would play a part in helping to avert the threat to Khufu's sovereignty, that the First Born—I believe this is a reference to Sokar, Khufu's half brother—suffers from great pain because of his misunderstanding of his fate."

"Thank you, Khem," Ani said. "That's the kind of information we'd hoped you'd be able to bring to us. Anyone else?"

The other women shook their heads and glanced in the direction of the nearest table, not wanting to be overheard. "Well, I have," Klea whispered cautiously. "I will tell you about it later, Ani."

"Have you been watching our nightly visitor, the comet?" Ani asked. "It is getting brighter every night."

Mention of the comet changed Khem's mood. The night before, she and Bast had gone out on the patio and gazed into the sky. "You should have seen Bast. She was looking right at it, like she knew exactly what it was," Khem said.

"She could feel its energy," Klea said. "Animals are very psychic." It was something they all knew, but the subject gave Khem the opportunity to share an experience she had had the night after Tiye left.

"I was surprised to see Bast looking at the comet. I never thought it would get her attention, that she would see it. But now I know she did, just like me," Khem stammered excitedly. "I guess it never dawned on me that she not only sees the same world I see, but is interested in what she sees!

She was not looking at the comet nonchalantly. She was really *looking* at it, studying it."

"You are kindred souls, and Bast is your 'familiar,' your animal counterpart," Klea said.

Khem looked at Klea, her eyes wide. "Yes. You are right! I know it. You know what I have been thinking? Does the lioness—you know, know about . . ." Her voice trailed off.

Ani answered quickly. "We must not speak about this now, not here."

"Oh, did I tell you, Khem," said Sheshat, "that I have a friend who is a scribe at the Temple of Sekhmet? We were in the House of Life together here in Heliopolis. Her name is Pakht. She is named for a lion goddess. Maybe Tiye will meet her. The temple in Memphis is small. That would be a way for Tiye to communicate with you, yes?"

Khem listened with interest. It would be nice for Tiye to have a friend at the Temple, but she knew the Nubian did not meet new people easily, and was inclined to keep to herself. But Tiye had changed a lot. What if she and Pakht became close friends? The thought sent a pang of jealousy through Khem. She already missed Tiye and felt her life would not be the same with her gone.

When the meal was finished they left the dining hall for Ani's quarters to discuss Klea's dream.

"I am not sure it was a dream," Klea began. "It was more like a vision. I was floating above my body on my bed. Then, I realized that I was no longer a human. I was a lion."

To Ani it seemed lions were appearing everywhere. There had to be a meaning to this.

"What happened next?" Khem asked, her interest peaked. Bast looked at Klea as if aware the conversation involved her.

"It felt funny, my body changing like that, very strange. But . . . but . . . I knew of a power inside me I was not aware of when I was just a human," Klea said.

Khufu paced the audience chamber, his mind in thought. Nemon and his labor force were at the quarry in Silsilis. It would be several days before the first load of stone would be shipped up the Nile, though Nemon had enough manpower to speed up the job, and this pleased Khufu immensely. He was committed to building the temple that would capture the precious predawn light of the Great Star. The temple would be his greatest contribution to Egypt.

Today Khufu would seek Shemshu-Hor's counsel. He trusted no one's judgment above his. He needed to relate his encounter with the "Congress of Osiris" to determine its meaning.

When the old man arrived he carried the "presence" with him, an air that always aroused Khufu's respect. Here was a living legend, the embodiment of Egyptian spirituality, knowledge, and history.

Shemshu-Hor sat erect, the stiffness in his bones an obvious discomfort. Fan bearers stirred the warm air around him, wine and sweet cakes were placed next to him on a table. Khufu offered the usual pleasantries, then came to his point. It was hard to know if the aged priest was listening or not. He sat with closed eyes, his folded, gnarled hands on the hilt of his cane. Khufu spoke about his dream in detail, pausing at times to gather his thoughts. He wanted his story to be accurate.

Shemshu-Hor sat quietly. Finally, he sighed deeply. "You are assured of your place among the kings of Egypt, descendant of Osiris."

The mention of Osiris brought an expression of respect to Shemshu-Hor's face. Khufu realized Shemshu-Hor had a long relationship in higher dimensions of reality with the Father God of Egypt, and that through this elderly man, Osiris still lived.

Khufu stood before Shemshu-Hor with a humbleness he had rarely felt for another. The old man's words were few, but always provocative.

"My place is assured, you say?" Khufu inquired. "Am I to take it that Your Eminence is saying that I am truly the rightful king of Egypt and that my having a place in the Congress of Osiris is proof of this?"

Shemshu-Hor slowly opened his eyes and looked at the Pharaoh. His craggy face bore a resemblance to the faces of the Congress members. "Doubt wears away at a man's soul, renders him helpless as a leader."

Khufu was surprised. He had not realized how much Sokar's threat bothered him. "You are right, Old One," Khufu answered quietly. "I will not doubt nor will I will forget my place and the responsibilities that go with it."

Tiye was full of expectations on her first day at the Temple of Sekhmet. Her intention was to allow her life there to simply unfold. She was where she needed to be, part of a magical operation that could lead her into circumstances no one could predict. Tiye's thoughts drifted to Heliopolis, to Khem, Akhi, and Bast. It had been a while since she had awakened alone in a strange place. She missed the enthusiasm the lioness exuded at the start of every day, the sound of Akhi's feet padding about the apartment as she served breakfast, laying out their clothing, pacifying Bast. Most of all she missed Khem. She now felt a bond with her roommate and fellow priestess that she had not felt for any of her peers, or anyone else for that matter, except Khaba. Granted, her relationship with Khaba was different, but there was love there. She felt that for Akhi and Bast too. They were the family she had never had. . . .

The desert air was as thick as soup. As the sun sank inch by inch into the horizon, it left swaths of purple and gold splashed across the sky. The last vestiges of Ra before he made his nightly journey through the Underworld graced the line between Heaven and Earth in a blaze of fading glory. Soon, stars appeared as the sky darkened. When darkness finally came, there was the comet, like an apparition from another world.

Khufu had received word that the first barge of granite had arrived from Silsilis. Nemon had sent a personal messenger to inform the king the work at the quarry was proceeding in advance of schedule, and that he planned to return to Memphis by Inundation. The floodwaters would make travel faster and more dangerous. Like all rivers the Nile was moody, but a good mariner could read its moods and navigate its twists and turns and the cataracts with little difficulty. Inundation was a time to celebrate the return of the life-nourishing, silt-laden water to the land, animals, and people. This year's celebration would, to the *fellahin* at least, be no different from any other, that is, until the predicted extraordinary events began to unfold.

Khufu had met with Kermit, the foreman of the workforce. The leveling of the land would begin soon since the first boatload of granite had arrived. Kermit would oversee the workers but Nemon would make decisions regarding the work. Khufu would spare no expense for this project. The result would be much more than an ordinary temple. It would be more advanced than any other in how it would capture starlight upon the altar carved from the finest stone by the most skilled stonemason.

Looking at the night sky, Khufu thought of Sokar. They had not been raised as brothers, yet they had the same father. He knew very little about Sokar or his mother other than she had been a royal concubine, and that Sokar was the first son born to King Sneferu.

Khufu questioned Sokar's motives again as he had done many times since learning of his jealousy and anger over being cheated out of what he believed was his rightful inheritance. Would he, Khufu, feel the same in Sokar's position? Did Sokar have a legitimate claim? Was Sokar a powerful enough magician to be the victor in a magical war?

"No, he does not have a claim," Khufu spoke out loud, his fists and teeth clenched tight. "I am Pharaoh. The gods have proven this to me, and they will soon prove it to all the people."

Khufu glared into the night. The muscles in his arms rippled as his fists tightened. His jaw grew square and firm. Legs apart and standing tall, Khufu spoke to the stars whom he knew to be the spirits of the blessed dead:

> Great Ones, who are eternity and everlastingness,
> grant me a path that I may walk in peace,
> for I am just and true.
> I have not spoken falsehoods knowingly,
> nor have I done anything with deceit.
>
> I am King of the Two Lands.
> I Khufu, Son of Horus,
> Brilliant Son of the Sun,
> the Living God,
> I am the Chosen One.
> This you have told me.
>
> I am the one who will come to you
> and merge with you
> so that I may be the Living Lord of Light
> walking on the soil of Egypt,
> the sacred Mother Land.
>
> None can change what you,
> the Star Gods, have ordained.
> None will be the victor save me.
>
> It is I who will conquer
> the demons of envy and jealousy
> and hunger for power
> for personal satisfaction and self-acclaim.
>
> I will meet the challenge,
> and I will meet it unafraid
> to claim the Warrior of Truth
> to be on my side.

Khufu poured his heart out to the stars, and he knew they heard him. Creeping doubt once again was expelled, and his heart felt strengthened. Sometimes it was too easy even for a living god to give in to the frailties of human nature. . . .

The next morning Khufu ate with Meritates and his son, Dejedfre, High Priest of the Temple of Ptah. It had been a while since he had spent time socially with his son. He informed the queen and Dejedfre that later that morning he would meet with the Sirius Council. It was an important meeting that would precede the annual ritual Khufu would perform in honor of Hathor. He would consult with the Council to determine if he should do anything different this year.

"Have you two been watching the comet?" Dejedfre asked.

"Yes, we have," Meritates answered. Khufu nodded.

"Then you know that it has given birth to another tail."

Khufu spoke up. "Yes, I noticed it but I didn't think much of it."

"Oh, but I think it is an omen, my father. In fact, I am sure of it," Dejedfre said with conviction.

The remark intrigued Khufu. Dejedfre was not known as a prophet or seer, but he was a priest trained in the esoteric traditions. "What do you know?" Khufu asked.

"Well, it is a long story. It begins in a legend told for generations. I first heard it during my school years from a colleague copying an old text for the presiding High Priest of Ptah. The tome was said to have been written by Thoth after its contents had been told to the Holy Three during the First Time. A number of prophecies concern Egypt. One is about a celestial apparition that would come at the time of the rising of the Great Star Sirius. This 'visitor' first would come in a blaze of white light; then the light would change to blue and be seen and would forever be known as the Blue Star. It would bring two messages, one of war, one of peace. The prophecy says that the war would be fought in the Duat, but the peace earned by fighting the war would rain down like starlight upon Egypt."

Khufu knew what the prophecy meant. He knew the forecast had to do with him and these times. The Blue Star prophecy reminded him of the comet racing through the night sky with its spectacular blue tail. That's it, he thought. The comet is the Blue Star.

"Is that all of the legend, Dejedfre? Or is there more?"

"No, not really," Dejedfre replied, with a slight smile. "It says the One in the Heavens will change places with the One on Earth."

The portent of the Blue Star foretold *his* ascension, his initiation into the Greater Star Mysteries, and the return of the Sky Gods, Khufu reflected. Or, was it *the* Star God? Was the prophecy foretelling the Second Coming or the return to Earth of one of the Star Gods? *Which* Star God?

Meritates touched his forearm in a gesture of comfort. She realized the prophecy was about Khufu, but she did not understand all its implications.

Khufu went from breakfast into his antechamber adjacent to the Throne Room. As always, the room was cleared of everyone except his two royal guards and a trusted scribe. Soon the members of the Sirius Council gathered. Khufu related the prophecy of the Blue Star, then asked, "Are you familiar with this statement from the old text, any of you?"

"Yes, at least I think so," said Meri-ib. "I remember the prophecy being among those in a transcript I studied while I was serving as a teacher many years ago in the House of Life. Yes, yes. I am sure of it."

Meri-ib's remembering confirmed that Dejedfre was right. The prophecy did exist. But did it refer to *these* times? Did it concern *him?* Was he the one who would bring a reign of peace? Was Sokar the one who would go from Earth into the Duat so that evil would prevail?

Then Shemshu-Hor spoke. "Prophecy speaks of times and events that are not necessarily destined to happen. It is not of truths etched in stone that cannot be averted. What is prophesied can be changed. It is a message telling you something. The prophecy about which you speak was first spoken by *me* a very long time ago. I received it in a vision sent to me by the Star Gods. I am the 'guardian' of the Blue Star prophecy. I am here to see to it that you, Khufu, Lord of the Two Lands, have the choice as to whether it will be fulfilled. The fate of Egypt depends on *your* decision, which you have already made."

"There *is* a divine plan!" Khufu finally said, both awed and certain.

Chapter Fifty-Two

An Ancient Scroll of Spells

Sokar had spent a quiet evening on the patio outside his bedchamber, watching as the sky turned from red to gold and finally indigo. The comet's appearance shortly after sunset captured his attention. As the sky grew darker he saw that the star with the long, sparkling tail had changed. It now had two tails, one white, the other blue. He knew the change was significant.

Time passed slowly as Sokar sipped palm wine, thoughts of kingship and power on his mind. Sokar examined the mace he had carved, its design appealing in the flickering light of the torch. The intense thoughts and feelings the amulet evoked in Sokar did not go unnoticed by his perching hawk, its eyes reflecting the light, his head turning now and then in response to the sounds around him.

Sokar thought of the ghost. There was something about her. Her face, Sokar realized. He thought of women he had known who were now deceased. He ruled out his mother and a younger sister who had died at two and other distant family members, even ladies of the court of Sneferu. That face was not of anyone he could recall, not someone close to him. Still, he was convinced he had seen that face before encountering the ghost.

Sokar's memory threw up a scene from the past. He saw himself standing outside the doorway of the classroom in the House of Life in the Temple of the Sun. He was engaged in one of his many conversations with Meri-ib, the two of them exchanging polite barbs. Three young women arrived together. Khem, the Nubian Tiye, and Bakka, the daughter of the wealthy merchant Ali Gabri. Bakka. The female ghost who was petitioning him to find a body was Bakka, deceased.

Lady Taret and Meri-ib had declared Bakka's death a suicide based on the evidence. Egyptian religion did not view the taking of one's life as a way of entering the world of the Neters; it could in fact jeopardize a soul's immortality. This surely would make a deceased person desperate for another chance at life, for an opportunity to right a wrong done in a moment of despair. Bakka evidently saw herself, forced into Temple life, separated from the man she loved and had hoped to marry, as a state of irrevocable sadness to endure for the rest of her life, unless. . . .

Bakka's spirit had become earthbound. Her only ambition now was to possess a physical body, *any* body, so she could be among the living again.

Sokar felt sorrow for the dead girl, yet it was mixed with anger and cunning. Now that he knew the ghost's identity, he had an angle from which he could bargain. It might not be necessary for him to steal Kheti's body after all. Sokar felt a new power over the ghost. Female spirits were greatly feared by the common folk. Dedi had taught him that even seasoned magicians should be careful not to underestimate their power to get what they want from the living as they could bring bad luck or hauntings.

Sokar sensed the ghost was with him now. The presence of the other-worldly entity immediately caught Horus's attention. The big bird stiffened, his wings spread as if poised for flight. A piercing shrill rang out, causing Sokar's body to tense. The hawk glared at the vision, its beak open, wings flapping to keep his balance. Sokar faced the ghost and spoke in his mind, "You want me to provide you with a body among the living so that you might live again? Yes?"

The ghost's features formed into a face, its eyes fixed on Sokar, tears sliding down her cheeks, as if weakness and sorrow had overcome her. But then the sadness turned to anger. The spirit's eyes flashed red, her teeth bared in defiance. Words spewed from her clear and sharp, causing the air to crackle. "You *will* obey me! You *will* provide me with what I desire! Or your days will be filled with terrors and your nights with dreams of endless battles with the great serpent, Apep!"

She was cursing him! The sound of the spell electrified the air around him.

Sokar watched as the pitiful, angry phantom faded into the mists of the spirit world. The experience left him in a mild shock. He slowly regained his senses, and sat on the rim of the lotus pool. Bending over, he put his elbows on his knees and rested his head in his cupped hands. He had to think this through. His first encounter with a hostile spirit perhaps, but he had no doubt about his ability to deal with this. He would battle Bakka and be victorious.

Sokar stood and laid his hand on the hawk's sleek feathered back. He felt its muscles tightening. Having his familiar beside him was reassuring. Horus made Sokar feel strong, more confident than by himself. Thoughts flowed from his mind to the hawk's:

Horus, my partner in fulfilling the wishes of the Neters. Engaging in a battle with a pitiful ghost who has created her reality by her own misguided, impulsive actions is not worth the time and energy I would forfeit. It would draw away attention best spent on getting the kingship. No, my battle with Khufu is more important than the problem of one lost soul. But I have gone too far to back off now.

Cocking its head to one side as it always did when it was listening, the hawk let out a shrill sound in seeming agreement.

Sokar held out his right forearm for Horus to step onto. Before going into his bedchamber, Sokar gazed up again at the comet. Thoughts of Nut came to mind, and he recalled words from an old spell: "I am your Mother Nut. I spread myself above you in my nome of the sky. Having entered my mouth, you go out between my thighs, like the Sun each day."

He had learned this from Dedi. He had watched many times as the old magician invoked the power of Nut, and became himself a personification of the sky goddess. Sokar knew well the flights magicians take into the sky. He was aware also of their desire to connect with Osiris and be judged impeccable practitioners of the arts. Sokar's desire, when his life was over, was to be reborn as a star, a favor granted only to Pharaoh, the living Horus, Lord of the Two Worlds.

At moments like this, Sokar felt strongly the rightness of his ambitions to be king, his righteousness as a priest, the power he possessed. He would not do Bakka's bidding, at least not the way she wanted. He knew about spirits who could possess a human. All magicians had to banish such entities in the course of their magical practice. So would he. No ghost was going to cast a spell upon him or rob him of his power.

Staring at the stars and dwelling on the ghost altered Sokar's consciousness. Soon he was on a journey into the Duat, standing before the palace he had built in vision. Yet here again was Bakka, her presence stronger than before. Again she transmitted to him the image of her form merging with a human body. She had come for Sokar's decision.

He would make the ghost think he had chosen to do her bidding, and as he relayed the thought he watched the phantom fade away. She had his message. In her desperate desire to have a body she had not demanded any details. All the better, for he had a plan in which Horus would take care of this distasteful business once and for all.

Accompanied by Sheshat, Ani stepped onto the teacher's platform. "These are times of growth for Egypt. Such times have perils that challenge the priesthood but bring opportunities to stay in closer contact with the Neters. When we truly look and listen, we realize that the Neters are revealing themselves to us in many ways. I have been aware of the goddess Hathor. She is of particular importance to Star Priestesses as one of her names is Ruler of the Sky."

Ani paused to take a sip of water. She was an expert at instigating pauses that allowed her audience time to digest what she had said. "You all know that Hathor is a Neter who has the power of joy and love and music and dance. Her temples echo with the sounds of the music played during her rituals."

No sooner had Ani spoken about the music when sounds rang out, filling the room with uplifting energy. The doors opened and in came a dozen women, wearing beaded *menyet* necklaces and gold-colored leggings that bloused out before clinging to the gold, bespangled ankles of their bare feet. The same filmy linen covered their arms and shoulders and chains of turquoise nuggets draped around their necks. Long braids of shiny black hair whipped around in the air as they danced, two by two, clapping their hands as they wove their way to the foot of the dais.

The air tingled. Melodious sounds of their music and chants held the audience spellbound. With graceful ease, the leader of the troupe lifted her arms, her many bracelets clinking as they slid from her wrists to her elbows, and called out the titles of Hathor:

"Our beautiful Mother goddess, Hathor, Mother of the King, Lady of Happiness, Mistress of all the gods, Patroness of Love, you are within us all. Hail to you who shines as gold, and to your power that evokes a joyful response inside and among us, your followers. We offer up praise to your majesty. We invite you to come and be with us."

Just inside the door at the back of the room stood a tall beautiful woman, her full lips slightly open in a smile. Her almond-shaped eyes, outlined in blue kohl, seemed to look through the priestesses. She wore a linen sheath interwoven with gold; on her feet were white linen straps. She was redolent with perfumed oil of lotus. She held a lotus blossom in her right hand, a bronze sistrum in her left.

Khem was drawn to the magnificent *menat* on her neck and shoulders, the collar that represented Hathor's power of rhythmic expansion and contraction. The *menat* was also a musical instrument, a conduit through which Hathor channeled her power. The front of the *menat* was a mass of turquoise-colored beads that hung from a chain of larger blue and red beads arrayed in a crescent. The counterweight at the woman's nape was a thin, flat piece of bronze molded into an image of Hathor's *ba*, her visible form.

This must surely be the High Priestess of Hathor, Khem thought. Her thought was confirmed when the leader of the group introduced the mystery woman.

"Daughters of Nut, all assembled here, the person of the Mistress of all the Gods, Lady of Heaven, the Cow Goddess, Lady of Happiness is present in your midst."

All eyes fixed on the exotic priestess who made slow, graceful steps towards the front of the room. She appeared to glide above the tiled floor. When she arrived at the foot of the dais, the other Hathor priestesses formed a circle around her, their feet tinkling from the tiny ankle bells. The air filled with the sound of sistrums and lutes. Surely that is Heaven's music, the music of the stars, Khem thought.

The music stopped. The circle of musicians and dancers dropped their arms by their sides and bowed their heads in deference to the central figure who faced the audience, her dark eyes sparkling. She detected a slight stiffening of the woman's body as her eyes closed and she stood still as a statue. Khem saw a wave of energy ripple down from the ceiling and enter the top of the priestess's head. Her features changed, her face now that of Hathor.

Khem had seen deities come through humans on numerous occasions such as High Priestess Taret when she spoke for the goddess Nut. This was different, more physical perhaps, as Hathor was present physically. Then, in a clear, soft voice, the Lady of All spoke through the woman:

"I have come that I might kiss the Earth. I am come that I might spend these moments with you in pleasure. I am come to exalt Ra, who shines without ceasing. His heart rejoices. He rides high in the firmament, in peace. He turns and takes his course. I ask you, Star Priestesses of the Holy Order of Nut, to live each of your days in a good way. Speak Ma'at, do Ma'at, for she is mighty. She is great and enduring. Her power rests in the minds, hands, and hearts of those who use her.

"Ma'at, I, Hathor, the eternal Isis, all the goddesses will lead you to sacredness. The doors of the sky are open to you and to your beauty. In your times of need come to me, rise up to me, turn to me. Always stay awakened to the breath of life within you. See daybreak. Rejoice every night when you are with the unwearying stars."

As quickly as the goddess had entered the priestess's body, she left in a cloud of smoke that lifted out of her head. Her eyes closed slowly, and her body relaxed. It was over.

Arriving at the dais, the first two Hathor dancers shook tambourines that tinkled loudly while the second two snapped copper cymbals, and the rest made sounds with rattles, lyres, bells, and reed flutes. Then all the followers of Hathor recited in unison:

> Joy to the Spirit of God,
> and sweet praise for
> The Lady of the Two Lands,
> that She may bring life,
> that She may endure.
> Come, rise, Goddess of the Sky.
> Come, rise, O Hathor.
> You are exalted in the light of Ra.
> To you belongs everything,
> all people love you.
> Great is your majesty
> when you shine forth in the sky.
> To you have been given
> the sky, deep night, and the stars.

Ani addressed the apprentices. Her voice reflected the soft hoarseness of one who is struggling to return to consciousness after a journey in the Duat.

"I honor Hathor and her spirit of excitement that is so is alive and awake in the music. Your movements and your mesmerizing sounds mirror the eternal dance between Earth and sky." Then, motioning to the lead dancer of the group, Ani invited her to address the group. "Come, Teyet. Please share your thoughts with us."

"Music-making and moving our bodies in rhythm with the fire of life is what we live for," Teyet said. "It makes our lives an offering to our beloved Hathor, Lady of Heaven, Mistress of the Night, Mother of Horus, Goddess of Love and Joy. On the surface it appears we are mere entertainers who enjoy what we do. But I assure you there is more to it. Much more. Using the body as an instrument of magic generates power that must be guided. Music intoxicates, like wine. Both are magical instruments, and like all such instruments, have a dangerous side.

"This sistrum is my wand of power and my instrument of praise. Priestesses, even goddesses, have used this to accomplish miraculous things. Isis could cause blindness with her sistrum. Others used it to fight Typhon. These are surely great feats. But this modest object is great in power, for it is also the instrument that perpetually keeps creation in motion. It shows that everything that exists should shake and never stop moving. Stories about the sistrum's power to ward off evil and do deeds of revenge show how its power can halt decay and ruin, even death, undo limitations on the mind. The power of creation sets us free and restores each of us by means of movement. The sistrum is power to control the rage and violence of wrathful deities.

"The king, His Royal Highness, Khufu, Son of Horus, Lord of the Two Lands, knows of these things. When Pharaoh enters Hathor's Temple on festival days carrying her musical instruments, he brings the power to control the turbulent divinities residing there. Contact with powerful beings is dangerous, my sisters. If you have not yet learned this firsthand, you will. One has to be trained well and properly, no matter what god or goddess one serves. The time will come when your knowledge and skills will be tested.

"The sistrum," Teyet said as she shook the instrument in her hand, "is a rod of power to petition a deity to cast a merciful face towards you instead of a face of vengeance. In the face resides the deity's power. The power revealed in the face, be it of a deity or demon, is the power of *sekhem*, which is also one of the names of the sistrum. It is also one of the names linked to Sekhmet, the powerful, ominous one.

"Anyone, including Hathor's priests and priestesses, who enters the presence of the king of Egypt must hold their hands before their face to shield themselves from his countenance. He possesses this power because he is a living god. He is the great lord Osiris. The power he manifests as the one ruler under the authority of Ra can strike down the unprotected and those who may have knowledge but not the skill to apply it. Witness of this kingly power is written in the oldest of the sacred texts which says 'On whom my Pharaoh's wrath falls, his head shall not stay in place.' This is why the frontal aspect of a deity is rarely depicted in paintings, sculpture, or reliefs. Such a power is not displayed openly or revealed in a trivial manner, for it is a force that must be approached with caution. If so, it transforms into a beneficial energy.

"Egypt is coming into an important time, the beginning of a new year. This event is heralded by a sky phenomenon, the predawn rising of Sirius. Many among the *fellahin* fear this time because of its potential for disease, pollution, and fevers. Yet it also brings the promise of renewal, fertility, and prosperity. The appearance of Sirius is bittersweet, with destruction and death and creation and life interwoven.

"For Hathor's priests and priestesses, the rising of the Great Star has another meaning. Hathor is a giver and taker of life. She is linked to fertility and agriculture, to growing. She is the goddess of moisture and vegetation. At the time of the rising of Sirius on the first day of the month of Thoth, we will celebrate the festival of Hathor's birth."

Teyet's speech finished, she descended the dais and took her place among her sister priestesses. The grace of her body testified to the beauty and power of the deity she served.

Ani walked to the center of the platform. With a glance toward the Hathors, she smiled. "The great and mighty goddess you serve brings much joy to the people of Egypt. She brings overwhelming joy to Ra, whose deep love for her inspires him to cross the sky each day. Her power motivates the journey of the Sun, and for this we are grateful." Looking at the audience of priestesses, Ani closed the occasion with a deep sigh and a pertinent reminder. "Remember, my sisters, what you have seen and heard today. You are dismissed."

The first dozen loads of granite had arrived at the building site where the massive labor force had begun construction on what Khufu vowed would be the most beautiful and magical Temple in the Two Lands of Upper and Lower Egypt.

The morning heat was already scorching and cast a haze over the desert. Mornings like this made Sokar grateful for his station in life, for it afforded him the coolness and comfort of his lavish quarters. Though this morning seemed no different from any other, little did he know that before Ra had finished his journey across the sky that blithe assumption would be proven wrong.

Sokar strolled onto the vine-covered patio. Its soft trickle of the water and the fresh, sweet scent of the lotus pleased him. Sitting down on the cobalt rim, he leaned over the pool and touched a blossom. Sokar studied the delicate flower, tilting it from side to side. What a beautiful flower you are. Sokar spoke to the blossom telepathically. You are like me. You seek out the light of Ra. I do so with my mind. But you, a flower—I don't know. Perhaps you seek light for the same reason, to renew your life every day, someday to reach immortality. If you, beautiful flower, have another reason, then you possess a great mystery. At noon, when the Sun is highest in the sky, you spew out your seeds just as the Sun god throws out his life-giving rays.

Sokar released the flower, turned around on the rim of the pool, put his head in his hands, and rested his elbows on his knees. He sighed deeply. He felt his soul was naked. It was almost time to take the magical steps to fulfill the demands of the ghost. She was desperate, and that could only mean problems for him, problems he did not need. It was time for his new plan, time to rendezvous with his magical partner, Horus.

Kheti walked onto the patio carrying a tray of breakfast food and drink. "Good morning, Master," Kheti said, his body bent at the waist in his customary bow. "Your breakfast."

When Sokar looked at Kheti he felt relief about his change of plans to rob his faithful valet of his body. Sokar felt the force of loyalty tug at him. Kheti had always been there; his loyalty at times bordered on adoration.

"Will you be going out today, master?" Kheti asked. "Shall I get out street clothing?"

Sokar did not answer. His mind was far away.

"Master?" Kheti spoke again, a puzzled look spreading over his face. "Are you all right?"

Sokar snapped out of his reverie and looked at Kheti. "Oh, yes, Kheti. I will be going out after the Sun has gone past its zenith when it is cooler. I will go to the Temple of the Sun. I have business there, and later I will be spending time with Horus. There is work to be done."

By the time Sokar reached the gates of the Temple of the Sun, a breeze had taken the edge off the blistering heat. The great palms on each side of the colossal cedar doors, as old as the gateway they guarded, swayed in the light wind. Sokar walked through the gates and crossed the tiled pavilion. This was what made a temple a Temple: the beauty of the hand-painted tiles that formed a mural of the Sun, the majestic lotus-crowned columns, the statues of Ra and his family carved from red and black granite and alabaster.

Sokar made his way to the library, pausing at the foot of a gilded statue of Ra to offer a prayer. Entering the lobby of the main scroll room, he approached a scribe seated at a table. With his customary smile and pleasant tone of voice, Sokar asked in the name of the royal family that he be let into one of the library's antechambers. He knew rare old texts were stored there. The scribe led the way.

Sokar relied on his intuition to guide him to the text that contained what he sought. Closing his eyes and biting his lower lip in concentration, he felt pulled to a particular scroll in a clay jar. The scroll was tied with embroidered linen. Sokar glanced around the room to make sure he was alone. Taking the scroll, he sat at a table with an oil lamp. The small Temple room was dim in the afternoon light even so.

Sokar immediately saw the scroll was very old and would not survive rough treatment. He unrolled the yellowed papyrus. The title read "Pert Em Hru." Sokar realized he had chosen a book of spells. He felt energy flow through him, a sensation he always interpreted as confirmation he was in the right place at the right time.

Sokar came to a table of contents. Scanning the list rapidly, he saw a spell for inflicting a dreamless sleep upon an enemy. After reading the first part of the enchantment, he spurned accepting it. Sokar would not use such a spell to accomplish his purpose. This was revenge.

Another passage caught his eye. This script was a copy of the *Book of Coming*. This was a spell of transformation for moving from one level of existence to another, the success of which depended upon the magician performing the rite. The ritual was performed as a "journey" through the Duat, beginning in the West and through the Duat until the end of the Darkness of Night. The operator went into the region of the Duat behind the Earth, where the Sun passes on its sojourn from East to West.

Sokar drank in every word of the script. No magician would dare attempt a rite such as this alone. He needed to make sure the one he designated to assist him was qualified and confident. Sokar thought of the second most powerful magician he knew, his hawk. Horus could help Sokar demolish the threat of interference that Bakka's ghost presented to the important magic to come in a day or two, and for which he needed his full powers.

For a human practitioner alone, the ritual would take twelve hours to complete. It would not take Horus and Sokar that long, however, as one of the bird's powers was his ability to travel through time at incredible speed. Powerful spirits were involved, but Sokar had confidence in his familiar. Reading further in the manuscript, he saw there were preparations to make. The ritual had to be done at night and consisted of twelve visualizations, meaning Sokar's magical tool would be his imagination.

Sokar closed his eyes and sighed. How could he get this scroll out of the library without being detected? He would bully the High Lector priest, Eucrates. If there was anything Sokar was a master of, it was intimidation. He would only need the scroll for a few hours, and would guarantee its safe return, he'd tell Eucrates.

Sokar rolled up the papyrus carefully and put it back into its jar. He left the room and strolled out into the main hall and on to the doorway to Eucrates's office, where he encountered several apprentice scribes waiting for an audience. Seeing the three apprentices gave Sokar an idea. He exchanged pleasantries, then, singling out the youngest, he introduced himself as Sokar, half-brother to the Son of Horus Incarnate, the venerable Khufu, and as a priest of the Temple of the *Benu*. The formality of Sokar's demeanor and the weight of his titles accomplished what he hoped.

"I need a special favor," he said, "and I would like to have it done without bother to Eucrates. I know he is a busy man." Sokar's charm was, as always, mesmerizing to the unsuspecting apprentice. "Please forgive me, but I do not believe I know your name."

"Atef," the lad replied in a friendly tone.

"Ah, Atef. I am pleased to make your acquaintance."

Sokar vaguely remembered having met the young man before. There was no sign that Atef remembered ever meeting Sokar.

"What is the favor you would ask, honorable one?" Atef asked, a puzzled look on his face.

"There is a manuscript I wish to have delivered to the Temple of the *Benu*, to the House of Life there, so that a copy can be made to replace one that I accidentally destroyed when I caused an oil lamp to overturn. Since the unfortunate event was my fault, I wish to rectify the situation by having the loss replaced as soon as possible before my clumsy deed is discovered. Will you help me?"

Without saying the words, Sokar's demeanor transmitted to Atef the acute anger and even embarrassment he had suffered due to a quirk of fate that robbed him of his rightful position as Pharaoh. Atef concluded that there would be no harm in offering to make the copy Sokar requested. Besides, he was proud to be asked to do a favor for a member of the royal family. Atef's naïveté allowed the magician the leverage he needed to take advantage of the apprentice scribe.

"Pardon me, sir, but I cannot remove the scroll from these premises. I have no such authority. But I can help you. I will make the copy for you."

"How kind of you, my lad. I am in your debt," Sokar said, visualizing a shield of authority to assure Atef that the request was not out of line. The apprentice had no reason to suspect being singled out to perform a simple job for a high-ranking citizen and priest who might someday return the favor. He did not see how he could get into trouble or jeopardize the library or its safety, but he also didn't know he had been conned into believing what he saw, which was precisely what Sokar wanted him to see.

Chapter Fifty-Three

Omen of Danger

Egyptians woke to the blinding burst of the sun rising above the horizon. The air hung heavy. It was going to be one of those days when the heat would test the endurance of every man, beast, and fowl.

The building of the Star Temple at Giza was going well. Even Nemon was surprised, and his promise of a bonus to the laborers if the construction proceeded efficiently and smoothly might have to be awarded. The workers had been so inspired that they had decided to work in shifts, so the project moved ahead of schedule, as if aided by the gods.

When Khufu awoke, he thought of Osiris, remembering a journey on the royal barge as a boy with his father and the royal entourage to the Temple of Osiris in Abydos. It was the first time he had witnessed the ritual of the Priests of Osiris attending to the needs of the god. After a purifying bath in the Temple's sacred pool, a dozen priests had entered the main gate, proceeded through the courtyard, and, after breaking the seals on its door, gone into the sanctuary. At the moment the Sun first cast its rays over the horizon, a priest had swung open the doors to reveal the effigy of Osiris. The chanting of prayers sounded in the fresh morning air already scented with sweet incense.

Khufu had stood proudly by his father, bearing the position of crown prince with honor, even at ten. The priest removed the statue from its niche, divested it of its garments, and cleansed it with tremendous care. When the statue was dressed with a fresh, perfumed raiment, it was put back in its place. The priest presented the god with food and drink before resealing the sanctuary and leaving. . . .

This scene had made an indelible impression on Khufu and now replayed in his mind. It would soon be time for him to perform that same task. The court Nile reader had reported a rise of several feet in the river. The flood waters were coming; Mother Nile was turning green.

Manetho arrived in the Throne Room with his daily report. The Pharaoh listened with particular interest to his summation that began with the water level measurement and ended with word that the last barge of stone from Silsilis had arrived at Giza. Khufu was pleased and grateful. Everything was on schedule.

"Majesty, while all the news is good," Manetho said calmly, "there is reason to suspect that all may not be as well as it seems."

"What do you mean?" Khufu inquired, anxious.

"Well, nothing really, I mean nothing that constitutes hard evidence, that is," Manetho replied. The vizier walked closer to the great chair with a look of apprehension. "I had a dream, Your Majesty, a disturbing dream."

"Well, out with it. What was your dream?"

Manetho was clearly troubled as he turned to pace the floor and wring his hands. "There was not much to it, Majesty, at least as I remember. I saw you, sitting like you are now, on the throne. There was an aura of bright, golden light around you. Out of nowhere came a huge hawk, its talons outstretched like knives, its eyes flashing!"

Khufu regarded his vizier with a puzzled look.

"I know. It does not sound like much of a dream, my lord, but what happened next bothers me." Manetho told Khufu how the giant hawk had flown into the king's body through the top of his head. "It possessed you, my king. It became you! It did not seem right, not a good sign. The hawk seemed vicious. It invaded your body and your mind."

"Do you think the dream is an omen?"

"Yes, I do," Manetho answered, serious. "I think the hawk was from the Underworld, sent by a magician *or* was the magician himself in a bird's body. I am not sure which. I am not a seer. But I am sure of one thing, Majesty. I am sure the hawk was not an innocent visitor."

Sokar. "If your dream is an indication that a magician is attacking me in the Duat, then I need more protection," Khufu said. "Send a message to Lady Taret to come right away."

Sokar stood by Horus's perch and gently stroked the hawk's head. The afternoon sun cast a light on the feathers that made them glow with the color of smoldering embers. His thoughts were on the ritual, on the scroll he had talked Atef into copying and delivering to him. The time had come for him to prepare Horus for the ritual that would obliterate the ghost from his life and from the Duat for good. Inundation was close, the first day of the season of Thoth and the start of a new year, and the energy was building.

"You have done well, my friend." Sokar was remembering the last "assignment" he had given Horus, to enter Khufu's mind and plant the thought that whenever he encountered the hawk he would know it was Sokar. Soon he would force Khufu's hand. The Pharaoh would be engaged in a war. He would have to defend the sovereignty of the Throne, but not before the people. Sokar would weaken Khufu by engaging him in a battle most could not see. He would prevent Khufu and his government from being sole rulers of Egypt, and he would do it with magic. His thoughts were interrupted by Kheti coming out onto the patio.

"Master," Kheti said, with his usual bow. "I am sorry to disturb you, but you have received a message from Memphis. The scroll the courier has brought has the seal of the royal palace."

"A message? From the palace?" Sokar's mind raced. "The palace. Then I must see to its contents right away."

Sokar tried to sound as if a message from the royal palace was nothing out of the ordinary, and that he was not anxious about its contents. "Fetch the message scroll, Kheti. I may be needed in Memphis. These are auspicious times."

Taret's house servant wakened her from an afternoon nap. Khufu had sent for her, and she should report to the Throne Room right away. She expected Meri-ib and Shemshu-Hor there too, but found herself alone with the king.

Khufu greeted her respectfully. "Thank you for your prompt response to my summons, Lady Taret."

Bending in a customary bow, Taret replied, "Of course, Your Majesty. I detected an urgency in your request."

"Yes, you are right, Madam Taret." He then turned to the royal guards and fan bearers, and motioned to them with a swift wave of his hand. "Leave us in privacy. Go."

Khufu went straight to the point. "Manetho has had a dream that has alarmed him regarding my safety in the Duat. If there is a threat to my safety, I am certain I know who it is: Sokar."

Taret's lips tightened and the muscles in her face twitched. She knew he was right. "It is time to make a move, Your Majesty. There is a priestess named Tiye, a Nubian, who possesses an ability to make powerful amulets. With Your Majesty's approval I will send for her immediately."

Tiye was preparing for her afternoon rituals. Her life at the Temple of Sekhmet was becoming easier. She had spent the last few afternoons with the High Priestess Amenti. She found her kind and gentle, and Tiye sensed strength in her. Amenti had questioned her about her relationship with Sekhmet and the goddess's alter ego, Hathor. Amenti said it was time to take the Nubian under her wing and teach her more about the lioness-headed deity. Tiye recalled her first teaching from Amenti.

"I know you are aware of the destructive powers of our beloved goddess. But there is more you do not know about her. Sekhmet is the beloved of the great god Ptah, the Master Mason. She is a fierce destroyer, yes, but she is also the goddess of renewal. Sekhmet brings changes by tearing things down so that Ptah can rebuild them on a more solid foundation. From destruction and rebuilding, a third is born, a son, Nefertem, the god of healing and medicine."

Just as Tiye was about to start her daily prayer ritual before Sekhmet, a knock came at the door.

It was Mutirkis delivering a message that had come by courier from the palace. Tiye was summoned to meet with Taret the following day, and she was to say nothing to anyone about it. . . .

When Tiye arrived at the gates of the royal mansion, she was met by two guards and carried by enclosed litter to Taret's wing of the complex. After a gracious welcome, servants brought beer and fig cakes. Tiye drank the beer thirstily, but was too nervous to eat. Taret sent the serving girls and her fan bearers away so she and Tiye could be alone. "I know you are anxious to know why I have sent for you, Tiye. So I will get straight to the point. There is reason to believe that King Khufu is under psychic attack."

"What has happened?"

"The vizier Manetho had a dream that disturbed him and left him with a fear for Pharaoh's safety and the sanctity of the Throne. The king must be protected in every possible way. That is where you are needed, my child. You must employ your skills and make an amulet for Lord Khufu, one for each of his family members, and three others for key members of the court. One will go to Manetho, the other two will be in safekeeping until the need arises, the Neters forbid that such be so."

Taret's straightforwardness inspired Tiye. She saw she was relied upon and trusted by no less than the king of Egypt. The pride and self-confidence that welled up in her was something she had never felt before. It caught her off guard. "I don't know what to say, Mistress Taret, but yes, yes, I am at your service," Tiye said.

It was class time again for Khem. Today Ani's teaching centered on the imminent rising of Sirius. "Like people, stars are not always as they appear. When you see a star, its bright light looks like one big star. But with some stars, this is not so. The Nile Star that embodies the power of Isis is really three stars. Three star worlds. I will tell you about the smallest and most obscure of the worlds, the home of the Star Women of Sirius.

"To us as Star Priestesses, the third star world of Sirius, the Star of Women, is present, though our physical eyes cannot see it. We can see it with inner vision. On the planet that resides within that star world exists a holy order of Star Priestesses." Ani's words brought a gasp from the apprentices when they realized they had "counterparts" in another star system. "It was from them that during the First Time a Star Woman came to Earth, bringing the knowledge we now possess and the celestial magic we now practice.

"The Priestess of Sirius was among the First Coming of the Star Gods to Earth. She brought peace and civilization. She is the soul of every woman. She is in each of you and you are in her. In the old language, the Star of Women is represented by an equal-armed cross outlined by three points surrounded by seven dots. The power of the symbol pertains to the four female and three male powers that make the sacred seven. So this symbol represents the members of the Council of Seven, four Star Priestesses, three Star Priests.

"It is time now that one of these Star Priestesses returns to Earth. She will be the first of the returning Star Gods. She brings her power and prophecies for Egypt."

Khem could not contain her excitement. "May I speak, Madam High Priestess?" Shocked that she had interrupted Ani's teaching, she would not have blamed the High Priestess for reprimanding her.

"Yes, Khem? What do you wish to say?" Ani replied.

"I think I know what you are going to say. I saw it in a vision. The Star Woman will come in the body of the comet!"

Khem felt her soul was bared. She had revealed her vision on the gamble she was correct. With her eyes fixed intently in anticipation of Ani's expression, she was relieved to see that it was approval.

"Yes, Khem. Your vision is indeed accurate. The Comet Woman looks down at us even as I speak. The comet brings her, and soon she will appear to us all."

Khem was thrilled. Her communication with the Comet Woman was valid. She was more confident now about herself and her intuition than she had ever been.

"The Sirian Star Women," Ani resumed, "who are the ancestors of all the women of Earth, comprise the original Holy Order of Nut from which our order was founded. The Sirian Star Woman and the Comet Woman"—looking at Khem—"are the same. She comes to bring a higher knowledge to us and to initiate a new generation of Star Priestesses."

Khufu was awaiting Lady Taret and Tiye. If this young apprentice is as adept as she is touted to be, I will be happy to have her make protection amulets for me and my loved ones, he thought. Standing by the window of the Throne Room and gazing out over the desert, Pharaoh remembered the Sirius Council he had "seen" in the secret chamber beneath the Sphinx. Khufu had dismissed his servants and guards so he could be alone, yet he felt a presence. The west corner of the room began to fill with a swirling yellow-gold mist. Just as the vortex of energy seemed it would take a form, a strong, deep male voice spoke out:

> I am Osiris, perfect before the gods.
> My body is perfect, made so by suffering and trial.
> The scent of the dying rose is like the sigh of my suffering,
> and the red fire is the energy of my will.
> The bread and the salt are as the foundations of my body,
> which I destroy in order that they may be renewed.

> I am Osiris, the Triumphant, the Justified One.
> I am He who is clothed with the body of flesh
> yet in whom flames the spirit of the eternal gods.
> I am the Lord of Life, victorious over Death.
> Whoever partakes with me shall arise.
> I am manifest in matter for those who dwell in the invisible.
> I am the purified.
> I stand upon the universe.
> I am its reconciler with the eternal gods.
> I am the perfector of matter,
> and without me, the universe is not.

The voice faded, leaving an echo as the swirling yellow-gold mist floated to the throne and took form. Before Khufu's eyes, the heavenly king took shape. Upon the great chair sat Osiris, the Double Crown of Egypt on his head. The Crook in one hand, the Flail in the other crossed on his chest, the wooden beard of Pharaoh strapped to his chin. The figure sat perfectly still. Then, the deity was gone.

Khufu was jolted when the chief servant of the Throne Room entered, bowing, and spoke in a low tone. "The Lady Taret, former High Priestess of the Temple of the Sun, Star Priestess of the Holy Order of Nut, and venerable member of the Sirius Council, has arrived. She is accompanied by a Nubian named Tiye. Begging the pardon of Your Majesty, I did not mean to interrupt you," the servant said, bending again in a deep bow.

"No, no, I mean—it is all right. I was lost in my thoughts. Please, do send them in." He withdrew himself from the vision of Osiris. There was business to attend to, though he heard more words, "Whoever partakes with me shall arise. . . ."

As Taret and Tiye entered the chambers, Tiye was in awe of the King of Egypt. The energy in the room was electric with his presence, but she sensed a greater power. It was the first time Tiye had been before a living god.

Khufu graciously welcomed the priestesses, saying to Tiye, "I am pleased to meet you, Daughter of Nut and the Great One of the Flame, the beloved Sekhmet. Your reputation as a maker of amulets precedes you." Khufu said this warmly, a slight smile softening the chiseled lines in his face.

Tiye was speechless, but gathered her wits enough to kneel at his feet.

Taret spoke. "Your Majesty's power is both gracious and overwhelming to one who has never looked upon the countenance of the Son of Horus. Please, you must forgive Tiye's loss of words."

"Yes, of course, I understand," Khufu replied. Then, turning to Tiye, he said, "I am sure Lady Taret has informed you of the reason you have been summoned."

The Nubian cleared her throat, now as dry as the desert air. "Yes, Your Highness. I am aware."

Pharaoh stepped up onto the royal dais, sat down, and rested his chin on his right hand, his elbow propped on the arm of the great chair.

"Your Majesty, I shall be brief," Taret said. "At this point, my best judgment is to have Tiye make an amulet that will protect you in the Duat and your dreaming from the hawk. I associate Sokar with the hawk, Majesty. After all, a great bird is his magical familiar, the one that does his bidding. If Sokar intends to threaten the Throne in any way he is likely to do so with the aid of that hawk."

Tiye hung on Taret's every word. It was unnerving to hear such extraordinary and secret affairs being openly discussed.

"One trained in *heka* might automatically think that an amulet made in the likeness of a hawk would be the likely image for dealing with a hawk in the Duat," Taret said. "But I do not think it wise to use this form. I prefer Tiye make the special protection amulets in the image of the goddess Sekhmet.

"Your Majesty, she is the mighty one, the warrior. I, for one, believe that this is an occasion that calls for a warrior. She is all powerful, especially here in our beloved Memphis. Here the amulets will be made. Sekhmet, as you are well aware, my king, is the provider of strength to pharaohs who go into battle. As I see it, you are going into battle, a magic battle."

Khufu absorbed the High Priestess's words. "The divine one, daughter of Ra, beloved wife of Ptah, is a warrior," Khufu said as he left the throne and began to pace slowly in front of the dais. "She is impatient and hotheaded for a fact, but the passion, though it can be destructive, does not rage ceaselessly. She is also merciful, for she is capable of using her power for healing and preserving others."

"Exactly my point, Your Majesty. Sekhmet can protect and heal, but she can also destroy. She is without question the choice I would make. With passion for the beloved goddess, I am certain Tiye's power will be at its peak. The work will surely provide an opportunity for our Nubian to join forces with the Lady of the Flame."

Tiye stood silently in what, to her, was a surreal scene. She would play a role in protecting the King and Egypt. Even as she thought of Sokar, that man with the hawk on his shoulder, surely a formidable foe, her strength did not waver. She felt Sekhmet inside her.

Khufu trusted Taret's judgment. He would leave the task of the amulet-making with these two. Turning to Tiye, he said that he could feel Sekhmet's power in her. "Sekhmet and Bastet are alive in you. The wicked fear Sekhmet's destruction and loathe the love of Bastet, whose light dispels the darkness where evil dwells. Go in peace, Tiye. Surely the power of the Neters is with you."

Chapter Fifty-Four

The Goddess-Bearing Comet

When Lady Taret and Tiye left the Throne Room they went to Taret's private chamber in the palace. Tiye had never seen such splendor as she strolled through the hallways of the most celebrated building in all of Egypt. Its walls depicted the lives of the pharaohs, including Khufu and his royal wife, and there were many gilded statues of Ptah, Sekhmet, and Nefertem, the divine trinity of Memphis.

Tiye lagged behind Taret as she studied the wall leading into the palace's residential wing. Its artwork depicted the Lady of the Flame in the most beautiful female body Tiye had ever seen. An orange sheath clung to her body from breasts to ankles. Braided gold straps from the sheath's bodice snaked between the breasts, and crossed over her shoulders to tie at the back of her neck. The goddess had a lion's head out of whose crown rose a golden cobra with emerald eyes. The golden solar disk hung above the head of the magnificent figure; a male lion lay at her feet, its paws crossed one upon the other. The great serpent of the underworld, Apep, lay dead in the background, along with seven demons of Seth, the brother of Osiris, Isis, and their sister Nepthys. Apep and the demons had been slain by the avenging Sekhmet.

Taret did not want to interrupt Tiye's link with the goddess. The High Priestess herself had had numerous such experiences with her own beloved Nut, Isis, and others. But time was pressing and there was a great deal of work to be done while the Moon was waxing. Taret put her hand gently on Tiye's arm. The touch snapped Tiye out of her trance.

"I am sorry, Mistress Taret," Tiye said quickly and nervously. "I got caught up in the Lady's image."

"I understand, my Star Daughter. Come, let us have a cool drink in my quarters. We must talk."

Khem lay in her bed reviewing the events of the day, especially the Comet Woman. High above Egypt's parched soil the comet sped through space bearing the Star Woman of Sirius on her return to Earth to walk among her human children again.

Bast purred in a restful state and the soft sound lulled Khem into sleep. Khem soon found herself floating over the Temple of the Sun, watching a procession of initiates walk onto the shore after a rite of purification in the Sacred Lake. The two priests leading the procession were dressed as the jackal-headed gods Anubis and *Wepwawet*, the Openers of the Way. The rest wore white linen robes. The procession came to the doors of the Temple where the initiates were blindfolded, then escorted inside. Khem saw a huge cow with a litter on its back bearing a statue of Isis in her form of golden cow. The image was enshrouded in black linen. The initiates led the cow and her precious cargo around the Temple's precinct seven times.

Khem came into the presence of Isis in her guise as Sopdet, wearing the Double Crown of Egypt, a star on its apex.

The dreaming Khem recognized Isis as the Comet Woman.

"I am Isis, the eldest daughter of Geb and Nut, wife and sister of Osiris, mother of Horus," the figure said. "I am she who rises with the Great Star, the goddess of women, who revealed the map of the stars, who commands the journeys of the Sun and the Moon. I am the queen of river, wind, and sea. I rise beyond destiny. Fate listens to my voice and obeys my wishes.

"I deliver evildoers into the hands of those they injure. I protect the guardians of truth. With me, the justice of the gods prevails. I destroy tyrants and cause truth to prevail and shine brighter than gold and silver. Words of an ancient spell have been delivered by your earthly brother into the hands of an evildoer! Make this known."

Khem awoke with a start. Earthly brother? Atef? Could it be? Surely her brother was innocent of such wrongdoing! But what else could Isis mean?

The noonday sun was unrelenting, the heat stifling. In the House of Life, Atef was copying an old text when he received the message that his sister was waiting in the foyer of the scroll room. Thoughts of their parents' well-being raced through his head as he grasped Khem's shoulders and kissed her on each cheek. "Sister, what is it? Is something wrong? Are you all right?"

"Yes, Atef. I am fine," Khem answered firmly. "I have come to tell you about a dream I had. No, it wasn't a dream; it was a vision of Isis."

Atef knew that Khem would not have come to the House of Life, most likely missing her class, if it was not important.

"Did you give anything to Sokar, the king's half-brother?" Khem blurted out.

Atef was surprised. Yes, he had copied the spell for the magician-priest to replace a manuscript that had gotten damaged while in his possession. He had done it as a favor, and had not given it much thought.

"Why do you ask? It was a favor, and it gave me the opportunity to read from one of the oldest scrolls in the Temple."

Khem took a firm hold of her brother's arm. "Tell me what kind of spell it was," Khem asked in an urgent, low whisper.

Atef was beginning to get annoyed at being questioned about something he thought trivial. What could make it a cause for his sister's alarm? "Wait, slow down, Khem. Tell me what this is all about."

Khem related her dream to Atef. She placed particular emphasis on what the goddess had communicated about "an evildoer," and Atef's role in providing that "doer" with a spell. Atef listened intently, his facial expressions shifting from annoyed curiosity to a frown. Could an "innocent" favor lead to a spell to cause harm? Atef realized he had been duped and used by Sokar to obtain information that could cause harm to a trusting person.

"You have done nothing wrong, my brother. Your generous and kind nature has been betrayed," Khem said. "What is done is done. But do you remember the contents of the spell?"

"Yes, I remember. It was a transformation spell. Something about changing levels of existence in the Duat."

Atef, a downtrodden look on his face, said, "What is done is done. I cannot change that." Then hope spread across his face. "Wait! Maybe there is something I can do. There must be a spell that will counteract the one I copied for Sokar. If there is, I will find it."

The rising of Sirius was imminent. The High Priestess was supersensitive to the energy of this time of year. No time was more sacred than this, no event more special than the predawn rising of the Nile Star. When such energies peak, events that occur, good or bad, are enhanced. The same is true for magical acts, Taret knew.

Taret led Tiye into her palace quarters. The task ahead required magical precision and nothing and no one would be allowed to compromise that. "I assume you understand my reason for drawing upon Sekhmet to empower the royal amulets?"

Tiye looked at the elder priestess with confidence. "Yes, I understand that, mistress, and I am honored to do this work with the goddess. Are you certain I am worthy of the task?"

"It is not for me to pass judgment any further than my actions have displayed," Taret said. "The question is whether you believe yourself worthy. Let's get started. What does your inner voice tell you is the most appropriate material to use?"

After a moment of thought, the Nubian answered. "The amulets will only be used temporarily, but we cannot know how long that will be. They should be made of something that will hold up to being handled under the crisis of the situation. I would choose clay from the Nile, clay I can mold into two deities with three heads."

"Two Neters, three heads? I do not understand. Explain."

Tiye told her a story Khaba had related about the double-headed lion god Aker. "Aker was a guardian of the Underworld and he watched over the entrance and the exit to insure the safe passage of Ra on his nightly journey," Tiye replied, giggling. "When I was bad, Khaba would tell me Aker was watching me. It would scare me."

"I see," Taret said thoughtfully. "Your three heads are Aker and Sekhmet, two deities. Aker has two heads, Sekhmet one."

"Yes, yes, that is right," Tiye answered eagerly. "I can mold them into one image for His Majesty's protection. It will invoke the power of all the lion gods and goddesses. They will represent and embody the awesome power of Sekhmet."

Tiye's eyes blazed with the passion she felt from Sekhmet inside, her rage and splendor. Taret was spellbound by the power emanating from the Nubian. It was as if Tiye *were* Sekhmet.

"Yes, you are right. Clay from the Nile. I will have it brought to you right away," Taret said.

"No, please, Lady Taret. Let me. Permit me to gather it myself," Tiye replied anxiously. "I will go now."

"All right. Go, but return here to my quarters before Ra has begun his nightly journey. I will send guards with you if you wish."

"Thank you, holy mistress."

Tiye rarely ventured outdoors past sunset, but this dusk would be different. She knew she should go to the Nile when Ra's life-draining hours of searing heat were over. Even though Taret had instructed her to return before dark, Tiye needed to see the river by the light of the stars so she agreed to the guards. It was not the invisible dangers that a priestess could face that concerned Taret but the visible ones for a young woman.

With two palace guards a short distance behind her, Tiye went to the banks of the river where the purple and gold sunset was reflecting in the water, casting up the same colors into the desert air. The river marshes were alive with activity. Fragrant lotuses floated in the wake of ripples made by frogs leaping into the cool water. Egrets, white wings fluttering, took flight. The smell of the river refreshed Tiye and bought back memories of playing in the pools that often collected between stones and the tributaries of Mother Nile.

Today Tiye began filling a jug with mud and thought of Sekhmet as the Goddess of the Setting Sun. This is why I had to come to the river at sunset, Tiye thought. You are here with me. I see your reflection in the sky and water. You are all around me, everywhere. You are displaying yourself in the Heavens, and the waters of Mother Nile.

Tiye was exuberant. Everything in her life was culminating in this very moment. There was enough light for her to see her reflection in the water. In that fleeting moment, Tiye caught a strange glimpse of herself. The face was not hers, but a mighty lioness with eyes like gold nuggets. A faint smile spread across her face. Seeing herself transformed into Sekhmet was an experience she must get used to for she sensed it would occur time and again for the rest of her life.

A dream awakened Sokar and a clammy sweat covered his body. He had dreamed of a woman. This time it wasn't the female ghost who invaded his sleep. It was a woman *in* the comet.

Sokar went out onto his patio. The night air chilled his skin, still damp from his sweat. Sight of the blue-and-white-tailed comet brought the details of the dream back. He was flying alongside the comet when it transformed into a woman, strong in body and beautiful to behold, a goddess of the night sky. Nut? Surely he must have been in the presence of the Sky Mother. But. . . .

"No, you are not Nut!" Sokar's words hissed between clenched teeth. "You are a Star Priestess. You are Isis! You are She returning!"

Sokar knew he was right. His dream vessel had been in the presence of Isis, most powerful of all magicians, including the Great Father Ra.

What does this mean? Sokar asked himself. What is the message I am being sent? He recalled the prophecy of the Second Coming of the Star Gods. The priesthood had always known that time would come, though no one had known precisely when the Star People who had brought the ancient knowledge to Egypt and entrusted it to the hands of the Followers of Horus would return. Was this now the time when the Great Ones would reappear among men and she would be the first? It had to be. It was the only answer he could find for the Star Woman making herself known to him. But why to me?

He could not look at the comet in the same way again. No longer would it be a mere feast for the eyes or a beautiful, glowing ball of light transiently gracing the firmament. The "visitor" is the living Star Woman, Isis. So the Second Coming was at hand. What did it bode for him, the bastard son of a long-dead king, struggling to lay claim to his heritage? Was the great goddess an ally or foe?

Shemshu-Hor sat quietly in his tiny room in the *Benu* Temple, in the shadows of the dim light put off by a sputtering oil lamp. Night was when he communed with his fellow Star Gods, his brothers and sisters who had returned to the sky world leaving him behind among humanity. For ages he had been the "watcher" and the "protector" of the teachings brought to the Earth during the First Time.

He knew the time for the long-awaited return of his celestial brethren was at hand. Now, in the stillness of the night he surrounded himself with ceremonial objects spread on a linen cloth yellowed with age. The cloth was embroidered with symbols like hieroglyphs, but they were not. These were taken from a cuneiform known by no one else on Earth but Shemshu-Hor. Nine tools of magic lay on the beautiful cloth. Shemshu-Hor thought of them as instruments, and he kept them finely tuned at all times. Each linked his mind with minds of the Star Gods.

This night the Elder felt a calling from the goddess Isis. Shemshu-Hor picked up one of the objects and held it in his hand. It was a small diamond wand. Circling the cap of the shaft and attached by a thick strand of gold was a chunk of meteorite.

The wand felt warm to the touch and pulsed with the life of a being with whom the old man had shared a relationship since the First Time. It was his link with Isis, his peer and fellow Sirian. He always communicated with Isis at the time of year when all Egyptians witnessed the rising of the Great Star. But this time Shemshu-Hor would connect minds with the goddess for a special reason. He felt her presence as nearer than he had in a long time, and he anticipated that his "conversation" with her would confirm what he already knew.

The Old One put the diamond and meteorite wand back on the cloth and untied a flaxen bag from the sash around his waist. Inside, wrapped securely in palm leaves, was a piece of myrrh; he dropped it gently into a small brazier large enough to hold but a few glowing embers of sycamore wood. A wisp of smoke went up from the brazier and filled the room with fragrance.

He took up the wand again and this time, after taking a deep breath, he held the meteorite capstone to his brow. As he exhaled, he whispered, "Isis, my Star Sister, take me to where you are now." Shemshu-Hor removed the wand from his brow and placed it in his lap. His eyes remained closed in anticipation of an answer in the form of a vision.

The Old One's keen mind focused upon a location in space and the image of a blazing comet came into his consciousness. The Wise One knew that his fellow Star Gods would adapt to any form necessary for their journeys through the universe, so he did not question the revelation. The contact made, Shemshu-Hor began sending thoughts to Isis. "I greet you, Glorious One of Many Names. I trust your journey is a safe and pleasant one that is nearing its end."

Isis replied: "I am safe within the shining eyes of my son, Horus, whose flame burns away the shadows in the heart of humanity and makes their light shine more brightly than ever. My coming soon will illumine the heart of every human. I am the first to come. The others will follow."

It was as Shemshu-Hor had thought. Isis would be the first Star God to return.

The morning sky was ablaze with Ra's first light. Khufu had sat most of the night in his gilded saddle chair in his bedchamber. His thoughts roamed the night as the small brazier beside him cast faint, dancing shadows on the walls. Leaving his quarters, the king joined Meritates on the patio for breakfast.

"Could you not sleep, my husband?" The soft voice of the royal wife cut into Khufu's thoughts, bringing him back to the present time and place. He was always amazed at how Meritates seemed to know what was going on inside him. "Tell me, my king? What kept you from your much needed rest?" Meritates was sure she knew but she wanted to hear it from Khufu.

With a deep sigh, Khufu faced his wife. "Nothing and everything is on my mind, Meritates. Truly, it is just that there is so much to think about, so much that is expected of me. And with the events to come, well I . . ."

"Yes, I know," Meritates said. "There is no reason for you to explain. It is as I thought. You are a god, yet a man too. Any man's sleep would be interrupted under the circumstances you face, my husband."

Khufu smiled faintly and strolled over to the lotus pool on the patio. The sweet smells of the royal garden filled the air. Meritates followed and changed the subject, reminding him of the comet that sailed in the heavens in silent splendor the night before.

"Did you see the beautiful omen the Sky Gods have sent?"

"Yes," Khufu answered somewhat hesitantly. "It is a beautiful sight indeed."

Picking up on the trepidation in Khufu's words, Meritates said, "But you are not sure if the omen bodes well for Egypt, yes? Or are you suffering from the tensions of self-doubt?"

Meritates's words struck a nerve. How many times would Khufu need to be reassured that he was up to all the tasks at hand? Why did self-doubt dog him? He intended to fulfill his commitment to Egypt and he knew he possessed the power of the god, that he was a living deity. It was his mind that was giving him trouble, not his heart. He was giving in to the all-too-human shortcoming of letting his mind and heart conflict. His human self was battling his soul.

"Is that not a natural reaction, my husband?" Meritates said. "The One would not place itself in a physical shell if it did not serve our country and show the Great Lord of the Two Lands is god and man. The god inside you strengthens the man you are. The man in you is fit as a house for the gods."

Chapter Fifty-Five

Incident in the Holy of Holies

Amenti was up before sunrise, making prayers and seeing to the needs of the goddess statue. She and four other Sekhmet priestesses went to the sanctuary, broke the seal, and entered. The stuffy air inside was uncomfortably warm and smelled of incense. The gold statue glowed eerily in the nearly spent flames of two oil lamps on each side of it.

Two priestesses refilled the lamps with oil, while the other two cleaned the four copper censors. Old flowers and stale food were replaced with a fresh lotus bouquet, a bowl of figs, a jug of honey, and bread. When these chores were completed, the priestesses took out cymbals and sistrums and began to play in praise of the goddess. Afterwards, Amenti recited prayers:

> All hail, jubilation to you, Golden One,
> Heaven makes merry,
> the temples fill with joy and song,
> all of the Earth rejoices because you live.
> Goddess of magic,
> Wife and sister of Ptah,
> mother of Nefertem, and child of the dawn.
> Hail, Sekhmet.
> Blessed are you as one of the seven wise beings
> who assisted in world creation.
> O, most powerful One, defender of divine order,
> destroyer of the king's enemies.
> Lady of the Flame, Goddess of the Setting Sun, we honor you.

Amenti took a bowl of scented water for washing the golden body of the goddess. This was the Neter she had devoted her life to, and there was nothing the High Priestess would not do to bring honor to Sekhmet's name. She was aware of the Great One's temperament as a warrioress and as the gentle Bastet, of the fiery avenger of Ra and her association with the joyful Hathor, goddess of love and jubilation. Amenti saw these goddesses herself and in other women.

Doing the daily toilet of Sekhmet had long been Amenti's favorite task as High Priestess of the Sekhmet Temple. It was something she looked forward to every day, and of which she never tired. She saw it as her personal time with Sekhmet, and here in the Holy of Holies she felt the presence of her beloved Neter more than anywhere else.

On this morning, like many others, Amenti requested to be alone. She knelt before the statue. She had a keen feeling this morning that she needed private time, though she did not know why. She had stopped second-guessing the wisdom of following what her feelings led her to do. As she knelt reverently in the stillness of the chamber, Amenti's eyes went to the base and the feet of the Golden One. In an instant, the small room was alive with the actual presence of Sekhmet.

The figure towered above Amenti's crouched body. The human part of the goddess was clothed in skin as white as milk, and unblemished by ages of time. A sheath of the finest red linen clung to her from just below her breasts to her ankles. A border of lapis blue braid went around the top of the dress, crisscrossed between her breasts, and up over her shoulders.

The goddess's head was that of a magnificent, mighty lioness. Its features were clearly that of an animal yet were strangely human in the eyes and in the animation of the muscles in the soft, pink mouth surrounded by the same golden strands of hair that covered the head. A radiant disk of starlight glowed orange-red above her, and in the middle of it sat a cobra, its eyes ruby, hissing in protection of its charge. The lioness-woman held an ankh of gold in her left hand; in her right, a was scepter, carved from ebony, displaying a forked tail and long shaft, topped by the head of a dog.

Sekhmet looked at Amenti with strength and compassion, and with a gesture for her to stand, the Neter spoke:

"Do not be afraid or turn away from me. I have come so that you may look upon me with eyes that before now have beheld me only through your faith. I am come so you will have no doubt that the task I give you comes from none but me, Sekhmet, Daughter of Ra, of the lineage of Sky Women."

Amenti felt as if her body was lifted off the floor by Sekhmet. Word-thoughts flowed from the mouth of the feline goddess, and every word sent a tingle down Amenti's spine. Amenti not only *heard* the words being spoken to her; she *felt* them in her being. She gazed at the majestic figure. "I have sent the Nubian. She was called by me so that no one impure in heart may disrupt Egypt's royal house. She will come to you soon. Assist her in protecting the One. Do so without doubt or question."

Sekhmet faded away; the warmth her presence emitted gave way to a chill. Amenti had never felt more alive than at this moment. She knew she must keep Sekhmet's appearance in the Holy of Holies a secret. The words had been meant for her alone. Tiye, her newly called fledgling apprentice, was in truth a powerful "chosen" magician.

The Nubian's room in the palace was lit by flickering oil lamps. Tiye evidently had not slept. Her mind had been filled with excitement about where she was and why. The meeting with Pharaoh had given her a deep sense of the responsibility laid upon her, of making protection amulets for the royal family. She was surrounded by magicians, priests, and priestesses, all of whom had more knowledge and experience than she. Even the Pharaoh was a seasoned magician. This made it hard for Tiye to understand why she had been recruited for such an important task. She had only been told that she possessed a special power to make amulets and that her ability was needed for this.

"I assume your journey to the Nile was a successful and pleasant one, my dear," Taret said, entering her room.

Tiye smiled, slightly nervous, and nodded her head. "Yes, it was, Mistress Taret."

"But?"

"Oh, nothing is wrong. I have all the ingredients I need to fashion the special amulet for the king and the others," Tiye replied, as a look of peace spread across her face. "It's just that I brought another important ingredient with me from the river."

Tiye looked at Taret with a confidence she had never displayed before. It was one soul looking into the soul of another, what Taret recognized as the most powerful connection two magicians could experience: respect, equality, and trust.

"And what would that ingredient be?" Taret asked, her eyes twinkling.

"I saw myself differently. I was her, Lady Taret. I was Sekhmet, the Lady of the Flame."

A slight smile curved the lips of the older priestess. She knew her trust in Tiye had been validated. All was proceeding as planned. Tiye was up to her part of the task.

Chapter Fifty-Six

In the Presence of Sekhmet

As Khufu began his day, the court was hectic, and it stayed that way. Taxes were being paid, squabbles settled, reports came in from the building projects, as did updates on revenues of exported goods. Nemon's report concerned the Sphinx temple project and was welcome news to the king. With a low bow, and true to his flamboyant nature, Nemon stood at the foot of the great chair in the Throne Room of the palace, a grin dancing across his face.

"Your Majesty, Wearer of the Double Crown, Mighty Bull of this very Egypt, I, Nemon, your Chief Architect and most humble servant, bring you word your ears have longed to hear. Indeed, what I have to say is timely and in keeping with these most auspicious times."

Khufu, with his vizier and other court officials, listened with interest as Nemon proclaimed the outline of the Sphinx Temple was completed. "The essential structure itself is set and sound, though much more work remains. There are also many details yet to be finished, Your Majesty, and artwork that cannot be rushed. I have inspected the premises, and find the construction acceptable, up to the standards set forth by the venerable king of Egypt."

Khufu did not just hear Nemon's words; he *felt* them. It was more than he could have hoped for to have a working temple available, however skeletal, by Inundation. It was as if the gods themselves had helped speed the work. The sacred light from the rising of the Great Star would shine on the new temple's high altar this year. Yet the building would be a testament to Khufu's dedication to the Nile Star and its power to effect change on the land and people.

"Majesty?" Nemon said, tilting his head in an inquiring way. "Did you hear me?"

"Oh, yes, ah, no, I am sorry, my cousin. My thoughts were off somewhere. I apologize. Please, go on."

"That is no problem, my lord. I was saying that much of the labor force has been sent back to their homes and families. The artisans are at work. The cedars have arrived from Punt, and they will be carved into the great doors. But, tell me, Your Majesty, how shall the doors be designed? What theme? Or what—"

Before Nemon could finish, Khufu answered. "Isis, the Mother and First Queen of Egypt—in her honor the Temple is built."

"Yes, of course," Nemon replied.

Khufu rolled his eyes and tapped a finger to his lips as he pondered. After a few seconds, his mind was made up. "I wish that the doors be plain except for a seven-pointed star whose north and south points reach to the top and bottom of each door and whose eastern and western points span the full width of each door panel. This will designate the Temple's purpose to capture the power of the Great Star."

Nemon used a small portable ink palette and a reed paper upon which to draw the design Khufu described. He showed the figure to Khufu, who, after studying it briefly, took the stylus from Nemon and drew a vertical line down the symbol's middle.

"Look at this, Nemon. If the Great Star of Isis is divided in this manner, half on each door, when the door is opened to the temple, every time it will be as if the star is opening for all to receive its power. What do you think?"

"Yes, I see what you mean. In the name of Ptah. I think you have a good plan, cousin. I will put the woodcarvers to work right away. May their hands be guided by the power of the beloved Ptah, god of all artisans."

Nemon packed away his scribe's palette in his waistband, and bowed, then clamped his hands on the king's shoulders, and kissed each cheek, a sign of love and respect for this man who, in Nemon's eyes, towered above all men. "I will be on my way," Nemon said. "I will report back very soon."

Khufu's next report was delivered by Atur, the palace engineer, whose task, as a member of the civil administration, was to watch the rising of the Nile as Inundation approached. The stout man waddled into the Throne Room, huffing under the weight of his body. Though Khufu valued the man, whose duties were always performed with timeliness and precision, he found Atur comical. Bowing awkwardly and spilling his papers, Atur, by his very presence, added gaiety to the serious atmosphere of the court.

Hustling to gather his papers and regain his composure, he announced that the Nile was indeed on the rise.

"Your Royal Highness," Atur spoke breathlessly, "the first waters of the river's rise, exceptionally green and foul, have come. My trusted aides have checked all of the nilometers along the banks and I myself have checked those in the capital. As I see it, the height may be expected to reach or even exceed fourteen cubits by the time the final flood comes."

The glee in Atur's voice was matched by the murmur of approval his good news generated. Khufu spoke, his voice rising above the buzz of the court. "Splendid, Atur! Splendid indeed. With your sound prediction I would say that Mother Nile, in her guise as a winding serpent, will deliver her life-giving waters throughout Egypt. This is good, very good. There is no reason to consult the oracle or to fear famine this season."

Khufu's pleasure and relief were evident in the upbeat tone of his voice. After commanding Atur and his aides to continue their vigilance, the king told them of the feast for the evening of the rising of the Great Star. "Invitations have been sent out and are being delivered even as I speak. It will be a feast fit for these auspicious times to celebrate Egypt's good fortune."

The thought of the feast brought Sokar to mind. Khufu was sure that his half-brother would have received his invitation scroll by now. Would Sokar appear? His intuition told him that he would. To be with Sokar would allow Khufu to monitor his mood and maybe provide answers. It would be better than speculating.

During a break in his busy morning in court, Khufu reflected on the previous night. He had spent most of it in his lotus garden. The chilly night air had been a welcome relief from the day's blazing heat. These days his attention was on the heavens more than the Earth. On the patio, the stars had seemed close enough to touch.

The construction of the Sphinx Temple had been occupying his thoughts last night when the darkness was lit by an orange-yellow flash. Khufu jumped to his feet as a boom of thunder sounded. A shooting star had blazed towards the Earth. It was the second time he had witnessed such an event, the first being the night King Sneferu died. Upon the rising of Ra the next morning Khufu had been elevated to the highest position in the land as king of Egypt.

"An omen," Khufu whispered. "The Star Gods have sent me a message. But what is the message you bring, mighty fallen star?"

The sound blast from the meteor had interrupted Meritates's sleep, who woke to find herself in bed alone. Alarmed, the queen rushed onto the patio in search of her husband. "My husband, are you all right? What has happened?" Meritates said breathlessly.

"Nothing, my dear. Do not be frightened." Putting his arm around her, he drew her close. "It was a falling star. I saw it, Meritates. I saw the heavens send a messenger to Egypt."

Khufu and Meritates silently stood arm in arm, her head resting on his shoulder.

"Look! It is the comet!" each said, before bursting into laughter. "What a beautiful sight it is," Khufu said.

Taret helped Tiye empty the jugs of the wet river mud. Its rank smell filled the room. The two women dumped the mud onto a flat wooden tray carved out of acacia. Clay was not the typical material used for amulets. Gold, bronze, glass, and stone were far more common. But Taret had not questioned Tiye's choice.

Tiye had decided to fashion the identical amulets as pendants to be worn over the heart under a garment. These would be cippi, a miniature form of a magical object, coupled with the power of Sekhmet with which each would be inscribed. On such an amulet, the combination of image and the words generates the magical effect, so it was precisely this coupling that made the cippi the most powerful of amulets.

Magical work requires a certain atmosphere, Taret knew well, so she had lit all the oil lamps at her disposal and placed them at various places around the room adjacent to her bedchamber. A mat of sweet-smelling reeds covered the floor. Pillows of fine linen lay on the floor. Taret's altar stood against the west wall of the little chamber and held a small brazier with glowing coals. The scent of myrrh filled the room.

The work table was draped in a black cloth and upon it sat a bowl of myrrh ashes from previous rituals. The ashes would be mixed with river clay as a natural adhesive. Beside this bowl was another, beautifully gilded and inscribed with symbols; it contained Nile water scented with myrrh and night jasmine. There were two gold chalices, one for each woman. One held date wine, the other water. A bowl of sand had been placed at each end of the table, and in the sand stood a candle. Magical acts required this type of votive focus and each had been endowed with power to protect the magician.

Tiye invited Taret to set the tone for the magical working by invoking Isis. Taret, her linen sheath wrapping her body in folds of luxurious embroidered fabric, stood at her altar on the far side of the room. She would leave the central table solely for Tiye's work, so only the Nubian's energy would be involved there. A peculiar quiet fell over the room. Tiye had not worked in this private way with a woman who had been her teacher since Khaba.

As Taret spoke her body seemed to grow taller, and her usual meek voice became louder and stronger:

> Mother Nut, Mother of Isis, Osiris, Nepthys, and Seth.
> Great Cosmic Mother whose divine body
> stretches from horizon to horizon.
> Supreme Sky Goddess,
> She Who Wraps All in Her body,
> enfolding and containing everything.
> Beautiful divine Sky Goddess,
> whose laughter is the thunder,
> you who gives birth to the Sun
> and the rest of the heavenly bodies each dawn,
> the dawn whose red glow is your very daughter.
> Beloved Nut, whose body is the Celestial Nile
> which flows from east to west,
> and upon which all the heavenly bodies travel.
> You who protect us from chaos,
> come to me now in this sacred place.

Taret lifted her arms from her side and let her head tilt backwards to rest between her slender shoulders, then spoke again:

> Mother Nut, spread your wings over me,
> encircle me with your arms
> that I and Tiye, humble servant
> of the Great Lady of the Flame, Sekhmet,
> may be inside you, that you may be our protection.
>
> I am your daughter, Taret.
> O Star Mother, guide the hands of this servant
> as she fashions the amulets
> to protect the incarnated Horus,
> Ruler of the Two Lands,
> Wearer of the Double Crown.
>
> Let her see visions in the darkness.
> Make her firm in her resolve
> and mighty in her power over evil.
> I, Taret, like you over the heavens,
> stretch my body out over this daughter of mine
> in your name.

Then, turning to Tiye, Taret said:

I, Taret, protect you.
Isis protects you.
The Brilliant One who lives forever
among the indestructible stars,
Nut, protects you.

Tiye felt peace descend upon her. The room seemed transformed from a tiny cell into a boundless arena, vast as space.

Taret walked away from the altar to a corner. Tiye was on her own. Reaching down into the flat, wooden tray she had placed on the floor beside the table, Tiye took the partially dried Nile mud in her hands. She felt the cool, soft clay, and sensed it had life in it, eager to be molded according to her will. Holding the clay, Tiye spoke.

I am Tiye. I am come to you,
Sekhmet, Lady of the Battles and Lady of Healing.
Do you recognize me?
O Sekhmet, I call you!
I call you with my body,
I call you with my heart,
I call you with the utterances of my mouth,
I call you with the thoughts of my mind,
and with the feelings living has earned me.
O Sekhmet, I call you.

Expectation gripped Tiye. Long seconds passed. An orange pinpoint of light appeared a few feet above the little table. Flickering unsteadily at first, the tiny light burst into a yellowish-orange flame. Within this heat-less fire Sekhmet formed, her radiance drawing Tiye's and Taret's attention like a lamp. Tiye gasped as she felt herself drawn to the beautiful light that was the goddess. She had never gazed upon a more frightening yet welcome sight. She felt the goddess's light stimulating, igniting creativity within her. Every cell in her body came alive with the power of the deity. Then, a voice came:

I am Sekhmet, the Radiant One,
who has called you forth.
With the irresistible desire of an impassioned lover,
you come to me.
I want you, as you want me.
Be aware that you bear the light and fire of me,
Sekhmet, within you.
Open the door of your heart
so that the deity of *heka* can come in.

Tiye was elated. Here at this very moment was Sekhmet before her. Then the lion-headed goddess communicated again, sending thoughts into Tiye's mind.

"Your path is now open into the realm of the mysteries, my star daughter. All is in readiness. I, Sekhmet, Lady of the Flames, Daughter of Ra, wife of Ptah, and mother of Nefertem, am before you unveiled. Your life as it was is no more. Yet what shall be has not yet become. If it is still your heart's desire to become my beloved, then affirm it to me now where your vow will echo throughout the star systems of the universe. Say 'I, Tiye, Nubian sorceress trained by the wise woman Khaba, Star Priestess of the Holy Order of Nut, the Sky Goddess, ally myself forever and a day with the divine Sekhmet.'"

"I do so ally myself with you, the divine Sekhmet," Tiye said.

The apparition of the lion-headed one continuously emitted light from its dimension into the tiny temple.

> True of voice you are, my beloved one.
> This day you have taken your place
> in the secret place of the Lion Neters.
> Go about your work in peace.
> By your handiworks shall you be known and judged.

The room returned to what it had been, a simple antechamber in the great palace in Memphis in which a Nubian and her teacher made amulets to protect Egypt's Pharaoh and family. Tiye took Sekhmet's appearance in stride. This was no time for traces of girlhood or fear or heady excitement to dissolve the magical energy now built up. This was a turning point in Tiye's life. She was a woman now, a mature, responsible priestess and prophet of Sekhmet.

As Tiye focused her attention on the river clay still in her hands, it seemed to take on a life of its own and mold itself. Her fingers rolled and shaped the substance into a miniature Sekhmet. Her notions of a three-headed double deity were quickly abandoned. The heka flowed through her and as her hands moved, one thought kept repeating itself. "I release the magic of Sekhmet from myself and into this amulet." In less than an hour, the king's amulet lay finished in Tiye's hand.

Chapter Fifty-Seven

The Two Hawks Deal with Bakka

While Tiye labored on her amulets, Sokar's world was closing in on him. The time of Inundation was here and so was the time when he would challenge Khufu and make his announcement to all Egyptians regarding his alternate government. Sokar worked best under pressure. It was time to execute his plans, which he would begin by summoning Kheti.

No sooner had this thought crossed his mind than Kheti entered Sokar's quarters with cool refreshments to take the edge off the searing heat. After setting down a tray of beer, fruits, and dried fish, Kheti fluffed up the floor pillows and smoothed out the linens on Sokar's bed.

"Kheti," Sokar said, an edge of sharpness in his voice. "Never mind your chores. We must talk."

The servant, detecting the urgency in his master's voice, promptly bowed. "Yes, my lord, is there something you need?"

"No, Kheti, nothing other than your undivided attention, and your loyalty." Sokar said this in case Kheti became hostile upon learning of Sokar's prior plan to steal his body.

"Yes, of course, my lord," Kheti replied, confused by the remark about loyalty.

Sokar motioned for Kheti to sit down, while he stood by Horus's perch, where the bird was mute in the heavy air. Kheti watched every move, anticipation building.

"Summer is fit only for snakes and jackals, eh, Horus?" Sokar said.

Kheti waited patiently until Sokar had poured himself a cup of beer and sat down. Painstakingly, Sokar told Kheti about his encounter with the female ghost. He explained in detail how she had struck a bargain with him to provide her a living body to occupy at her will, in return for her guarantee of his success in becoming a respected ruler of Egypt, fulfilling his lifelong dream.

Kheti listened intently, his expression reflecting surprise at one turn, and terror at another. He remained silent, frozen to the spot.

When Sokar came to the point in the story where he confessed that he had planned to fulfill his agreement with the ghost by pronouncing an ancient spell to rob Kheti of his physical being, the servant's eyes widened with fear and disbelief. Sokar stood up again and walked over to the door leading to the patio. Looking out over the lovely garden and lotus pool, he said in a moment of rare revelation and genuine caring, "But I decided against going ahead with that plan."

Turning to face his servant again, Sokar admitted it was a tough decision, one he had not made until the last moment. His recognition of the identity of the vile apparition had changed his mind and caused him to decide that with Kheti's help, he could dispatch the ghost. He had not believed her promise nor had he reason to think he needed her help, he told Kheti.

His master's words brought relief to the disturbed servant, who had been unsure of what the conversation was leading to. He wasn't sure whether to relax or if there was something even more terrifying in store. Sokar noted his apprehension and went on.

"I can and I will deal with Bakka's ghost. I do not intend to owe my soul to some unfortunate, desperate wraith who could in any way cast a shadow over my forthcoming triumph!" Sokar's voice had become firm with an edge of defiance. "The enemy—the *only* enemy—of a skilled magician is the foolhardy rebel who seeks to go against the order of things provoking an adept to anger and crying with a loud voice for evil to be summoned into action." Turning to look at Kheti, Sokar added, "The evil I intend is going to benefit *me*, and not some lovesick ghost who brought her fate upon herself."

Kheti took his first relaxed breath since Sokar started talking. He was beginning to feel more at ease, though his guard was still up. "What will you do, my master?" Kheti asked, swallowing hard to rid himself of the lump in his throat. What with his dry throat, dry mouth, and his nervousness, Kheti started to gag. Sokar granted him permission to drink from his jug of beer. Kheti accepted, his hands shaking as he lifted the jug to his lips and swallowed big gulps of the cool liquid.

"I will challenge, no, I will *defeat* Bakka's spirit. I will command the force within her to be gone, forever banished into a realm of nonexistence. And I will not, and neither will you, Kheti, show any fear or remorse or the slightest weakness in so doing." Sokar spoke with conviction and Kheti knew he was committed to the task. "But I will need your help," the magician said. "You will serve as my assistant and you will do so willingly and with the utmost loyalty to me and my cause."

Kheti knew his life had been spared. There was no request Sokar could make now that the servant would even consider refusing.

Sokar took out the papyrus scroll Atef had prepared for him. Seeing it again made him think of the visit the young scribe had paid him shortly after copying the spell. Atef had asked for an audience with Sokar to express his dismay at copying the scroll. He was not accusing Sokar of deceit, but the nature of the spell had alarmed him. Why had Sokar "borrowed" the spell if he had not intended to use it?

Sokar had dealt with Atef's inquiries by pulling rank as a member of the royal family, putting his actions beyond question, telling him the spell was relevant to his training as a magician-priest. The apprentice scribe had seemed embarrassed that Sokar would view his suspicious attitude as an affront. Atef did not want Sokar as an enemy.

Sokar scanned the images on the scroll. The contents of the spell, even now, made the hair stand up on the back of his neck. He was viewing the details of the spell for clues only the most skilled of practitioners might discern, searching for hints that would show him how to banish the ghost to the realm of the nonexistent. If such clues existed, he would find them in the part that warned the magician and the ghostly petitioner of the consequences of failure. Sokar stopped at a sentence and read it carefully.

"That's it," he said. "This tells me *exactly* what I need to know." A smile formed on his face that resembled a hawk's.

"Woe be to the petitioner who misjudges who is petitioned for the forbidden deed." This was the sentence Sokar read over again. Bakka, pitiful ghost, had misjudged Sokar. She had thought that he would do anything to become a king, and in that judgment she was right. What she was wrong about was that he needed *her* help, or anybody else's, to "guarantee" his success.

Kheti had completed the transformation from manservant to magical assistant by the time Sokar was ready to confront Bakka.

A *menes* of white linen sewed with gold threads held Sokar's black plait in place close to his head. He was bare except for a loincloth. The magical operation would require Sokar to go into a deep trance, gain entrance into the precise place in the Duat where earthbound spirits reside, and send Bakka's ghost into a dimension from which there was no escape. Sokar would work with Horus on this and shape-shifting would make the process quick and tidy.

As evening approached, Sokar and Kheti slipped into the ceremonial room near the inner sanctum of the Phoenix Temple. Aside from a small brazier with hot coals to burn incense to help Sokar enter an altered state and an amulet of protection to wear around his neck, the two carried nothing else except Horus. Once safely inside, Sokar stripped naked, wearing only the bronze amulet fashioned after Seth. It was a figure that resembled a griffin with a long, curved muzzle, tall ears, and bifurcated tail. The amulet hung on a braided linen cord around his thick neck. Sokar had attached a smaller version of the same amulet to Horus's right leg. Seth, red god of the desert, was familiar with all domains of ghosts and demons. Kheti had his own protection amulet, a green and black faience figure of a multiple wedjat eye. He had had the tiny amulet since he was a boy, given to him by the midwife who attended his birth.

Sokar looked around the room to see what furniture might be useful for the operation. In trance work, physical comfort was a main key to success. He spotted a chair with a high back that would serve as a suitable perch for Horus. Several large floor cushions would provide comfortable seating for himself. Kheti let it be known that he preferred to stand. As was always the case prior to magical work, once they settled in the room, communication consisted only of gestures.

Kheti dropped a few chunks of incense onto the coals in the brazier. The fumes quickly spread through the closed space, filling it with the sweet fragrance of night jasmine. The aroma always helped Sokar enter an altered state. Sokar was ready, settled on the floor. The shape-shifting was about to begin. Sokar's relaxed body began to twitch and stiffen, then jerked. His torso began to shrink, taking on the form of a hawk, his arms spread out on each side, turned into wings, calves and ankles now short, large feet with talons. Raspy, guttural sounds emanated from the magician's throat; then an ear-piercing shriek tore a hole in the veil between dimensions and Sokar and Horus flew through it in a flash of light.

Kheti saw it all. Now he had to maintain the psychic shield he had placed at the entrance of the chamber to guarantee no one would be attracted to investigate. This was a part of his work as Sokar's magical assistant.

Once free of the physical world, the hawks pinpointed their destination by picturing the place in the Duat where earthbound spirits reside. The "twelve hours" normally required for this ritual passed in an instant, the Star Goddesses of the Duat met and dealt with by Horus, completely out of Sokar's awareness. Sokar saw a place of pitiful wraiths, alone and in despair. The hawks flew into the lowest realm of the Underworld, the realm of the living dead. Sokar formed the image of Bakka, and she appeared as an undulating reddish-yellow firelight, the color suggesting the misery of a frantic specter. Then the two hawks aimed themselves at this light, their bodies flying into it like arrows of fire, shattering it instantly. It was over. In a flash, the hawks sped out of the Duat, soaring through the spirit world, and returned to the chamber, where Sokar regained his human form.

Stepping from the shadows, Kheti held out a flask of wine. It would help Sokar ground himself. The servant stood quietly, knowing that to speak to Sokar before he was fully back in his human body was inadvisable. Sokar's eyes opened slowly and caught Kheti's gaze of nervous concern. With a slight smile Sokar said, "I will have no more problem with my unwanted ghost from the spirit world."

It was not usual for the palace guards to allow a visitor an audience with Pharaoh after court hours. But when they recognized the woman standing before them, a message was sent to inform Khufu that Taret of Heliopolis wished to see him. Taret knew the men were completely trustworthy, and that word of her evening visit with Khufu would not get around the palace or beyond its walls.

When the High Priestess was allowed entrance into the foyer of the royal apartment, both the king and Meritates met her. Taret bowed deeply, nodding to each. An apology fell immediately from her lips.

"Please, Lady Taret, your presence is most welcome. Tell us," Khufu said as he glanced at his wife. "What has brought you here?"

Before answering, Taret also looked at Meritates, unsure of how much she should say in front of the queen.

"Is it the amulets, Mistress Taret?" Khufu spoke up, seeing the woman's uncertainty. By his words, Taret realized that the queen knew everything.

"Yes, Your Majesty. It is about the amulets that I have come," Taret answered. "They are done. I have brought them."

Taret untied a sash that hung around her waist, revealing three bags that contained the fetishes Tiye had made. She placed one in Khufu's hand. The king looked at the bag in his palm, wondering what the image inside looked like.

"This is yours, my king. It is the first made, the prototype of the others born from it." Taret still held the two remaining bags.

Khufu thought he might feel the energy of the amulet through the linen. But it was not until he took out the miniature image of Sekhmet that its power made itself known as a tingle through his hand and arm. Khufu slipped the amulet over his head, so the clay ornament hung near his heart.

Taret gave the queen an identical linen pouch. Following the king's lead, Meritates took her amulet and placed it around her neck, then cupped the fetish in her hand, took a deep breath, and closed her eyes to absorb its power into her body.

"These are smaller amulets made for your sons," Taret said, referring to the last bag. "It is advised that they be worn during these times should peril from any source seek to befall the princes."

Khufu took the bag from Taret's hand and tucked it into the waistband tied around his midriff. "I will see my sons get them. Thank you, Lady Taret."

Taret bowed and turned to leave when Khufu spoke again. "Thank Tiye. Her deed will be remembered, I assure you."

Chapter Fifty-Eight

Final Preparation for Inundation

After Taret left, Khufu retreated to the confines of his royal apartment in the palace, where his family was busy preparing for the trip to Giza. It felt good to remove the crown. It could feel heavy in the heat. He admired the amulet on his chest.

After dinner, Khufu and Meritates walked into the garden. "Look, my love," Meritates spoke. "The day has come to an end. The lotus flowers are drawing in their petals."

"Yes, I see," Khufu responded, a smile bringing a gentleness to his usually stark face. The king turned to face his wife, putting his hands on her, gently brushing a wisp of her hair off her brow. "I remember when we were wed. You wore the longest, most beautiful, blue lotus in your hair. You and the flower were beautiful, and you both still are."

Khufu was in a calm and collected mood, unusual given the hectic circumstances of his recent life. It warmed Meritates to see her husband so at ease.

"The god of the blue water lilies is pleased to have all these lotus hearts to sit in," Meritates said wistfully, making reference to an old story about the flower concealing a young god sitting in its golden center.

The couple relaxed as twilight draped its cobalt cloak over the land. "Tell me, my husband," Meritates said, "are you ready for what the next days will bring?"

"I am King of Egypt now, and it happens to be in the most extraordinary of times. I will represent the country and the people in whatever ways I am charged by the gods, and I will do so to the death, if need be."

Tiye sat in her room at the Temple of Sekhmet reviewing what had happened. Confidence in her magical ability had increased a hundredfold since she witnessed the manifestation of her beloved goddess while she made the amulets. A bond had been created, one that would never be broken. She was anxious to speak to Amenti of her experiences.

Tiye's thoughts turned to Khem. She felt alone and missed her friend and fellow priestess. On the day of the rising of the Great Star, there would be an initiation ceremony at the Temple of the Sun in Heliopolis. The annual rising of Sirius had long been of special import to the Star Priests and Star Priestesses of Heliopolis. Since Isis was viewed by the Holy Orders as the mother and heart of the universe, her reappearance after an absence of seventy days was a time to rejoice.

The initiation, an offering to Isis, would take place in a special ritual hall. An altar would be set up, oriented to the East. Tiye had witnessed this rite shortly after her arrival in Heliopolis. It had made a deep impression on her such that she knew she had come to the right place and that being a Star Priestess was the right choice. Tiye would attend the initiation this year too, even though she now served Sekhmet.

Tiye felt more mature now. She had always seen herself as a girl-child, as Khaba's girl. Now she felt different. She was aware of what had been a fact all along, that she was no longer anyone's "child." She was a young woman in her own right, a budding Star Priestess and magician. Khaba had taught Tiye well, but now her teacher was not a human, but a Neter, her beloved Sekhmet. . . .

Sokar lay in bed listening to chirping insects and the rustling of breezes. The defeat of Bakka achieved, Sokar saw the road ahead as a clear path to the Throne. It was as if all his yesterdays were over, gone to a place inside him where everything else he had forgotten resided. All his tomorrows were not yet born. He realized he was living in the eternal moment that is now. He saw no need to look back on his past; he knew what it held and was ready to forget it. With Kheti, he would journey to Giza to witness the rising of Sirius and would gather with royalty and commoners to witness the celestial vision.

How sweet it would be to see the look on Khufu's face when he, Sokar, stepped onto the dais that was erected for the royal family to view the rising of the Great Star and proclaimed himself a legitimate, viable ruler, the first-born son of Pharaoh Sneferu. Equally sweet to him would be the faces of Meri-ib and Taret, those vile, gullible sages whose judgment would be called into question, as would anyone's who had served the wrong

Pharaoh for all these years. He would command his glory as he stood before them all; he would be outshone by no one save the light of the Star of Isis. The people would *see* and *feel* his power, Sokar's. The rising of Ra that morning would bring more than a new year. It would be the dawning of a new era in Egypt.

Darkness cloaked his bedroom in shadows. Sokar lay in the dim room, relishing that his time had come, until he fell asleep. Floating gently out of his body into the freedom of his dream vessel, Sokar drifted as an invisible observer into a young girl's dream. The scene was Nubia. An old woman with gnarled hands knelt over a piece of fabric on the hot, desert sand. On top of the cloth lay two strips of black dyed linen and a purple candle. Kneeling on the sand beside her was a dark-skinned, naked girl. Sokar knew the girl had only moments before emerged from a purifying dip in the Nile. The old woman anointed the girl's body with lotus oil.

After the anointing, the old woman tied one piece of the black cloth around the girl's wrist, and then the other around her waist, then anointed the purple candle with the same oil that she had rubbed on the girl. She placed the end of the candle into the sand so it would stand upright, and told the girl to gaze into the flame, without blinking as long as she could, while visualizing the goddess Isis as coming out of the fire into her presence.

In an instant—for time has no rule in the dream world—that deity formed before the two humans. Sokar heard the girl ask the goddess to send a dream to teach her about the mysteries. The candle was then blown out as the deity departed and the images of Sokar's dream faded into oblivion.

Chapter Fifty-Nine

The Cycle of Life

Egypt's summer is merciless. The only hope of survival for man or beast is the coolness brought by the flooding of the Nile that drives away the oppressive heat, replacing it with dampness and the sweet breath of fertility. But with relief comes a new anxiety, for the fate of the country depends on the river, and all wait to see if it will rise too high or not be high enough, or not rise at all. Anything other than just right could spell devastation.

The yearly sky omen, the heliacal rising of the Great Star, let the people know Inundation had come. The rising of the star marked the reappearance of the Mother Goddess of Ten Thousand Names, Sothis, Sopdet, Isis. Egyptians knew that the events in the sky are "letters" from the Neters, messages pertinent to the land and people. Sky omens signaled changes in the climate, predicted matters of political import, and told about dramas in the lives of celestial beings.

So on this special dawn on the eve of Inundation Khem was awakened by the pacing and low growling of Bast. The city was so uncommonly quiet that the gentle rushing of the river's water could be heard even above the lowing of cattle, the bleats of sheep, and birdsongs.

"What is it, Bast?" Khem asked the lioness in the shrill, singsong tone she often used when communicating with the cat. "What do you hear?"

Bast looked at Khem, now sitting up in bed, and sniffed the air with two snorts. Her pacing stopped and her body froze, her tail straight and stiff. It was obvious she was sensing energies, but as quickly as the lioness had become excited, the spell was broken and she became calm again, strolling over to Khem's bed, laying her head down to be scratched. Khem gave the cat's head a couple of rakes with her fingernails. "You are spoiled!" Khem said, pushing Bast's head off the bed in jest. "It is too early to play."

Khem got up. She had to go to Ani's. When Khem and Bast reached Ani's quarters in the House of Life, Klea and Sheshat were already there. Klea seemed to have an edge today, rather than her usual calm demeanor. There was also a nervousness in the room. Servants had placed trays of fruit on a low table, and Khem took a cluster of grapes and popped one in her mouth. Bast sat like a sphinx with her paws stretched out in front of her, eyeing Klea. Ani invited them all to sit on cushions around the food table. She then had Sheshat relate a recent dream.

The image had consisted of a giant "egg" flying through the sky. The egg sparkled like a star, throwing off particles of light as it flew. The egg landed on the ground and cracked open. From it stepped a humanlike figure composed of light. Ani was of the opinion that the image of an "egg" was not an egg at all, but rather a star or other kind of celestial body en route to Earth. The light being was either literal, from another time and place, or symbolic of the same.

"So, Sheshat has reported an interesting dream," Ani said, "yet neither you, Khem, nor you, Klea, have done so. Am I to understand your silence means no significant dreams have occurred?"

Khem and Klea nodded yes.

"I did not have any dreams of any import, but that seems rather strange, don't you think?" Klea said.

"What do you mean?" Ani asked.

"It may mean nothing at all, Mistress Ani. But it has been my experience in the past that, prior to magical work, my dreams are usually filled with images that relate to the matter at hand. I mean, at times like this, I usually dream all the time."

Ani leaned forward to be closer to Klea. "Do you suppose your dreaming vessel has been blocked in a psychic blackout?"

"Yes. I know what you mean, Ani. That is *exactly* how I have felt." A look of concern coupled with relief crossed her face.

"But we cannot jump to conclusions. Your statement has a serious implication," Ani said.

"What do you mean? What implication?"

Ani pointed her finger to emphasize her answer. "For a black magician bent on undertaking the boldest act of heka in a lifetime, he would have to *know* the identity of everyone in collusion to prevent him from succeeding. So, for your dream vessel to be deliberately blocked, the magician would have to know precisely *whose* dreams he should block. And that would mean that he would know *you*, and you, and you," she said, pointing to Khem and Sheshat.

"And what's more, he would be crafty enough to have detected the rest who are involved—Taret, Tiye, and me. He would have to know the entire plot of who was out to stop him, maybe even sense the role of Pharaoh himself."

It seemed obvious to the priestesses that Sokar did *not* know of their plot against him in defense of the sovereignty of the Throne. "He could not know," Ani said, a flash of excitement showing in her voice. "Because not all of you have experienced such a lack of dreams of any kind, significant or otherwise."

"You are right," Khem spoke out, while Sheshat nodded in agreement. "If all our dreams were blocked, none of us would have dreamed about anything. But we did. At least Sheshat did."

"That is right," Ani replied. "If he knew about us and our operation, not one of us would have dreamed."

The matter was resolved. The Star Priestesses agreed that Sokar was not on to them yet. Their work, so far, was in the clear. Though no one had noticed, the conversation had been tracked by Bast. The animal somehow knew the seriousness of what was discussed, her gold eyes focused on Klea the entire time.

"Bast, you are staring," said Khem. "It is not nice to stare," Khem added, breaking the animal's trance. A sweeping wag of her tail and a flop of her head as she sought to lick Khem's face was evidence that the spell had been broken.

Khem, looking at Klea, smiled and laughed. "Maybe she sees a spirit with you."

No sooner had the words come out of Khem's mouth than the four priestesses realized that was it. Bast was seeing a spirit with Klea, and they knew what spirit it was: Sekhmet!

The collective thought power of the four women opened the veil between dimensions and in a flash of light, the lion-headed goddess stood in the corner of the room. Her radiance filled the room with a power and a humming sound just like the one Khem had heard coming from the obelisk on the island in the Sacred Lake at the Temple of the Sun when Khaba had appeared.

In a visitation of this sort, communication takes place through the eyes. Thoughts and feelings are transmitted as energy. The spectacle of the deity's body and garments captured the priestesses' attention, as did her lioness's head and its huge golden-orange eyes. The goddess transmitted thoughts of amulets, the royal family, Tiye, and Lady Taret to the Star Priestesses. Her message was clear: the amulets were done and in the hands of the royal family. The first step in the magical battle between them and Sokar had begun.

Shemshu-Hor woke to daylight on this Eve of Inundation in a palace guest room. He had awakened many times to this day in his long life, but he knew this time would be different. He stirred on his bed, the soft, damp linens sticking to his body in the predawn heat. The wooden headrest had been hard on his neck so he had lain on his side using his arm as a pillow, but this had not helped. He was aching and sore.

The Elder's stirring brought Mery-Ptah, the valet-servant who was also a royal physician. Khufu wanted the elder priest's every need to be met, especially when it concerned his comfort and health.

Bones creaked as the old man struggled to sit up after the long night. Mery-Ptah helped pull him upright, and held a cup of cool water to his lips. Mery-Ptah thought, as he had so many times before, how intriguing was this job of taking care of the holy man. He had never tended one whose body was so much in the physical world, yet whose consciousness was on a level whose qualities Mery-Ptah could only imagine.

Reaching for a plate of food, Mery-Ptah felt a slight push against his arm. The sky blue eyes focused on him, kind, gentle, penetrating eyes that seemed to hold the memories of life itself. Shemshu-Hor shook his head. "Thank you, but I want no food."

"Very well," Mery-Ptah replied. "As you wish."

While the process of the morning's toilet and getting the old man dressed proceeded, every step seemed to revive the elder from his almost trancelike state into one of reasonable vigor and acute awareness. This old man is truly an enigma, Mery-Ptah reflected.

After being bathed and dressed in a plain sheath secured at the waist by a sash embroidered with gold symbols of the wedjat—the Eye of Horus—Shemshu-Hor waved Mery-Ptah away so he could make his morning prayers to Horus and Isis. After seeing to it that the water and wine jugs were filled, and placing fruits and small fresh-baked loaves of bread on a nearby table, the valet left him alone.

Shemshu-Hor contemplated the coming events. The Old One was accustomed to spending his time in double consciousness: in the physical world, and the Duat, and he was comfortable in both. The part of him awake in the Duat went to the familiar counterpart of the *Benu* Temple, where he had passed vast amounts of time. Shemshu-Hor's Body of Light ascended the starlit stairway that led to the rooftop of the Duat Temple where he drank in the sight he had seen so many times before. All around him was the star-filled Duat. Every ray of light from every sun communicated its glory to him as if to honor his presence.

This was a frequent haunt of Shemshu-Hor and the priesthood of the Followers of Horus. Here, more than anywhere else, he met his fellow Sirians to discuss their work on Earth with humans. Moored at the east side of the roof of the Duat Temple was the Boat of a Million Years. Shemshu-Hor knew this as the Barque of Isis and although Isis was not here, he knew he could use it to make contact with his Sirian sister. On the roof of the barque in the center of the ship was an empty throne, canopied by a pair of persea trees whose every leaf and stem trembled with light.

The Old One climbed aboard the barque and it began to slowly ascend into the heavens of the Duat. Stars and galaxies passed by as the ship glided through space. Shemshu-Hor saw the three belt stars in Orion that point to Sirius and as the ship's prow turned to align itself with the Great Star, coming ever closer, Shemshu-Hor made his psychic connection with Isis. The Old One's thoughts reached the goddess within the comet, causing her spirit to stir gently.

"Sothis, my sister, my mind and heart call you. It is time to talk."

Caravans of crude land conveyances and small fleets of various types of river crafts on the Nile were moving by the time Ra had reached the midway point in his journey across the sky. All were headed to Giza. Soon the desert floor would be speckled with tents, blankets spread out on the sand, and lean-tos providing the barest of shelters. Smoke from cooking fires would curl heavenward, and countless beasts of burden would bray and holler their distress against the heat.

The palace was buzzing with preparations to transport the royal family and key members of the court and the Sirius Council to Giza. Khufu had so many things to focus on, it was hard to stay on one topic for long. The long-awaited day was here. Khufu had felt calm since putting on Tiye's amulet. Before departing for Giza, Khufu called a meeting of the Sirius Council. Taret had no dreams to report, except for Sheshat's "egg."

"The scribe's dream was the only one necessary to reveal everything to you," Shemshu-Hor said. "It tells all."

"The Star God, Your Majesty," Taret said. "The Star God comes to us in an egg." Taret turned to Shemshu-Hor with expectation that the Elder would fill in the blanks.

"The comet provides a life and soul-sustaining chamber, a 'womb' for the return of the Great Mother of Egypt," the Old One said.

Chapter Sixty

Awaiting the Dawn

Sokar awoke on the Eve of Inundation to the sound of Kheti's feet padding softly about the room. "I am sorry to disturb you, my master, but Ra is rising quickly and there is much to be done."

"Yes, you are right," Sokar responded sleepily.

"Shall I leave you to your privacy for now, master?" Kheti inquired, embarrassed that he had needed to rouse Sokar.

"No," Sokar replied hastily. "Just bring my fresh kilt and my leopard-skin shoulder drape. I am ready to be bathed and dressed. This is an important day, Kheti."

"As you wish, Master," Kheti answered with a low bow and disappeared into another part of the quarters.

Sokar rarely asked for the mantle of the priesthood, the leopard skin cape worn by the priests of Heliopolis. Although Sokar valued the garment and respected what it represented, he felt too orthodox when he wore it, and orthodox he was not. Still, there were a few occasions when the magician felt that it was to his advantage to appear that he was indeed orthodox in his views, and this was one. He wanted his presence at the Rising of the Great Star to be noted, but only as a member of the priesthood.

Sokar examined the leopard skin. The sight and the feel of it brought back memories of the day it was presented to him at his ordination. Voices sounded in his head, one of which was Meri-ib's, High Priest at the time. Sokar was presented before Ra, touted as an excellent, brilliant young man. He had been introduced to the Horizon of Heaven at the Sacred Lake and ritually purified of the ills within him. He was led into the Holy of Holies to face the god and experience power. He was confirmed in the power to "charm the sky, the netherworld, the mountains, and the waters, the Moon and all the stars."

Yet it had not purified Sokar of his "ills." They were too deep. To him, the Temple was merely a building, an indifferent setting. He had not seen the Temple as a microcosm of the universe even though that view of it was explained to him. An induction into the priesthood was not what he wanted. It should have been coronation as king of Egypt, first-born of Sneferu. Notwithstanding, in secret rooms of the House of Life, Sokar was inducted as a practitioner of the magical arts and reader of sacred texts used in ceremonies.

There had been a time when Sokar felt perhaps he would accept his lot as a bastard child, of a long dead king, and work his way up to become High Priest of Heliopolis. He would become the great seer, one who sees the great god, the supreme master of the secrets of the sky. This high office would give him prestige and honor and a legitimate place in society. But no, he would not settle for less than what he deserved. As Pharaoh, he would be chief of *all* magicians and priests, not just the High Priest of one temple, no matter how important a temple it might be. Tomorrow was the day, and it would be *his* day.

When Sokar was dressed, he rummaged through his ebony jewelry box. As he picked around at the armbands, chokers, and anklets, he quickly withdrew his hand! There was a scorpion in the box. "Mother of the Gods!" Sokar yelled, slinging the deadly creature off the back of his hand. The thing hit the wall and fell to the floor, then scurried under a clothes basket. This was the one creature Sokar feared.

Khufu and his family traveled by barque to Giza. The Giza Plateau always evoked pride in Khufu. He was proud of having unearthed the body of *Harmakhis*, the Great Sphinx, so it could again look out over the eastern horizon and stand guard over the holiest ground in Egypt.

Yet so much weighed on Khufu's mind: Sokar, the threat he posed, the Second Coming, Isis, Inundation, his living ascension. Khufu noted that on this day before the festival the landscape around the Giza complex was dotted with campsites. Children played ball and tag, darting in and out of the many monuments under the sweltering sun. Music came from the largest contingent of tents, including the two erected for the royal family. Hathor priestesses were singing in accompaniment to a troupe of dancers. Even from the barque, Khufu could hear them.

Celebrate this joyful day!
Let sweet odors of oils be in your nostrils,
Wreaths of lotus flowers for you,
Let song and music be made before you.
Celebrate this joyful time
with contented heart and a spirit full of gladness.

The royal barque docked and litter bearers were waiting to transport the royals and guests to the temporary palace. Khufu was surrounded by splendor. He and his family left the boat and climbed into a rich sedan-chair, flanked by fan bearers. Others in the court boarded other litters, and the caravan set out in the direction of the pyramids and their quarters. Two priests walked in front of the litter burning incense as they went, while a third read aloud all the customary titles and praises of the king. Soldiers followed behind for protection.

The words of the rector-priest, though shouted in a stout voice, could be heard dimly above the clamor of the celebrants:

Incline your ear towards me,
Here is the One who reigns over the Two Lands
with beauty and power unmatched by any living man among men.
Hail to the sunshine of humanity,
Hail him who chases darkness out of Egypt.
Honor and glory to the One
whose form is that of Ra riding in the heavens.
Honor to him whose eyes are clearer
than the stars of the firmament
Great is he who sees farther than the Sun.
The rays of your countenance penetrate
beyond the borders of Egypt.
Hail to you, Khufu,
Lord of the Two Lands,
who, when resting in your palace,
hear the words of all the people,
for indeed as surely as the sky hosts millions of stars,
you have millions of ears.
Your eyes see every deed that is done, good and evil.
Hail, king of beauty who gives breath to all.

Later in the day, Khufu and Nemon ventured out of the royal campsite to the fledgling Sphinx Temple. Khufu felt this was somehow the first step, the triggering, that would unleash the powers of magic upon the land and people, powers that would shape the future. What kind of future would depend on the power wielded by the ablest magician.

It was not easy for Khufu to go to the Sphinx Temple since it was known he was present in Giza. Going incognito was the only way, so he dressed himself as an ordinary priest, the leopard skin thrown over his shoulder. This would also work well for Nemon, since he too was a member of the upper class and needed a disguise. They could wear wigs that would make posing as priests work.

The tour of the temple, still under construction, was deeply satisfying to both men but for different reasons. Nemon was filled with the pride of a job well started and with the pleasure it brought his royal cousin; Khufu was satisfied because he had begun to erect a beautiful, inspiring sanctuary in honor of the great goddess Isis, the Star God who would be the first to return to Earth at this auspicious time in the history of Egypt. Khufu could picture what the building would look like when the work was done. He was pleased. The joy of that alone was almost enough to make him forget about Sokar and his threat even when Manetho told the king that Sokar had arrived at Giza and had been spotted with his valet strolling among the monuments. . . .

Sokar, accompanied by Kheti, had hired a sailing vessel to carry them to Giza and, in an unusual gesture, had taken Horus. A priest-magician with a hawk on his forearm definitely stood out in a crowd, making Sokar's presence easy to spot.

Kheti had set up two small tents for himself and his master. Sokar's was lavish. Overnight jaunts like this were unusual for Sokar. Truth be told, the elite classes did not like the carnival-like atmosphere of prefestival activities. Tomorrow would be different, for the celebration would change from frivolity to orderly respect for the sacred event that had brought the people together.

Sokar strolled among the people, drawn to the area of the plateau where the royal camp was located. Not wanting to be seen, Sokar stood in the shadows cast by the setting sun upon the assortment of tents and lean-tos pitched on the desert floor. He sighted Meri-ib and Taret in conversation with several other priests from Heliopolis. Their demeanor suggested that they were engaged in small talk, but the sight of the two gave Sokar pause. He knew they had been advisors to Khufu, although he was not aware to what extent.

Sokar watched the priest and priestess, all the while sorting out his thoughts. Taret left the group, so Sokar concentrated on the priest. Meri-ib—Sokar had known a thousand like him: loyal to the Throne, a traditionalist whose view of the priesthood was more fraternal than political, about religion, not power. Sokar had often wondered what motivated priests like Meri-ib. He *knew* what motivated magicians like Dedi.

Dedi was motivated by power and control; he liked the "taste" of the highest, most refined energies, and the "smell" of victory over weakness of any kind. It was this that made priests like Dedi good magicians. If the "weakness" was illness or disease, he thrived on the thrill of defeating it and becoming a powerful healer. For Dedi, it was not about healing the sick person; it was about the thrill he got from the defeat of his opponents. Like Dedi, Sokar knew the more power one has, the more power one can wield.

It did not go unnoticed by Sokar that the hawk on his arm, although hooded, was also watching the scene, evident by the tightness of its muscles. Horus had "met" Meri-ib before, had been in his dreams, was familiar with his energy imprint.

Sokar merged with Horus's mind for a moment and tuned into Meri-ib. Does Meri-ib know this is the time I will make my move against Khufu? Does he know what Khufu's plans are? Does Khufu have a plan?

So in the middle of a conversation with a colleague from the House of Life at the Temple of Thoth in Hermopolis, Meri-ib's train of thought was interrupted. Due to his extraordinary sensitivity to psychic events around him, Meri-ib was aware someone was injecting himself into his mind. He felt his body stiffen and a slight current of electricity shot through him. He quickly turned around on his stool to see who might be doing this.

Sokar ducked behind a tapestry hanging from a cross-pole and disappeared from Meri-ib's sight. Touching the hawk's hooded head firmly was Sokar's way of communicating the message to "stay still and quiet." Horus got the message. The two stood perfectly still and shut off their minds so as not to be sensed telepathically.

Meri-ib went to Taret's tent to inform her of his experience. "He is here, Lady Taret," Meri-ib spoke softly. "Sokar is here, and his energy is vengeance."

Chapter Sixty-One

The Eve of All Tomorrows

Ever since Khufu had received word from his chief intelligence officer that Sokar was present at Giza, the king felt what could almost be called relief. It was time for the confrontation to occur, the matter settled. Though he was sure of the loyalty of the Egyptian people and of his claim to the Throne of the Two Lands, Khufu was not so foolish as to underestimate the destructive power that could be wielded by a lone magician bent on revenge and power. He knew that Meri-ib and Taret were aware of Sokar's presence, and he was confident in his cadre of magicians.

In the privacy of the royal campsite, Khufu, Nemon, and Meritates sat under the glittering night sky, the comet above them. Khufu could not now remember a time when it wasn't visible, though it had only been for a short time. It seemed as if it had always been there and always would be. Maybe this was the nature of its power, to bring a part of the distant universe into one's everyday life.

Meritates sat nearby, listening to the conversation between her husband and his cousin. She liked Nemon. He brought out the best in Khufu, including his humor. Khufu always seemed more light-hearted when he was with Nemon, more confident. Nemon never displayed envy, never disrespected Khufu or took advantage of his position within the royal family, and Khufu trusted Nemon.

"Do you ever wonder what it is like up there?" Khufu said.

Nemon, surprised at the question and Khufu's mood, exhaled heavily, then laughed. "No, I cannot say that I ever have, cousin."

"You do not say much about the Neters, my cousin. Do you not believe in their existence?"'

"Yes, yes, of course I do." Nemon's tone was defensive. "You know that. Surely you do, Your Majesty."

Khufu stood and walked a few paces away before turning to face Nemon and the queen, a grin on his face. "Tell me, cousin. What god is your god? To which among the Neters do you pledge the greatest allegiance?"

Nemon responded without hesitation, "Thoth, my lord, consort of Ma'at."

"Ah, I see. Thoth."

The king straightened his posture and put an index finger to his lips in contemplation. "I suppose that makes perfectly good sense for an architect."

"What do you mean 'for an architect'?" Nemon questioned.

"I suspect my conclusion has less to do with Thoth than Ma'at," Khufu said. "I view Ma'at as the progenitor of order who oversees the patterns by which all live. An architect's world is about patterns, harmony, and balance, is it not?"

Nemon was impressed. This showed the king had insight about architecture. Nemon stood, his legs spread slightly, his arms crossed over his bare chest, and looked up at the stars. "Yes, now that I think about it, I suppose I have thought about what is 'up' there. I think in a way different from you. You are king of Egypt, a living god. It is part of who you are as Chief Priest and chief magician to know more about these things than a common man like me would."

"You are right. It is part of my job to know more than perhaps I care to know," Khufu replied pleasantly. "But you, Nemon, are far from ignorant. This I know. I am very interested in knowing what you think is 'up' there beyond the stars we can see."

"The comet seems especially bright tonight," the queen said, her voice soft and melodious. "Strange, but every time I see it I think of the House of Eternity." Her comment seemed out of context from the direction in which the conversation had been going, Khufu thought.

"The House of Eternity?" Khufu asked, not recalling Meritates ever having said much about religious matters. "What do you mean?"

"Oh, I don't know. Looking at it makes me think of mysteries, star mysteries. It makes me think about . . . about my soul, I suppose. About the cosmic intelligence. I think a lot about the Star Gods, the 'gateways' in the sky, even about becoming a star when I die, becoming a part of the landscape of the imperishable stars."

"Well, my dear. It sounds as if you have been giving this a lot of thought."

Meritates smiled and apologized for interrupting the conversation.

"No, do not be sorry, my queen," Nemon said, taking a step towards her. "I find what you are saying most interesting. I too have had thoughts of living in the House of Eternity and what it must be like to be a part of that—that is, provided it is something a soul would be *conscious* of." Turning to Khufu, Nemon asked, "What do you think, cousin? Does a king ever think about such things?"

Khufu did not answer at first, his thoughts distant. A nudge from his wife brought him back. "Yes, of course a king thinks about things like that. At least *this* king does."

The topic was getting close to what had been on Khufu's mind for some time, facts which Nemon did not know. Khufu recognized the irony in the discussion.

Anxious now to change the subject, Meritates suggested that a cup of palm wine would be soothing to a dry throat. "And it will help you sleep, my husband."

"I don't think I will have any trouble sleeping, my dear," Khufu said, stifling a yawn with his hand over his mouth. "In fact, I *know* I won't."

That same night, Shemshu-Hor sat in his tent in meditation. It was his method of leaving the physical world and existing in a dimension where "his world," the Sirius star system, was accessible. The Old One spent the majority of his time in this altered state in order to move freely between the world he occupied in Egypt and his world of origin. There the Temple of the One Star in the Sirius star system was the place where the Neters worshipped and interacted with the divine force.

Shemshu-Hor transported himself into the Duat to the Temple of the One Star to connect with Osiris. Consort and brother of Isis, Osiris would be the second of the Star Gods to return to Egypt, and his return would mark the beginning of the next level of teachings that would allow humans to enter the starry realms beyond death. Shemshu-Hor continued to play a major role in conditioning humanity to be ready to receive the teachings and to handle the energies associated with this next step.

Eldest of all the Sirian Star Gods, older even than Shemshu-Hor, Osiris now existed as pure light. To Shemshu-Hor's eyes, however, the deity appeared in his human form, yet with an extraordinary aura of golden light surrounding him. The two Star Gods in the Temple of the One Star acknowledged each other, then settled in for an exchange regarding what would befall the children of Egypt. When Shemshu-Hor voiced his concern for the future, Osiris explained the mission of Isis.

"It is time for humanity to have knowledge that will, over time, bring it deeper understanding of reality," said Osiris. "This knowledge will take humans beyond physical, emotional, and intellectual life. It will help them take part in divine experiences by becoming aligned to the underlying principles, of which they are still mostly unaware."

Shemshu-Hor knew what Osiris was speaking about. "It has been decided then that the teaching of the Law of Synchronicity shall be transmitted?"

"Exactly," Osiris answered. "The Law of Simultaneity. This teaching will inform them that every event, everything that happens in any cycle of time, is purposeful and happens at the same time on more than one level of reality."

In his wisdom, Osiris had determined what humans needed to learn at this point, and to whom the wisdom would be entrusted. The Old One realized that it would be "given" initially by Isis to the priesthood of Egypt, and from their teachings it would eventually spread to all cultures and peoples on Earth. In the centuries that Shemshu-Hor had been in Egypt, due to the teachings given to humans at the First Time, he had witnessed a nearly barbaric society transform itself in search of a "path" of life that would ultimately lead to the divine.

The gods are potent, yet human free will always has to be taken into consideration, Shemshu-Hor reflected. The new teachings would guarantee advancement, but how long that would take, or if humans would *choose* to learn, was uncertain, and the process could not be interfered with by the Star Gods.

"The teachings our Star Sister brings to the priesthood of Egypt—" Shemshu-Hor began, but Osiris cut him off.

"The teachings will be revealed to the trustworthy minds of the priesthood of Heliopolis. They will then disperse them by teaching the advanced apprentices in the House of Life at the Temple of the Sun."

Shemshu-Hor was not surprised. He knew that the priesthood in Heliopolis was capable of receiving the teachings and giving them the respect they deserved. "Very well. I see the wisdom in this choice, my brother." The Old One made a slight gesture of acquiescence. "They will receive the 'seed' of Osiris consciousness."

"Yes, so they can be eligible to participate in these cycles during life and see that any and all experiences, positive or negative, difficult or easy, are transformative in nature."

Night was upon them as Ani, Khem, Tiye, and Bast arrived at Giza and joined Sheshat and Klea. The priestesses had decided to visit the site of the festivities rather than remain in Heliopolis. Word had been sent to Taret of their change of plans, and she had told Meri-ib, Taret trusting that the presence of the priestesses at Giza had been divinely ordained. . . .

In the last hours of that night before the rising of Sirius, Meri-ib lay awake. It was not Sokar who was on his mind, but the rumor of the appearance of two magicians. The names being bantered about were Dedi, the old adept from the South, and Anpu the Jackal, a mysterious desert-dweller who was rarely seen in populated areas. Not much was known about Anpu, a fact that amplified his reputation as a magician to be feared. Some said that Anpu could charm the cobra and tame the most rabid jackal, that he could "speak" death to a human, that he was a skilled necromancer. So why were these two sorcerers now in Giza?

Before returning to her makeshift bedchamber on this night before Inundation, Taret had spent a short time with the four priestesses from Heliopolis. But Taret was especially interested in another "priestess." Bast. Khem's pet lioness. The animal had an air about her that Taret had not sensed before tonight, an air that suggested divinity, the kind ascribed to special animals such as the Apis bull and the Delta crocodile. Bast was no ordinary lioness. The cat possessed a power that would soon be revealed, Taret intuited.

Taret's reflections on Bast led her to consider a Neter she had not thought about in some time: Mut. There was little mention of Mut in the texts of Taret's day. Her name, which means "mother," could be considered a clue as to her identity, but nothing about Mut was certain. She was rarely referred to in the star teachings at the Temple of the Sun, but when she was, she was portrayed as a celestial cow closely associated with Ra and other luminaries of the sky, such as the Moon.

Mut's concern was the integrity of the state and the ruling monarch. Apep, the great serpent who embodied all the enemies of the Throne, himself had but one enemy: the cat, often portrayed as a lioness. Mut as a crone goddess wielded power and influence as Mistress of Heaven, and her hieroglyph was that of the vulture. When depicted in her "human" form, the goddess wore a vulture-shaped cap, complete with wings and a head. Mut and Bast—were they connected, Taret wondered.

"Could it possibly be? Could Bast be an incarnation of Mut?" Taret whispered, her voice sounding loud in the quiet of the night. Had the troubled atmosphere generated by Khufu's peril summoned Mut? Did Mut need a physical form at this time to walk among the men and women of Egypt?

Across a small sand dune, in a one-person tent that had been set up for each of the visiting Star Priestesses, Khem lay half-asleep. She was in a keen psychic state, aware of Taret's thoughts about Bast and Mut. Khem was aware, from her training in the House of Life, of feline deities, and she understood feline power, and a lot about Sekhmet because of her relationship with Tiye.

With images of cats and cat deities in mind, Khem finally fell asleep. She was soon floating in her dream vessel, on a small planet, green with vegetation under a bright blue sky. She knew she was on a planet that revolved around the Star of Women in the Sirius system. She encountered a tribe of lionlike females who possessed great powers of healing and medicine and yet who were also warrior women, defenders of their realm. Theirs was one of three life-bearing planets that comprised the Sirius system. Khem saw several Amazonlike women, masculine and physically strong. Their bodies were human, bronze in color, their skin leathery, but their heads were leonine—beautiful, regal.

Khem felt her own body become a lion-woman. Now she could understand their language and listened to a conversation that concerned the Holy Order of Nut. She realized she was dreaming about the Sirian counterpart of her own order of Star Priestesses. She was one of them, and they were one of her. The lion-women appointed her their ambassador to the Order of Nut on Earth.

She woke up. Her dream over, Khem lingered in the experience of her transformed body. Beads of sweat formed on her neck and scalp. Her head always seemed more sensitive to the heat, and was the first part of her body to respond to it. Tonight was no different, and the discomfort of the warm night drew her thoughts back from the heights and focused them on how hard it was to sleep. She hated that feeling of restless, fitful napping and the disjointed images that came with it.

Khem sat up, her feet dangling off the cot. She had spent only a few nights in a tent in her life and had found the experience unpleasant each time. The netting that protected her from insects gave her an almost claustrophobic feeling, like being wrapped in a cocoon, and an even greater uncomfortable feeling of closeness. She wondered if Tiye was asleep.

Khem's fretfulness woke up Bast. The cat lifted her head and peered at her mistress in the darkness. The dying embers of a small brazier reflected the orange globes of the cat's eyes, eyes of a lioness and of a soul aware of its mission in life. . . .

Tiye lay asleep in a tent next to Khem's. Her body was tired, her muscles sore from stress and a lack of rest, and she had fallen into a restful sleep. Just before sleep came, however, her thoughts too had focused on Bast.

What a magnificent animal she has become, Tiye reflected. Her features are so expressive, the golden color of her fur luminous. But it was Bast's inner magnificence that enchanted Tiye. The animal's eyes seemed the embodiment of wisdom. She marveled how the cat's mind-to-mind connection allowed her to communicate with humans, how her presence seemed to calm human feelings. Bast was certainly one of the most psychic creatures Tiye had seen, and the lioness seemed even to have knowledge of human psychology.

What if there were a race of beings like Bast? Maybe they live on one of the wandering stars or maybe on every one of them, Tiye thought. Maybe they can travel around the universe. . . .

Khufu was always surrounded by luxury. On this night before the momentous day, the king lay on his gilded cot, his head resting comfortably on a carved wooden headrest. He had fallen into a light sleep, but that had lasted only an hour and he was again wide-awake. Had any man before him lain in bed contemplating ascending into the starry realm of Osiris while alive?

Every cell in Khufu's body was expectant of what would begin at dawn. Surely neither god nor man could sleep under these circumstances. He could hear Meritates's gentle breathing, and somewhere in the distant hills the howls of jackals, which led the king to reach for the Sekhmet amulet around his neck. He had not been without it a moment.

He thought of the Mysteries, of human nature and the subtle bodies, the part of him that was the *akh*, the spirit, the highest, most refined essence. He had little experience of this. He had been taught it was his imperishable Body of Light, not bound or restricted in any way to time and space. What power that body has, Khufu thought.

Pharaoh rolled over and sat up on the side of his bed. He felt both alone within himself and filled with the presence of countless gods, demigods, and spirit forces. He was aware somewhere in his consciousness of possessing knowledge of all beings, and he knew he could access it if he needed to. He wondered if his experience of living ascension would result in his attaining a transcendent, superconscious state. He thought about the symbol of the *akh*, the *Benu*, associated with Isis as she manifested through the light rays of the Great Star. In a few hours, Sirius would make its appearance. So many had come to Giza to witness this most celebrated of celestial events. Did fate gather these witnesses together? Did each have a role to play in this auspicious event? Where was Sokar? What scheme did he have in mind?

Thoughts of Sokar started to lead Khufu into fear, but it was not a precipice he would allow himself to fall over. He would not allow fear to taint his clarity of mind and heart. He would be open to whatever experience was to come, and he would deal with it with his full power.

The feeling you get when you think you are being watched came over Khufu. He turned around to look behind him. In the darkness stood a shadowy figure so real that Khufu could hear its breathing and smell its sweet perfume. The dark shadow became a silver woman. The Silver Woman was iridescent. For the moment, to Khufu, there was no one else on the planet except him and this mirage. Thoughts began to be exchanged between Khufu and the Silver Woman.

"Soon, Khufu, first true born of King Sneferu, Wearer of the Double Crown, Uniter of the Two Lands, you will learn what it is like to assume your place among the stars. To go beyond knowing with your mind that you are a star and to experience *being* a star. A solitary, eternal star king who will someday join the ranks of the celestial rulers. You will look upon Osiris as he commands the Star Gods. You will feel his divine qualities, taste of the nectar, touch the energies of the masters of wisdom, the Star Gods. Your body will be the body of a god. It will not decay or be destroyed. Once again your flesh will be born to life and your years will exceed the years of the stars. This is to be a hallowed rite performed only for you and upon you, and you shall never perform it on anyone, not your sons or your sons' sons. It is truly a secret of the gods."

The silvery light faded slowly, leaving nothing more than a dark shadow before disappearing completely. The experience left Khufu calm and secure. He had nothing to fear.

Chapter Sixty-Two

The Rising of the Great Star

Silence loomed over the towns, countryside, and the Nile, as Egypt slept, yet the night was nearly over. Servants throughout the royal campsite awoke hours before dawn on Inundation day, preparing breakfasts, gathering necessities for morning toilets, laying out the clothes the elite would wear for the day's festivities. Darkness cloaked the land in an indigo robe spangled with stars, and the comet, still distinct, dominated the heavens. The Royal Family was dressed and ate a meal of figs, sweet bread, and goat's milk. Khufu was anxious to go to the viewing outpost erected up on the eastern side of the Great Pyramid for the family and their guests.

When the king emerged from his tent, Nemon was waiting and Khufu saw in a nearby campsite that Meri-ib and Taret were preparing to board litters that would take them to the viewing dais. Sweeping the panorama of people and tents scattered nearby, Khufu saw him, fifty yards away. It was Sokar. An impressive sight even in the dim light, Sokar stood in front of a brightly dyed tent, the hooded hawk Horus on his right forearm. Even in the dim light, the two men's eyes locked for an instant, Sokar and Khufu.

Khufu joined Nemon and the two walked over to the royal litter and climbed in. Royal guards escorted them onto the dais, where they sat and sipped milk. People assembled on the plateau, congregating around the Sphinx and pyramids. The festival-goers were quiet and orderly, awaiting the rising of the Great Star of Isis.

A thousand thoughts rushed through Khufu's head. There was no denying Sokar's feelings. They had been transmitted to Khufu through their fleeting eye contact. The king knew he was in for the battle of his life. He also knew that this would not be a physical battle, but one fought in the Duat with weapons inaccessible to the uninitiated.

Sokar, for his part, had awakened refreshed from sleep, ready to meet the day and his fate, whatever the Neters deemed that to be. Kheti gathered a few of his master's personal effects that Sokar had requested—the mace, a hammered copper sunburst necklace, his leopard skin vestment, and a linen bag that contained a few special stones, cowrie shells, and a variety of diamonds, rubies, and garnets. Sokar knew the rising of the star would release cosmic energy into the fabric of physical reality and that such power could be harnessed for magical operations. Sokar knew how to use that power to his advantage, and he would.

Kheti saw to Sokar's morning toilet and got his master dressed in the outfit he had chosen. Bare feet were protected from what would become scorching sand by sandals that laced up to his calves and tied below the knees. A stiff linen kilt wrapped around his waist, secured by a sash of jewel-studded leather. It was against tradition for priests to wear leather, but Sokar was not in a priestly frame of mind. Today he was a magician.

Kheti had driven a stake in the ground as a perch for Horus. The hawk sensed the tension in the air, much of which had nothing to do with the celebration of the rising of the Great Star. He was so attuned to Sokar he knew things were coming to a head.

Sokar watched the *fellahin* and elite arrive on the east side of the Great Pyramid. He observed two figures different from the rest, not in their physical appearance for it was still too dark to see all that clearly, but in their energy. Magicians, no question about it. One was Dedi, but the other was not familiar to Sokar. What was Dedi doing here? It was uncommon for magicians to be present at this sort of public celebration; they preferred to perform their own private rituals on such occasions. Who was with Dedi and why? Sokar surrounded himself with a psychic shield.

The two magicians were coming close to Sokar's campsite. Not wanting to be seen or engaged by them in any way, Sokar slipped back inside his tent to watch. Finally he saw who the other magician was—Anpu the Jackal. Anpu was assumed to be Egyptian, but his mother was said to be a full-blooded Nubian and among the most respected and feared of magicians. Called Nefer, she was said to have been so beautiful that the very sight of her enchanted king and commoner alike. Anpu's father had been an advisor to several high-born men, including King Sneferu.

Word had it that Anpu had spent the majority of his life in the legendary land of Punt, reputed to be a semitropical coastal land by the Red

Sea and a "land of the gods." It was said that Anpu could talk to the animals, spoke the language of every living creature, and could transform himself into any life form he chose, even trees. Anpu was tall and thin, and his body was hairy, reminiscent of the animals he was said to live amongst and communicate with. He wore only a loincloth, leather sandals, and a jackal pelt slung over his right shoulder.

Meanwhile, Khufu's standard bearer went to the dais carrying the Double Crown and the Crook and Flail. It was time to adorn the King with the symbols of his office as everyone was gathered on the east side of the Great Pyramid and sunrise was now but half an hour away.

Three litter bearers approached the dais. Meri-ib and Taret were the first to disembark from their individual litters. Side by side the former High Priest and High Priestess of Heliopolis were escorted to their places. Before the third litter was emptied of its occupant, another litter arrived bearing Meritates and other members of the royal family.

The other litters were opened. Two royal guards flanked Shemshu-Hor. Servants straightened his long kilt and held onto his arms to prevent him from falling. Shemshu-Hor was carried up the two steps to the dais. His presence did not go unnoticed by the two magicians standing unobtrusively nearby. Neither Dedi nor Anpu had met Shemshu-Hor in person, yet they were both aware of him, knew what he was rumored to be.

Shemshu-Hor gestured to be put down to stand on his own. He turned to the two magicians, and let their eyes meet. A slight nod of recognition moved the old man's head, though no words were said by any of the three. Shemshu-Hor shuffled over to a small chair that had been placed for him, leaning against the servants for support. What was going on in the elder's mind was anyone's guess.

The entourage of Star Priestesses and apprentices was the last to join the company of dignitaries assembled on the Royal Dais. Ani was leading the small group of priestesses. Walking obediently beside Khem, Bast seemed to sense the tension in the air. The women ascended the dais and took their places beside the contingent of priests from the Temple of the Sun in Heliopolis and the Temple of Ptah in Memphis. Khem, Klea, Ani, Sheshat, and others were all present, but Tiye was not. Though the Nubian's absence was troubling, even irritating, to Khem, she was certain that Tiye would join them momentarily.

The moment of sunrise was finally at hand. Across from the dais stood Khem, Bast, Klea, and Ani, but Tiye had slipped away. The moment assumed an air of grand drama, all players visibly in place. Except Sokar.

There were no more preparations to be made, no last minute details to be addressed, no more instructions for Sokar to give Kheti. The stars were still shining, and the comet was brighter than ever in the moments before dawn.

A procession of priests and priestesses from various nomes now appeared, winding their way to the east side of the Great Pyramid and the royal dais from the opening between the paws of the Sphinx. Flares made from thatched palm fronds, symbolizing the renewed lighting of the sacred fires in temples across the land, lit their way. Chanting voices became more audible as they got closer. Sistrums and small hand drums gave rhythm to the words.

> We call you, O Starry One,
> from the place beyond the horizon.
> We call you, Sothis, O Beautiful One.
> We call upon you to rise up and fill this place.
> Isis, rise. Isis, rise. Isis, rise.
>
> We call upon you, Great Sothis,
> Goddess of Creation and Renewer of Abundance.
> We long to know you, to see you.
> Open to our eyes as the lotus opens to the Sun.
> Enter in, O Goddess,
> O Lady of the Silver Light, enter in.

The clerics at the end of the procession were followed by servants with trays for Pharaoh and his guests: bread, beef, wine and beer, incense, and a large amphora of sanctified water sprinkled on the ground as they proceeded.

When the offerings came into sight, Khufu remembered that this Opening of the Year festival was also his traditional birthday. Though it was not the day of his actual birth, the ceremonial date corresponded with the birth of Ra. This reaffirmed the divine paternity of the king and the embodiment of the divine on Earth. Khufu had had little time to reflect on this. The procession stopped at the foot of the dais and its members laid down their offerings of food, wine, and flowers, everyone bowing. Khufu nodded in appreciation.

The horizon began to flush pink. Then, all eyes focused upon it, the Great Star appeared, its rays streaming in all directions across the predawn sky. For a few moments, Sirius shone with an unmatched brilliance representing the beautiful goddess Isis, robed in light.

All observers rose to their feet. In a loud voice, Khufu shouted forth the customary praise:

Behold, Beautiful Lady of All
Welcome Lady,
Welcome Goddess,
Welcome Isis,
Your son calls to You,
You have come.
You have come.

The uraeus on Khufu's crown caught the glint of Sirius's light, and the faint light of dawn cast an eerie, beautiful glow on the sea of faces gazing upward.

Khem watched, her hands in tight fists, muscles taut, Bast still as a stone beside her. The other Star Priestesses were also glued to the spot, enrapt in the star's appearance.

In the predawn desert plateau, Khem felt the lingering night chill. Images floated through her mind, pictures of her life. The thought of being guided by fate caused her to remember events and people since coming to Heliopolis; she remembered the awe she had felt the first time she met Taret and Tiye. How exotic she had thought the Nubian then. She understood now it was the heka that flowed through her.

Khem remembered their afternoon on the tiny island in the sacred lake of the Sun Temple when Khaba's spirit had appeared to them. Images of the Spirit Woman in the water of her ceremonial bowl came up, and she saw the writhing priestesses of Hathor and could hear again the tinkling of the finger cymbals and the clinking of the sistrums.

Khem noted Sokar was not on the dais. It would be extraordinary for him to miss an occasion like this. Then she spotted him several feet away from the dais at the edge of the crowd. The sight of him chilled her.

Taret stood with her arms folded across her chest, her eyes closed. This was the most sacred moment in the life of a Star Priestess, the star nourishing her with its light. She felt herself being renewed, participating in one of the greatest moments in the star religion of Egypt.

Each savored the experience in their own way. Some smiled and lifted their arms towards the heavens; others wept for joy and thanksgiving; others stood motionless, humbled. The atmosphere crackled. Sirius hung there in glory until suddenly the horizon split like a burst seam. Ra was coming. Before long, the Sun's light absorbed that of Sirius, and the fires of the two stars were as if blended into one flame that began its journey across the sky. Sirius had risen, its promise kept.

The excitement generated by the rising of the Great Star had drawn the people's attention away from the comet that had lit up the night sky. After a brief disappearance in the surge of sunlight, the comet reappeared brighter than ever. Yet the comet should not be visible during the day, thought Khufu, who realized the foretold events had begun, and that the comet's visibility must be the first sign of the Second Coming of the Star Gods.

Two hawks swooped hugely above the Great Pyramid and the royal dais. Soaring in a circle above the dais several times, the birds landed on an outcrop of rocks a hundred feet away.

Thinking the incident strange, Khufu turned back to the comet. Gradually, its head became a ball of bluish-white light. The great ball began to slowly descend. The comet was now a sphere of blue-white flames.

The two hawks leapt into the air again to circle high above the plateau. Sokar was about to make his stand. His plan was that he would appear as a hawk, with Horus in his hawk form, then shape-shift back into human form for all to see. What better way to show his power of a magician who possessed the powers of a god.

Awe turned to apprehension in the crowd as people sensed evil and darkness. The air became stifling, with an odor of singed hair. The sky seemed to be pierced with four holes through which blew the cosmic winds. Hostile forms appeared, serpents, crocodiles, and scorpions, even deformed humanlike beings, from the Underworld.

The appearance of the hawks and the otherworldly forms alerted every magician present. Dedi and Anpu were the first to react. The two transformed themselves into big jackals. Teeth bared, they ran to the dais. At the same moment, out on the eastern edge of the plateau, Tiye felt herself taken over by Sekhmet and change into a lioness with fangs and sharp claws. Her eyes fixed immediately on the two hawks. Sensing their target, she raced towards the King of Egypt. Bast jerked free of her leash in a burst of power that almost knocked Khem off her feet, and joined Tiye, now like the lion goddess Sekhmet. On the dais, Khufu grasped Tiye's amulet.

Sokar's and Horus's confidence made them oblivious to danger or interference in their mission. The strange beings from the Duat surrounded them in a vile mist and added to the strength of the hawks. Meanwhile, Bast joined Tiye-Sekhmet to defend the king against the hawks, the two lions running side by side. This was a goddess, a devourer of evil. No one could stop Sekhmet.

The massive hawks swooped toward the desert and landed, sunlight flashing like gold on their feathers. Horus lit a few feet from the Sokar-hawk, his wings spread wide to gain his balance. The Sokar-hawk let out a piercing shriek as his talons gripped the rocky ground, his wings spread wide and flapping wildly, kicking up dust.

The jackals arrived at the base of the royal dais to avert the threat to

Khufu. They crouched, teeth bared, snarling, and the power the two emitted caused the hawks to freeze, beaks open. But before the jackals did anything, the attack came from a different source, the two running lionesses.

The two lionesses then merged into a single wild lion. Hind legs and paws of the single charging lioness became legs, a muscular bronze woman. Front legs and paws became arms and hands, each bicep surrounded by a gold armband. The naked body was human from the neck down, but had the head of a magnificent lioness topped by a golden disk. It was Sekhmet in full glory!

The lion-woman ran with all her might, chest heaving, the muscles in her thighs rippling. From out of the solar disk atop her head reared a hissing cobra, its hood spread wide, jaws gaped open. The uraeus on Khufu's crown came to life, and its snake reared, eyes like diamonds, creating a barrier of protection around the royal dais. Sekhmet leaped, claws tearing into the Sokar-hawk.

The huge bird reverted back into a human. Sekhmet and Sokar fell as if through a tear in the sky into the Duat and were gone. Horus flew away. Still crouching in readiness, the jackals rose on all fours, and ran into the distance.

There would be no announcement by Sokar, no demonstration of his power. Sokar was gone, defeated, having risked his all for the power of the Throne, and lost. He was now in a place where he would have to deal with the consequences of his actions in the presence of the demons he had created. He would trouble Khufu and Egypt no more.

Chapter Sixty-Three

Into the Path of Stars

The morning air was hot, but no one noticed. Purple and gold light broke the darkness of the eastern horizon and Ra's rays would soon be blindingly bright, but no one would complain this day. The aroma of warming sand, campfires, and incense wafted through the air and a kind of purity permeated the crowd, and no one spoke.

Khufu, Nemon, and the rest of the royal family and dignitaries stood in awe of what they had just witnessed. Sekhmet had saved the Pharaoh. The Great Lady of the Flame, Daughter of Ra, had raged in power as the defender of the king and avenger of the Sun god when he was disrespected by humans. They had watched Sokar be thrown out of the physical world, into some other time and place. Not suprisingly, most people had been distracted from the descending comet which now appeared as a glowing sphere of blue-white ice. With Sokar gone, all eyes focused again on the miraculous event unfolding before them. The comet slowly began to disintegrate, emitting bright particles, and in seconds, the comet's shell dissolved.

Khufu felt a surge of energy through his body, thrilling every cell. The moment of the Second Coming had arrived. Meri-ib and Taret were wide-eyed with expectation, and Meri-ib reached out to take hold of Taret's hand. Years of dedication to the Neters were about to be rewarded.

As the comet came apart, radiance sparkled in every direction. Gradually, out of the comet's light filaments, the form of the goddess took shape. Surrounding her, the Boat of a Million Years formed, the barque of light.

The bow and stern of the celestial ship curved towards the heavens, as if inviting the sky itself to come on board. Physical and astral worlds overlapped at Egypt's holiest site as Isis, a Star Woman, came back to Egypt.

Out of the massive crowd came shouts of praise and prayers. People fell prostrate to the ground, their foreheads to the hot sand, then sat up on their knees, arms waving in gleeful gyrations.

On the dais, Khufu and the royal family and members of the court were dazzled by the spectacle. The goddess was veiled in swirls of bluish light, but within that she wore a white garment embroidered in shimmering gold in symbols and hieroglyphs. Her long, dark hair curled over her neck and streamed over her shoulders. In her right hand, she held a Rod of Power, a scepter of bronze surrounded by a serpent whose head with emerald eyes reared in the stance of intimidation to enemies. The bottom of the scepter was a blue lotus blossom, age-old symbol of dawn, new beginnings, and renewal.

Following Khufu's lead, everyone on the royal dais knelt in respect. Then Isis spoke:

> I am Isis, ruler of this land.
> I gave the sacred laws to humanity
> and ordained what no one can change.
> I am the eldest daughter of Time,
> wife and sister of Osiris who will soon join me,
> and mother of Horus.
> I am She who rises within the Great Star.
> I have traveled the path of the stars to be with you.
> I separate the Earth from the sky
> and regulate the course of Sun and Moon.
> I have participated in the initiation of humans into the Mysteries.
> I am the Mistress of the winds, rivers, and seas of Earth.
> I am the Daughter of the Sun;
> I shine forth in His mighty rays of light.
> I am Isis who conquers destiny;
> destiny obeys me.
> I come to bring the future destiny of Egypt to you.

Suddenly, the Sun, which had barely climbed above the horizon, looked as if Apep had taken a bite out of it. Darkness descended. An eclipse had begun. The figure of Isis cast an eerie glow across the landscape as it became predawn again. Hanging above the horizon like a diamond pendant was the Great Star.

Khufu rose to his feet and it seemed to him that time was standing still. The act of standing up could have taken six seconds or six million years. Isis was silent, and all of Giza was in suspension. Shemshu-Hor stepped forward to stand beside the king. Khufu realized that Shemshu-Hor would be his companion as starwalker in this long-anticipated moment.

Khufu raised his arms as if reaching up to the starry realm. A cloudlike funnel of wind descended over him and Shemshu-Hor, lifting them both into the air. Their bodies spun in the tornado cloud that carried them toward the star bridge. In a flash they were gone, into the Duat of Osiris and the Star Gods.

Khufu often had imagined walking among the stars, seeing the stars up close, but the reality was far different. He felt part of every star at once.

Spiraling upward, the physical structure of his body seemed to disintegrate and become radiant light causing Khufu's mind to be at one with the cosmos. Everything that existed seemed to dissolve into undulating light waves in every direction. He was aware of being a part of it all, all-knowing, omnipresent, omnipotent in this realm.

He was beyond the grasp of death, beyond analyzing his thoughts, beyond fear. He was in bliss, free in his soul, in perfect balance. Walking among the stars is walking in the Light, Khufu understood. It is being everything and nothing at once. In the Light is the Darkness, the Darkness being but the dark side of the Light, that which is hidden from human eyes and incomprehensible to human intellect. Every star revealed itself as a cell of the universe as he felt himself to be everywhere at the same time.

Khufu perceived the Star Gods. He knew them as the universal ambassadors, as galactic spiritual leaders. Khufu encountered Osiris and saw the god was *his own self.* He encountered Thoth among the Star God scribes, the record keepers of all times. He saw Hathor, Isis, Ra: all were he, he was they.

He saw the souls of the great suns. Each Star God was clothed in robes of silver light; and one by one Khufu merged in awareness with each of the Star Gods.

"I am a Body of Light," Khufu thought. "A body of stars, of the souls of great suns. All these bodies of light are the same." Khufu was linked with Osiris, not a star, but *starry. . . .*

Khufu felt his body transforming back into a physical human. Unlike the kings before him, death had not been a prerequisite for him to experience star consciousness. This had been his living ascension. The funnel that had conveyed Shemshu-Hor and Khufu into the stars now brought them back to Earth. The force that had blocked the Sun's light slowly relinquished its hold and gradually the light of day returned. Yet the light of the Great Star still shone as a diadem over the head of Isis.

Khufu stood again on the royal dais. Meritates and Nemon approached him to reassure themselves he was all right. He was.

Shemshu-Hor stood, his frail and stooped body seeming to have new strength and life. He seemed younger. The holy man's voice was audible across the plateau, yet another manifestation of the magical day. "We welcome you, O Great Lady Isis, Lady of the Mysteries, Beautiful Shining One of Sirius, our home in the world of the stars. We greet you and praise you for connecting us all once again to our star. Isis, my star sister, giver of life, you are the one who pours out the precious waters of Inundation. I, along with all the souls of this sacred land, welcome you who make people live and plants grow. We celebrate your coming, Lady of Sirius, Lady of the Underworld, Mistress of Heaven, you who created what your heart conceived, you who are the living soul of all that lives. Come now to the Temple prepared for you."

Khufu asked the royal valet to fetch his leopard skin robe, which he then laid across his shoulders. The golden armbands around each of his biceps glinted in the sunlight, his white pleated kilt shone brightly against his dark tanned skin, and the Double Crown sat proudly on his head.

Cries began to swell among the ranks of the *fellahin* and elite alike, "Hail Khufu, King of Egypt. Hail, O Great One."

Over and over the words poured forth in waves of devotion. Khufu stood proud and tall on the dais. He lifted his hands in humble acceptance of the praise and motioned to Meritates to stand by his side. The royal couple basked in the light of Ra and public devotion.

An entourage of attendant priests, Followers of Horus, led Shemshu-Hor from the dais. The old priest and Isis, who had assumed the form of a human woman, met members of the royal family, the priesthood, and the Sirius Council on their way to the Sphinx Temple. When the entourage arrived, Isis stood at the Temple gateway. Khufu took charge of the dedication ceremony. "A temple is a sacred place existing in many dimensions other than the physical," he declared. "A temple is a place that links the Earth and sky. This temple will serve that purpose for as long as it stands. Egypt, our sacred land, is a mirror of the divine regions. The Two Lands of Egypt reflect the celestial sphere. So this is a special place. Temple construction here has one objective, to create a place to communicate with the Sky Gods at auspicious times. Today is one of those times. This temple is designed to collect the light of Sirius, which we shall do today."

Isis, her voice sweet and melodious declared, "I am aware of the purpose of this temple, to capture the sacred light of the Great Star. It has already done that."

The group moved inside the temple to the entryway of a long, narrow shaft. The high altar of red granite was flanked on each side by miniature obelisks etched with the ten thousand names of Isis and capped with a pyramidion made from meteorite. When completed, light from the Sun could be let in at any time through tiny portholes that could be opened, but otherwise, the shaft would remain dark.

The entourage, led by Isis, went to the high altar. Isis pointed her finger at the Tet symbol that appeared to have been burned into the red stone. Resembling an ankh and the knot that ties the belts of the gods, the Tet symbolized the union and combined power of Isis and Osiris. "It is put here by heka for all to see and be reminded of my bond with Osiris. And with you, King Khufu, and with the people of Egypt," Isis said. Then Isis dedicated the Sphinx Temple:

> I am Mother Isis,
> I am she who fights not,
> but who is always victorious.
> I am in all things, and all things are in me.
> I dedicate this place as holy ground
> for as long as the pyramids stand,
> as long as the Great Sphinx sits guarding the East,
> for as long as this consecrated place is pure and is kept pure.
> By my magic it is so.

With a wave of her hand over the altar, the goddess released the fragrance of ten thousand blossoms to fill the place with the aroma of paradise.

Chapter Sixty-Four

The New Initiations in Heliopolis

Later in that tumultuous day: at Giza, Tiye and Bast wandered in from the desert. Khem ran out to meet them.

"Tiye! Are you all right? What happened?"

Tiye was dazed. "I don't know. I was going with you and the others to the ceremony, then it was as if something, or *someone*, called to me. I remember a surge of power and that's all."

Khem smiled at her friend and gave her a hug. "Never mind, I'll tell you all about it later. But come, you must hurry or we'll miss our initiation."

There was a network in the universe that connected all things. Although the average person was unaware of the existence of this, it was common knowledge to those who studied in the House of Life. Nowhere was this truer than among the learned sages of Heliopolis.

One of the purposes of the network was to link the minds of the Neters, so the cosmic network would be lively at this time, as all the Neters had been monitoring the comet that bore Isis. One of the Star Gods was particularly interested: Thoth, the messenger of the gods and original teacher of the knowledge to Egyptians during the First Time. Thoth and Shemshu-Hor were brothers, sages, wisest of the wise, whose forte was knowledge gathered from numerous sources through time. Their extreme longevity qualified them to be the keepers of this wisdom.

The new teachings were brought to Egypt with Isis, but the teaching of them would be by Thoth. In the days to come, Thoth would return to Egypt and enter the House of the Sun in Heliopolis to teach initiates about humanity's role in the universe. There was a legend that pieces of the original teachings of Thoth were missing. Only Shemshu-Hor knew where they were and now they could be restored. The teachings had to do with humanity's extraterrestrial origin and what that knowledge implied for the future.

Shemshu-Hor was the only human who understood these teachings that the elite sector of the Priesthood of Heliopolis was about to be taught. The Old One had earned the right to return home to Sirius, and it was now time for Thoth to return to Egypt for the new teaching to begin on subjects such as architecture, design, mathematics, and astronomy.

Shemshu-Hor had one last decision to make before departing. He would select one from among the Star Priestesses to serve as the counterpart of Thoth during the god's time in Egypt. This one would have the responsibility of serving the Father of All Scribes. Shemshu-Hor's choice was Sheshat. She would work closely with Khufu and future kings. Only she would know how many days would be allotted to Khufu in life. She would be in charge of the royal library and the Great Library at the Temple of the Sun. She would assist the Pharaoh in the Stretching of the Cord ceremonies having to do with laying the foundation of temples. The appointment would be a continuing initiation for the able priestess and scribe. And Sheshat would have an assistant, Khem.

It was unprecedented to have a novice priestess in such a position, but Shemshu-Hor knew his decision was the correct one. Khem would assist Sheshat.

The initiations of the priestesses would take place in a special ritual hall in the Temple of the Sun where Star Gods and humans could meet as citizens of the universe.

Khem, Tiye, Sheshat, Ani, Klea, and their religious sisters would have an unprecedented opportunity to experience this initiation in the presence of a Neter, the Great Mother Isis. Taret would preside over the ritual as High Priestess, and Ani would pass the Rod of Power to each initiate as she touched a large pyramid carved from meteorite. As a result the initiate would never be separate from the star ancestors.

So on this epochal day of Inundation, the Isis procession entered the ritual hall. The Star Priests entered first, their long white kilts, leopard skin capes, and bald heads shining in the flickering light of the torches made for a resplendent sight. Chants filled the hall with heavenly sounds. The entourage of priests mounted the dais and took their places behind the high altar that held the Rod of Initiation. They were followed by the physical representative of Nut, the Sky Goddess, Lady Taret. She was carried to the base of the dais on a flat gilded litter borne on the shoulders of four Nubian servants. She wore a linen garment stitched at the seams with threads of pure gold, and a diadem made of spikes of gold with a star on each point rested on her head.

Taret was Nut as she ascended the dais to take her place on a gilded chair. Two additional chairs reserved for Meri-ib and his successor, were placed to her left. Ani, the current High Priestess, would sit on Taret's right.

Isis was borne on a golden litter dotted with stars carved from electrum. The Star Goddess wore a plain linen sheath with a linen cape around her shoulders, the hem of the dress and cape embroidered in gold hieroglyphs, a sash of gold cloth around her waist. She wore a thick, black shoulder-length wig crowned by a set of gold wings pointed downward to cover her ears. Tall, inverted cow horns rested atop the hood of the headdress, embracing a red solar disk. The Star Goddess stood for a moment in silence just below the high altar before turning slowly to look into the eyes of those present.

Khem and Tiye were next to appear in the hall. This brought a gasp from those gathered; they knew the important roles these two had played. Two female servants, one Egyptian, the other Nubian, led Bast on a gold-chained leash. The cat's fur was clean and coarse, causing it to fluff out more than usual. The animal walked with her head held high, her tail curled over her back. Right behind Bast and the servant girls attending her was Ani, followed by a priestess from the Temple of Sekhmet in Memphis, wearing a lioness mask and carrying a papyrus scepter in her right hand. She had come in honor of Bast and to represent the goddess Sekhmet's role in the day's magical battle.

Ani took her place beside Taret. Khem, Tiye, and the other apprentices stood in a line at the base of the dais. All were dressed in plain white sheaths and simple reed sandals.

The ceremony was extraordinary. The transfer of power that flowed into Khem from the Rod of Initiation sent a jolt of warmth surging through her and propelled her into space, where she walked among the stars.

Tiye stepped onto the dais to receive her initiation. She would stay in the Temple of Sekhmet as a servant of the Lion Goddess and chief amulet maker. These were honors bestowed upon her by Khufu himself in gratitude for her magical skill and for helping to save his life. Tiye possessed a lioness soul, which her initiation and the extraordinary happenings of the day confirmed.

The inductions into the Holy Order of Nut and their reception of energy from the Rod of Power assured the immortality of the priestesses honored. They were now Star Priestesses, women who knew their destiny, who would live their lives with purpose. Each person involved in this great drama had a path to follow, work to be done. And Khufu? He would serve Egypt as the unchallenged king, and he would do so with a deep wisdom unmatched in the long lineage of Egyptian star kings.

Glossary

Stars, Gods, and Goddesses

Aker	double-headed lion god who watches over the entrance and the exit of the Duat to ensure safe passage for Ra on his nightly journey
Anubis	son of Nepthys, consort of her brother, Seth; a primordial form of the lord of the dead, who later became subservient to Osiris
Anukis	goddess seen with Isis, who with Satis, became one star
Apep	dragon of the Underworld
Apis	the sacred bull of Memphis; Ptah's oracle
Apophis	serpent, most evil of those who dwell in darkness
Ap-uat	Opener of the Ways in the Duat
Aset	Isis
Athor	see *Hathor*
Atmu	god of the setting sun
Bastet	also Bast, cat goddess of joy
Benu	The Egyptian mythical sun bird of Heliopolis, connected with Ra
Bes	dwarf god who protects against evil spirits; associated with the power of the breath of life
Echinda	consort of Typhon
Geb	Earth god; son of Shu and Tefnut; consort of Nut with whom he sired Osiris, Isis, Seth (Set), and Nepthys (Nebthet)
Grand Ennead	the nine original Neters; Ra, Neith, Tefnut, Shu, Geb, Nepthys, Seth, Isis, and Osiris
Hadar Beta Centauri	northern star in the Southern Hemisphere
Hapi	one of the four sons of Horus; represents the cardinal direction north; symbolized by a mummified man with the head of a baboon; he and his brothers were given the duties of mummification by Anubis
Hapi	god who personified the Nile River; pictured as a fat man to signify abundance, with either a crown of lilies or a papyrus plant circling his head

Hathor	goddess symbolized by a cow with a solar disk on its head and hawk-feather plumes; originally a Nubian war goddess who took the same lioness form as Sekhmet and drank her enemies' blood
Henkhisesui	god of the East invoked by Sokar
Heru	Horus
Horakti	Horus aspect of the Sun god; the rising Sun
Horus	son of Isis and Osiris; Sun god
Hutchaici	god of the West invoked by Sokar
Imhotep	see *Nefertem*
Isis	Aset, daughter of Ra; sister of Seth and Nebthet; sister and consort of Osiris. mother of Horus. See *Osiris*
Khepera	Ra; the scarab god
Khonsu	Moon god
Ma'at	daughter of Ra; goddess of fundamental truth and order
Mehturt	Sky Goddess associated with the primeval waters from which Ra was born
Melha	one of the Sirius Star Gods
Mestha	one of the four sons of Horus; depicted as a human; guardian of the cardinal direction south
Mut	principal female counterpart of Ra, the king of the gods; Mut was believed to possess both the male and female attributes of reproduction
Nebthet	see *Nepthys*
Nefertem	son of Sekhmet and Ptah; Imhotep
Neith	mother of Sebek and Ra, the Sun god
Nekhebet	the vulture goddess who looked after the ruling pharaoh; goddess of childbirth; portrayed as a vulture wearing the white crown of Upper Egypt, while Uatchit wore the crown of Lower Egypt
Nepthys	also *Nebthet*; youngest daughter of Nut; sister of Isis and Osiris; sister consort of Seth; mother of Anubis; also goddess of childbirth; friend of the dead, she is depicted as "riding the night boat" of the Underworld, meeting the deceased king's spirit and accompanying him into "Lightland." She is also called the companion who gives guidance to the newly deceased; "Mistress of the House" (House of Horus, i.e., the sky)
Neter	Deities, gods and goddesses; Neters and Neteru are plural forms
Neter-Khert	magical dimension
Nut	daughter of Shu and Tefnut; twin and consort of Geb; Sky Goddess and mother of Osiris by Geb; married to Ra, she also took Thoth for a lover; goddess of cosmic order
Ogdoad	eight gods and goddesses who predated and caused creation; Nun and Naunet (the primodial water); Huh

	and Hauhet (infinite space); Kuk and Kauket (darkness); and Amun and Amaunet (representing hidden powers)
Osiris	son of Geb and Nut; brother and consort of Isis, brother of Seth and Nebthet. He and Isis had a dual function as fertility gods; she saw over love and union; he was the god of growth. He was drowned and dismembered by his jealous brother, Seth. Isis used her medical skills to impregnate herself with the last drop of semen from her consort's penis. This resulted in the birth of Horus. Osiris became the ruler of the Underworld. Isis vowed revenge on Seth and encouraged Horus to kill him.
Ptah	also *Ta-tenem*, the Primordial Mound; the Great Creator, the god of crafts and skills, the guardian of all knowledge; son of Nun and Naunet; he made the first gods by imagining them and then naming them, so they were creations of both intention and the breath-of-life
Qebhsenuf	one of the four sons of Horus; depicted as a falcon; guardian of the cardinal direction west
Qebui	god of the North invoked by Sokar
Ra	also *Re*; son of Neith; sun god
Re	see *Ra*
Satis	goddess seen with Isis, who with Anukis became one star
Seb	son of Ra; father of Osiris; consort of Nutpe
Sebek	same as Sobek; son of Neith, brother of Ra; crocodile god associated with death and burial
Sekhmet	daughter of Ra; sister of Seb; wife of Ptah; mother of Nefertem, Imhotep, and Maahes; goddess associated with divine vengeance and war. She is depicted with the head of a lioness. Ra (Re) sent Sekhmet to slay mortals who were plotting against him.
Sekti	Re
Selket	scorpion goddess
Shebbui	god of the South invoked by Sokar
Shu	one of the first pair of gods to be created by Ra (along with Tefnut); Shu and Tefnut were parents of twins, Geb and Nut, who sired Osiris, Isis, Seth (Set), and Nepthys (Nebthet)
Sirius	Isis; Star of the Nile, whose rising ushers in the new year; marks the beginning of the season of Inundation, the annual flooding of the Nile
Sobek	see *Sebek*
Sopdet	Isis
Sphinx	Image carved from a natural rock depicted with the body of a lion, wings, and a human face; head represents intelligence and wisdom
Ta-tenem	see *Ptah*
Tefnut	one of the first pair of gods to be created by Ra (along with Shu); parents of twins Geb and Nut, who sired Osiris, Isis, Seth, and Nepthys

Tet	a healer spirit
Thoth	divine patron of wisdom; said to be son of Ra; staunch defender of Horus in his battles against Seth as rightful claimant to the Throne; mediator and peacemaker; present at the final judgment, weighing the heart of the deceased in a balance, as Osiris sits as judge; messenger of the gods
Tuamutef	one of the four sons of Horus; symbolized as a jackal; guardian of the cardinal direction east
Typhon	mythical beast; fire-breathing giant with one hundred serpentine heads, serpentine legs and thighs, with a feathered and winged body; with Echidna, he fathered the Sphinx and many other beasts.
Uatchet	a serpent goddess, often associated with Nekhebet
Wepwawet	a jackal-headed Neter; Opener of the Ways; associated with processions for both religious and military purposes
Zeno-sothis	Star Woman

Characters

Akhi	Khem's servant
Ali Gabri	businessman; Bakka's father
Amen	Sokar's stepfather
Amen-tep	calendar-maker
Amenti	high priestess of the Temple of Sekhmet
Ani	Chief Dream Priestess, teacher of magic
Anpu	the jackal magician
Ant'en	prophet, leader of the priests of various divinities, succeeds Meri-ib as High Priest of Heliopolis
Atef	Khem's brother, scribe apprentice
Atur	palace engineer in charge of recording the rising of the Nile
Ba-ba	Amenti's house steward
Bakka	young woman in training against her will to be a Star Priestess
Bast	name of lioness cub raised by Khem
Bata	Khem's mother
Caliph	Chief Star Priest
Cephren	youngest son of Khufu
Dak	priestess, the chief amulet-maker
Dedi	magician; Sokar's teacher
Dejedfre	Khufu's eldest son; crown prince; High Priest of the Temple of Memphis
Eucrates	high lector priest in temple library

Hap	sacred bull
Haroun	chief scribe in the Temple of the Sun
Harum	Nemon's chief foreman
Heba	Khaba's Star Sister
Heka	Khaba's Moon Sister
Henna	Khem's paternal grandmother
Her-bak	contemporary of Sokar; scribe; head of mathematics division in the Temple of the Sun
Her-mon	importer of woods and resins
Heru	the Offspring, a divine name for the Pharaoh
Hetepheres	wife of Sneferu; mother of Khufu
Horus	name of Sokar's falcon
Kasut	in training to be a Star Priestess
Kermit	foreman of work force at the Sphinx Temple
Khaba	Tiye's mentor and teacher of magic
Khem	teenage girl called by a vision to be a Star Priestess; confidante of Tiye
Khufu	Pharaoh
Kunum	most feared and respected sorcerer in Nubia
Lucius	chief astrologer
Mafdet	young woman attracting Sokar's interest
Manetho	chief executive; vizier
Mebak-her	Mafdet's mother
Menet	in training to be a Star Priestess
Men-kar	the Elder; Sokar's teacher
Menkar	Mafdet's father
Men-ka-re	Nemon's chief assistant
Mentu	oracle priest
Meri-ib	High Priest of Heliopolis
Meritates	wife of Khufu; mother of Dejedfre and Cephren
Meretneith/Meret	a dream-talker; Star Gods speak to her through her dreams
Mery-Ptah	valet-servant to Shemshu-Hor
Mutirkis	receptionist at the Temple of Sekhmet
Neba	Morning Star Priestess
Nebseni	court astronomer
Nedjemou	the chief of the physicians and priests
Nefer	Tiye's ren (magical name); means "good," "beautiful"; associated with Nubia
Nefer-er	Sokar's mother
Neith	wife of Amen-tep
Nemon	chief architect; Khufu's cousin
Neqet	Khem's ren (magical name); means "magician"; another name for Isis
Nerah	Tiye's servant
Nita	Kasut's servant
Pakht	friend of Sheshat; scribe at temple of Sekhmet

Pepi	servant of Senna
Pepy	chancellor of temple instruction house
Petosiris	High Priest of Hermopolis
Ra-hotep	overseer of temple treasures
Rama-se	mentor of Lucius, the astrologer
Rashid	Khem's father
Remy	assistant to Shemshu-Hor
Seku	Chief dream priest
Senna	priest
Shem-hotep	chief of Khufu's army
Shemshu-Hor	oldest living being; priest; sage; prophet of prophets
Sheshat	Taret's scribe
Sinuhe	Ani's courier
Sneferu	Khufu's father
Sokar	magician; half brother to the Pharaoh, Khufu
Taret	elder Chief Priestess
Teyet	lead dancer in ritual at the Star Temple
Tiye	Nubian girl, trained as a magician, called to study to be a Star Priestess; confidante of Khem
Urthekau	Ani's ren (magical name); she who is knowledgeable, rich in magic spells; one of Isis's names

Objects and Places

Abydos	city of Khem's origin located in Upper Egypt (South)
akh	spirit
Al Kemi	Pharaonic Egypt
amphora	decorated earthenware jar with two handles and an oval body with a flat base, used to hold wine and water
amulet	a symbol worn as a talisman against evil or injury; often wrapped with mummies to protect them on their journey through the Duat
ankh	a hieroglyphic sign for life similar to a cross but with a loop in place of the upper arm, which was also often produced in solid form and worn as jewelry
aufu	the physical body
ba	the eternal divine soul
barque	royal boat used to transport statues of gods or mummies
ben-ben	the hill which was the first land to rise from the waters
benbenet	pyramidion; capstone of a pyramid
B'ja	iron meteorite
cenotaph	a symbolic tomb honoring the dead, but not containing the body
cippi	miniatures of objects with hieroglyphs; for protection of a single person

crook and flail	royal emblems that symbolize the position of Pharaoh; symbols of kingship
cuneiform	a script originating in Mesopotamia; usually written using a stylus on clay tablets
diorite	igneus rock similar to granite, but with less quartz; has a salt and pepper appearance
djed	an enigmatic hieroglyph and amulet linked to Osiris's back bone and resurrection
double-ka	mind
Duat	the netherworld, Underworld, the Starry Realm of Osiris in the constellation currently known as Orion
electrum	an alloy of gold and silver, often used on the tips of obelisks
evil eye	casting a harmful spell with the use of the human eye
fellahin	plural for peasant
galabayya	a long robe worn by Egyptian men
haidit	shadow; the unconscious
Harmakhis	Horus of the Horizon; the Great Sphinx
heka	magic
hekau	magician-priestesses
hekau	term for magical formulae used to energize amulets
hieroglyphs	the picture alphabet used for writing the Egyptian language
ibis	wading bird related to the heron, distinguished by a long, slender, downwardly curved bill; sacred to the god Thoth
ka	body of "experience"
khabs	divine component within each person
khai'bit	the Shadow, unconsciousness
khat	the physical body
khu with sahu	bodies appropriate for magic work
kohl	chalklike pigmented substance used as eye makeup
ma'at	truth; justice, right
medjty	keeper of robes
mehit	see *utchat*; amulet
mekt	amulet for protection
menat	a necklace with several rows of beads that gather into a counterweight at the back of the neck; worn by the goddess Hathor and symbolized the divine powers of healing
menes	head covering
menyet	beaded collar
naos	inner temple, the most sacred part of a temple, where the emblem or likeness of the god is kept and from which the core teachings or qualities of that god emanate
natron	a carbonate salt used for desiccating mummies; also used in making soaps and lotions
natronade	soap made from natron
natronella	cleansing lotion made from natron
neshmet	barque
nilometer	a measuring device that shows the height of the Nile waters
nome	district; area
Nubia	land south of Egypt; inhabitants were black; distinct culture and religion

pectoral	a large piece of jewelry worn on the chest
pyramidion	capstone of a pyramid
ren	a secret, personal, magical name
sekhem	power or might
sistrum	a percussion instrument made up of disks that rattled when shaken
tetamulet	representing tree trunk in which Isis concealed the body of Osiris
udjat	icon symbolizing the eye of Ra or Horus; depicted with the long tail and brows of a hawk; means prosperous, sound, whole
uraeus	symbol of kingship represented by a cobra in an upright position worn as a head ornament or crown
ushabti	clay figure made by a person to represent him/herself; capable of storing power
utchat	eye of Horus; the White Eye is the Sun, the *utchat*; the black Eye is the Moon, mehit amulet worn around neck for strength, vigor, protection, safety, and good health
vizier	chief executive
wadjet	depicted as a full cobra, or the head of a cobra, rearing up in protection on the forehead of the Neters and rulers
was	power
wedjat	eye, small amulet worn for protection, wealth, and good health

About the Author

A former radio and television talk-show host, Page Bryant is the author of ten books, an intuitive counselor, and a seminar facilitator. She and her husband operate the Mystic Mountains Retreat Center from their home in Waynesville, North Carolina.

Hampton Roads Publishing Company
. . . for the evolving human spirit

Hampton Roads Publishing Company
publishes books on a variety of subjects including
metaphysics, health,
visionary fiction, and other related topics.

For a copy of our latest catalog,
call toll-free, 800-766-8009,
or send your name and address to:

Hampton Roads Publishing Company, Inc.
1125 Stoney Ridge Road
Charlottesville, VA 22902
e-mail: hrpc@hrpub.com
www.hrpub.com